AUTHOR	CLASS
MACALLAN, A.	F

TITLE

SUCCESSION

SUCCESSION

Andrew MacAllan

HEADLINE

034921613

British Library Cataloguing in Publication Data

MacAllan, Andrew
Succession.
I. Title
823'.914[F]

ISBN 0-7472-0094-7

Typeset in 11/12 pt Plantin
by Colset Private Limited, Singapore

Printed and bound in Great Britain by
Richard Clay Ltd, Bungay, Suffolk

HEADLINE BOOK PUBLISHING PLC
Headline House
79 Great Titchfield Street
London W1P 7FN

To the Memory of
Sir Franklin Gimson,
Hong Kong 1941–1945.
A Man of Honour in a
World of Dross

Cut-purses, miles of cheats, enterprises of scoundrels, delicious disgusts, foolish decisions, crippled hopes, virile women, effeminate men, and everywhere the love of gold.

Giordano Bruno (c. 1548–1600),
a former monk, about his own life and times

Quidquid agunt homines, votum timor ira voluptas
Gaudia discursus nostri farrago libelli est.
(All that men are engaged in, their wishes, fears, anger, pleasures, joys, and varied pursuits, form the hotch-potch of my book.)

Juvenal (A.D. 60–c.130) – *Satires*

Contents

Preface

The Present

Nassau

The inauguration of the new international headquarters of Trinity-Trio, the vast multi-national conglomerate, was, as the Senior Minister of the Bahamas said in his speech, more than an event of financial and economic significance, enormously important as these were. It marked the move from the East, where the company had first started trading in the nineteenth century, across the world to the West, which would now benefit immeasurably from its ever increasing success in the twentieth century and into the twenty-first.

The Senior Minister did not add that on his retirement he would also personally benefit, some unkindly said immeasurably, by becoming a non-executive vice-president. Nor did he refer to the company's very early days in the East when it had traded almost exclusively in opium, and indeed had forced this pernicious commodity upon China, to the extent of provoking war with this country when her rulers attempted to stop the trade.

Such origins were best left in decent obscurity. The huge present-day traffic in drugs from the East and South America to North America through the Bahamas accounted for the enormous wealth of many in the distinguished audience in Trinity-Trio's stratospheric penthouse hospitality suite. Wisely, the Senior Minister felt no need to touch on such a sensitive issue. People who had been unwise enough to do so publicly had frequently lived to regret it; many had not even lived.

But the irony of the situation was not lost on everyone. From forcing the Chinese to buy a drug they did not want because of its deadly qualities, the Western nations were now desperately seeking to prevent it being imported into their own countries. But instead of dwelling on the theme of full circle, the Senior Minister, on the advice of his speechwriter, an earnest young Bahamian graduate of Yale (where he had enjoyed a generous Trinity-Trio bursary), had likened their new thirty-storey gold and glass headquarters to a signpost pointing the way on and up towards a new era of unparalleled prosperity. The past was behind them, he declared dramatically, rising to the moment like the actor he sometimes wished he had been. It had, he admitted, been a past of booms and slumps. Former Bahamian boom times had included running guns in the American Civil War, and rum during Prohibition, while the slumps had been largely caused not by human error but by natural disasters, such as hurricanes, or the inexplicable failure of the local sponge industry.

Ahead, the future was bright. Trinity-Trio was one of the world's largest and most important commercial companies. Bahamian prosperity would now be linked with the destiny of a company whose annual revenues were far greater than the gross national products of many countries. Respected city editors and financial commentators argued most forcibly that if all Trinity-Trio's subsidiaries around the world were included, it could even lay claim to being the world's most important trading group. Any criticism that might be levelled at it was instantly met by a hostile return barrage from the TV and radio stations, the newspapers and magazines it controlled through an international subsidiary, Enquirer Media, Inc. Not many critics could risk strident recapitulations of their private lives and associations. It was more prudent to accept that Trinity-Trio was a power in many lands and wielded more influence than ever appeared in any company prospectus.

Similarly, the Senior Minister did not add how the arcane, complex and sophisticated maze of master shares and nominees and beneficial trusts, prudently registered in Vaduz, the Caymans and the Dutch Antilles, meant that seemingly only one man knew the precise extent of its real wealth and influence. He was Lord Jackson of Gravesend, Trinity-Trio's chairman and the lineal descendant of one of the company's three founders, Dr Richard Jackson.

Everyone knew that Lord Jackson never publicly discussed matters relating to the Group: he had no need to explain or to excuse. His family motto, 'Beyond the dreams of avarice', was said by the envious to be apt, because he did indeed have wide artistic interests. For example, he personally owned the world's largest collection of paintings by George Chinnery, who had specialised in early Chinese scenes, and by Thomas and William Daniell, whose portrayals of life in eighteenth-century India were equally sought after.

Others, of a more acid outlook, declared that Lord Jackson's motto really referred to his forebears' indefatigable and supremely successful efforts to amass wealth on a magnificent scale by any means whatever, regardless of the consequences – whether to themselves or those who stood in their way.

After the Senior Minister sat down, perspiring from the efforts of oratory, and having declared the headquarters formally open, toasts to prosperity, to the future and to the memory of the company's three illustrious founders were drunk with enthusiasm and respect. Then Lord Jackson, grey-haired, wearing a lightweight suit of impeccable cut, a cream silk shirt and Sulka tie, smiling benignly as though at some subtle and secret jest, moved easily among his guests.

Slightly behind him, and on either side, walked two younger, heavier men with unusually light tread. They could have been relations but were, in fact, his bodyguard, former SAS captains. Having left the British service, they preferred this agreeable existence to soldiering on in the private armies of some Middle East sheikh. Trinity-Trio paid more highly, and such were the ramifications of T-T – as the company was familiarly known world-wide – that one day they could be in Bonn and the next in New York; then south to Mexico City, or east to Singapore, Sydney, Tokyo.

On Lord Jackson's right was his beautiful wife Corinne, the only daughter of the professor in charge of the Dr Richard Jackson Medical Foundation; on his left, Lord Jackson's equally elegant but rather younger Chinese mistress, Anna Lu-Kuan.

Both women smiled at each other when they had to, but never with their eyes, although Anna could claim to be present in a legitimate professional capacity; she was executive vice-president of Trinity-Trio's aircraft-leasing subsidiary in New York. They had already hung inflated mental price tags on each other's clothes and jewellery, which would be a matter for subsequent discussion (and possible financial adjustment) with his lordship at a more intimate and private time.

Lord Jackson greeted people he recognised (and some he did not wish to see) with the same effortless charm and apparently genuine pleasure. A word here, a smile there, the tilt of his glass of Perrier water – he never drank alcohol – in the direction of someone else; the laying of a reassuring, superbly manicured hand on the shoulder of a prince, a president, a potentate who might just have seized power in some black African dictatorship – or who was, most unhappily, just about to lose it, and so, possibly, his life.

Lord Jackson's passage among his guests had all the dignity and significance of a medieval royal progress. This was his court; these his courtiers, his creatures. Such was his power and personal magnetism that everyone who strove to catch his eye and failed, instantly felt humiliated, cast down, deprived. Guests who did exchange a few words with him would embellish and elevate the banalities actually spoken into the wit and wisdom of a Socratic dialogue, in which, naturally, in their recollections, they took the part of the sage.

Those on the fringe, the majority, invited for reasons of policy or mass reciprocal entertainment, because individually they would not merit the expenditure of a moment of Lord Jackson's enormously valuable time, and who rightly suspected he had no idea who they were and cared as much, noted sourly that in a certain light he did have a slight look of the East about him.

But that was wholly understandable, surely, because had not the original Richard Jackson married a Chinese girl? Or if not, she had been his mistress and borne him a son. Plain wives, in middle age, with less than successful husbands, assured each other that this would doubtless account for his relationship with this Lu-Kuan woman.

(Of course, there must be lots of other odd relationships in the family background, too, if only you could find them out. But you never would, would you? Not with all that money and muscle. It wasn't right, really, was it, that one man could be so rich and powerful and even appear to enjoy this situation, when there was so much poverty in the world? No wonder he had to have guards.

It was all *monstrously* unfair, but then life was unfair, wasn't it? And if you wanted to know what God thought about money, well, you just had to look at the people to whom He gave it. Yes, thank you, waiter, I *will* have a little more champagne. Oh, I didn't mean a *full* glass. But since you have filled it, I'll just have to drink it slowly, won't I?)

The crowds surged slowly through the huge air-conditioned suite like a tide of many colours, past the Nassau Police Band playing soft music on a dais, in their white pith helmets and red and blue uniforms; past enlarged floodlit colour photographs of Trinity-Trio's quays and docks and assembly plants in a dozen countries.

Aerial views of acres of saw-toothed factory roofs, oil rigs, super-markets, all showed the familiar Trinity-Trio logo in glass or concrete or bright metal. It shone in red neon from the top of high-rise buildings; was emblazoned boldly on the funnels of the company's cruise liners; flowers spelled it out on company airfields.

A few guests, but not too many, also noticed an early nineteenth-century print of an English river. Some fishing boats rode at anchor, and smoke spiralled from the chimneys of cottages snuggled together beneath a church, close to the shore. The print had little artistic merit, all agreed on that point, and it seemed singularly out of place here, literally more than a hundred yards in the air above the flat, sun-hardened harshness of New Providence Island. Only the inscription gave a clue to its interest: 'A View of Gravesend, Kent'.

Wasn't that the town Lord Jackson had selected to use in his title? Odd place to choose, surely? One or two guests had actually been there. Gravesend was totally unlike that print now, they said: new housing estates and shopping precincts and industrial parks. This showed that he held some sentimental feelings – or else his public relations people had dug the picture up from somewhere.

At the far end of the vast room stood another unlikely addition, also seemingly out of tune with modern architecture and brushed aluminium furniture: a glass case on a stainless steel stand, about shoulder height. Brightly lit by spotlights in the ceiling, it bore an unexpected and incongruous warning: 'Electronically protected. Do not touch'.

Who would want to touch it? All that the case contained was a single copper penny lying on a red velvet cushion like a jewel. Nothing else. No explanation. This protected splendour gave the penny all the significance of a religious totem. Ridiculous, really, unless it was a symbol of some sort – but what?

A young journalist, unused to champagne and worried in case he could not find a story that would have what his news editor quaintly called 'an angle' to it, saw Lord Jackson approaching, and forgot his natural diffidence in the presence of the wealthy to put this question directly to his host.

'What does that represent, sir?' he asked him. 'Why is that penny in such a prominent position, all lit up and guarded?'

Lord Jackson smiled, and nodded almost imperceptibly to a hovering waiter to recharge the young man's glass.

'For the very best of reasons,' he replied courteously. 'That particular coin, although of course obsolete for many years, and possessing no value now whatever as legal tender, is to me and to my fellow directors – and should be to every one of our shareholders world-wide – quite simply the most valuable coin in the world.

'That penny was the reason why the company started. It is the foundation of all its fortunes. Dr Richard Jackson, one of our three founders, called it his totem, his symbol of good luck. And so it has proved. Without that coin, we would quite simply not exist today. Does that answer your query?'

He paused, as though expecting a reply, and when the young man, confused by alcohol and his own temerity in asking such a leading question, only nodded and mumbled an affirmative, Jackson moved on, hand outstretched to greet the wife of the chairman of Trinity-Trio's Japanese subsidiary.

The journalist shrugged, not quite certain whether he should have replied, or if he had done, what he should have said. You could never tell when these tycoons were joking or serious. He drained his glass quickly and held it out to be refilled. How could T-T have started with one penny? What the hell did the man mean? Lord Jackson must have been making fun of him. Perhaps he should have laughed? A rich man's jokes are always funny – at least to the rich man.

He'd have a couple more glasses – this champagne was really extremely good – and then be on his way. There was no story here for him. A lot of publicity photographs on the walls, an absurd print of some forgotten village on the Thames, and an old penny in a show case; they did not add up to much.

But, in fact, they did. They added up to everything. Trinity-Trio was the total of these parts. The long, often bitter, sometimes bloody, sometimes terrible story of the growth of a company now so powerful that it could lean on the policies of a hundred countries, bring down or promote governments and even hold the balance between peace and war, was encapsulated in this print and this penny.

And as Lord Jackson moved on to greet more guests, he had been prepared to tell how, just as he had heard his father tell the story to him, as he in turn had heard it from *his* father and grandfather, and the sons and grandsons of others who had lived, and sometimes died through it or for it. The story was more than in his blood, he thought, as he gave a diplomatic and passionless kiss to the daughter of a Bolivian trade minister. It *was* his blood, his bone, his being.

As soon as he could, he turned away from the chattering prattle of cocktail conversation, bright and brittle as pretzel sticks, and stood looking out of a wide, high double-glazed window at the sea glowing like a lake of lapis lazuli. The name Bahamas came from the Spanish word *bajamar*, meaning a shallow sea. But beneath that serene surface lurked poisonous fish and dangerous creatures. The appearance was deceptive; a mountain top can seem to be a harmless, snow-covered peak, but deep within, fire can be raging, ready to erupt without warning in flame and white-hot liquid lava.

Was Trinity-Trio as secure as he had described it? Had all the efforts of lawyers and accountants succeeded in making it impregnable to any take-over bid? There had been attempts, of course, but all had been beaten off, although at an ever increasing cost in treasure and time. And just recently he had been surprised and concerned when his senior attorney in Geneva, Laurens Gustav, had, without any warning, resigned his position on the grounds of ill-health.

Lord Jackson had instigated the most specific enquiries and found to his concern that the man was apparently in the best of health. So why had he resigned? Had he been threatened or suborned in some way?

And only one month previously, a car in which Lord Jackson should have travelled from Athens airport to his hotel had suddenly caught fire while actually on its way to meet his plane. Police were convinced that some concealed incendiary device had been set in action through a faulty timing mechanism.

Was the device flawed and so set the car on fire too soon, before he was even in it? Or was this a deliberate warning to him? But if so, from whom and why? These questions remained unanswered.

No mention of the fact that the car was on its way to meet him had appeared in any newspaper or on any news bulletin: that was ensured by T-T's control of the media, but equally no comforting answers could be found to satisfy Lord Jackson, hence his concealed unease. And he had heard rumours about the Occidental-Oriental Bank, to which T-T owed billions – all thoroughly secured, of course, but still a debt. Not that it really mattered if the bank's ownership did change, he was one of O-O's biggest clients, but even rumours of change could prove unsettling.

This new headquarters bristled with security devices, and security men, dressed as diplomats or journalists, mingled with the guests. But still the old question remained that had worried the powerful since the days of the Roman Empire: *Quis custodiet custodians?*

Far beneath the penthouses, among pink roofs and palm trees, Lord Jackson could see a statue, erected two centuries earlier to Woodes Rogers, the first successful Governor of the Bahamas, who, in the eighteenth century, had driven out the pirates – Morgan, Teach and the rest – who then infested the islands.

'Pirates expelled; commerce restored', claimed the statue's laconic inscription. Dr Jackson would have been amused by the directness of that simple statement, just as he would have appreciated Rogers' family motto: *Dum spiro, spero*, While I breathe, I hope.

Life had been much simpler then, Lord Jackson thought, almost wistfully; so much more natural. Progress moved in those days at the pace of a man or a horse or a sailing ship beneath the winds of heaven. Then, under the first hammer blows of steam-engine pistons, the world steadily began to shrink. Soon, the car, aircraft, radio telegraphy, made it smaller still. Now he could talk to anyone almost anywhere as clearly as if they were beside him in this room – probably more lucidly, with the noise these buffoons were making. And satellites, space stations, computers, processors of words and minds and thoughts, memory banks, the mighty silicon chip, were continuously diminishing the world even more. Dr Jackson would not have cared for that, he thought.

When news took weeks or even months to reach one continent from another, one could use the time to redress a balance, correct a mistake. Now there was no time; the report and the action it reported were virtually simultaneous.

Sometimes Lord Jackson wondered what the first Richard Jackson would have done in a problem or a crisis. At those times he felt especially close to that doctor; he could almost imagine that in some way *he* was actually the founder of Trinity-Trio, not simply a fortunate descendant who had picked up the golden baton in succession, and run with it in a kind of relay race to even greater riches.

At such times he almost believed in rebirth, reincarnation, the return of a spirit from the past in another body to complete what had been left unfinished in a previous life. His long association with the East had familiarised him with the teachings of Hinduism, Buddhism, Confucianism, Shintoism; religions that subscribed to some belief in reincarnation – if only to atone for past misdemeanours. Could they *all* be wrong?

People had wondered why T-T had endowed a new chair of parapsychology at Oxford. Lord Jackson had never revealed the real reason, his own interest in the subject. But otherwise why would he have chosen this particular date, September the fourth, out of season in the Bahamas but of crucial significance to him? For on this day, long long ago, Dr Richard Jackson had started out on an unplanned, unsought, unmapped journey that would take him across the world and, in succession, bring to his descendants wealth and power and influence beyond all imagining. . . .

Part One

The 1830s to the 1890s

Gravesend

Sometimes, when the capricious autumn winds blew the spiced scents of an ancient land off Calangute beach in Goa, or when sunset etched the shark-fin sail of a Chinese junk beyond Hong Kong, Dr Jackson would also wonder why and when he had been chosen to make this journey.

Had it really started on that September evening in the shabby front room of a fisherman's cottage at Gravesend, with an old woman dying on a straw bed? Richard Jackson was twenty-three then: He had recently qualified as a physician and surgeon. The parchment scroll describing him as one learned in the arts of healing, newly framed for him by the local carpenter, hung in the surgery he rented above Mr Stapleford's apothecary's shop, overlooking the Thames.

Jackson had served his apprenticeship with the local doctor, jogging around with him in his pony and trap, copying his actions, even the way he frequently and prudently refrained from committing himself to any precise diagnosis.

'If you are wrong, my boy, you can frighten yourself. If you are right you may frighten the patient – and then they will not pay your fee. Always remember, patients do not like to be frightened. They are paying you to reassure them.'

'But what if you are right, and you cannot help them, and they're going to die?'

'Then that is a matter for the Reverend gentlemen, my boy. That i God's business, not ours.'

Jackson had watched the old doctor set limbs and administer aid a childbirth; he knew when to remove leeches from their jar of salt, when t place them on the flesh of those requiring to be bled – and when t refrain. He had sat examinations at the College of Physicians in thei splendid new buildings in Pall Mall, and been granted their licence t practise. He felt proud of belonging to a college founded in the sixteent century by Thomas Linacre, Henry VIII's court physician, in his ow home near St Paul's Cathedral, as only a young man can feel proud whe

12

he has no illusions to lose, no disappointments to bear, no backward glances to the fantasy land of might-have-been.

Looking down at the exhausted face of this woman, Mrs Gray – he would never forget her name – a widow before her time, with her life now to be counted in days, if not only in hours, Jackson wondered what real use were all the specifics with their false Latin names; the mercury, the salts and syrups of the East, bought at great expense from his landlord. What so many of his patients had really needed over many years had been good food and warmth, hope for the future, love and affection in the present – and all had been denied them.

It would be pointless to bleed her. What Mrs Gray required was not less blood but more: beef steaks, chops, a leg of lamb, with rich gravy and a pint of porter, or, even better, claret. But how could she ever afford any of these necessary things when she had not one halfpenny in the house, or indeed in the world?

As he had soon learned to do when visiting poor patients, Jackson put his hand in the back pocket of his tweed trousers, ran his thumb around each coin it contained until he found one with a milled edge. He took out the florin, handed it to her. Mrs Gray clutched it greedily in a hand thin and wrinkled as a vulture's claw.

'Your son is looking after you, I understand?' he said. She nodded. 'Then send him out to buy some bones to make broth for you. Give him a jug for a gill of porter. You will feel better then, that I can promise you.'

The old woman looked up at him in pleased surprise; a tear of gratitude coursed down her cheek. It had been years since anyone had given her anything.

'You are a very kind young gentleman,' she said. 'Thank you for the money.'

'Money,' Jackson replied as cheerfully as he could, 'the root of all evil. Or so the Good Book says.'

'You are wrong, doctor,' she replied. 'I was once second housemaid in a clergyman's house, so I *often* heard what the Good Book says. It is not money, but the *love* of money that is the root of all evil. The lack of it can be equally as bad. I know.'

She smiled at the thought and closed her eyes, as though to compose herself to sleep. Jackson tiptoed out of the room, glad to breathe fresh air after the foetid atmosphere inside, heavy with wood smoke and the sweat of terminal illness.

The old woman called him back unexpectedly, her voice thin and querulous as the cry of a distant bird.

'I also have a gift for you,' she said shyly. Jackson looked down at her. The candle cast flickering shadows on her old, lined face.

'Give me your hand.'

Jackson held out his right hand reluctantly. Two scaly claws gripped him. The flesh felt dry and hot with fever.

'I can see into the future, doctor. But only for others. Never for myself – else I might have profited by it.'

'What do you see now?' Jackson asked, to humour her.

'A strange land, doctor, where the sun burns like a furnace in the sky. I see men's faces, not white like yours and mine, nor black like the Lascars' on the ships that anchor here from the East, but yellow as parchment, and they wear strange flat hats, like plates.'

'Am I there with them?'

'You are there, doctor. And so is a great ship with many masts, not just one, like the Thames barges here. And I see two other men. One has a red beard and red hair, and his face is raw with the heat. The other is dark and does not come from England. I see crates being carried ashore on the heads of servants and he is cursing them. The crates are packed with rows of white puff balls, like pastry from the baker's shop in the High Street. Yet they are not pastry.'

'What do you think they are?' Jackson asked her, not really caring: her mind was wandering. It must be the thought of food.

'I do not know, doctor. I can only tell you what I see, not what or who the pictures represent.'

She paused. In the silent room, shadows leapt on the walls like terrified ghosts. Jackson felt suddenly uneasy. Perhaps Mrs Gray had really opened a door on to his future – and she did not want him to know what it concealed?

'That is all?' he asked her, eager to be away. Maybe the dying, or some of them, did possess powers not given to others in the prime of life?

'Yes,' she agreed quietly. 'That is all.'

But Jackson sensed she was lying; he could tell it from the tone of her voice, from the way she turned her head away from him. What else had she seen that concerned him in this strange vision of his future?

Had she seen his death, as he would soon witness hers? He shook the thought from him; he was becoming morbid. A clatter of hooves outside on the cobbles made him turn in surprise towards the front door. A cottage like this did not attract many visitors.

He heard the creak of a leather saddle, the blowing of a horse that had been ridden too hard, then firm footsteps on iron-shod heels, and a peremptory beating on the door. He opened it.

A man wearing livery stood outside. He had a mean, sharp face, like a vole; his cross-eyes raked the room.

'Ah, doctor,' he said, with the half insolent, half servile familiarity of a bad servant. 'Mr Stapleford told me you were here.'

'Who are you?' Jackson asked him shortly; he did not like the visitor's appearance or his attitude.

'From Mr Piggott, sir,' said the man more smartly. 'He requests your attendance.'

'What is the matter? Is he ill?'

'He did not confide in me, doctor, but he said it was a matter of great urgency. I was to fetch you back with all convenient speed.'

'I am attending a patient. I will come as soon as I am able,' Jackson replied. 'Be so good as to give Mr Piggott that answer.'

The man bowed, went back to his horse, swung himself up into the saddle. Jackson listened as the clip-clop of hooves diminished, then turned back to Mrs Gray.

'You think I can see more than I say?' she asked him, continuing their conversation as though there had been no interruption.

'Perhaps.'

'You are right, doctor. I see – *mud*. Nothing but mud, grey and stinking, like the shore here when the tide goes out. *Mud!*'

Jackson nodded. Clearly, her mind was wandering.

'I will call in the morning,' he told her.

'If I am here.'

'You will be here,' Jackson assured her with the professional confidence of the physician, assuming she meant, if she were still alive.

'I may not be. Mr Piggott wants me out. He has increased my rent, and I cannot pay. He knows that – which is why he put it up.'

'I'll speak to him about it,' Jackson promised. 'Do not worry.'

'You are very kind, doctor. Very kind. And all I can see for you is mud, a sea of mud. . . .'

She shook her head sadly, and the fluttering candle flame flung the movement, hugely magnified, against the wall. A giant and grotesque head nodded as she repeated the word: 'Mud.'

Jackson closed the front door, untethered his horse from the hitching post, and turned the animal's head in the direction of Thursday Hall, the largest house for ten miles around. The hall took its name from the hill on which it stood, Thursday Hill, so called because after market, on every Thursday of the year, horses pulling carts laden with merchandise found the hill a challenge. A smith nearby kept half a dozen shires ready to help tow these wagons up and over the crest.

Most of the property in and around the town belonged to the Piggott family. The largest inn, The Piggott Arms, displayed their recently-designed family crest, for the Piggotts were without one until they came to wealth. The mailed fist, clenched, with three scallop shells, azure, and dagger unsheathed, symbolized violence and action.

'I hate the man,' Stapleford the apothecary had once admitted to

Jackson. 'I fear him, I suppose. That's the real reason. He is so unpredictable, so bullying. There is no chance to discuss any dispute in a
rational manner. If he cannot attack you through your rent, then he has a
gang of roughs who owe him favours and he will literally set them on you,
like curs. I know. I have seen it happen, and, shame on me, I did not raise
a hand to help the poor man they set about. I was afraid, doctor. Mortally
afraid.'

Jackson rode in silence through the muddy streets, wondering why
Percy Piggott should suddenly require his presence. When doctors had
been needed before at Thursday Hall, they came down from London
either by fast post-chaise, or on the recently opened London to Chatham
railway that reduced the time of the journey from three hours to one.

A gusty wind blew a fine mist of rain from the river, sullen a
unpolished pewter beneath the half moon. Thames barges, red sail
furled, and moored in rows near the quay, swayed slightly, holding
leeboards close to their hulls like the folded wings of great black sea-birds

Lights glimmered aboard the Indiaman *Coromandel*, a three-maste
schooner. Ships from India and the spice islands of the East favoured a
anchorage at Gravesend. The river ran deep there, and victuals wer
easily obtainable at a reasonable price.

A few fishermen rowed out to the centre of the river to lay their nets
the incoming tide usually brought in a shoal of fish from the sea, some
times even salmon. Next morning, these men would fight for a place o
Piggott's quay to sell their catch to Piggott's men – at whatever price
Percy Piggott decided. He owned their houses, he fixed their rents – an
then he set a limit on what they could earn.

Jackson reached the tall iron gates of Thursday Hall. The lodgekeepe
unlocked them, raising a flaring tarred torch above his head to examir
Jackson's face and make certain he was neither unexpected no
undesirable. The gates clanged behind him, and gravel crunched lik
broken glass under the hooves of Jackson's horse. He dismounted at th
front door, tugged a long brass bell-handle. A bell pealed faintly and fa
away within the deep recesses of the great house. Footsteps, the creak o
shoes, and a footman opened the door.

'Doctor Jackson.'

'The back door please, doctor. Tradesmen's entrance.'

'But I come here at Mr Piggott's urgent request.'

'It is his strict instruction, sir. Tradesmen and physicians to the bac
door.'

The servant closed the front door in Jackson's face; he heard th
insulting slam of bolts. Jackson's right hand tightened instinctively an
angrily into a fist at this boorish reception, and his left gripped the hand
of his bag. He would leave at once. Then he relaxed. He had come th

far; he might as well go through with his visit, which could be worth a crown or, if he called again, half a guinea.

He tied up his horse at a ring on one side of the front pillar, walked around the dark house and through a latticed side-gate. A dim glow showed an open kitchen doorway. He went through this to a yellow-painted corridor, where the smell of stale cooking fat and sea coal hung sourly on the air. One of the new gas lamps blazed on a wall; the flame sent eerie shadows trembling along the tiled floor.

The footman was waiting for him.

'This way, doctor,' he said, more civilly.

'Did I not treat your wife the other day?' Jackson asked him, seeing the man's face clearly for the first time under the gas light.

'You did, doctor, and my thanks to you. She is now in much better health.'

'I hope she keeps that way. She has a weak chest, you know. This poor weather is not good for people with consumptive tendencies.'

The man shrugged, suddenly not bullying but pathetic in his white wig, his pale blue breeches and stockings, his velvet coat with its golden epaulettes.

'I know that, doctor, but what is a man to do? I do not earn enough to keep her and our four children in food, sir. She must work, too. She's in the laundry room now, weak as she is.'

He tapped on a door. A voice inside called: 'Come.'

The footman bowed deeply, and opened the door. Jackson went into a warm room walled with leather-backed books, red and green and brown, lettered in gold, on white shelves. Busts of Roman emperors regarded him with stony eyes from the tops of fluted plinths; Caesar wore a garland of laurel leaves.

Percy Piggott was seated in a leather armchair at the fire. Flames, glowing red through the diamond fretwork of the polished brass fender, made his face seem rough and raw as uncooked steak. He was a short, fat man with small, bad-tempered eyes. He nodded towards Jackson, but did not leave his chair.

'Ah, doctor, you took your time, I see,' he said, shortly. 'A more pressing engagement?'

He pulled out a watch from his waistcoat pocket, looked at it and frowned, as though feeling the hands might somehow lie to him.

'I was attending another patient,' Jackson explained. 'Old Mrs Gray. One of your tenants, I understand, and under some apprehension that she is about to be evicted.'

'Really? I have so many tenants, and to my mind most of them are wretched, lying scum.'

'Not to mine, sir. Mrs Gray is a most respectable widow who is looked after by her son, Tom, a fisherman. I promised I would speak to you on her behalf.'

'Really? Well, you have. But I cannot concern myself with such a petty matter. If she is being put out of her dwelling, there must be a good reason. Either she cannot pay the rent, or she will not. Now, to a matter of importance. The reason for calling you here.'

'Before we discuss that, sir, if I may speak further on the subject? To be put out of her cottage at her age, and ill and lonely, is to Mrs Gray not a petty matter but a question of the most supreme importance.'

'For God's sake, man, desist! I called you here to see my sister, Miss Amelia Piggott, not to discuss the status of some tenant I have never even heard of until now.'

'Very well, sir. Where is Miss Piggott?'

'In bed, of course. Where else? You know her condition?'

'I know nothing about her. I have not attended her before.'

'Well, you will attend her now. She has the vapours, man. One of these damned feminine things. She is deliberately acting as though she is mad, or she may *be* mad – I do not know. She cries out hysterically, beating her pillows with her fists. This afternoon she made as though to attack her own maid, so I decided to send for you. Not that I like to use a local country doctor, but needs must. It would take a London man time to get here, and her condition demands instant attention.'

'Then I had better see her at once.'

'You had indeed, man. You have already tarried long enough.'

Mr Piggott pulled a tasselled bell-rope irritably. The footman, who had been listening in the corridor, opened the door and again bowed low.

'Take the doctor to Miss Amelia's room. Fetch for him whatever he may want. Hot water, wine – for the patient only, of course – or whatever else is needed for his professional purposes. Then wait outside Miss Amelia's door to take his instructions.'

Jackson followed the man along a carpeted hall, up a veined marble stairway that curved gently to another landing, heavily curtained and carpeted. The flunkey tapped lightly on one door, put his ear against the panel and listened. There was no answer. He glanced nervously at the doctor. Jackson pushed by him and turned the handle.

The door opened into a large bedroom. A coal fire burned low in the grate, and thick brocade curtains had been drawn across white wooden shutters to seal out any draught from the windows. Two small gas flames burned in frosted glass globes, one on each side of the wall above the four-poster bed. Drawers in a dressing table had been wrenched open and clothes were strewn across the floor, together with little sachets of lavender.

From the bed, wild-eyed, hair matted and damp with sweat, Miss

Piggott stared at him with all the alarm and antagonism of a wild animal at bay. Jackson closed the door behind him, bowed, and put down his black leather bag on the top of a side table.

'You are Doctor Jackson?' she asked him.

'The same. I hear you have not been well, madam?'

She looked at him again and suddenly, unexpectedly, she smiled. All trace of wildness vanished from her countenance. She nodded towards the door.

'Open it,' she whispered. The footman, who had been on his knees outside, one eye at the keyhole, almost fell inside the room.

'Tell him there is no need for him to stay. I know he wants to spy on me. And if he remains for one moment longer, I will have him and his wife and their family removed from their cottage within the hour.'

'You heard that,' the doctor told the footman. 'Please leave us.'

'Mr Piggott's orders are that I am to stay. You heard him, sir.'

'You heard *me*,' retorted Amelia Piggott coldly.

'Very good, ma'am.'

The man bowed, and shuffled miserably away down the corridor. Jackson watched him out of sight before he closed the door.

'Now,' he said, sitting on the edge of a chair near the bed, 'tell me what is causing this upset.'

He had heard that she had been thrown from her horse when out hunting during the previous autumn, shortly before he arrived in Gravesend. The animal had rolled on her, but although its weight had not broken any of her bones, she had been left without any feeling in her legs and could not walk.

Specialists had travelled from London to examine her. They had prescribed treatment as varied as bleeding to pummelling her legs with damp knotted towels. One had even attempted to shock her system by connecting bare wires to her ankles and tying the ends of the wires to a pole erected outside her window, in the hope of attracting lightning during the winter storms, a remedy in which he claimed great confidence. But all treatments were without effect. Jackson had followed the case at one remove, because some of the visiting specialists purchased drugs at Mr Stapleford's pharmacy and he passed on medical details to his tenant.

'There's nothing broken, nothing that they can *see*, doctor,' Stapleford had explained. 'Her muscles appear to be in order, but apparently there exists no means of activating them.'

'Perhaps some nerve is severed internally?' Jackson had suggested.

The chemist shrugged. 'That may be so. But then I would have thought that these clever physicians would have discovered it. You know what *I* think? It's a punishment from the Almighty on the whole family.

Her father, old man Piggott, was a gambler – and a cheat. His nickname was The Fox, he was that sly and cunning. He won the whole estate at a game of cards that went on for two days and a night. After that, Lord Quendon, whose family had owned everything around here for hundreds of years, was so upset, so full of grief, that he went out and hanged himself. Then old man Piggott moved in. Now the Lord has seen fit to punish his daughter in this way. A pity, for she is a kind lady, by all accounts. Not like her brother Percy.'

Jackson stroked his chin as he considered the position. How could he, newly qualified, hope to cure her when the greatest medical experts in the land had failed?

Amelia explained that she could only move about her room on crutches, and with two maids to support her. The estate carpenter had made a special chair on wooden wheels for her, and her personal maid would push her in this up and down the corridor outside the room. If she wished to leave the house, two servants had to carry her downstairs, and then place her in this chair in the sun or the shade.

'You are suffering pain now?' Jackson asked her.

'Not from my legs, doctor. But I must tell you, I *am* in pain. From my heart.'

'You have palpitations?'

Jackson leaned across the bed and placed his ear against her chest. Her heartbeat was fast, but regular. She seemed healthy, apart from this extraordinary and crippling disability. At her age, she should have been married for years and carrying her second or third child by a husband who was a landowner, a Member of Parliament, or a successful barrister.

'I *think* I can trust you,' she said at last, almost asking a question instead of stating her opinion.

'I hope so, Miss Piggott. We physicians take the oath of Hippocrates. Nothing we hear in confidence is ever repeated to any third party.'

'I am relieved to hear that. The footman you sent away has told me how much time you have spent helping his wife – although she cannot afford a penny piece in payment for your treatment. I am, as you can see, virtually a prisoner here. If I go out – or rather if I'm taken out by others – my brother knows where I go and who I see; often what our conversation has been. I felt I *had* to talk to someone in private, person to person, out of the hearing of any third party.

'You are the only person I could think of to whom I can mention a matter about which I dare not even hint to others. That is the reason I pretended to be out of my mind, so that my brother would send for you in a hurry rather than wait a day until a specialist could attend from London. I am not mad, doctor, but I am distraught. Now, tell me, do you know the conditions of my father's will?'

'I have no idea whatever of them,' Jackson replied.

'Then I must tell you. They are of significance in this situation. I am the elder child. Everything was left to me until Percy was born. Then, of course, as the son, he had to inherit, and so the will was changed in his favour.

'But Father did not like Percy's ways. He did not approve of the type of women he would bring to the house, or of his gambling friends, or his habit of being disgustingly rude to anyone he considered to be his social or financial inferior. Perhaps these ways reminded him of his own early life. Father had little money of his own until he won the estate at a card game, as you may already know.'

Jackson inclined his head.

'So Father changed his will. He left the estate in the hands of trustees, all men of substance and probity. The trust possesses a curious clause. If I, his only daughter, should marry a man of whom *I* felt Father would have approved – no one else, not even my brother or the trustees, doctor, just *me* – the trust would at once be broken, and all would be left to me. Except, of course, for an annuity of £3,000 a year for my brother.'

'Does your brother accept this, Miss Piggott?'

'He has to. But, understandably, he bitterly resents this clause. He has tried on several occasions to have the trust broken and these strict conditions set aside, but always unsuccessfully, for the will contains a further clause.

'If he disputes it, and should the trustees be unwise enough to uphold his plea, the entire estate will at once revert to the family of the man from whom my father won it at the card table, the late Lord Quendon, with just enough property left to bring *me* an income of £3,000 a year. There would then be no provision whatever for him. Not one penny piece!'

'I can appreciate his feelings, Miss Piggott. It is a harsh will.'

'My father was a harsh man, Dr Jackson. My brother takes after him, I feel.'

'But you do not intend to marry, Miss Piggott?'

'As I am, it would be quite impossible, and even improper, for me to do so. Whoever married me, doctor, would, in my opinion, do so for one reason only – to gain access to my money, so that he could spend it as he wished. I would simply become his source of income. The sort of man who would contemplate such a liaison is not one I could respect, let alone love. He would remind me constantly of my own brother.

'Until a month or six weeks ago, doctor, I was prepared to accept that fate had thought fit to strike me down in this way. I thought that perhaps I could make some sort of future for myself in good works, in embroidery, or in making clothes for the deserving poor. Then, by total chance, I met a man who I believe *could* love me for myself, not for my money, were I able to accept his love. Never have I experienced such joy and happiness as when I have been in his company.'

'So you *do* wish to marry, Miss Piggott?'

'This gentleman wishes to marry me, doctor,' she corrected him firmly. 'But he is fit, healthy – a man of vigour, a sportsman, recently retired as a major in the Lancers, with property in Lincolnshire bequeathed to him by his late father, and interests in commerce of various kinds. He is wealthy and has no need whatever of any money of mine. But, of course, the whole idea of accepting his hand is impossible.'

'Nothing is impossible, Miss Piggott. All I will accept is that *you* feel that this happy prospect is impossible. But that is only your personal view, not the view of this gentleman. How did you meet him?'

'A friend of my brother saw him standing by his carriage one evening, at the side of the London road. An axle had shed a wheel and, since he was travelling to Gravesend, my brother's friend gave the traveller a lift here. Percy grudgingly offered him hospitality for the night.

'He owns a clipper ship, *Coromandel*, presently lying off Gravesend. She is engaged in the India trade and has been here for several weeks owing to some fault, I know not what. He came from London to oversee repairs to it himself.'

'I had been carried downstairs at the time, and so was introduced. I was immediately impressed by the kindness in his face. We have met several times since at a friend's house. That he must soon go out of my life is what I feel I cannot bear. It would have been infinitely better never to have experienced the shining warmth of happiness I have known, even at our few meetings with others present, than to see this prospect die.'

'Is there anything I can say or do to make you change your mind, or at least persuade you to think again?' Jackson asked.

'I could not marry him as I am, doctor. You must see that. My brother spreads gossip about me that I am not in my right mind. He wants to discredit me.'

'Let me examine your legs now, Miss Piggott, and form my own conclusions.'

Jackson pulled back the silk sheet, lifted her nightgown, crossed one of her legs on the other, and tapped the knee cap gently with a bamboo mallet from his bag. Her leg jerked slightly. There was some small reflex action. He felt the muscles, soft and flabby from lack of use, but he could not find any serious internal damage.

The machinery of the joints and muscles appeared sound, if wasted; what was lacking was any means to co-ordinate them, to set them in motion. He pulled up the sheet again, pondering the problem.

'With such a superficial examination, I can find nothing seriously wrong, except that – for some reason quite beyond me – your legs do not respond to your wishes. Are you having any treatment?'

'There is no real treatment, so I am informed.'

'I find it difficult to go against the diagnosis of experts. I am a local practitioner, not a specialist. But sometimes even the most puzzling case can be reduced to its basic, much simpler components.'

'Is there *anything* you can do, doctor?'

'At present, I just do not know. I will consider the problem,' he replied guardedly. 'Then I will return and tell you what course we will adopt. And now, since you are understandably upset, I will give you a little laudanum, which will compose you to sleep. In the morning, events will look less melancholy.'

'In the morning, unfortunately, they look much more so. When the light is bright, I see in the mirror the face of a bedridden cripple, a woman doomed to spinsterhood.'

Amelia began to sob. Jackson poured a little milky fluid into a beaker, added water from a carafe on the bedside table, and handed the beaker to her. She drank it obediently, grimacing at the taste, and then motioned to Jackson to open a small drawer of the bedside table. It contained an unsealed envelope. She shook out ten golden sovereigns and gave them to him.

'This is far beyond my fee, I assure you,' he told her, embarrassed at such prodigality.

'I can do what I please with my own money, doctor,' she replied shortly. 'This is, after all, one of the few actions I can still take unaided. I await with the liveliest interest the results of your deliberations.'

Jackson bowed to her, let himself into the corridor. The flunkey was waiting for him, just out of earshot.

'Mr Piggott would like to see you, sir,' he announced. Jackson followed him down the stairs into the library. Piggott was standing in front of the fire, hands clasped behind his back. A decanter of port and two glasses reflected the fire. Piggott filled one glass, drained it, refilled it. He did not offer a glass to the doctor.

'You have taken your time,' he began accusingly, wiping his lips with the back of his hand.

'I had to examine the patient, Mr Piggott,' Jackson replied mildly. 'You surely would not propose that I should hurry such an examination?'

'She's a damn' good-looking girl, my sister,' said Piggott. 'I don't know if it's delicate for a young man like you to examine a young lady on her own.'

'I have delivered many young ladies of babies, and on their own,' retorted Jackson.

'But with a midwife present?'

'Not always. But what did you wish to see me about? To discuss my professional conduct or medical etiquette?'

'I don't know if I altogether like your manner, doctor.'

'I could say the same of yours, Mr Piggott. You summon me here in great urgency, and when I present myself at the front door you send me, like a tradesman or a debt collector, to the servants' entrance. Now you criticise the examination you asked me to give your sister as a matter of great urgency.'

'You are being damned insolent, sir,' said Piggott. He took two paces towards Jackson. 'I have a good mind to give you a hiding to beat some good manners into you.'

'Then why do you not follow your inclination?'

The flunkey looked in horrified astonishment from one man to the other as Piggott thrust his sweating face towards Jackson: pig eyes, flecked with matter at the corners, yellow teeth in slimy gums, individual bristles where his razor had slipped around his jaw. Jackson did not move.

'I could not waste my time,' said Piggott slowly, taking a pace back towards the fire.

'So why do you wish to see me?'

'In my opinion, there is nothing whatever wrong with my sister. Only the damned vapours some women get – or pretend they get.'

'She is unable to walk, Mr Piggott.'

'She doesn't *try* to walk, damn it!'

'I understand that she has frequently tried and failed.'

'You understand too damned much,' retorted Piggott. 'You are all the same, you sawbones. Long on talk, and short on cures. What treatment have you prescribed for her fits of madness, pray?'

'I have given her a specific, and I will call again shortly to see how she is responding to my treatment.'

'You will not come into this house again,' declared Piggott angrily. 'Of that I can assure you.'

'She is my patient, sir. In my care. She has invited me to return.'

'I own this house,' retorted Piggott. 'You will stay away.'

'That is for Miss Piggott to say. But one thing I can promise you, sir, I will stay out of your way. I am not accustomed to such discourtesy from a man of any class, let alone from someone who purports to be a gentleman. Goodnight to you.'

Jackson picked up his bag and left Piggott standing there, glaring after him.

He was back in his lodgings, and his horse in its stable, within half an hour. He took out the ten coins, laid them in a row on his dressing-room table, side by side. The gold glowed in the lamplight, more than he earned in a month treating poor people – yet this was the price for ten minutes' talk to a rich patient. The incongruity disturbed and excited him. He had never possessed so much money of his own.

Money, enough money, he realised, represented freedom, independence. He could do much good with great wealth – as well as live in the style of a prince: but he was never likely to have the opportunity, for the profession he followed was notoriously ill-paid. But if he could be paid so much for so little time with Miss Piggott, what would his fee amount to for a cure?

On impulse, he left his lodgings and walked down by the edge of the river to consider the problem. There must be an answer somewhere; of that he was certain, but how to find it?

The fishing fleet was going out now, their dim lights reflected on the rippling surface of the tide. He walked past cottages where chained dogs barked warnings. Warehouses stood shuttered, blank walled, with only a watchman warming his hands by a fire of salty driftwood. Jackson paused outside a hovel where a light glowed dimly behind a ragged curtain. It took him a few moments to realise that he had arrived outside Mrs Gray's house. He knocked on the door. It opened quickly. A man of his own height and age, dressed in blue serge trousers, thick boots and a heavy turtle-neck blue sweater, looked at him enquiringly, then with relieved recognition.

'You are too late, doctor,' he said sadly. 'Just by minutes, but still too late.'

'Too late? What do you mean? I saw your mother barely an hour ago,' Jackson replied, recognising her son Tom.

'Mr Piggott's agent has just left. He has given us notice to be out by morning. If you had been here, you might have made him change his mind.'

'But I have just come from Thursday Hall, where I was called to Miss Amelia. I spoke to Mr Piggott about your mother. He must have acted at once.'

'We were owing rent, I know, doctor, because Mr Piggott owed me for a week's catch. But I pawned some of my fishing nets and raised the money. Now his agent says it is too late. We have been dispossessed.'

'But where can you take your mother?'

'To my cottage. There is nowhere else.'

'But you live in two rooms, with your wife and child. There is no place there for an ill old woman.'

'Doctor, there is no place for an ill old woman or an ill old man anywhere in this world – if they lack money.'

'Let me see her.'

Jackson followed Tom Gray into the shabby room. Mrs Gray was propped up in bed, huddled in threadbare blankets and an old woollen shawl. Despite the driftwood fire in the grate, the room felt chilly. Thin fingers of wind stirred the ragged curtain at the windows. The old woman did not recognise the doctor. Jackson felt her pulse; it was slow and heavy and feeble. One glance at her face showed she had not long to live.

There was a faint cry from the next room. Jackson looked inquiringly at Tom.

'My daughter, Joanna,' he explained. 'She's a very nervous child. She's losing her milk teeth and there's one that is worrying her. She won't let me pull it out. Screams if I go near, and I don't want any disturbance with my mother here.'

'Let me see her.'

Jackson went into the next room. A child of nine or ten sat on a stool facing the fire, sucking at her tooth. Jackson took a penny piece out his pocket.

'A present for you to buy a bag of sweets,' he explained as she turned towards him. 'But let me look at that tooth first. A tooth like that does not deserve any sweets.'

The girl obediently opened her mouth, her eyes on the copper coin in the doctor's hand. He could see the loose rootless molar in her lower jaw; a touch and it could be detached.

'Shut your eyes and hold my hand very tightly, and the penny passes to you,' he told her. She gripped his hand strongly. Suddenly he jerked her arm and at the same time twisted the loose tooth with his other hand. It came out instantly. The girl opened her eyes and smiled up at him, turning the penny over and over in her hand. She had forgotten all about the tooth.

'Thank you, doctor,' said her father.

'It is nothing.'

Jackson put his hand into his pocket again and this time took out two of the sovereigns Amelia Piggott had given to him; there seemed to be a certain kind of justice in giving them to the man her brother was evicting.

'Take these,' he told him. 'Buy your mother some comforts she might not otherwise enjoy. I fear she may have little enough time left for them: fruit, a capon, a flagon of brandy, anything she fancies.'

'I cannot take charity,' said Tom hoarsely.

'This is not charity, it is a gift. And one day I may call upon you for help.'

'You call on me, doctor, and I swear to God and on my heart I will not let you down.'

Early next morning, a messenger, smart in his pillbox hat, blue uniform and polished boots, presented himself at Mr Stapleford's shop. He had a sealed letter to deliver to Dr Richard Jackson personally. Jackson opened the envelope, glancing at the heavily embossed heading '408, Harley Street, London'. The letter was from his late examiner in surgery, Mr Johannes Beech.

> My dear Jackson,
>
> I wonder if you hold for me the warm regard with which I remember you as a student?
>
> This communication is to apprise you of a situation in which I seek your help. Would you be so kind as to visit me in my rooms here, at your earliest convenience? In the earnest hope that you can accommodate me in this request, I will keep free tomorrow morning, all Thursday afternoon and all Friday morning.
>
> Pray be so kind as to write the time and date when you will be able to wait upon me on the bottom of this letter so that the messenger can bring your answer to me. Your journey will not be wasted.

Dr Jackson carried the note into his room, wrote 'Eleven o'clock' on the paper, and paused. It would not be wise to admit he had so few calls on his time that he could visit Mr Beech at any hour on all three days if need be. He therefore added the word 'Friday', resealed the envelope and handed it to the messenger.

Mr Beech's chambers were rather more commodious than Dr Jackson's. A butler, wearing a black swallowtail coat and striped trousers, opened the door; a maid bustled into the waiting room carrying coals for the fire; leather chairs were heavily studded with brass dome-headed nails. The room had more the appearance of the smoking room in a gentleman's club than a surgeon's home.

The butler ushered him into Mr Beech's consulting room. On a small table stood a tobacco jar, bearing the crest of a Cambridge college, and a rack of pipes. Skeletons of rare African apes and other animals were displayed inside glass-fronted cases. Beech, avuncular, plump, smiling, looked like the genial bishop of a fashionable see.

He had not changed since Jackson had attended his lectures and demonstrations on the bodies of the two criminals hanged for murder the college was allowed each year for such purposes. Against this background of opulence, as opposed to the austere surroundings of the dissecting room and the stench of decomposing viscera, Mr Beech appeared an enviable figure.

'My dear Jackson,' he said warmly, striding across the room to grip his former pupil's hand. 'How typically kind of you to come and to come so speedily.'

'I hope that all is well, sir?' Jackson replied.

'Very well indeed, dear fellow. But you may be surprised when I tell you why I invited you here: I wish you to conduct an operation for me.'

'For you, sir? But you are one of the foremost surgeons in the land. Your speed is a byword. Three minutes to remove a leg, two for an arm. Although I understand, sir, from reports in the newspapers, there may be rather less need for such swift action in the future. Some American doctors are claiming to have discovered a means of putting the patient to sleep before an operation.'

'These claims are as yet not highly regarded in serious surgery,' Beech replied. 'Something of the same sort, little better than a parlour trick, has been invented by a so-called scientist, Humphry Davy, in Cornwall, of all places. Hardly a centre of surgical research, eh? Davy discovered that if he introduced 200 grains of compact nitrate of ammoniac into a glass retort and applied a slow spirit lamp, a gas, known either as nitrous phosoxyd or gaseous oxyd of azote, or, as I prefer to call it, nitrous oxide, would be released.

'He drew this off into a bladder, applied it to the patient's nose, and instructed him to inhale. The patient became pleasantly drowsy, and in several cases fell totally asleep. Afterwards, he would recover with a stupid smile on his face as though he had been to some happy land. Davy called it laughing gas. I call it bloody nonsense!

'Serious practitioners of the art and craft of surgery have a name for this sort of demonstration – "ether frolics". I have attended private parties where sealed bladders of this gas have been introduced. The guests were invited to open them and breathe deeply. They would then jump about and fall over insensible, often in a most degrading and disgusting fashion. I operate in the old British way. Fast, incisive, decisive.'

'But in America, sir, so I have read, a dentist, William Morton, with two medical colleagues, Horace Wells and John Warren, of the Massachusetts General Hospital, has also been experimenting with ether gas.'

'Yankees will experiment with anything, dear fellow. I am past such tricks.'

'I would have thought, sir, that in due time, when experiments are over, there could be a use for some such system to relieve the pain of women in child-birth.'

'Then you would have thought wrongly, Jackson,' Mr Beech retorted. 'Would you go against the teaching of God: "In sorrow thou shalt bring forth children"? Does the Holy Bible mean nothing to you, eh?'

Jackson could see that Mr Beech was finding the conversation irksome. As with many men of his age and wealth, the prospect of any change was not pleasant to contemplate. He knew what he knew, and to him this knowledge was sufficient.

'What is the operation you say you wish me to perform on your behalf?' Jackson asked, diplomatically changing the subject.

The older man turned away for a moment, selecting a cigar from the humidor. He offered one to Jackson, who declined it. Mr Beech lit the Havana and regarded the glowing end thoughtfully.

'I have never gone against my instincts in a lifetime devoted to the practice of surgery, Jackson,' he began pontifically. ' I cannot afford to risk any hints or rumours that might be circulated, either about my professional capabilities or my ethics.

'I honour my good name more than the prospect of money, and I must now be especially circumspect, for a reason dear to my lady wife. There is the possibility, and I speak to you in the strictest confidence, that the sovereign may honour me with a knighthood. But should my name in the meantime attract any criticism or contumely whatever, then this high distinction could easily be put in jeopardy.'

'I am pleased that you have the expectation of the honour, sir,' said Jackson, 'but what criticism could conceivably attach to your name?'

'Let me explain. I have been offered a huge sum to conduct an operation which, to be frank, I am not happy to perform.'

'Do you mean an abortion, sir? To terminate an unwanted pregnancy of some daughter of the aristocracy?'

'I do not. Nothing like that at all. Indeed, you may find nothing strange in the request the patient makes. But see him for yourself.'

'Where is he, sir?'

'Waiting in an outer room. I should add, Jackson, that should you proceed – as I greatly hope you will – I will pay you handsomely from the fee I have been promised. I will give you one hundred sovereigns.'

This was generous indeed; nearly twice the annual salary of the surgeon to the Royal Navy in Chatham, four miles from Gravesend.

'Pray let me see the patient and hear from his own lips what operation he wishes to be performed.'

Beech pulled a bell rope. The butler entered. Jackson followed him into a smaller room. A man was standing with his back to them, looking out on to the foggy street. The clop of horses' hooves, the clang of hand-bells from muffin sellers bearing trays of pastry on their heads, came faintly into the room, muffled by glass and distance. The man turned and looked at Jackson enquiringly. He was just under six feet in height, of thin build, slightly bald, with a gingery beard. His shoulders were narrow, and he had a nervous twitch in his right eye. He clasped and unclasped his hands, as though forcing himself to reach a decision. He was clearly under great strain.

'I am Dr Jackson, sir. Mr Beech advises me you wish a consultation?'

'You are correct. You do not know my name,' said the other man, 'and forgive me if I do not acquaint you with it until a later date. For the time being, let me be Mr Brown. But you seem young to be a surgeon?'

'It was said of William Pitt, when he was Prime Minister, that he was guilty of the crime of being a young man. It is a crime for which time has its own punishment.'

The thin man smiled; his face was friendly but austere. He did not have the appearance of a man of the world, yet he was obviously a man of means. His suit was of good cloth and cut, his linen expensive, and his boots of the best and most supple leather.

'I wish you to operate on my right leg.'

'It is giving you pain? You have broken a bone that has been set badly?'

'No, sir, it is not giving me pain and I have never broken any bone in my body. Allow me to suggest you examine the leg before I explain my reasons.'

Jackson had the impression that the man was testing him in some way, making up his mind about his capabilities. Brown lay down on a couch and Jackson felt his right ankle gently but expertly, then the bones and joints in his leg and foot.

'Does this give you any pain?'

'Certainly not.'

'Then what operation do you wish me to perform?'

'I want you to amputate my right foot.'

'Cut off your right foot?' Jackson repeated in amazement. 'But why? You would have to wear a false foot, a crude, painful, wooden thing, with a cavity like an egg-cup to be strapped to fit the stump of leg remaining. And that stump would bleed and rub raw in a walk of more than a hundred paces. You would always need two sticks, maybe crutches, for the rest of your life. Are you joking with me, sir? Is this a jest or a wager of some kind you have with Mr Beech?'

'Certainly not. It is a most serious request. I have the money, and you have the skills – or so Mr Beech assures me. He speaks most highly of your competence.'

'I am flattered by his opinion, which I value greatly. But such an amputation would be madness. I see patients every day who wish to be cured of all manner of infirmities – goitres, cancers, haemorrhages of blood, broken limbs, loss of sight. They would give all they possessed simply to be whole and healthy. And you, sir, fit and well, wish to be mutilated and join their company?'

'I have my reasons.'

'Then I suggest, Mr Brown, that you explain them to some other surgeon. I cannot do this. My calling is to help people, not to deform them.'

'You would be helping me, sir.'

'That is not how I see the matter.'

'I have offered Mr Beech a large fee to perform this operation for me.'

'He has told me. But he is unwilling to attempt it. So am I.'

'I admire you for your directness, Dr Jackson. I have seen many eminent medical gentlemen besides Mr Beech, all holding the highest qualifications, and they gave me the same answer.'

The patient sat up, swung himself off the couch, and began to put on his clothes and boots.

'Where will you go now?' Jackson asked him. 'Do not put yourself into the hands of quack practitioners. Such dangerous paths can lead to poisoning and death in agony.'

'But surely I would endure agony enough having my foot removed by the swiftest surgeon in the land?'

'Not necessarily. There is now a means of sending a patient to sleep, so that an operation can be carried out with minimum pain. But to remove your foot without such merciful oblivion would require you to be strapped to a table and held down by strong men, with a leather gag in your mouth lest you bite out your own tongue. Have you considered this, sir?'

'I have.'

'Then what do you seek to gain by undergoing such a terrible experience?'

'You are a younger man than me, doctor. Although I was fortunate to be born with wealth sufficient to afford virtually anything I wished to buy, I have never known real happiness. I bought a commission in the cavalry. I commanded a squadron of horse in the West Indies. I have visited both Americas, and the Far East. I have been able to buy anything I wanted – except the one thing beyond all cost, because it is priceless: happiness with the woman I wish to marry.'

'I am indeed sorry to hear that, sir. But how would undergoing such a serious and unnecessary operation improve your chances of finding such happiness?'

'You may wonder, doctor, why Mr Beech called on *you* especially to see me?'

'He told me that it was because he had been my instructor in surgery, and he had warm recollections of our association.'

'So he has. But there is another reason. You practise, I understand, in the fishing village of Gravesend on the River Thames?'

'I do indeed.'

'I believe you have been called to see a patient there, one Miss Piggott, who as a result of a riding accident is unable to walk?'

'I have.'

'Is it your opinion that she will ever walk again?'

'I would not like to say, sir. I do not feel it fitting to discuss any patient's ailment with a stranger – as you doubtless would not wish me to go out into the street and advise passers-by of the nature of the operation you wish carried out.'

'It would not matter one whit to me,' Brown replied with a sad smile. 'You do not know my real name, so whatever you said, whoever you told, could not harm me.

'But I will tell you why I wish to be made a cripple. I love Miss Piggott. She refuses to marry me because she feels she would be unable to be a proper wife, since she is now virtually confined to bed. I take a different view. I believe that if I were to marry her and devote my life and fortune to her welfare – and, of course, take her away from that disgraceful scoundrel of a brother – our life together could be totally fulfilled.

'Since she will not wed me whole, I am prepared – willingly – to undergo this deliberate surgery in the hope and expectation that it would convince her of my feelings. Then she might change her mind.'

'So you are seriously contemplating an amputation, with an effect totally impossible to reverse, in the hope that a lady, who I understand you have only met on a few occasions, will marry you?'

'Who told you I have only met her a few times?'

'She did. She had resigned herself to her condition, until by chance she met you and realised, as I think from your own words you do yourself, how different life could be – if only. . . .'

' "If only", doctor! The two saddest words in the English language. But, enough. I have been frank with you. Now that you know my reasons for seeking this operation, will you reconsider your refusal and carry it out?'

'I appreciate your situation, but I could never condemn an active man to become a cripple.'

The thin man turned away for a moment and kicked a loose coal in the fireplace. Sparks flared up. He turned back to Jackson.

'So you refuse to help me?'

'I did not say that,' Jackson corrected him, and paused. An idea was forming in his mind; a vague plan seen in the distance like a faint light far off in a dark forest.

'Do you mean you can help me in some other way?'

'I can try to help you *and* Miss Piggott. As on the river or at sea, if a vessel founders and another goes to her aid, the agreement is: no cure, no pay. I would, however, seek reimbursement for some essential expenses, which I will itemise, and which should not amount to more than ten sovereigns at the outside. I can offer you nothing but a possibility of success, Mr Brown, not a certainty.'

'The only certainty that life offers is that one day we are all required to lose it,' Brown replied.

'Then, sir, this is my proposal. . . .'

Joe Dover, the landlord of The Piggott Arms at Gravesend, was a former sailor; the backs of his hands were liberally tattooed with blue and red palm trees and faces that could smile or frown as he flexed his fingers. He took a liberal view of his responsibilities as innkeeper, and was always prepared to hire out a spare room in his hostelry for a cock fight, or an outhouse for a match between bare-fist pugilists on whom the wealthiest tradesmen in the town, and even the gentry, placed their bets. He fully realised the value of discretion in some of the arrangements he made. Jackson knew this and believed he could trust him; greed, if nothing else, would ensure his silence.

Dover listened respectfully, nodding from time to time, while Jackson outlined his requirements.

'Two quiet bedrooms – your best, Mr Dover, with a communicating door. I also wish the services of two strong potmen. Their aprons to be freshly washed, their hair combed and faces shaved. I need a table, strong enough to bear the weight of a six-foot man, sheets to place on this table, a pillow, and above all, your utmost circumspection.

'I am prepared to pay you two sovereigns now, the same amount when we arrive, and the same amount again one week later on the absolute understanding that not one single word of these requirements, or who may occupy these rooms, will be spoken to any third party.'

'You have my word, doctor,' said Mr Dover, impressed with the sums mentioned. 'Is there anything else you require?'

'There is. At a time to be agreed, you will attend with your potmen in a pony and trap where the road to Dartford crosses the Greenhithe road. A closed carriage will approach. You will follow it. The carriage will drive directly into the yard behind your inn here. You will all lift out the passenger travelling in the carriage, an invalid, and carry this person up the back stairs to one of these rooms. You will already have lit a fire in the grate and placed a warming pan in the bed. I also wish a firm, high-backed chair to be in the room. The curtains will be drawn and you will ensure that nobody else is upstairs at this time. You understand?'

'Perfectly, doctor. May I ask, who is this person?'

'You may ask, but I shall not answer. That is no concern of yours. Should you, by chance, catch a glance of this person's face, or recognise any other part of them, you will not pass on the information to anybody. I will personally see to it that any breach of this essential secrecy will be met with harsh reprisals. This inn is owned by the Piggott family, and you are a tenant landlord?'

'I am, doctor. My lease comes up for renewal next quarter day.'

'In the unhappy event of any of these arrangements being discussed publicly, that lease will be terminated forthwith.'

'I give you my word, doctor, no one will seek to discover who this person is.'

'Now, to continue. A gentleman will arrive at your front door, giving his name as Brown. He is tall and thin and he will wear a scarf around his face. No attempt whatever is to be made to discover his true identity or to observe his face closely. I can tell you now that he is not from this neighbourhood. You have never seen him before, and you will probably never see him again. He is Mr Brown, and that is all. Understood?'

'Understood, doctor.'

'You will take him upstairs to the second bedroom, where I will await him. We will shut and bolt the outer doors of these rooms but the connecting door between them will be left fully open, unless I say otherwise. I will bandage Mr Brown's eyes and face to preserve his anonymity. Your potmen will put on their aprons and assist him to undress to his shirt.

'He will lie on the table you have prepared and they will each hold his arms. I will place straps around the lower part of his body and the table so that he will be totally incapable of any movement on the table.'

'But why, doctor? What do you seek to do?'

'I will perform an operation with results that may affect others besides Mr Brown. I cannot carry it out at his residence, or in a hospital, where secrecy would be impossible to achieve.'

'You are not going to kill him, sir?'

'Of course not. My business is to heal, to help. Do you fully understand my requirements?'

'I do, doctor.'

Jackson opened his purse, took out two golden sovereigns and handed them to the innkeeper. Dover bit the edge of each coin to check it was not counterfeit, nodded his approval and slipped them into a pouch on his belt. They shook hands.

'Is this to be the first of many operations, sir?' he asked jocularly, cheerful now that he had received money.

'It could be,' replied Jackson with a smile. 'Perhaps we should set up in business together?'

The innkeeper roared with laughter at the suggestion; the doctor was a card all right. Jackson heard Dover's laugh echo along the corridor as he walked to the tap room. He hoped they would both be laughing at the same time on the following day.

Piggott stood in the library of Thursday Hall, thumbs in the pockets of his waistcoat, gold watch-chain stretched tightly across his stomach. The two footmen bumped the chair in which they were carrying his sister down the stairs, and set it down in front of him.

'I did not know you were going out, my dear,' Piggott said softly. 'You id not inform me of your intention.'

Just for a drive,' Amelia explained.

'Alone? It is usual, surely, for your maid to accompany you on all your excursions?'

'Sometimes I wish to be on my own with my thoughts.'

'I would have assumed you were alone enough in your room?'

'You make many wrong assumptions, Percy,' she retorted, nodding to the footmen. Piggott followed them out. The coachman opened the door of the carriage and helped to lift Amelia from the chair and set her on the buttoned leather seat. A maid wrapped a rug around her useless legs. The coachman closed the door, saluted Piggott, climbed up on the box and flicked the whip. The polished iron wheels struck sparks from the gravel. Piggott waited for the carriage to disappear down the drive, then turned to one of the footmen.

'Send the head groom here at once,' he ordered.

When the man arrived, Piggott gave him his instructions.

'Go out on one of the cobs and follow the coach. Do not get too close. Just keep it in sight.'

'And if it stops, sir?'

'You stop, too.'

'You have reason to fear there is something afoot, sir?'

'I have reason to fear nothing. Do as I order and get you gone.'

Piggott turned back into the house. Amelia had never been out on her own since her accident. She always took a maid in case she felt unwell. He wondered why today she should wish to travel on her own. He would soon know.

Richard Jackson sat astride his horse, concealed by trees inside a small wood a few yards off the main Gravesend to London road, half a mile before it crossed a lane to the fishing village of Greenhithe. The land sloped gently down on one side, and rose on the other through fields to embrace a handful of small farm buildings. As he waited, hoping that nothing had happened to delay the timing of his plan, Tom Gray came out of one of the thatched shacks behind the main farmhouse and walked slowly along the track towards him. Jackson could tell he was the bearer of bad news from the droop of his shoulders, his hesitant pace.

'I was on my way to your lodgings, doctor,' Gray explained, 'to tell you my mother has just been called to higher service with the Almighty.'

'Where is she being buried?'

'I regret, in a pauper's grave.'

'But that is unthinkable, Tom!'

'The sovereigns you kindly gave me, doctor, were seized by Mr Piggott's agent. He claimed we had left our house by the river in bad repair and would bring me before the magistrates if I did not pay. And Mr Piggott, as you may know, is chairman of the bench.'

'So your mother did not get any extra food at all? Nothing?'

'Nothing, doctor – not even a crust and dripping. I will even owe the good wife who has come to lay her out.'

'How much would a proper burial cost?' Jackson asked him.

'I believe, one pound, doctor.'

'Here are two more sovereigns,' said Jackson, handing him the coins. 'I cannot stand by and allow a good woman like Mrs Gray to be buried in a nameless grave.'

Tom, close to tears, touched his cap in salutation and thanks.

'I told you before, doctor, if I can ever pay you back, in any way, you will ask? You promise me, doctor?'

'I promise,' Jackson assured him.

As they were talking, Jackson saw a two-horse carriage coming towards him at a smart pace. Behind this, in a pony trap, sat the innkeeper and his two potmen.

Jackson hailed the coachman.

'To the rear of The Piggott Arms,' he told him. The man raised his whip in response and flicked the oiled thong about the horses' ears. The carriage clattered on.

Jackson urged his horse back into the thicket by the side of the road, turned to face the road, and sat, listening. Soon he heard the clop-clop of another horse's hooves. A groom approached, riding an old cob. Jackson recognised the green livery of the Piggott family and hailed him.

The groom reined in the cob.

'What is your business, sir?' he asked Jackson.

'I put the same question to you.'

'That is my master's affair.'

'And I see from your livery that your master is Mr Percy Piggott. I will therefore make my own assessment of your commission,' continued Jackson amiably. 'You are under orders to follow a certain coach to see where it goes. A coach that contains Mr Piggott's sister. Am I right?'

He could see from the expression of astonishment on the groom's brutish face that he was. The man said nothing but made to dig his heels into the horse's side. Jackson moved his own horse ahead of him, reached out and grabbed the bridle.

'Let me go, sir,' said the man angrily, raising his whip.

'Before you use that whip foolishly in an act that could end in your being transported for life for blatant highway violence, listen to me. Miss Piggott is taking a ride on her own. She does not wish to be followed.'

'I have my orders, sir.'

Jackson put his hand in his jacket pocket.

'And I have here one golden sovereign. It is yours if you wait here. She will return within the hour.'

'But what shall I tell Mr Piggott?' asked the man, staring at the coin covetously. He ran a furred tongue over his lips.

'That she went into town, which is true. You will then be able to follow her back, thereby earning your master's approbation – and my sovereign. Do we understand each other?'

The groom touched his hat and held out his hand.

Jackson tossed him the coin. The groom grabbed at it and missed. The sovereign fell in the dust. As he dismounted to retrieve it, Jackson dug his spurs into his own horse's flanks and caught up with the carriage as it entered the inn-yard.

He motioned Dover to close the high gates. Then he picked up the carriage rug, covering Amelia's head and shoulders with it so that her face was totally concealed from view. The two potmen carried her carefully up the back service staircase to one of the two bedrooms Jackson had rented. He instructed the two men to place her in the high-backed chair, then told them to leave the room.

When they had gone, he locked the outer door of the bedroom and removed the rug from Amelia Piggott's face, afterwards handing her a mirror. She examined her face and hair critically, then looked at Jackson enquiringly, as though to ask a question. He shook his head.

'Please do not speak, Miss Piggott,' he told her gently but firmly. 'You are about to witness a sacrifice for love which I think is unique in all medical history. It calls for quiet contemplation, for thought, for a prayer of thanksgiving that a man is prepared to do this to demonstrate his love for you – and, I must admit, I have done my utmost to dissuade him.'

'You must hear me, doctor, before it is too late,' she said desperately. 'When you came to see me, you said you wished to meet me in secret, for you planned something that would help me immeasurably. Then you told me that the man who has honoured me by asking for my hand in marriage was preparing to undergo an operation to remove a foot as a token of his feelings for me. I said I could not – and I *cannot* – allow him to do such a thing. But I had no means of communicating my feelings to him, except I came to this place.

'Now you tell me that nothing I can do or say will persuade him to change his mind. I *must* see him before this amputation, which he will regret every day of his life.'

'Of course you will see him, Miss Piggott. He is coming here to meet you. I am to perform the operation in the adjoining room. But I repeat that nothing you may say will make him waver from his firm resolve.'

'But the pain,' she protested. 'It will be unbearable for him, as for me.'

'Pain can be a pleasure where love is concerned,' Jackson assured her. 'I have also a most modern and ingenious apparatus, producing a soothing gas, which should send him to sleep, so that all should be carried out painlessly.'

'*Should?*' she asked him quickly. 'You are not certain?'

'The science of such things is still imperfect, Miss Piggott. Now please compose yourself. The gentleman will be here directly.'

Downstairs, Mr Dover was drawing a pint of strong ale when a shadow darkened the frosted door of the taproom. A tall man entered. He wore a black coat and hat; a silk scarf muffled his face. Mr Dover could only see his eyes, bright and unwavering as coals of fire.

'Mr Brown?' he asked. The man nodded.

'The surgeon is expecting you, sir.'

Dover led the way upstairs.

In the nearest bedroom, the two potmen, unusually smart in stiff aprons and clean shirts, well shaven, hair drawn back neatly from their foreheads, stood to attention like soldiers on either side of the table. This was covered by a white sheet with the folds ironed into it. At the far side of this table was the machine Jackson had obtained for dispensing gas.

It was slightly different from the one Mr Beech had described. A red rubber bladder with a long rubber tube, sealed by a spring clip, was attached to the mouth of a glass retort. Under this, a small spirit lamp burned with a blue flame. Gas fumed and writhed cloudily inside the glass, like a genie eager to be free. Through the half-open connecting door, Jackson could see Miss Piggott regarding the scene with dismay.

One of the potmen helped Mr Brown off with his coat, his scarf and his jacket. At a nod from Jackson, he went into the second bedroom.

'Thank God I am here to stop you,' Amelia said in a tremulous voice. Tears were pouring down her cheeks; she made no effort to check them. Her hands were trembling, her grief uncontrollable. Mr Brown took out a newly laundered Irish linen handkerchief and gently dabbed away her tears.

'You will not stop me,' he replied quietly. 'No one can – unless the surgeon has suddenly refused to do what he has solemnly agreed and given me his hand on?'

'I am ready to proceed,' Jackson answered him.

'You must not go through with this terrible operation,' Miss Piggott insisted. 'There is no sense whatever in such a thing.'

'I do not agree, my dear. It is my wish, my decision.'

He smiled rather sadly. 'And my leg,' he added.

'I can *never* be worthy of this sacrifice.'

'This is no sacrifice, dear Amelia. This is the only way in which I can ever approach someone as good and kind and beautiful as you.'

He picked up her hand, kissed it gently, bowed and walked back to the bedroom. Out of sight of Miss Piggott, he removed his shoes and socks and his trousers, swung himself up on the table and lay on the sheet, both hands folded across his chest, a man determined and a man at peace.

Jackson half closed the door to Amelia's room. She could now see a part of the table and Mr Brown's head and body, but not his feet.

'I am sorry, Miss Piggott,' the doctor explained. 'I would not wish you to be a witness to what I have to do. There will be sights from which it would be wise to turn away your eyes, and sounds I would not wish you to hear, but it is necessary to keep this door slightly ajar to provide a sufficient flow of air for this new gas to work properly.'

Amelia Piggott nodded; she was now completely beyond speech.

Mr Dover slipped the leather belt from his trousers and strapped it around the patient's legs below the knees, pulling it tight until Brown gasped at the constriction.

'Now!' Jackson ordered. The two potmen gripped Mr Brown's arms, leaning forward on him, putting their weight on his chest and stomach to prevent any movement of his body. He began to choke and gasp for breath.

'No tighter, I beg of you!' he cried.

Jackson removed the bladder from the apparatus, blew out the spirit lamp and held the tube at the end of the bladder near the patient's face. Then he put the bladder under his right arm, and squeezed. The gas burbled and rumbled through the narrow aperture.

'Breathe out, then in,' Jackson instructed his patient. Brown did so, choking at the strange odour of the gas. He began to fling his head wildly from side to side to escape from it. Jackson handed the bladder to Dover.

'See that he breathes deeply,' he told him. Amelia watched in fascinated horror as the doctor opened his case of instruments. On a padded, red plush bed, silver-plated saws, probes and pliers and forceps, glittered coldly in the afternoon light. He picked up an amputation saw and ran one finger cautiously along its serrated teeth, frowning as though displeased and disappointed that they appeared blunter than he had expected. The essence of successful surgery, whether with this new sleep-inducing vapour or without, was speed; the less time the operation took, the less chance of anything going wrong.

As Jackson tightened the blade with its thumb-screw, he happened to glance up and see Amelia regarding him with horror, mesmerised by the blade's glittering jagged teeth.

'Please look away, dear lady,' he advised her. 'This will not be something for untrained eyes. When I was a student, I often saw strong men faint at the sight of their first major operation. This saw is not as sharp as I would have wished. But he should feel no pain. Or, rather, little pain.'

Jackson saw Amelia wince at his words. He spun the saw easily in his hand to make sure he had the correct grip on its handle, and then twanged the blade with his thumb to test its tightness. It sang like a violin string.

'Scalpels,' he said briskly. 'And a vessel for the blood.'

'Will there be much blood, doctor?' Dover asked him anxiously. 'I am concerned about my carpet. It was new last Easter.'

'There must be some blood shed, man. After all, I am about to sever the foot of a grown man. The main artery is as thick as my little finger. If I cut it accidentally, blood will flow like a fountain of red wine until I can staunch it. I will have to work quickly, or our patient will lose not only his blood, but his life. Fetch some towels to cover your carpet.'

He turned to the patient.

'Now, sir,' he said, 'are you sleepy? Is this new gas taking effect? Do you feel *this*?'

As Jackson spoke, he suddenly reached out and seized the patient's right hand and twisted it sharply.

'Aaah!' Brown cried out in surprise and discomfort.

'I wanted to see whether you could still feel pain, sir.'

'I most certainly felt that.'

'There is something wrong, gentlemen,' said Jackson gravely, addressing Dover and the potmen as equals, not as subordinates. 'Something is seriously amiss. The gas is not coming through strongly enough. I suspect that this may be the fault of the crystals. They can quickly lose their potency. And I regret I have no more with which to recharge the retort.'

'Then I beg of you, delay the operation!' cried Brown in a voice thinned by terror and entreaty. 'I cannot endure it unless you give me something to ease the pain. You promised me I would feel nothing.'

'I am truly sorry, sir, but we must go through with it now, or else abandon the operation completely. As you know, the most discreet arrangements have been made. They cannot conceivably be repeated in a small town like this without grave risk of discovery. You must see that?'

'But the pain?' Brown screamed, all manly reserve deserting him. 'You told me, you *insisted*, it would simply be a matter of falling asleep, and when I awoke, all would be finished. Now I am to endure the agonies of hell. This was not the arrangement to which I agreed.'

'Do not concern yourself. I will cut quickly. Three minutes is my aim.'

'No! No! In the name of mercy, stop! Help me, oh, *help me*!'

Brown began to thrash about so furiously beneath the strap that the table legs lifted from the floor.

'Do not touch me with that saw! Do not dare to touch me with that blade! Untie me, gentlemen. I *order* you, *untie this strap!*'

'Calm yourself, sir. Bear this like a man. I will be swift, that I promise you. Now, to work.'

Jackson nodded to the innkeeper, picked up the saw and bent over his patient. Through the open door, Amelia could see the backward and forward motion of his right shoulder and arm, but mercifully could not actually see it slice into the flesh of the man she loved.

Brown screamed hoarsely: 'I beg of you, desist! Oh, the pain, the pain! I cannot bear it. Blood! I am bleeding to death! Amelia, my darling Amelia, help me! I implore you, *help me!*'

He began to shout incoherently in an extremity of terror and pain, writhing on the table against the strap and the combined weight of the two potmen. And, all the while, Amelia watched as Jackson's arm sawed away steadily. She could hear the rasping of each stroke and the patient's agonised, animal-like cries of pain and entreaty. She imagined the spurting spouts of his lifeblood, the tearing of tendons and sinews, the saw's cruel teeth biting through red pulpy marrow within its white-pink circle of bone.

'Hold him!' shouted Jackson, suddenly alarmed, as the table heaved and bucked like a living thing. 'If this blade slips, I will cut the main artery, and he is a dead man. Hold him, you fools! Damn you, hold him, I say!'

The table now rocked furiously from one side to the other under Mr Brown's ferocious struggles. His cries filled both rooms. The nearest potman shouted in horror: 'I *cannot* hold him, sir! The strap has gone! Stop, in the name of mercy, stop! You have cut the artery. May God be my judge, he is bleeding to his death.'

'Amelia! Oh, my beloved, *help me!*' Brown entreated her.

At that moment, they all heard a scream from the adjoining room. Amelia Piggott was down on her hands and knees in front of her chair. Her long hair trailed on the floor as her body shook with uncontrollable spasms of grief.

Jackson raced to her side, the saw still in his hand.

'Get up!' he commanded roughly, and seized her right arm. Dover gripped her left arm. Together, they jerked Amelia Piggott to her feet with as little ceremony as if she had been a sack of potatoes. For a moment, she stood uncomprehendingly, swaying slightly from side to side, head on one shoulder, eyes closed, her forehead soaked with sweat like a person in a trance.

'Go to him!' Jackson ordered in firm tones. 'He needs you. *Now!*'

Amelia nodded and, eyes still shut, took one tentative step towards the door with her left foot, another with her right – and then collapsed. Gently now, the two men held her upright and guided her back to the chair.

'You can walk!' Jackson told her triumphantly, as she sat down. 'You have broken the spell. Miss Piggott, you are cured.'

'But too late! It has all been a terrible waste, a tragedy.'

'Not so, Miss Piggott. I would not describe it as that.'

One of the potmen came into the room holding a small log of firewood and a hacksaw. He was grinning sheepishly. Out of her sight, he had been sawing the log to synchronise with Dr Jackson's movements. This was the sound she had heard so clearly.

Mr Brown untied the strap, wrapped the sheet modestly about him like a kilt and hurried to her side.

'But I do not understand,' she protested weakly as she put out her hands to hold him. 'You are not cut at all. There is no blood. What is happening? Is it all a dream?'

'It has been a nightmare, but that belongs to the past. Our concern now is the future – our future.'

'But I was told I would never walk again. The specialists all agreed, *no one* could cure me.'

'And no one did cure you, Miss Piggott,' Jackson replied. 'Love cured you. Your love – and the love of this brave gentleman I still only know as Mr Brown, who was prepared and even eager to lose his leg for love of you.

'Your feelings for him were so strong that when you thought this was actually happening, you *had* to go to him because he needed you. Then, as with the crippled man in the Bible story who took up his bed – you walked. Your disability has been swept away by the warmth of your feelings for each other.'

'And we owe this outcome entirely to Dr Jackson's ingenuity,' Brown pointed out. 'He persuaded me to mount what, at first, I must admit seemed to be a foolish charade in poor taste, with all of us acting the parts he gave us. But he convinced me that I should place myself in his hands with these totally successful results.'

He took a visiting card from his pocket, scribbled something on it, and handed it to Jackson. Then he turned to Amelia Piggott.

'Now, my dear, in front of these good people who have all diligently helped you in your recovery, will you marry me?'

'I will, I will,' she cried, weeping with sheer happiness. Then she looked up at him shyly.

'But if the ploy had *not* succeeded?' she asked him.

'It did succeed, my dear. That is what matters. But if it had not, then would willingly have gone through with the operation. Love, my dear Amelia, can conquer all things.'

And then he took her in his arms.

Mr Beech walked across the thick carpet in his consulting room to shake Jackson warmly by the hand.

'A most astonishing cure,' he said in a hushed voice. 'Amazing. Had I only heard of this from someone else, without knowing all the facts, quite simply I would not have believed it.'

'I am glad you are pleased, sir,' said Jackson. 'I feel very satisfied myself, because there has been a most happy outcome. The patient I knew as Mr Brown is actually Major the Honourable Reginald Forster. He and Miss Piggott have announced their engagement. They plan to marry at the earliest possible date. He was kind enough to inscribe his card for me.'

'I congratulate you, Jackson. Pray tell me, what gave you the idea to attempt the ploy which has been blessed with such felicitous results, eh?'

'A little girl, Mr Beech, the grand-daughter of a patient. She had a troublesome milk tooth which she would not allow anyone to touch, let alone pull. I directed her attention elsewhere and so made her forget all about her tooth, which I easily removed. I decided to attempt a rather more dramatic diversion for Miss Piggott.'

'And an equally successful one, eh? Capital, sir, capital. Now, to a matter of business. Mr Forster has paid me the sum he promised, exactly as though I had conducted the operation he requested. He is clearly a man of honour. You will doubtless remember that I promised you one hundred sovereigns if you conducted this for me? Agreed, eh?'

'Agreed, Mr Beech.'

'But, in fact, you did not conduct the operation?'

'That is so, in point of fact. But I cured the lady, sir, and so rendered unnecessary what we both felt would be a most dubious operation.'

'That is not in question. But again, as you say, in point of fact, you were not *asked* to cure the lady. You were asked to amputate the limb of an adult male patient – and no amputation took place. I think, therefore, you will agree that I am within my rights in not paying you the fee I promised if you had performed such a major amputation, eh?

'Indeed, friends learned in the law assure me I am not bound to pay you anything at all. But I am a generous man, Jackson, and you are a former student of mine. We have that bond in common. I would not therefore wish to appear eager to abide by the narrow letter of the law. Accordingly, I intend to give you not one hundred sovereigns, but fifty. What do you say to that, eh?'

'I think that your decision, while doubtless according to the law, is not according to the spirit of our agreement.'

'But surely you do not deny you did not carry out the operation you were asked to do?'

Jackson shrugged. It would be pointless to argue. This fee, and the hundred extra sovereigns Major Forster had promised him, would be recompense enough; he must not be greedy. Even so, the realisation that his former tutor, rich and successful beyond his imagining, soon no doubt to be honoured with a knighthood and admitted to an ancient order of chivalry, should stoop to act in this way, depressed and disturbed him.

'I have the sovereigns here in a bag,' Mr Beech continued. 'Would you care to count them?'

'In these circumstances, I would.'

The surgeon handed him a small blue canvas bag. Jackson slit its neck with his penknife and poured out the coins on Mr Beech's desk. He counted them, then put them in his pouch.

'You appear a little chilly, sir,' said Mr Beech, in a rather hurt tone of voice.

'If I do, Mr Beech, it is the chill of surprise. Yet I have learned much of value from this experience, possibly cheap at the price of fifty sovereigns. First, I have proved how the human mind can overcome what would appear to be insuperable malfunction of the body's muscles. I have also learned that it is prudent to have every agreement in writing, before any work is done, so that there can be no misunderstanding on either side about what each person will receive.'

'That is all you have learned, eh?' Beech asked him.

'One more thing, Mr Beech. Never to trust anybody, no matter how much I may have previously admired them. As my father used to say, an honest man has hair growing in the palm of his hand.'

'I do not greatly care for your attitude, Jackson. Avarice is an ignoble trait. Remember the teaching of the Good Book. Money is the root of all evil.'

'You are wrong, sir. It is not money, but the *love* of money.'

Even as he spoke, Jackson remembered Mrs Gray correcting him on the same point. And with this thought came another that shocked him: this love of money could easily become his love. He had been poor for too long; as a student and as a young physician and surgeon, being shown to the back door on Percy Piggott's orders, being beaten down by Mr Beech.

From now on, all this was going to change. *He* was going to change. He would become his own man, able to speak his own thoughts with no concern for what others might say. He would go his own way, because he would be rich.

From now on, Richard Jackson suddenly realised, the love of money would be his only love.

* * *

Shortly after seven o'clock on the evening of the following Tuesday, Jackson unsaddled, fed and watered his tired horse. He slipped home the two bolts on the stable door and paused for a moment before he went up to his rooms.

He had been on duty since the first call that morning, shortly after dawn, attending the premature birth of a dead child to a shrimp fisherman's wife. And he realised ruefully he had not yet taken any obvious steps towards his goal of becoming rich. The fisherman had no money to pay him; all he had earned that day from his other cases could be counted in small coins.

He picked up his bag and walked slowly across the yard to the back door that Mr Stapleford preferred him to use instead of coming in and out through the apothecary's shop. This back door opened into a small hallway with a wooden flight of stairs leading to the two rooms he rented. He turned the brass door-knob, pushed the door. It did not move. This surprised him. The door had never been locked before. Mr Stapleford always left it on the latch when he was on his rounds. Now it was locked or bolted from the inside. But why? Jackson hammered on a panel with his fist. The noise echoed from the passage and the kitchen. The house was empty. Had there been an accident? Had Mr Stapleford suddenly been called away? For some reason he could not fathom, Jackson suddenly felt uneasy.

He walked round to the front of the shop and peered in through a small glass pane let into the front door. The inside of the shop was in total darkness. He rattled the door, then tapped on the glass with the edge of a coin. Still there was no answer, no response.

He knocked on the door of the house next to the shop. An old man opened it a few inches. He had been eating his supper. A dirty napkin was tucked into the collar band of his shirt. His jaw was still moving.

'Where is Mr Stapleford?' Jackson asked him. 'He appears to have locked me out.'

'He and his wife went off in their trap in a great hurry.'

'Do you know why?'

The old man shrugged; he did not care to become involved in other people's lives, other people's problems.

'I have a key, doctor,' he said. 'Mr Stapleford doesn't know I have it. His predecessor gave it to me.'

'I am much in your debt,' said Jackson.

The man produced a key and opened the door.

'Shall I lock it?' he asked.

'No, I can bolt it from the inside.'

'You have a good name around here, doctor,' the old man told him. For a moment it seemed as though he had more to say, then he thought better of the matter and shuffled back to his supper.

Jackson struck a match to see his way through the shop, then lit a candle lantern, bolted the front door and stood for a moment, listening. Not only the shop but the whole house appeared silent, except for mice scuttling to and fro behind the wainscot.

The tiny flame reflected blue and green and amber and red from the giant glass bottles of coloured liquid Mr Stapleford kept on the shelf behind the counter, as much the mark of his calling of apothecary as the striped pole that used to signify the home of the barber surgeon. A faint not unpleasant scent of cinnamon and other spices sweetened the air.

Jackson picked up the lantern to guide him through the back premises to the stairs. He tested the back door. Not only was this locked, it was bolted top and bottom. Mr Stapleford was taking no chances. But against whom – or what? A tapping at the front door, urgent and timid, and thus somehow disquieting, made him turn.

A pale, disembodied face was peering into the shop, framed by the wood around the glass panel. Jackson undid the bolts and opened the door. Tom Gray stepped into the shop.

'Thank God I have found you, doctor,' he said breathlessly. He had been running; in the flickering light from the lantern, his face shone with sweat.

'What is the matter?' Jackson asked him. 'Why this haste?'

'Come upstairs,' said Tom urgently, ignoring Jackson's question. 'It will be safer there.'

'Safer? In what way safer?'

They climbed the back stairs to the doctor's bedroom.

'Is the back door locked?' Tom asked him, ignoring his questions.

'Locked and bolted,' Jackson replied. 'Fortunately for me, the next door neighbour had a spare key to the front.'

'Perhaps not so fortunate for you, doctor!'

'What do you mean, man? Why this mystery? Where is Mr Stapleford in any case?'

'He will have removed himself, if I know him. He is a cautious man. He does not relish commotion of any kind, and there is going to be trouble here, doctor. Percy Piggott plans to pay you a visit. I had the word from one of his scurvy servants in the tap room at The Arms. He was boasting his master was going to teach the doctor a lesson.'

'There must be some mistake,' said Jackson, puzzled. 'Perhaps he meant some other doctor?'

'You are the only doctor in this town,' Tom pointed out.

'But I have cured his sister, Miss Amelia Piggott, who has been confined to bed for months. She is now perfectly well and about to marry.'

'Maybe he did not wish her cured – or married?'

'Ah,' said Jackson slowly, remembering the clause in her father's will that Amelia had mentioned. 'Now I understand. So just what sort of lesson is he intent on teaching me?'

'I would say a painful one, doctor. They plan to break your bones, so servant said, which is why the prudent Mr Stapleford has absented self. No doubt they told him they were coming to find you. Mr gott is his landlord, remember. Mr Stapleford knows what side his ead is buttered on, doctor. His own side.'

'Then I had better go and see Piggott myself right away.'

'I beg you not to do that. You may never come back if you do. He will ave given his men plenty to drink. They may not personally wish you ny harm, but he will make sure they are spoiling for a fight – any fight. Do not give them such an opportunity.'

'But I cannot remain here, waiting to be assaulted by his ruffians, Tom. Attack is always the best defence – sometimes the only one. You an never run away from your fate.'

Tom suddenly turned and put a finger to his lips, nodding to Jackson o blow out the lantern. Both men heard footsteps in the yard. Someone vas trying the back door, gently at first and then more roughly.

'They are here,' whispered Tom grimly.

'I will meet them,' replied Jackson stubbornly. 'I have nowhere to go o, in any case, and retreat is not in my character. Also, I practise my rofession here. This is my home. Wherever I ran, I would still have to ome back – and they could be waiting for me.'

'I beg you to reconsider, doctor. Try the front door. They are probably l at the back. If you don't go now, you may not have another chance. If ey find you here, they will beat you to death.'

'I am staying.'

'Then at least pack what you can carry, before they destroy it all. uickly!'

Even as Tom spoke, he began rummaging round the room. Jackson abbed his carpet bag, tossed in a few clothes and his instruments. He at the hundred and fifty sovereigns he had received into a pouch, uttoned down its flap, and placed this in the bag, wrapped inside a shirt. hen he looked around the room for some weapon, but there was othing, nothing at all.

Carrying the bag, he followed Tom down the stairs, and into the othecary's shop. Behind the front door, he saw Mr Stapleford's walk- g stick, and picked it up. This was a poor enough weapon, but anything uld be better than bare fists against a mob. The two men stood in the op behind the counter, backs to the row of flasks of coloured liquids. ow they could hear footsteps outside the shop. Tom looked frantically r a chair, a wooden box, anything to block the door, but there was thing. Beneath the counter, Jackson saw the apothecary's store of

specifics: wooden barrels of bicarbonate of soda and saltpetre, huge glass
carboys of hydrochloric and sulphuric acids and magnesia milk.

As he stood up, the glass pane in the door shattered with a tinkle like
tiny warning bells. A chill evening breeze blew in from the river. A h
came carefully through the jagged hole in the door. Fingers moved
serpents' heads as they searched for bolts they could not reach.

Shoulders now pressed heavily against the door. Suddenly, wo
panels splintered, and the door swung open. The shop was instantly fu
of men. The sour smell of their unwashed bodies mingled with the sharp
and unmistakable scents of fear and danger.

One held a lantern above his head.

'Ah, doctor,' he called when he saw Jackson. 'We have come to se
you.'

His speech was thick and slurred; he had obviously been drinking
heavily.

'It is not necessary to break the door down to see me, surely?'

'Mr Piggott thinks it is. He has urgent business to discuss.'

The throng parted. Percy Piggott came through the gap, and stoo
facing Jackson across the counter. He was smiling.

'I owe you a debt, Dr Jackson,' he said. 'I do not like owing peopl
anything. Especially someone like you.'

'And I do not like the front door of my home being broken down
especially by someone like you,' Jackson replied.

'*Your* home, doctor? I own this house and shop, remember. I can do
I wish with my own property. And I have the most serious reason fc
being here. You have performed some necromancy or devil's experimer
on my poor, demented sister. You claim to have cured her. *You,*
common country practitioner! When the greatest medical men of the a
have pronounced her incurable!

'No doubt you have swindled her out of money for your fee, and no
this dear lady, towards whom I entertain the warmest feeling, claims s
is about to marry a man she hardly knows! My God, doctor, I owe you
great debt indeed – a debt of honour. I am going to thrash you like t
swine you are.'

The men fell back on either side; if there was to be a fight, the comb
ants would need room. Jackson was surprised to see naked hatred and
glow of anticipation darken their rough, unshaven faces. Several we
strangers to him, but others had been his patients, with their wives a
families. To most of these, he had never presented a bill for his servic
because he considered they were too poor to pay. All this appear
forgotten in the imminent expectation of violence. He had seen the sai
gloating looks on men's faces at a dog fight, a cock fight, once even at t
baiting of a chained bear in the backyard of The Piggott Arms. T

prospect of seeing pain inflicted excited them. In the suffering and fear of another creature, animal or human, they could temporarily forget the misery of their own unspeakable existences between the grindstones of 〔 ..sh landlord and low pay.

'You threatened me in your house, Piggott,' Jackson said easily, as though he was engaged in nothing more serious than a friendly discussion about a trivial matter. 'But when I accepted your challenge, you declined to match your words with action. Only now, surrounded by men whose whole lives are in pawn to you, do you feel sufficiently courageous to attack me.

'Your concern is not for your sister, but for yourself. When she marries, you lose your inheritance. How brave you are when you break into a tenant's house, surrounded by your creatures!'

'There was someone else here with you, doctor. I saw him. Who is he?'

Jackson glanced quickly behind him. Tom had gone, and so silently he had not even noticed him leave. Jackson felt a sudden, almost overwhelming sense of disappointment and betrayal. Tom Gray had come here to warn him, but now, at the moment of his greatest need, his resolution had failed. Was there no one he could trust?

'I will not demean myself by fighting a swine like you,' said Piggott. 'You are not a gentleman.'

He turned to the men around him.

'Teach this apothecary's runner a lesson in manners he will remember. And be quick about it.'

The nearest man, a huge black-bearded labourer, wearing a belt studded with horse-brasses, lunged at Jackson clumsily with a fist the size of a ham. Jackson ducked. The blow missed his face and smashed one of Mr Stapleford's bottles. A gallon of cold blue liquid cascaded over Jackson's shoulders, with a faint smell of camphor. He turned for a second, shaking the coloured, scented water out of his face. In that moment, three men rushed him.

One tried to leap across the counter, but it collapsed beneath his weight. Jackson brought down the edge of his hand on the back of the man's neck in a hammer blow as he lay on the splintered planks. He slid sideways to the floor. Jackson drove the end of his walking stick like a lance into the stomach of the second. Then, gripping the stick with both hands, he brought it up with all his force beneath the chin of the third. Bone snapped like a dry larch twig. The man screamed in agony.

But already others behind were elbowing these bodies out of their way. Within seconds they would overpower him; he could be beaten to death. Jackson dropped down to dodge a blow from an axe handle, and saw the barrel of bicarbonate of soda. He tore off its lid, picked up the drum and threw it into the middle of the crowd. The men scattered for a moment, choking, half-blinded by the powder, their faces white as millers' in the flickering flame of the lantern.

Jackson bent down for a second time and picked up the carboy of sulphuric acid. He raised this slowly above his head with both hands.

'Get back!' he bellowed. 'Back, or I will blind you all!'

He could see their eyes fixed on the giant amber bottle, not quite certain whether he was bluffing, but unwilling to put their doubt to the test.

'He's lying!' screamed Piggott. 'Kill him!'

Jackson edged around the end of the counter, still holding the bottle.

'Back!' he shouted and leaped forward. The men drew away from him hurriedly, scattering as he approached, raising their hands to shield their eyes in case he threw the bottle at them. He reached the open door, and in the street turned to face them, now holding the huge carboy with both hands like a trophy above his head.

'Kill him!' bellowed Piggott again, but he backed away with the rest. They were all out in the street now, watching Jackson warily.

'I will give you to three to leave me, or I will blind you all, every one of you,' Jackson told them, and began to count.

'One. . . .'

Piggott bent down to pick up a stone to throw at Jackson, and a bearded man with a spotted red handkerchief around his neck raised a huge ash branch cut from a hedge and swung this at the bottle like a club. Jackson saw the danger and threw the heavy bottle towards him. The branch shattered the glass.

For a moment there was silence, and then screams of horror and pain filled the air as the acid ate into the flesh of their faces. They began to claw desperately at suddenly blinded and burning eyes, as though they could somehow tear the agony out with their finger nails. Then they all started to race across the road towards the river, desperate to plunge their faces into the water. As they ran, they threw away sticks and stones and other weapons, shouting in pain and bewilderment, bumping into each other and tripping over the cobbles in unexpected blindness.

Piggott had kept slightly behind them for safety and the acid had not even splashed him. Suddenly he was on his own. He turned, bewildered and then started to follow them to the river, away from the shop. Jackson reached out with his stick and hooked him back by his neck, as a shepherd hooks a straying sheep.

'You called me a swine,' he said. 'You threatened me. So stay and fight like a man – if you are one.'

'I will see you pay for this,' threatened Piggott. 'Damn your blood doctor, but I will.'

Jackson hit him hard in the stomach. As Piggott lurched forward gasping for breath from the force of the blow, Jackson brought up his knee. He heard Piggott's jaw crack as his teeth snapped together like a rat-trap. Piggott reeled to one side, went down on his hands and knees, spitting out blood and broken teeth.

'You bastard!' he shouted in a paroxysm of rage and pain.

Jackson saw him fumble at the band of his trousers, then the glitter of a knife blade.

From down the road came the drum of running feet. Piggott's men had dunked their faces in the river and wiped the acid away on their sleeves. Now they were coming back for revenge. Jackson would expect no mercy, and this time there would be no escape. They were coming back to kill him.

For a moment that seemed timeless, Jackson stood, feeling warmth from the bricks of Mr Stapleford's shop wall through the thin stuff of his jacket. Ahead, as still as painted ships upon a painted river, fishing boats lay at anchor, the East Indiaman *Coromandel* towering above them. A few lights burned on the far Essex shore. It was as though the scene was not real, but somehow etched with fearful clarity on his mind; as though nothing had any significance for him any more. They will kill me, he thought, as though accepting the fate of a stranger. I am about to die.

At that moment, he heard a great, unexpected roar of shouting from the beach. Newcomers suddenly swarmed up from the shelter of rows of shrimp boats and fishing smacks drawn up on the shingle. They were fishermen in leather boots, with heavy fustian trousers and thick blue sweaters. Most were black-bearded, with woollen hats pulled down on their heads so that they could not be recognised. They gripped marlin pikes, oars, mud anchors with four hooks, and yard lengths of tarred rope and chains. As they ran, they roared threats at Piggott and his men.

'We are with you, doctor!' he heard Tom shout reassuringly, and relief surged through Jackson's body like a warm, welcome tide. Thank God, he was not alone; Tom had not deserted him.

The next few minutes were a phantasmagoria of fists and boots and clubs; the iron rattle of chain links, gasps for breath, and screams of pain as hooks bit into flesh and oars crashed down on skulls and arms. This totally unexpected commotion had momentarily distracted Piggott. Now, taking advantage of it, he drove his knife up towards Jackson's chest.

The doctor dodged, but not quite quickly enough. The blade sliced through his shirt and scored his skin. The blow concentrated all the latent hatred and contempt he felt for Piggott.

Jackson flung away his stick, gripped Piggott's right wrist with both hands, twisted it sharply to the left and then the right. The knife clattered noisily down on to the cobbles. Jackson swung Piggott around, rammed him up against the shop wall and hit him with a straight left and a right to his jaw. Piggott collapsed on his hands and knees.

Suddenly, the street was filled with running men. Two bent down and picked up Piggott as they passed, and dragged him away. Eyes burning from the acid, unable to see anything clearly, his men had lost all stomach for further fighting. To attack one man under the leadership of their landlord, primed by his drink and promises, was altogether different from facing an equal number of tougher men, better armed and angry. Within seconds, Jackson was left alone with Tom.

'Thank you, friend,' he said shakily, thinking as he spoke how totally inadequate the words were. 'You have saved my life.'

'They will be back,' warned Tom. 'Piggott will serve a warrant on you with some charge or other. Assaulting him, attempted murder maybe. Anything. He is a magistrate, you know. There is no staying here for you now, doctor, none at all. Look at that shop – ruined. Piggott will make sure that Apothecary Stapleford presses charges for that. After all, he is Piggott's tenant and has to do his bidding like the rest of them. You will be transported, doctor – if you are not hanged.'

'I cannot believe that,' began Jackson stoutly, but even as he spoke, he did believe it. What Tom said was quite true; he should have heeded his earlier warning. He could not afford to ignore his advice a second time. He had to go while there was still time to escape, while he was still free to move. If he waited until the town constable arrested him, who would speak in his favour when so many witnesses would willingly swear against him? But where could he go?

'The river,' said Tom. 'That Indiaman, *Coromandel*. She's sailing at high tide. I have a boat. I will row you out. Her master will sell you passage. She's probably calling at Dover. You could disembark there.'

'That will not be far enough away,' Jackson replied. He realised he would not be safe anywhere in the kingdom when Piggott recovered. He walked back into the ruined shop to collect his bag. The lantern lit a scene of wrecked bottles, spilled powders, the smashed counter. Jackson hurried down to the beach with Tom. They waded out into the cool water to his rowing boat and climbed aboard. Tom cast off, put his single oar over the stern, leaned on it, first from one side, then from the other. The tiny coracle moved out slowly through the ripples of the river, to the Indiaman. As they drew close, Jackson could see her tarred hull rise like a sheer black shining wall; her masts dipped slightly against the sky.

'Ahoy there!' a sailor on watch called down at them warningly. 'Who are you?'

'A visitor,' Tom called back. 'Lower a ladder directly.'

Wooden rungs rattled against the vessel's side as the man threw down a rope ladder. Jackson shook Tom's hand.

'Will you be all right?' he asked Tom anxiously.

'I will be safe, doctor. I was born here, remember. I have many friends

I may have to face some hostility, but it should not last long. It is different for you, doctor. You were a stranger here, and strangers need powerful friends – or great wealth.'

'That I realise,' Jackson agreed. 'And both I intend to acquire.'

Tom fumbled in his pocket.

'Something for you to remember Joanna by,' he said.

'Joanna?'

For the moment, Jackson could not put a face to the name.

'Yes, my daughter. You gave her a penny, remember? When I told her tonight of the trouble I knew was facing you, she handed it back to me to give to you. She said you needed it more than her. Here it is, doctor.'

Tom passed over the penny, warm in his hand. Jackson turned it over.

'I cannot take it,' he said.

'You must, doctor. She wants you to have it.'

Jackson nodded and put it carefully in his fob pocket.

'I shall never forget this,' Jackson told Tom, his voice thick with emotion. 'I will keep it always as a talisman. And one day I will come back and repay her kindness – and yours.'

'God shield you wherever you may be, doctor. You will prosper. My mother saw it in the stars and in your hand. She told me as much.'

'All she told me was that my future was mud,' retorted Jackson, smiling. He had even looked up the word in Dr Johnson's dictionary in case it had a more agreeable meaning, but the definition was plain: 'The slime and uliginous matter at the bottom of still water.'

He climbed up the rope ladder. As he put down his bag on deck, Tom was already pulling away strongly to the shore.

'Pray call the captain,' Jackson told the sailor.

'Who are you, sir? What is your business here?'

'A physician and surgeon. I wish to take passage in this vessel.'

'We are not carrying passengers on this voyage,' a voice behind him informed him in a strange, nasal accent. Jackson turned. A man wearing blue canvas trousers and a jersey, with long black hair down his back and rings glittering in his ears, regarded him with some amusement. He was tall and broad-shouldered, but Jackson caught the whiff of a woman's scent on the evening wind. For all his masculine appearance, the man was an effeminate. No matter; many sailors, caged for months within the narrow confines of wooden ships, sought satisfaction with each other. As a doctor, he did not criticise; he had learned to accept that what may be abhorrent to one person can be solace to another.

'I am Captain Ross, Marvin Ross,' the man announced. 'Citizen of Boston, in the United States of America.'

'Dr Richard Jackson, Captain. Until now, of Gravesend, England. At your service.'

'I am sorry I cannot be at yours with regard to your wish to sail with me. But we can take no passengers. Owner's strict orders. From Major the Honourable Reginald Forster himself, no less.'

'I have lately done that gentleman a great personal service. I have his card. It may help you to change your mind, Captain.'

He showed the captain the visiting card that Forster had inscribed to him. Captain Ross looked at it intently, read Forster's scribbled inscription: 'The bearer is my friend', and handed it back with a shrug of his shoulders.

'I stand at your command, doctor. But friend or no, the Major's orders are that I must not carry any passengers on this voyage. Cargo only must occupy all space. We sail on the evening tide to Dover. There we take on cotton goods. Then we sail down the coasts of Spain and Africa, to the Cape of Good Hope where, God willing, we land and take on provisions and fresh water. Then it is across the warm Arabian Sea, south of India, and up to the port of Calcutta.'

'How long will the voyage take?'

'Possibly three months, maybe less if the winds are favourable, as they can be at this time of year. But the information is of no use to you, doctor, because, I repeat, we are not carrying passengers.'

'I have fifty gold sovereigns in my pouch,' replied Jackson with a smile. 'They all tell me you are carrying one. Me.'

The captain paused, stroked his chin, and then smiled.

'They speak with such eloquence that I stand corrected, sir. We *are* carrying one – yourself. And what the gallant Major does not know will never distress him.'

Captain Ross roared with laughter as he shook Jackson's hand, and motioned to the sailor to pick up the doctor's bag and carry it to a cabin. Again, Jackson smelled the sweetness of the captain's scent. Now he wrinkled his nose in distaste – and at the knowledge he would have to endure it for many months to come.

Coupar Castle, Perthshire

Even with his head bowed against the driving spears of rain blown in on the late autumn wind from the Grampian hills, Alec Douglas towered over all the other mourners at the edge of the new-made grave.

His stepfather, John Pomfret, a head shorter, pudgy-faced and pot-bellied, his nose pitted like a red bathroom sponge from years of whisk drinking, stood facing him across the open trench. Rain varnished his bared, bald head, accentuating his age and the deep disagreeable calipers of temper on either side of his mouth.

Their indoor and outdoor servants, some in family livery, others wearing the deep green tartan of the Douglas clan, stood to one side, slightly apart. The men had doffed their hats and wore black arm bands. The women shielded their faces with black veils. They knew their place. They might be with the family mourners, but socially they were not of them.

Alec Douglas watched six foresters from the estate lower his mother's coffin into the raw, dark grave. He felt a sense of numb bewilderment as the ropes rasped against its rough peat-lined sides. He might be watching something that did not concern him at all, a piece of play-acting; reality could come later. But he saw from the gentle way in which these rough men handled the coffin carved from trees that lined the loch, that they honoured his mother's memory.

The shocked faces of the other servants showed clearly how they shared Alec's surprise at her sudden death – and especially the manner of it. Alec had been fishing, away from Coupar Castle for three days, living rough as he liked to live, with a bag of oatmeal and a sporting gun to shoot rabbits, on the bank of a river filled with salmon. He returned to find the castle in consternation. Late on the night he left, apparently, his mother had tripped on a high stone staircase. She had fallen down two flights. When the servants found her hours later, she was dead. The local physician, Dr Drummond, who had known and attended her for many years, admitted he wept when he gave the news to Alec's stepfather, who had not shared the doctor's obvious grief. Perhaps he mourned inwardly, thought Douglas. Perhaps.

This ancient castle, set in two hundred thousand acres, ringed by heather-purpled hills, had been his wife's property, not his. It had been in her first husband's family from the fourteenth century when James Douglas, the closest confidant and most loyal supporter of Robert the Bruce, had commanded part of the victorious Scots Army at the Battle of Bannockburn. For this and for subsequent services in wars against the English, he had been presented with the estate.

When Robert the Bruce died, his last wish was that his heart should be carried to the Holy Land. Douglas immediately volunteered to lead this crusade, from which he never returned. The Douglas family had always been one of Scotland's most powerful; ruthless, proud, loyal, unforgiving, and with their origins curiously shrouded in mystery. Of them it was written: 'Men have seen the stream, but what eye ever beheld its source?' The Douglas crest, a salamander surrounded but undevoured by flame, with their French motto – *Jamais derrière*, 'Never behind' – was carved in the castle. The Pomfret name was nowhere. Who was he, anyway? Not a man of valour or tradition or culture. He had brought little to the union except a taste for whisky, which had increased markedly over the few years of his marriage to Alec's mother, and a disconcerting habit of roaring requests like a bull, as though the sheer volume of his voice could somehow conceal the empty impotence within.

Alec Douglas recalled too many overheard arguments between his mother and his stepfather, often centring on his prolonged and mysterious visits to Edinburgh and London, and the resulting expensive bills he presented to her to pay. How different were these jagged, abrasive recollections to boyhood memories of his father: a kindly red-haired bear of a man who had suddenly fallen ill with a disease that neither the local physician nor specialists brought from Perth and Edinburgh could cure.

His widow had been lonely, and John Pomfret, the antithesis of her late husband, physically, mentally and morally, had amused her. At first, at least. After she married him, she realised that his charm was as thin as his hair; that he was cruel, corrupt, lazy, only interested in himself – and regarded her simply as a source of income to be spent far away from home.

Alec had been against the marriage, but his mother misinterpreted his feelings. She imagined he must be resentful of a strange man taking the place of his father. Too late, she realised the truth and the strength of his arguments. But all that was past now; she was dead, beyond all discussion, all dispute, all further unhappiness.

Douglas drew himself up to his full height as the minister threw a handful of wet soil on the coffin top, intoning the ancient words of the burial service: 'Earth to earth, dust to dust . . . The Lord giveth and the Lord taketh away. Blessed be the name of the Lord.'

Over his stepfather's shoulder, Alec could see the road to the castle across the moors shine like a river in the rain, and two closed carriages waiting. The servants, of course, could walk back to the castle. The minister and he would ride with Mr Pomfret in one carriage, while the strange young woman who had arrived with her brother by hackney from Perth only that morning would travel in the second.

'This is Mrs Cochrane, Mrs Jane Cochrane,' his stepfather had introduced her with a barely concealed smirk. 'She was a dear friend of your mother.'

'She is much younger than my mother,' Alec had replied, looking at the new arrival. She was possibly twenty-five, big-breasted and bold-eyed. In an instant, animal reaction, Alec neither liked nor trusted her, but had to admit her allure. Years ago, when he was a boy, he had come across a deadly adder in a copse on the estate. Instantly, a ghillie had struck the snake's head from its body with a single blow from his axe. But in that second, seeing the serpent, Alec knew he was in the presence

danger, beautiful though it might appear. He had experienced this same
feeling of unease, and yet a curious and very strong attraction, as he
bowed politely to Mrs Cochrane and took her hand. Her brother was
several years younger than Alec; thin, tall, spotty-faced. They had disliked
each other on sight.

They all trudged in silence across the soggy heathery peat to the
carriages. A footman held open the door for Pomfret, who ignored him
and instead opened the door of the second carriage and steadied Mrs
Cochrane as she put a dainty foot on the step.

'I want to talk to you privately, Alec,' he said, as they climbed into the
other carriage.

'I thought the minister was riding with us?'

'I asked him to walk back.'

'He will get very wet, and he is not a young man.'

'That is his concern.'

'What do you wish to discuss in private, Stepfather?'

'Your mother's will.'

The carriage jerked forward. Iron wheels crunched damp granite chip-
pings. Alec said nothing. He knew from many talks with his mother that
she wished to leave the whole estate to him, but that an agreed income
from several farms would be paid to his stepfather for as long as he lived.
He said nothing now; he did not wish to embarrass the older man by
admitting that he knew of this arrangement. It would be more fitting to
listen as though he were hearing the details for the first time.

Pomfret took a silver flask from his pocket, snapped open the cap, put
the neck to his lips and drank deeply and noisily. Some whisky dribbled
down his chin on to his shirt. He shook the last drops from the flask into
his mouth, and wiped his chin with the back of his hand.

'Now, Alec,' he began more briskly, fired by the spirit, 'you well know
that your late mother planned at one time to leave the estate to you. Last
week, while you were away, she changed her mind – as women tend to
do. She called a Writer to the Signet here from Edinburgh and told him
she wished to make over everything to me, to dispose of as I wish. Of
course, the understanding is that, if nothing else happens, it would come
to you. In the end.'

'What else could happen?' asked Douglas in amazement.

'I might marry again.'

'But that need not affect the continuity of the estate?'

'It need not, agreed. But since it is mine to do with as I wish absolutely,
it *could*.'

'You mean you would leave it to a stranger, some woman – not this
Mrs Cochrane, surely?'

'Mrs Cochrane, as I told you, was a dear friend of your mother's.'

'I have never seen her before. Nor did I ever hear my mother mention her name.'

'There is no reason why she should. After all, you doubtless have friends she knew nothing about. I have friends – and so did she – of whom you are in equal ignorance.'

'She does not look the sort of woman my mother would choose as a friend.'

'Who are you to judge that? She is an honourable widowed lady, with a brother.'

'I did not like the look of him, either.'

'You are being rather petulant, Alec. I understand your distress at your mother's death. I personally am prostrated by grief, but life must go on. That is why I wanted this opportunity of speaking to you in private, in the confines of my carriage, where no damned servant can listen. Then, when the Writer reads the will, you will not show surprise or make any unseemly comments because you do not inherit all you had hoped.'

'What do I inherit, if I may ask?'

'Five hundred pounds. In Mr Hoare's bank in London.'

'And that is all? Nothing about the family silver, houses on the estate? *Nothing* else?'

'Nothing else, Alec.'

'And virtually on the night after my mother made this extraordinary will, she dies as a result of what seems a very strange accident? I would like to see the will.'

'You shall, Alec. This evening.'

And so he did. There was no doubt about it; everything seemed perfectly legal. His mother must have changed her mind – or had it changed for her. The whole situation was as disturbing and inexplicable as his return home from a few days on the river to find her dead, a funeral planned, a grave already dug.

He went up to his room, deep in thought and concern. Candles had been lit in his bedroom, and a fire burned low in the grate. He had not eaten any supper, but was not hungry. He felt cold and wretched and alone. He wanted a friend to turn to, and there was no one. He sat down on the bed, undressed, and washed in the basin from the ewer of warm water.

He stood for a moment, as men do on their own, examining his face in the mirror. He was tall, twenty-five, red-haired, broad-shouldered. His whole life had been spent in expectation of one day owning the estate. He knew by first name every crofter, every husband and wife, even their children, who lived in the little white-washed houses where peat fires burned almost constantly, as much to drive out the damp as to give warmth. He had deliberately served a harsh apprenticeship to fit himsel.

for the task of running so large an estate. He had cut heather, felled trees, sawed logs, dug peat, helped to bind stooks of corn, always willing to learn every separate aspect of its working. Now there was no job on the land he could not undertake; no problem he could not say should be solved this way rather than that.

But now what was to be his future? To wait here until his stepfather died – or until he changed his mind?

Alec threw himself back on the bed and lay for a moment, his mind miles and years away. Dying embers of the fire dropped into the grate with a sudden flurry of sparks, and the wind's thin fingers rapped on loose window panes.

He must have slept, because suddenly he was awake, listening. The room felt very cold and dark; the fire was out. He raised himself on his elbow, hearing the usual faint scuttle of mice behind the plaster, the myriad creaks that are the night voices of every old building. Then he heard something else: a muffled laugh. Someone must be awake at his end of the house, where usually he was the only one to sleep. This bedroom had been his since his boyhood; it was small and out of the way.

The nearest guest rooms, with thick curtains and drapes to keep out the draughts as much as for privacy, stood perhaps twenty yards away at the end of a long stone corridor. Alec swung himself out of bed, pulled a blanket around him (he always slept naked), opened the door and tiptoed down the corridor. He could see a faint fan of light on the stone flags from a half-open door. So far as he knew, that room had not been used for years, but like all bedrooms in the castle, with an inside staff of forty, beds were always made and fires laid *just in case* – as his mother used to say, stressing the words – they might be needed unexpectedly.

Whoever was in that room would not know that anyone else was on the same floor. He approached the doorway, surprising himself at his own stealth. There should be no need of concealment, surely, in his own house, near his own room?

But then, as he cautiously put his head round the door, he realised here was every need.

Alec's stepfather faced him across the desk in the smoking room next morning. Behind him, through wide windows, acres of heather trembled beneath the morning wind like a purple sea. Pomfret did not offer his stepson a seat. A flask of whisky was on the desk. Pomfret's face was flushed and his eyes shot with tiny red veins. His fleshy lips hung slack and moist and drooling.

'You wished to see me?' Alec asked him.

'I do not wish to see you now, or at any other time, but the nature of our disgusting behaviour makes it imperative I do so.'

'I do not understand you, Stepfather.'

'You may be unaware that it is my intention to seek Mrs Cochrane's hand in marriage?'

'I was not aware, but it seemed a strong possibility.'

'Despite that, you deliberately insinuate yourself into her room. You make foul and lewd advances to her. To be blunt, you attempt to copulate with the lady who will, God willing, shortly be your stepmother.'

'I never *attempt* to copulate. I either do, or I do not. And in this instance, I did not. I was asleep in my own room, and was awakened by the sound of laughter – rare in this house since your arrival.'

Alec could see the older man wince. He poured out more whisky; the neck of the flask rattled on the silver beaker.

'I saw that a bedroom door along the corridor was half open. I walked towards it and there discovered this woman, who you say you wish to wed, naked on the bed with her brother. To be blunt, he was mounted on her, and she was giving every evidence of pleasure – an incestuous union, punishable under law by death.'

'A damned lie!' shouted Pomfret hoarsely, standing up with such haste that he upset the whisky. 'You lying blackguard! If I were younger, I would thrash you as you deserve to be thrashed, like the lying, lecherous swine you are. We shall see what her brother has to say.'

He stormed to another door, pulled it open and shouted: 'Claude, *Claude*!'

'Yes, Mr Pomfret?'

The pale youth came running, a newspaper in one hand, one of Pomfret's Havana cigars in the other. He stared insolently at Alec.

'This damnable swine has accused you and your sister of a disgusting offence.'

'What do you mean?' asked Claude, looking sharply at Alec.

'You know exactly what I mean. It is a change – marginally for the better – to see you clothed and perpendicular rather than naked and horizontal, rutting like a stag on your own sister.'

Claude dropped the newspaper on the carpet, and picked up a heavy glass paperweight the size of a small cannon-ball from Pomfret's desk.

'You bastard!' he said slowly. 'You dare to insult my sister's name – and mine.'

He flung the paperweight into Alec's face. Alec ducked, but no quickly enough. The ball caught him on the cheek. He staggered to one side, momentarily dazed by its force, and put up one hand to his face. His fingers came away stained with blood.

Claude saw his advantage and kicked at Alec's shins. Alec side-stepped and hit him hard, first in the stomach with his left fist, then on the jaw with his right. Claude seemed suspended for a moment, like a human question mark, his face distorted with pain and disbelief. As he sagged forward slowly, mouth open, eyes wide, Alec hit him for the third time. He fell, face down, between the ink-stands and the spilled whisky on Pomfret's desk and slithered to the floor.

'So much for a whore's champion,' said Alec, flexing his fingers.

'Get out of my sight!' shouted Pomfret.

'I will stay here as long as I wish,' Alec replied. 'This has always been my home. It should by right now be mine. I will engage the ablest Writer to the Signet in Edinburgh to plead my case, and, by God, when I win – as I shall – I will have you, old as you are, flogged off the estate, *my* estate. I will also tell the Writer what I have seen.'

'You have no proof. You have no money, no influence. *Nothing.*'

'I have right.'

'*Right?* What is right? *Which* right? *Whose* right? The will is in my favour.'

'Do not waste words on me, old man. Go back to your whore. You are well suited.'

Alec turned away. Pomfret followed him to the door, suddenly conciliatory.

'You cannot stay here, and you know it. Your life would be a misery. You know that, too. Your mother is dead. The castle and lands are mine. You are unwanted, an interloper, a trespasser on my property. If you do not leave, I could have you thrown off – legally.'

He paused and regarded Alec slyly through half-closed eyes.

'On the other hand . . . if you leave now, I will make you a generous offer. I will buy you a commission in any regiment of your choice. But in India, out of this country, in the army of the Honourable East India Company.'

'That is exile forever.'

'For a time. Until you can see things in a different light.'

The Honourable East India Company had been formed more than two hundred years earlier by merchants with a taste for high profits, no matter what the risk. They traded with Sumatra and Java, the so-called Spice Islands, bringing back spices for sale in Europe. At that time, so Alec Douglas had learned at school, the sole means of preserving meat was to salt it. Herds of cattle could not be kept alive throughout the winter months, so any other means of making rancid meat edible was of great value. Only the relatively rich could afford to eat meat, of course, and naturally no one was greatly concerned with the diet or tastes of the poor.

Spices from these faraway places could cunningly disguise the foul taste of putrid meat, make even the stalest fish palatable, and so commanded huge prices. Pirates soon realised the potential of this trade, and regularly attacked the East India Company's ships, usually in the Indian Ocean, as they sailed home slowly, heavy with their valuable cargoes.

To provide bases where these vessels could re-victual, and where they might escape from pirate attacks, the Company rented small enclaves of land in Bombay, Madras and Calcutta. Here, by agreement with the local maharajah or other ruler, they built what they called factories, really large warehouses where they could store stocks of spices from individual ships and release them as needed.

The Dutch drove the British out of Java and Sumatra at the same time as Indian rulers demanded more for the privilege of allowing Europeans these facilities. The French were frequently at war with the English, and since Dutch, French and Portuguese trading companies all rented similar enclaves in India for the same reasons, it became prudent to recruit Indians from races of martial disposition to guard factories from attacks by any alien business competitor.

Each trading company – English, French, Dutch, Portuguese – dressed these guards in the distinctive uniforms of their country's army, largely so that they could recognise them easily. The British called their guards sepoys, from the Persian word *sepahi*, meaning a soldier.

The Indian rulers knew of the strong rivalry between the different European trading companies and accordingly played them off against each other. For example, they made it a condition of continuing their arrangements with the British that the Company's sepoys, trained by retired regular British NCOs and therefore remarkably smart and well-disciplined, could be used in any private disputes they might have with other maharajahs. Gradually, and with increasing reluctance, the East India Company found itself involved in controlling huge areas of India, with a correspondingly large private army.

It became in many ways a government, unelected and unwilling, but forced into this role by circumstances it could not control. The British government of the day recognised the dangers in this situation and posted regular British troops to India with the avowed intention of guarding British subjects and investments, but with the covert aim of making sure that the East India Company did not become too powerful, because of its huge profits, and eventually independent of all elected government control.

Regular British officers looked down on their East India Company counterparts. Aristocratic British officers often refused to serve in India when their regiments were posted east. They did not wish to abandon the social whirl that revolved around London and Brighton, nor were they eager to expose themselves to the fevers and other incurable diseases from which so many Europeans died in India, often within months of landing.

All Army commissions and promotions were bought, so richer officers paid other officers, who lacked private means, to serve in India in their place.

Officers in the East India Company's army resented the contempt in which regular British officers held them, and hated their epithet of 'black officers'. They also realised that a passage to India was often one-way – which increased their wish to become rich by any means as quickly as possible, and then to buy an estate in Britain and retire early while they still could.

Some went into commerce. Others found consolations of a different sort. They 'went native', with Indian concubines and an addiction to the hookah, or hubble-bubble pipe, and hot curries; and finally, for the failures, lonely and far from home, there was always the sweet and comforting oblivion of opium.

This was not a prospect to attract every ambitious young man, especially someone like Douglas, who was being ordered off his family estate. But what was the alternative?

'You do not like the idea of India?' asked Pomfret softly, guessing the turmoil in the young man's mind. 'You could make a fortune out there. Everyone else does. You are good-looking and, more important, you are well hung. I know. I have seen you naked, bathing in the river. That means a lot to women in the East. Heat always has a powerful effect on women. Three hundred guineas to go now, *and* I will buy you a commission.'

'Five hundred,' replied Alec quickly.

'It is done.'

Pomfret went to a safe, opened it with a key that hung from a chain at his waist, and took out a small black metal box. This he also unlocked and counted out ten fifty-pound bank notes, issued on Alexander's Bank in Edinburgh.

'Here you are,' he said. 'Now, go!'

Alec put them in his pocket, buttoned down the flap.

'I will be back,' he told Pomfret, and to himself he added in silence: 'To claim what is rightly mine.'

He walked out of the room, along the corridor, up the stairs towards his bedroom. As he approached Mrs Cochrane's room, the door opened and she stood framed in the doorway. She wore a thin white cotton shift. Her hair was unpinned and streamed down her back, almost to her knees, giving her an oddly vulnerable, almost innocent appearance. She looked at him with surprise tinged with alarm. She had heard footsteps and obviously expected her brother or Pomfret. Seeing the angry, resentful expression on Alec's face, she quickly retreated into her bedroom, hairbrush in one hand, tortoiseshell comb in the other. He followed her inside, shut the door and locked it behind him.

'I saw you fornicating with Claude last night,' he began bluntly, his voice still thick with anger. 'And you must have known I saw you. You told my stepfather these lies about me, I suppose, in case I informed him what had really happened?'

'I do not know what you mean,' she replied nervously, without conviction, not meeting his eyes. Her tongue darted nervously around her lips. 'I do not understand you.'

'You will be relieved to know he still means to marry you. You may have a future, of a kind, with him. But only until I return to take possession of all that should be mine. Until then, you will have to pay the price of his impotence, his soft, sickening old man's drooling. A high price, even for a whore!'

'You hate me, don't you?'

She made the question sound a statement of fact.

'You are not worth hating,' he replied simply.

'Possibly not – to you. But I have feelings, too. I have known your stepfather for several years, long before his marriage, when he worked in London. He has many virtues.'

'Which he has always successfully concealed from me. What did he do in London? It was always vaguely referred to as his business.'

'He was a linen draper. In Cheapside.'

'I can imagine him fingering rolls of soft cloth, bowing and scraping to rich women customers, fawning over them. What a thought!'

'And now he owns this castle and two hundred thousand acres of land.'

'I would describe him as a tenant, not an owner. And his tenure lasts until I come back, and only until then. A point to bear in mind.'

'So you are leaving?'

Douglas nodded. As they spoke he realised, almost unbelievably, his initial dislike and distrust of Mrs Cochrane were evaporating. She was so damned good-looking it was impossible not to find her desirable and attractive. She possessed a powerful magnetism Douglas had never previously encountered. She moved to put brush and comb on a side table, and the dark points of her breasts danced slightly, tremulously, behind the fine, almost transparent, stuff of her shift.

'He wormed his way into my mother's affections when she was widowed and lonely,' Douglas said. 'You never knew my mother, did you? Despite what he says about your being friends?'

'I never knew her, may her soul rest in peace.'

'Are you married, Mrs Cochrane?'

'No. I have never been married.'

'So, like a housekeeper or a cook, you prefer to be referred to as Mrs rather than Miss?'

She did not reply, but her face coloured slightly.

'So how did you come to know my stepfather so well that now he seeks to make you his wife?' Douglas continued.

'He used to come to our house in London.'

'*Your* house? Your parents' house – or yours?'

'Mine. Or, rather, I lived there. With other girls.'

She paused, temporarily too embarrassed to continue.

'A whore-house?'

'You could call it that, yes, but I did not know it when I first came to London. My sister, a friend and I had come up from the country to take positions in great houses. It had all been arranged, so we were told before we left home, and we were met at the station by a woman who said she was housekeeper to the noble lord who was to be our employer. We believed her. There was no work for us in Dorset.

'She took us to a house off Jermyn Street and there *was* no noble lord, of course. At least, not then, although later on we encountered several lords, even earls. She gave us our meals and provided us with new clothes. We had no money at all. Nothing. We thought our prospective employer was doing this for us. But, when she asked us to pay for the food and clothes and of course we could not, she threatened to send for the constable to put us in jail. But there *was* an alternative, and we took it. Wouldn't you, in our place?'

'And that is where you met my stepfather?'

'Yes. Most of us had our regulars. Men of all stations in life. Noblemen, as I said. Rich City merchants, a minister of the crown, even a bishop.'

'Is that creature Claude really your brother?'

'No.'

'You told Pomfret he was.'

'What else could I tell him? The truth? That he is my fancy man? That he looks after me?'

'You keep him?'

'Yes. Every woman in the house had someone like Claude. They are not really interested in what we do, so long as we buy them clothes, meals, wine. They are usually on the game themselves – sodomites, catamites, they will do anything with anyone.'

'I saw him doing his best with you last night.'

She smiled, more confident now. They stood looking at each other. Douglas had not imagined any of this, and he knew he should feel outraged and disgusted, but, oddly, her honesty had somehow disarmed him. Or was it just her honesty? Could it also be the extraordinarily strong aura of sexuality she exuded, her scent of crushed violet petals, the tiny beads of moisture on her upper lip?

He saw her in a different light now, hating himself for his feelings and yet trying to rationalise them in his mind. She was unlike any woman he had ever met. Country girls he had fondled or lain with in the hay on hot summer afternoons in some part of the grounds, had all been quite different; fresh-faced, red-cheeked, buxom and boisterous, with a curious innocence.

Mrs Cochrane was not like this. She had come from the country, agreed, but she had long since ceased to be a country girl. She lived by her looks, by her ability to please men, not one, not even two, but any man with money and a mind to be pleasured. Her looks and her clothes had the style and polish of the big city; they spoke of money and experience. Before Douglas tasted malt whisky he had been content with beer, but not afterwards. He knew that after Mrs Cochrane, simple girls would be similarly unsatisfying. *After* her? He knew then, too, that he had already made up his mind about her.

She seemed to have moved closer to him, without actually moving at all. She was actually watching him warily, wondering whether the clouding of his eyes signified anger – as she knew from experience it did with some men; whether she could avoid a sudden blow if he struck her, as she had often been struck by men who she would never have imagined could be violent. Or was this a sign of desire that, as with a fire left low and smouldering, could erupt into flame?

She could not afford a mistake; too much was at risk. She was playing for high stakes, to become the wife of a man owning two hundred thousand acres and heaven alone knew what income every year. And did old Pomfret believe what this young man had told him about her and Claude – or did he believe her story, thin as it sounded?

Alec Douglas could see the dark brown stains of her nipples through the shift, seemingly larger than before, pointing out at him. She saw him looking despite himself, and smiled. Her confidence grew with his obvious need and admiration; this was well-mapped territory where she was in command.

She said gently: 'It is a pity I hadn't met you before I met Claude. A great pity.'

'You would never keep me,' Douglas retorted.

'I would not need to keep you – financially,' she agreed. 'But I could keep you happy, satisfied, relaxed. That I *do* know, Mr Douglas.'

She moved even closer to him, so that he could now feel her firm breasts through the thin cotton brushing his shirt and, through his shirt his chest as her body moved gently from side to side against his. One of her hands went up and ruffled his hair gently, the other moved down adroitly to the swelling in his loins. Douglas knew his weakness and his strength. Other women had been amazed at the size of his phallus, and uneasy lest it should pain them on entering, and yet willing to put th question to the test. And then they had remarked on his recuperative powers. A husband might spend before they had begun to enjoy the session: Douglas could keep on, like a rider in a long, long race, until they literally cried in their ecstasy, and then, and only then, confident in his supremacy, he reached his climax.

Such an ability was undoubtedly wrong, he was sure, at least according to the preaching of the minister in the kirk every Sunday; pleasure for itself must be a sin because it was so enjoyable. Only bad-tasting medicine could hope to cure any patient.

It was always easy to condemn, and only those who could not experience – or give to their partner – the supreme gift of satisfaction of two bodies joined as one, would ever wish to criticise. And had not the Apostle Paul been too vehement in his castigation of all sexual activity simply because he personally was impotent and so could never know the exquisite sweetness of the act he declared a wickedness?

Men, Mrs Cochrane thought, half contemptuously, half amused, were all alike; all children to be bowed and bent and turned by the touch of soft fingers; the sight and softness and warmth of something hitherto unseen, untouched. They were like great ships of the seven seas. No matter their size or importance, they could all be steered in any direction by the movement of a small rudder.

So long as a woman knew and accepted this, she would always stay in control. If this was a man's world, women made it turn. She stroked his risen member with expert fingers, light as a butterfly's wings.

'Let us go to bed,' she suggested gently, knowing that however much Douglas might feel he should resist, he would not do so now, could not do so. Her suggestion was turned by his urgent need into a command. As a client with a wry way with words had once remarked to her: 'A standing prick has no conscience.' And from her stroking hand, the message was that Douglas was now beyond all thought or matters of principle.

The Writer to the Signet was a small tubby man, bald-headed, with a beak of a nose. He reminded Douglas of a brooding eagle as he sat at his desk. On the ledge outside the sooty window, three black ravens crouched, fluttering their wings from time to time. Beneath them stretched rows of tall houses. Sulphurous smoke from countless crooked chimneys gave Edinburgh its local nickname of Auld Reekie; it hung like perpetual gloomy cloud over the straggling city. The Writer tapped his fingers together, coughed preparatory to speech, sat back on his chair. Spectacles with thick lenses magnified his eyes grotesquely to the size of blue poached eggs.

'I fully understand your concern, Mr Douglas,' he said, 'but it gives me sadness to have to tell you that I am unable to express any confident view that you can alter the wishes of your late mother as expressed in her will. I have examined the document closely and it appears to be entirely in order.'

'But surely there must have been pressure to make her change her mind about something we had discussed so often after the death of my father?'

'Not necessarily. Tell me, you are unmarried, Mr Douglas?'

'I am.'

'Then, as an older man, let me advise you that the mental processes of the fair sex do not always follow men's more rational lines of logic. Ladies are creatures of whim. They say one thing one day – and may even mean it – but next day they can espouse a totally different view, and will blame you for still holding to the first.'

'I accept that, but my mother was not young or easily influenced. She was unhappy with her second husband, as she admitted to me on several occasions, however reluctant she was to speak about such a private matter.'

'Consider the situation. I go away for a few days. Hardly am I out of the castle than she changes her will. Then, within hours, she is found dead. And this happens during the only time in the year that I have stayed away from the castle for a night. The servants were amazed.'

'The fact remains she had her will drawn up by an advocate for whom I have the highest professional regard. I am also on terms of friendship with him, and I asked him privately whether Mrs Douglas appeared distraught or under any other influence when she drew up the will. He said that she was perfectly calm. She knew exactly what she wanted to say, and she told him precisely how she wanted to leave her estate.'

'Did he ask her why she was changing her will?'

'He did not. We do as our clients tell us. In the legal phrase, we take instructions. What you have to say, Mr Douglas, is interesting and may be cogent, but it only concerns *opinions* – yours and those of unnamed servants. The law is concerned with facts, not theories. If you can *prove* that any coercion was used, any kind of threat – or forgery – then that i a totally different matter. But I need proof, Mr Douglas. *Proof.*

'Many people have sat here and told me how husbands, wives, fathers mothers, cousins promised to leave them all kinds of things. But when the will was read, they were not included. The wish is not always fathe to the deed.'

'This case is surely different. You mentioned forgery. Let me look a the signature.'

The Writer handed the document across the desk. Doulgas could no remember seeing his mother's full signature, Maureen Douglas. So far a he remembered, she signed what few letters he had received from he with the single initial M, either for Maureen or mother; he had neve really wondered about the matter. Now, for the first time, he saw she had signed the will as Maureen Pomfret. The clerk of the Writer she had consulted had signed as witness.

The older man tweaked his beaked nose between the thumb and forefinger of his left hand, as though to sharpen it, when Douglas handed the will back to him.

'I will keep the will, of course, and this problem will stay in the forefront of my mind,' he promised. 'Have I an address to which I can write to you in India?'

'Only the regiment. To be rid of me, my stepfather has bought me a commission in the 113th Regiment of Foot. The commanding officer is a Colonel MacTavish, whom I have yet to meet.'

'A letter, of course, will take months to reach you, and your reply at least as long to come back. Please do not expect quick results. At the best of times, the law moves slowly.'

'Understood. But I am a young man. I have time. The rich spend money to make time, but I will spend time to make money. You, sir, will also spend time – with my money – so that I will at the last recover my inheritance.'

The Writer smiled and put his head on one side, a wise old bird, tolerant of the certainty of the young. It was easy for this good-looking young man to make boasts. When he was older he would realise how far desire can outrun performance. Douglas leaned across the desk towards him.

'Think of your fees, man. And all the work you can do for me when the estate is mine.'

'I am thinking,' the Writer assured him. 'I am thinking.'

Barrackpore

Douglas looked out over Colonel MacTavish's head towards the Barrackpore parade ground that trembled in the burning heat of morning like a lake of liquid fire. Behind and beyond, distant hills and solitary palm trees shimmered as though in a hazy mirage.

On three sides of a square, the 113th Regiment stood at ease, each soldier holding his carbine. On the fourth side, Douglas could see eight Indian sepoys in a small and forlorn line. They were wearing their red tunics, but iron shackles gripped their ankles. They stood facing the sun and, even from this distance, Douglas saw that their faces were varnished with sweat. Now and then one or another of them would shake his head and then consciously brace his shoulders as though he had been on the point of collapse, and the discovery had suddenly brought him back to reality.

They must bear themselves like men, for within minutes, when the colonel gave the command, they were to die. It was not fitting that their comrades should see any fear or weakness in their faces or their bearing. They must leave life in the ways they had been taught to live as soldiers: with honour, dignity and courage.

The Regiment's old siege guns, usually only wheeled out on rare and ceremonial occasions, eight-inch muzzles intricately decorated with bronze serpents and fiery-tongued heads, had been specially sanded and polished for this specific parade. Barrels glowed gold in the sun, and black lacquer newly applied on the wooden spokes of their wheels shone like melting tar. All their barrels pointed to the sky, at the highest angle of elevation, and by every gun stood two sepoys.

One held a crudely-fashioned wooden cross of rough, unplaned wood. These, Douglas knew, would be placed against the mouth of each barrel. The prisoners would be lashed to the crosses with mule loading-ropes. On the command to fire, a gunner would apply a lighted taper to the touchhole in each barrel – and instantly the prisoner in front of that gun would be blown to eternity.

The second sepoy by each cannon was a regimental blacksmith. His duty was to hammer the shackles from each prisoner's legs. It would be extravagant to destroy them needlessly; metal was expensive and they could be used again.

Douglas could imagine the whole terrible picture: the raw, bloodied chunks of human flesh, the sweet stench of calcinated bones and bodies. Leather shields had been erected behind the guns, usually only in position when firing test charges to protect the gunners from any flashback. Now their purpose was more macabre: to protect the gunners being showered with the dismembered bodies of their former comrades. Already vultures wheeled expectantly above the tree-tops, scenting death and carrion.

Every soldier on parade would remember this day vividly, and would pass on his description to his sons and, in older age, to his sons' sons. Their accounts would lose nothing in each re-telling. By killing these sepoys in this fashion, copied from the Mogul rulers of an earlier age, they were about to add fuel to a fire of hatred and resentment that could one day destroy British influence in India as certainly as gunpowder would annihilate these prisoners.

Douglas turned to the colonel.

'I cannot order the gunners to fire, sir,' he said in a grave voice he barely recognised as his own.

'You cannot do *what*, Douglas? You are refusing an order, eh?'

'I am refusing to commit murder.'

'You damned young puppy!'

The colonel lay back in his cane chair, sweating with irritation. The sudden movement made him wince, for he suffered severely from gout. His right foot, with its knobbly, rusty-jointed toes, lay bare before him on a small stool. Behind him, an Indian servant stroked the air with a fan of peacock feathers. It was the hottest time of day, in the hottest season of the year, just before the monsoon broke. Tempers were thin and blood ran warm; the wrong reply, even the wrong accent, could provoke irrational anger.

The colonel regarded Douglas through half-closed eyes. He had been drinking since noon, which was madness in that temperature, but on some days the bitterness of being passed over so frequently for promotion became unbearable, unendurable. Alcohol ran in his veins like flame and offered a temporary antidote to disappointment. The contrast with what he had hoped to achieve when he was young, like Alec Douglas facing him, and what he had actually accomplished, was so great that only the constant comfort of claret and whisky could drive the roaring demons of remorse from his mind. But still they waited, on the threshold of memory, always ready to return.

'I will have you know, Douglas,' he began, and then paused. The words sounded slurred and indistinct, as though someone else altogether was speaking through fog or a thick blanket. He realised he was already slightly tipsy.

'I will have you know, Douglas,' he said slowly and deliberately, 'that your conduct since joining this regiment has been altogether unsatisfactory. Altogether.'

'You never mentioned this to me before, sir,' Douglas replied.

'I was making my own assessment,' the colonel told him. 'The fact is, I don't think you fit in. You are not quite – not quite one of us.'

'In what way, sir?'

'I need not particularise, damn it! The fact that you refuse a direct order, an offence which, for a ranker, would mean field punishment, being strapped to the wheel of a gun for a whole day, or even death, as it means for these mutineers, is surely enough indication. I am recommending to the commander-in-chief that you are relieved of your commission immediately.'

'On the grounds of refusing this order, sir, which if it were implemented, could cause unrest right across India?'

'You know nothing about India or Indians. You have only been here a few months. No time at all. I have served in India for twenty-two *years*. The only thing Indians respect is strength. Give them an inch, let them see you're soft, and they'll be at your throat like rats!'

'I am not against administering punishment appropriate to proven misconduct, sir. But these men have only refused to use new grease supplied for lubricating cartridges in their carbines because it is made – by an ignorant and defaulting contractor – from a mixture of pig's lard and cow fat. A more deliberate insult – to their minds – could not be imagined.

'The pig is totally abhorrent to Muslims, and the cow is revered by Hindus. So men of both religions are offended beyond measure if they use this grease.'

'I cannot become involved in their heathen beliefs. A lot of mumbo-jumbo.'

'You are a Christian, I know, sir, because you lead church parade. Would you not be shocked if some heathen sepoy used the chalice from the altar to drink his toddy?'

'Are you mad, Douglas? That would be blasphemy deserving of the most rigorous punishment.'

'Of course, sir. But these sepoys feel the same about *their* religions. I beg you, with the deepest respect, to think again.'

'You can beg all you like, Douglas, but the more you go on bleating and arguing, the more you convince me that you are totally unsuited to hold a commission in the army of the Honourable East India Company. An officer should be a man of action, not someone who refuses an order. You have one week to settle up your personal affairs.'

He struck a brass bell on the desk. An orderly opened the door and saluted.

'My compliments to the adjutant,' the colonel began.

The adjutant, Captain Edwin Bushell, was a plump forty-year-old bachelor, the second son of a Leeds brewer who, like Douglas, had been paid to leave home in a hurry. There had been some trouble over his association with married women. Nothing proven, of course, but rumours had been sufficiently insistent to become unpleasant; one of the women was the wife of an influential MP.

'Mr Douglas is leaving the regiment,' the colonel explained shortly. 'I am writing to the C-in-C giving my reasons. You will draft the letter. The culmination of months of unsatisfactory service and a direct refusal to obey my orders.'

'If I appeal, sir?' Douglas asked him.

'Appeal, damn you, and I will have you court martialled. For encouraging insurrection.'

Douglas looked with unconcealed contempt at the fat old man with his slack mouth and swollen bubble-belly, lying back in the chair. All three men knew quite well that although Douglas could appeal, to do so would be futile. Any appeal he might address to the directors of the East India

Company in London would take months to reach them, and as many more months for their reply to return – if, indeed, it did not somehow become mislaid on its outward journey. Such inexplicable loss had happened often enough before to critical reports.

Douglas looked at the colonel, and suddenly he smiled.

'You think this is funny, then, do you, damn you?' the colonel shouted, arching his back in rage.

'It may be serious for you, sir,' replied Douglas. 'I was thinking of something else.'

How could he admit that he was thinking of the long voyage east and what happened on it, and again and again since he had reached India? When the ship put in for fresh water and provisions, at the Cape of Good Hope, the colonel and Emma, his much younger second wife, came aboard.

They had been spending some months in South Africa on their way out from England. As was the custom, they bought cabin space, with all the furniture in that cabin and an ante-room, for the voyage across the Arabian Sea, around the southern tip of India and across the Bay of Bengal to Calcutta. When the ship docked, they would sell this space and the furniture to whoever wished to take passage home to England.

Douglas had seen little of them at first, for the colonel was a poor sailor, but Emma, possibly thirty years younger than her husband, had been one of the few women passengers who liked sitting on deck, even catching the sun on her face. Most European women feared the sun, convinced its rays could spoil their complexion or even cause insanity. Some believed that direct sunlight was fatal, if not immediately then within days. They told stories of people whose blood had literally boiled in their veins through staying out too long in the heat of the sun.

'You don't believe those tales, do you?' she asked Douglas as they leaned on the polished mahogany rail, watching flying fish dart like silver dagger blades from the crest of one wave to the next.

'It depends who you lie in the sun with,' he replied. She smiled, and said nothing.

'How did you meet the colonel?' he asked her.

'I was a nurse. He engaged me in England to look after his wife. She had caught one of these fearful fevers that seem so common in India. She survived the voyage home, but did not respond to any treatment. Specialists let blood, dosed her with bark, advised that she ate less meat, or more, even that she should sleep in a bed pointing north to south, then east to west. But all the time she steadily grew weaker. I doubt whether she wanted to go on living. She had somehow lost her will, her spirit. They all do with India fevers. It is hard for me to say, but I think perhaps her marriage was not a happy one.'

'And is yours?'

Emma did not reply, but looked down at her hands, twirling the wedding ring on her finger. When she did look up, Alec could see pain and unhappiness in her china-blue eyes.

'He means to be kind, my husband. It is just that. . . .' She paused. 'There is a great difference in our ages,' she said at last. 'But I have been fortunate. My mother is a widow. I was lucky to find such a position nursing his wife. And I had no position to go on to when she died.'

'How long have you been married?'

He was not really interested but conversation aboard ship was stilted, centring mainly on card games that had been played the previous evening, or discussions about the speed of the vessel, the likelihood of running into a typhoon – and was that strange shape momentarily glimpsed in the glittering sea a whale, a sea-serpent, or an hallucination?

'Six months,' she said.

The look-out cried down from the crow's nest: 'Wreckage ahoy, on the port bow!'

The helmsman threw his weight against the wheel. Creaking protest, the ship dipped sluggishly and turned. The unexpected movement caused Emma to lose balance for a moment. She slid along the rail so that her shoulder touched Alec's arm. He did not move away, neither did she.

From where they stood they could not see all the wreckage, only a few spars of raw splintered wood, for they were looking at each other, their eyes only inches apart.

Still with his arms folded on the rail, Alec released his right hand and stroked Emma's forearm. It was a scouting movement in the complex chess match of seduction. If, as a wife, she did not wish his attentions, she could draw away. If she appeared to resent them, he could then apologise with the explanation that he had not realised she was so close to him. Instead, she pressed slightly against his shoulder. They stayed like this for a moment, Alec suddenly conscious of the mounting beat of his heart. A new electric excitement lit the air like lightning in a summer storm.

Emma turned away and began to walk towards the companionway. She did not look back. He followed her, caught up with her at the top of the steps. She turned then and regarded him with a strange detachment, as though genuinely surprised to see him.

'Is your cabin on the starboard side?' he asked, his voice suddenly hoarse.

'Yes.'

'So you could not see the wreckage from it, then?'

'No.'

'I have a spy glass in mine – portside. We could see where the wreckage is from. Maybe a ship has gone down.'

She might not even have heard him. He took her arm to help her down the creaking wooden steps of the companionway, and in silence he guided her towards his cabin. She entered without a backward glance. He closed the door behind her, locked it. When she turned, she was smiling.

The room felt very confined after the breeze on deck, scented by the warm sweet smell of beeswax polish on its panelling.

'*Only* a spy glass, Mr Douglas?' she asked him. He smiled in response. 'It has been called other things,' he admitted.

They were close together now. There was no need for any concealment. He had sent his first cautious signal and she had replied: there was no doubt about her intention – or his.

Douglas trailed his fingers down her arm, feeling the warmth of her skin through the thin silk of her blouse. Her tongue, as they kissed, possessed a life of its own; hot, darting, exploring. With his mouth still locked on hers, he began to unbutton her blouse. She stood back a pace to make this easier for him. He kicked off his shoes, tore off his shirt and trousers. Her skirt and shift slid to the thick carpet. Her hand went down to his groin, gripped him, long delicate fingers stroking his throbbing phallus, hard as hickory.

'My!' she whispered in admiration and surprise.

For a moment, they stood thus, naked and unashamed as Adam and Eve, two people, all but one flesh.

Then, without a word, Alec carried her to his bed.

The colonel was talking angrily. . . .

Douglas did not hear him. He was remembering Emma's face damp with sweat, her lips parted, her hair spread like a dark mysterious fan across the white pillow. He felt the nipples rise on her breasts beneath his palms, and then the warm moist welcome of that other, secret, mouth as he entered and her body arched with longing to meet each thrust.

The thick glass in the cabin's port-hole magnified the sun's reflection on the heaving sea so that it shone hot as a burning glass on Douglas's bare back. She entwined her long legs about him, clinging tightly as if she would die if she released her hold. He heard her cry as the long, warm cream of life surged from him to her.

'You are *still* smirking, damn you!'

'I was thinking, sir,' Douglas admitted.

'Thinking?' the colonel repeated, sarcastically. 'You stand there grinning like an ape, and tell me you're *thinking*? I trust your thoughts are cheerful?'

'Memorable, sir!'

Emma MacTavish did not possess the sexual skill and dexterity of Mrs Cochrane, but then that was scarcely to be expected: one was a professional, while Emma was at most an enthusiastic amateur. However, this

was their first encounter. There were others, many others, afloat and,
later, ashore. If this old fool knew how many times he had taken his wife,
in what strange places and in positions he could not even imagine, he
would never believe it. People rarely gave credence to any experience out
of the narrow spectrum of their own lives, and Colonel MacTavish was at
best a day labourer in the matter of the arts and crafts of love.

'You are a damned insolent swine,' the colonel told Douglas, watching
him through narrowed eyes. 'I thought that the first time I set eyes on
you! I only entertained your application because I know your stepfather.
The regiment is well rid of you – as no doubt he was.'

He turned to the adjutant.

'My compliments to Mr Barker. He will take the parade.'

He turned back to Douglas.

'I will not forbid you the companionship of the mess, but I make it
clear that your presence there will not be welcomed. You will doubtless
wish to make other arrangements for your accommodation and your
entertainment.'

Douglas clicked his heels, bowed, took the regulation two paces back
and left the room.

Captain Bushell followed him out, bemused by the sudden turn of
events.

'You know what you are doing, I suppose?' he asked weakly.

'I am absolutely certain. I cannot serve for another hour under that old
fool.'

'I would say that the colonel's lady wife is one person who *will* be very
sorry you are leaving,' the adjutant said slyly, looking sideways at him.

'I will be sorry to leave the regiment in many ways,' Douglas agreed
carefully, looking him in the eyes. 'Mrs MacTavish has been friendly to
me. She has done me the honour of asking me to dine on several occasions. But life, my dear fellow, is made up of partings and new meetings.'

Unconvinced, the adjutant shook his head. Could those rumours he
had heard about Emma MacTavish and Alec Douglas be only bazaar
gossip, tittle-tattle put about by indolent servants hoping for a tip?

The fellow Douglas certainly looked straight enough. Yet he had seen
him bathing and had been impressed by the size of what, in Army terms
was always obliquely referred to as his short arm. If he was not involved
with Mrs MacTavish, then he knew of several ladies who would be glad
of the opportunity. No point in wasting any sympathy on Douglas. With
his build he was bound to be a winner, and did not his family own land in
Scotland? He would be all right for money. That was the main thing.

The adjutant's own private income was so large that he would sometimes learn with total amazement, almost disbelief, that other officers
could be less wealthy, and some were compelled to accept and swallow

the most scandalous treatment simply because they had no alternative. Mr Barker, for instance, a most able officer on whom much of the drearier work descended, had served in the lowly rank of lieutenant for twenty-five years only because he lacked money to buy a captaincy, a majority, or eventually the command of a regiment. Thank God, this would never happen to him.

As Douglas left the building, heat hit him like a blast from a suddenly opened oven. He turned away from the parade ground, and hurried between dusty palm trees to his own quarters.

He therefore did not see the old subedar, a native officer of nearly thirty years' service, standing out of the sun's heat under a high stone archway, watching the scene while tears ran unheeded down his face.

News of Alec Douglas's dismissal spread as rapidly as his bearers could pack his kit in his black tin trunks, so necessary against the ants of India, which could eat through almost any thickness of wood.

He winced as he heard the sudden angry rumble of the guns. Birds nesting in the rafters fled out through the unglazed windows in frantic terror. His bearers faltered briefly as they folded his clothes; they knew that with these sudden bursts of fire, their comrades had left them forever, doomed to eternal damnation. To die a warrior's death in honourable combat meant instant entry to paradise, but to die in mutilation meant the prospect of endless purgatory. It was one thing to be punished in this world, but what kind of man would condemn another to everlasting torment in the next?

The head bearer salaamed him with two hands pressed palm to palm and raised to his forehead; he wished to know Douglas sahib's instructions about packing his dress uniform. There was a knock at the door before Douglas could reply. A messenger brought in a folded note. Alec guessed it must be from Emma; bad news was always a swift traveller. There was no name on the paper, no signature, just the words: 'Nine o'clock – banyan tree'.

At a quarter to nine that evening, having stayed in his quarters all day, freshly bathed, shaved and wearing undress uniform, Douglas sauntered round the edge of the parade ground – for no one crossed it unless on duty – until he reached a cluster of trees on the far side. The night was alive with the croaks and twitterings, like rusty ratchets unwinding, of crickets and frogs, and the whirring wings of a myriad unknown insects. The air felt so humid that even the exertion of walking made sweat pour from his body and soak his shirt.

During daylight hours, this huge banyan tree, with its spreading umbrella of branches, was a favourite place for itinerant vendors of sweetmeats, money-lenders and snake charmers with cobras in baskets, or men who led red-eyed muzzled bears to dance at the flick of a cane. After dark, it was deserted. Locals believed that the tree was the haunt of evil spirits who only came alive when the sun went down and could be harmful if disturbed. It was therefore useful for any secret and brief meeting between those who did not share this dread.

Douglas drew on his cigar, hoping that Emma would see the red glow in the deepening dark and know he had arrived. She did, and approached him from the other side of the warm, gnarled trunk. He stubbed out his cigar, and could smell the heady aroma of the scent she wore: crushed violet essence she had brought out from England – from another life, another world, another time – that suddenly also recalled another woman, Mrs Cochrane.

'I heard what happened,' she said at once as they touched hands and kissed gently. 'I admire you for it. But those poor wretched Indians died just the same.'

'We are all born to die,' Douglas replied philosophically. 'Some are called early, others late. I did what I could to stop that charade, but your husband would not be persuaded. I am glad you asked to see me, because otherwise I would not have been able to say goodbye to you. It would have been unwise for me to send you a note.'

'What are you going to do?' Emma asked him miserably.

He shrugged.

'I do not know,' he admitted. 'I only wish I did. I have no private means. My stepfather bought my commission. I will have to make my own way – like most others of God's creatures.'

'I will miss you more than I can possibly say. You do know that?'

'And I will miss you, my dear,' he said, thinking: I will really only miss your warm pliable body pressed against mine, mine inside yours, mouth on mouth, legs entwined, two people as one, the beast with two backs.

He felt sorry for her. He knew how insecure and lonely she felt, and how worse than lonely, totally alone, with an old and impotent and cantankerous husband with whom she had nothing in common.

Douglas's feelings for her might be almost totally animal, but it was still impossible to lie with any white woman in India and not to feel a modicum of warmth and remembrance. He did not simply lust after her, he liked her.

'Will you remember me?' she asked anxiously, seeking reassurance that their relationship was not simply a passing affair – although, in all the circumstances, what else could it be?

'Of course,' he assured her. 'How can I keep in touch with you?'

'You cannot,' she replied. 'If my husband discovered how we feel, would be in an even worse plight than I am now.'

'Write to me then in Calcutta,' he told her, 'care of Mr Grindlay' bank, and mark the envelope "Personal". How long can you stay now? Do you not fear the colonel will miss you?'

'I told him I had a migraine. I came out through the servants' entrance.'

'Someone will have seen you leave,' warned Douglas. On every military station, there was always someone with sharp eyes and a ready tongue.

'In that case, let us give them something to talk about.'

Already raising her skirt, she led him into the deeper shade of the tree.

At that moment, the croaking of the insects ceased. The night was suddenly filled with silence. Against the warm bole of the tree, Douglas took her until, panting for breath, they clung together else both would have fallen, exhausted. In the distance a bugle sounded some military call. Emma was trembling, weeping uncontrollably because he was going out of her life, and she guessed forever.

Next day he travelled to Calcutta in a palanquin, a kind of elongated sedan chair with a couch inside where the passenger could sleep. This was borne by four coolies, one at the end of each carrying pole. His luggage followed on the backs of two elephants. His servants walked – a *khansama*, or cook; the *bhisti*, to draw water; a sweeper to take care of toilet arrangements; two bearers to look after his uniforms; a *dhobi* to wash his linen; a personal bearer to fetch and carry whatever Douglas might wish him to fetch and carry.

Some of these servants were married; their wives and families travelled with them. The women took it in turns to carry the smaller children and their few possessions. The men did not carry anything.

Douglas spent each night of the journey in a *dak* bungalow used by travelling mailmen, the *dak*-wallahs, and maintained by the Company with a permanent staff of servants for the use of travellers. There were no good hotels in Calcutta, and since he knew no one with whom he could stay, he had to rent rooms in a new building facing the Hooghly River. Here he paid off the baggage train, and pondered on his future.

He had a few hundred pounds saved, but life in India was expensive. Those employed in business firms or the law earned large salaries, and lived in a style that led them to be called nabobs. Military officers usually had private incomes from family estates in Britain or trust funds set up by relatives, and Douglas therefore had to maintain a certain standard.

He had visiting cards printed and paid his calls, a custom that stemmed from the earliest days of the British in India. After each monsoon, when the worst time for fevers and cholera and incurable maladies was thankfully over for another year, those who had survived called on each other – simply to show they were still alive.

What had originally been a necessity, gradually became a social custom by which newcomers could inform others of their arrival. As a result, he was invited to several dinner parties, but since he had no hostess to organise reciprocal hospitality, these invitations soon diminished, and then stopped.

Every morning, in a newly pressed suit and freshly starched linen, he presented himself at the offices of attorneys and merchants. He called at counting houses, and offered his services in any capacity for which the principals might consider him a suitable candidate. He was thanked with various degrees of courtesy, and heard nothing further from any of them. He possessed no qualifications, no introductions from important people, no valuable social connections, and worst of all, soon he had no money.

Douglas was on the point of dismissing his last personal bearer – the least any European required – when an Indian messenger, splendid in livery, with a white turban bearing a gold star, and wearing a red sash edged with gold, arrived and presented him with a sealed envelope. Puzzled, he opened it at once. The writer, one Mr Sodawaterwallah, desired that Douglas would attend upon him at his earliest. Should it be convenient, the bearer of this invitation would guide him to the writer' house.

Who the devil was Mr Sodawaterwallah? he wondered. How did he come by such an extraordinary name – and why should he want to se Douglas? There seemed only one sure way to discover the answers to al these questions. Since Douglas had nothing better to do – indeed nothing at all to do – he took his seat in the phaeton that waited outside complete with outrider and a footman up front with the coachman o the box.

The phaeton drove through the teeming city and into the walle courtyard of a property so large and luxurious that it could best b described as a palace. From the street, little had been visible; only a lon high white-washed wall and the roof of a house standing some wa behind it. Within the wall, however, he was surprised at the opulenc this drab exterior concealed, completely divorced from the brayir crowds and stink of Calcutta, the piles of rotting mangoes at stre corners, the ordure and dung that littered every pavement.

Servants, bowing low before him, ushered him into a high-ceiling room tiled with black and white marble squares. It had the appearance a giant's chess-board. Above his head, gold-edged punkahs, connected delicate silver chains, stirred the cool and fragrant air. Through archway a fountain cascaded into a circular pool, where golden ca moved lethargically from the shelter of one heart-shaped lily leaf another. Next to this pool, in a golden bowl supported on a slender sto pillar, a flame a foot high burned steadily.

Douglas was examining this when he heard a quiet footstep behi him and turned. A man of about thirty-five had followed him into the room.

'I am Mr Sodawaterwallah,' the newcomer explained briskly, and held out a limp, rather damp hand. As Douglas shook it, he noticed that Mr Sodawaterwallah exuded a strong smell of scent. He was plump and somehow soft but not dark-skinned, more the colour of a Levantine or a southern Italian. He wore silk pantaloons, a white silk shirt and silver slippers with pointed curled-up toes. Douglas was absurdly reminded of pictures in a children's book about the adventures of Sindbad the Sailor.

'I hear that you have resigned your commission,' Mr Sodawaterwallah went on without any preamble, as though directness was the best way to begin a conversation with a stranger.

'Your information, sir, is only partly accurate. My colonel required my resignation. It was his decision that I left, not mine.'

'May I ask why?'

'I refused to order eight sepoys to be blown from the mouths of cannon for what, amongst more understanding officers, would be considered a relatively unimportant misdemeanour.'

'I heard as much,' the other man said with satisfaction. 'But I found the news difficult to believe, because I know how little some Europeans know – or care – about the religious beliefs of those who do not follow their own faith. Now, to business. You are a single man?'

'I am.'

'Please forgive my asking what may be considered almost impertinent questions at a first meeting, but let us establish our relationship at once. It is important for both of us to do so. Without a commission, am I correct in assuming that you are now also without a job?'

'That is so.'

'Are you particular about the work you would undertake – work of, shall I say, a very unusual and unspecified nature?'

'I do not wish to do anything against the interests of my own countrymen or the Company or my sovereign. Apart from that, sir, I am prepared to hear details of any proposition.'

They were walking through the archway now and came out into the courtyard. The wind had changed, causing the flame to tremble, blowing spray on to the tiles. The air felt damp and fresh. They might be not in Calcutta, but in some far cooler, cleaner climate.

'You are but recently arrived in this country?' asked Mr Sodawaterwallah, as though still uncertain whether to come to the reason for his invitation to Douglas.

'About six months ago.'

'Then you may not realise that I am not an Indian – I am a Parsee. We take the name from Pars, a province in Persia. To many Europeans, all people in India are Indians, just as in China everyone of whatever Eastern race – Koreans, Japanese, Javanese, Siamese – must be considered to be Chinese. Because the colour of our skins is not the colour of yours, we can all be classed alike as Indians.

'That is a false assumption, Mr Douglas. We are not all alike, just as you as a Scot are not *quite* like any other man from the West, from France or Portugal, or even America.'

'So you are a stranger here, too?'

The man smiled.

'In a sense. We are all strangers, my friend, in life's short journey. Here for a brief season, then we part. As a Parsee, I follow a different religion to you, but I do not necessarily worship a different God from you or from a Brahmin or a Buddhist. We each worship a God in whom we can believe.'

Douglas nodded, wondering what the meaning of this discourse could be. Surely this obviously immensely rich man had not brought him out in such style to this sumptuous palace simply to discuss comparative religions?

'We worship Ahura Mazda,' Mr Sodawaterwallah went on, 'the God of Light, whose prophet was Zarathustra. This burning flame is alight day and night, to remind us that light banishes darkness. People not of our faith assume we worship fire. That is not so, although fire is beneficial. It represents light – as do the candles on a Christian altar. Darkness – in the form of charred wood or a burned candle wick – represents evil.

'If you are interested in matters of the hereafter – and we should always interest ourselves in them, my friend, because life itself is so short and the journey after death so long – it is prudent to remember that all religions teach the need to worship *some* god or force we cannot see, and the faithful are in perpetual combat with evil.

'Your God and your Satan derive from the God and Satan of the Jews. The Muslim faith has a similar origin. But all three religions are based on ours. Our god, as I have said, is called Ahura Mazda, and our devil Ahriman. The whole concept of angels and demons and heaven and hell come from Zarathustra's teachings.'

'I find this difficult to accept,' said Douglas, remembering the minister in the little kirk on the family estate, preaching the Gospels, earnestly expounding what he so sincerely believed was the one true faith.

'Very possibly, my friend. But look at any picture of Jesus or any Christian saint, and you will see a halo of light around their heads. This is from our teaching.'

'That may well be so, sir,' Douglas agreed, trying to conceal his impatience, ' but why bring me here to instruct me in these matters?'

'Because it is necessary for you to understand why I am going to send your assistance. You have a fair skin. You have red hair, the symbol of the eternal flame. You also have the physique of a warrior, the body of a man. I have made some enquiries about you and understand that your family owned great estates in your native country, that you are a man of culture. And also, according to my enquiries, a man of vigour and resilience in encounters of the couch, with an organ, my sources claim, not like the *zab* of an ordinary man but, how shall I say, a maypole. And that you have used it tirelessly – even, it is whispered, pleasuring the wives of other men? Is this true?'

'I have never thought of myself in those terms, Mr Sodawaterwallah.'

'Very possibly not. It is not given for us to see ourselves as others regard us. We have a saying, my friend – "The eye cannot see its own lashes." Now, to the matter on which I have brought you here.

'Look at my skin. It is darker than yours, agreed – but it is not black, like the flesh of an Ethiopian. Nor am I brown, like an Indian. It is imperative that Parsees have children with fair skins. We consider it a disgrace to be of too dark a complexion. For this reason, my friend, it is sometimes necessary for our wives to seek sexual connection with men from the north or the west, otherwise they might bear their husbands dark children. And darkness to us, as I have explained, represents the forces of evil.

'I have brought you here, Mr Douglas, to make you a business proposition. I have a young wife, barren by me. I wish you to put her with child.'

'If she is barren, it may be impossible for her to conceive,' Douglas replied.

'That is so. I know how, as a sop to male vanity, it is widely believed among your people that only the woman can be barren. Our teaching says that the man's seed can also be without life. It may be that this is the case in this instance, that I fear getting her with child in case our child might have a darker skin. My wife has been totally faithful to me, so this is a matter that can only be put to the test.'

'If she bears a child as a result of your proposal, her son or daughter will be yours?'

'Indeed. Mine and mine alone. Any hint or suggestion to the contrary would be repudiated with the utmost vigour. For this purpose, I am prepared to pay you two sums of money. Five thousand rupees if you agree with my proposal, and the same sum again if you put my wife with child. This second sum to be paid when she misses her monthly course, not when the child is born. So you could be ten thousand rupees richer within the space of weeks.'

They had reached the end of the courtyard, and turned and walked back past the fountain, towards the flame in the golden bowl. Brightly plumaged birds fluttered brilliant wings as they dived and swooped and turned in the sunshine.

'You are quiet, young man,' said the Parsee, looking at him enquiringly.

'No one has ever made a proposition like this to me before,' said Douglas. 'You make me feel like a male whore, a pander.'

Mr Sodawaterwallah put out a hand, soft as the pad of a tiger, and touched Douglas on the arm.

'My friend, that is a most unworthy thought. Please dismiss i instantly from your mind. I am paying you the highest compliment an man can offer another – I am offering you my wife, whom I love dearly. I wish to bring up your child as mine. If a girl, she will marry well with a large dowry. If a boy, he will inherit this house, and family businesses here and in Bombay. That surely is not the price of a whore?'

'Whatever it is,' replied Douglas, 'I will take it. But at twice the sum you mention. Ten thousand now, the same to follow.'

Mr Sodawaterwallah smiled.

'I read your mind aright,' he said triumphantly. 'Since you are English –'

'Scottish,' corrected Douglas.

'Of course. There is a difference, I know. Since you are Scottish – race which I feel has a great affinity with the Jews, in that they work hard to make money – I thought you would ask me to double my offer. So i that expectation, I put ten thousand rupees in my pocket for you.'

He handed a manilla envelope to Douglas.

'Open it if you wish. You will find that it contains a ten thousand rupee bank note.'

'I did not know one could get a single note of such high denomination from a bank.'

'It is not usual, agreed. But then, Mr Douglas, I own the bank.'

They shook hands.

'You have asked me questions,' said Douglas, 'and I have answered them. Now, sir, a question to you. How do you have such a strange name Sodawaterwallah?'

'It is not strange. That is my family's trade. I own a factory Bombay – the largest in India – where air and carbonate of soda pumped into tanks of water. This soda water, as you call it, is then bottl and sold under various names. You have probably drunk it in yo officers' mess, mixed with whisky or brandy or the juice of mangoes an oranges. I am the merchant – the wallah – who makes this beverag Hence my name. We take our names from our work, as I understand w once the case in your country – Smith, Cook, Butler, and so forth.'

As he spoke, he was leading the way through a small side door t

Douglas had not previously noticed, into a room with marble floor and walls. A sunken bath, larger than Douglas had ever seen, was half filled with warm water. Lotus blossoms floated through perfumed steam.

'I will leave you here. When you have bathed, servants will bring you warm towels. You will then go through to the next room where my wife, Savina, will be waiting.'

He showed no emotion, no embarrassment. A business proposal had been made, an offer accepted. Now all that remained was for the agreement to be honoured. He bowed politely and went out.

Douglas removed his clothes, folded up the envelope, tied it in his handkerchief and put this in his trouser pocket. Then he climbed into the bath. Ten minutes later, refreshed and relaxed, he saw two servants enter the room, each carrying a warm towel. He climbed out, dried himself, brushed his hair with silver-backed brushes he found on the side table and, with a towel wrapped around him, was bowed into another room. This was carpeted, with leopard and bear skins strewn on the carpet. There was a wide bed with peach-coloured silk sheets, a chaise longue, a dressing table with three mirrors. Across the window, white silk curtains, thin as gossamer wings, filtered the harsh sunlight.

A young girl barely out of her teens, it seemed to Douglas, stood looking out of the window through these billowing curtains. Her skin was the colour of very creamy coffee. She wore a white sari edged with gold, and slippers bright with tiny diamonds. Gold rings dangled from her ears; her finger-nails and toe-nails were painted cherry red. Douglas had never before seen a woman with painted nails; he found the sight attractive and erotic. She smiled a welcome to him. They might have been old friends.

He bowed formally to her, feeling like a Roman in a toga in his white towel. What did he do now? Shake hands? Introduce himself? The girl spoke in a small pleasing voice with a slight and attractive sing-song lilt.

'I am Savina,' she said, smiling reassuringly at him. 'I can imagine how embarrassed you must feel, so you will appreciate *my* feelings. Please sit down.'

Douglas sat uneasily at one end of the chaise longue. She sat down gracefully at the other. Glasses and a huge flask of crushed fruit juice, with cubes of ice and flower petals floating on it, stood on a side table. She filled a glass, handed it to him. He raised the glass in a toast to her, and drank. The liquid tasted agreeably cold and sharp.

'You must think we have strange customs in the East?' said Savina.

'They are – or at least, these are – rather different from anything I have known in my own country.'

'But you have a saying I read in an English book: "Variety is the spice of life." Am I right? Yes?'

'Yes. This is so.'

Silence hung uneasily between them.

'You are hungry?' she asked him.

'Not really,' Douglas admitted.

'Tell me about your home, then.'

He shook his head. How could he explain to this lovely creature in this scented boudoir how he lived in a cold castle that had many windows without glass, fires which burned logs as long as a man, how dogs could gnaw bones beneath the dining table? It was an impossibility.

'I would rather hear about you,' he replied.

'There is very little to tell. As you may know, I am fortunate among women. I have everything here any woman could wish for. A husband who loves me dearly, loyal servants, anything that money can buy. Except the one thing that is without price, so far denied to both of us – a child with a fair skin. Can *you* give me my heart's desire?'

She looked at him with the appealing, pouting face of a beautiful child, half innocent, half petulant.

'I can try,' he said hesitantly. He felt desire grow with confidence as he slid across the silk of the sofa. He put out an arm and drew Savina towards him. She did not resist. He could smell the subtle scent of her hair. His lips brushed her ear, and all the while his right hand was stroking her shoulder through the silk of her sari. She turned towards him, so close that her face seemed to fill his whole vision. He saw her lips, reddened in a way he had never seen any woman's lips reddened before, and the glisten of white teeth, her smile and her enormous liquid eyes.

He kissed her then, gently, and the kiss was totally unlike the savage biting of his stepfather's mistress or the naked need of Emma MacTavish. Savina's tongue was not darting like a sword, but soft and warm as the wing of an elusive night moth. They drew apart and he began to unbutton the jacket above the sari with eager fingers. She gave a sigh of content and wriggled free. Her breasts felt warm and firm in his hands; two round worlds, it seemed, with life of their own. Her nipples were reddened with some dye, like her lips, the twin peaks of fairytale hills in an enchanted land.

She moved against him. Her sari, like his bath towel, fell away. Slowly as though in the predestined movement of a delicate minuet, beyond all measurement of time, their legs entwined. They were not two people but one, and suddenly overcome by his need, Douglas was rearing like a beast, thrusting as though he must die if he ceased, heedless of her first half cry and then the soft moans of pleasure she uttered.

Her hands grasped his bare shoulders, digging into his hard muscle like firm claws, and then the long, hot throbbing thread of human life passed from him to her, and they subsided, sobbing for breath, side by side

They lay quietly until the thunder of his heart receded from his ears, and he could hear sounds he had forgotten: the tinkling of the fountain in the courtyard, the cawing of the birds outside as they spun and soared up again in the shining air.

Savina was the first to move.

Her eyes were luminous, like stars shining at him, and she smiled a soft and secret smile.

'There is something I also read in an English book, about rushing like a bull at a gate. Here, in the East, we have less haste, more time. There is a saying, "It is pleasant to smell the blossom and pick the flowers before we eat the fruit." It is written.'

'As it is written, so shall it be,' Douglas assured her solemnly, and once more emparadised her in his arms.

Douglas slept, and as he slept, dreamed uneasily, and not of Savina.

He was standing in a church, in a side vestry, and above his head, unseen in their tower, the bells were pealing joyfully for a wedding. But he had no joy in his head, only a deep sense of foreboding. By his side stood a man whose face he could not see.

Douglas watched through a slit window as guests arrived, stepping down from their carriages, coming into the church; friends of the bride on the left, friends of the groom on the right. Who were they all? Why was he where he was and not with them? Then someone asked him to take his place in the body of the church with this man by his side, and he realised that he was not a guest: that this was *his* wedding. But who was he marrying – and where and when?

Even in his dream Douglas knew it could prove ill-omened for him to look over his shoulder and see the bride approach, and he suddenly became aware that she was standing by his side. Then, as he turned to look, she made to raise her veil.

At that moment, he awoke. He was sweating, his mouth was dry, and his heart thumped heavily like an overloaded steam engine. He was conscious of a feeling of immense relief: he was still free, he was still single. Thank God, it had only been a dream.

Time and again, since he left Scotland, he had experienced this fantasy, and each time he awoke just before he saw the face of the woman he had married in his sleep. And each time, too, he experienced the same enormous relief, the feeling he had somehow barely escaped a snare from which there could only ever be one means of securing freedom: death. But whose – his or hers?

Douglas started up in horror. He was lying on a straw palliasse, gasping for breath, soaking with sweat in a humid, foetid room. For a moment, he was not quite sure where he was, or even who he was. He was standing in the rain by his mother's grave, watching his stepfather, hating him; he was leaning over the ship's rail with Emma; lying on the silken bed with Savina, mouth on mouth, his body hard within hers. The images faded and bitter reality burned his soul with the harshness of etching acid. He was in a squalid rented room in the village of Alipore, three miles outside Calcutta.

In an attempt to give the impression that he was wealthy – believing this might encourage someone to offer him a worthwhile job – he had spent the money Mr Sodawaterwallah had paid him. Now, only weeks later, Douglas was on his own, without a single servant, a poor sahib in a native house. He could sink no further.

No one wanted an indigent European in India in that year of Our Lord, for the valid reason that there should be no poor Europeans in India. They should have stayed in Europe. If they were poor and white and in India, then they were an unwelcome, almost impossible anachronism, and like lepers, they should be carefully avoided. Failure could also be contagious. Eventually, they must accept total ostracism, and if they had any shreds of honour left would take the only decent course left to them, and remove themselves. In the last analysis, this could mean suicide. Other, richer Europeans would then come to their funeral and nod approvingly when the preacher spoke of treasure in Heaven.

Someone was banging urgently on the door. Douglas stood up and wrapped a blanket around his bare body, cursing the interruption and the insistent droning whine of mosquitoes. He pulled back the wooden bolt.

There was no window in his tiny cell, and he was surprised how bright the light seemed outside on the landing. It was nearly noon. He must have overslept, drugged by the stinking air. He blinked until his eyes grew accustomed to the naked glare of morning.

An Indian was standing in the doorway, a man of medium height with grey hair, soberly and neatly dressed. There was something military about his appearance. He raised his hand smartly to his turban.

'What do you want?' Douglas asked him shortly. He had no time for mendicants now: he was almost one himself.

'I wish to see Mr Douglas, sahib, formerly an ensign with the 113th Regiment.'

'I am Douglas. Who are you?'

'I was, sahib, a subedar in that regiment. I am now a pensioner.'

Douglas looked at him more closely. He recognised his face, but could not put a name to him. There had been several subedars in the regiment. He had not served with the 113th for long, and he did not know them all.

'What do you want with me?' he asked less brusquely.

'I seek your help, sahib.'

Douglas laughed.

'I am in no position to help myself, let alone anyone else, however much I might wish to do so. I have no money, no influence, no friends.'

'*I* am your friend, sahib.'

'I am pleased to hear that. But I cannot even ask you into my room, I am too ashamed of it. Why have you sought me out in this wretched place?'

'Because, sahib, you have a gentle heart. I was present when those men were blown from guns on the colonel sahib's command. I know you refused to carry out that order. I stood and watched you as you left the regiment forever, and my heart travelled with you. You see, sahib, my only son was one of those the colonel condemned to die. The regiment had been his mother and his father, as it had been mine since I joined as a drummer. When my son died, something in me died also. There is no one left to carry on my name.'

'I am very sorry to hear of this, subedar sahib. But how can I possibly help you?'

'I will tell you, sahib. I am a member of the Imfalli Muslim sect. Our spiritual leader has been murdered as he paid a visit to the holy places in Mecca.'

'I am also sorry to hear that,' replied Douglas. 'But please be brief. How can I help *you*?'

'Not with any money, but with your knowledge of the English mind.'

'As a Scot, that has not done me a great deal of good so far, subedar sahib. You can see that by looking at me now.'

'Deeds are measured by intentions, sahib. You followed the path of honour.'

'I followed the path of my own temper. In my home country, men with red hair are known for their fiery tempers. They pride themselves on it. In military terms, we have short fuses.'

'It is well written, sahib, "He who lives in a cave with a tiger must learn to stroke a tiger's fur the right way." And you did not do that?'

'I have never been one to learn that skill,' admitted Douglas, smiling. 'But please, once more, how can I help you with whatever knowledge you think I possess?'

'Is there nowhere we can speak in private?'

'Nowhere. I even owe money on this single filthy room, in which I would not keep an animal.'

'Then I will be brief, and speak quickly lest other ears are long. There is no god but Allah, and Mohammed is the Apostle of God. Allah, who knowest the weight of the mountains and the measure of the seas, and even the number of the raindrops and the leaves on the trees, has decreed that the Muslim faith is split into many sects. It is the custom of the

Imfalli sect, to which I belong, to weigh our leader or Imam every year against precious jewels, just as the Aga Khan is weighed in gold by the Ismaili sect. And as with that ceremony, so with ours. We then sell his weight in jewels, which are given by generous believers, and present the money to the poor and the needy.'

'I approve of that. Especially since I became one of them,' said Douglas.

'It is not a matter for levity, sahib. Our Imam, may Allah rest his soul forever and give him eternal comfort, was murdered because he refused to accede to the wishes of some richer, greedier members of our community. They wanted him to divide the money received from this sale with them.

'He would not entertain such a proposal so, on their instructions, he was killed at the hands of an assassin, a poor wretched creature who believed he was earning a place in paradise by this deed. The Muslim faith assures us that all who die in battle against the infidel are assured of endless bliss in paradise. His mission was falsely explained to him as a blow against a non-believer. He was a simple man and he believed what he was told by men of high position.

'Of course, the crowd tore him into pieces as soon as he stabbed the Iman, may Allah the ever merciful show unbounded mercy both to the killer and the killed.'

'But since the Imam is dead, the merchants will get nothing, so what was the point of killing him?'

'I will explain, sahib. Allah in his boundless wisdom, wider than all the oceans of the world, can look on a crowd of people and select one of them as the new Imam. It could be any male person of the faith, young, old, or middle age. In fact, it is said that a boy ten years old has been chosen.'

'Who just happens to be related to one of the merchants, I suppose?' asked Douglas ironically.

'Ah, sahib, you suppose correctly. If this boy is enthroned as Imam, how wretched will be the future for the poor in our community! The faithful will still give the jewels, of course, but a huge proportion of the money they fetch will fatten the purses of our sleek merchants. It is to prevent this evil thing that I seek your aid. I petition you, sahib, and as the Prophet has said, petition is the weapon of the believer. I believe you can help me.'

'But *how?*'

'By giving me your advice, sahib. This young boy, Ahmed Khan, was in the habit of playing childish games with my granddaughter, Fatima. The merchants discussed their plans for murder in a deserted room in the house of Ahmed's father. They did not know that Ahmed and Fatima had been playing there, and Fatima was hiding behind one of the curtains

She planned to jump out and surprise her friend. But when she heard the grave voices of these money-lenders and rice merchants, men of immense wealth and power, fear overcame her. She stayed where she was, in case they discovered her and punished her.'

'So she heard everything?'

'Everything, sahib. But somehow they discovered she had been there, and they arranged for a child marriage between the two young children. They did this on the advice of a lawyer, because under the law of England, which of course is paramount in India, a wife cannot give evidence against her husband. If this child spoke of what she knows, she could denounce them for what they are: murderers, swindlers, misbelievers, men without the faith. But she will be married the day after tomorrow, and then her silence will be assured. Forever.'

'Can you not stop the wedding?'

'That is impossible. It has all been agreed. The child is now in my daughter's house preparing for the feast that follows the ceremony.'

'Can you not go to the Governor General before she is married?'

'He is out of Calcutta, sahib, until the day after the wedding. He would not see a poor man like me, but he might see you – if only he were here.'

'Then can you not postpone the wedding – if only by a day?'

'That is impossible, sahib. The stars have been consulted. It would be the most auspicious time for a wedding, so the merchants say – not for my grand-daughter's happiness, but for their gain. And for their liberty, possibly even their lives, should she be free to speak against them.

'I am also in turmoil, sahib, because my son-in-law will be put to great expense. He cannot afford to pay a dowry suitable to such an occasion, and to give a feast worthy of the wedding to the boy born to be Imam.'

'How is he raising this money?' asked Douglas.

'From the merchants, of course. He knows full well why the wedding must go ahead, but he is not a rich man. He has no powerful friends, no influence.'

'Has he already arranged to take this loan?'

'It is now in progress, sahib, but nothing will be signed until I return. I have searched for you for days. Allah has been kind that he directed my feet to this place.'

Douglas looked closely at the older man.

'There is something else. You are not telling me everything,' he said. 'What do you hold back from me?'

'Sahib,' said the subedar, raising his hands above his head, as though appealing to heaven, 'I, or my ancestors, must have sinned grievously, because truly Allah in his wisdom has punished me more than anyone else I know. I have lost one son, blown from the cannon's mouth. The man who was so wickedly persuaded to kill the Imam, he was also the son of my loins.

'Now I have my daughter's daughter about to be married to a boy with whom she has little in common, and who in all innocence will become part of the murder of a man blessed above men, an instrument of the Messenger of God.'

'I have a theory, subedar sahib,' said Douglas. 'Just as we are all supposed to eat so much dirt in our lives, so we all suffer the same amount of tribulation and rejoice in the same amount of pleasure. But sometimes it happens, as with you now, that all these tribulations come crowding one upon the other at the same time. May hereafter your life be one of peace and content.'

'I pray you are correct, sahib.'

'Pray also that we can thwart this scheme. Who will be Allah's next choice as Imam, if we can?'

'A most worthy man, sahib, rich in years and experience. Abdullah Said, a man of honour, a farmer whose heart is enlightened with the light of faith.'

'Wait for a moment while I dress. I have a friend who may help you.'

'A Muslim, sahib?'

'No.'

'Thrice blessed will he be, sahib. Allah is merciful, even to unbelievers.'

Douglas went back into his room, lit the candle that supplied its only illumination, poured water into the metal basin, washed, shaved, took down from the highest shelf his last clean shirt and suit, where he had placed them out of the way of mice or rats.

'What is your plan, sahib?' the subedar asked as he rejoined him.

'It is best you do not ask,' Douglas replied, falling into step beside him, as they walked the teeming streets. 'If you do not know, you cannot lie should anyone question you.'

They walked through Calcutta until they came to Mr Sodawaterwallah's house.

'Wait here,' Douglas told him and beat on the burnished brass door. A servant opened it.

'You have an appointment, sahib? He is busy at this time.'

'I am a most intimate friend,' Douglas replied and handed him his card. 'Please say that this is a matter of the greatest urgency.'

The servant bowed Douglas into a small courtyard. Doves cooed soothingly. Through an open window, he could see the flickering flame. He thought about Savina and wished he could see her again, lie with her again, not once or twice, but for years ahead. He forced such impossible thoughts from his mind.

The servant re-appeared.

'Please to come in, sahib,' he said.

Douglas followed him into the room where he had first met Sodawaterwallah. He was standing at the far window.

'You have an urgent matter to discuss?' the Parsee asked coolly.

'I have, sir,' said Douglas. 'I seek your help.'

'You wish for money?'

'We all wish for money as we wish for eternal life,' replied Douglas, 'but now I only seek your advice and your opinion.'

He repeated what the subedar had told him. The older man nodded his head.

'I have heard rumours about this,' he said. 'If this marriage could be prevented, who would be the new Imam?'

'Someone highly regarded, according to the subedar,' Douglas replied. 'One Abdullah Said. And doubtless he will look benignly on those who help his selection – in a material if not a spiritual way.'

'There are things of the spirit and things of the body,' Mr Sodawaterwallah agreed solemnly. 'I could no doubt come to an accommodation with him. It is a possibility, a chance I am prepared to take.'

'Then, sir, if you will help us, this is what I propose.'

Douglas outlined his plan; Mr Sodawaterwallah nodded approvingly.

'I will do as you suggest,' he said, 'and I will help you.'

He clapped his hands. A servant entered. The Parsee ordered his phaeton. As it bowled out into the street, the coachman slowed briefly to allow the subedar to jump aboard. They drove on in silence to the bazaar, stopping outside a small house decorated with pieces of coloured paper that fluttered in the warm morning wind like the tiny wings of captured birds.

As the subedar led the way into the house, Douglas caught a glimpse of a woman in her early twenties. A child peered at them from behind a door. Somewhere, a baby was crying. The man of the house came in from a back room and bowed gravely in salutation.

Mr Sodawaterwallah took charge of the conversation.

'Your father-in-law tells me you wish to arrange a loan to pay for the happy celebrations surrounding the marriage of your daughter Fatima?'

'I am already in the process of negotiating such an accommodation.'

'Can I ask, sir, at what percentage?'

'Ten per cent. Forever.'

'Does this interest, which seems to me to be high for such a happy purpose, bear on the whole amount of the loan, even though you pay part of it off?'

'I am borrowing three hundred rupees, sir,' the younger man explained. 'I pay ten per cent on this sum, although I may owe only one rupee.'

'Truly you have fallen into the hands of the *bunyars*. Come back with me in my carriage and I will write you a loan for five per cent, diminishing with every rupee, every single anna you can repay. And on the security, not of your house, or its furnishings, but of your good name. The wise lender lends only on such security. Without it, all other charges and agreements are useless.'

'That is a fine offer, sir.'

'You will not get a better one,' Mr Sodawaterwallah assured him. 'Come, and bring your child with you.'

He turned to the little girl who stood watching the grown-ups from behind the door.

'Tell me,' he said to her, 'have you ever seen a fish of gold?'

She looked questioningly at her father, at Mr Sodawaterwallah, at the subedar, at Douglas, and then slowly and doubtfully she shook her head.

'Never have I seen a golden fish,' she agreed solemnly.

'I can show you fishes of gold swimming in a pool. Would you like to see them? Better still, would you like me to give you a present of two fish of gold in their own little bowl? They will swim for you for as long as they live. It will be as though the sun shines perpetually on you from their golden scales. Would you like that?'

'I would. I would very much,' Fatima replied fervently.

The plump merchant Nasrullah Khan sat cross-legged on a cushion of purple silk in the back of his shop. Bales and rolls of brightly coloured cloth, some with gold threads interwoven in crimson and yellow and blue, lined the walls. Their softness filtered noises from the street outside: the crunch of the bullock carts' wooden wheels, the hoarse cries of sweetmeat sellers and *bhistis*, who naked but for loin cloths, carrying huge glistening hog-skins of water, repeated as they ran, '*Mussulman pani*' – water for Muslims. It was unthinkable that they could drink water from the same source as Hindus or anyone of another religion.

Nasrullah sighed, and the soft folds of flesh beneath his silk robe gave forth a sweet perfumed exudation. He looked at his young nephew, Akbar, who stood regarding him uneasily.

'When you are married,' Nasrullah said, as gently as he could, for he was not by nature a marrying man, preferring the brutish advances of rickshaw wallahs and rough sailors from the river boats, who would beat and bruise him, to the soft caresses of women, 'when you are married, you, of all males in our community, will have a very special part to play. You will not only be joined with your bride, you will be a person apart. No longer a boy, not yet a man, you will be Allah's manifestation to all Imfalli Muslims in the world. Blessed be the name of Allah, forever.'

'I would rather stay as I am, Uncle,' the boy replied miserably. He had already endured days of long talks by grave men, pulling on straggly beards; exhortations by elders with high, cracked voices and dirty finger-nails, whose hands sometimes, and no doubt quite accidentally, brushed his thighs and bottom in an embarrassing manner.

He did not understand their extraordinary claim that he would now be different from other boys. He was not different, he had never been different. He had a brother and a sister, yet now he felt alone, set apart, as his eldest brother, who had died of fever, had been set apart, lest his coughing of blood and sputum should infect others.

There seemed no one to whom he could turn. His mother would veil her eyes as she looked at him and he knew that she wept behind her veil; it was not fitting for a son to see his mother weep. His father appeared nervous and ill at ease in his presence, as though he felt he should give counsel or comfort, but could not find the words.

'It is too late to draw back from the destiny of the Almighty,' said Nasrullah, thinking of his share in the sale of the jewels, not only this year, but every year, for the rest of his life. Originally, he and the other merchants, who had organised the murder of the old Imam, had considered that one-tenth would be a fair proportion. But when blood had been spilled and much put at risk, it seemed foolish to give a child nine-tenths of several lakhs of rupees, to present to the poor. How could he conceivably know who of their number were deserving and who was a rogue? It would be far better to split equally whatever the jewels fetched between the poor and the merchants who had organised everything, who had engaged an assassin and accepted the risk of discovery.

They could then put this money into ventures which would help the poor indirectly: new godowns to store grain, for example; more carts to carry rice to new points of sale; even new vessels to ply the river trade. And some, of course, would go on their own incidental expenses.

Here he was thinking particularly of a poor Pathan he had recently engaged, a pleasing young man who wore cotton trousers as tight on his thighs as another skin, so that the full outline of his magnificent organs and his bottom, rounded as a divided water melon, were plain to see. Was he not a living example of the Pathan saying, 'A woman for children, a boy for pleasure, a melon for sheer delight'?

How agreeable it would be to dress this lover man in white oiled silk, to place a gold chain around his neck, rub camphor-scented oils into his flesh. The prospect disturbed Nasrullah deeply; he moved on his cushions to ease discomfort in his loins. At that moment, a man entered his shop. He brushed aside the salesmen who bowed obsequiously and prattled about special offers and new cloth lately arrived from Europe or China or Afghanistan, and strode towards Nasrullah, who recognised the lawyer, Musjib.

'*Salaam,*' said Nasrullah, standing up.

'*Aleikum, salaam,*' replied Musjib, but without his usual smile of greeting. 'Let me speak to you privately.'

Nasrullah led him into a room behind the shop, pulled the double curtain and looked at him enquiringly.

'This wedding,' said Musjib, and stopped.

'What about it? Everything is planned for this afternoon at three o'clock. It is the most propitious time. The stars in their courses all point to the hour.'

'They point to nothing at all,' retorted the lawyer. 'The bride has disappeared.'

'But I saw her only yesterday with her grandfather. Where can she be?'

'No one knows. Apparently the girl's grandfather arrived at her home with a Parsee banker and an Englishman. The Parsee offered better terms for a loan than we could give, and they set off in his carriage to his counting house. Here, they transacted their business and then went on to the Parsee's house. There was some talk of giving the girl a present of two gold fish. On the way, they ran into a procession and had to wait until it had passed. Suddenly, the Englishman jumped out of the carriage and ran off with the girl.'

'Who is this man?'

'No one seems to know. The Parsee says he has only met him once before and does not even know his name. The girl's father and mother and her grandfather are demented with worry. It is a most extraordinary situation.'

'Was it planned, do you think?'

'I do not know what to think. All I know is that the girl has vanished.'

'What if she talks?'

The lawyer answered his question with another.

'Who would believe a child? Under English law, there are all manner of restrictions about children giving evidence.'

'Maybe that is the law,' agreed the merchant, 'but you know that any hint of collusion would not only imperil our whole plan but damage our standing, our credit, our incomes – everything.'

'We have three hours,' Musjib replied. 'After that, the elders will vote as they wanted to vote originally – that Abdullah Said is chosen as Imam.'

'There is no extension?' asked Nasrullah anxiously. 'The stars will surely not have changed so much in one day or one night?'

'You and I know that,' agreed Musjib. 'But the mass believe what we have told them – that this is the most auspicious time for the wedding. We cannot retain credibility if we go against what we have been preaching so strongly. Three hours, maximum.'

'This is a big city,' said Nasrullah reflectively.

'But there are only so many places, surely, where a child can be hidden? She will be distinctive because of the Englishman with her. They make an unusual couple to seek.'

'I will close the shop,' said Nasrullah at once. 'I will send my staff out to search for her and promise a reward of one hundred silver rupees to whoever discovers her, unharmed. You pass the word to your informers – all those men you employ as friendly witnesses to any accident or crime of which your clients are accused. Make them work for their money for once. Now, let us to our task.'

Nasrullah clapped his hands to show the discussion was at an end. At this sound, his serving men came running through the shop towards him.

Mr Sodawaterwallah was waiting in his courtyard, the spraying fountain behind him, as Douglas and the subedar arrived.

'I understand the ceremony for choosing the new Imam was successful?' Douglas nodded.

'The right man, I hope, in the right post. And the little girl?'

'After you brought her back, she stayed here for two days. No one thought of looking for her here. She is now at home with her parents.'

'Is any harm likely to come to her?' Douglas asked the subedar. 'These merchants lost a lot of money through this.'

'They know that we know,' the subedar replied enigmatically. 'They also know that I will no longer keep silent if any threat is made to her.'

He turned to Mr Sodawaterwallah.

'I have outside, in a carriage, the new Imam, Abdullah Said. May the one true god bless all his works and every hour of his life and yours.'

'I would be honoured to meet him,' said Mr Sodawaterwallah gravely.

The subedar left the courtyard and returned in a few moments with another man, tall, grey-haired, of aquiline countenance. He bowed towards Mr Sodawaterwallah, who held up both his hands, palms pressed together in greeting.

'I owe you a great deal,' said the Imam. His speech was resilient, strong. Douglas instantly realised the beneficial effect this reassuring and confident voice could have on a congregation, and not only on the faithful, but on waverers; on the multitude who longed to believe. It was the voice of authority, it could indeed be the voice of Allah's chosen.

'I am glad to have been of service,' replied Mr Sodawaterwallah modestly. 'Although I did not know Mr Nasrullah personally – indeed, I do not recall ever meeting him – yet his path has sometimes crossed with mine, not always to my advancement. Now, as in a game of chess, I feel I have scored a point.'

'You will know, sir,' the Imam continued, 'that Mr Nasrullah and his colleagues planned to take half of whatever sum the jewels might fetch. Soon, I fancy, they would have seized it all. I could not agree to this any more than could the Imam who died at the hands of their hired assassin.'

'And rightly so,' replied Mr Sodawaterwallah. 'One half is too much. Ten per cent is my fee.'

'This was never mentioned before,' said Douglas sharply.

'I was never asked before what I would require. I was simply asked to help. Is not the labourer worthy of his hire?'

The Imam's face hardened. His eyes narrowed and he turned to Douglas.

'And you, sahib, have you a request to make, a percentage to take from the gifts of love to the needy and deserving poor?'

'No, Imam,' replied Douglas, 'I have no request for any fee. In my country, I am the son of a landowner, a *zamindar* as you would say. In this country, I followed the honourable profession of arms. I am not versed in the ways of business. Money to me is only currency to buy whatever I may need. I have never worshipped the golden calf.'

'My family, too, owns land,' said the Imam. 'It is under crops. I understand that you are now without a place in the Company's army?'

'You understand correctly,' said Douglas.

'Then please let me put my home at your disposal for a visit. We have elephants which you can ride. Tigers to shoot. Fish in the rivers.'

'I would welcome the opportunity of visiting the country. Cities are not for me,' said Douglas. 'Tell me, what do you grow in your fields?'

'A crop which may be strange to you. I have upwards of fourteen thousand acres covered entirely with flowers. Poppies, to be precise.'

Calcutta

Captain Ross was in the cuddy when he heard the look-out from the crow's nest give the most welcome final call of the long voyage east: 'Land ahoy!'

He hurried up on deck. The wind had dropped and *Coromandel* was scarcely moving; her sails rattled and flapped like huge flags above his head. On the far horizon, he could make out a faint dim green smudge. His telescope showed marsh with a faint haze of heat hovering above a rash of white buildings along a shore. The sea all around him was yellow now, churned up by sand brought down by the Hooghly River. At last, after three months, they were within sight of India.

Theirs had been a relatively routine voyage. Off the Canary Islands they had been followed by a shoal of sharks, turning and diving and baring serried rows of teeth in a menacing way. At the sight, the more religious among passengers and crew crossed themselves and said their prayers. Sharks, to all sea-farers, were a portent of death, the jaws of death in fact. Sure enough, the sea cook went mad that same afternoon, seized a meat cleaver and set about one of the crew who had entered his galley without his permission.

The sailor fought back furiously and struck the cook on the head with an axe handle. The man collapsed and Ross pronounced him dead. He had not been a very popular sailor, or even a very good cook; Ross did not bother to charge his assailant with the slaughter of a man. It was simpler to enter in the ship's log that the cook had slipped when the ship rolled, and hit his head on a bench.

The ship hove-to for the moment, rocking and dipping on the endless swell of the ocean as they slipped his body overboard, wrapped in a blanket (the cost of which Ross deducted from the amount of pay due to his next-of-kin at the end of the voyage).

As the grey woollen bundle hit the water, it moved and appeared to writhe, as though the body within the blanket was not dead, but simply stunned, and was now revived by the shock of being flung into the sea.

'He is alive, I tell you! He is not dead! Put out a boat and bring him back!' a passenger shouted in horror. But it was too late; the ship was already moving and so were the sharks.

'You should have asked me to attend him,' Jackson told Ross angrily. He had come up on deck to enquire why the ship was stationary.

'Bodies often move like that when they're buried at sea,' the captain assured him, lighting a cheroot.

'Even so, he might not be dead.'

'He is now, that's a certainty,' Ross replied shortly.

The sharks had returned to butt the corpse, which, despite a weight of tones as ballast, stubbornly refused to sink. The more squeamish of the passengers turned away quickly as the teeth ripped through the thin blanket, and ruptured bowels and entrails suddenly reddened the sparkling sea.

The captain's main worry had been to find another cook; passengers could become greatly agitated if standards fell too far. Fortunately, one passenger had bought a Kaffir servant at the Cape of Good Hope for fifty guineas, a huge sum it had seemed at the time, but now well spent, because the man could cook and spoke good English.

Soon, now, Captain Ross would pay off his crew, open a sealed envelope that contained his orders for the next destination, take on provisions and set about re-selling cabin and deck space to new passengers.

He hoped the letter would instruct him to go farther east; the opportunities for profit were greater in that direction, and he enjoyed these voyages on charter to the Company. There was less risk of trouble than in the West Indies, running a slaver, where over a period of years, first as mate, then as master, he had experienced a surfeit of violence.

Each trip would begin when he put his ship into the ironically named Freetown in West Africa, and negotiated with blacks ashore for them to go inland, carrying ropes or chains concealed in sacks, and little useless trinkets such as beads, or sheath knives carefully blunted so that they could not be used as weapons against them.

They would parley with each local chief, and give him as little money or as few beads as they could, in return for his permission to roam his territory and round up likely young men and women as slaves. No one suffering from any obvious disability – lameness, blindness, lacking a hand or foot, or with sores on their body, or any noxious discharges – was wanted; nor were pregnant women, if they were near their time.

The primitive natives, naked except for a leaf or leather thong around their loins, welcomed the visitors – often the first strangers they had ever seen. They listened with awe and envy to their stories of wealth and adventure and the promise of as much toddy as they could drink every day, knives for the men, beads for the women, and payment in gold for their services, if only they would come back with them to Freetown.

When they reached the docks, they were taken to an open square of land, fenced in with high metal spikes. Here their hands were tied and loose ropes put around their ankles, on the pretext that this was part of an important initiation ceremony. Then a sailor led them up the gangplanks aboard ship. If any faltered or hung back, another sailor whipped them on their way.

If anyone fell or jumped into the water, they were left to struggle. Since none of them had ever seen the sea before and could not swim, these usually drowned. If they managed somehow to reach shore, they were dragged aboard at the end of a rope, like cattle.

With each voyage it became more difficult to find a new section of territory which slave traders had not previously visited. Young men and girls fled as the slavers approached, running into caves, up trees, anywhere to escape. This made the slavers more brutal; they were paid by results.

Ross would then sail north with his live cargo, to Lagos in southern Portugal, a port named after the other Lagos in West Africa, where the main trade for generations had been in human beings. Merchants in Portugal paid a good price for young boys to be trained as servants. They were marched ashore in chains to a market, to stand in lines while potential buyers felt their muscles, and sometimes, with other activities in mind, closely examined their private parts.

After this, Ross would head west, with his ship crammed with unhappy, shrieking, weeping black people who had not found buyers. They had no proper bed spaces, but lay on deck; between decks; beneath decks; down in the steerage, where stinking bilge swilled around their ebony bodies, and rusty anchor chains scored their naked flesh. The men's hands were free, but around their legs blacksmiths hammered metal shackles so that they could only take small paces.

This was a most necessary precaution to minimise the risk of mutiny or insurrection. There had been ugly scenes aboard some slave ships when unshackled slaves had murdered captain and crew and sailed away, hoping to return home. But lacking anyone to navigate or who could read a compass or the stars, they had perished of hunger and thirst, often eating the dead in their desperate attempts to stay alive.

Throughout the voyage, they ate, slept, defecated, copulated or buggered each other, while the mercury in the ship's thermometer rose steadily. Frequently, slaves would fall ill, and lie for days or even weeks, wretched in their own mess of vomit and excrement. If they died, their manacles were struck off ankles now red and festering where raw rough metal had eaten into the bone. These irons could be used again and again. The corpses, unweighted, unwrapped, unshriven, were flung into the sea for fish to finish.

Sometimes, the voyage west lasted for so long that women, not pregnant when it began, gave birth. Many babies were stillborn. Day and night, Captain Ross and his officers would burn joss sticks, bought on previous voyages to India, in an attempt to mask the foul stench of human putrefaction and misery. The saying among sailors was that you could smell a slave from two miles distance downwind. Sometimes, the distance was much greater.

Each ship's captain received a share of whatever price the slaves fetched when they reached the Caribbean or North America. It was therefore in their own interest to keep as many as possible alive, but conditions under which they travelled weakened all but the most hardy. Ross was not a squeamish man, but as he watched these pathetic exiles shamble down the gangway on to some dock in the New World, with bodies, once glistening with health and youth, now covered with scabs and sores, shoulders hunched in despair, excrement caking their legs, he hated to see their eyes. They frightened him: he knew he was staring into the depths of hell, and one day these slaves or their descendants would wreak a terrible vengeance on the white races who had tricked them into bondage.

He was always glad when the last slave had gone ashore, and the crew had finally swilled out their quarters with sea water. Frequently, they discovered a rotting body, usually of some unwanted child, or a baby a mother could not bear to lose, even in death. The rewards for this traffic were good, but the money seemed tainted. Curiously, all who handled it tried to be rid of it as soon as possible, on drink or women or boys.

On trading trips east, the business was altogether different. The captain had the right to what the East India Company called 'private trade', which meant that on his return trip to Gravesend he could carry lashed to the deck whatever cargo he could afford to buy out of his own purse, to sell on his own behalf. Many captains had made fortunes by shrewd purchases of rubies and other gems from primitive natives with no idea of their value in Europe; they would willingly exchange them for a polished copper penny or even a clay pipe.

In Canton, on the shore of the vast Chinese empire, there was a most lucrative trade in opium. A few more voyages, a few prudent buys, and he could retire altogether from the sea, buy a house in Leicester Square, perhaps an estate on the Thames beyond Chiswick, and most of all, enjoy the companionship he craved of young, soft-skinned, clean-limbed, freshly-washed boys.

Dr Jackson came up on deck and stood beside Ross as he mused on these future pleasures.

'How far inshore do you take the ship?' he asked him.

'No farther. The river is silted up and very dangerous. We wait here for a pilot to take us to an anchorage.'

'How do I reach shore?'

'In this boat, now drawing alongside.'

Ross pointed to a curious craft, broad in the beam, with a mat covering held up from the flat deck on half a dozen short poles. Jackson climbed down a bamboo ladder and his bags, tied with ropes, were dangled after him on hooks. Six Indians, three on each side, held the craft hard up against *Coromandel*'s hull, while others lashed his trunks to the upright poles. There was not enough room beneath the roof to stand upright, so Jackson squatted uncomfortably, cross-legged like a tailor, as the rower pulled away.

At last the unwieldy boat, known, so one of the Indians explained in halting English, as a *paunceway*, bumped against the quayside. Several Europeans were waiting, obviously expecting more passengers. All but one drifted away as Jackson climbed out stiffly. Coolies lifted out his luggage and stood about expectantly with the oarsmen.

'You have no India coin, sir?' the last European asked him.

'Not a penny – or, as I understand the word here – not one single anna.'

'Then let me change some English money for you, and welcome you to this strange but not altogether disagreeable land.'

He dug into his pocket, pulled out a handful of coins and scattered them on the ground like grain before chickens. The Indians went down on their hands and knees to pick them up, respectfully touching their foreheads with the coins as a sign of thanks.

'How much do I owe you, sir?' Jackson asked him.

'Shall we say two guineas? Now, sir, I am Elijah Potiphar. Have you a residence in Calcutta, friends who are expecting you?'

'Unfortunately, neither. I am a physician and surgeon. I wish to set up a practice here. Dr Richard Jackson. At your service.'

'Then maybe I can also be at yours. I own two houses. In one I live, and I rent the other, with a full complement of servants, of course. One hundred pounds a month. Payable in English or Indian money, in advance.'

'You have a tenant for one month at least,' Jackson replied, shaking Potiphar's hand warmly.

'There is one small condition,' he added. 'That you give the address to these boatmen, so that when they go out next time to *Coromandel*, they can give it to the captain, so he will know where to find me.'

'Done in a trice, sir.'

Captain Ross watched the *paunceway* out of sight, then went back to the cuddy. He took two keys from the chain he wore around his neck, opened the double lock of the safe and lifted out a sealed envelope that had been brought down by personal rider from Major Forster in London when *Coromandel* lay at anchor off Gravesend. The envelope bore the inscription in black copper-plate 'To be opened only by the captain on arrival in Calcutta', and the Major's signature.

He ripped it open impatiently with an ivory paper knife, and read the brief message it contained: 'Report to the East India Company office on arrival for further orders.'

This office was in a square white building with two small brass cannon at the gate near the centre of Calcutta. In front stretched the *maidan*, a wide open space extending for several miles in each direction, running towards the river. It was late afternoon when Ross called, and two-horse carriages, sporting chariots and four-horse phaetons were driving up and down the dried grass. European women in loose gowns sat with their friends, white silk parasols raised against the weakening sunshine, but all taking care that the parasols did not entirely obscure their faces. They were there to be seen and admired, and the wealth of husbands and lovers envied; and some, to show that they were available – at a price.

Young bachelors rode to and fro at a great pace, sweeping off their hats in exaggerated salutation to women they knew or would like to know, now and then reining in sharply. Their horses reared up violently on their hind legs so that their riders could bring them down gently to show their prowess. If a man was so strong and sure on horseback, would not he display the same desirable and all too rare masculine qualities astride a softer, gentler mount?

Ross presented himself to the duty manager, a Welshman with thinning hair, who read the opened letter from Major Forster that Ross showed him. He rang a bell for an Indian clerk to bring in a file.

'*Coromandel*?' he asked, when it appeared.

'Yes.'

'Then the orders are you pay off the crew. The voyage is over, the commission ended.'

'But is there no cargo for me to take back to England? No instructions to sail on to Canton?'

'Nothing here, Captain. You have sufficient funds to pay off the crew?'

'In my safe, yes. But the ship – does not the owner wish her to earn money for him?'

'It is not for me to say, Captain, nor for you. She is his ship. His instructions are as I have given you. Here are his exact words. "The vessel to ride at anchor until further orders, or offered for sale." '

'That is damned preposterous,' said Ross angrily.

'Maybe – from your point of view, Captain, but not from his. The ways of the wealthy are inscrutable to those of us without such funds.'

'What if someone wished to buy *Coromandel*? She will rot at anchor here during the monsoon.'

'We have later instructions that she could be sold for the equivalent of 5,000 English pounds, over 65,000 rupees.'

'I can't understand it,' said Ross, shaking his head in bewilderment. 'Ships always take back some cargo: jute, tea, teak, spices.'

'Things are changing, Captain. These cargoes are not so easy to sell in England now as they were. Anyhow, that is entirely academic. Those are my orders, sir. I regret I cannot help you further.'

Ross stormed out of the office and stood on the pavement, irresolute and furious. Two Indians trotted past carrying a palanquin, slowed, and looked at him enquiringly. He nodded, climbed inside and gave them the address of Jackson's house.

This was an imposing building with a Palladian portico supported by six white pillars and approached along a driveway of brushed dust. As the Indians padded up to the huge front door, Ross could see gardeners watering shrubs from glistening hog-skins strapped to their backs, directing the water through the hog's neck, held between their body and elbow. Jackson had seen Ross arrive from an upper window, and pushed aside the servant who opened the door.

'Welcome,' he said warmly. 'Come and sample some Madeira. It is uncommonly good, especially in this climate, I understand. And fresh bread. A luxury after months of ship's biscuit.'

'I could use a bottle, not a glass,' said Ross thankfully, and explained what had happened.

'So you are without a job?'

'Without anything! A job, a place to rest my head, or a future. I will have to go back aboard ship, call the crew together, pay them off, and then God help us all.'

'They will not take this well, doctor. The ports of India are thick with sailors who have been paid off and spent their money and now are ready for any villainy: piracy, larceny, even murder.'

'But you will not be reduced to such straits?'

'Not immediately. But if trade is bad, as the manager told me it is, I will not be the only captain seeking a ship. I had hoped to obtain a full cargo and sail back to England with some private trade.'

'What have you carried in the past on your own account?'

'Tea, largely. There is, as you know, a heavy tax on it, so I anchor off the two-mile limit. There are at least half a dozen fellows with fast cutters along the south-east coast of England, looking out all the time for East Indiamen coming up channel. They sail out to meet us. First come, first to deal. We strike a bargain, and the revenue cutters can do nothing about it.'

'Do they not arrest the smuggler on his way in?'

'No. He either outsails their cutters, or they do not cram on sail enough. After all, he has them in his pay. How would they live on their income otherwise?'

'So what do you propose to do?'

'Deplete the stock of your Madeira first and think about it. This is an uncommonly good wine, I must say.'

'It is. And then?'

'Try to find some merchant who will buy the ship – and me with her. I have my ticket and a crew, and he puts in the money. We can share the profit, which could be considerable.'

'How much is required?'

'They are asking 65,000 silver rupees, though I reckon I could buy her for half that sum. But, damn me, doctor, how can a sea captain raise such money? It may be little enough to merchants here, but a fortune to me.'

'You were slaving before. You must have made a fortune, surely?'

'Yes, and by God, I spent it! I had every woman, every boy I wanted, and where and when I wanted him or her. Name your price, I would say and they did so. And I would do that all again, everything, and damn you, doctor, I *will* do it again! Now, what about that second bottle?'

As the Imam Abdullah Said came out from under the shade of the rattan roof behind his huge house, a great cry went up from more than a hundred labourers who had gathered to await his appearance. They dropped to their knees and bowed three times, rubbing their faces gladly in the dust. Douglas stood to one side, still in the shade, watching this extraordinary spectacle.

'Blessed is the Lord,' they chanted. 'There is one God. Allah is his name. Mohammed is his prophet. Peace be to the Apostles of God. And blessings on you and on your sons forever.'

The Imam bowed.

'Peace to you all,' he replied. 'Peace and forgiveness and love.'

They repeated the words in a kind of chant, then stood up and, still half bowed, backed reverently out of his presence.

The Imam turned to Douglas.

'My people are very loyal,' he said. 'They believe in me. I must never let any one of them question that belief. That is my charge. However, I did not bring you here for a demonstration of religious loyalty, but to show you a crop about which I think you may know little, and which could possibly interest you, as a visitor of perception. It is the source of my family's wealth, great profits for the East India Company, and hence for your countrymen, too. Poppies!'

Fields of red and white poppies stretched to foothills trembling and hazy blue in the distance. The fields were sown in giant squares, one red as newly shed blood next to another white as Highland snow. The effect was of an enormous chequer board, waiting for giants to move the pieces, repeated and repeated as far as his gaze could reach. The sight had a curiously mesmeric effect.

As Douglas's eyes grew more used to this dazzling prospect, he saw that the poppies were planted in long straight rows a foot apart. Up and down these unsown strips walked labourers wearing loin cloths and huge white turbans against the cruel heat of an overhead sun. They carried hog-skins of water, bending over each poppy carefully to release their grip on the throat of the skin.

'We water them every morning at noon, and again when the sun goes down,' the Imam explained. 'In between times, the labourers break up the soil with hoes.'

'You take more care over the plants than over the labourers?'

'Of course,' agreed the Imam instantly. 'They need greater care. They are also more expensive to acquire, more difficult to maintain and inf nitely more valuable and productive than any of the men who look after them.'

'Where do you sell them? For decoration? Or are the seeds used for food?'

'You are unacquainted with what we call the Forbidden Trade, and in China, the Coast Trade?'

'Totally,' said Douglas. 'I do not know what you mean.'

'Then I will explain. Beautiful as the poppy appears, its flower is the least valuable part of the plant.'

He plucked the head from the nearest poppy, pulled off the white petals and threw them away. Beneath the stamen was a green fleshy bulb the size of a small onion. The Imam clapped his hands together. A servant came running and produced a knife with a curious hook on its blade. The Imam split the bulb expertly with four vertical cuts. Then he squeezed gently. A few drops of white juice, like milk, began to bleed from the four wounds.

'We make opium from this,' he explained.

'And where do you sell that?'

'Some goes to your country. It is used in medicines, to kill pain and provide sleep. That trade is not forbidden, but encouraged. The trade east to China, *that* is forbidden. By the Chinese.'

'Who owns the farm?'

'My family and I. But we sell most of our crop to the East India Company. Because the Chinese take so much – and all illegally – the East India Company – very wisely in my view – refuse to have anything to do with it *officially*. They are the only western company that the Chinese emperor allows to trade with his country. Naturally, they would not wish to do anything to prejudice such a monopoly, although they do not make a great deal out of their legitimate trading activities with China. A matter, often enough, of simply bartering cloth from England or India for tea and porcelain. But they have hopes of extending this one day. In the meantime, they make a fortune from opium.

'To transport it, they hire ships. Often, these vessels are chased by cutters of the Chinese authorities and the crews are incarcerated. They can even be strangled if they come before a harsh magistrate. Sometimes, they meet slower and more terrible deaths. So the crews have to be very well paid. They risk their lives with every voyage.'

'How much opium do you get from these fields?'

'A great deal. We plant according to the demand. There have been criticisms of the Company's policy of producing what many of your countrymen consider is a vile and dangerous drug. When Warren Hastings was Governor General here, he declared that opium was so pernicious it should not be sold at all in India – and it still isn't. Stamford

Raffles declared that in Java it degraded people's character and enervated them completely.

'The Company naturally takes note of such remarks, and from time to time tries to restrict its sales – by keeping up the price. Whereas the Turks, our only real competitor, produce an ounce from so many poppies, we produce a pound weight from the same number of pods. The Americans take the Turkish stuff, and run it into China, too, but not so profitably. They would buy ours, my friend, if we had any to spare, but we have not a grain. At the moment, we cannot grow enough. A few years ago, we cultivated about seven thousand acres. Now we have twice that amount. Next year we will increase it by as much again.'

'And the profit?'

'Enormous, my friend, enormous. The Company sells more than two million pounds sterling worth of opium to China every year. That is half of all government costs in India – the army, the civil servants, everything. If the Company was deprived of this revenue, then who would pay for the loss? There would have to be more taxes in your country, on tea, tobacco, everything. That would not be a popular move, my friend.

'If I sowed this ground with other crops, the earth here is so poor and lacking in nutriment that I doubt if we would make enough to pay for the seed. But it is perfect for poppies. We sow their seed every November. By March, the petals drop and the poppy's life is nearly over. I then send out teams of men with these hooked knives to cut the bulbs.

'These knives, by the way, are their own. I insist on that, otherwise they would steal them. Sometimes they are so poor, they cannot afford to buy a knife, so they sharpen the shell of a freshwater mussel or even a piece of stone. They are very keen to work, Mr Douglas, although this is not a trade at which they can expect to grow rich. Our harvest lasts for only two weeks, and during that time we pay them the equivalent of three English pennies a day. Dawn to dusk, of course.'

'And for the rest of the year, how do they live?'

'My dear friend, if we wondered how other people lived, we would have no time to live ourselves. They *do* live, as you can see. They may work as coolies, or labourers, perhaps. I do not know. That is not my concern. We do employ a few all the year, though. We use them to pull ploughs.'

'I thought bullocks did that here in India?'

'They do, but men can be cheaper. They also eat less – and are more intelligent. They plough shallow furrows to plant the new poppies, and they repair irrigation ditches to hold rainwater when the monsoon comes. Bullocks cannot do that. And their work is not finished then. They cut each bulb as late as possible in the afternoon, for example, to give it chance to drain through the night, when the air is cool. Next day, the sun will harden the juice. The men go out with iron spoons very early to collect it in buckets before that happens.'

As they talked, they were approaching a huge wooden building, like a giant English barn, sixty or seventy feet high and at least twice as long. From inside, Douglas could hear the muted sound of singing and chanting, a repetitive rhythm like a monotonous dirge. He sniffed the air; there was a strong, sweet smell, not altogether unpleasant.

'The scent of money,' the Imam explained. 'Opium, to be exact. Poisoned honey, we call it. You can become addicted just by its smell, without ever taking a grain of the drug.'

He led the way through a small door into the building. Two huge pyramids of green balls faced them, reaching almost to the roof. Each ball was the size and colour of a small water melon, taking its colour from the poppy leaves wrapped around it to prevent one from sticking to the next. Twenty or thirty naked Indian children ran to and fro in relays along the earth floor, chanting as they ran. Each removed two opium balls from the pyramid, and carried one under each arm to the far end of the building. Here, bamboo ladders had been set up against racks of the kind Douglas had seen used for storing apples in Scotland. More children, standing on alternate rungs of the ladders in a human chain, handed up the balls, one at a time, to others who squatted high in the racks and set them down gently, so as not to disturb the wrapping. As with apples, they left a small space between each one.

Here, the smell of sickly deadly sweetness was almost overpowering, and the children's faces bore a look of glazed happiness. They were already addicts at the age of five or six.

'How long do they do this work?' Douglas asked.

'Until they are ten or eleven. Then they are too big to climb up and down the ladders quickly – or they become drowsy and lack interest – so we retire them. Fortunately, there are always plenty more. They grow very skilled, my friend. If you weighed any one of those opium balls, you would find that each one is almost exactly two pounds in weight. They cannot count or read, of course. They do it entirely by eye and feel. Remarkable, I call it. Remarkable.'

'How long do you store them here?'

'Until they are needed. They would rot if they were left in one position for too long, so we employ other children up on the racks – you cannot see them from here – to keep turning the balls over, dusting them with dried crushed poppy leaves if they look damp. There is a fortune under this roof. More than half a million pounds of mud.'

'Mud?'

'That is what we call the stuff. You cannot get arrested, even by the

Chinese, surely, for carrying a cargo of mud, can you? That is what appears on the manifest.'

'And all this is bound for China?'

'Most of it. We pack the balls in mango-wood crates, because that wood smells sweet and helps to disguise the scent of opium if any officials our people have not been able to bribe come aboard to check the cargo. We put seventy balls in each box, rather like a chest of drawers. That is enough to keep seven hundred addicts happy for a whole year. And when one remembers there are around three hundred million people in China – at the least – demand always exceeds supply, which, of course, is very much to our advantage.'

'How much does an addict smoke a day? I know absolutely nothing about the habit.'

'And if you value your health, my friend, do not experiment. It is so easy to begin – and almost impossible to stop. Usually, people will start with ten grains a day, puffed in a little clay pipe. That quickly moves up to twenty or thirty. At forty grains a day, smokers are not much better than walking corpses. They lose all impetus. They cannot work, they cannot think, they just squat, whether they are smoking or not, dreaming. That is one of the reasons why the Chinese forbid the trade. It is ruining their workers, weakening their troops.'

'But these children are breathing it all the time.'

'They are only children.'

'They will never grow up to be anything more than just creatures?'

'Agreed, my friend. But life is at best a compromise. At least they have food and work. If they did not work here, they would probably starve, because their parents could not afford to feed them. They are coolies' children, remember. Many parents actually put their offspring to death because they cannot feed another mouth.'

Douglas was about to express amazement at infanticide so casually accepted, when he remembered much the same happened in Scotland when a kitchen maid in a big house was got with child, as not infrequently happened, often by the son of the house. They were dismissed immediately, of course – no one could continue to employ someone with such loose morals. Equally, no one would then employ a single girl of that class with an illegitimate child, so she or a member of her family might deliberately smother the baby. This was widely known, but such cases rarely came before the courts. And when they did, the excuse that the child died during a brief absence of the mother, or from some disease or abnormality, was invariably accepted.

Douglas was relieved to return to the open air. He did not speak until he was out of earshot of the eerie, doomed chanting and the sickly smell that had the cloying sweetness of hot-house blooms at a funeral. H breathed deeply, looking away from the red and white chequer board of poppies which had suddenly lost all beauty. The sight was totally distasteful to him.

'You have been very kind in showing me all this,' he told the Imam carefully, not wishing to offend his host. 'But let me ask you one more question.'

'Anything, my friend, anything.'

'You are a holy man, a leader in your sect. I have seen people here bow down and worship your god and theirs through your presence. How can you equate that position with what seems to me to be the deliberate destruction of thousands, perhaps eventually millions, of Chinese peasants, simply for gain?'

'I do not look at the trade in that light at all. These wretched Chinese peasants, whose welfare so concerns you, may your God reward you, spend their lives working in rice paddy fields up to their knees, often their thighs in water. This causes the most excruciating pain as they grow older. Their joints lock like rusted hinges on a gate. Frequently, they cannot move without agony. They are as good as dead, although they still breathe.

'In Burma, the men tattoo their legs in the belief that this will prevent such pain. It does not, of course. Nothing can comfort them or soothe their torture – except opium. With a pipe of mud, they can sleep and dream and forget their miseries – at least for a time. They are transported miraculously to the past – or to the future. They speak with their ancestors. They meet their children's children, as yet unborn. They dine with kings and lie with the loveliest women of their dreams. They stand on the steps of paradise for an hour, or a day. Is it not something to give them such a magic passport, my friend? I think it is.

'Now, let us withdraw from the heat – and from such discussions that tax the mind as heavily as governments tax their richer citizens. In the evening, I will show you our special elephants, trained to hunt the tiger.'

They walked in silence along the hard dusty path to the big house. Douglas had believed the subedar when he assured him that the wrong person was about to be chosen as his religious leader. He had taken him at his word and helped him, and now this sleek, satin-skinned man was Imam. Would a leader who had allowed a proportion of charitable gifts to go to businessmen be any worse than one who deliberately traded in dust that led from delusion to death? Or was he being foolish and weak-minded even to entertain such thoughts?

Captain Ross paid off the palanquin outside the gates of a square stone house in Park Street on the edge of Calcutta, where the proud stone buildings suddenly and alarmingly disintegrated into bamboo and wattle shacks, and then the dangerous darkness of the jungle. The night was alive with the twang and hum of a million tiny insects. Crickets crackled, bullfrogs croaked throatily from unseen marshes.

Ross had drunk a bottle and a half of Madeira in Jackson's house, and the strong thick wine was fuming in his blood, exacerbating his bitterness at being paid off so summarily. In an attempt to cheer himself up, he had suggested to Jackson that they should visit this discreet house, which he knew from past trips. There were girls here, boys if you wanted them, but more important, *life*; people drinking strong liquor, eating fresh food, not making do with rain water and stale ship's biscuits and salted pork. There was the feeling of belonging to a group out to enjoy themselves. He desperately needed to be wanted, the man in charge, not the man who had lost command.

A servant in a freshly laundered *dhoti* opened the cedar door; another bowed them to a table; a third asked their wishes as they sat down.

'Roast fowl,' Jackson told him. 'And two pints of claret.'

He trusted a roast in preference to the more customary curry, because the curry was served so hot it could disguise the most disgusting flesh: dead dogs and cats taken from ditches; even, it was rumoured, the flesh of unwanted babies.

'We have some very special prawns, sahib,' said the waiter.

'And you can keep them,' Ross retorted crossly. He turned to Jackson.

'Those bloody prawns! Look at the Hooghly River and you will see it is full of dead bodies floating past. Cows, horses, bullocks, men. They all have white birds squatting on them, pecking at them, taking a voyage and a meal. And underneath, if you turn over those stinking carcasses, millions of prawns are tearing away at the flesh. That is why Calcutta prawns are so big – they are far better fed than the fishermen! I do not want your carrion feeders. Might as well make a meal from the worms in a corpse.'

The waiter fled, and returned with the claret. Jackson sipped appreciatively, and looked around the room. It was the size of a tennis court, dimly lit with candles on each table. Overhead, half a dozen punkahs swept the air; smoke from pipes, cheroots and cigars swirled in blue wraiths above their heads. The atmosphere felt very hot; his shirt clung damply to his back, and the faces of all the other diners shone with sweat and alcohol.

Indian girls in Western dresses, faces heavily powdered to make them appear more European, walked between the tables, their finger-tips deliberately brushing the head or shoulders of a possible client. Sometimes, a man would elbow them out of the way angrily, while other men stood up and engaged them in conversation, and then followed them out of the room.

'Half of those girls are boys,' said Ross knowingly. 'I have a special friend here,' he said. 'Evelyn.' His eyes followed them all, searching for one.

'Get your poxy arse out of it,' said a growling voice behind them both. Jackson turned in surprise. A huge man, wearing rough fustian trousers held up by a leather belt with a buckle the size of a saucer, his blue cotton shirt ripped open to his navel, was standing behind them, a bottle of red wine in his hand. His face was contorted with rage.

Ross started up in pleased recognition.

'Why, Bill!' he shouted.

'Don't Bill me, you bastard!' shouted the bearded man thickly.

'Who the hell are you?' asked Jackson, annoyed at this interruption. Then he recognised the bo'sun from *Coromandel*.

'Join us,' said Ross warmly, pulling out a chair at the table and signalling to the waiter to bring a third glass.

'I'll not join you here or any other place, save in hell,' retorted the bo'sun, and swigged loosely from his bottle. Wine dribbled down his chin and ran like blood through the matted black hair on his chest.

'What the devil do you mean?' asked Ross, all his irritation instantly returning. Why should a drunk address him in this rude way? Men had been put in irons for less, very much less.

'You know damned well what I mean, Cap'n. You go ashore on your own. Last words to me were, "We are all going to sail on – or back to England." But what do they tell me at the Company's office? That we are going *nowhere*. We're being paid off. Abandoned. And you knew all along.'

'I swear to you I did not,' said Ross earnestly. 'I was only told this today at the office.'

'Don't swear to me, you bastard. You had a sealed letter. I saw you read it. You knew then. I have sailed with you before, and I know you for what you are – an arsehole bandit who cannot be believed. And, by God, I'll never sail with you again.'

'By God, you will not, nor with any other captain I know,' Ross roared furiously. 'You mutinous, foul-mouthed dog!'

The bo'sun did not reply. Instead he kicked away the nearest leg of the table. Claret spilled from the glasses. Then he smashed down his bottle of wine on the wooden board and lunged at Ross with the jagged edge.

Ross ducked, but too late. The bottle scored his ear; blood spurted down his neck. He put up one hand to the fearful wound, then picked up his own glass of claret and flung the wine into the bo'sun's face. The man staggered back, half blinded for a moment. In that instant, Jackson saw the glitter of a knife grow like an extension of the captain's right hand. With a swift, practised, curving motion, Ross plunged the blade into the bo'sun's gut and ripped it up and out above the man's navel. Bowels spilled over his wrist like a huge nest of red and steaming serpents. The bo'sun collapsed, screaming in mortal agony, vomiting blood and wine and bile.

All around them, the room instantly erupted into violence. It was as though drinkers at every table had only been waiting for such a cue. What had at one moment seemed a room full of apparently good-humoured men was immediately transformed into a wild crowd intent on vengeance. No matter that most of them neither knew nor cared the reason for the bo'sun's screams, the fight provided an essential catalyst for release from months of boredom, cooped in cramped quarters below decks in rolling leaking merchant ships. On all their voyages they were denied liquor in case it encouraged mutiny, and they survived on dry weevil-filled biscuits and slices of salt pork, cut from the hanging carcass of a pig.

Their voyages were without women, without release, except for that found furtively by buggers, sodomites, catamites. Now, free of the foul confines of life below decks, full of wine, with women and boys and transvestites eager and willing to be pleasured, the prospect of a brawl was too exciting to ignore.

What did it matter who they fought? This was action, the chance to unfetter pent-up fury against lives of misery and degradation. If Ross and the bo'sun had not lit this fuse, someone or something else could easily have done so. Whores screamed and waiters fled, as chairs, tables, sideboards turned over. Jackson leapt up from his own chair, swung it in front of him, his back to the wall. He dug one leg of the chair in the eye of a man who came at him, swinging a club. Then someone hit him in the stomach, and momentarily he went down on his knees and lost sight of Ross.

This was a case of every man fighting for himself: drinking companions, friends, messmates were discounted. Jackson suddenly saw Ross, his face pale, one hand at his ear, desperately trying to staunch the flow of blood that streamed down his bare forearm. Other men were moving around the far side of the room, coming towards them – kicking chairs, tables and fallen bodies out of their way, trying to reach the door before Ross and Jackson could find it and escape.

Jackson stood up, still gripping the chair, part weapon, part shield. He had nothing against any of the men he hit, as possibly they had nothing against him. It was simply an animal, brutal contest: the options were survive, or die like the bo'sun. They tripped over his body, trod and slipped on his exposed and steaming bowels, cursing him for being in the way.

Ross, weakened from loss of blood, slumped down in a corner, head on his chest. Hammer blows rained down on him and he was powerless to avoid them. Someone gripped the chair Jackson held, twisted it out of his hand, then drove the leg with all his force into Jackson's stomach. As lunged forward, gasping for breath, he heard a Scottish voice shout: 'Out of the way, you bastards! Make way for the Douglas clan!'

From the back of the fighting sailors, Jackson saw, through a red roaring mist of pain, a man larger than all the rest, hair bright as a furnace flame, fists seemingly the size of pickled hams, fighting, kicking, kneeing, butting with his head.

If he hits me, I'm dead, thought Jackson, but mercifully, inexplicably, the man paused, only feet away.

'There's a side door!' the Scot was shouting. 'To the left, man! Away with you!'

As he spoke, he bent down and picked up Ross by the neck of his shirt, dragging him like a corpse towards a doorway the doctor had not seen. It was shielded by a blue curtain. The Scotsman ripped this down, threw it over the head of a man who rushed at him with a knife, brought up his knee into the man's stomach, seized the curtain pole, broke this over the shoulders of a second attacker, and then they were all through the door into the sweating humidity of a Bengal night.

'This way!' the red-haired giant shouted. He lifted Ross and slung him over his shoulder like a sack of sand. Jackson followed. They reached a row of palanquins and gharries. Horses stood, heads down in nosebags; candle-lights flickered in the gloom; dark faces hovered around them like disembodied ghosts.

'Where is your house?' he asked Jackson.

Jackson gave him the address. They piled into the nearest palanquins.

'As fast as you can go for double money!' the Scotsman told the bearers. He turned to Jackson.

'How's your friend?' he asked.

'Poorly,' Jackson replied. 'But I am a doctor. I will treat him when we can get some light.'

They reached Jackson's house. Bearers carried Ross up to his room and pulled off his clothes. Jackson ripped a sheet into strips of linen, and ordered a servant to fetch salt and warm water from the kitchen. He bathed the captain's wound and bound it up tightly with the sheet. Then Jackson turned to the Scotsman.

'You saved our lives,' he said simply.

'I like a fight,' Douglas replied. 'I had just arrived from a trip up-country. wanted to drink on my own, to get my thoughts straight. A fight blows the gloom out of a body. It's better than whisky for that – and cheaper! Let me introduce myself. I am Alec Douglas, late of Perthshire, and even more lately an officer in the 113th Regiment of Foot. Now, unemployed.'

'This is Captain Marvin Ross of the merchantman *Coromandel*, with whom I sailed out here. I am Dr Richard Jackson. Unemployed, you say you are, but you certainly employed yourself very well tonight.'

He clapped his hands for a bearer.

'Two bottles of claret,' he told him. 'And quickly.'

Ross stirred uneasily. Jackson handed him a glass of wine. He drank deeply; colour returned to his face.

'Unlikely place to find a doctor, in a whore-house,' said Douglas, raising his glass in a toast. 'Unless you are treating the customers?'

'My friend had some bad news,' explained Jackson, as though this was an unarguable reason.

'He is not the only one.'

'His was especially serious. He has been paid off from his ship. *Coromandel* is to stay at anchor in the river, unless she can be sold.'

'Who would buy her?'

'I would, if I could,' said Ross weakly, stirring into consciousness. 'But the price is too high. The owner wants 65,000 silver rupees.'

'If you raised the money, Captain, what would you do with her?'

'First, to show a return on the capital, I would sail to China, load up with tea and sell it beyond the two-mile limit in England. I'd make a clear profit of two thousand per cent.'

'A big return,' said Douglas, impressed. 'What if I found the money for you?'

'You are a rich man?' Jackson asked him.

'No, but I know a rich man, a Parsee. Say we went splits,' said Douglas. 'Down the middle.'

'And what about the doctor here?'

'You are a ship's surgeon? Or maybe you practise your profession in Calcutta?'

'I would like to do so, but I have just arrived in India.'

'But you would not be averse to trade?'

'For a time, yes, I would join you. But not forever. The practice of medicine is my first aim.'

'Good. A three-way split, then – if I can raise the money. I will visit the Parsee tomorrow.'

Mr Sodawaterwallah nodded his head patiently as Douglas explained his proposition. If he would consent to finance the purchase of the ship, the would give him an agreed proportion of all profits. Then the Parsee shook his head sadly from side to side, as one who has listened to the prattle of a child.

'You are not a business man, Mr Douglas. You are a man of war, a man of action.'

'I am neither of those things, but you understand the world of commerce,' said Douglas. 'I thought that this would interest you in a business sense.'

'I regret to have to tell you, it does not, although what you propose to me may seem eminently attractive to you. After all, you and your companions will have to find items to sell at a profit. You will also endure the hazards of each voyage – shipwreck, piracy, mutiny – while, by your understanding, all I would put at risk is a small part of my fortune, in the expectation of a large return. Am I right?'

'Perfectly,' agreed Douglas. 'So why is the idea unattractive to you?'

'Because I can put out such a sum of money at loan or in any other investment, and it will earn me fifteen per cent at the very least, without any worry, any commotion, any risk whatever. And if you cannot trade successfully? After all, this is your first commercial venture. What if pirates seize your vessel or she runs upon the rocks? I have then lost my total investment.'

'We could have lost our lives,' Douglas pointed out.

'Agreed, but in the matter of business I am not concerned about your lives. What concerns me is the safety of my capital. I am sorry, but I cannot advance any money for such a speculative venture in the hands of, if I may say without disrespect, a disparate trio. A doctor of medicine without a practice, an officer who has just been relieved of his commission, and a sea captain of dubious reputation who has been dismissed his ship. A trinity of inexperience in the art of making money, are you not? I am sorry, but that must be my last word on this matter.'

Mr Sodawaterwallah did not add that an even more important reason for refusing to help was that, under another name and with a different branch of his family, he already owned a controlling interest in a company trading with China. Why help competition when it could be stifled?

Douglas explained this refusal to Jackson and the captain, now greatly recovered from his wound.

'Doesn't surprise me,' Ross said. 'To extract money from a rich man is like tearing flesh from a roaring lion. Almost an impossibility.'

'You have been here in Calcutta on previous trips,' said Jackson. 'Do you know of any other source?'

'None.'

'What about the banks?' suggested Douglas.

'Useless. Banks only lend money to those who do not need a loan. If our venture proves profitable, they will shower us with money – and on our terms. But not a single anna, one-sixteenth of one rupee, will they advance before they know that it *is* profitable.'

'Well, the Parsee was my only rich acquaintance, and unless you have others, gentlemen, I propose we abandon all hope of acquiring the vessel.'

'I will endeavour to interest Portuguese and French traders I know, and take a commission on her sale,' said Ross sadly. 'That is my only course. Perhaps a new owner will retain me as captain.'

A servant entered, bowing.

'There is a visitor in a closed palanquin to see Mr Douglas sahib,' he announced.

'Who?' asked Douglas.

'A bearer tells me this, sahib. I do not know the personage. He requests you to come and see for yourself.'

Douglas shrugged. He could think of no one who knew he was here; but he might as well discover who the caller was, and the nature of their business. He walked down the front steps to a palanquin which had been set down by its four bearers to one side of the base. The curtains were still drawn, and the bearers were nowhere to be seen. He approached the palanquin cautiously, and coughed outside the curtains.

'I am Douglas,' he said. 'Who is within?'

A hand with cherry-red painted finger-nails reached out and drew one curtain back slightly. He climbed in through the gap, closing the curtain behind him. In the scented dimness inside he could see Savina, sitting up on the long couch.

'What brings you here?' he asked her in surprise.

'No one must know it is me,' she replied nervously. 'But I wished to tell you something personally. I am with child. Your child.'

'Does your husband know?'

'I will tell him this evening. I wanted to tell the boy's father first.'

'You are sure the baby is a boy?' Douglas asked her.

'I have consulted the sages. They have their secret ways of knowing. They tell me I am carrying a son. Your son.'

'I am very pleased,' said Douglas warmly, and yet as he spoke he felt a curious spasm of sadness. He had never really thought about fathering children, but to realise now that his son, born of his loins, his love, was already in the body of this beautiful woman – and that he would never know the boy, never walk the heather with him, teach him how to cast or to shoot, to play the pipes – these thoughts touched his heart. Was a fee of ten thousand rupees – twenty, a million – enough to pay for such a loss? He had sold a soul, and not even his own, for a tiny sum, already spent.

'You are sad,' Savina said and put out her hand to touch his.

'I am pleased for you, very pleased,' Douglas assured her again. 'I hope your husband will share this joy.'

'He will. To have an heir, and an heir with a light skin, is something all Parsees desire. But I wanted to tell you first, because he is yours as much as he is mine.'

'Will I ever see him?' asked Douglas.

'That would not be wise. We are moving back to Bombay within the month. My husband's father is ill. My husband is his eldest son and he must take over the business there. It is much larger than his business here in Calcutta.'

'Could I see you – and the boy – in Bombay, if I passed through?'

'No,' she said, shaking her head. 'My husband would not be pleased. I hear you have already called at my house today?'

'Yes. About another matter. I had hoped to interest your husband in making an investment.'

'Oh. Nothing to do with me?'

Savina sounded disappointed.

'Nothing. But I wish it had been.'

'Since you will not see your son, but possibly you may think about him in years ahead, as he grows from boyhood to manhood, and as I will think about you, seeing you in him, your smile – perhaps even with your red hair – I would like to make you a small gift, a remembrance.'

'I could not accept it. Your husband was very generous to me.'

'I am not being generous. This is just for you,' she said. 'Because of – everything.'

As Douglas looked at her more closely, he could see she was crying. Tears ran unchecked down her cheeks.

'Can you not understand? I am carrying *your* son. He is within me, blood of my blood, and blood of *you*. That is no little thing for a woman to know, Scotsman. I dream of you. When my husband lies with me, and enters me, I close my eyes and think it is you. When my son – our son – is born, he will be you in a small compass. Every time I look at him, I will be looking at you.'

They sat in silence for a moment. Savina wiped away her tears with a scented silk handkerchief.

'Now,' she said, making a great effort to compose herself, 'partings are only a rehearsal for death. They must be brief. If they are prolonged, it is as though our hearts die a little within us. Here is my gift. Do not look at it until I have gone. Do with it what you will. Maybe one day you will give it to some woman you love, a woman of your own kind and colour, and what you call your class or clan. And when she wears it, and thinks you are looking at her and admiring her, I hope you will also be remembering me.'

Savina took a small pouch from the recesses of the cushions and handed it to Douglas, and then looked away quickly, her shoulders already trembling with the extent of her sadness. He put the pouch in a side pocket, drew her towards him and kissed her gently on the forehead, then on the tip of her nose, her ears and then her mouth. She clung to him tightly for a moment before she pushed him away.

'Please go,' she said miserably. 'I beg of you, go. And do not look back.

Do not think of me now, weeping. Remember me as I was when I was happy with you. As I will always remember you, Scotsman.'

Douglas stepped out of the palanquin, drew the curtains together slowly and walked up the steps. Four bearers appeared from the shadow of the house, salaamed silently towards him. Each one went to his pole, bent down and lifted up the palanquin. In step, they marched away into the suddenly deepened tropical twilight. For a moment, Douglas heard their feet on the gravel, and then there was silence and the dark, and a sudden disquieting emptiness in his heart that he knew nothing and no one would ever completely fill.

Canton

Dr Jackson was still asleep when *Coromandel*'s anchor chains screeched out into the Pearl River with a roar of rusty metal. He dressed quickly and hurried up on deck.

A hot lazy wind, heavy with spice and the smell of dung dried in the sun, drifted out from the Chinese mainland ten miles away. All around them bobbed junks and sampans. The high sing-song calls of men, shouting in unknown tongues, sounded as incomprehensible as the cries of shrill tropical birds. Captain Ross climbed up the companionway and stood next to him, leaning on the ship's rail, already warm under the early morning sun.

'Well,' he said. 'Destination Canton. Or, to be exact, Whampoa Island off-shore and as near as we are allowed to approach, being what the Chinese charmingly call Red-Bristled Barbarians.'

All around them other ships lay at anchor, large vessels of upwards of 1,500 tons, flying the flags of Holland, Sweden, France and Denmark. As they watched the morning activity aboard them, the sound of music suddenly and surprisingly encompassed them; it was as though *Coromandel* lay at the centre of a trained brass band, several bands in fact, for martial music blared at them from every direction.

Jackson borrowed the captain's glass and trained it on the decks of each ship in turn. Aboard every one, he could see a band playing to greet the new day.

'For a moment,' he said, smiling, 'I thought this was just in our honour.'

'Not yet, but it will be, doctor, it will be. We'll have the largest ships – *and* the best bands aboard 'em.'

'You think so?'

'I know so.'

'If you are so sure then, Captain, what is the next move?'

'To find someone to sell us tea cheaply and get out as quickly as we can.'

'Why such haste? It has taken us weeks to reach here.'

'Because the sole trading concession belongs to the East India Company, and although we fly their flag, we have of course absolutely no right to do so, for we have nothing whatever to do with them. This deception is dangerous, but necessary. It is our only hope of being allowed to anchor. The Chinese officials recognise it. Later, we can pretend we are diplomats and fly the flag of Tuscany or some such unlikely place.'

'Why not France or Germany?'

'Other wily dealers have already thought of that and fly their flags as though they had actually visited those countries. Do not worry, doctor, we will find some spare flag or other. I have a locker full of them. But first we have to trade in a small way, test the water so to speak, and that is why we are here.

'If the Company discovers what we are doing, we will be in very great trouble. The Chinese customs officers here are corrupt as a counterfeit guinea. The Company will suggest that they earn their huge bribes. It is at best evens that they will then board the ship on the excuse that we are carrying opium – and seize it in the Emperor's name.'

'Not with my money,' said Douglas, who had joined them. 'No one seizes this ship while I am alive and aboard her.'

He and the captain went for'ard to check on the anchors; they could drag very easily on the muddy bottom of the river. Jackson watched Ross out of sight. The man irritated him, yet he had to admire his professionalism. He knew how to navigate a ship, he could keep discipline among a rough, cut-throat crew, but there was a dark side to his character. In a tight spot, could he trust him?

He remembered the sea-cook's body, splashing into the sea and its sudden convulsive squirming. *Had* the man been dead? Was that simply a muscular reaction with the shock of the water? Or had he still been alive, fighting desperately for air? He remembered the sudden glitter of the captain's knife when the bo'sun had attacked him.

'You deliberately killed that man,' Jackson told him afterwards, when he staunched the captain's wound.

'I had to,' Ross replied at once. 'He damn' nigh killed me. We have only one life, and I'll thank you for saving mine, doctor. You would not have had the chance if I had let that swine live.'

Jackson's whole training had been to save life. This casual, cavalier attitude was disturbing, but there was no doubt that in these faraway and foreign seas Ross would be a good man to have on his side – so long as he stayed there.

Douglas cast his mind back to the excitement that had marked the weeks before they sailed. Savina's present was a ruby, even redder than his hair. He took it to Mr Grindlay's bank in the hope that he would accept it as security for an advance. This the chief clerk was unwilling to do, and directed him instead to a Portuguese Jew in a small house behind one of the mansions overlooking the *maidan*.

'How much would you advance me on this stone?' Douglas asked him. The Jew, small and wizened like a shrunken manikin, screwed an eye-glass into his right eye and examined the ruby, turning it over and over slowly with a pair of tweezers.

'It is unflawed,' he said in amazement. 'Perfect.'

'Which must reflect on your price?' said Douglas.

'Ah now, *senhor*,' the other man replied quickly, 'it is better for a jewel to be flawed, as a human being is flawed. Even so, I can offer you ten thousand rupees.'

'Too little,' said Douglas, shaking his head.

The dealer pushed the jewel across the table to him. It glittered on the white cloth like a fallen star. The dealer ran his tongue around dry lips, already caked white with salt.

'Twelve thousand,' he said shortly.

'For a perfect gem, twenty thousand,' replied Douglas, watching the other man's face for his reaction. 'With the promise of redemption at that sum within a year.'

'Impossible.'

'Then I will take it elsewhere,' said Douglas.

'No one will pay you twenty thousand *and* redeem it.'

'Then I will make it easy for you,' said Douglas. 'You are Jewish and I am Scottish. I was brought up to believe that we Scots are descended from one of the two lost tribes of Israel. We will not argue over the value of a tiny stone, which either of us could in this instant swallow and lose forever. Why, in a desert we would willingly trade it for a glass of water. It is only a bauble. Twenty thousand now, and *I* pay *you* twenty-one within the year for redemption.'

The Jew smiled and held out his hand, dry and scaly as a vulture's claw.

'I cannot deny you,' he said with relief. 'We are of the same blood, if not the same faith.'

He rang a bell. A servant brought in a bond form, which the Jew made out with his quill pen for the agreed sum. Next, on to the East India Company's office to buy the ship, using the extra ten thousand rupees the Parsee gave him when his wife assured him she was with child, to buy victuals. The manager accepted his offer of thirty thousand with such speed Douglas regretted he had not offered less.

Next, they went to the offices of the most prestigious lawyers in Calcutta, Groves, de Souza and Bortwith, and signed a partnership agreement. Each would be entitled to one-third of all profits. Should any of them die, he could only leave his share to his other two partners, or to his widow if he were married. This, Mr Groves proposed as a means to prevent any dilution of the company's equity, and to keep out unwanted shareholders. Then back to Jackson's house to tell Ross he could engage a crew. Several had sailed with him before; others were newcomers. All were young and willing to take low pay for a percentage of any profit.

They had sailed almost immediately. Now they lay off the only port on all the China coast where the Emperor reluctantly permitted Europeans and Americans to land, but only briefly and for certain specified and very limited trading purposes.

Already, junks and other sampans were bumping against the far side of *Coromandel*'s tarred hull; all cargoes had to be loaded into these local vessels and rowed in to Canton.

Jackson saw a Chinese official nodding and gesticulating as he spoke to Ross. The man bowed deeply, then climbed down the rope ladder to a sampan.

'The Hoppo has given us permission to land,' Ross explained. 'We are a new vessel he has not seen before. He probably wants a closer look to see our style, and guess what he can squeeze out of us in bribes.'

'Who is the Hoppo?'

'The Emperor's man here in Canton. I don't know what his damned title really is – that is the nearest we can get to pronouncing it. Canton has a Viceroy, who also reports to the Emperor, but the Hoppo is the most influential man here. He has the job of controlling all foreign trade for three years and then he has to step down, and someone else takes over.

'This is to try and keep a check on his honesty. All it means is that in these three years he has to make his fortune in bribes from us. The Emperor does not want any of us to be here at all, so the Hoppo has to think up convenient excuses for our presence, and they have to be good excuses, or he can easily end up a head shorter than he is at present.

'He has to spend another fortune to be appointed in the first place, so he squeezes us every way he can. He charges absurd mooring fees, heavy duties on everything he can think of, taxes on loading, others on unloading. And all the while, on his back, he has every kind of petty official and senior ones, too, right up to the Emperor's court in Peking, all wanting their share for turning a Nelson eye.

'If the Hoppo is in a bad mood, he can stop us loading for a week, a month, or indeed forever. And all the time we have to pay out large sums simply to lie at anchor off this poxy island. We were fortunate to find him in good humour. He had just taken a huge levy from an American ship, so was disposed to be relatively helpful.'

'Why is his job necessary, if he simply pockets the money or gives bribes to other people?' asked Douglas.

'Who knows?' replied the captain enigmatically. 'It is the Chinese way. The Emperor believes that all foreigners sail to China – on his seas, by the way, for by his reckoning, he controls all the world – simply to pay tribute to him. As a concession, he therefore permits trade – of a kind. China will sell us tea and silk and silver – always provided we buy cargoes of rhubarb from them.'

'We grow that back home,' said Douglas. 'I hate the taste of the stuff.'

'So do I, but the Chinese feel that unless they sell us rhubarb, we in the West will all die of constipation. It is a kind of salve for their conscience in doing any trade with us. We buy the stuff, then dump it in the sea as soon as we are out of sight of land. They want to keep our bowels open, and we want to keep the trade routes open.

'That is why I wish to take a cargo of tea. Britain's total imports of tea, exactly a hundred and fifty years ago this month, were just over two pounds in weight. Now, they are worth three and a half million pounds sterling every year – plus Government tax. It suits us well to deal in tea, because it is harmless and bears no taint of the other trade, the Forbidden Trade, which is where real wealth lies. Foreign mud. Opium. But it is death to be caught handling a grain of the stuff, let alone a casket, so we must feel our way carefully here.'

'What about the Hoppo?' asked Douglas.

'He is involved, too, of course. The business is now so big that his predecessor amassed the equivalent of ten million pounds sterling – and in only three years. He makes a profit buying from us and selling it on When you consider that the annual rent for a cottage in England is only two shillings and sixpence, and a servant's wage is five pounds a year, we can all live like kings on what we will make in a couple of years, i we don't go down with the pox or at the end of a rope.'

'I will keep away from the first,' said Jackson firmly. 'I have treated to many patients for it.'

'Possibly. But the second possibility becomes more difficult to avoi with every voyage,' said Ross.

'You have been on this coast before?'

'Several times, but as first mate. Never commanding a vessel.'

'Why didn't we get into that trade at once?' asked Jackson. 'Make fortune and then clear out?'

'Too risky,' replied Ross. 'It is safer to buy tea, and at the same time t approach the Hoppo and others who can help us. See what they requir from us. What protection they can afford in return. Then, on our second trip, we trade in mud, like the rest.'

'Mud,' said Jackson reflectively, remembering the hovel on the edge of the Thames with Mrs Gray dying.

'I can see mud,' she had told him. 'Nothing but mud.' Could she really see his future? Could this mud turn to gold, as the strengthening morning sun was already transforming the filthy oily river into a channel of flowing gold?

'I would rather we stayed as traders in tea or silk or silver, instead of dabbling in mud,' said Douglas unexpectedly. 'I saw opium poppies growing in India. Children, already drugged by its smell, were packing it on shelves. I would not like to grow rich by that means.'

He was thinking of Savina carrying his child beneath her heart. What future could there be for any young boy or girl doomed to labour in that scented charnel-house?

'I thought you wanted to get rich,' said Ross contemptuously. 'After all, you found the money to buy the ship. You still wish to cover your expenditure, surely?'

'I do. And I need money to fight for the lands of my family, back in Scotland. But somehow – I cannot explain my feelings more explicitly – I do not wish to make money by condemning others to a lingering death.'

'We'll not ask you to,' said Ross cheerfully. 'Most of the peasants who smoke the stuff would already describe their lives in those terms, if anyone asked them.

'We'll be doing them a great favour, I say, and ourselves one at the same time. I tell you what we'll do, Douglas. The doctor here and I will keep your share of the money we make running mud. You can make your money from the tea. What do you say to that?'

He roared with laughter at what he intended to be a ludicrous proposal, to show Douglas how absurd his attitude was. He stopped laughing and stared in amazement when Douglas immediately agreed – and gave him his hand on it.

They climbed down the rope ladder in silence, each busy with his own thoughts. The ship's barge awaited them, *Coromandel*'s crew, smartly turned out in white shirts and black caps, sitting at the oars. Half way across the river, several sampans came out of a small inlet known as Lob Lob Creek. The nearest vessel drew alongside and a man stood up on the prow; behind him sat several young Chinese girls.

'Wantee girl?' he enquired hopefully. 'Wantee girl?'

'Don't be a fool,' said Ross before either of the others could answer. 'They are all poxed up to their eyes. Six girls to service every merchantman at anchor. Get out!' he shouted. 'Take your scabs elsewhere!'

The man grinned, turned, bent forward and bared his bottom at them to show his opinion of the captain. Then the little craft crossed the choppy water to the next ship.

'It's the only place they can ply their trade,' Ross explained. 'You'd make your fortune here, treating sailors of pox, doctor.'

'Possibly, but I'd still rather try my luck with honest trade.'

'I would not call hawking opium honest,' said Douglas sarcastically.

They approached a quay, green-bearded with seaweed, and jumped ashore, instinctively steadying themselves on solid land after weeks aboard a rocking, rolling ship.

On the shining stones, six Chinese, naked except for long blue drawers, crouched dangling looped ropes into the filthy river. They totally ignored the newcomers. Their attention was fixed on the bloated carcass of a pig, mouth open, eyes staring, skin shining with putrefaction. It moved on the sluggish tide towards their loops. As with a co-ordinated drill movement, they positioned them until they surrounded the rotting corpse, and then heaved it up, bursting with gas and decay.

'They will serve it tonight with spices,' said Ross. 'I have eaten all sorts of things here – not knowing what they were until afterwards. Frogs' legs, fish heads, the nests of birds, the fins of sharks, the feet of ducks, eggs a hundred years old. The spices they treat them with are so so strong they make anything taste good, which is why, of course, spices fetch such high prices back home.'

A crowd had silently gathered around Ross. Now he pulled from his trouser pocket a brightly coloured silk handkerchief. He carefully tied one corner of this around his belt, then replaced the handkerchief in his pocket, taking care to leave visible half a foot of brilliant red and green silk that trailed from the pocket like a pennant.

'What's that for?' Douglas asked him.

'You will see in a minute,' he replied. 'In the East, face is everything. Foreigners have the peculiar right of being allowed to belabour – on the spot – any Chinese who attempts to steal anything from them. They are great pickpockets, and someone is certain to try and steal this. If they do, I will know – and take action.'

'But why set a trap for them?'

'Because they guess we are new here. If we do not establish our position immediately, we are worse than worms, lower than the bellies of serpents.'

A crowd of children clustered around them, hands outstretched or patting their pitifully thin stomachs. Some Englishmen, wearing black jackets, black stovepipe hats, and white, freshly laundered trousers, nodded a distant greeting. It would not do to be too forthcoming; one never knew exactly what sort of people new arrivals were until one had been properly introduced.

In the background stood a row of proud white buildings with pillars and porticos. Flags fluttered from masts set in strips of lawn between them and the road: Dutch, French, Danish, the American Stars and Stripes, the British Union Jack.

'This is the main street,' explained Ross. 'Thirteen Factories Street, because these buildings are called factories or manufactories. There used to be thirteen. Now the number has diminished. When we establish a base here, as we will, my friends, we will reverse that trend.

'On the ground floors there is a warehouse, with a counting house, and a treasury with granite walls and double iron doors to discourage theft. These factories have to act as their own banks because no Chinese bank will do any business with Red-Bristled Barbarians.

'Foreigners, by the way, are only allowed in this street and along the three alleys that run up from the sea – Hog Lane, Old China Street and New China Street. If you try to enter the main part of Canton, you will be stoned by everyone in sight. They will throw shit at you – and as you can see from the state of the streets, they are not lacking in ammunition. You will be lucky if you are not also flayed with bamboos – so keep out. Remember, if you disappear in Canton, no one will ever come looking for you.'

Suddenly, there was a great commotion, a wailing and crying, and the crowd surged to each side of the road, where they stood, heads bowed, not moving, seemingly not even breathing.

'Quick,' said Ross urgently. 'Off the road, and do what I do.'

'Why?'

'Because it could be death not to. Do not speak until I speak.'

They stood, heads lowered. Jackson peered up under the rim of his hat. He saw a sumptuous palanquin, lacquered purple and red, and supported by twelve servants, three on each end of the gilded poles. Ahead of them marched men with shaven heads and long drooping waxed moustaches. Each carried a whip of hide which he flicked from side to side indiscriminately. The leather thongs, tipped with metal, cut into the naked legs of children or the faces of any they considered did not bow their heads deeply enough.

'The Hoppo,' whispered Ross in explanation.

He was a large plump man, with a sallow face the size of a ripe melon, his eyes tiny horizontal slits set in a soft mass of fat. He sat on a gilded chair in the palanquin with his hands folded, and his fingers deliberately stretched out so that all could see the length of his lacquered nails. Each finger-nail was sharpened to a needle point to demonstrate that he never undertook manual work of any kind.

He wore a purple robe shot with gold and bearing the design of a quail. His hat was round like an inverted soup plate and on the top was his mark of rank, a single round gold button. Other officials of lower degree wore buttons of different colours but gold was the badge of the highest grade.

After the procession passed, Ross counted to ten, and then said it would be safe to speak, but in whispers. All around them, the crowd of peasants, labourers, touts and minor officials, began to walk again.

'I reckon that is an omen,' said Ross. 'Remember, he takes a percentage of *everything* that comes ashore from every ship and everything that is loaded on to them – even the drinking water we have to buy. If a stupid fat man like that can make a fortune, what have we to fear?'

'According to you, death by strangulation or decapitation,' remarked Jackson drily.

'We will not fail,' Ross assured them. 'I can feel it in my bones and water. We are going to be rich, my friends, very, very rich!'

At that moment, he felt a slight tug from the region of his belt, and turned just in time to see a thin man with a long pigtail pulling at his silk handkerchief.

'Ho! You slit-arsed swine!' Ross shouted with the utmost geniality, and swinging his cane, brought it down upon the shoulders of the pickpocket. The man stared at him in amazement and obvious disbelief: how could this red-bristled one know his intention so swiftly? Had he an eye in his pocket? He clung on to the handkerchief, pulling it vigorously, all pretence at stealth now vanished.

Up and down went Ross's cane with the regularity of a housewife beating a carpet. Then, at last realising he could not remove the handkerchief, the man fled, with Ross in quick pursuit, belabouring him about the legs and shoulders until the thief vanished up a narrow alley.

To the amazement of Jackson and Douglas, Chinese in the street roared with laughter and cheered Ross as he returned.

'You see?' he said triumphantly. 'They'll know now that we three will never be made fools of. The three of us make a trinity – a trio. Let us go by that name and become known to West and East alike as Trinity-Trio.'

'That calls for a toast,' said Douglas.

'Several,' agreed Jackson, and led the way into a grog-shop.

Fifteen hundred miles to the north, in the centre of a flower garden cunningly designed around the peak of a small hill known as Beautiful Autumn Hillock, within distant sight of the Great Wall and the dust road to Inner Mongolia, the panels of a silken parasol fluttered gently in the morning breeze, like the translucent gossamer wings of a giant and captive moth.

Beneath its shade sat a weak-faced, middle-aged man, his hands folded in his lap. His fingernails were even longer than the Hoppo's nails. His lips moved in silent speech as he watched the slow graceful movements of three golden carp in a crystal bowl on a table before him. As they swam around and around, they opened their mouths, as though they also were talking without words, and he opened his in return, wondering at their thoughts as much as at his own.

This man was Tao-Kuang, the Emperor of all China. This garden, built by his great-great-grandfather, K'ang-Hsi, as a summer retreat from the dust and stench and pestilence of the cities, was aptly named The Paradise of Countless Trees, because around dainty flowerbeds were planted rows of apricot and walnut, apple and pear trees, and corianders that stretched away on every side with military precision.

Willow trees dipped long pale green branches around an ornamental lake, where lotus blossom and water lily flowers opened blushing petals to the sun. The architects of this garden had incorporated streams spanned by bridges, with pavilions and summer-houses. Porcelain dragons and lions stared with blue and bulging eyes from the shade of ornamental shrubs.

Such was the Emperor's eminence that no one could ever physically look down upon him, so his palace stood on the highest promontory. From this, he could look down on other summer-houses, built for his queens and courtiers and concubines, that dotted artificial hills created over many years by thousands of toiling slaves, to give the appearance of a natural landscape.

The air hung heavy with the scent of acres of flowers. A busy hum and buzz of bees from hives built in the shape of tiny pagodas added to the agreeable sense of peace and warmth and leisure. Yet he knew that this feeling of safety and serenity was an illusion. Even in this tranquil garden, teams of guards kept a constant watch from the tops of high towers for the approach of any strangers, lest they could cause harm to the Imperial Presence.

Far beneath the Emperor, from his own favourite place of observance near the Temple of Universal Joy, he could see the outline of two dust roads. One was travelled only by the feet of bearers carrying his palanquin as he journeyed to or from his main palace in the Forbidden City of Peking. On such ceremonial occasions, an immense procession of palanquins, camels and pack animals, with his attendant mandarins, eunuchs, musicians, guards, and his various queens and concubines, could extend for several miles.

The second road was of inferior design and construction, and only used by infinitely lesser personages. Messengers would ride along it with intelligence from other cities, and envoys bringing gifts and tributes from the outer marches of his Empire.

Tao-Kuang, like many weak men with inherited power and no personal aptitude for authority, was also parsimonious. He enjoyed receiving gifts; silver ornaments, amber, musk, ginseng. Even if he had no personal use for such presents, he could pass them on to others and so save having to buy presents with his own money. His huge and avaricious staff had therefore to take every advantage of any opportunity to enrich themselves, for none could live on wages the Emperor considered adequate.

His palaces were run by eunuchs of different grades, from those who worked in his kitchens, to those who served his person. His favourite dish was macaroni soup, but when he ordered the Chief of the Imperial Household to prepare this, he was informed that not only would a new kitchen have to be built to make such soup, but special cooks would need to be engaged, and naturally a special official appointed to oversee them. This would cost an initial 600,000 taels – around £180,000, as the Barbarians counted money – and would in addition involve an annual expenditure on ingredients of another 15,000 taels, or about £5,000.

The Emperor refused to sanction this, and instead sent a eunuch every day to buy a bowlful of soup from an eating house for workmen along the Secondary Road. It cost him 40 cash a bowl – roughly the equivalent of a Barbarian penny. His household officials, deprived of a new and hitherto unexplored source of revenue, closed down the eating house in the Emperor's name and exiled its owner.

The Emperor frowned at the thought of such indignities, which he personally felt powerless to alter. Of course, he could have ordered the officials responsible to be castrated, disembowelled or handed over to the torturers to be killed by a variety of slow methods.

They might be strapped naked to a bench and suffer their flesh slowly to be combed from their bodies by a torturer using an iron comb with sharpened curved teeth. By combing a small part of the prisoner's body each day, death could be postponed indefinitely, but the agony of the festering sores, black with flies, would increase with every hour.

Again, he could have ordered them to be cut into a thousand pieces or burned alive or beaten to death, and his predecessors had frequently ordered such punishment for relatively small offences, but to do any of these things demanded resolution, a definite decision. And decisions of any kind he was always reluctant to make.

It was the Hour of the Snake – nine o'clock in the morning as the Red-Bristled Barbarians strangely counted the passing of the hours. He frowned anew at the thought of these pestilential people with their raw sweating flesh, their hog-like faces, their long noses and pale eyes, and their peculiar walk, like prancing ponies, instead of the smooth glide of mandarins. They clustered on his coast, seeking his trade with all the perseverance of blue-tailed flies around the orifices of a rotting corpse.

He put contemplation of their presence, fifteen hundred miles away, from his mind. It belonged with other unhappy matters, such as the streets of Peking, inches deep in excrement and thick with flies, and vague uneasy rumours he had heard at second and third hand of insurrection and resentment among his people.

How best to deal with rebellious subjects? He thought of one such man, Nien Keng-Yao, who long ago had been brought in chains to the Imperial Palace at Peking by his predessor, Yun Cheng. Nien Keng-Yao's prosecutors claimed that he had so many accusations against him that, if placed one upon the other, the pile would reach higher than Mount Tai, and his proven offences would reach deeper into the deepest sea than ever a plumb-line had dropped.

He had committed gross and unpardonable acts of treason and usurpation. He had ordered that roads should be sprinkled with yellow earth and cleared as though for an Imperial procession when he went about the streets. He had sat before the Dragon Tablet of the Emperor, instead of *kow-towing* on his knees. He had even worn the Emperor's Dragon Robes, and sat, as only an Emperor could sit, facing south, to receive congratulations from his loathsome subordinates. He had appropriated millions of taels of government money, promoted the unworthy and demoted those of greater account.

The sentence could only be death by dismemberment. His father, brothers, sons, grandsons, and all other male relations above the age of sixteen must also be decapitated. All women members of his family were to be sold as slaves to families he had dishonoured.

But the Emperor had been unexpectedly merciful; he had graciously allowed the prisoner to commit suicide. He had only banished for life his male relatives to the most malarious regions of Yunnan. Now, Tao-Kuang feared that what might in the past be accepted as mercy and a sign of strength from a strong ruler would in his case be interpreted as another token of weakness.

His wives knew he was feeble; so did his concubines. He was unable to pleasure them. He had heard from his eunuch informers how slightingly they spoke of him. Oh, to be likened to his illustrious predecessor, the Manchu Emperor K'ang H'si, who had sired thirty-five sons and could pleasure so many women in a single night that songs were sung in his praise and to honour his Personal Sword with the Head of a Purple Plum which he wielded so adroitly and without fatigue. He remembered the harsh prophecy of the poet Yang Chen, who, sixteen hundred years earlier – as the Barbarians counted time – had written:

If the hen announces the dawn
Instead of the cock,

If the affairs of State
Are in the hands of women,
If the prince in bed
Is the one to be mounted,
Then will the Empire fall apart.

How true these words were, only the Emperor knew. His Celestial Mist and Rain was thin and weak; his Imperial Jade-Thruster found difficulty in penetrating the Flowery Path of his most experienced and willing concubine. How long would it be before whispers of this grievous inability would reach beyond his palace walls?

As Tao-Kuang sat on his throne looking at the two distant roads, he felt rat's teeth of fear and despair gnaw within him as he sensed personal and political humiliation. The foreign Barbarians had ships armed with guns that could destroy targets at great distances, and although ships of his Imperial Navy had pictures of such guns painted on their hulls, these could cause no damage to an armed enemy. Also, the Barbarian sea captains could traverse the oceans accurately by means of a curious needle that always pointed to the north, while his captains had to make do with eyes painted on their ships' bows to see which way they were going. Clearly, the Emperor needed to be strong, and to show this strength in some dramatic way, and quickly.

Among the many jugglers and contortionists who, for a few cash, exhibited their strange skills in the dust at the roadside to entertain travellers, was one man whose abilities fascinated the Emperor. This man could be bound with thongs and ropes and chains, hooded, even placed in a tank of water, but somehow he managed to escape.

But at his most recent performance, which the Emperor in disguise had seen, the bonds had been too strong, or the contortionist was too old. He had not been able to escape; he had died choking in chains, because he had left his escape attempt too late. This seemed to Tao-Kuang to be an omen, a portent. One more sign of his own weakness and it might also be too late to restore his waning authority.

As he sat brooding on past and present, seeking a solution, any solution, his eyes were drawn to the passage of a cloud of dust along the lesser of the two roads; a rider was approaching at speed. He saw his guards go out to meet him with whips and sharpened bamboo staves, ready to strike him from his horse if he was a person without honour. Then he saw the man being brought towards him through flowers that nodded waist-high blooms.

Even from this distance the Emperor could see that the rider was caked with red dust. It was neither fitting nor seemly that he should approach the Son of Heaven in such a condition. There was a pause while servants led him to the Royal Bath House to be washed and ceremoniously dried. Then, barefoot, as befitted a man in the Emperor's presence, he was escorted before Tao-Kuang and threw himself full length on the polished marble tiles. Even when the Emperor graciously gave him permission to rise, he stayed on his knees in the position of a supplicant at prayer.

He was the son of a mandarin of some standing, proud at being selected to bring news one and a half thousand miles. He handed up a roll of vellum on which the Viceroy of Canton had painted a long letter. The Emperor frowned as he read the characters. This was not news of business bargaining between Barbarians from beyond the Outer Seas, but the arrival of a personage the Viceroy referred to contemptuously as the Barbarian Eye and later with the ideograph of Laboriously Vile. It appeared that from the country of England this personage had arrived at the Portuguese enclave of Macao on the frontiers of the Celestial Empire.

He was apparently a man of rank in his Barbarian country, a lord, previously an admiral, named in the Barbarian tongue, Napier. He claimed to be an ambassador, not a merchant. The Emperor frowned at such a presumption. For far too long these Barbarians, like hogs with thick skins and blunt snouts, had butted their vilely bristled bodies against his kingdom. He had no wish for ambassadors, less even than for merchants. All other countries were his vassal states and owed allegiance only to him.

This lord had arrived in a vessel heavy with guns, and sought permission to meet the Emperor forthwith. What an insulting wish! What made this crude buffoon feel he was worthy to see, even from a great distance, the celestial presence?

Tao-Kuang ceased reading, ordered a secretary instantly to his side and dictated a reply, which the man, bowing low, painted in flowing characters on a long vellum sheet as the Emperor spoke.

'Let all with trembling awe obey,' the missive began. 'This Laboriously Vile must be kept from the Celestial Empire! Action must be taken against further encroachment by Barbarian merchants! Delay not! Instantly obey! Imperial edict!'

He nodded dismissal to the secretary and turned now to the young man and motioned him to his feet.

'You have ears,' he said briefly. 'You have heard our Imperial Command.'

The messenger bowed his head in acknowledgement. The Emperor looked at him for a moment. This young fellow must personally have seen Barbarian merchants; he must know what was happening in Canton, whereas the Emperor had to rely on his own officials, and he had heard constant and most disquieting rumours of corruption among them. Periodically he ordered routine decapitations, but alarmingly the rumours persisted. Why were these strange, snouted people so intent on trading with his Celestial Empire?

'Have *you* seen this Barbarian Eye?' he asked him.

'No, Your Most Celestial Majesty, but I am told by those who have gazed upon his disgusting features that he is like the rest – detestable. His body is thin and long, his skin is raw.'

'Tell me more about the Bristled Barbarians you have met,' the Emperor commanded him. He could not, of course, admit any ignorance, so he added casually: 'We will weigh your opinions against those of others.'

'Your Most Celestial Majesty, in my humble understanding they come, in the main, from two distant and unimportant islands. First, many dwell in the island of England, which is divided into two provinces. The north province is Scotland, from where the worst Barbarians have sailed.

'There is another island many days' sailing to the west, known as America. The English colonised this island, which is also small and without consequence. There was a war, and although both sets of Barbarians speak the same language still, they are not linked. The Americans are known for considerable mechanical ingenuity.'

He paused, not certain how to proceed. He did not wish the Emperor to think he was exaggerating, nor did he feel justified in extolling inventions he had not personally seen. And had not the Emperor himself declared that he was not interested in such toys, that China was supreme in all areas of invention?

'In what dimensions?' the older man asked him.

'It is said, Your Most Celestial Majesty, they have ships that need no sails. They claim their engineers light huge fires within their hulls and this makes wheels with wooden paddles to turn with the force of steam. Our admirals, Majesty, do not accept this. They believe that these wheels with paddles are actually turned through teams of oxen below decks, as peasants here turn grinding wheels for grain.'

'We accept the view of Our admirals that this is fiction. How can a tub of boiling water make a vessel progress through our seas? What are the trading habits of these despicable liars?'

'They have several small buildings on the coast, Most Celestial One, where they trade under the flags of nations hitherto unknown and obviously so small they are beneath Your Celestial Majesty's consideration.'

'Do *all* trade under such flags?'

The man bowed.

'Sometimes privateers arrive and take aboard our goods or bring stores from their own islands, and are away before the vigilance of Your Celestial Majesty's officials can catch and punish them.'

'How is this allowed?'

'They have the guile of serpents. They arrive and leave by night, like sea creatures of the dark. They are men altogether without honour of any kind.'

'Are there any such in our port now?'

'One such vessel arrived, Celestial Majesty, on the day I left with the honour of conveying your illustrious Viceroy's message. This is a ship with three merchants aboard. One is an American who appears to be captain of the vessel. The next is a physician from England, but only qualified in western medical arts, not the true medicine of the Golden Needles of Acupuncture and the Herbs of Heaven.'

'And the third?'

'The third is a man of fearsome appearance, nearly four cubits tall, with hair the colour of blazing flame. He has a crude appearance, and comes from the northern province of Scotland.'

'So, young man, in one vessel the wisdom and generosity of Our Ancestors has delivered to us representatives of the three nations who cause Our Kingdom most inconvenience and anxiety?'

The messenger inclined his head.

The Emperor thought for a moment, reluctant as ever to make a definite and conclusive decision. Then he made up his mind: this must be the opportunity he had been seeking to show firmness.

He called back the secretary.

'An edict!' he told him brusquely. 'To the Viceroy in Canton. Delay not! It is Our express and Aweful Command that the Barbarians lately and illegally arrived as described by your faithful messenger are to be seized! Make of them an example to others who would seek to follow their wrongful ways.

'They are to be castrated and decapitated in the most public place! Out of Our mercy, we will spare them the ultimate punishments of the lingering death or dismemberment. But others cannot assume that such merciful treatment will be extended to them by Us. Let all regard and obey! It is Our wish! Instantly to be carried out! Let all with trembling awe obey!'

Captain Ross sat well back in his palanquin, the concealing bead screen lowered in front of him, partly because he valued privacy, partly because he secretly dreaded the hostile shouts and sneers the Chinese gave at the sight of any Red-Bristled Barbarian travelling alone.

Locals would line the streets and laugh at them, puffing on their pipes, opening their fans and pointing in derision at the long nose, pale skin and large eyes of any European who passed by. Often they would draw a finger across their throats and bare their teeth in a gesture of deadly hatred for the foreign devils. If Ross did not see and hear these signs of almost universal animosity, he could nearly persuade himself that it did not exist.

The sheer size of China frightened him. The few Westerners allowed to land there – and then not to travel more than a few yards from the sea – were outnumbered millions of times, and yet they behaved as though the reverse was the case. This was simply an exercise of will, he thought, an inborn belief in Western political and mechanical superiority, and their physical size. In any such equation, numbers on their own had no meaning. But they had a harsh meaning for Captain Ross; he had incurred mute hatred in slave ships for too long not to recognise and fear it instantly.

The knowledge of being execrated ate like acid in his mind, eroding resolution. And as it dissolved layers of protective, selective memory, he remembered one voyage made special by a boy, a voyage that also marked the real beginning of this unreasoning terror.

Ross, and other avaricious captains who commanded slave ships, where conditions were so harsh that as many as eight out of ten of their unwilling passengers would die before they reached Kingston in Jamaica from West Africa, understandably endeavoured to select only the fittest human cargo before they set sail. That way they minimised the risk, not only of loss of life but, more importantly to them, of profit.

Ross would usually ride a few miles inland from Freetown to watch newly-caught slaves being brought in from the countryside. It was often possible then to mark those who were strong, as against those who might not survive the fearful voyage. Dead men paid no dividends, but once the slaves were brought into the town square, dealers could revive the more exhausted by throwing buckets of cold water over them, and for a brief time thereafter, even the weak and diseased would give the illusion of health and virility.

They had all marched in single file for days, sometimes weeks, through pampas and elephant grass. The men wore loincloths and were marched in pairs, each couple close behind the next. They were linked together by logs of wood, tied on their shoulders with stout creeper to form the shape of an X. This was to prevent any newly-captured slave making a sudden bolt for freedom, for the swine were wily and strong and wild as beasts. Their hands were also bound behind their backs as a further deterrent to any escape attempt.

To these bindings was tied a rope, with its other end in a noose around the neck of their woman. She was often carrying a child, or a totally naked piccaninny would run alongside, like a dog, bound to the mother by small cord.

The drovers, half-castes or Portuguese soldiers of fortune, would march to one side of these long and mournful columns that could stretch for hundreds of yards. They carried rifles in the crook of their arm, but understandably were reluctant to fire. The loss of even one slave diminished everyone's profit, and the discomforts and dangers of their own lonely lives required a large return to make all this worth while.

The slaves defecated and urinated on the march. To stop for such matters could delay them all immeasurably, and the quicker they were delivered to Freetown, the less chance of any mishap. There were no arrangements for washing, and the women's legs were often caked with blood from their monthly courses.

Ross carried chalk in his pocket when he rode out to meet new arrivals, and as the likeliest slaves marched past him, he marked them with a cross on a thigh, a breast or a shoulder. The best prices, of course, were for the men who could work in the sugar plantations. Women had their value as domestic servants and washerwomen; sometimes as the secret mistresses of plantation owners. The children, if healthy, would grow up, and so a small outlay for a child could mean a large return within a few years.

On this particular occasion – which, for reasons Ross could not understand, he frequently relived in dreams – he had noticed an extremely strong slave marching at the head of his particular column. He was a proud man, well built, with muscles that rippled like smooth serpents beneath his oiled flesh. He had a small beard and his eyes, deep sunk and brooding, looked down at Ross with scorn and contempt and a depth of hatred that the captain had never previously seen in the eyes of any man. His physique meant he would fetch a prime price.

By his side marched a young boy. He was perhaps fourteen years old; it was difficult to be precise. Children aged quickly in these hot, heathen climates, and girls were frequently mature by the time they were ten. These two were on their own, without a wife or a mother.

The boy instantly attracted Ross. He had a fine figure and was naked as the day he was born. Ross's eyes dropped instinctively to his genitals. The lad possessed an unusually large member for his age and a tight cod. His firm thighs and rounded bottom excited Ross so that he felt his own masculinity harden against the hot roughness of his trousers. By God, he'd buy them both. He had frequently selected young boys or girls, the offspring of slaves, for his own pleasure aboard the ship. Many of the crew did the same, of course, but the captain's rank assured him of first choice.

Ross rode back into town, and just before the auction on the following day, when the slaves stood stinking and sweating in the baking heat, so that the entire marketplace, innocent of any shade, shimmered like a mirage, a lake of liquid fire, he approached the auctioneer.

'I have marked the one I want,' he said knowingly.

'I have to make a fair price,' replied the auctioneer, a shifty man with wall eyes. He had a damp straggly moustache which he sucked as he spoke.

'How much?' asked Ross.

'Five guineas on top,' said the auctioneer at once.

'Make it four,' said Ross; he was not a generous spender.

'It is a deal, sir,' agreed the auctioneer through his sodden moustache. 'As I call their names, I will put them down to you.'

'Have they names?' asked Ross in surprise. In his experience, most newly-caught slaves were without names. These were added afterwards by their new owners.

'They are only blacks, heathens, so they do not have names as we understand them, Christian names,' the auctioneer agreed. 'We generally call them after the area from where they were taken. Congoes, Nangoes, Mongolas, Ashantis, Ibos.

'That big fellow, I shall call him John Ibo, then. The boy, call him Jack. There's years of hard work in both of those, Captain. I can tell you. But he is a dangerous bastard, that big black one. I know the type. You will have to watch him.'

'I am watching the boy,' retorted Ross, grinning lasciviously.

'I thought you were.' The auctioneer smiled knowingly, slapping Ross on the back. 'Got a fine arse on him. Though personally I do not care for a bit of black. I see too much of it in the way of business. And, if I am honest, I cannot abide the smell of black meat.'

The slaves were marched aboard Ross's ship that night and crammed beneath decks. Some had brought drums aboard – and why not? They could provide a harmless amusement on the voyage for people now without freedom or hope. Although the men were shackled at their ankles, their hands were freed, and soon the drums beat from one end of the vessel to the other. Ross recognised them; Africans called them talking drums, because by such drumbeats natives could transmit messages for hundreds of miles, one drum speaking to another, across forests and hills and plains.

What they were saying now, though, he had no idea, but the tapping of the tight skins made him uneasy; it was as though they were somehow measuring out time – his time – an idea that was manifestly absurd. He took a long swig of rum from the flask he always carried, and the spirit gradually quietened his unease.

He waited until the ship was two days out and then went down into the main hold. John Ibo was standing, his back against the mast tree that extended down to the ship's keel. Ross was not a small man but this giant towered above him.

'You speak English?' asked Ross.

The slave shrugged, shook his head.

'What's that in your hand?' Ross asked him, indicating a piece of wood he was holding. The man shrugged again, and reluctantly held it out; a slice of some African softwood tree. The Ibo must have found a nail or a sharp stone, and with this he had carved a likeness of his son in the wood. The carving was not done head on – these people were too primitive for that – but sideways, as Egyptians had carved heads and figures thousands of years earlier. The likeness was unmistakable; the man had talent.

'You have others?' Ross asked him, his voice as kindly as he could make it, which was difficult because he detested these people and their stink. They were not humans, of course, but animals, monkey men.

The man said something in his own language and the boy produced another piece of wood. On this was carved the face of a woman, proud and not unbeautiful in a native way. Perhaps his mother?

Ross wished later that he had destroyed these carvings then and there, but instead he handed them back and held out his hand for the carving instrument. A nail could be dangerous and become a weapon or an instrument to open the lock of a shackle. The man hesitated, then reluctantly put his hand down inside his loincloth and took out a half-inch nail.

Ross pocketed it, and as he did so saw a red flash of hatred in John Ibo's eyes; and mixed with this a curiously tragic sense of loss. The man was a bloody artist in his own way, thought Ross, but that of course was his concern.

Ross now tapped the boy on the shoulder and nodded his head towards the companionway. The boy looked appealingly at his father and lowered his eyes. Ross could see the father's chest heave and knew it could want but a moment before he struck him. But the Ibo realised the consequences in this – he would immediately be lashed to the mast and punished to a pulp – so he did nothing. Ross marched the boy up to the bridge. He saw leers and sniggers on the faces of the crew. The bo'sun, who despised him, remarked contemptuously: 'Supper in bed tonight, Captain?'

'Shut your bloody mouth, or I will have you in irons,' retorted Ross through clenched teeth.

The bo'sun grinned at the useless threat. He was another insolent swine, thought Ross. He should be taught a lesson – and one day would be. Ross took the boy to his cabin, and shot the bolt on the door, because he did not care to be disturbed.

The boy stood, absurdly young and defenceless in these alien surroundings. He peered with wonder and incomprehension at the metal wash-bowl, the mirror above it, the narrow bunk and the tiny desk where the captain wrote his log each day.

Ross took out a bottle of rum from the cupboard, and poured two inches into two metal pannikins. This was a quick way of relaxing nervous people, he had found previously. He gave one pannikin to the boy to drink. He sipped the fiery liquid cautiously, wrinkling his face, not knowing what it was, but appreciating the unexpected warmth and well-being it brought to his miserable brain.

He was probably a virgin, thought Ross, pouring himself another drink. These blacks did not usually go in for the kind of indulgences he liked. They were too primitive, too basic. Well, there was no point in delaying things; his need was great and growing.

He took a second swig of rum and then turned the boy to him. He opened his medicine chest, poured a little olive oil on the palm of his right hand and gently smoothed the boy's pudenda and genitals with his hand, moving slowly. He saw a startled fear in the boy's face and then felt the rush of blood and the involuntary stiffening of his member. Ross saw approvingly that it beat as with a heart and life of its own; the head glowed purple like a ripe plum.

There was nothing said between them; they did not speak the same language, but Ross could see from the boy's face how, under the influence of rum and his expert fondling, fear was gradually giving way to pleasurable anticipation. Now Ross splashed some oil on his own parts, and turning the boy away, still gripping him, pressed against his cleft. In the mirror he could see the boy's face as he was bent forward under the older man's grip. Then he entered.

The boy gave a brief cry of pain and alarm. He had not been expecting such action. He tried to pull himself away, but there was nowhere to move, so Ross held him, manipulating his impudent organ with one hand and gripping him with the other until the surge. And then he leaned over him, smelling his black sweat for the first time, mingled with the warm wheat scent of his discharge.

Lust grew again, and he had the boy twice more in different ways. He felt he should give the lad something for the pleasure that had been his but all he could find in the cabin was a ship's biscuit in a tin, so gave him this. The boy clasped his hand over the biscuit and looked at Ross. There was something in his eyes the captain did not like; a glint of wildness and hatred; he was his father's son and had his father's temper. He had been violated and humiliated against his will; he would remember this. Suddenly, Ross was repulsed by the overpowering animal smell of sweat in the tiny airless cabin and disgust at his own coupling with a black slave.

'Get out!' he told Jack roughly.

Afterwards, he washed himself carefully. You never knew with the blacks; you could easily catch pox or some other of their filthy diseases if you were not careful.

Ross went out on the bridge, and the cool night air soothed him. H breathed deeply, and then in mid-breath, he stopped. He had heard a faint rattle, like wind in the dry fronds of a dead palm tree, but there were no trees, no shore within miles. These were the drums, and the drums were talking with a lighter, more urgent, beat than he had ever heard. He guessed their message; the slaves in the ship would now know what he had done. His mouth dried at the thought. They would hate him, but what did that matter? They hated him already, and after all, they were harmless, manacled, shackled; a high proportion would never even reach the shore. In any case, he would never see them again, but he would have that boy again, and every day, as he wanted, in any way and manner, until they docked in Kingston.

Next day, the bo'sun reported that John Ibo had been shouting in his own tongue, cursing the captain and the crew.

'How do you know?' Ross asked him. 'You do not speak his lingo.'

'One of the slaves speaks some English. He told me. Come and see him for yourself, Captain.'

'I do not wish to,' Ross replied.

'I think you should,' said the bo'sun. 'I do not like the look of the fellow at all. If anything happens to him, the others may lose heart and die. He seems to be some kind of leader. Maybe he was a chief in his own country.'

Ross reluctantly followed the bo'sun down the wooden companionways into the main hold. The smell here was so strong that he choked, and would have thrown up if he had not swallowed hard and pinched his nose between his thumb and forefinger.

There seemed to be excrement, vomit and urine everywhere, and not a porthole open, in case a slave jumped overboard. A woman in a corner had given birth on the bare boards to a dead baby and the tiny cadaver still lay in a pool of congealing blood. The mother was sobbing and screaming and being consoled by others, who were trying to wipe her with dirty rags. He passed two men delirious with fever. Their frenzied straining at rusty shackles had cut through the flesh to their bones. Raw wounds swarmed with busy black flies.

Ross came face to face with John Ibo, who stood up with a clanking of chains. The other slaves stepped back. A smaller slave appeared from somewhere. He had a limp and he bowed nervously to the captain and then looked up at the Ibo. They spoke in their own tongue. The second slave clearly did not wish to translate and shifted his weight uneasily from foot to foot.

'Come on,' said Ross sharply, to conceal his own unease. Why the devil was he lumbered with a cripple in his cargo? He would make nothing on the man. 'What does he say?'

'He says you have humiliated him, his son, his ancestors and those yet to be born, sir. He says you have done with him that which is unseemly.'

'Tell him to shut his mouth,' said Ross coarsely.

The man was equally unwilling to interpret this to the Ibo, but eventually he passed on the message. The Ibo suddenly lunged at Ross and hit him a tremendous blow, like a mule kick, on the side of the face. Ross rocked on his feet, and went down on his hands and knees. He stood up shakily. Teeth had cracked in his jaw, his mouth was full of blood, dribbling down his chin. He would have to show these swine who was boss or they would all be in an uproar.

'Give him the stave,' he ordered the bo'sun, mumbling through broken teeth.

Two sailors came running, with a long bamboo pole and a length of rope. One dug the end of the pole like a spear into the Ibo's stomach. As the giant doubled forward, they pulled one leg from under him so that he fell heavily on his side, and lay writhing, his face contorted with pain.

Veins stood out on his forehead, large as knotted cords; his eyes bulged like onions in his head. Ross saw to his surprise that the soles of the man's feet, like the palms of his hands, were white. He had never noticed that in a native.

As the Ibo lay, knees drawn up to his chest in an attempt to ease his agony, the two sailors passed the pole behind his knees and bound his arms and ankles to it. He was now trussed like a chicken, brought down in the dung and the filth, unable to move. And there the bastard would stay until Ross decided he was willing to allow him to stand upright again.

Ross returned to his cabin, washed out his mouth, drank a pannikin of rum – and fell into a drunken sleep on his bunk.

He awoke at dawn, but it was nearly nine o'clock – two bells in the morning watch – before he ordered the Ibo to be released. Such a long time in this cramped condition, with consequent constriction of his blood vessels, had grievously weakened the man. When the pole and ropes were removed, he still lay on his side, limbs twitching feebly. For a moment, Ross thought he would be permanently crippled, and cursed his folly in sleeping so soundly.

He ordered slaves to swing down buckets into the sea on the end of ropes and dowse the Ibo with salt water. Gradually, he began to move his limbs, and within an hour he could crawl away, moving slowly and painfully, like a giant black and wounded crab.

By the time the ship docked, the Ibo appeared able to walk, but Ross feared he had unintentionally diminished the man's value to a slave master. He gave orders that the Ibo was to be kept in what little shade they could find in the market. His weakened condition was more likely to become apparent if he was forced to stand for hours under the pitiless sun. Fortunately, the rainy season had just begun. There was n doubt that the rain refreshed him, and he made his price – fifty golden guineas.

Ross could do with some rain now, he thought, as the perspiring runners bearing his palanquin grunted and cursed their way through crowds of beggars and hawkers and street salesmen. Some sold tea, and others crouched by heaps of birdseed laid out on mats. All watched his progress with bright button eyes, their yellow faces drained of all emotion.

Ross hated this inscrutability; you never knew what they were thinking. He had received a message from the Hoppo: his distinguished presence was most earnestly and respectfully sought with all convenient speed. He knew that his concern at this request would show on his face. He wondered at the reason for such a summons, and hoped there was nothing sinister in it.

But then why should there be? The Hoppo had been paid his bribe, more indeed than Ross, Douglas and Jackson could reasonably afford, but you could never really tell with these slit-arsed swine. They were greedy and they were cruel. It would be terrible ever to find himself at their mercy.

Suddenly, he moved even further back into the palanquin. He had just noticed three Europeans standing on the quay. One was tall and red-haired. His two companions had dark, greasy hair hanging in ringlets round their ears. Ross's heart fluttered like a captive bird at the sight, because he recognised them as members of the crew he had paid off in Calcutta.

He had last seen them when the bo'sun had attacked him in the tavern. Their angry shouts and curses re-echoed in his ears. He knew he had only escaped death at their hands because Jackson and Douglas had saved him. Now, he was on his own. One to one was fair; two to one he might manage, for he was a hard fighter, but three to one, with them hating him – these men must hate him, and he was dead.

What the devil could they be doing here? Surely they had not come in pursuit of him at such a distance? In this tiny enclave of Canton, their paths must eventually cross because his ship was not due to leave for a week. This was time enough for them to find him: there were only a few bars and grog-shops in the town, and every stranger was instantly remarked on. His present crew might even mention his name, and then these three would be waiting for him in the shadows; three to one, with sharpened knives.

The captain's mouth dried in the extremity of his alarm. He peered through a crack in the bamboos and saw them start to walk slowly in the opposite direction. He sweated with relief at the sight. They could not have seen him through the bead screen, so he was still safe – but for how long?

The bearers lowered his palanquin gently to the ground, bowing their heads respectfully to their knees so that their unworthy eyes would not see him descend. A liveried servant, wearing an elaborately embroidered tunic, also bowed low as he opened an outer gate to the Hoppo's house. Another, equally obsequious, guided him into his master's presence.

The Hoppo sat at his ease, legs crossed, on a silken cushion on the floor. He puffed a pipe of forbidden opium. Inferior persons faced death by strangulation for such a heinous crime, but superior persons who administered the laws understandably took a more liberal view of the practice.

'You wish to see me?' said Ross.

The Hoppo nodded genially and waved his hand, indicating another cushion on the carpet. Ross squatted down like his host.

The Hoppo did not come to the object of the meeting as soon as Ross wished. There was a long and complex etiquette to be followed in such conversations. How was the captain's health? What were his views on the coast trade? When did he propose to sail? And when would they be favoured with his illustrious return?

Then the Hoppo clapped his hands together. A servant entered through a curtained doorway carrying a long parchment scroll. The man immediately prostrated himself full-length at the Hoppo's feet, beating his head three times on the floor in ceremonial *kow-tow*. Then he stood up and unrolled the scroll, holding it in front of the Hoppo so that his master could read the printed characters. The Hoppo nodded, dismissed the man, and turned to Ross.

'An edict,' he explained. 'From the Celestial Throne, the Son of Heaven, the Emperor. I wished to refresh the lamp of my memory, lest in my unworthy way I had somehow misunderstood his divine command. But, no.

'It has been brought to His Celestial Notice that three strange Barbarians have arrived in his Empire for the purposes of trade, and have landed here without his express permission.

'One Barbarian is tall, to the height of four cubits, with hair as red as flame. Another claims to be a physician, although of only a Western kind, totally unversed in the true Chinese arts of healing. The third is a sea captain from the island of America. Do you know anything of these men?'

The Hoppo allowed himself a frosty and cynical smile as he looked quizzically at his visitor. Ross already knew the answer, but he replied cautiously: 'Nothing whatever, Your Excellency.'

'Are you certain?'

'It is possible that the characteristics you describe are shared by Mr Douglas, Dr Jackson and me. But that is a coincidence of total absurdity

'Who could be so base as to doubt it?'

The two men sat for a moment, not looking at each other.

'What is the Emperor's wish?' asked Ross, speaking first to break this sinister silence that hung between them.

'The Emperor does not *wish*, the Emperor *commands*. He commands that two of the three shall be executed as a warning to others who might otherwise foolishly be tempted to follow their disgraceful example.'

'And the third?'

Ross's mouth was dry with horror.

'To show the Divine Compassion of our Celestial Ruler, the third shall be spared, but gelded.'

'You mean, castrated?'

'I do. But that is surely a fate that shows the everlasting mercy of the Son of Heaven. We may geld a horse, but it can still work. We cut a bull and its anger dies, yet its strength remains. Cut a dog and he will cease to roam, but will follow his master loyally. And, of course, in our country eunuchs are among our richest citizens. They become powerful in the court. Great administrators. Men of high ambition and achievement.'

'Who chooses which of these unfortunate Barbarians will live or die?'

'His Celestial Majesty has been graciously pleased to honour me with making this decision.'

'And the man who offers the greatest gift is also the one most likely to live?'

The Hoppo inclined his head; there was no need for words. Even a Barbarian like this uncouth and craven captain must understand the basic principles involved.

Ross bit his lower lip to stop himself cursing. This bastard could steal their ship, their cargo, everything – and then doubtless kill them all when they had nothing left to give. Yet they were in no position to bargain. Mercy to Barbarians was not a Chinese characteristic – and he knew that if the Hoppo did not carry out his Emperor's instructions, he could forfeit his own life.

Angry, desperate thoughts fluttered madly through Ross's brain like frightened birds in a tiny cage. Then an idea began to form. The Hoppo was totally corrupt, of course. All he sought was a safe solution that also brought him a fresh bribe. Ross cleared his throat, and spoke as casually as he could, treating the matter as of little consequence.

'The edict does not name these men!'

'It does not, because their names are not known. But descriptions are better than names. You recognise a hog or a serpent or a monkey by their appearances, not their names. And I recognise these three very clearly. So will others, when this edict is made public.'

'If, purely for the sake of academic discussion, Your Excellency, three other Barbarians with exactly similar characteristics, one with red hair, all recently arrived and so on, could be found, could they meet this fate instead of others of the same description?'

'Entirely for the sake of discussion, an art so dear to our ancestors in greater times than these, that would be possible. But where could you find three such men?'

'I know three men exactly as you describe,' said Ross, remembering the red-headed man and his two companions on the quay. 'Kill them or castrate them, and you have carried out your Emperor's edict, with all honour to you. We can then go forward together, the four of us, to riches as yet unimagined.'

'How do you propose to honour such a whimsical and altogether extravagant undertaking?'

'We possess only one vessel now, *Coromandel*. But when we return to Calcutta, we intend to buy a second. Soon there will be a third, a fourth, and maybe more. And you will enjoy a share of all their profits. If, however, you decide to punish us, you deny us all this prospect. What is Your Excellency's answer?'

The Hoppo pursed his lips as he considered the proposition. A servant appeared, carrying a tray of beaten silver, with a small china pot and a single fragile cup without a handle. The man poured out scented tea, bowed to the ground while the Hoppo tasted it and sipped delicately. There was no cup for the captain, an omission which Ross knew was deliberate to emphasise the gulf between them.

Ross watched this pantomime impatiently. It would not do to interrupt the Hoppo, to press for an answer; there must be no hurrying in the East. Finally, the Hoppo wiped his full fleshy lips with a silken square, and pushed away the empty cup.

'I am inclined towards your proposal, Captain, but as you will appreciate, to take such a course will involve me in enormous personal risk. The humblest servant is entitled to his reward. Even a day labourer is paid. What have you in mind for your unworthy servant?'

'We are already paying you the largest proportion of our estimated profits that our modest budget will stand,' Ross pointed out bluntly. 'We simply cannot afford to pay more.'

'Not even for your lives – or your manhood?'

'As the Chinese proverb truly says, "There is a limit to the amount of flesh on the back of the fattest hog," ' said Ross. 'And this hog is now very thin. I will pay you, however, out of my own resources.'

The Hoppo raised his eyebrows politely. What did the captain mean?

'As you may be aware, captains in the service of the East India Company, and some other English companies, are allowed to engage in what we call private trade. I have a secret hold in the vessel packed with mud.

will offer that to you, not for tea or silver, but for our freedom.'

'How much are you carrying?'

'As much as five strong men can bear on their backs,' said Ross.

'It is agreed then,' said the Hoppo quickly, impressed by the captain's reply. 'You must now point out to my steward these three insolent Barbarians who have so insulted the Son of Heaven, blessed be his name always.'

Ross stood up. He felt sick. His back was soaked with sweat, and his hands were wet, as though he had just washed them. Only by a great effort of will did he not vomit his disgust at what he had agreed to do. Cold-bloodedly and deliberately, he was about to order the murder of three former shipmates. Yet if he did not, he could die himself, or at least have his stones cut out as a public spectacle for slit-eyed slaves and beggars. He bowed to the Hoppo and went outside.

The air was thick with the hoarse parrot cries of sweetmeat-sellers. Coolies trotted barefoot between the crowds, vast bundles and bales of cloth on their bent backs. In the background he heard a constant metallic clatter like loose chains rattling, a sound peculiar to this road. It came from rows of Chinese clerks who squatted cross-legged on the ground in front of local banks, which were little better than open-fronted shops. On either side of each clerk stood small pyramids of coins. They passed individual coins, left to right, from one pile to the other, snapping their teeth on each one to test for forgeries. Years of practice had made them astonishly adept.

Soon they would be counting his money, but the thought gave him less pleasure than it should. It would be blood money. Judas had betrayed Jesus for thirty pieces of silver. He was betraying three men for his own survival. The price was different, the principle of false witness remained.

Ross was surprised at the intensity of his feelings; it was unlike him to feel sorrow or remorse or regret over any action he took. One of those accursed fevers and agues of the East, no doubt. Yes, that must be the reason.

He climbed thankfully into his palanquin. As the coolies raised it up to their shoulders with much chanting, a lithe, slightly-built Chinese servant jumped in beside Ross, pulled down the bead curtain, and they set off. Several hundred yards up the road, sitting on benches in an open grog-shop, Ross saw the three men, now joined by half a dozen others whom he did not recognise.

They were drinking toddy and smoking clay pipes. The red-headed man was roaring with laughter. Ross drew back in the palanquin in case they should see him. He gripped his companion's thin, bony arm, and nodded towards the bench.

'The three on the left,' he said.

The Hoppo's steward nodded. As the palanquin passed the grog-shop, he jumped out and was instantly lost in the crowd. Ross covered his face with his hands, swallowing hard against the lurching jog-trot of the conveyance in case he vomited. When he reached his ship, he went straight up the gangway to his cabin. He poured himself four fingers of neat rum, drank the draught in a gulp, and poured himself another four. Only then did his uneasiness temporarily subside.

Jackson put down his empty glass of rice wine and turned to Douglas. They were sitting at a table in the grog-shop, shielded from the sun by a bamboo screen, and unnoticed by other drinkers who sat outside on benches facing the quay.

'You see those three men on that bench? I'm damn sure they were with the bo'sun when that trouble started in Calcutta.'

'What of it?' asked Douglas. The wine and the warmth had made him feel pleasantly drowsy.

'If they see us, they might remember, and continue where they left off.'

'Let them see. Let them remember. They will never continue that fight here. They were drunk then. They aren't now – yet.'

'Perhaps not. But they still seem to attract trouble.'

Half a dozen Chinese, wearing blue tunics and carrying metal-tipped staves, had suddenly surrounded the three men, pounding the flagstones with the metal ends of their staves. The Europeans stood up, pipes still in their mouths, glasses in their hands. They looked at one another in bewilderment, hoping someone would explain the meaning of this pantomime, which was clearly hostile and threatening.

Then, so quickly that neither Jackson nor Douglas could see the movement, other Chinese, who had approached from a different direction, slipped rope loops over their shoulders and pulled them tight. The men's arms were now strapped to their sides, useless as the pinioned wings of chickens that farmers carried to market. Glasses and pipe clattered to the ground. Within seconds, they were being dragged away shouting, cursing, bellowing for help.

Douglas took a step forward. Jackson pulled him back quickly.

'There is nothing you can do here. We do not speak a word of the language.'

'But those men were doing nothing wrong.'

'How do you know?'

'You saw them. They were just having a drink.'

'Now, yes. But you do not know what they have just done – or are planning to do. The Chinese hate us here. They seek any excuse to start trouble. They would kick us all out – if they could.'

'So what do you propose?'

'That we get back to the ship in double time. Some of the crew may know the reason for this.'

A small boat with four oarsmen ferried them out to *Coromandel*. As they approached the ropeladder, they saw another larger boat, of the type known as a fast crab, with half a dozen rowers, pulling strongly towards the shore. Her stern sat low in the water, laden down with several large canvas bales.

'What the hell are those?' asked Douglas.

'Ross will know.'

They paid off their ferry, climbed the ladder, and went down to Ross's cabin. He had by then finished half the bottle of rum and was sitting on the edge of his bunk, bleary-eyed, shoulders hunched dejectedly. Douglas stood looking down at him with displeasure. This was no way for the captain of a merchantman and a partner in Trinity-Trio to behave. A pederast he undoubtedly was, and could be accepted as such. A drunken pederast, probably now incapable of managing his ship, was infinitely more serious.

'Who is on watch?' he asked Ross shortly. Ross shrugged.

'Better go up and see.'

'We've just come down.'

'Well, then, why ask me? I've been here for the past half hour.'

'So it would appear,' said Douglas, lifting the rum bottle and putting it on a side table, out of the captain's reach.

'There's no one on watch,' said Jackson. 'And a fast crab packed with goods has just rowed away from the ship. Are they thieves?'

'No,' said Ross in a surly voice. 'They are not thieves.'

'So who are they? And what are they taking out of our vessel? I understood we had discharged all our cargo, and taken on silk and tea and that useless rhubarb.'

'You understood correctly. That boat was removing something of mine.'

'*What* of yours, exactly?'

'Is that any of your business?'

'Yes,' replied Douglas. 'They could not all contain your possessions, such as clothes. They looked like bales of mud to me.'

'They were bales of mud.'

'Where from?'

'My private store.'

Douglas put out a hand, gripped Ross by his lapels and pulled him to his feet. He stood, swaying unsteadily. A little rum had trickled down his chin and stained his shirt.

'Your private store?' Douglas repeated angrily. 'What the devil do you mean? You should have no private store. We are partners. We share everything equally. On that basis, two-thirds of that mud is ours. And why the hell was it not in the hold?'

'It was in a hold, *my* hold.'

'What do you mean, *your* hold? Explain yourself, man.'

'I'll tell you exactly what I mean,' said Ross, pushing away Douglas's hand roughly. 'And what I have done. I have just saved your lives. I did have some mud, kept for my own purposes in a small hold aft. And if I had not, you two would either be about to be killed or, at best, lose your balls.'

'What the devil are you talking about? You are drunk.'

'Maybe,' replied Ross, 'and so would you be drunk if you had done what I had to do. I was called before the Hoppo. He read out some edict from the Emperor ordering three Barbarians – one with red hair, the second a doctor and the third an American sea captain – to be punished immediately.

'Two were to be executed, the third castrated – the Hoppo to decide who lived or died – and all for trading here without permission. As an example to any others who might be thinking they would do likewise. That's what the Hoppo said. And if he did not obey, then that could be the end of him.'

'Are you serious?'

'Of course I'm bloody serious! I had to think quickly. I had some mud aboard I hadn't told you about, because in my calling you learn to look after yourself. No one will do that for you. I let the Hoppo have my mud.'

'How will that allow him to square things with the Emperor?'

'Because I saw three men on the quay who had been with the bo'sun in Calcutta. One, unfortunately for him, has red hair. On the spur of the moment, I suggested to the Hoppo that since the Chinese do not know one Barbarian from another – any more than we can differentiate one Chink from another – those three could be punished in our stead.'

'I saw three men arrested just now,' said Jackson. 'In a grog-shop.'

'No doubt. And I pointed them out, like Judas. That's why I am drinking.'

'Cannot we stop this?' asked Douglas in horror.

'How? We have nothing left to pay more bribes to the Hoppo. You know that as well as I do. And he does not just want a bribe, he wants to survive. If he cannot show three Barbarians punished as the Emperor ordered, then he will be punished with equal or greater severity. He wants to keep his head – and his balls. Cannot you understand?'

At that moment, there was a knock on the door.

'Come,' said Douglas. A sailor entered and addressed Ross.

'A deputation of Chinese to see you, sir,' he announced. 'A big boat with a dragon's head on the bows. One man speaks some pidgin. The Hoppo sends his compliments and wishes to see all you gentlemen ashore.'

'Did he say why?' asked Douglas.

'You know why,' said Ross irritably. 'It is to witness the punishment being carried out, of course. They make a spectacle of that sort of thing here, just as we used to at Tyburn. It settles the minds of any others who might be unwise enough to consider a bit of free enterprise on their own account outside the Emperor's rules.'

'Do we have to go? Let us up anchor and be away. Send our regrets.'

'What happens when we come back if we do that?' replied Ross. 'We would not be allowed to trade here again, gentlemen. Ever. We would have insulted the Hoppo, and through him the Viceroy in Canton, and everyone else, up to the Emperor. We would be finished.'

'How do you know we are not going to be finished – in a different sense – if we accept the Hoppo's invitation?'

'That is a risk we have to take. There is simply no other way. I think it is an acceptable risk, because the Hoppo is greedy. He knows if he gets rid of us, he will lose an enormous potential income over his three years in office. He is not a fool.'

'We are the fools,' said Douglas bitterly. 'Two of our countrymen are going to die, and another be castrated. For nothing. We *must* stop it.'

'Tell me how,' said Ross, crossing the cabin to the rum bottle and pouring himself another drink.

'Tell the Hoppo this cannot go ahead.'

'If you do that, then we have to take their places. Do you *really* want to do that?'

The Hoppo, at that moment, was being carried in his palanquin, wearing his hat with the gold button and an elaborately woven court uniform. Ahead of him marched lictors with metal-tipped whips to strike out of the way any inferior persons who dared to slow their passage, however unintentionally. The Hoppo had dined well, and drunk several agreeable glasses of strong rice wine. With his blood thus warmed and enriched, he contemplated an agreeable session with one or other of his favourite concubines after the public punishment.

He was thinking of the hour he would spend performing what in the Chinese vernacular was known as the Bamboo Bridge to the Jade Pavilion. He and the woman of his choice would stand facing each other, naked and embracing, their tongues bridging the tiny space between their scented lips. Soon the Jade Root would rise and form a firm Lower Bridge, stretching out towards the Jade Gate. This would open and the

Jade Root would proceed on the Jade Steps, and into the welcome warmth of the secret Love Pavilion.

This agreeable prospect brought the Hoppo's thoughts, by progression, to the fact that the survivor of the three barbarians would, within the hour, lose all interest or indeed participation in such delectable pleasures.

There were three ways of performing the operation to make a man what in the vernacular was called 'a flapping crow, a court rat'. The Hoppo had seen them all performed many times, but they never lost their fascination.

The first method involved total loss of testicles and penis, achieved with a single swift stroke of a knife so sharp that it could sever a human hair left to float down on the wind against the blade. This was the kindest way, and might be carried out today, to show the Emperor's infinite mercy towards inferiors, no matter how base they might be and how grievous their transgressions.

The second operation was less drastic and involved the removal of the penis alone; the third, simply the testicles.

When the first technique, known as *hsing ch'en*, was practised, a bamboo or hollow straw would immediately be inserted into the heart of the wound to allow the patient to urinate. Such a straw was also introduced into the body of a man who had suffered castration by the second procedure, because in his case it also permitted the life force, the Vital Essence or *tseng*, to drain away.

When total removal of all genital organs had been achieved, the eunuch would experience only relatively mild erotic feelings. But when the testicles were not removed, he could burn with maddening and unslakeable lust. He would cry out that his blood vessels were about to burst, but still he would have to endure this agony; there was no means of relief. In such a case, the Hoppo had known a eunuch strap himself to the back of a lusty youth. At his command this young man would mount a woman and with each thrust of the young man's body, the eunuch would attempt to achieve pleasure by proxy.

As with a half-cut horse, a type that Barbarians called a rig, sufferers from this type of operation could never be trusted. Their tempers were violent and as unpredictable as a summer storm at sea. They were victims of melancholy, and their deliberate cruelty and sheer brute strength appeared to increase in proportion to their loss.

Of course, the Hoppo could not say what would become of the Red Bristled Barbarian who was cut. He was unacquainted with the savage and heathen customs of their remote and unimportant island, but in his own country, young eunuchs frequently formed attachments to rich men. They managed their harems, because they could be trusted, even with the most beautiful women.

There had been cases, of course, when a eunuch had wickedly and unlawfully manufactured an imitation Jade Stem with a fine Turtlehead from bamboo and wax, to pleasure these concubines, but this was rare, because discovery meant instant execution.

There were other advantages from controlling the harem of a very rich man, or, best of all, at the Celestial Court. They could help the advancement of one concubine against another, with consequent personal enrichment. At the highest level, in the harem of the Son of Heaven, they could even select which girl was to be honoured by Regal Coitus, and grow wealthy as a result.

Because of their own deprivation and their constant need to prove their superiority in other ways, they invariably took a perverse pleasure in their influence, nearly always evil. The ancient Book of Odes declared: 'Not Heaven, but Women and Eunuchs bring Misfortunes to Mankind. Wives and those without Balls bleat with similar Voices. . . .'

The Hoppo's bearers set down his palanquin gently. A servant who had run behind it from his house now prostrated himself at full length on the ground and then arose to open the curtain. The Hoppo stepped out, hands folded within the ends of his wide sleeves in front of his ample stomach.

Behind the lictors, he walked on through the narrow alleyway where black-shuttered shops leaned towards each other, apparently deserted, but inside seething with customers. The alley led to an open square, already crowded. Here dogs barked and scuttered about, nervous at the unusual commotion and the sense of electric anticipation in the air.

In the centre stood the three Barbarians, hands still bound to their sides. From the other side of the square, the Hoppo saw Ross and his two companions approach, hemmed in by their escort.

'It is Captain Ross,' cried the red-haired man in relief, as though greeting an old friend. 'My God, Cap'n, it is good to see your face, sir. I beg you to help us. Why are we strapped here like hogs? We have done nothing wrong, sir. I swear it.'

Ross did not reply. He pretended he had not heard, that he had not seen them.

'I saw you two gentlemen in Calcutta,' shouted another of the sailors to Douglas and Jackson. 'Can you speak the lingo here? There has been a mistake, sirs, a terrible mistake, but we cannot seem to make anyone understand or even listen. Speak for us, I beg you!'

Now it was the turn of Douglas and Jackson not to reply; they felt too shamed to look the men in the eyes. They were, in any case, outnumbered by hundreds of Chinese, who had suddenly pressed in from their tiny paths and unseen doorways and formed a ring around them. They were grinning and chatting cheerfully among themselves. Douglas recognised the mood and atmosphere. He had seen it before at an illegal cockfight in a remote Scottish glen, or at a bare-knuckle match between two prizefighters, fists pickled in brine and vinegar, pledged to fight to defeat, even death, winner to take the purse.

The Hoppo bowed slightly in the direction of Captain Ross.

'An edict from the Emperor,' he announced slowly and in English. 'Listen! With meekness and humility! These miserable Bristled Ones have landed here on our Celestial Shores without permission from the Ruler of this Heavenly Realm.

'Within his embrace lie ten thousand kingdoms. The oceans of the earth are at peace beneath his rule. But these serpents have seen fit to insult his hospitality. The Sword of Heaven is slow to smite, but justice never leaves a debt unpaid. An edict! The decision of the Son of Heaven! Two barbarians to die! One to lose the source of his Dragon Spirit!'

The Hoppo held out one hand. A servant placed an English penny in his palm. The Hoppo turned to the red-haired sailor, as the leader.

'You have a custom in your heathen land of throwing a coin to see whether the woman's head turns towards heaven or not. Now, Red-Bristled Hairy One, call when I throw.'

The man called: 'Heads!' He was bemused by the request, not understanding what hung on the toss of the coin. How could they have landed here without permission? They did not control their vessel; they were only insignificant members of her crew, three of many others who had also come ashore. Why pick on them in this extraordinary way?

The coin landed in the dust, tails uppermost. The Hoppo turned enquiringly to the next man and spun the coin for a second time.

'Heads!' the sailor called in a high nervous voice.

This time – and when the third sailor called – the coin landed face uppermost.

The Hoppo nodded towards the red-haired man. At once, two Chinese servants stepped forward, pulled him roughly to one side. They slipped off his ropes and began to rip his clothes with curved knives with the skill of men skinning a wild beast. He fought back ferociously, kicking, punching, butting with his head, his elbows, his knees. But other Chinese came to their aid, and they were many and he was on his own, heavy with rum, crazed by fear, dry-mouthed in the sweltering sun. The more he struggled, the more they allowed him to tire himself until, exhausted, panting, shoulders hunched, his red hair matted with sweat, he stood like a weary giant surrounded by smooth-faced yellow-fleshed pygmies.

Now, with their knives, they slit away the buttons and slashed the seams of his clothes. Within seconds he was standing naked, hands clasped modestly in front of him. Again the Hoppo nodded. Somewhere out of sight, a gong struck once, twice, three times. The men pulled aside the sailor's hands so that all could see his total nakedness, and admire the size of his Male Peak and his Secret Pouch. Then they bound his hands behind him. Others now brought in a table on trestles, and they stretched him out on his back on this. They prised apart his legs and fixed a bamboo reed, sharpened at each end, between his ankles, slipped a looped rope across his legs. He squirmed in an attempt to escape, and cried out in pain as they tightened the rope so roughly that the bamboo spikes speared his flesh to the bone.

Two men carried in a copper cauldron of boiling water, which they set down on the ground. One of them poured red pepper from a horn container into the water, stirred the mixture. The peppery steam was so strong that Douglas choked and sneezed when the wind blew it in his direction. The red-haired man cried out in alarm.

'What is happening? Oh, God, *help me*! *Help me!*'

One of his companions leaped towards him, but was immediately tripped, his hair gripped and his face smashed twice into the hard earth. He lost consciousness, and when he was dragged to his feet, he had to be supported, his head lolling to one side like a sawdust dummy.

Now another Chinese approached, bearing a long knife curved in the shape of a sickle. He sharpened this against a stone, held up the blade for all to see – and immediately plunged it deep into the red-haired man's testicles.

For a second there was silence, as a beast in the slaughter-house will cease all noise in that brief split instant before it dies. Then a sigh of appreciation escaped the onlookers – and the hoarse, despairing shriek of the red-haired sailor drove flocks of tiny birds out from the eaves of houses in terror at the noise, wings outstretched like black parentheses in the burning sky.

Blood spurted like a fountain from the terrible wound, reddening the hand of the man who gripped the knife as though it had been suddenly submerged in red paint. A helper pressed a sheet of white rice-paper against the gorging wound. Two other men released the looped rope and the bamboo that pressed into the victim's ankles, and, supporting the sailor, they dragged him to his feet.

He stood unsteadily, bent double, gibbering with pain. A long stream of saliva dribbled from his mouth. He gasped for breath and for mercy as they began to walk him around the square. Sometimes his feet did not even touch the ground, only his toes. He was nearly delirious with pain, unseeing of his surroundings, choking, sobbing, his face contorted like the face of a gargoyle in his agony.

'They will walk him like that for two hours,' explained Jackson in a whisper. 'Simply to keep him alive. It is like cutting a horse. You have to walk it about, to keep the blood circulating.'

'And then what happens?'

'They take him away, bind him up for two days. All that time, he cannot pass water, so his bladder will swell to the size of an ostrich egg. When they release the bandages, they push a fine bamboo tube into the hole – if they can find it – and at last he can relieve himself. But sometimes the wound will have swollen and closed and will not accept this tube. Then his bladder must burst and he will die. But not quickly, not quickly. No punishment in China is ever quick or merciful.'

The Hoppo now turned to the red-haired man's two companions. The sailor who had attempted to rush to the aid of his colleague was still bewildered and unsteady on his feet, clearly now not comprehending what was happening.

'You,' the Hoppo told him sternly. 'Who dared dispute the edict of the Emperor, shall die the death of the cuts.'

Two men, each holding a long knife, now approached him. One slashed him across the forehead. The blade was so sharp, it left a line as thin as a red pencil stroke. Then blood welled out, and as the sailor put up a hand to touch it, the second man slit upwards and downwards on both his cheeks, once, twice, three times, so that strips of flesh, dripping blood, hung down.

Now, one after the other, with the precision of long practice, they hacked in a kind of minuet of murder at his arms, his shoulders, his hands, his chest. Soon his whole body was covered with blood; strips of flesh hung down like tongues. He was beyond crying out; he stood, moaning and swaying. Then, at a brief command from the Hoppo, the two men decapitated him. A gout of blood shot two feet in the air and the headless corpse collapsed. As the head rolled to one side like a cannonball, a slave grasped it by the hair and hurried away; the brain would be gouged out to provide a tasty dish for his master, a middle-aged eunuch of importance.

The Chinese now drove their knives swiftly into the third man's belly. As he bent forward in an extremity of agony, one removed his knife with a left and right motion, and cut off his head. His death had been altogether swifter, as though the executioners did not wish to prolong the spectacle.

Jackson found himself considering the operation from a surgeon's point of view. The sharpness of the knives had impressed him; he wondered at the temper of the metal blades. A great cry from the crowd concentrated his thoughts on his own predicament. What if they demanded more deaths, more castrations? But the tension was gone from the scene. Justice had been done. The Red-Bristled Barbarians from beyond the Outer Seas had been punished for whatever their crimes had been, and about which they knew nothing and cared no more. Such matters were the concern of superior persons. They were satisfied with what they had seen – and the two Barbarians who had lost their heads were indeed doubly chastised.

Decapitation denied them the blessing of burial rites. This, in turn, would prevent reunion with their ancestors, because their bodies would not reach the next world complete, as they had arrived in this. Truly, the ways of the Son of Heaven were wise beyond all understood wisdom. Blessed and honoured was his name. His exalted shadow would never grow less, but, like his power and influence, must spread ever wider, world without end, time beyond all reckoning.

The Hoppo climbed into his palanquin and was borne away, behind his lictors, with people on either side prostrating themselves as he passed.

Ross lit a cheroot with shaking hands. The headless bodies of his two former shipmates were carried past on bamboo stretchers, the red-haired man propelled away out of their sight and hearing.

'Now you will understand what my quick thinking saved you from,' Ross said in a voice he did not recognise as his own.

'I do,' agreed Douglas. 'And I hate myself for acquiescing in the public murder and humiliation of two of our fellow men, and our Queen's subjects.'

'There was nothing we could have done to stop it,' said Ross.

'Maybe. I feel I should have tried to do *something*. I know not what, but something. I will always hate myself for this.'

They began to walk back slowly towards the quay.

'You wanted to change places with them then?' asked Ross sarcastically.

'Do not be a fool,' said Jackson. 'But I know how Alec feels. I feel the same.'

Ross grunted.

'You will soon get over it,' he assured them. 'Getting rich out here does not leave time for regrets and soft feelings. It is either them or you. So long as I have any say in the matter, it is going to be them – until I have made enough to leave this business forever.'

'The trouble is,' said Jackson quietly, 'one never can make enough money. However rich one becomes, there is always someone richer. I can sense already what is happening to us. We seek material possessions, to own them. And we could end up with them owning us.'

Next morning, early, Jackson went to see Douglas in his cabin.

'I slept badly,' he said. 'I keep thinking about yesterday. I am going ashore to see if I can do anything to help that poor wretched red-haired sailor.'

'I will come with you,' said Douglas at once.

Jackson went back to his own cabin and shook out two white pills from a phial in his medicine cupboard, which he locked carefully.

Ross was reluctant to accompany them. He knew they were grateful because he had undoubtedly saved their lives, but equally they felt – however irrationally – he should not have betrayed three other men. After some argument, they persuaded him to come along, on the excuse that he had arranged the entire matter with the Hoppo, whose permission they would need before they could see the prisoner. This permission was readily given, and a guide led the three partners through a maze of tiny alleys so narrow that their shoulders brushed the walls of houses.

They came to an opening covered by a screen, and followed the guide into a small room. Its roof was so low, they had to bow their heads. A strong smell of sweat and dung and dried blood hung in the air as though a large animal was caged there. As their eyes grew accustomed to the dimness, they saw the red-haired man stretched out on a bed of rushes. He was naked except for a crude bandage around his loins, soaked in blood and excrement. He groaned and writhed feebly as he lay. A bowl of some gruel, now a focus for flies, lay untouched by his side. His lips were caked with salt. Sweat had matted his red hair to his skull, and he was breathing heavily, unevenly, as though he had been running up a long, steep hill.

A Chinese servant bowed to them.

'He has not recovered,' their guide explained.

Jackson knelt by the man's side, felt his pulse, his brow. He did not open his eyes. Jackson ran his fingers across his groin.

'His bladder is hugely extended,' he said. 'He is poisoning himself with his own urine.'

He started to undo the bandage, but the keeper seized his wrist and shook his head.

'That would be unwise,' explained the guide nervously. 'His Excellency would not wish any interference.'

'The man has been punished enough,' Jackson retorted. 'The sentence was not of death, only mutilation. I am trying to save his life.'

'What is your prognosis?' Douglas asked him.

'He is going to die unless we can release that urine. If he cannot relieve himself, he will be dead before nightfall. At present he is in a kind of coma, but the pain will drag him out of that. Then he will tear his own flesh with his hands, trying to be rid of the bursting agony in his bladder.'

'Have you any physic you can give him?'

'There is no physic in the world to help him unless he can be rid of his water.'

'But you brought two pills with you,' Douglas pointed out.

'I did. One was to send him to sleep for a time if he was conscious and in agony – but not to cure him.'

He paused.

'And the second?' Douglas asked.

Jackson looked at him with a grave face.

'When I qualified as a doctor,' he said, 'I took the oath of Hippocrates, the Greek physician we revere as the father of medicine. I swore to help any patient who came within my care, to keep pure my mind and my art, to treat the sick according to my ability and judgement. But never to administer poison to anyone when asked to do so, nor to suggest such a course of action.

'Nevertheless, I have brought with me this second pill – a poison pill. Physicians use cyanide and arsenic and other poisons in very small amounts to cure people, but this pill is different. This will kill whoever takes it.'

'But you cannot administer it yourself?' Douglas asked him.

'I cannot. It is totally against my oath and my profession. Yet if I do nothing, this poor man will die in unspeakable pain.'

Ross stubbed out his cheroot on the wall of the room.

'I will administer it to him,' he announced. 'While you two are arguing about some bloody Greek, God only knows what is happening out of our sight here. I would not trust that Hoppo as far as I can piss. If we are not careful, we could find ourselves in more trouble.'

He held out his hand. Jackson shook the white capsule into it from the phial.

Ross knelt down by the side of the red-haired man, prised open his clenched teeth, and dropped the pill into his mouth. The man choked slightly, then swallowed. Suddenly, his body arched, his arms shot out as stiff as a scarecrow's limbs. He choked, retched, and his head jerked back. He opened his eyes and saw the three men around him. In that split instant on the narrow bridge between life and death, he recognised them.

'Captain Ross!' he cried in a cracked, delirious voice. 'I curse you and all who bear your name, forever! May you rot in hell, you Judas bastard!'

His throat rattled, he coughed. A gobbet of green phlegm, flecked with blood, dribbled down his chin, and then he sank back. Two Chinese men knelt by his side, shook him, and spoke rapidly to each other.

'Give them some money,' said Ross sharply. 'Then they will forget about the pill. They know he would have died in any case, but their silence – at least until we up anchor – is essential.'

Douglas handed each man a gold sovereign. They tested it with their teeth, bowed their thanks. The guide led the three partners out into the alley and back to the quay.

As he walked, Jackson realised that he had clenched both his fists tightly, partly to stop himself from crying out, partly to help brace himself against the reaction to what he had just seen, what he had not attempted to prevent.

He became aware that he was gripping something in his right hand. He opened his fingers. He was holding the penny that the little girl, Joanna Gray, had given him on his departure from England. A lucky penny, her father had said. Now he believed that this was true: he had survived while three others had died. If this was not good luck, what else could it be?

Edinburgh

The clerk, stoop-shouldered and bow-legged, as though carrying on his back a great if invisible weight, opened the door of the Writer to the Signet's inner office.

'Mrs Pomfret to see you, sir,' he announced gravely.

The Writer stood up, shook hands with his visitor, and then sat back in his creaking chair, tapping the tips of his fingers together, head on one side, like a wise old bird. Outside his window, the ravens still sat on the ledge, as though reluctant to spread their black wings above the smoke from Edinburgh's myriad chimneys. Jane thought that they looked like the Writer: dark, brooding, wary. The room felt dusty and smelled of lamp oil and candle grease, the scent of learning and the law.

'To what do I owe the pleasure of this visit, ma'am?' the Writer asked her. 'Your late husband did not favour me with his legal instructions.'

'He did not,' Jane Pomfret agreed, as she sat down. 'But I intend to favour you with mine.'

The Writer inclined his head and regarded her quizzically. She wore the black dress of a woman recently widowed, but a dress cut to show off her full, firm figure, a hat with a broad brim and a lace veil. As she unfolded her hands, the Writer's hooded eyes caught the glint of diamonds in her rings. She was wearing a fortune on her hands, he thought enviously. How much of that fortune could be transferred to his private account with the British Linen Bank in Princes Street – and how soon?

'I have come to see you about a personal matter,' Jane Pomfret continued.

The Writer nodded. To him, in this office, all matters were personal: gambling debts, estates cripplingly mortgaged or bought or sold unwisely, madness, perversion, despair and suicide.

'My late husband promised me that I would inherit everything on his death – the castle, an estate of two hundred thousand acres, Long Glen whisky distillery, farms, houses, other properties, everything.'

She paused.

'He was a very rich man, I know,' the Writer agreed. 'But may I ask why you are not consulting his legal adviser? I would not wish to trespass on what is his preserve. You understand me, ma'am?'

'Perfectly,' Jane replied. 'But I must tell you that while my husband promised me all this, and drew up the will in my favour – he neglected to sign it. I would thus like an independent legal opinion of my situation. In addition to my young daughter Fiona by Mr Pomfret, there is also, as you may know, my husband's stepson by his first marriage. He is at present serving in India as an officer in the East India Company's army.'

'Have you any idea why your husband neglected to sign the will?'

'None. And now, naturally, I would like to inherit what he promised.'

'Unless, of course, there is another, later will, you shall, as a widow, inherit something.'

Jane Pomfret leaned across the desk, so close to the Writer that he could smell her heady, expensive perfume. Her wide, worried blue eyes and sensual mouth, her rounded breasts, were within inches of his face. He swallowed heavily; his throat suddenly felt constricted.

'Something is not enough,' Jane told him quietly. 'He gave me his *word*. I believed him. He has left me with a daughter to bring up. I want his promise honoured. For her sake, even more than mine.'

'What we want and what we sometimes receive in this transitory life, dear lady, are not always the same thing. Your daughter – your husband's child – should, of course, share in the inheritance.'

'Should?'

'Will – if this was his final will and testament – but it appears otherwise.'

'There must be a way to help me, to help both of us. The fee for such a service could be very attractive.'

'You are most kind, ma'am, but I must make it clear that I only administer the law as it is laid down,' the Writer replied gently, his mind racing ahead of his tongue. Would – *could* – part at least of his fee be in kind rather than cash? For a fleeting delectable instant, he imagined his body pressed against hers in some silken, scented bed, and as quickly drove the thought from his mind.

'I cannot alter the law, much as one may sometimes wish to do so. Now, Mr Pomfret's stepson. I have an address for him in India.'

'Please give it to me.'

'How would that help you? Surely he would then claim a prior right to his father's estate? He is the only male heir.'

Jane pursed her lips and then, as if on impulse, asked unexpectedly, 'Can I seek your help, not just as an advocate, but, if I may use the word after such a brief meeting, as a *friend?* I cannot do what I plan on my own. I need someone on whom I can rely totally.'

'You are speaking to such a person now,' the Writer replied, also leaning forward, all pretence at casualness gone. An unsigned will, a fortune at risk, a despairing and lovely woman, the prospect of a fee of unprecedented proportions . . . what Scottish lawyer could wish for more?

'This is what I have in mind,' Jane Pomfret said. 'I am not learned in the law, but it seems that this proposal could present a solution satisfactory to my husband's stepson and daughter – and to me, his widow.'

She began to speak in a low voice, in case anyone should be listening on the other side of the door.

The Writer did not interrupt until Jane had finished, and then he sat back, pulling his beaked nose between his thumb and forefinger. Outside the window, the ravens fluttered their wings briefly, moved their weight from one thin leg to the other, then settled again, as though they also had considered the situation and reached a conclusion.

'An interesting proposition, Mrs Pomfret,' the Writer allowed carefully. 'But it will require considerable funding to have any hope of success.'

'I have nothing,' she admitted. 'Except these few jewels I wear. If I accept what may be my due in law, as a widow, then I might prejudice my chances of gaining the whole estate, which I claim. Could I borrow against that expectation? The interest would be high – and could I trust the usurer?'

'No to both questions,' the Writer told her firmly. 'And there is no need to take such a course. I must explain that Mr Alec Douglas, your stepson by marriage, has put me in funds to safeguard *his* interests.'

'You should have told me!' said Jane angrily, standing up. 'You have led me on deliberately!'

'Not so, dear lady. Pray do not jump to false conclusions. Nothing you have said leads me to believe there need be *any* conflict whatsoever between your best interests and his. Rather the reverse, or I would have informed you.

'I will therefore take it upon myself to advance you sufficient monies from these funds – against the value of your jewellery – for you to take passage to India. Today I will also write to Mr Douglas and send the letter east by the fastest clipper, to inform him that you will be arriving. But I will not, of course, give him any reason for your journey. I leave that to you.'

'But will he not have heard his stepfather is dead? You have not told him?'

'I have not told him – yet. I think it unlikely that he has heard, even if h received the Scottish newspapers. Mail by ordinary vessel takes at least three months to reach India, often longer. You will see him before the papers arrive. You can then explain his stepfather's death to him. In view of our discussion, that would be more fitting than for me to write and inform him, which I was planning to do. I will also give you a sealed letter to deliver to him personally.'

'Thank you,' Jane said, and held out her hand. 'I feel that in you I have indeed found a friend, a true friend.'

The Writer bowed at the compliment. He did not reply. He felt that in Jane Pomfret he had found more than a friend; he had found a fortune.

Outside the office, Jane Pomfret hailed a passing hackney, climbed inside and sat wrinkling her nose in distaste at the smell of camphor and dried saddle-soap from the cracked leather seats. The words 'Hackney Cab' on the oval porcelain plate in front of her brought back memories of the seedy, sour area of Hackney, east of London, she had seen when she visited the home of another girl in Mrs Jones' house.

Used to the open Dorset countryside, the squalor had appalled her. Gypsies reared ponies and horses on Hackney Marshes. Because the animals had continually to keep pulling their feet out of the mud, they developed a peculiar high-stepping trot that became highly regarded in the more fashionable parts of London. Hackney, and a cab such as this pulled by a Hackney pony, represented to her the cruel underside of life to which she could so easily descend again if her plan failed.

Since her marriage, Jane had become accustomed to travelling in a carriage and four, with two liveried coachmen up front on the box, two liveried footmen standing behind, and a trained spotted Dalmatian carriage dog running obediently beneath and between the axles. Today she had thought it wiser to tell her maid she was going for a walk, and then to hire a cab to take her to the Writer's chambers, rather than to instruct the groom to prepare a town carriage.

Servants talked too much, and to anyone. She knew this; she had once been a servant herself. Now she would dismiss the cab half a mile from home, and walk the rest of the way. The exercise would help to clear her head; she had much to remember that she wished she could forget.

First, there had been the shock of realising she was pregnant. She had always assumed that Pomfret's seed was dead. That had been the rumour, and she had believed it. Now she felt herself trapped. He had to marry her quickly, because within weeks, months at the most, her condition would be obvious. A brothel-keeper would never employ a pregnant harlot, and no one save a tinker would marry a girl with an illegitimate child.

Jane begged Pomfret to advance the date of their wedding, assuring him that so great was her love for him, and her passionate need of him, she could not bear to wait until the day they had originally set for the ceremony. Pomfret had been flattered, as old men are by any show of endearment from a young and lovely woman, but he was still surprisingly reluctant to accede to her wish.

He agreed in the end, of course; she could be very persuasive, and he was a vain man. They married quietly, and within weeks, Jane told her husband the good news that she was carrying a child. Pomfret appeared absurdly proud of this, as though it somehow confirmed his masculinity. And, Jane thought now, with a wry smile, that proof might otherwise have been difficult to establish. He was not interested in what she considered was a straightforward attitude to sex; his fancy lay in exploring devious side tracks.

She had initially tolerated his fumbling, wet-mouthed approaches in the house in Jermyn Street, just as she accepted the strange wishes and practices of other clients. One required to be bound with thongs; another, with chains, and masked; a third had to put on her clothes, as soiled as possible, before he could perform.

Men were like that, Mrs Jones, the madam, had warned her.

'You are being paid to pander to their whims and wishes. You may not enjoy them all. Some may horrify or even disgust you, but you must conceal your feelings, dear, and pretend to pleasure. You are being paid, remember – which is more than married women can say when they have to endure their husbands' often equally loathsome approaches.'

Now Jane knew what Mrs Jones had meant, for, married to Pomfret, she belatedly realised with some surprise, for she was not inexperienced in such matters, that he greatly preferred men partners to women. This he had carefully kept concealed from her, but it would at least in part explain his reluctance to wed her. Worse, she then discovered Claude's attraction for him.

'*I* am married to the man,' she told Claude furiously. 'For God's sake, don't ruin everything.'

'I am not ruining *anything*,' Claude replied haughtily in his mincing way. 'He gives me presents because he *likes* me. Only this week, a gold watch and a signet ring – of his own free will. Am I to refuse them? *And I* am having a new suit made to measure at the very best tailor in Edinburgh.'

'You bloody fool, I brought you here to help me!'

'I am helping myself, dearie.'

'And in doing so, you are putting everything at risk. I am playing for the highest stakes – the estate, the castle, *everything*. And you go to bed with this man – my husband, remember – for a new suit, a watch and a ring.'

'That is only a beginning,' Claude replied tartly. 'If you think you are playing for high rewards, so am I.'

'What do you mean?'

'Just what I say, dearie.'

He left her then, and she had waited alone in the big room in front of a dying fire, unwilling in her present mood to ring for a servant to replenish it, and to do such a thing herself was now beneath her dignity. What could Claude mean?

That night, she discovered.

Pomfret had told Jane he had work to do in his study, and he retired there with a decanter of port and a box of Havanas. Jane went to bed early, thankful to be on her own. If she was not asleep when her husband came upstairs, she would pretend to be and trust he did not demand what he termed his rights. But she fell asleep early – and then some sixth sense of awareness awoke her.

She lit a candle and glanced at the clock. Half past midnight, far beyond his usual bedtime. She climbed out of bed, put on a pair of slippers and a robe, and went along the corridor to the head of the stairs.

Oil lamps burned in sconces on the walls, spreading streaks of soot towards the ceiling. A larger lamp illuminated the centre of the hall, turning the tiled floor into a pool of mellow light ringed with darkness. She went down the stairs silently, consciously holding her breath, walking on tiptoe as though she sensed it was imperative that her presence was not discovered. She paused in the hall. Her mouth was dry and she felt unaccountably nervous as she walked towards the study door. It was closed.

With infinite care, Jane turned the handle and pushed gently on the heavy panels. As the door opened, she could see one light burning on the far side of the study, not on her husband's desk, but on a table by the side of a huge leather couch.

On the floor lay two naked men, their flesh pale and shining with sweat in the glow of the single flame, her husband behind Claude, both in full and splendid erection.

Jane flung open the door, not really intending to do so, but in an automatic reflex muscular reaction of disgust and anger. The two men started up in horror at the interruption and stared at her as she stood framed in the doorway. Then Claude picked up a shirt and tossed it to Pomfret, who held it bashfully in front of him. He was sweating from his exertions: his chest heaved with each beat of his heart.

'You should have knocked,' said Claude reproachfully, not bothering to conceal what Jane had already seen many times. 'Did your mother not teach you any manners down in Dorset, dearie?'

'Go!' she told him shortly, her voice hoarse with rage.

'I do not take orders from you, dearie, but from the master of the house. You and I have been friends for a long time.'

'Friends? To conduct yourself in this foul and unnatural manner with *my* husband, in *my* house, puts an end to our association.'

'Not quite *your* house, dearie,' Claude corrected her. 'Your husband's house.'

Pomfret stood, shrivelled now, pot-bellied and thin-haired. His face trembled in anguish, like a wax effigy melting near an unexpected flame.

'What are you going to do?' he asked Jane nervously, in the voice of a little boy expecting to be punished. She despised him then, not so much for what he had been doing – her time in the house in Jermyn Street had made her tolerant of all searchings for sexual satisfaction – but, having been discovered, for this pathetic, pitiable response. A man would have bluffed it out with some excuse, however outrageous, but her husband was not a man, he was a creature.

'I am going to call the butler,' she told him, 'as a witness.'

'A witness?' asked Claude sharply, reaching for his own shirt. 'Of what?'

'Buggery carries sentence of death in Scotland,' she replied. 'I know that you, Claude, are anything to anyone, man or woman, and I have suspected my husband is of the same stamp. This may not be the first time for him but, by heaven, while married to me, it will be his last.'

Jane reached towards the tasselled bell rope by the side of the door. Pomfret stepped forward.

'No,' he pleaded, 'I beg of you, no. I can explain everything, Jane. I will give you. . . .'

Suddenly he choked. Both hands went up to his throat. His shirt fell unheeded to the carpet. He began to sink down on his knees, naked, coughing, retching, gasping for breath. A little saliva seeped from his mouth. He kneeled now, head down, as though in supplication, begging for forgiveness, for time to explain. Then Pomfret's face turned purple, and he rolled forward slowly. His body arched like a drawn bow and he gave a cry as one suffering unendurable agony. Then her husband lay at her feet.

'You were right,' said Claude, looking down at him without pity or interest. 'That *was* his last time.'

'Shut up and get dressed,' Jane ordered him. 'Then help me to dress him.'

'Oh, so you need my help now, do you, dearie? Friends again, are we?'

Jane struck him across the face with the back of her hand. For moment, Claude stood, eyes narrowed in hatred, as though debating whether to return the blow. Then, with a shrug of his shoulders, he kne down by Pomfret's side, moved his legs, pulled the dead man's drawers and trousers over his limbs, dressed him in shirt and jacket. Only then did Jane pull the bell rope. She was standing, head bowed, hands pressed together as though in prayer, when the butler arrived, holding a candle in one hand, a thick ash walking stick in the other. He wore a woollen nightcap.

'Something terrible has happened,' she explained in a matter-of-fact voice. 'My dear husband has suffered a seizure, mercifully without pain. My brother here heard a noise and came to my room, but too late. Together, we found him on the floor.'

'Shall I be calling the doctor, ma'am?'

'He is beyond the aid of all physicians now. No power on earth can help him. May God have mercy on his dear, gentle soul.'

'You are *certain* he is dead, ma'am?'

The butler knelt down and peered into Pomfret's face. His candle dripped wax on to the body. The butler closed Pomfret's eyelids and then stood up.

'Wake a footman and between you carry my husband to his dressing-room,' Jane Pomfret told him.

She followed the corpse up to the room, watched the two servants stretch out the dead man on a bed and cover him with a blanket. Idly, she saw that it bore a crest embroidered in one corner; the arms of the Douglas clan, a burning fire above a salamander and the motto, *Jamais derrière*. Never behind. At least Pomfret's habits would never contradict that claim again, she thought, half-amused at its incongruity.

She went downstairs to the study. Claude was already there. He put a full glass of claret in her hand.

'You have seen his will?' he asked her, without sarcasm or hostility. They might be business partners.

'Yes. Everything comes to me, apart from a small bequest to Alec Douglas, his first wife's son.'

'Then take a second look at it. A closer one this time, dearie.'

Claude pulled open a drawer in Pomfret's desk, removed two folded parchments bound with pink ribbon. He untied one, kept the other in his hand.

As she unfolded the will, the words seemed to leap out of the careful black copperplate: 'Two hundred thousand acres, both banks of the river for three miles . . . Twenty-three farms, with all stock, live and dead . . . Villages . . . The castle . . . The distillery . . . All unencumbered . . . To my beloved wife Jane. . . .'

'It is here,' she said excitedly. 'All listed. And all mine.'

She turned over the pages, skimming legal phraseology she did not understand, then suddenly she cried out in anguish.

'My God, he never signed it! The bastard *never signed it*! But he *promised* me. And it's all written here.'

'Everything. Except the most important part. His signature. But I can forge that. I have forged before.'

Claude dipped a quill pen into an inkhorn.

'No,' Jane said urgently. 'I don't know how he signed his name.'

'But you *must* know. Are there not any letters here he has signed?'

'I have not seen any,' she said. 'He may have signed with his initials or with a Christian name. He had three. His lawyer would know instantly that it was a forgery.'

'He'd have to prove it.'

'Probably he could. And there is Alec Douglas, remember. He is no fool.'

'You are the fool,' said Claude savagely. 'You married this pederast because you wanted what he had – wealth, a position in society. You did not care a fish's tit for him as a person. And he probably realised that and thought he would wait until he saw how things worked out before he signed his will. He was not too eager to wed you in the first place, as I recall. To be brutally blunt, he fancied me more than you. Yet you blandly accepted his assurances, and now – nothing!'

'There is nothing for you, if I have nothing,' Jane reminded him.

'We shall see about that,' Claude replied. 'In the meantime, I am taking off what I can carry. Now.'

He picked up a small silver vase, a cigar ashtray, a pen-stand, and crammed them into his pockets.

'You have some jewels, have you not?' he asked her.

'Yes.'

'Do you know where his first wife's jewellery is kept? Then put that in your bag, too. Take all you can before the lawyers move in. They are like vultures. They will make you prove title to everything. And if you cannot, they will take it themselves – and still charge you a fee.'

'My God,' said Jane bitterly. 'What a fool I have been, what a bloody stupid idiot.'

But Claude had already gone. She was alone in the big room with the single flickering candle flame casting long shadows on leather-bound books on the shelves. Only then did she realise that Claude had taken the copy of the will with him.

She had not told the Writer to the Signet of the events of that night: she had not told anybody, because she could not trust anybody. But now that she had informed the Writer of her plan and intention, she had one thing still to do. She must sell enough of Pomfret's first wife's jewellery to pay for her daughter Fiona to be boarded out with some local family for at least a year. She had a family in mind, the Macduffs, decent hones people. He was the tenant of Long Glen Farm. They already had a son, Alastair, and she knew they would look after her daughter if she provided them with money.

A passage to India could prove difficult to find, because swift vessels were in great demand, and even the fastest ship would take months on the voyage. She would then have to allow for more time there to carry out what she planned, and possibly another three months for the homeward voyage.

With Fiona looked after for a twelvemonth, she should have time enough and the peace of mind necessary to pursue her purpose without haste, for undue hurry could ruin her chances.

The prospect of seeing Alec Douglas again recalled that afternoon of love after his mother's funeral. Here was a man she could admire and respect; here was a man she could enjoy, time and again, tirelessly. At the thought, she flicked up her skirt and her hand strayed down to caress that soft, moist secret place in the way which always brought her pleasure.

En Route for Calcutta

On the voyage back to Calcutta, the atmosphere between the three partners stayed strained and unnatural. Douglas and Jackson felt guilty about what Ross had done, yet realised that, but for his quick thinking, they would all have been either killed or castrated.

This did not absolve them from the feeling of being an accessory to the murder and mutilation of three innocent men. Ross sensed their ambivalence and resented it. To show his displeasure, he reminded Douglas sharply how he had once declared he wanted no share in any profit from opium.

'I stick by that,' Douglas replied. 'I will take my share of profit from the tea we are carrying, which must be around five thousand pounds each.'

'We can make five or more times that amount with mud,' said Ross. 'Why are you being so yellow-bellied?'

'Because I do not like the idea of making money from poisoning thousands of people I have never even seen,' Douglas replied. 'I do not care who they are, heathen or Christian, Chinese or European. They are human beings, and once they start smoking opium, they never give up. And that means they die.'

'Agreed,' said Jackson. 'But so do we all in the end. And opium possesses considerable therapeutic qualities. I have used many medicines in England that contain it in various amounts – sometimes as much as half a grain in every fluid once. Nannies feed children with McMunn's Elixir, Godfrey's Cordial and Mother Bailey's Quieting Syrup to send them to sleep or soothe them when they are teething.

'It helps Chinese labourers, who have to work all their lives in the rice paddy fields. They just could not endure the pain of their joints without it.'

'I agree that it can be useful,' Douglas replied, 'but when I first saw poppy fields in India, I thought the smell of opium was the smell of death. Nothing either of you can say will alter that opinion.'

'But any medicine can be harmful if taken in excess. Most can kill more quickly than mud. It is not *our* concern what people do with the stuff. All I am interested in is selling it.'

'I agree one hundred per cent,' declared Ross enthusiastically. 'I do not give a damn about these Chinks or the blacks or anyone else. We have all only seventy years on this earth, so the Good Book says, before we go to heaven or hell.

'None of us is even sure *where* we are going – or when. But we all have to leave one day. So let us enjoy ourselves while we can. No one cares *how* you get rich, only that you *are* rich.'

He went below decks to finish a bottle of rum. He had been drinking more heavily on this voyage. For all his bravado, he could not forget the curse of the red-haired man. He heard his voice each night in tortured dreams, and saw his face thrust into his, and despite his loudly voiced disclaimers, Ross was afraid. Only rum, and still more rum, could quiet his unease and allow him to sleep, and even then but fitfully.

Jackson walked along the companionway to his cabin to open a bundle of letters and newspapers, many months old, which had been delivered before they left Canton.

Douglas stayed on deck, hearing the thunderclap of the sails as the wind changed, listening to the creak of the vessel, the groan of her masts under their huge spread of canvas. He leaned over the stern rail, smoking a cheroot and watching the long white wash they were leaving behind them, his mind in confusion.

Was he being a fool, as the others thought, in not accepting his share of the mud, or had he genuinely little interest in business and the market place? How much more rewarding to be out on the moors of home purple with heather, and the air fresh as new wine, on an August morning, than arguing about selling a deadly drug to people he would never know, never even meet!

He remembered, as a schoolboy, learning the quotations of Anarcharsis the Scythian philosopher who made many acute observations on Greek society. One seemed apt to his present situation: 'The market is a place se apart where men may deceive each other.' Was Douglas now simply deceiving himself?

There was no question that Trinity-Trio *could* grow immensely rich by selling mud, but in his opinion there was equally no doubt that other merchants who were ahead of them in this field had already established a lead it would be impossible for them to challenge. They could never hope to overtake them, and there was always the risk that these pioneers might appear to tolerate Trinity-Trio with faintly contemptuous amusement – and then suddenly unite to crush them.

Douglas believed that, given the same opportunities, and starting at the same time, Trinity-Trio could at least have equalled the achievements of these first-comers, but this was not now a race against equals; Trinity-Trio were starting years after their rivals had become entrenched.

The first individually successful European trader in China had been Daniel Beale, the purser of an East India Company ship. His employers held the monopoly then for trade in India and China, and would not permit any outsiders to squeeze more than the barest living in competition with them.

Beale calculated that this strict ruling, while accepted reluctantly by British subjects because they had no alternative, could not possibly extend to foreign nationals, or even to British citizens who might trade beneath the protection of a foreign flag. He therefore made his plans accordingly.

He persuaded the friend of a friend in the court of the King of Prussia to advance to him papers naming him as Prussian Consul. Beale then opened one office in Macao, the island off Canton which the Chinese had allowed earlier Portuguese voyagers to acquire, and another in Canton. He described himself diplomatically as Agent to the Government of Prussia. He was nothing of the kind, of course; he was a British merchant, but this loophole allowed him to prosper.

Then a Scot, David Reid, sailed east, and immediately appreciating the huge potential for trade, decided to follow Beale's example. He bought himself a commission as an officer in a Danish infantry regiment, and joined Beale in his Canton office. More recently, Dr William Jardine, who at the age of eighteen had been a ship's surgeon with the East India Company, and James Matheson, the son of a Scottish baronet, had joined forces in Canton.

Jardine originally worked with another partner, but this man unexpectedly married his coloured mistress, and it was felt that by such behaviour he had forfeited his interest in the business. Jardine then became sole owner. Initially he rented living quarters from James Matheson, and then the two men decided to work together. Matheson had previously been employed by a Spanish company owning some minor trading concession farther up the coast in the port of Amoy. For some reason, this company had never used these privileges to the full, and Matheson now decided to do so.

His first major deal was to sell a cargo of opium for the enormous sum of £33,000 sterling. This was the start of the Coast Trade, the Forbidden Trade, and of fortunes beyond accounting for all Europeans involved.

Matheson realised that the East India Company might decide to put them out of business, and to prevent this, he became Danish Consul. This meant that his ships would fly the Danish flag, and if ever a British naval vessel or a ship of the East India Company approached one of his vessels, they could not investigate the cargo because he sailed under the protection of a foreign flag.

The Chinese respected these two men, even if they did not warm to them. They called Jardine The Iron-headed Old Rat because once, when he was being interviewed about some trivial misdemeanour, Chinese officials had set about him, beating his head with staves. Jardine totally ignored their blows, and simply smoothed back his hair until they stopped.

He was an extremely able man of business; possibly the shrewdest in the East. To show his dislike of time-wasters and visitors who indulged in useless small talk, he did not keep a chair in his office for the use of callers. He kept them standing, because then they would not stay so long.

Jardine and Matheson were not content to ship mud, as Ross and Jackson would be happy to do, at huge profit; they also traded in all manner of legitimate merchandise. They would bring in machinery from Scotland; camphor and birds' nests from Malaya; cotton from India; fur from the North American continent. And they were ingenious in finding ways to transport goods more quickly and cheaply than their rivals.

Jardine knew from his own experience of East India Company vessels that many of their ships' officers were allotted cabins far larger than they needed. He persuaded them to rent space to him in these huge cabins and then filled this space with goods for sale.

Matheson imported bales of blue cotton bandanas from Lancashire mills for sale in China. The first consignment arrived with white spots woven into the cloth, and sales were slow. Matheson investigated and discovered that the Chinese preferred stripes to spots, so from then on the mills wove striped cotton to his exact specification – and every consignment was sold immediately.

Some European traders were content to ship their goods from Calcutta to Canton in vessels literally two hundred years out of date – built seventeenth-century designs for Portuguese caravelles, with a short way for guns. These ships, displacing possibly 800 tons, were known country wallahs, because, like people who lived in the country, they were slow and dull and heavy.

Jardine and Matheson realised that faster, more modern vessels would be far more efficient, so they ordered new ships, displacing only 240 tons each and based on plans for American privateers. These were noted for their speed, and against all tides and the most hostile winds they could make the journey from Calcutta to Lintin Island within three weeks. At Lintin, opium was stored in old ships especially kept there as floating warehouses. Country wallahs took at least three months to cover the same distance.

Again, the shrewdness of these partners was shown in the way they cleverly side-stepped another East India Company monopoly: the right to sail direct from Canton to British ports. They simply arranged for their vessels to call at Singapore, where they quickly unloaded cargoes on the quayside and then reloaded them. Technically, this meant that new cargoes had been taken aboard, and the East India Company had no legal case against them.

Clearly, it would be impossible for three amateurs arriving late on the scene, and as disparate as Douglas, Jackson and Ross, to survive against such established professionalism. Their best hope was to make as much money as possible, and then branch out into other ventures – perhaps not in the East at all. Douglas was thinking about possible new areas of expansion when Jackson came on deck and hailed him. He was carrying a copy of *The Enquirer* newspaper.

'I've been reading something here about your place in Scotland,' he said, with the surprise someone invariably expresses when they discover in print the name of a person they know.

'Really?' Douglas asked in surprise. 'What about it?'

Jackson handed him the newspaper and pointed to a paragraph:

Sudden death of Scottish Landowner
The death was announced this week of Mr John Pomfret at his home, Coupar Castle, in Perthshire. It is believed that Mr Pomfret, who had only recently inherited the castle, died of a heart attack. He is survived by a widow and an infant daughter, Fiona. The funeral of this gentleman, who hailed from London, is expected to take place next week.

Douglas checked the date on the top of the page.

'That was more than a year ago,' he said. 'So who inherits? His widow, s child, or me? Or all of us?'

'That depends entirely on the will,' Jackson replied. 'Usually the widow ould get everything. But perhaps he left it over her head to you?'

'Unlikely. But he damn' well ought to have done! She was only a tart picked up somewhere.'

'What people ought to do and what they do,' Jackson reminded him, 'are often two totally different things.'

Douglas did not reply. He stubbed out his cheroot on the ship's rail and went below decks to his cabin. The news was so surprising, so unexpected, that he could not decide on his best course of action. The Writer to the Signet in Edinburgh would no doubt have already advised him of the legal situation, but letters took months to arrive. Perhaps there might be one waiting for him in Calcutta? Then he remembered that it would have been sent to his regiment, and so very likely could have been destroyed or lost, because they had no forwarding address.

As soon as the ship reached Calcutta, he would send a messenger to the adjutant asking him to give the man any letters that had arrived in his absence.

But if there was nothing, should he abandon his enterprise with Trinity-Trio, at least for the time being, and return to Scotland immediately to find out for himself what had happened? Coupar Castle had belonged to his family for centuries; he could not bear to see it spirited into other ownership by the whim of an evil and perverted man.

If the estate had been left to Jane Pomfret, then could he overturn that will, or at least come to some accommodation with her? This might be unlikely because it was always impossible to over-estimate another person's greed, but to have any hope of success, was it not imperative for him to be there, on the spot, not here, on the other side of the world?

The other alternative was to remain in the East, make his fortune, and *then* to return. Money did not speak; it shouted. Money could buy the best advocates, the strongest arguments.

There and then Douglas made his decision. Whether any letter awaited him or not, whether he had inherited the castle and estate or not he would stay in the East until he had acquired sufficient wealth to overwhelm all opposition.

Then he would return, either to enjoy what he believed should be rightfully his – or to fight and fight again until he had won it all back.

London

The cab dropped Claude outside Mrs Jones's house in Jermyn Street, London. He gave the staff recognition tattoo of knocks with his cane on the front door. A maid opened it and looked at him enquiringly. Claude pushed past her into the front sitting room.

Mrs Jones, the madam, was sitting in a red velvet chair to one side of the fire. Flames glinted on the polished brass fender and coal tongs, turning them briefly to gold. She had a pot of coffee and a full balloon glass of brandy on a small table by her side, with an open cash box of black lacquered metal. Inside it, Claude could see white ten-pound notes and gold sovereigns. She was totting up the previous week's takings on a pad, and looked up, frowning at the interruption.

'Forgive me,' said Claude nervously.

'I should think so,' Mrs Jones replied sharply. 'You've made me miss a column. What brings you here? I thought you were in Scotland, fortune hunting?'

'I have come back,' he explained. 'I need your help.'

'Your type are all the same. You only come back when you want something. What do you want, then? Money, I suppose?'

'No. The name of a lawyer you would recommend for a delicate matter.'

Her eyes narrowed shrewdly.

'How delicate?'

'It concerns Mrs Pomfret's inheritance.'

'Oh, *Mrs Pomfret*. We *are* moving up. It was Jane in the old days, was it not? As keen a learner on the game as ever I saw. You require a gentleman learned in the law who will use his knowledge to your advantage, whether what he advises is strictly legal or not?'

'Precisely.'

Mrs Jones sipped her brandy, looking at him. She did not offer him a glass or some coffee, or even a seat. Claude had never been a favourite of hers. She liked men to be one thing or the other. Back-scuttlers she had to bide as necessary to her profits, but not when they would also pleasure a woman simply for a fee. She had her standards, she told herself.

'All right,' she said at last. 'There are two or three I know who might help you, but where money is involved, Macnamara is your man.'

'I have heard of him. But does he not deal only with the very rich?'

'Yes. And the well-born. Several of my clients he's helped, in different ways.'

Claude nodded. He remembered some of the more delicate cases: a prince of the blood whose pleasure was taken with children, and who had experienced the misfortune of having a child die under his gross attack. Somehow, Mr Macnamara had smoothed things over with the child's parents.

Another case involved a duke who had died while actually mounted on the woman of his choice in the most expensive room of the house. There had been the deuce of a job uncoupling them. Again, Mr Macnamara's services had proved of inestimable value to the duke's family, who had their good name to protect – and gladly paid a fortune to ensure that it was protected.

'He has another name when he deals with people like you,' said Mrs Jones sharply. 'O'Hara.'

'Why?' asked Claude.

'Because he has another practice. In Lincoln's Inn he deals with the wealthy. In Seven Dials he deals with matters that Mr Macnamara would not touch, but which can be equally as lucrative.'

'Will he see me?'

'If I write him a letter, yes. But first, what's in it for me?'

'What do you want?'

'For an introduction, I cannot ask money from you *yet*. But, shall we say, I would expect you to be available here – when you are in London, of course – for a period of, say, three months from the time you arrive. For helping male clients with tastes to which you pander so well.'

'I suppose so,' said Claude without enthusiasm. If he were successful in his plans, he hoped to rise above this sexual servitude. But at present he was in no position to refuse, or even to argue.

'I may not be back in London for some time,' he added carefully.

'You will come back eventually,' prophesied Mrs Jones, nodding her head sagely. 'When you have to. Now, I will write you a letter.'

She crossed to a writing desk, dipped her pen into a horn of ink and scribbled a few lines on a piece of headed paper. Then she scattered faint powdering of sand to dry the ink, blew surplus sand away, folded the paper, slipped it into an envelope and sealed the envelope carefully using a signet ring given to her by an earl's second son in payment of debt he could not otherwise honour.

'What can you tell me about Mr O'Hara?' Claude asked her.

'He is a bachelor, but not your sort. Not anyone's sort, really. A curious fellow. Claims to love animals. He has a charity of some kind building horse troughs in towns, at the bottom of hills. St Agnes' Fountains he calls them, after the saint, you know. I've never found out the connection between her and animals. She was not like St Francis of Assisi. So far as I know, she was a Roman virgin who was sexually assaulted and then beheaded when she was twelve, because she became Christian. Perhaps Mr O'Hara likes little girls, or just virgins – you never can tell. Even he must have had his peculiarities, once. But not now, only money now.'

Mrs Jones paused and sipped her brandy thoughtfully.

'Whenever I see a horse trough, I always read the inscription. It's usually given by an alderman, or by some rich widow in memory of a dear dead husband. There are dozens of such fountains, of course, but I've yet to see one dedicated to St Agnes.'

'He sounds a kindly enough man,' said Claude.

'Kindly? You have no notion what he is like. He has an old fellow working for him, Ebenezer. A sort of clerk, but not learned in the law. A poor wretched deaf mute, who sits on a high stool wherever O'Hara or Macnamara may be, scribbling away with a quill pen. If Ebenezer could speak, poor man, I wonder whether he would describe his master as "kindly". But then Ebenezer is not a beneficiary of St Agnes. Nor, I imagine, is anyone else. Except Mr O'Hara.'

'Why tell me this?'

'As a warning never to under-estimate him. Ebenezer, so I am told, is the third son of a noble house. O'Hara knows something dubious about him or his family. For this reason, he keeps the man virtually as a slave.'

She wrote an address on the envelope.

'Take that to him and he'll see you. Then you will have to strike your own bargain with him.'

Claude read the address: 'Mr O'Hara, Pim's Buildings, Seven Dials'. This lay between Holborn and Covent Garden and took its name from a pillar with a clock possessing seven faces that stood in a place where seven roads met.

It was generally considered the vilest area in all London. Here lived murderers on the run, thieves maintaining kitchens of young boys and girls, usually orphans or unwanted illegitimates, but all desperate for food. Their masters sent them out daily to steal or pick pockets, relying on their nimble feet to escape retribution.

Here dwelt fences who bought silver, gold, jewels, anything at a fraction of its cost, and swiftly sold them on at a huge profit. No policeman would enter Seven Dials alone. If a thief being chased could reach its safety, he was assured he would never be pursued within its mass of lanes and alleys and congeries. Some who had been imprudent enough to attempt such pursuit had not come out alive. Their bodies had been found mutilated, as a warning to others. Yet no one had ever seen what had actually happened in these cases; no one knew anything; no one heard anything or saw anything. Claude put the letter in his pocket.

'Not a very nice address,' he said reflectively.

Mrs Jones nodded agreement.

'Mr O'Hara, my dear, is not a very nice man.'

Claude's cabby refused to take him into Seven Dials and would only deposit him on the outskirts. It was not safe to go inside, he said. The people were so light-fingered they would steal the lamps off his cab or the bit from his horse's mouth if he so much as turned his back.

Pim's Buildings sounded more impressive than it appeared: a sooty brick structure, like a warehouse. Claude reached Mr O'Hara's office up a steep, wooden and uncarpeted stairway. The walls were sticky and slimy with filth. On a landing, the stench from a blocked privy in a yard below filtered chokingly through a cracked window stuffed with sheets of newspaper. Behind the privy, Claude could see lines of grey and tattered washing, a dog chained in a backyard. A gibbon, used by a professional beggar to perch on his shoulders on his pitch in Oxford Street, crouched miserably on a wall, a rope around its neck, chewing a cabbage stalk. Claude knocked on a door marked, in chalk, 'O'Hara'.

'Come,' commanded a deep Irish voice.

He entered. Mr O'Hara was standing with his back to a small fire that burned low in the grate. He was a tall, thin man wearing a black suit of good cut. His hands were folded behind him and he cracked the joints in his long fingers as he stood. Claude thought that they sounded like dry twigs breaking.

'Who are you?' asked O'Hara, looking at him quizzically.

'A friend of Mrs Jones, in Jermyn Street,' Claude replied, putting on his best accent. He had had his suit pressed, his linen washed, his shoes cleaned. He prided himself that he looked like a young man about town.

The lawyer slit open the envelope with a silver knife, read Mrs Jones's note and put it beneath a silver paperweight on his desk. Claude noticed that all the ornaments in the room seemed to be silver: a framed cheval glass, reading lights, inkwells, penholders. In the far corner, away from the window, a man sat on a high stool before a high desk, shoulders hunched, back to the room. The sound of his pen-nib on a pad of paper was like the scratching of a tiny, frantic mouse. He did not look up, and gave no sign he was aware of Claude's entry. This must be Ebenezer, writing by the light of a candle in a holder caked with wax.

'What is the matter on which Mrs Jones has recommended you see me?' asked O'Hara.

'A private matter.'

'All matters are private within these four walls.'

'This is one I would particularly prefer to discuss with you alone, sir.'

'You mean my colleague Ebenezer here should leave? Never! He i deaf, he is dumb. He can hear nothing, so he can repeat nothing.'

O'Hara picked up a silver handbell, crossed the room impatiently an jangled it furiously within inches of Ebenezer's left ear. The old man di not flinch. Only when O'Hara leaned into Ebenezer's face did he tur and start, apparently surprised that someone had come close to him s swiftly and unawares. O'Hara replaced the bell on his desk.

'Now are you satisfied? Please, to the point. I am a busy man.'

'So am I,' replied Claude with unexpected firmness. When he wa rich he would not be spoken to like this. 'I wish to discuss the matter a will.'

'You have it upon your person?'

Claude placed the parchment scroll he had taken from Pomfret's study on O'Hara's desk. The lawyer skimmed it rapidly with an expert eye, and pushed it back towards Claude.

'Useless,' he said. 'A declaration of intent, maybe, but unsigned and therefore invalid in any court.'

'I appreciate that. But may I tell you the background?'

'If you wish. But for whom do you wish me to act? Mrs Pomfret?'

'You will act, sir, for me, Claude Cartwright. If you take the case.'

'Proceed.'

O'Hara leaned back in his chair, eyes half closed, assessing Claude. You could never tell with these deviants: they often attracted extremely wealthy friends. He was glad he had no time for such a useless pursuit as sexual satisfaction. Who needed such brief moments of pleasure and release when you could enjoy a lifetime of power once you had amassed a fortune?

'Mrs Pomfret is the second wife,' Claude began. 'She has a young daughter by Mr Pomfret. There is a grown-up stepson by his previous marriage. This son's mother, already a widow, died shortly after she married Pomfret.'

'I remember,' said O'Hara surprisingly. 'Was she not found dead at the foot of a long flight of stairs?'

He had a filing cabinet for a mind, in which he stored details of any unusual or bizarre circumstance involving anyone of wealth or consequence which he might conceivably exploit to his own future advantage.

'Yes,' said Claude. 'A tragic affair.'

'For the first Mrs Pomfret, certainly,' agreed O'Hara drily. 'Pray proceed.'

'Mr Pomfret was much older than his second wife. He died suddenly of a heart attack. He had frequently told her he was leaving everything to her, but he simply forgot to sign the will.'

'Forgot or declined? This is a matter for the widow's legal advisers to decide. How do you come in?'

'Like this. With you,' said Claude. He sat down facing O'Hara and leaned forward, elbows on the desk. Then he nodded uneasily towards Ebenezer.

'Are you *certain* that old man cannot hear a thing?'

'You have my word, sir. And you have witnessed my demonstration of his total deafness. Pray proceed, or let us go no further. As I said, I am a busy man.'

'I want you to draw up a will in *my* favour which will be signed and dated after the unsigned document here, which was in Mrs Pomfret's favour. I will then inherit the estate, and will give her what is due to her as a widow under Scottish law.'

'You are asking a lot, sir. You are seriously suggesting that I forge a will for an estate that must be worth a huge sum of money? Do you realise the penalty for this? A lifetime in gaol. My God, sir, you have a nerve!'

'And you have a wish to make money, Mr O'Hara. Now you have the opportunity.'

'I am a professional man. I could not entertain such an action. I would never stoop to it.'

'Money – enough money, of course – has the ability to relax even those of ramrod conviction and allow them to unbend occasionally.'

'You speak from your own experience?' asked O'Hara sharply.

'Possibly. Let us not waste time in such protestations of integrity. I am addressing Mr O'Hara now, not Mr Macnamara.'

O'Hara looked at him coldly.

'Who else have you discussed this with?' he asked at last.

'No one. I am not a fool.'

'About that, I cannot give an opinion. But if you do mention this to another soul, I give you my word, you will regret it. And not only through the processes of the law. Do I make myself clear?'

'You do. And so am I to assume that you will take my instructions?'

'I will consider what you have to say.'

O'Hara stood up, walked to the fire, cracked his knuckles, and looked at Claude.

'A new will would almost certainly be strongly disputed unless I could come to some accommodation with the lawyers representing other interested parties. And that is most unlikely. Where is the stepson?'

'In India, serving with the East India Company's army.'

'He would fight such a will. But it might be that to do this successfully he would have to return. Perhaps the will could be proved in his absence.'

'We could, of course, make provision for him, and for Mrs Pomfret' daughter.'

'And what about my fee – assuming that we can find a solution to thi problem?'

'I can give you nothing now, Mr O'Hara. There is no point in pretend ing that I can, but I promise you a large sum when the will is proved.'

'Ah, *when*. A sad word, Mr Cartwright, a sad word. I see from M Jones's letter that you were, as she puts it delicately, on intimate term with the late Mr Pomfret?'

'I was.'

'If I understand the meaning of that phrase aright – you know t sentence for such intimate relationships in Scotland?'

'I am aware of it. But you could not prove it.'

'Naturally I would not wish to. I simply feel it prudent to examine every possible aspect of the case. We might find ourselves against those who have less scruples.'

He turned and faced the fire, warming his thin, withered palms before its scanty flames. Then he turned back to Claude.

'For the sum of ten thousand golden guineas, paid to a charity of my choice, when the will is proven in your favour, and ten per cent of the agreed value of the estate, I will accept your instructions. No fee whatever to me.'

'What is the charity?' asked Claude.

'St Agnes' Fountains. We build drinking fountains in many cities, both for travellers to refresh themselves, and for dogs and horses that are all too often poorly treated.'

'It is a great sum, Mr O'Hara.'

'And a great principle, if you like. Principal meaning a capital sum, and the principle of helping dumb creatures.'

He paused and looked slyly at Claude.

'I assume that the late Mr Pomfret first became acquainted with you intimately – on Mrs Jones's premises?'

'Yes.'

'So there we have the reason for him to come and consult me. He was in London and came to seek advice from Mr Macnamara. This could mean that, like many husbands, and even some bachelors, he wrote more than one will. But this must be his last. We will date it on his last visit to London, virtually the eve of his death. Now, sir, if you will give me some more particulars as to your full name and address?'

He began to write as Claude dictated. In the corner, on his high stool, Ebenezer's nib scratched away like a rusty claw.

Calcutta

Jane Pomfret stepped ashore in Calcutta and looked about her in bewilderment and dismay.

She had had no clear idea in her mind what the city would be like, but the crowds, the cruelly bright sunlight, the heavy smells of spice and dung and incense, and the hoarse incessant cries of Indian sweetmeat-sellers, their mouths red with betel nut juice giving the loathsome impression they were full of blood – all this was totally outside her expectation.

She stood irresolute on the stone-flagged quay. How could she possibly find the 113th Regiment of Foot when she did not even possess an address for them? For the first time since Jane left Scotland she began to appreciate the vastness of the country to which she had sailed. The voyage had been strange enough, but aboard ship she still had the comfortable feeling she was in an extension of her own land. Now, she realised she had left all familiar things behind her – and a fear grew within her that perhaps she might never see them again. She knew that the average lifespan of a European in India was measured by two monsoons; perhaps a year, possibly eighteen months.

Her cabin had been deep in the heart of the vessel, a bonus, so she had been informed, because that meant she would experience less rolling or pitching in rough weather. But she shared this cabin with a huge gun which could be run out through a concealed porthole if the ship faced pirates. The porthole was usually kept closed, and when the ship entered the tropics, the heat became excessive. Jane's discomfort increased because bilge water was pumped through an open sluice in the cabin floor. When she objected to this stench and to the lack of fresh air, she was told brusquely by the captain: 'Madam, that is simply the smell of the vessel.'

Above her head, on some inner deck, poultry was kept in coops to provide eggs and flesh, and the clucking of hens and the crowing of cocks became a continual irritation. It had been a relief when the vessel called to take on fresh water and victuals at Madeira and the Cape. As the voyage progressed, live sheep and pigs, carried elsewhere in the vessel, were killed off like the chickens. Finally, the passengers were reduced to a diet of salted mutton, boiled potatoes and rice.

Everything would change in Calcutta, she had assured herself, but now this strange city, shimmering like a mirage in the noonday heat, with a noise that assaulted her eardrums and an intensity of light that already hurt her eyes, made her wonder whether she had only exchanged one extension of purgatory for another.

A cheerful voice broke into her depression.

'Come along, my dear, we will soon see you on the way to your regiment.'

She turned with relief to see a companion on the voyage, Mr Armitage, a widow from Tunbridge Wells, who had joined the ship at the Cape on her way to stay with her brother, a colonel commanding the 90th Dragoons. As she spoke, a tall young man pushed through the crowd and bowed to her.

'My brother's adjutant,' Mrs Armitage explained thankfully. 'He knows everyone and everything, so my brother says. He will put you right.'

The officer turned, bowed to Jane Pomfret, and looked at her enquiringly.

'She is visiting a relation in the 113th,' Mrs Armitage explained. 'Mr Douglas. Do you know him?'

'Only of him, ma'am. His regiment is encamped at Barrackpore, Colonel McTavish commanding.'

'How can I reach Barrackpore?' Jane asked him.

'It will be my pleasure to organise transport, ma'am. Have you much luggage?'

'Two cabin trunks.'

'That's nothing here in India. Why, I have known a regimental baggage train extend for twenty miles, with camels and elephants. We will have you in Barrackpore by this time tomorrow.'

'In the meantime,' Mrs Armitage told Jane, 'you must stay with me. My brother has booked me into a private house that takes paying guests. They will have room for you, I am sure.'

'You are very kind,' said Jane gratefully. 'Can I make arrangements at Barrackpore for my accommodation? I assume there will be no hotel there?'

'You assume correctly, ma'am,' said the officer. 'There is little there except the regiment, a lot of natives, most of them disagreeable, and a pestilential climate. But their regimental adjutant, Captain Bushell, will see you provided for. I will give you a letter of introduction to him.'

And so, within a day of landing in Calcutta, Jane Pomfret was in Barrackpore, in a house that Captain Bushell assured her would be as inexpensive as it was commodious. This Jane doubted, but she was grateful for his help. The ceilings in the house seemed unusually high – for coolness, Bushell explained – there was no glass in the windows, and birds flew in and out in a way that at first disturbed her.

The adjutant, plump and curious as to the reason for her arrival, appeared friendly.

'If I can help you in any way, ma'am, it will be my pleasure,' he assured her.

'Thank you,' said Jane, smiling at him. 'I have come out to see one of your brother officers to whom I am related by marriage. Lieutenant Douglas.'

Captain Bushell's smile froze on his face; he coughed deprecatingly.

'I am sorry to have to tell you, ma'am, but Mr Douglas is no longer with the regiment.'

'What do you mean? Is he on detachment – on the staff?'

'Neither, ma'am. He has relinquished his commission.'

'Resigned it?'

'No, ma'am. Relinquished it. Several months ago. Nearly a year, in fact.'

'Why did he do that?'

'It was the colonel's decision, ma'am. Pray do not think me unforthcoming, but I am in an awkward position in discussing regimental matters with you.'

'I can see that, Captain Bushell. But you will appreciate the awkwardness of my position also. As a widow, bearing news for Mr Douglas of the utmost importance to him personally, I have been travelling for months. Can you tell me where I can contact him now?'

'I think you should address your questions to the colonel, ma'am. I am sure he will help you if he is able.'

The following afternoon, a bearer brought a note for Jane from the colonel; he and his wife would be pleased if she would take tea with them at four o'clock. A carriage would attend at her residence.

The colonel's house was a square whitewashed building with a flat roof. A tapestried punkah beat the humid afternoon air in his drawing-room. The room was sparsely furnished: cane chairs with holes in their armrests to take glasses; cane tables.

Two servants wearing white pantaloons, long white jackets with thick belts, turbans in the regimental colours, and polished brass buckles in the shape of the regimental badge, stood by the door. Jane had the uneasy feeling that, although they stood so still they might have been ebony statues, they were watching her critically, weighing her up.

A slightly-built woman wearing a white dress that reached to her ankles, with a necklace of pearls which she kept twisting nervously in the fingers of one hand, came into the room. She had once been very pretty, Jane thought, but the heat had faded her good looks. She appeared oddly nervous and ill at ease.

'You wish to see my husband, the colonel?' she asked. 'I am Emma McTavish.'

Jane Pomfret introduced herself.

'I am seeking the whereabouts of one of your husband's officers, Alec Douglas.'

Emma McTavish drew back half a pace. Her hand tightened around the pearls. Her face was suddenly white and drawn.

'You know him well?' she asked.

'I am related to him by marriage.'

'Oh.'

Jane Pomfret could sense relief in the other woman's voice.

'Captain Bushell tells me he has left the regiment.'

'It was most unfortunate,' Emma McTavish began, and then paused

The colonel had just been wheeled into the room by an orderly. His right leg had swollen with gout to such an extent that its muscles had lost all strength. The limb was merely a puffy, useless appendage. Regimental carpenters had fashioned a chair on wheels for him, with a long extension on which he could rest his leg, stretched out and discreetly covered by a cloth in the regimental colours.

Such incapacitation was not unusual. Some colonels and generals were so gross they had to be lifted on to their chargers. Others had become so sodden with drink they could not even ride, and were wheeled out to the edge of the parade ground, where they whispered orders through an intermediary.

McTavish regarded Jane Pomfret with appraising eyes.

'I understand, ma'am, that you have come in search of Mr Douglas. I am sorry to have to tell you that he and I had a serious disagreement. He refused to obey a direct order, and relinquished his commission to go to Calcutta to seek his fortune. A number of letters have arrived for him since his departure, but I have no address for him.'

'So I have no means of contacting him?'

'None at all, ma'am, I regret to tell you.'

'In this unhappy situation, what do you advise, sir?'

'Advise? I do not *advise* young ladies at my time of life. But since you ask, I would say you should go home to England and not waste any more time in this damn' climate.'

'But I have only just arrived here. It is most important that I find him. A matter of an inheritance is involved.'

'Hm. I'm damn' sure he would like to see you in that case. He always was one to live up to his means.'

McTavish attempted to find a less uncomfortable position for his swollen leg and winced at the pain.

'This must be a very grievous shock for you,' said Emma gently.

Jane nodded. That Douglas would not be there at the end of her journey was a complication she had never anticipated. Letters took so long to travel, ships were so slow, distances so vast, and Douglas could be anywhere. He might, by supreme irony, even be on his way back to Scotland.

After tea with the Colonel and Emma, Jane excused herself early and returned to her rented house. She took off her white hat and gloves, and sat down in a cane chair on the verandah overlooking the scrubby garden, not much more than a patch of reddish earth fissured with cracks by the sun. Around the few shrubs, the *mali* or gardener had scratched circles with a pointed stick, and *bhistis* were filling them with water from vessels fashioned out of animal skins sewn together. They glistened like glass in the blazing sunshine.

Surely there must be some way of tracing Douglas? But on her own, weary, suffering from reaction after the long voyage and the disappointment of not finding him here, she could not think of any. She passed a hand in front of her eyes; the sun was giving her a headache.

She went into her bedroom and lay down on the wide bed. Even here, the sun reached through the unshaded windows with a scorching, blinding strength.

She considered her situation. She had several hundred pounds remaining of the money the Writer to the Signet had advanced to her. That had seemed a fortune in Edinburgh. Now, on the other side of the world, it seemed very little. She would have to leave this house; it was obviously too expensive for her, with bearers, servants, gardeners.

She was not accustomed to dealing with servants, and she did not trust these men. She could only communicate in the simplest terms with the bearer, who then passed on her instructions to the others.

But before she decided anything, she must calculate exactly how much money she possessed. Mrs Jones in Jermyn Street had always stressed the importance of listing assets against expenditure, and keeping an accurate balance between profit and loss.

Jane swung her long legs off the bed, lifted the mattress, took out the envelope where she kept the money. She opened it, and shook out the contents.

A few pieces of blank paper fluttered on to the bed. But where were the bank notes? She plunged one hand deep into the envelope, thinking they might have become stuck to it by sweat or humidity. But the envelope was empty.

She heaved at the mattress in a panic, ripped it off the bed, tore away the sheets and threw them on the floor in case somehow the notes had become dislodged and hidden. But there were no notes. They had gone. She was penniless.

Jane looked up and saw the bearer standing in the doorway. In that instant, she sensed instinctively he had stolen them.

'My money!' she cried. 'Where is my money?'

'Memsahib?'

He looked at her, deliberately pretending he did not understand her question.

'You have stolen the money!' she screamed.

She seized him by the arm and shook him. His head rolled like a rubber doll's, but he stood there, grinning foolishly at her.

'Not understanding, memsahib,' he said. 'I am just now not understanding anything.'

Jane released him, and at that moment she heard the grind of steel rimmed wheels on the drive, the clop of hooves, the cry of a coachman

Who the devil could this be? She gave her hair a quick brush, and went out into the hall.

Captain Bushell was standing hesitantly in the doorway.

'You must excuse me, ma'am,' he said, 'but I thought I would bring you the correspondence that has arrived for Mr Douglas.'

'Thank you.'

Jane put up one hand to smooth her forehead, surprised that it was damp with perspiration.

The adjutant came into the hall.

'Are you all right, ma'am?' he asked her solicitously.

'Yes, yes,' she assured him. 'It is just this heat.'

'You look very pale.'

He clapped his hands and spoke to the bearer. He disappeared and returned with a glass of *nimbu pani*, a cool drink of lemon juice, water and sugar. Jane sipped it gratefully.

'Please sit down for a moment, ma'am. This change of climate, especially before the monsoon, is always difficult to endure, even for those of us who are used to it.'

They went out on to the verandah, and sat down. Jane looked at Bushell appraisingly over the rim of her glass. She did not greatly like his face. It was too soft for her taste, and lacked character. His uniform was well-cut, though, and the cloth expensive, and his boots were of the most supple leather, very highly polished. He wore a ring engraved with a crest on the little finger of his left hand. She had seen such signs of wealth often enough in Mrs Jones's house to recognise them instantly. She had captivated rich men there when nothing was at stake. Surely she could do the same when her whole future depended on it?

'Captain Bushell,' she said, 'you are right in saying I appear unwell. I have just made the most fearful discovery. I have been robbed of all the money I brought out with me!'

Bushell's face showed his incredulity.

'I put the bank notes in an envelope beneath the mattress before I came to see you. I thought they would be safe there.'

'Nothing is safe in India, ma'am. They are very light-fingered, these people. Of course, they are poor. That makes a difference, I suppose.'

'A great difference,' agreed Jane. 'In many ways, I can sympathise with them, but now I seek sympathy for my own plight. To be blunt and frank – and at a time like this, I have no alternative – I am without funds. I have no money at all.'

'What are you going to do?' Captain Bushell asked, as if he had not already formed an answer in his mind.

His voice was soft, barely above a whisper, as though the walls of the house might have ears and hear the proposition both knew he was about to make.

So by mutual agreement, Jane became the adjutant's mistress for an indefinite time. All her living expenses would be paid and he would also transmit an agreed sum every month of their association to an account he would open in her name in Grindlay's Bank in Calcutta. Jane would appear as his consort at occasions like a regimental ball or that held by the local governor, and accompany him to the races. But both would be discreet in their relationship. She was a rich widow of gentle birth, so everyone would be told. As a middle-aged bachelor of immense wealth, Bushell distrusted any closer attachment between them. He was proud of what he claimed was his freedom.

He had no wish to marry, and Jane knew how strongly other wives, and perhaps even Captain Bushell, would react to her if her true background ever became known. So long as she appeared a woman of means in her own right, who had come out to India to seek a relation formerly with the regiment, they both believed that the subterfuge could be kept alive for as long as it suited them.

But in their willingness to come quickly to such a mutually satisfactory arrangement, the adjutant had neglected to consider one other interested party about whom Jane knew nothing – his Indian mistress, Rani.

It was the custom for unattached British officers to have some association – always at a discreet distance, of course – with an Indian woman. She was usually kept in a modest establishment in the bazaar or the city, where most Indians lived, and certainly not near the cantonment where Europeans had their houses.

She would receive visits from the officer from time to time, and presents commensurate with her social station. If she became pregnant, as sometimes happened, the child might be adopted elsewhere, but nothing would ever associate her or any children she might bear by her lover, with that lover. One was from the East, the other from the West. Between them lay a gulf of colour, prejudice, religion and social mores too wide to be permanently bridged.

The bearer whom Jane correctly believed had stolen her money instantly assessed the situation between her and the adjutant, and informed Rani accordingly. At her request, the bearer bored a tiny hole in the ceiling, near an oil lamp suspended by a chain. Through this, Rani could watch her rival, concealed and silent, but with hatred burning in her heart. She had an elderly widowed mother, and a sister with a seriously ill child, totally dependent upon her. Rani was in her thirties, old for an Indian concubine, and she realised that if this relationship between the adjutant and this new memsahib, so much younger, so much more voluptuous, and of his colour, his country, should become permanent, even to the extent of a month or more, she might never find another protector. What would then become of her and those she was committed to support?

She thus had to be rid of this interloper as soon as possible. The bearer agreed. With the arrival of the adjutant, he feared the memsahib might dismiss him and, in addition to his wages, he would then lose another considerable source of income: on everything bought for the household in the bazaar, he extracted, by custom, a very large percentage.

The quickest way of removing Mrs Pomfret would probably be to poison her. They discussed the possibility of introducing a poisonous serpent into the house, but agreed there was no certainty it would sting the memsahib.

The bearer could easily poison her food, or introduce chips of glass or the whiskers of a cat, cut up very small, which irritated the intestine and caused death. But this would be risky, because some of the British doctors who treated patients with stomach ailments had been openly critical of Indian standards of cleanliness, and the bearer might be blamed and punished.

There was another means of harming Mrs Pomfret, however. The results would be apparent within weeks, and then the adjutant, no matter how enamoured or impassioned he might be, would immediately abandon her, and Rani could return. Of this, both were certain.

The following Sunday evening, after an afternoon spent in bed with the adjutant, with the sun beating on the drawn blinds and the room scented by joss-sticks, Jane Pomfret lay alone. Bushell had visited her earlier, but had returned to his own house. Jane was thankful he had gone. His clumsy, panting advances repulsed her. He was incompetent as a lover, eager only for his own quick pleasure. But he was a means of survival, and at present her only one: she had to endure him.

Jane thought, with a wry smile, that although she had moved from Mrs Jones's establishment in Jermyn Street to the other side of the world, only the background had changed. Yet if she could find Alec Douglas, surely everything *must* improve?

The letters the adjutant had brought her were those the Writer to the Signet had sent, bearing his name on the envelope. She had not opened them, because they were sealed. If they had not been, she would have succumbed to the temptation and steamed them open with a kettle, but she could not replace the wax. It was better to keep them unopened, and to find Douglas. Thinking about this, and what they could do together in bed when they did meet, she stroked herself gently until relief came, and then she dozed.

Suddenly something woke her, a slight movement against her naked limbs. The room was dark now and she put down a hand, half expecting that Bushell had returned and crawled into bed, intending to surprise her. But instead, her fingers touched the head of a child.

The child kicked her smartly. She felt a painful scratch on her thigh from a finger-nail or a toe-nail as sharp as a bird's claw. What was happening? Who *was* this child?

She threw back the sheets and jumped out of bed. She struck a tinder, but for some reason the lamp would not light. Now she cried out in alarm and someone came running, holding a candle lantern: a woman she had never seen before, wearing a white sari, the sort *ayahs* or nurses wore.

She put down the lantern on a side table and seized the child. Jane saw its face for a second: horribly, almost unbelieveably mutilated, eyes tightly closed as though blind, the eyelids damp with some yellow secretion, mouth only a tiny orifice, dribbling and foul. The flesh was wrinkled and dry and covered with raw scabs. This was a horrific mask, not a human face at all.

'Whose is it? *Who are you?*' Jane shrieked in terror and disgust.

The woman did not answer, but fled away carrying the child. Jane picked up the lantern, looked at the bed and sniffed. The sweet afternoon scent of joss-sticks had long since gone. The room was filled with a strange cloying smell of decay and death; of old corpses, putrefying. Then, almost as quickly as she breathed, it had gone. She managed to light the bedside oil lamp and glanced down at her naked thigh. The child had somehow cut her. The wound on her thigh was not deep, but about two inches in length, and bleeding. She stared at it in disbelief. Could it be a snake bite? What a terrible country this was when a stranger could walk into your house and a loathsome child could actually creep into your bed!

She hated India then and feared it, because she did not understand it, and she was lonely and afraid. She called for the bearer, but he was not in the house. She was alone.

She went out into the next room, where a tin bath and a basin hung from nails on one wall. The floor was green with damp and smelled of stagnant water. From holes in the base of the sodden wall, rats watched her with bright pinpoint eyes.

Jane bathed her wound in a basin and bound a gauze bandage around it. Somehow she did not want to go back to that bed. It seemed horrible unclean. She moved into another bedroom, but it was a long time before sleep came. And when she slept, she dreamed of that deformed face next to hers, and smelled again the fearful rotting stench of an opened grave.

Hong Kong

Everyone in Hong Kong agreed that the most impressive road in the colony at that time was the Praya.

Fifty feet wide, and running for more than four miles, the entire length of Victoria City, except where a military barracks and the naval yard jutted into it, the Praya seemed to symbolise the colony's commercial prosperity and military impregnability under British rule.

On its harbour side was a reassuringly strong retaining wall of granite, and facing the harbour stood the imposing storehouses and godowns of merchants, shippers and traders. Parallel to this ran Queen's Road, the principal business thoroughfare where banks and major trading companies – including Trinity-Trio – had their offices.

But despite the colony's astonishing growth and prosperity in the years since the Chinese had ceded it to Britain, and the presence of British troops ashore and warships in the harbour, Hong Kong still seemed to Jackson to be dangerously indefensible, perched like an impudent pimple on the edge of a huge and potentially hostile Chinese mainland.

Business everywhere was brisk, of course, and increasing. Whereas only 694 foreign ships had docked there in its first year as a British colony, now nearly as many appeared every week. The Australasia and China Telegraph Company accepted cables to Britain, and to the United States, Russia, Japan and Australia. Five new hotels advertised electric light and hot running water in their bedrooms, with flower gardens shielded by awnings. Some even had hydraulic lifts to all floors.

There were photographers' studios, makers and purveyors of aerated water, drapers, a newspaper – *The Chinese Mail*, dealers in foreign stamps, even a horse repository. The well-known wine merchants, Caldbeck Macgregor, of Leadenhall Street in London, had a branch here and others in Shanghai, Canton and Amoy.

Because of Jackson's doubts about Hong Kong's viability in the event of war, which were totally ridiculed by others, he had persuaded his partners to maintain only a small office there. Trinity-Trio's main office was in Calcutta, where he did not feel an interloper, tolerated, but never really accepted, as he always felt in Hong Kong and Canton.

Some of the names in Hong Kong amused him by being brutally direct – or totally inapposite: American Town, Stone Cutter's Island, Gin-drinkers Bay and Malatoon – a corruption of the Chinese *ma-lau-ung* – on the ridge of a hill east of the Lion's Head. The name literally meant Monkey Pond – so called, said local wits, because it did not possess a pond nor even any monkeys.

Whenever Jackson was in Hong Kong he remembered one visit made years earlier and important to him and to his partners because it had marked a great step forward in their company's growth.

He had come ashore at Pedder's Wharf, the main landing pier, which extended for 250 feet out into the harbour. As the launch brought him in from his steamer, he noticed a ship at anchor, lighter and faster than *Coromandel II*, with raked masts and a long steam funnel and rear paddle wheel.

He entered the harbour office to present his card.

'Who owns that ship?' he asked the managing clerk, a pale Englishman of middle age. 'The vessel with a gold line around her hull.'

The clerk evaluated the stitched cuffs on Jackson's suit, his perfectly polished crocodile-skin shoes, his gold watch and chain. His deferential tone indicated the respect he felt was due to such clear signs of success.

'*Sea-Sprite*, sir, owned by Major the Honourable Reginald Forster. Operating out of Gravesend in England. She is for sale.'

Forster. It was a long time since Jackson had heard his name. He wondered how the Major was, and his wife Amelia. And in remembering them, he remembered Mrs Gray, and how her son, Tom, had saved his life, and the penny Tom's daughter, Joanna, had given back to him. He still had this, of course. He regarded it as some kind of talisman, a link with a half-forgotten past that once he had earnestly promised to remember – and had so readily and unforgivably forgotten.

He frequently found himself using this coin as a means of deciding quickly which of two courses he should take. He would withdraw from a meeting with bankers and traders, and outside the room toss this penny three times. Two heads out of three and he would go ahead with the deal. If tails came up twice, he would not.

Now Jackson put one hand into his fob pocket and ran his thumb around the smooth face of the coin. Why, after his pledge on the night he left England, had he never been in touch with Tom again? What miseries, or possibly punishments, might Tom not have suffered at Piggott's hands, while he, their cause, had blithely sailed away and lacked even the basic courtesy to write a single letter to him?

Had the pursuit of gain completely obliterated all finer feelings of obligation and gratitude? Mud. . . . He remembered old Mrs Gray' prophecy.

'The Major is eager for a speedy sale, sir,' the clerk went on, breaking into Jackson's guilty thoughts. 'He will accept ten thousand Englis' pounds.'

'Take me out to her,' Jackson told the clerk.

A rowing boat was ordered with two oarsmen. They ferried Jackson t' *Sea-Sprite*. She was not so fast or so light as the new Jardine an'

Matheson ships, maybe, but still far more competitive than the country wallahs, and cheap at the price. And he guessed that not too many people in Hong Kong would be in the market for such a ship. He took out the penny and tossed it three times. The clerk saw that the coin fell head upwards on each occasion. Jackson put it back into his pocket, his mind made up.

'What are you empowered to take?' he asked the clerk.

'As I say, sir, the Major is asking ten thousand pounds.'

'Asking and receiving are different things, my friend. I am prepared to offer seven thousand. Cash. Not this evening. Not tomorrow. *Now.*'

'It is very little, sir, for a ship of this size, in such condition, with a good crew.'

'Seven thousand. Until we reach the shore.'

'You put me in the most difficult position.'

'Then get yourself out of that position and take my offer.'

The clerk consulted some papers, bit his lower lip and ran his tongue around his mouth. He knew that Forster was asking eight thousand, and had intimated he would take less. The clerk had personally set the price at ten, hoping to make two for himself. How was it that some people had the gift of making money, when all he could do was to earn so very little of it? Could it be that because he did not know the answer, even because he had to ask the question, he was still a clerk?

'For settlement today, sir, I will accept on the owner's behalf,' he said reluctantly.

'You have a deal,' said Jackson, shaking hands. 'Now take me back to shore. I have partners to discuss this with.'

Ross and Douglas agreed to put part of their profits from the sale of their last cargo of tea towards the purchase. She was ready to sail within the week. But this time, while *Coromandel* carried a legitimate cargo of cotton, *Sea-Sprite* was packed to the gunwales with mud.

Canton

Douglas stood in *Sea-Sprite*'s bows as, behind *Coromandel*, she turned in towards Whampoa Island off Canton. Here, *Coromandel*'s legal cargo would be loaded into junks and riverboats with matted sails, slatted horizontally like giant fans, and ferried into Canton. *Sea-Sprite* would not unload her mud, but after a brief period to revictual she would sail on to her special destination.

A longboat ferried Douglas to the shore. He passed girls sculling sampans heavy with oranges and bananas and other fruit, crying, 'Olanges! Flute!' Houseboats and junks were lacquered so brightly that their hulls reflected half a dozen glittering colours in the yellow water of the river.

He overtook anchored war junks with eyes painted on their bows to enable their captains to seek out enemies miles ahead. On their sterns, painted demons flexed blue talons and poked crimson tongues from gaping jaws to frighten any who might dare to approach them from the rear.

As Douglas landed, gongs boomed and the band of a funeral procession played its way brassily past the factories. As much noise as possible was required to frighten away evil demons; the louder the noise, the farther away such devils would be kept. But no amount of music or drumbeats could ever exorcise from his mind the memory of the three men he and his colleagues had watched die in their stead in Canton.

This memory was what the Chinese called 'bad joss' – a corruption of the Portuguese word for god, *deos*. The passing of years, the acquisition of fortunes, did not dim the memory of those sights and sounds. And Douglas knew that Ross still dreamed of it, still heard in his sleep the red-haired sailor cursing him, and would awake sweating and dry-mouthed. And then, with racing heart, would reach out thankfully for the rum bottle.

In the background, fireworks crackled and flared constantly. They were far brighter and louder than any fireworks he had encountered at home when election results were declared, or at celebrations to mark the visit of a Royal personage to a provincial city. Idly, he wondered what powder they contained that was missing from British fireworks. He decided it could be instructive to discover the secret: there might be a market somewhere for an explosive powder so much more powerful than any he had come across elsewhere. He gave instructions to buy several pounds of this powder and deliver it to the Calcutta office.

Douglas had sailed on *Sea-Sprite*'s first voyage under Trinity-Trio's flag because he wanted to see for himself how opium was off-loaded and how deals were arranged. All knowledge of the Forbidden Trade was useful, even though he personally did not wish to profit commercially from it.

He had adopted the curious way of speech that traders called pidgin English. When the first British traders had landed in the days of Beale they proclaimed their intention to do business. The Chinese found this word difficult to pronounce, just as the letter 'r' was almost an impossibility for them. They called business 'pidginess', and the strange hybrid language, neither Chinese nor English, but easily understood by both nationalities, became pidgin.

While coolies carried stores aboard *Sea-Sprite*, Douglas dined off large grilled prawns, served with roasted snails and saffron rice. He drank a green wine made from peas, still to the background of booming brass gongs and the flash of fireworks, now not concerned with a funeral but announcing the departure of their two ships.

They sailed on the evening tide. The current was running fast, and *Sea-Sprite*'s decks dipped and creaked and her sails hammered protests against the masts as the wind changed. When the captain started the engine and lowered the sails, the vessel surged forwards.

They were carrying 250 chests of opium, worth about 75,000 Spanish dollars, a currency in which some merchants still traded, the equivalent of £20,000 sterling. At least three-quarters of that sum would be clear profit to Trinity-Trio.

At dawn, *Sea-Sprite*'s golden figurehead, with her streaming blonde hair and unnaturally red cheeks, pointed her carved wooden breasts at Lintin, a small island with a curious rock formation pointing to the sky, which gave it the name of the Island of the Solitary Nail. Several other ships were already there, anchored fore and aft so they would not turn with the tide, and deliberately placed parallel to the shore, to allow their cargoes to be unloaded on the far side of each vessel, without any interested watcher ashore being able to see the nature of the trade.

These ships had gun ports, and carried large heads of sail. They could be pirate vessels, and in a sense they were; they were used to land opium direct from India or to transport it for sale farther along the coast.

Douglas came up on deck in time to see two Chinese war junks sailing down towards them from the north. Immediately, several of the ships slipped anchor and took off under all sail in the opposite direction, with the junks in pursuit, but rapidly falling behind.

Douglas asked a sailor the reason for this pantomime.

'Simple, sir. Those Chinks are trying to catch them smuggling mud.'

'But they are much faster than the foreign ships. Why don't they clap on more sail?'

'Aha, sir, they haven't got the spirit.'

As the man spoke, Douglas saw puffs of white smoke coming from the junks, and seconds later, heard the crack of their cannon.

'They're firing at them,' he said. 'But they're so far out of range, the shells are simply landing in the sea.'

'Of course, sir. That's what is meant to happen. It's all a big bit of play-acting. The Chinese are bribed not to catch the smugglers. But they have to put up a show, otherwise the Viceroy in Canton, maybe even the Emperor in Peking, thinks they're not doing their bit. And that means nasty deaths for all. Very nasty deaths, sir.'

'But they'll never catch them like this.'

'Of course they won't, sir. How can they? They are well paid not to.'

This was, of course, exactly the same charade that took place off the south coast of England when clippers came in sight packed with tea. The revenue cutters arrived too late to intercept them. Captains and crews would not have it otherwise because their bribes were much larger than their pay.

Sea-Sprite dropped anchors at bow and stern near a row of curious vessels, half houseboat, half barge. These hulks lacked masts of any kind and so were without sails or rigging. Flat roofs had been built out over their decks and on these roofs stood lines of newly painted flower pots filled with bright flowers. These vessels were store ships, simply floating warehouses. Opium was kept aboard them and released as required elsewhere.

'Are we discharging all the cargo?' Douglas asked the captain.

'No, sir. About a quarter, just to pay our expenses. We will then go up the coast to test our fortune.'

'Under the British flag?'

'Never, sir, oh, no. The flag of Imperial Russia is what we fly today. It's not often they see a Russian vessel here with the white, blue and red flag of the Czar, so they'll not fire on it. But even if they did, I'm sure they would miss.'

Next day, they sailed north, and dropped anchor in the Bay of Swatow, off the port of Namoa. Here, as elsewhere along the coast, it was forbidden for any Red-Bristled Barbarian or Foreign Devil to land.

'How do you get the stuff ashore then?' Douglas asked naively.

'They come out for it. We don't need to go to them. And if I may give you some advice, sir, even if you have the chance of going ashore, do not take it. You would very likely end up a head shorter than you are. The mandarin who is coming out now to see us has to show *some* results, and he is never too careful whose head he cuts off. After all, he knows others will still want to do business – and because of his vigilance, he will still be here to treat with them.'

As the captain spoke, Douglas saw a flat-bottomed sampan, rather larger than the usual kind, being rowed energetically towards *Sea-Sprite*. In her stern, beneath the shade of a white silk umbrella held by a servant sat a fat man with a shining, contented face. He looked like a Buddha in a red silk robe, stretched at ease in an armchair. Servants waved delicately painted fans to keep him cool as the sampan drew alongside.

Sailors helped the mandarin to climb the gangway. He bowed stiffly to the captain and sat down thankfully on a chair placed on the after deck under a canvas sun awning. A steward had already set out on a side table a bottle of Madeira and two glasses, one for the mandarin, one for the captain, with a large box of Havana cigars. At once, the mandarin signalled to an orderly to take the cigars to the sampan. The steward poured out the wine. The mandarin sipped appreciatively, then addressed himself to the captain in English. He spoke in a high-pitched, sing-song accent.

'Why this ship flying flag I no-one seen before, anchoring off Namoa? Is not known all ships from all foreign shore can only anchor Cantonside?'

The captain nodded gravely.

'That is true, Your Excellency,' he agreed. 'I am indeed grateful to you for raising this matter, which I will endeavour to answer to Your Excellency's complete satisfaction. We are aware we can only land at Canton, but such is the age of our vessel and the feebleness of our steam engine, that the contrary strength of the winds of heaven have most regrettably blown us off our intended course. We seek therefore Your Excellency's gracious indulgence in granting us permission to remain here only long enough to take on fresh water and supplies of food.'

The mandarin nodded.

'It is our wish you should be so provided,' he replied magnanimously. 'His Majesty, our most illustrious Emperor, being ever desirous his extreme compassion is made manifest, even to least deserving of such benign generosity, cannot deny to you in distress from adverse winds, necessary means to continue voyage. But when supplied, you must not linger one hour, but put to sea at once.'

'That is understood, sir,' the captain assured him solemnly.

As the mandarin finished his glass of wine it was instantly refilled. The mandarin drank, and then spoke again, this time in a more relaxed tone of voice.

'How many chests foreign mud you carrying topside?'

'Two hundred and fifty, Your Excellency.'

'All for here?'

'If you so wish, Your Excellency.'

'I wish. Not safe venturing farther up coast. Not any way safe. Officers all new at Amoy, very keen to show sterling worth. Several foreign dealers already lost heads. Safest not go. You wish to land chests quickly now, here?'

'With Your Excellency's permission.'

'Ah,' said the mandarin, finishing the second glass, and holding it out to the steward. 'Permission, as you know, always depending on kindness.'

Douglas, who had watched this scene from the side of the deck, now tiptoed away. He did not wish to know the size of the bribes or how they would be paid. But as soon as the mandarin had been helped down the gangway, his face slightly redder than before, his bearers fanning him more vigorously, other little craft bumped alongside to collect bales of opium. Before the mandarin had reached shore, a string of small craft were following him, all piled high with wooden crates. Douglas watched them go, heavy in the water.

'A very good morning's business, sir,' the captain told him approvingly. 'A far better way of making money than working for it.'

There were other trips; many other trips. Trinity-Trio's two ships grew to four, five, six, the last four powered entirely by steam engines, driving screws not paddle wheels, and so totally independent of adverse winds and currents.

Douglas did not venture on these later voyages. He accepted that his partners could make huge fortunes quickly from the trade, but he was content with the less spectacular but still important profits of legitimate commerce.

All this time, he wondered what was happening about his family's estate in Scotland. Then he received a letter from the Writer to the Signet; it had been following him about for many months.

> I am sorry to have to inform you that the will of your late stepfather was proved in favour of Mr Claude Cartwright.
>
> I have examined the document. It was drawn up by Mr Pomfret's solicitor in London, Mr Macnamara of Lincoln's Inn, and witnessed by his clerk, Mr Ebenezer, and is totally in order. For this reason I have not previously communicated with you.
>
> You ask whether there is anything to be gained by your returning to Scotland. While it would be my personal pleasure to meet you again, and to take your instructions, I am bound to inform you, with regret, that I do not consider your presence here could influence the reversal of the terms of your late stepfather's will – unless, of course, you could prove it was a forgery, or could produce a later will in your favour. Both these suppositions seem unlikely.
>
> I personally feel sorrow at your situation, and I know that this sorrow is shared to an even greater extent by your former tenant farmers. Some have been driven from their crofts because they could not pay the increased rents demanded by the new owner. All are depressed beyond degree at the way he runs the estate and, in particular, at the disgusting and immoral manner in which it is said he conducts his private life.

Douglas had read and re-read the letter until he knew it by heart as an actor learns his part in a play. The Writer was correct; he could gain nothing by returning – yet. His best hope, as he had already decided, was to remain in the East until he had acquired a fortune. Then he would return and put his suspicions to the test.

With each voyage to sell mud, the danger of death to captains and crew increased. So did their earnings, for none were willing to risk ritual disembowelment, beheading, or public castration for a pittance. The Chinese Emperor had embarked upon a far fiercer and more ruthless extermination of the Forbidden Trade than his weaker predecessor had ever attempted. Tao Kuang, which translated in Chinese meant Glorious Rectitude, was of the family of Manchus who had ruled China for two hundred years. But time moves sluggishly as the Yellow River in the East, and many still felt he was some kind of interloper. He was not one of the Old Kings, and they pointed out that under his rule, China had suffered many grievous calamities; floods of the Yellow River, famines, droughts.

The most recent drought had also been the most severe. Thousands of head of cattle died of thirst; crops simply would not grow; rivers ran so low, they barely contained enough water to keep alive the smallest fish.

Not even the Emperor's public prayers in the Altar of Heaven, which stood between the Palace of Heavenly Purity and the Hall of the Blending of Heaven and Earth, had brought the divine blessing of rain. So what was the reason for this celestial displeasure? Why were the gods so angry? Surely the reason must be the continued and unwanted presence of Barbarians? The Portuguese had been the first Barbarians to trade with China three centuries earlier. They were overtaken by the Spanish, who had previously seized the Philippines, and in the course of trading between Mexico and Manila, received permission to call at the Portuguese enclave of Macao to replenish their ships.

The Dutch had been the next Barbarians to arrive. Barely had they subdued the island of Java, which they re-named Batavia, than their envoys were at the gates of the Forbidden City, saucily seeking the use of a port in China where they could trade. The Emperor naturally refused such an insolent request. He believed that the Dutch were simply pirates; in any case, he felt concern at allowing Barbarians from yet another country any concessions whatever.

He explained cautiously that while he accepted the willingness of the Dutch to pay homage to the Son of Heaven, and to admire the great and immeasurable advantages of everything Chinese, he did not wish to trade with them. Nor did he wish to receive their ambassador, and he certainly would not grant them the use of a port.

Hardly had the Dutch been repulsed, than the British landed, and then the Americans, known from their national flag as Flowery Flag Devils. The Emperor could not understand how men from these two countries spoke the same language, yet claimed to be two separate peoples from two distant islands.

Of the two he feared the British most; they were devious. He had made enquiries about them, and learned that the island from which they took their name was small, insignificant, and rain fell on it almost constantly. They were an industrious race, however, and like the Portuguese, they had sailed in tiny craft around the world to discover countries many times the size of their own – and then claim them for their Sovereign.

In attempts to buy the Emperor's favour, they presented him with brass cannons and telescopes through which a man could see ships miles away as clearly as if they were in harbour. They had even given him carriages, which he found amusing, because they were hung on springs, and everyone knew that carriages had no need for springs because Chinese conveyances did not possess them. Rather than have springs, the Emperor employed sixteen strong men to carry his palanquin, in which he sat on a golden throne, its legs carved in the shape of an eagle's feet.

And what an absurd anachronism it was for the Barbarians to set the coachman in front of the owner and actually physically above him, so that such an inferior hireling could literally look down on a totally superior person. But then, what could one expect from people who belched after drink and not to show their appreciation after food?

These lunacies might be tolerated, as one must stoically bear the unmannered habits of inferiors, so long as they could be turned to advantage, but the mud in which they traded so assiduously was seriously weakening the vigour and resolve of his troops, and sapping the energy of the country's labourers. Indeed, opium was corrupting his whole kingdom, and especially was it corrupting officials he had personally appointed to guard the outer approaches of the Heavenly Kingdom: the Viceroy in Canton, the Hoppo, the customs officers.

The Emperor knew from his spies that these men took huge bribes – but did they also bribe his spies? In whom could he trust? He felt alone, solitary and afraid. The only solution in such a sad situation was to strike fiercely without mercy.

In this, he would follow the matchless example of Chou-Hsin, a king of the Yu'i dynasty who, built like a bull, still possessed the lithe strength of a tiger. Chou-Hsin kept himself fit by fighting with wild beasts in a specially built arena, and by jousting with six of his strongest knights at the same time. Here, indeed, was a man to revere and emulate.

Such feats of strength were beyond the ability of Heaven's present Son, but he would show his resolve in another way; he would appoint a new Viceroy in Canton to deal with the utmost harshness with all Foreign Devils. His Imperial Edict was that all opium dealers would now be liable to instant death if discovered engaging in this illegal trade.

Word of this swiftly reached the three partners in Trinity-Trio. Ross was inclined to ignore the edict. There had been similar alarms before doubtless, there would be others. Jackson tended to agree with Ross over this, but in the meantime accepted Douglas's view that it would be prudent to extend their trading activities into other areas, other countries. They had amassed capital that could be put to work for them, profitably and with total safety. Now seemed a good moment to do so.

Trinity-Trio's legitimate trade had already prospered exceedingly. Douglas had built up a thriving business with scrap iron and cotton from Britain, and camphor and rattan from Malaya. Tea and silver went back in Trinity-Trio ships to Tilbury and Gravesend. And now a time had come when the three partners, meeting in their upstairs office in Hog Lane in Canton, decided to leave clerks in charge at their offices in Calcutta, Hong Kong and Canton while they followed their interests elsewhere.

For years they had met regularly in Hog Lane, and, like other Western merchants, had never considered the incongruity of having their company's office in an alley crammed with grog-shops and windowless shacks, where sailors from visiting ships were plied with blinding amounts of home-made liquor laced with sugar, tobacco juice and arsenic. These concoctions had the reputation of being ferociously aphrodisiac, and were therefore greatly in demand.

The sexual prowess of the Chinese was legendary, and Americans and Europeans did not wish to appear at a disadvantage. But when they were drunk, they were then either robbed or attacked. Sometimes these fights, often outside Trinity-Trio's office, would develop into a minor riot, with sailors wielding studded leather belts to defend themselves against Chinese armed with whips and poles.

Drunken shouts and curses and cries of pain, the constant beating of gongs, the crack and swish of fireworks and rockets had become so much a part of the partners' lives over the years they had been here, that they barely noticed them. Now, they did, and it was time to go their separate ways. They had exhausted their Eastern experience.

Douglas planned to take ship from Calcutta for Gravesend, and then to travel north to Scotland. He was determined to win back his estate – even if he had to buy it at whatever inflated price Claude Cartwright might demand.

Jackson wished to start a medical practice in Calcutta. This was now a city of great palaces, and he would not lack for enormously wealthy patients, European and Indian. He had ordered supplies of crystals to manufacture ether, and the latest anaesthetic equipment from America which would be waiting for him in the company's godown.

Ross wished to return to the United States; he had been away for too long. He still called that country home, although he had not lived there since boyhood, and he had no surviving relations. He would discover whether Trinity-Trio could branch out into new business ventures in the States.

There were all manner of enterprises that could present themselves to a sea captain. He knew how a fellow American, Captain George Busch, had once sailed from Port Maria in Jamaica to Boston with bananas as ballast. On the trip north, the green bananas ripened. He made a small profit on selling them – a point speedily taken by another seafarer, Captain Lorenzo Dow Baker, who shipped 1,450 stems to Boston and made a clear $2,000 profit. Dow Baker realised the potential of this totally new trade, and organised locals in Jamaica to plant bananas and collect them. This one-man enterprise had become the Boston Fruit Company, registering prodigious profits. The wily captain did not sail his ships back empty from Boston to Jamaica. He advertised berths for rich American tourists who wanted to winter in a warm climate – and even built a hotel, the Titchfield in Port Antonio, to accommodate them.

But first Ross had some business of a most private nature to transact in Calcutta. So, leaving everything in the hands of their Chinese clerks, Ross and Douglas set sail in *Coromandel* for Calcutta. Jackson, aboard *Sea-Sprite*, planned to follow by way of Macao.

The three men had arrived unknown and without money. They were leaving with a reputation as successful merchants and men of means. They had sailed East with dreams of wealth. They were going back West with fortunes. Money was better than dreams.

Macao

Jackson sat beneath a scrubbed canvas awning on *Sea-Sprite*'s afterdeck off Macao, smoking a Havana. This had been a Portuguese colony since the sixteenth century and originally named by them Cidade do Santo Nome de Deos en China – the City of the Holy Name of God in China. It was still referred to as the Holy City, but now ironically: gambling houses and whorehouses greatly outnumbered its cathedral and four parish churches.

Jackson always found something appealing and forlorn about its appearance; especially that of the forts, once proud and impregnable, now old, run down. A single shell from a modern gun could demolish every one, but when built they were intended to last forever, part of a world wide Portuguese empire that extended from Brazil in the West to China in the East.

Then the British had challenged Portuguese claims, and now the Union Jack flew in all corners of the globe, so that when the sun sank over one British possession, it was rising on another. For this reason, the flag was always lowered at dusk: the sun could never be allowed to set on the flag or, by inference, the Empire.

But one day, not in Jackson's lifetime, perhaps, he knew that other nations would challenge British authority, which would dwindle in importance, like the forts in Macao. Which country would then take its place? The thought often concerned Jackson; it seemed somehow bound up with the fortunes of Trinity-Trio. Who would run the company when its founders retired – or died?

Along the Praya Grande, the colony's main thoroughfare, past great houses built in the Portuguese style with florid cherubs and carved stone pineapples on gate posts, Chinese servants pushed their masters in huge wheelbarrows, each barrow richly painted, carved and ornamented in keeping with its owner's status.

High-stepping horses, reminding Jackson of London hackney ponies, overtook them, pulling open carriages. Reclining on brocaded seats beneath silk parasols, pretty women pretended to ignore each other but mentally assessed the prices of the clothes and equipages of their acquaintances as they all bowled along to enjoy coffee and gossip with other wives and mistresses.

A faint, tentative cough behind Jackson interrupted his musings. A young Chinese man was standing only feet away, head bowed in respect.

'What do you want?' Jackson asked him roughly. The ship's captain dealt with all matters regarding loading and unloading; he did not wish to become involved with such boring details. The man raised his head.

'Forgive this intrusion, sir,' he said in English. 'My name is Kuan Chung. I have come to ask a favour of the only European I know who may even consider granting it.'

'You speak our language extremely well,' said Jackson suspiciously.

'I have the benefit of knowing a Scottish missionary.'

'There could not have been many about when you were young,' replied Jackson; the man was in his late twenties.

'When one craves a drink of water, sir, a single glass suffices. One does not require a lake to slake an individual thirst.'

'Well put,' Jackson agreed. 'And what is the favour you think I can grant?'

'To introduce myself – I am, sir, a physician. I wish to marry a young girl related to the Manchus, the royal family. It is the tradition, as you may know, that all ladies of high birth must have their feet bound.'

'I do know. As a physician myself, I deplore that custom.'

'I agree, sir, but some in China also think that the convention of encompassing the bodies of young ladies with stays and strait-lacing and other unnecessarily tight constrictions, to the extent that they sometimes faint and have to be revived with smelling salts, is also not in the best interests of their health.'

'I accept that,' replied Jackson. 'But what is this favour you mention?' These Chinese took the devil of a time to come to the point; although he had spent years in the East, he still found this irritating.

'I wish that my future wife may be excused the painful and crippling necessity of having her feet bound.'

'But how can I possibly help you there? Surely that is a matter between you and her family?'

'I wish it were so simple. The only way she can avoid what we both consider a humiliation is to leave China.'

'And cannot she do that?'

'On her own, it would be unthinkable. Even if she were my wife, we would still have to leave illicitly. I am therefore asking for the indulgence of secret passage in your ship. I will pay for this, of course, and it does not matter how lowly the quarters may be, we will welcome them with infinite gratitude.'

'I see. We are bound for Calcutta. When would you wish to leave?'

'Whenever it should be convenient to you, sir.'

Jackson drew on his cigar, eyes half closed against the sun and smoke, trying to make up his mind. He rather took to the fellow. This doctor wished to escape from the East by ship just as, so many years earlier, Jackson himself had escaped by ship from the West. Events were about to repeat themselves. He took out his penny, tossed it three times; two heads out of three.

'I will take you,' he told him. 'But, tell me, why is it essential for ladies of high social standing to have their feet bound?'

'Usually, it is done in childhood, but for various reasons my future wife most fortunately escaped this. When the feet of a young girl are bound, the toes and the muscles in the feet can never grow to their full strength. Then she cannot walk properly and requires maidservants to help her because, being of low and inferior birth, their feet are free – a fact that separates our social classes most effectively.

'Women who cannot walk unaided therefore become totally subject to their husbands – a situation that many men prefer. It gives them a sense of superiority they might not otherwise possess.

'Next, men are sexually attracted towards women with small feet, just as, I understand, in the West, there is a liking for women with large breasts and narrow waists.'

Jackson nodded his understanding. *Chacun à son goût.*

'Tomorrow evening then, after dusk, come here and I will place two cabins at your disposal.'

'I assure you of my lasting gratitude, sir. How much are we in your debt, in money?'

'In money, nothing. As for payment in kind, I would like to discuss the healing arts of China. I wish to know whether I could ever practise them myself.'

So it came about that on the first evening of their journey West, Kuan Chung and Jackson sat on canvas chairs on the afterdeck. Kuan's wife-to-be stayed below in her cabin; it was explained she was shy and an indifferent sailor.

'I understand that, in the West, a patient in need of surgery can breathe in some gas or vapour that makes them fall asleep,' said the Chinese physician. 'Then a surgeon can literally cut off their arm or a leg without them feeling pain. I find that difficult to believe.'

'Nevertheless, it is true,' Jackson replied.

'I can carry out operations with equal lack of discomfort to the patient – simply by pricking their skin with two or three gold needles, so fine they are little thicker than a hair.'

'Now *I* find *that* difficult to accept,' Jackson replied, and then paused before he became too dogmatic in his disbelief. He remembered, in his student days, reading in *The Lancet* how a general practitioner, one Dr John Tweedale of Lyme Regis on the Dorset coast, had successfully treated a patient suffering from anarsarca, more commonly known as dropsy, by this extraordinary means.

At the Royal Infirmary in Edinburgh, other experiments with golden needles had produced remarkable cures, and a Dr John Elliotson reported that in St Thomas's Hospital in London, he had helped nearly one thousand patients suffering from rheumatism by using similar needles. Of course, other physicians had immediately ridiculed these claims. One had written sarcastically: 'I refuse to have my "seat of honour" used as a pin cushion.'

Jackson knew that medical men were often strongly resistant to change. But all life was subject to constant change, as day turned to night, and winter followed the longest, hottest summer. It was foolish to react in such a rigid manner.

Only a few years previously, who could have ever seriously believed that houses, streets, even cities, would soon be lit not by gas but by filament bulbs in which a current of electricity passed through a fine wire which glowed with such heat that each globe became a tiny blazing sun?

Jackson personally believed that the wonders of electricity and the electric telegraph, which could transmit a message across a continent in the time it took to write these messages, were only the beginning of far greater discoveries. So he nodded for his guest to continue.

'The practice of healing with needles is at least five thousand years old,' Kuan went on. 'Physicians then, who were also high priests, discovered the treatment largely by chance. Those were times of many wars, and after a battle, they found that a wounded soldier would frequently tell them how another ailment in a different part of his body had also been cured – without any treatment whatever.

'For example, after binding up a sword wound in a soldier's leg, the patient could mention that he had suffered severe headaches from boyhood, but after being wounded, these headaches had totally disappeared.

'By a long process of calculation and the diligent study of many such cases, they concluded that secondary benefits could follow a wound, and the severity of the original wound was unimportant. What mattered was where the wound was in relation to any other ailment that might have previously affected the patient.

'They therefore began to treat civilian patients suffering, for example, from backache, by deliberately inflicting a very slight wound in their knee. They used fishbones at first, or bamboos sharpened and filed to a point, and then gold needles, because these can be used again and again.

'Eventually, they calculated that the human body contains twelve meridians, like the lines of latitude or longitude you in the West draw on an atlas or globe. Where these meridians crossed were points which could relieve pain elsewhere in the body if pricked gently with a needle. They called this art acupuncture which, you will doubtless know, comes from an even older Latin word, *acus*, meaning a needle, and *punctura*, meaning a hole.

'Our priests were not alone in making this discovery, of course. Men in all fields of learning and discovery around the world will often reach identical conclusions at the same time, even though they have not heard of each other's work.

'Egyptian doctors, and medical men in South America and Africa, discovered the powers of the needles. In Brazil, physicians would fire tiny sharpened arrows from blowpipes at specific parts of the patient's body. Bantu natives in Southern Africa would scratch the same points with a sharpened knife – in both cases, with encouraging results.

'Our Yellow Emperor became so convinced that acupuncture was the best means of curing diseases that he decreed that all other medical teaching should cease throughout China. Every case in which acupuncture had cured a patient was then recorded, so that a huge accumulation of histories was compiled.

'In the Sun Dynasty, the Emperor Wei Te went even further. He decreed that every doctor must possess a bronze cast of the human body in his consulting room. On this cast each acupuncture point was clearly marked.'

'We have much the same idea in the West,' Jackson told him. 'Charts on the walls of our hospitals and surgeries show the body's muscles and sinews and veins and arteries.'

'You see, sir,' said Kuan Chung, 'East and West are like two halves of a globe. Together, they can make a whole. I think we could possibly learn much from each other.'

At that moment, there came a warning shout from the lookout in the crow's nest: 'Man overboard!'

Jackson and Kuan ran to the rail. The ship heeled as the captain put her about; twenty yards out, they could see a sailor threshing feebly in the water. Another man dived into the sea, carrying a thin line. He swam to his companion with strong vigorous strokes, slipped the line around his body, and then others pulled them both aboard. The captain came down from the bridge to Jackson and presented his compliments.

'I fear he is badly injured, sir. If you could look at him in a medical way, I would greatly appreciate it.'

Jackson and Kuan Chung followed the captain on to the main deck where the sailor lay in a pool of water, the rope still around his waist. He appeared conscious and was moaning slightly.

'He hit his back a mighty blow on the rail as he fell, sir,' a sailor explained.

Jackson knelt down by the man's side, and gently rolled up his shirt. He had clearly dislocated his back. When he attempted to set this the pain would be unendurable and Jackson had no ether aboard ship. The only crude soporific available was rum.

'A pint of rum and a mug,' Jackson ordered. A sailor raced off to fetch them.

'If you give him alcohol, doctor,' said Kuan hesitantly, 'might not his later situation be worse than his present?'

'Then what do you propose?'

'My golden needles.'

'Will they work?'

'If they do not, you still have your rum.'

As he spoke, Kuan knelt down beside the injured man, took out a small leather pouch from his shirt pocket, and opened it. Jackson saw four slender gold needles inside, with their points embedded in a piece of cork. Kuan selected one, removed the man's right boot and his sock, and stuck the tip of the needle gently beneath the skin above his ankle. It hung, trembling, like a tiny barb. Then he pressed in a second needle behind the sailor's right ear, a third above his left eye. The sailor gave a groan, and relaxed as though deeply asleep.

'Bloody magic,' said another sailor in amazement. 'The Chink's put him out.'

'There, sir, I have done my part,' said Kuan. 'When you are ready, you may carry on with your treatment.'

Jackson had finished by the time the sailor returned with the rum.

'You are too late with that,' he told him. 'Fall in with two other men and carry this fellow on a door or a board to his quarters.'

'And put him in his hammock, sir?'

'No. It will be impossible for him to sleep in that for some time. Make up a bed for him on the floor – and keep the rum for yourselves.'

He waited while they carried away the injured sailor, and then turned to Kuan.

'You have convinced me. But if I had not seen it myself, I simply would not have believed it.'

'If I may quote your Holy Book, Dr Jackson, there is a story about a disciple called Doubting Thomas, because he would not believe until he saw. Now you have seen, I am honoured that you can believe.'

As Kuan spoke, Jackson heard a soft footstep behind him. He turned. A Chinese girl was standing there, smiling hesitantly at both men. She was in her early teens, with eyes like almonds and skin soft as morning mist. She was quite simply the loveliest and most alluring creature Jackson had ever seen. He was so entranced that he barely heard Kuan introduce her proudly.

'This is the girl I will marry – T'a Ki. Can you wonder why I wish to spare her the pain and humiliation of having her feet bound?'

Jackson shook his head. He could not find words to say what was in his heart, nor could he trust himself to speak at all.

No matter the cost in money, honour or friendship, he knew he could never rest until T'a Ki was his – and his alone.

Jackson invited them both to dine with him, and afterwards Kuan went up on deck to check the ship's progress by the stars, or so he said. Jackson and the girl, T'a Ki, whose name, she bashfully explained, meant Heavenly Beauty, stayed talking in his day cabin.

To the doctor's surprise and delight, she spoke almost perfect English and her voice was gentle and well-modulated. She sat modestly, eyes downcast, hands folded in her lap. They talked first of her wish to avoid having her feet bound. She explained that these bindings, often of splendid linen, would extend from the feet up to mid calf. They were known as Golden Lilies.

A woman might allow her lover – or even her husband – to strip h of all her clothes, she explained with a smile, but always she would keep on these leggings. In erotic prints and manuals of sexual behaviour, known as Pillow Books, which circulated among the rich and the high born, showing innumerable positions involving two, three or even more partners in the sexual act, the women always wore their Golden Lilies.

If a man met a young woman for the first time and wished to express his feelings – and intentions – the easiest and most direct way to inform her that he wished to make love was to touch them, as if by accident.

T'a Ki explained shyly that such a move must be made subtly. The man might drop a snuffbox or a pen on the floor when seated near the woman at some social gathering. As he bent down to retrieve it, the back of his hand could brush gently against the bindings. If he was very bold, he might take the opportunity to whisper that he wanted to walk between the Golden Lilies.

But, as Kuan had already told Jackson, the real value of the Lilies was that they ensured that the wearer, whether wife or concubine, stayed at home. Since she could not walk without assistance, she could not leave of her own volition to meet a lover, and her fidelity was therefore assured. After all, T'a Ki explained with a diffident smile, 'Not every husband has the abilities of the great Chou-Hsin.'

'And what set him apart?'

'His prowess as a lover. He was Emperor of my country hundreds of years ago. His physician, Fang-nei-pu, told him that to live for a hundred years, Chou-Hsin should pleasure ten women every night, always without losing a single drop of his Vital Essence.'

'And could he?'

'For a time, yes, so it is said. Then his brave Warrior Stem refused to rise and assault the Jade Gate, even when he was with his favourite concubine, well-versed in all the arts of love. So the Emperor ordered his physician to be beheaded for prescribing false treatment.'

'As a physician, I sympathise with Dr Fang-nei-pu,' said Jackson drily. 'And what was the concubine's name?'

'T'a Ki. I was named after her.'

T'a Ki was the first Chinese woman with whom Jackson had ever had a serious conversation, because despite his years in the East, he still knew little of the vernacular tongue, and relied on interpreters. Now T'a Ki began to teach him her language.

Days passed and Jackson became obsessed by her, infatuated by her gentle charm and the seeming contradiction between her outspokenness on the subject of sexuality and her personal reticence. He would allow her the rare privilege of joining the captain on the bridge to see how the vessel was controlled. Kuan Chung appeared to feel that it was important for T'a Ki to be on the friendliest terms with the man on whom they both relied for their passage, and would discreetly remain in the background. He courteously refused all invitations to join them.

It was for Dr Jackson but a short step from conversations on sexual matters to practising the arts of which they spoke. Jackson was delighted, but secretly surprised that T'a Ki displayed no reluctance. It was as though she was without loyalty to the man she was about to marry – or was this an example of Chinese liberality?

He felt guilty, but this did not prevent him from making love to her in his cabin several times a day. And all the while, he remained oblivious to the fact that the crew realised what was happening. As with many men, he thought that since no-one remarked to him personally on his behaviour, he was above and beyond suspicion.

Because Kuan Chung did not speak of it, and because his face presented its customary inscrutability, Jackson assumed that he also had no inkling of the situation. But then, three days out of Calcutta, Jackson suddenly learned the truth.

For most of that afternoon and evening, he and T'a Ki had made love in the different positions for which she taught him the Chinese names: Two Swallows with a Swift Heart; Leaping White Tigress; Making Fire behind the Mountain.

Later, he walked back with her across the deserted deck, where masts and starboard rail were silhouetted against fading moon and silver sea. The ship dipped and rose slowly, and her timbers creaked in the rhythm of all vessels. Her engine pounded reassuringly like an iron heart. They reached the companionway that led to the girl's cabin, and T'a Ki went down the wooden steps.

Jackson planned to take another turn on deck on his own, to enjoy a cigar and then to sleep the deep untroubled slumber of total relaxation. As he walked, he heard a faint movement behind him, a kind of scutter, as an animal might make with its claws on the deck. He turned. Kuan Chung was standing with his back against the port rail.

'I did not see you,' said Jackson, wondering whether Kuan Chung had followed him, whether he had watched him kiss T'a Ki and smooth her small firm breasts with both hands, as had become his custom before she went to her own cabin.

'I have seen you,' Kuan replied quietly. 'I have also seen the light o longing and of love in T'a Ki's eyes, as in yours. I have watched you together. I have seen you reach out and touch her tenderly, your hand o her shoulder, while you would both stand by the rail and watch flying fish jump like knife blades in the sea. And what I saw struck sharpe knives of misery and dismay in my heart.'

'Please,' said Jackson earnestly, 'you are becoming overwrought. I ar fond of your fiancée, as I am fond of you. I look on you both not just passengers here but as my friends. There is nothing more in my relationship with T'a Ki than friendship.'

Even as he lied, the words sounded hollow as the beating of an empty drum. Kuan shook his head.

'I have tried to ignore what I have seen, doctor, because T'a Ki and I owe so much to you. I have told myself that when ships reach land, such infatuations die, as wind dies in the sails of every vessel at anchor, as the hottest boiler cools and the engines are still. But I know in my innermost heart that in this instance it will not be so. The wind may not read, but I can read the signs written on it. Her feelings will not die when we reach harbour.

'She was my woman, betrothed to me. For her, and for what I believed was her love returned, I left the land of my ancestors, to which now I will never be able to return.

'I willingly committed myself to life in a strange and alien country with a black-skinned, unknown people, speaking a tongue that is not mine. I was willing to learn their ways and their speech, and to practise my medicine with them. But all this was dependent on T'a Ki being with me. We would share our lives and our future, together.

'Now I know that we will not do these things. Now I cannot go back, and I have no heart or wish to go on alone. It is meet that I leave life here, where the waters are neutral, neither belonging to my country nor to the country to which I had wished to sail. I will join the spirits of my ancestors, and perhaps with them I will find the fulfilment and content which I can never now enjoy in this world.'

Kuan Chung moved away from the rail. By moonlight, Jackson saw that he had bound his wrists together. Another rope was tied tightly around his ankles. This would account for the odd scraping sound Jackson had heard. Kuan could only shuffle half a pace at a time.

'I tell you, Kuan Chung, you are wrong,' Jackson answered him hoarsely. 'Quite wrong.'

He did not recognise his own voice, rough as a rasp, taut with emotion. He approached Kuan as though the nearer he was, the greater conviction his words would carry.

'Stand back from me,' said Kuan Chung sharply. 'At least let me have dignity in my departing, without false excuses that deceive neither of us.'

Kuan Chung turned to face the moon. In its light, Jackson could see tears glisten on his face.'

'I assure you . . .' he began seriously. He did not finish the sentence, because with one lithe movement, Kuan Chung placed his elbows on the rail, swung his feet up and was over the side. Jackson rushed to the rail and peered down at the shimmering sea. A wide rim of foam framed the ship's hull, and now, farther out, a white phosphorescent circle began to spread. At its centre, he could make out Kuan Chung's head and shoulders.

'Man overboard!' Jackson shouted. 'Overboard, I say!'

The lookout in the crow's nest took up the cry.

'Overboard! Man overboard! Portside!'

The night was instantly loud with shouted orders. The beat of the engine eased and *Sea-Sprite* turned to port. A vast white phosphorescence churned in the sea as she came around. By the time *Sea-Sprite* had turned, however, there was no sign of Kuan Chung. Boats were lowered and sailors searched the area, but they all came back without him.

Jackson went down to T'a Ki's cabin and tapped on the door. She opened it still dressed, although she had left him at least an hour previously.

He said gravely: 'I have to tell you something terrible has happened.'

'I know,' she replied. 'I felt it within me. It is Kuan. He is dead.'

'He jumped over the side,' said Jackson. 'He knew about us.'

'Yes,' she said. 'He must have seen his future – perhaps our future – in the stars. He used to stay up on deck at night reading them like a book. He said they told him the story of his life: when it began, when it would end.'

She opened the door wider. Jackson went into her cabin. An oil lamp glowed above a small dressing table. Through the open circular porthole, the gleaming sea stretched towards a dying moon. Her scent was sweet as wild honey on a summer night.

'I am terribly sorry,' he said, conscious of the total inadequacy of his words.

'What is meant to be must be,' T'a Ki replied philosophically. 'We cannot alter what is decided long before we are born.'

'Who decides it?' Jackson asked, already fondling her, his mouth seeking hers.

'As the Lord Buddha said: "From affection comes grief. From affection comes fear. Whoever is free from affection knows neither grief nor fear." And Kuan was never free from grief for his homeland, or fear that he would lose me.

'I did not feel so deeply about him, although I tried. I simply wished to escape being deformed, being made into a cripple. He was my means of escape, the key to my freedom. I will pray for him – and for myself.'

'Pray for me, too,' said Jackson. T'a Ki's candid admission sharpened his desire, as spice can heighten the flavour of the richest dish. He had her then and stayed with her for the short time remaining until dawn lit the cabin with the risen sun.

Next day, Jackson realised with horror and dismay that everyone aboard ship appeared to believe that Kuan Chung had deliberately killed himself because he had learned the doctor was sleeping with the woman he wished to marry. Perhaps the lookout had heard them talking, or the officer of the watch, or some other unseen person on deck, waiting in the dark shadows, had noticed them. Possibly they had known, or suspected, his feelings for T'a Ki all along.

Jackson felt a wave of condemnation, solid as a wall, rise against him. No-one said anything to him directly, of course; they did not dare to do so, because Jackson was rich and powerful. There was always one law for the very rich and another for the poor. The dispossessed might have to accept this, but they strongly resented it – and hated people like Jackson who could apparently make their own rules, and do exactly as they pleased because they had the wealth to crush all opposition.

For the second time since Jackson had sailed east, he felt uneasy. The first occasion had been when he had accepted Ross's arrangement that three innocent men should die in the place of the partners. That had been easier to explain away, but for what had happened now there was only one explanation: Jackson's scandalous behaviour had caused a young brother physician to take his own life.

Perthshire

Long Glen Farmhouse, a single-storey stone building with a grey slate roof, stood at the head of the glen from which it took its name.

Like many small farmhouses in the district, it was stoutly built and contained three rooms; two bedrooms and a large kitchen with an open fire. Rush mats covered stone-flagged floors. The plain wooden chairs in the kitchen had been made by the farmer, Stewart MacDuff.

On winter evenings, during the first few years after Jane Pomfret sailed for Calcutta, the farmer, with his wife and their son, Alastair, and Fiona, who had been boarded with them, would sit together around the fire by the mellow light of two oil lamps.

Sometimes, Mrs MacDuff would read aloud to the children from a book of Bible stories, or from a collection of fairy tales about princes and princesses, with knights in silver armour who rode white chargers – not at all the type of horse her husband used on the farm to pull the plough or put between the shafts of their cart to go to Perth.

Fiona would sit on a wooden stool MacDuff had made especially for her, because she was the smallest, and although she was accepted into the family, somehow she never felt one of them.

Looking into the heart of the fire, into red-hot caverns made by glowing blocks of peat and logs burned hollow, Fiona would imagine she could see the tesselated towers of a fairytale castle, or an enchanted forest; even the face of a handsome prince come to claim her.

This had been the homely, comfortable evening routine until Alastair had gone to work at Coupar Castle. His father had been reluctant to see him go, because he was strong for his sixteen years, and especially useful at lambing time and with the sheep in winter. But Claude Cartwright had paid them an unexpected visit one morning, and asked for the boy. As the laird, his wish was every tenant's command.

Fiona, curtseying to him, following the custom of Mrs MacDuff, had been surprised by Cartwright's soft, almost lisping voice and the petulant way in which he impatiently tapped the ground with the toe of his fancy, London-made shoe when MacDuff argued that he could ill afford to lose his son.

'It's promotion, my man,' Cartwright reminded him sharply.

Another young man with him, whose face was painted in a way that recalled a clown Fiona had once seen in a travelling circus, sniggered at this, and walked a few mincing steps to one side, swaying his plump bottom. Fiona did not know whether to laugh at him or to express surprise: was he being deliberately comic, like the clown? She was about to ask him, and then, catching Mrs MacDuff's eye and seeing the sudden desperate shake of her head, Fiona said nothing and quickly suppressed her smile.

That had been nearly a year ago, and since then Alastair had only come back to the farmhouse on a few occasions. Each time he called, he appeared more like a stranger than the familiar son of the house. He had grown withdrawn, his face pale and no longer ruddy-cheeked; he looked as though he breathed too little fresh air and ate too little fresh food. He did not laugh and joke or whittle tiny heads with his knife from cherrystones for Fiona, and offer to play hide-and-seek.

Several times after his visits, Fiona had come across his parents talking solemnly together, but when they saw her, they immediately changed the subject. She would leave the room uneasily, hoping they had not been discussing her, hoping that Alastair would return and then everything would be as it had been. But he had not returned and now, when the MacDuffs sat with her, looking into the fire, there was no reading of fairy stories or from the Bible. It was as though both had experienced a sorrow too great to express. Gloom and despair hung like a thick mountain fog over the farmhouse.

'Who is Mr Cartwright?' Fiona asked them once, really trying to mak conversation; she thought it so depressing to sit in silence, night after night.

'A swine,' replied MacDuff shortly. 'No, I must correct myself. No beast, not even the lowest hog, would behave as he has behaved.'

'You must not speak like that in front of the bairn,' his wife said nervously.

'I'll speak as I please in my own house.'

'But it's not our own house. It's Cartwright's.'

'Would he put us out?' asked Fiona anxiously.

'He might,' said MacDuff. 'He could. If he wanted to.'

'That won't happen, child,' Mrs MacDuff answered Fiona wearily. 'Not now, it won't happen.'

But she added in a whisper, almost to herself, 'I hope I am right. Dear God, please do not let that ever happen to us.'

That night, Fiona went into her room, undressed for bed, said her prayers, and then opened the threadbare curtains and looked out across the glen. Heather that by day lay across the hills like a purple robe was now drenched with moonlight. She could see a stag move gracefully across the skyline, confident that no-one would hunt it at such an hour. The moon touched the granite towers of the castle with silver; lights glowed like jewels from a dozen windows. Mr Cartwright must be having one of his parties, with guests all the way from London.

Fiona never tired of looking at the castle, especially from this aspect. She liked it equally when the old building basked in a mellow afternoon glow of sunshine, or when spears of rain poured down and made the granite walls glitter like glass.

Sometimes, during the day, after school, she would stand at the castle gates and look up the long drive, careful always to bow or curtsey if Mr Cartwright came by in his carriage, or the new, bright red phaeton he had recently bought.

MacDuff had told her how all the carriages on the estate, even pony carts and farm carts, used to be painted in the dark green livery of the Douglas clan when old Mr Douglas was alive. Now this upstart fop from London had ordered them to be repainted in garish colours – bright red, yellow, blue, gold – quite out of keeping with Scottish countryside tradition.

This was wrong, in some way she did not really understand. She also sensed that Cartwright was somehow wrong and did not belong here. She had heard MacDuff, talking to his wife, refer to him as effeminate, a pansy. But surely a pansy was a flower? Perhaps she had misheard the word?

She knew, too, that the MacDuffs were not her real father and mother, and she also shared another secret with them: her hair was not really blonde. Mrs MacDuff insisted she should wash it every week with a special bleaching powder she bought from the apothecary in Perth.

'I like a girl to have fair hair,' she would say in explanation. But somehow this did not ring true. Mrs MacDuff had dark hair herself, as did her husband and Alastair. Secretly, Fiona wished her hair was not as pale as corn, but darker and more determinate in colour. She liked vivid colours, and people who were positive in their approach – like the tinkers who called to sell pots and pans, or to sharpen knives, always with a joke and a wink, and sometimes a sweetie wrapped in paper, presented to her with all the panache of a rich and precious gift.

Fiona did not like being blonde because in some strange, inexplicable way the colour seemed to symbolise Cartwright and his friends. It was weak, a colour without character.

'What *did* my father do?' she sometimes asked Mrs MacDuff when they were on their own.

'He was a gentleman. They don't *do* things, gentlemen. They don't need to work. They just have money without it.'

'And my mother?'

'A beautiful lady. She left for India shortly after you were born. That is why you came to us. Until she returns, that is.'

'*Is* she coming back?'

'Oh, certainly. She will be back.'

'She has been away a long time. Do you have an address in India for her?'

'Well, no, I haven't, child. India is a very big country and she is probably moving about a lot.'

'Why? What is she doing?'

'Seeing people,' Mrs MacDuff replied vaguely. 'She had business interests.'

'What sort of business? Who with?'

'Ah, don't you be bothering your pretty head with questions like that, Fiona. When she comes back, you will be the very first person she comes to see, mark my words. After all, she specially asked us to look after you. She gave us enough money to buy you clothes and food, and now you are really one of us. Well, *almost*, aren't you?'

'Almost' was a word Fiona did not like. She wanted to belong totally, completely, not to be *almost* anyone's girl. When she grew up, if her mother still had not returned, she would make sure she never again *almost* belonged to anyone, however nice they seemed. She would belong to herself. Totally.

Barrackpore

Douglas met Jackson as he came down the gangway when *Sea-Sprite* docked in Calcutta. *Coromandel II* had arrived only hours previously, and a crowd of itinerant vendors, who had watched both vessels approach, now gathered around the partners.

One touted a house to rent; another, a carriage for hire. So many petitions, prayers, professional cards were thrust into their hands from all sides that it was only when they reached the house Jackson originally rented from Elijah Potiphar, and which he had long since bought, that Douglas had the opportunity to examine them all.

Most, he threw away. Several, he handed to his Indian clerk to keep for possible future use. One sealed envelope, marked with the crest of the 113th Regiment of Foot, was addressed in a spidery hand using cheap ink to 'Mr A Douglas'. He opened it, wondering with mild curiosity who from the regiment had bothered to keep in touch with him.

Inside, was a single sheet of paper. On this was written, in capital letters, presumably by a professional letterwriter in the bazaar employed by someone unable to write, MRS JANE POMFRET IS AT INVERNESS HOUSE, BARRACKPORE. There was no signature, no date. He turned it over. On the back were three more words: SHE HAS LETTERS.

Has she? he thought. To him? From whom? It was a long journey to make from Perthshire to Barrackpore simply to bring him letters – if that was Jane's only reason for coming to India. He turned to Jackson.

'According to this note, the woman my stepfather married has turned up in Barrackpore. I want to see her so I will arrange transport. If you are free, we can leave tomorrow.'

So it came about that, two days later, Douglas and Jackson called at Jane Pomfret's house. Douglas presented his card. Jane came out on to the porch, her face radiant.

'How *did* you know I was here?' she asked delightedly. 'No-one had any address for you.'

'This note was given to me in Calcutta,' he explained. 'So someone knew where to find me.'

Jane turned the sheet of paper over.

'I have never seen this before,' she said in amazement. 'But whoever sent must have known you were coming back. Could they not have told me?'

'Questions, questions,' said Douglas easily. 'Now, what about these letters?'

Jane went into the house and returned with two letters.

Douglas and Jackson sat down on the verandah. A bearer brought them whisky and seltzer water, while Douglas read then carefully folded the letters, finally putting each one back in its own envelope.

'Do you know what they contain?' he asked Jane.

'The Writer to the Signet told me he was writing to introduce me,' she admitted.

'That is one of them,' said Douglas. 'But do you know what the other is about?'

'I have no idea.'

'It is from another lawyer, a Mr Macnamara in Lincoln's Inn, London, with extracts from a will left by your late husband, my late stepfather. You know, I suppose, that the whole estate, which has been in my family for centuries, was left to Claude Cartwright?'

'Not him, surely?' cried Jane hoarsely. 'It cannot be!'

Her face was white with horror and disbelief. She had suddenly aged: he was looking at an old woman with a pinched mouth and sunken cheeks. For a moment, he thought she would collapse, and then she rallied.

'All this has happened since I left,' she went on. 'Look at the date. My daughter was a baby when I left. Now she is a child.'

'Your daughter?'

'You did not know? Fiona was born after my husband died. I have boarded her with people in the village, the MacDuffs.'

'I did not even know my stepfather had sired a child. To be blunt, I did not know he was capable of such an act of procreation.'

'Come, come,' said Jackson disapprovingly. 'That is an ungallant remark to make to a lady.'

'I do not feel in a very gallant mood,' retorted Douglas.

'Under the law, does not the son of the family inherit – or the widow?' Jackson asked him.

'I would assume so – unless, of course, there is another later will. As appears to be the case here.'

'I came out to India in the hope we could come to some accommodation together,' Jane explained. 'My late husband made a will in my favour – but he did not sign it. Now I just do not know what to believe or to think.'

Jane put her head in her hands and began to weep.

Douglas felt sorry for her. He reached out to comfort her. To his surprise, Jackson took his outstretched hand. He shook his hand warmingly, and held one finger to his lips for silence. Douglas sat back perplexed.

'If this will is genuine,' he said, 'then this fancy man Claude has inherited what I regard as my property. I find it difficult to believe that there is not some foul work here. It smells, doctor.'

As he spoke, a smell of death and decay, the stench of a rotting corpse, drifted across the verandah. He looked at Jackson enquiringly. Had he smelled this, too, or was he somehow imagining it? Strangely, the odour disappeared as quickly as it had arrived.

Jackson stood up, not meeting his gaze.

'We should leave, ma'am.'

'So soon?' asked Jane, looking at them in surprise. 'But Mr Douglas and I have much to discuss.'

'We will consider what this says, and perhaps seek a lawyer's opinion in Calcutta.'

As Douglas spoke, he heard a movement behind him. Captain Bushell was standing in the doorway.

'Ah,' he said. 'You have found us. Mrs Pomfret came all the way from England to meet you.'

'And met you first?'

The adjutant's plump face reddened somewhat.

'I am proud to say I have been of some slight assistance to her.'

'And I hope her presence has been of some assistance to you, sir,' said Douglas drily. 'I will bid you good day.'

'No hard feelings, are there?' asked the adjutant anxiously.

'About what?'

'About leaving the regiment in the way you did.'

'None,' Douglas assured him. 'I have made a new career.'

Jane and the adjutant watched their two visitors climb into their hired carriage and go down the drive. The adjutant sniffed the air. A peculiar odour, which he had never previously noticed in this house, offended him. Some damn' sweeper, who looked after the latrines, had probably been lazy in his duties. Wrinkling his nose in distaste, he followed Jane into the drawing room. A punkah creaked above their heads. They sat down on a settee.

Bushell felt unusually grateful for the seat. He had been feeling what he called 'under the weather', for some time. He lacked energy, felt depressed, nervous, ill at ease. He would awake in the night with a throat so swollen and constricted that breathing was difficult. The regimental medical officer told him it must be due to this accursed climate, this benighted country. He had probably caught one of the fevers that came and went like mists above a marsh.

He had served out here for too long, that was the real reason. In every other country where the British settled – Canada, Australia, New Zealand, South Africa – colonists *belonged*. The country of their choice became theirs, and they would live and eventually die there. Britain became the old country; their future lay with the country to which they had sailed.

India was the exception. Here, Europeans were not colonists but sojourners. They stayed for as few years as possible, made their money, and then, if they survived the climate, cholera, typhoid, plague and a dozen unnamed fevers, they returned to a cleaner, cooler land. Westerners could never belong here; they would always only be people of passage. Never could they become Indians as elsewhere they might have become Canadians or Australians or citizens of the Cape.

Bushell looked at Jane, who sat dabbing her eyes with a silk handkerchief. It seemed that she was suddenly older than she had appeared on his last visit. She looked unusually grave and unhappy. Perhaps, because he felt ill himself, he was seeing her through the eyes of a sick man? Or maybe she was disturbed at Douglas arriving unannounced. Could there have been something between them?

Bushell had to admit that in the time he had known Jane, he had come to like her as a person in so far as his cold, narrow spirit could like anyone, and he felt concerned in case she was sickening for something. She was not simply a woman to pleasure as and when and how he wished – Jane was a companion in a sense he had never thought a woman could be. This was the highest praise of which he was capable.

'Jane,' he said as tenderly as he could, 'what are your plans? Do you go back home to England?'

She shrugged her shoulders as though the decision was immaterial.

'I have no means, as you know,' she said simply. 'I wanted to see Alec about the matter of his inheritance. But apparently the whole estate has been left to someone else. If Alec pays my fare, I will return. But to what? To fight a law suit without money?

'And if I stay here – as I would like to do, with you – what is our future? There have been other women in your life before me, and when I grow older, there may well be others after me. For a widow in India, without private means and with a daughter at home to support, life will not be easy.'

For a moment, that very brief moment, Bushell considered proposing marriage to her, taking her in his arms and offering her comfort and freedom from financial worries for as long as she should live.

But his natural caution swiftly overwhelmed the instinct. He had never met her daughter, Fiona; he might not like the girl. He had never been at ease with other people's children – and why should he now complicate his life unnecessarily? Also, he had not been feeling well. Before he took such a serious decision, he should consult another doctor, perhaps this fellow, Jackson? Then, when he had received physic to restore his strength and energy, then he *might* propose to Jane Pomfret.

Having reached this decision not to decide, Bushell felt indescribable relief. He had not compromised himself, his fortune or his future. And Mrs Pomfret would still be here when he did decide what he meant to do – in his own best interests, of course. After all, where could she go without means – and who would want another man's leavings?

Dr Jackson lit a cheroot and stood thoughtfully at the window of his sitting room while Captain Bushell dressed in the adjoining bedroom.

He had given the adjutant a thorough examination. He had considered his symptoms and consulted the medical books he always carried with him. There was no doubt now about his diagnosis – but how to tell the patient? Bushell came back into the room with the false heartiness of a patient facing his doctor for a verdict on his health which he fears may be unfavourable.

'Sit down,' said Jackson. 'I have to give you some good news, and some that is not so good. First, you appear in good health for anybody who has lived as long as you have out in this climate. You have nothing to worry about in your general condition.'

He paused.

'What about my particular condition, doctor? The feebleness I feel so frequently?'

Jackson drew on his cheroot. Its end glowed red as he strove to find the least hurtful words.

'We are both men of the world, Captain,' he said at last, 'and there is no point in my beating about the bush. As a soldier, I am sure you would like the truth?'

Bushell's face tightened with concern.

'Is it *that* serious?'

'I am sorry to say that it is serious,' Jackson replied. 'I have made every test and examined every symptom in the hope that I could be wrong, but I must tell you, there is only one diagnosis. Bluntly, you are suffering from leprosy.'

'*Leprosy?* What the devil do you mean?'

'What I say.'

'But there's no cure for that!' Bushell cried in anguish.

'There is no cure in the end for all of us,' Jackson replied carefully. 'Death is the cure for all diseases.'

'But how could I catch leprosy? There's no-one on this station suffering from it, I'll swear.'

'Then you would swear in vain, sir. Tell me, have you had sexual connection with any Indian women?'

'*Indian* women?'

Bushell was about to deny the charge vehemently. Then he remembered Rani. This was a time for truth, if ever there was one.

'Not since Mrs Pomfret arrived,' he said. 'And before then, only with one woman.'

'And I assume you have had connection with Mrs Pomfret on a regular basis?'

'Yes. Usually several times a week.'

'Where does this native woman live?'

'I maintained her in a house some way out of the cantonment until I became – ah – friendly with Mrs Pomfret. But she is not there now. She is staying with her sister in the bazaar. Her sister's son has not been well.'

'I think we should see her. Together.'

'How will that help me?'

'We may be able to find which kind of leprosy she has passed to you – if indeed she has. Some types are within the scope of treatment, so we have hope. And hope is always the best medicine I know.'

Bushell ran a hand shakily across his forehead. It came away damp with sweat.

'Have you a brandy, doctor?' he asked Jackson hoarsely. 'I feel you have passed on me sentence of death.'

Jackson produced a bottle and a glass. Bushell ignored the glass and put the bottle to his lips. He drank greedily. Spirit trickled unheeded down his chin.

'It is unwise to drink too heavily in this heat,' said Jackson warningly.

'When you tell me I may already be a dying man?' Bushell retorted, and lifted the bottle once more.

Jackson called for his carriage, and they drove in silence to the edge of the bazaar. The street stretched away, lined on either side with huts and shacks. Naked children played in the dust among cow-pats. Native women crouched at the doors of the hutments they called home, picking nits out of their babies' hair. The adjutant motioned the driver to stop, took another swig from the bottle he had brought with him, and nodded to Jackson. They had arrived.

They climbed down, and he led the way between the huts. The ground, dry in the main thoroughfare, and fouled by horse droppings, was damp here. A purple putrefying liquid moved sluggishly along a deep ditch, a *nullah*. The smell of faeces and rotting vegetables was chokingly strong. How could a man of breeding, wealth and education seek a sexual companion from such surroundings? Jackson wondered, and marvelled anew at the strength and folly of masculine lust.

They stopped outside a hovel apparently no different from the others, and without any distinguishing mark or number. Some bright metal pots were piled outside, and a crude curtain hung across the doorway instead of a door. They could hear a child crying somewhere inside the little building. A yellow-eyed cur, covered with open sores, grovelled at their feet, lips drawn back from its pointed teeth.

The curtain was suddenly pulled aside and a woman in her early thirties stood framed in the doorway. Jackson had to admit she was beautiful: dark-skinned, wearing a deep blue silk sari, with a bodice edged with gold; a crimson caste mark glowed on her forehead between wide, kohl-darkened eyes. She looked surprised at seeing two Europeans in an area they very seldom visited, and then, recognising the adjutant, pleasure showed in her face.

'This is Rani,' Bushell explained. 'She speaks some English.'

'Can we go inside?' asked Jackson.

A number of children, thumbs in mouths, noses running with phlegm and mucus, had already gathered outside; most were naked, all barefoot, oblivious of the filth and the flies.

The hut was divided into two rooms. Curtains had been drawn across small unglazed windows. The main room was thick with pungent scent from a joss-stick burning slowly in a brass holder on a table. A garland of faded flowers draped a brass image of Ganesh, the elephant-headed god of good luck.

'I am a doctor,' Jackson explained, speaking slowly so that she could understand him. 'I believe that you may quite unknowingly be infected with leprosy.'

Rani looked at him in amazement. Then her eyes narrowed.

'That is a lie,' she said quietly. 'You take advantage of me because I am Indian. You would not make such an accusation to a woman of your kind.'

'I am not making it to you,' Jackson replied. 'I simply said what I believe. Am I right?'

'No. You are wrong. And in any case, if I were suffering from any unclean disease, Ganesh would cure me. He has that power.'

She bowed towards the idol, bringing up her hands, palms together, in front of her face.

Jackson pursed his lips. He could not very well forcibly examine Rani for leprosy, and for a moment he wondered whether they should leave. Why, indeed, he had ever suggested they should come and see her. It should have been obvious to him that she would deny she was a leper. Then he heard the cry of a child, the cry they had heard as they arrived outside. It came from the other room of the house; a faint, bubbling, gurgling sound as though the child was choking with a severe cold.

'Whose is that?' he asked.

'No-one's,' Rani replied quickly.

'Her sister is ill. She has a child who is sick. I told you,' said the adjutant.

'I would like to see the child,' said Jackson.

'He is sleeping,' Rani replied. She moved towards the doorway that led to the second room, to bar their entry.

Jackson pushed her aside and went in. A woman of about the same age sat on a truckle bed with an infant in her arms. Both men stood staring in horror at the child. It was impossible to see whether the infant was boy or girl, for the skin of its face was wrinkled and dark with fissures, rough as the grey hide of an elephant. The child's tongue protruded from the mouth, and a little yellow bile dribbled unchecked down its chin. The end of the tongue was thick with huge swollen nodules. Similar outgrowths, lichenous eruptions, suppurating with stinking pus, covered the child's hands, feet and arms.

The child's nose had almost collapsed into its face, and the fingers seemed unusually short and stubby. When they looked at them more closely, both men saw that their tips and finger nails had completely rotted away. The child urinated as it sat, but the stream that trickled steaming on to its mother's lap was thick and frothy, like the urine of a beast of burden, not a human being.

The stench in the tiny room was the stench of death; the smell of a rotting corpse, the sickening syrupy sweetness of decay that Jackson had noticed briefly on the verandah of Mrs Pomfret's house. He recoiled in horror. This was the odour of the living dead, when flesh literally decomposes on the bones; the reason why in times past lepers were compelled to carry a warning bell and cry, 'Unclean! Unclean!'

'That child is the source,' said Jackson, coming back into the outer room. 'Have you ever taken him or her into Mrs Pomfret's house?'

'Never,' said Rani.

Bushell seized her arm and twisted it roughly.

'Don't lie to me, you black bitch,' he said thickly. 'The doctor tells me I have this loathsome disease, and if I did not get it from you, it must have come from that foul child of your sister's. My God, it must have infected Mrs Pomfret! She told me how she awoke once to find a child in her bed. It scratched her. I will have you all flung out of here into a leper colony. You will die as you deserve to, with the rest of your kind.'

He turned to Jackson. 'Is it the curable sort?' he asked urgently.

'I fear not,' replied Jackson gravely. 'The symptoms are of the worst kind – tubercular leprosy. There is no cure.'

Bushell struck Rani across the face. She staggered from the force of the blow and then screamed at him, all pretence at gentility gone.

'Yes, I did bring the boy into the house!' she shouted. 'I hated your English whore. I brought him in, and scratched her leg and rubbed his poison on to her. I *wanted* her to die! Then I heard that some other Englishman was in Calcutta looking for her, but he did not know where she was. So I wrote him a letter.'

'You lie! You cannot write in your own language, let alone in mine.'

'I went to a letter-writer in the bazaar. He wrote – and the Englishman has arrived, yes?'

'Yes,' agreed Jackson. 'He has arrived.'

'Are you that man?' Rani asked him.

'No. But I have travelled with him.'

Suddenly she fell on her knees on the dirt floor.

'Then, sahib, I beg you, let him take the English mem Pomfret away. Leave my love to me! I beg you, sir!'

Bushell hit her again as she struggled to rise.

'Can't you see why I hate her?' she screamed. 'I did it for *you*! I love you! *I love you!*'

'Love!' retorted Bushell. 'You have killed her – and me.'

He turned to Jackson. 'Is there any hope for either of us?' he asked pathetically.

'Carriers can sometimes be immune,' Jackson replied, 'but not those to whom they transmit the disease.'

'You bloody bitch!' cried Bushell, and he kicked Rani in the face as she grovelled, screaming and sobbing, on the floor.

'Let us get out of here,' said Jackson. He wanted fresh air and cool water, an antiseptic to wash his hands. This was the festering underside of the East; the dark side of disease and lust and hate and terrible, lingering death. He had seen enough, too much; he could stand no more of it.

The sun seemed unusually bright after the dimness of the hovel, and by contrast even the air of the bazaar felt fresh. They drove back in silence to Jane Pomfret's house. Bushell finished the brandy in the carriage and tossed the empty bottle into the undergrowth at the side of the road. For all the effect the spirit had on him, it could have been water.

Before they reached the gates, Bushell stopped the carriage.

'I would like to see her alone,' he said. His voice was slurred with drink now, his eyes half closed. 'You understand my feelings?'

'Perfectly.'

'You are *certain* there is no cure for this? I am not a poor man, doctor. I would spend my fortune to be cured, and spend it willingly.'

'I appreciate that fully, Captain. But this is not a question of money. There is no cure that all the money in the world can buy. One day, this disease may be cured. But not yet.'

'One day,' said Bushell bitterly. 'That is no help to me. I have been very fortunate in my life up to now, doctor. Indeed, I have often wondered how some officers, without private means such as mine, managed to exist out here in India, while I enjoyed everything I wanted, and never expected otherwise. I suppose that now I have to accept what God has willed on me.'

'Not God,' said Jackson. 'Never God. Your own actions. There are neither punishments nor rewards in life. Only consequences.'

He climbed down from the carriage and watched it move slowly on and out of sight.

Bushell stopped the carriage halfway down the drive, and walked the rest of the way. He entered Jane's house by a side door, went up to the dressing room he used, and examined his face closely in his shaving mirror. It seemed much the same as always; a bit strained, perhaps, but he was tired, and damp with sweat from the journey. How long before it would become as disfigured and grotesque as the face of the child, shrunken and shrivelled, the flesh coarse and dark, like the flesh of a beast? How long before he also stank of the tomb?

He took a key from the end of a chain and opened a case he kept locked on a side table. Two pistols with polished barrels lay on padded red plush. He checked that they were both charged, then put one in each of the back pockets of his trousers. Next, he took several large swallows of whisky from a silver hip flask he kept in a drawer and went downstairs to the main drawing room.

The punkah still swung to and fro like a metronome, marking the passage of time. It would be swinging after he had done what he intended to do, he thought. The sun would still be shining, the child would still be coughing. The regimental bugler would sound 'Lights Out' and then 'Reveille' in the morning. But not for him; never again for him.

He swallowed, and the whisky tasted bitter as bile on his tongue. He put both hands behind him and fingered the comfortingly serrated handles of the pistols. Then he called: 'Jane?'

She replied from another room. She had been resting, with the blinds drawn against the heat and brightness of afternoon. For the past few weeks she had been conscious of a lassitude, a totally unusual weariness that not even sleep could completely cure. She rested when she could, usually for an hour or two after lunch each day.

Bushell came through the doorway. Her face was not quite as it had been; he was certain of that now. She must be carrying the disease. She had unknowingly infected him with a plague for which there was no cure, no antidote, no alleviation. Now it was killing them both slowly, by terrible degrees.

'I have reached a decision,' he told her.

'You have, darling?'

Jane came towards him, smiling. She had guessed that previously he had been about to propose marriage to her, and now he had made up his mind. At last her worries, her fears for the future, were all but over. She smiled, wanting to show surprise at the question she was certain he would ask.

As Bushell watched her, he thought he should accuse her of giving him leprosy, but as swiftly he changed his mind. What was the point of making such an accusation, only to have it denied, when denial was fruitless?

'One second,' he said. She was still two yards away, and she paused, slightly perplexed. What was he waiting for? Was he suddenly and uncharacteristically shy? Surely not, not after the things they had done together.

Bushell gripped the handles of the pistols. The weapons came out of his pockets easily; they might have been metal extensions of his arms.

Jane smiled again, more relaxed. He must be about to take out an engagement ring. She stood, hands outstretched towards him, waiting for him to put the ring on her finger. Then he withdrew the pistol from his right pocket and fired.

At that range, the ball blew away the top of her skull. The acrid whiff of gunpowder made him choke more than the sight of her mutilated body, still standing for a moment before it fell sideways. Blood spouted across the carpet. The adjutant swallowed, threw away the pistol and rammed the barrel of the second weapon against his own temple.

'I loved you,' he said hoarsely and tears ran unchecked down his cheeks. 'God forgive me, I loved you. And you did *this* to me. . . .'

Taking a deep breath, Captain Bushell squeezed the trigger.

Jackson and Douglas were taking tea on their verandah when a soldier messenger arrived. He reined in his sweating horse and saluted smartly.

'Colonel McTavish's compliments, gentlemen,' he began breathlessly. 'He requests your presence most urgently. There has been a tragedy.'

'A tragedy? What kind of tragedy?' asked Jackson.

'I'd better leave the colonel to inform you, sir.'

Douglas called to the *sais* to saddle two horses at once. They followed the messenger over the burning plain, their horses' hooves sending up long trails of choking, floury dust behind them. As they approached the colonel's house, Emma McTavish came out to meet them. Her shoulders stooped, her hair hung down in damp ringlets, her face was pale with misery.

'We have had frightful news. Poor Jane Pomfret has been killed, and Captain Bushell has died by her side, a pistol in his hand.'

'Did he kill her?' Jackson asked her.

'There is no other explanation. Yet they were so close. I fancied there might even be talk of marriage. I just cannot understand it.'

Jackson said nothing.

Two orderlies wheeled out the colonel in his chair.

'Damnable news,' he said hoarsely. 'I have lost the best adjutant the regiment has had in the last twenty years. He appears to have killed the widow Pomfret and then himself. An affair of the heart, doubtless.'

'I was just getting to know Jane well,' said Emma tearfully. 'It was so pleasant to have another young English woman here on the station. She was a most entertaining person.'

The colonel motioned her to silence.

'I believe Mrs Pomfret was of straitened means, although she never gave that impression,' he announced in a lowered voice. 'I know Bushell regarded her highly. I cannot understand how such a catastrophe could have occurred. I suppose we must blame this damned climate, this country. It unsettles people so. Have you any ideas, gentlemen, as to what could have caused this?'

Douglas shook his head.

'None at all. She came out to see me, bringing certain letters relating to private business. I was prepared to pay her passage home. Since you tell me she may have left little money, I will, of course, bear all expenses of a decent Christian burial and for a stone to be raised in her memory. Poor Jane.'

For the moment, he was not standing on an Indian verandah, feeling the sun's heat burn his back, seeing an aged colonel wince with pain as he moved his gouty leg, and his unhappy young wife sob into a silk handkerchief. He was back in Coupar Castle, closing the bedroom door of Jane Pomfret's room, seeing her smile at him, her breasts firm, nipples hard, her mouth moist with longing.

'She leaves a child, I believe,' he said, forcing this incongruous image from his mind. 'She was married to my late stepfather.'

'I did not know that, but she said you were related,' replied the colonel as though the matter was without importance. 'Well, gentlemen, even though it is not yet sundown, I suggest what we all need now is a large peg of whisky. A very large peg.'

The garrison church was packed for the funeral. A choir of Christian Indian boys and girls sang unfamiliar hymns in their peculiarly Welsh accents. The regimental burial party stood by the graveside with reversed arms, and the regimental band played the Funeral March from Saul.

Some mourners were surprised that a young Indian woman seemed so affected by grief that she collapsed and had to be carried from the church. No-one knew who she was, but someone said later that as she regained consciousness, she gave her name as Rani. No doubt she had been one of the adjutant's servants.

Because of the high esteem in which the regiment was held locally, and because the garrison commander had personally served in it, and considered that regimental honour was at stake, the fact that the adjutant had killed his mistress and then himself was not made public. Instead, it was spread about that there had been a shooting incident. Pistols, which in usual circumstances were always kept unloaded, had somehow been primed by hands unknown. While explaining their workings to a lady visitor from England, both had been fatally wounded. It was still a tragedy, but now at least a tragedy without dishonour.

After the funeral, Jackson and Douglas sent their luggage to Calcutta by baggage train. They had booked passage to England by way of the Cape of Good Hope and Madeira. Jackson went ahead to Calcutta on his own. Douglas stayed behind in Barrackpore for a further day. He ate a light supper of *bekti*, a river fish much esteemed in that part of India, rice, and a plate of peeled mangoes, with half a bottle of claret. Afterwards, cigar in one hand, glass of port in the other, he pondered on Jane's death, and how he could wrest the estate from Cartwright's control.

At the faint sound of a footstep, he stubbed out his cigar, and stood up. He had sent the servants to their quarters early and left the side door on the latch because he thought he might have a visitor. It was therefore no surprise when Emma McTavish came into the room.

She wore a dark veil to conceal her features because she had taken the considerable social risk of walking alone from the colonel's house to his. English women did not walk on their own after dark in India unless for the most compelling reasons. A wrong interpretation could so readily be placed on any such solitary nocturnal perambulations. Now Emma removed her veil and closed the door carefully behind her. They stood facing each other in the dimly lit room. Candles in glass globes threw faint, trembling shadows on the walls covered with incongruous scenes of English rural life; a hay wain waited outside a thatched cottage, a groom held a patient hunter.

'I had to see you,' Emma began nervously. 'There was no chance to talk at the funeral, and our house has been full of visitors ever since. You are leaving tomorrow?'

'Yes.'

'I want to come with you.'

'You mean, to Scotland?'

'If you are going there, yes. If not, like Ruth in the Bible, wherever you go, I want to go. I cannot bear the thought of living week after week, year after year, in this terrible place, sharing my life with a man who every day and night becomes more repulsive to me. I married him out of desperation, and ever since I have lived in increasing despair. I cannot go on any longer.'

'But what would you do in Scotland?'

'I have no relatives or even friends now in the old country, but I have you. I want to come with *you*. Can you not understand? Must you make me confess it? I love you.'

'Dear Emma,' said Alec gently, putting out his hands and holding her trembling shoulders. 'No-one has ever said that to me before. As long as I live, I will remember you and these words. I feel flattered that you could say them to me.'

'Do you mean that you love me too?'

The question was hesitant, disbelieving.

Douglas shook his head slowly, sadly.

'I am sorry, Emma. I sometimes feel that love is something which is not mine to give. I *like* you. I am fond of you, and I am honoured by your expression of your feelings. But I must be honest with you as well as with myself. Liking and fondness are not love. I do not love anyone, least of all myself.

'I cannot take you away to Scotland. I am not sure how long I will be staying there in any case. I may travel north as soon as I reach Gravesend, or I may go on to North America where my partner Captain Ross feels we should expand our company. I may even go back to China, I simply do not know. I am sorry. . . .'

He paused. He could feel her shoulders quiver as she sobbed.

'I thought you might say this,' she admitted disconsolately. 'But I hoped – I prayed – you would not. God has not answered my prayer. Perhaps He did not hear it?'

'Perhaps He did, and answered it in the best way. You may not love your husband, but in my experience, after several years, very few married people remain in love with their partner. It is not reasonable to suppose it could be otherwise. All most can hope for is mutual understanding and shared interests and respect. Sometimes they try to mould each other into the ideal person they *think* they should have married. But, of course, there is no ideal person. We are changing all the time.

'What and who appeals to us at twenty, by thirty can be less attractive, and by forty a bore. Your husband is not young and he is clearly not well. Looked at in the most mercenary way, he will not make very old bones, and when he dies, you will be a relatively wealthy widow. Then you can marry again, someone of your own age.

'If you came away with me now, we could not marry while you were married to him. You would therefore have no status. We would be like poor Jane Pomfret and Captain Bushell, co-habiting. Nothing more, perhaps even less. English society is even less tolerant than people here. We would be ostracised.'

Emma moved slightly away from him. As he released her shoulders, he saw tears glitter like crystals on her pale cheeks. She was looking at him closely, trying to store in her mind a picture of his face.

'I must go,' she said, her voice firmer now. She had tried and she had failed; this was a fact she had to accept with what stoicism she could muster.

'Wait,' said Douglas. 'I would like to give you something. Not charity, not a payment. A present.'

He scribbled a cheque, blew on the ink to dry the signature, handed it to her.

'One day you may need some money. You may wish to make a journey, or consult a lawyer. Then this could help you, for it is easier to open an oyster without a knife than a lawyer's mouth without money.'

He smiled, and Emma tried to smile, too, but her lips were trembling. He kissed her gently, and then she went out into the darkness and Douglas was alone.

Back in the colonel's house, Emma removed her veil, rinsed her face in cold water in a basin to remove traces of her tears.

'You have been out, dear?' her husband called from another room. His voice sounded thick and slurred with whisky.

'I had a headache,' she replied. 'I wanted some fresh air. I walked in the garden for a few minutes. I think I will retire to bed.'

McTavish did not reply. Emma went up the wooden stairs to her own room. By the light of an oil lamp a servant had left burning for her, she unfolded Douglas's cheque. It was undated, payable to bearer, for the sum of one thousand guineas.

Calcutta

White linen blinds shaded the windows of the huge drawing room that overlooked the Hooghly River in Calcutta, filtering and emasculating the sun's fierce, abrasive glare.

The mistress of the house, a woman in her late forties with a loose wet mouth and breasts large as melons that pressed unattractively against the tight cotton of her dress, sat in the most comfortable chair, as befitted her station. In a half circle around her were her guests, the wives of jute merchants, shippers, bankers, attorneys, in strict order of wealth and importance. To new arrivals, they would never simply be introduced as Mrs Brown or Mrs White, but as Mrs *Lawyer* Brown, Mrs *Merchant* White, so there would never be doubt or embarrassment as to where everyone stood socially and financially.

When the hostess spoke, the other women listened with respect and attention. Afterwards, among themselves, they might criticise her taste in clothes and her opinions on other matters, but never to her face.

'I hear this new doctor man – Jackson, I think his name is – has some revolutionary new treatment which literally works wonders,' she said. 'He makes you lie down on a bed – and then jabs you with a golden needle.'

The middle-aged wife of a tea planter, sipping a cherry brandy, wrinkled her leathery face in a refusal to be impressed.

'Usually men only want to prick you with something else, dear, and a rather blunt needle at that.'

The others smiled nervously, not sure of the hostess's attitude to remarks of this kind; she was known to be a strict Presbyterian. The hostess smiled mechanically.

'I have heard remarkable claims for his treatment, which is Chinese, so they say. Of course, he is a very rich man,' she added reflectively, as though this gave an extra benediction to his cures.

'It is unusual to find a doctor interested in commerce,' another guest ventured nervously. She was new to Calcutta and felt she should say something.

'There was Dr Jardine, of course,' a third pointed out to put her in her place. 'Jardine and Matheson both became prodigiously wealthy. *Prodigiously* so.'

'Last week I met Dr Jackson at a dinner party,' said the wife of a jute merchant. 'He struck me as being quite pleasant. A bachelor, I believe.'

'I have heard it said he keeps a woman here in Calcutta,' said the hostess, looking from one to the other for their reaction: surprise, distaste, interest, envy.

'He won't be the first man or the last to do that,' declared an acidulated woman with a straggling moustache and breasts thin as razor strops.

'Agreed, but his woman is Chinese, which *is* a bit unusual, don't you think?'

'Have you ever seen them together? At the races, or out in his carriage?'

'No. But I hear he has bought a house in Park Street for her. He does not live there himself – at least, not all the time. He has that magnificent place in Alipore, as well as keeping on old Elijah Potiphar's house. Dr Jackson really is a nabob now – and he lives like one. I have also heard it said this Chinese woman is carrying his child.'

'That would be a scandal,' said the hostess appreciatively.

'I do not know that I personally would like to be attended by a doctor whose Chinese mistress was bearing his child,' said the tea planter's wife, largely for something to say. She was not a natural conversationalist, and up on the plantation in Assam there were not many people to talk to or even about.

'Why not?'

'I think we have to keep ourselves to ourselves. Would you not agree?'

She looked around at the others, hoping for approval. It came from her hostess.

'As you do so well, my dear.'

'Well, then, I am sure you have nothing to fear from your husband going after Chinese women,' said the acidulated woman. She paused suddenly, remembering a rather unpleasant incident when she had discovered her own husband with their children's Indian *ayah*. She had sent the black baggage packing, of course, but every time her husband came into her bed – usually, they slept in separate rooms, she claimed for the sake of coolness – she would think of that black flesh opening to receive him, and shudder with revulsion.

The trouble with men was that you could never trust them. Old or young, they were all the same, like goats perpetually searching for what she could only bring herself to refer to as *it*; talking about it, imagining it. She poured herself another glass of cherry brandy to sweeten the recollection of her husband's infidelity. Who would ever have thought it of him? Why, he had always finished before she had even begun. But perhaps – hateful, horrible, totally unbearable thought – he had not been like that with the *ayah*?

'Do you think Dr Jackson will stay in Calcutta?' she asked hurriedly, to purge her mind of such ugly images.

'I hear he is planning to return to England shortly, to practise there.'

'Perhaps that is why he has bought her the house in Park Street. He is going to leave the woman there?'

'We will have to wait and see. In the meantime, I must tell you I am meeting Dr Jackson professionally on Tuesday. I have an appointment at ten o'clock. I will see what he says.'

'See what he does, more likely,' suggested the tea planter's wife, but under her breath, so as not to offend her hostess. Then she held out her glass for more cherry brandy; it really tasted uncommonly good.

Douglas and Jackson were in the smoking-room of Jackson's great house in Alipore. A punkah lazily stirred the heavy air above their heads. Jackson lay stretched out on the sofa, whisky at his elbow, cigar in his hand. Douglas was talking.

'You must see it from our point of view,' he said reprovingly. 'I have written to Ross in New York and he entirely agrees. As a medical man, apart from being active in business, you must always appear above the temptations of others. Caesar's wife and all that.'

'So what are you proposing?' asked Jackson, blowing smoke rings.

'That you give up this Chinese woman, T'a Ki.'

'She is the mother of my son, Robert.'

'That does not alter the situation. You can procreate a boy or girl in

seconds. It has taken the three of us years to build up Trinity-Trio. We do
not wish any scandal with you and this Chinese woman to harm its
reputation – or its profits.'

'Scandal? My dear fellow, scandal here is rife. Every English nabob
has one or two mistresses, and half a dozen illegitimates of various
colours. European women go mad in this heat. They will copulate with
grooms, gardeners. Any male with a hard prick will suit them. And you
accuse *me* of starting a scandal because I have a discreet Chinese woman
who has borne me a son?'

'It *is* a scandal,' said Douglas stubbornly. 'And as such can affect our
company. Most of the men we deal with are married. Their wives hear of
this and get on to them and say, "I wouldn't deal with Trinity-Trio.
There's a rather nasty fellow there, one of the partners, a doctor, living
with a Chink, even had a little yellow, slit-eyed bastard. He should know
better."'

'Remember, Richard, no-one is *obliged* to trade with us. There are
plenty of other firms they can do business with – who would all be
delighted to cut us out.'

'I am surprised at you, Alec, coming in on the side of morality,' said
Jackson sarcastically.

'Nothing I have done has ever harmed the company,' Douglas
retorted.

'We have always sold the best mud and we always give the keenest
prices for everything we import and export,' replied Jackson. 'It is hard
to beat us for prices or delivery. Anyone will tell you that.'

'I agree, but you can't beat these old women, needling away at their
husbands. Now, as you know, we have always agreed never knowingly to
do anything which could jeopardise our company – *in any way*. In Ross's
opinion and mine, Richard, your behaviour is doing just that.'

'You two are entitled to your opinions, but do not expect me to agree.
And if I refuse to abandon the lady – and my son?'

'Then we will buy you out. At cost.'

'Never.'

'Well, think again. And leave her. It is not love that is at stake. It is
money – which is much more durable than love.'

'You don't know what you're talking about,' replied Jackson shortly.

'I think I do. As Shakespeare put it, "Men have died and worms have
eaten them, but not for love." What the hell is the value of love? It is like
spirit poured on a hot glass plate. It can evaporate in seconds – and leave
a residue of misery. Travel on your own, Richard. Dump this bint and
the kid.'

'This is your last word on the matter?' asked Jackson, belatedly
realising the terrible truth of his partner's words. The cigar suddenly

tasted dead in his mouth, the whisky was like etching acid.

'That is *our* last word,' replied Douglas quietly. 'I am sorry to say this, but in your heart you must know we are talking sense, business sense.'

'Is that all you think about, money?' asked Jackson bitterly.

'In this case – yes. After all, what else is involved?'

Jackson shrugged. It was no use talking to Douglas, who he had imagined would understand how he felt about T'a Ki. Douglas and Ross were simply concerned with profit, and what people might think. He was surprised that they should take this view. Then he thought again. He had no right to appear surprised; secretly, he agreed with everything Douglas said.

Jackson was arguing largely to assuage his own conscience, to rationalise his feelings. He had been proud to sire a son, but now that satisfaction was diminishing. He suspected that T'a Ki cared more for the boy, Robert, than for him. That was not really surprising; he was tiring of her, a process that had begun with Kuan's death, and she must sense this.

Nothing, certainly not human feelings or frailty, must ever be allowed to harm what the three partners had constructed: a machine for making money in sums totally out of proportion to the effort entailed.

His personal feelings must not jeopardise its efficient working, any more than abstract considerations, strangely so important to Douglas, about the morality of making opium addicts of people they would never meet. But what exactly were his feelings? Jackson gave a sigh at the perversity of the situation, and at his secret relief. He was not voluntarily going to abandon T'a Ki and his son. He was being forced to do so under the terms of a prior agreement with his partners. His mind now made up and at ease, he rang the bell for the bearer to bring him another bottle of The Macallan.

It was the hour before dawn, before the cocks crowed, when even Calcutta still slept, a great, sweating, suppurating, uneasy city of ferocious, irreconcilable contrasts – uncountable wealth and unspeakable poverty, with tens of thousands who lacked even a roof from the monsoon rain.

In T'a Ki's sumptuous house in Park Street, she lay naked with Jackson in their great bed. He was awake. Through the wide windows, he could see mango swamps and paddy fields with palm trees in silhouette against the fading moon; hear faint calls of unseen, unknown animals in the distance and, nearer, the incessant cackle and croak of insects and dogs. The jungle lurked literally only feet away.

Jackson was thinking about his own future, and T'a Ki's. He did not really care how other people – his employees, or unimportant acquaintances – regarded him. If anyone was not content to work for him then he could easily bring them instant contentment, by dismissing them from his service. Experience had hardened his feelings; everyone enjoyed only a lease on life, not a freehold. We thus should make the most of each opportunity that presents itself; there will never be another exactly similar chance.

Nor did he greatly concern himself about the opinions of his partners: their private lives were far from blameless. Douglas, he knew, would bed any woman he could, regardless of the consequences, and before Ross had left for New York, he was becoming increasingly drawn to the dangerous courtship of young boys, and the pleasure of dressing them in outlandish clothes.

The moral opinions of two such men carried little weight with Jackson. What did concern him more were his own feelings towards T'a Ki and Trinity-Trio. There must be no cross-purposes, no concealment of issues at stake. So far as he was concerned, the sum of his achievement as a businessman and a fashionable physician in the Empire's second city was infinitely greater and more important than his feelings for any individual.

Did he *really* care for T'a Ki? And if he did, what would that logically entail? Not marriage, surely. This had been the grave error that Jardine's first partner had made, marrying his local mistress. Jackson had no intention of repeating such a crass blunder.

But sometimes, when he lay with T'a Ki and looked into her eyes, he was disquieted to imagine he saw Kuan's image reflected in them, not his. This was an illusion, of course – it must be – nevertheless it disturbed him, and did not increase his desire. Also, without the piquant element of possible discovery, he had to accept that much of the zest had drained from their relationship. He liked T'a Ki well enough, but he liked himself much more.

T'a Ki was always amenable; never once had he not enjoyed total satisfaction with her; never once had she failed him. But familiarity dulled every appetite, every taste. The Chinese had a saying that no-one could live happily on a constant diet of chicken and bamboo shoots. Other women possessed attractions of their own, and once free of his relationship with T'a Ki, he believed that a resilience of his spirit, which he secretly felt had been lacking for weeks, even months now, would return.

In his view, a single man was like a ship in full sail, able to travel wherever the captain willed. A married man was a ship of a different kind, with a cargo of commitments. And a married man with a child was an overloaded ship, stuck in harbour, perpetually straining against anchors and mooring ropes, yearning to be free.

Jackson made up his mind, and as he did so was conscious of a tiny stab of regret. Maybe his conscience, which once had been strong but which now seemed submerged beneath layers of self deception, was reacting in dismay, as the liver of a heavy drinker, despite years of alcohol, can still occasionally produce an unexpected spasm of pain.

As a young man, Jackson had been proud of his calling. Now the only achievement that gave him pride was the amount of money he was making every year, every month, every day. Relationships were on a lower scale of value. You became friendly with men, you might go to bed with women, but no-one must ever have any permanent hold on your loyalties or affection. You should always maintain your freedom. Like a swimmer against life's fierce currents, you must never allow anything – or, more important, anyone – to hold you back. Even as he assured himself of the truth of this, a question he did not care to answer echoed in his mind: Why not?

T'a Ki turned towards him. He did not look at her. Somehow, now that the moment of decision had arrived, he could not bring himself to act. Instead, he looked out of the window at the stars that always seemed so bright, so close, in these brief moments when night surrendered to another new day. If he wavered now, he could change course forever. All could be lost.

'You want to leave me,' T'a Ki said unexpectedly; she must have been reading his thoughts.

Jackson turned towards her then, forcing himself to look into her dark, fathomless eyes, and, for almost the first time, not seeing Kuan's reflected image but his own.

'I do not *want* to leave you,' he said carefully, wondering whether he was speaking the truth. But what was the truth? It was what you said, or believed, or pretended to believe, at one particular moment in life. But how long did that moment last? And when it passed, did whatever you thought was true dissolve with it?

So he said: 'I *have* to leave you.'

'Why?'

'It is not my wish, Heavenly Beauty,' he replied, calling her by the Chinese translation of her name, which he always used as a special term of endearment.

'As you know, I am in partnership with Douglas and Ross. When we began together we agreed that if any one of us did anything which, in the opinion of the other two, jeopardised our business in any way, he had to abandon his share in Trinity-Trio.'

'And they say that you and me and our son – your son – are threatening their business – your business?'

'Yes.'

'But how can this be so? Have you not told them they are wrong?'

'Of course I have. Our relationship, Heavenly Beauty, has nothing to do with business. But they point out we have to trade with other European. Most of them don't give a damn, if they even know about us. And why should they care? They know how things are in the heat. They have probably got mistresses somewhere, or amenable boys. But their wives take a different view – to protect themselves and their own position, of course.

'If a wife realises a man with whom her husband does a lot of business keeps a woman, she feels that this may tempt her husband to leave the path of virtue. And where would these dull English and Scottish wives be if their husbands went off after more attractive local women?'

'Men from the West are like ships turned by little rudders,' said T'a Ki contemptuously. 'I thought *you* were different, but I was wrong. You think so much more of things than of people. Your company. Money. Profits. What wives of other men might possibly say.

'It does not really matter to any of you who or what a woman is. Even if you do not care for her – perhaps even if you dislike her – you can still find her attractive enough to get her into bed.

'For a woman, contact with a man for whom she cannot feel love and respect is nothing. If a woman loves a man – as I have loved you ever since I first saw you aboard ship – she is thrilled, shaken with emotion. For us, love is all. For you Western men, lust takes its place. And then you cheat yourselves, as you are cheating yourself now – and me.'

She paused.

'Kuan was different. He knew how a woman feels inside herself. He loved me, and willingly gave up everything else in his life because he did. And still that sacrifice was not enough for me, because I had met you, and, like a foolish child, I wanted you.

'Meeting you was like one of your scientific experiments that creates a sudden flame – and now, so far as you are concerned, the fire has burned out. Kuan has gone, and you are going, and I am left. I have been foolish because I believed what you told me. So now I must accept the result of my folly. But you will not take our son, *my* son?'

'No, I will not do that. I will also leave you enough money for all you needs and for his. And I will make a will in his favour. That I promise you.'

'I do not care about your promises. I know what they can be worth. They are words spoken into the wind. What I want most of all is you. Now. Always. I do not care much for money. That is your god, not mine. I pray that this god – Mammon, as you Christians call it – will no disappoint you, as you have disappointed me. But I do not think my prayer will be answered.'

Jackson did not reply. The moment he had dreaded had passed more easily than he had anticipated. Already, he was rationalising the situation

He had done what he had to do for the best of reasons. Of course, it was in T'a Ki's best interest that he was leaving. Obviously, she could bring up the boy far more satisfactorily on her own. There would then be no clash of cultures, of East and West, or of colours, yellow and white. Everything was working out for the best for all of them; no question about it.

For a moment they lay in silence, bodies not touching, eyes carefully averted from each other. Then T'a Ki got up and went out of the room and left Jackson on his own. Outside, morning was already painting the sky pink. Most of the stars had died. Only a few of the brighter ones remained, fading gently into oblivion as he watched. Cocks began to crow, and he heard the first stirrings of people and traffic on the streets. The city of palaces and poverty was waking to face a new day. Jackson stretched luxuriously and turned on his side. Within seconds, he was asleep.

New York

At the same hour, by one of those chances which can affect equally the lives and destinies of people totally unknown to each other, two men on the other side of the world and separated from each other by over two thousand miles, as well as by colour, by background, language, race, country and ambitions, were reading the same advertisement in the same newspaper.

In the first-floor apartment of a tenement building off Mulberry Street, New York City, in the heart of the Italian quarter, sat a fat man in his late sixties, Enrico Pastellini.

The room was small, its white-washed walls hung with vividly col-oured religious pictures, a large ornamental gilt crucifix and a faded daguerrotype of his late wife. The apartment smelled strongly but not unpleasantly of garlic and aromatic herbs and spices.

Pastellini owned a small delicatessen shop on the ground floor, one of many in the area, selling Italian produce – cheese, salami, pasta – and their smells always drifted upwards like incense. He did not object. They reminded him of home in Southern Sicily; of hot sunshine and rich red wine, lazy days when he was young and every girl lowered her eyes bashfully under his bold enquiring gaze.

Enrico Pastellini was not an educated man, and even after years in New York, he still found reading English a strain. His lips moved to form

each word, and his weak eyes peered short-sightedly through
pebble-lensed spectacles at the hazy print.

> Captain Marvin Ross, formerly of Boston, Mass., latterly of
> Calcutta, India, and Canton, China, a partner in the Far Eastern
> trading company, Trinity-Trio, announces his arrival at the Fifth
> Avenue Hotel, Madison Square, New York, where he will be
> staying for some time.
>
> He is prepared to enter into business negotiations for the import
> and export of foodstuffs, medical supplies and objects of art. In
> certain circumstances, he would consider investing in serious
> manufacturing propositions, subject to an expert scrutiny of their
> potential.

Pastellini put down the paper, laid aside his spectacles, which these days
always hurt his eyes, and sat back in his chair, dreaming of the past as
clearly as if it were yesterday. If only *he* had met someone with such an
offer when he had arrived in this strange and enormous land, what a
different life he might have enjoyed! But perhaps, through the grace of
God, his only son, Leone, could benefit.

Leone was a bright boy, born late, and all the more precious for that. It
was as though Pastellini lived again through his son. Was this a kind of
immortality – perhaps the only one?

Pastellini wished he knew someone with whom he could discuss such
matters; knew someone educated, who would reason, argue, take a point
and give another. The parish priest always seemed too busy, and
attempted to calm every doubt with two words often repeated: 'Have
faith, have faith.'

But how could Pastellini have faith when, although he had worked
long hours, six days a week, year after year; although he had paid his taxes
and defrauded no-one, still the cold relentless tentacles of all that was evil
in the old country reached out to threaten him? And, like drowning
men's fingers, he knew that having gripped him, they would never let
him go.

No matter what name the evil went by in this New World, its aim
remained constant: to extract a percentage of all earnings every week from
anyone in whom they could instil fear. In Sicily, the custom was known
as wetting one's beak, *vagnari lu pizzu,* and went back centuries to the
time of the conquering Phoenicians. It had prospered under the rule of
Greeks and Romans, who had parcelled out the island into estates and
given them to local nobles – on condition they paid a tithe to the
occupying power.

Other foreign rulers continued these demands after the early conquerors departed. The Arabs strictly maintained this custom, and the Normans further divided the land after the feudal pattern common in France. Under this, landowners had virtually absolute sovereignty over the peasants, who were little better than slaves.

These landlords were not always in residence in the great houses on their estates. Life was more civilised and agreeable in Italy or elsewhere. They hired local Sicilians to patrol their properties when they were not in occupation. Frequently, these guards were ex-convicts, tough and ruthless. In the owners' absence, they promoted themselves to stewards, cultivating the estates and in return guaranteeing the owners a certain annual revenue.

The workers were now completely enslaved, because these stewards, who took the embracing title of Mafia, controlled the estates totally and could decide who would work – and who would starve. No-one was absolutely certain of the origin of the word. Some said it was an acronym of the fighting cry of Sicilian peasants who slaughtered their French overlords in the thirteenth century: *'Morte alla Francia Italia anela'* – 'Death to the French is Italy's cry'. But who cared where it originated? What mattered was its continuing and growing influence.

Central Government in Italy lacked the power and the will to break their rule. Gradually, landowners found themselves forced to sell their estates to people they or their fathers had intially engaged to guard them. No-one could run an estate by remote control, and attempts to administer it in person always failed. If an absentee landowner returned and tried to do so, he soon found that he was an unwelcome stranger in an alien land. No local would help him. They feared to speak against what became known ironically as 'the honoured society'.

Lawyers were afraid to prosecute the Mafia; judges were equally reluctant to pass sentence. And if any Mafia members were jailed by a judge less craven than his colleagues, then jailers would mysteriously mislay their keys, and the prisoners would walk free.

Should some owner from overseas still foolishly imagine that he could actually stay and run his own estate in an efficient manner, he would be presented with a series of graded warnings.

First, a hundred olive trees would be cut down overnight on his land, or an entire vineyard ruined. If, despite this initial sign of displeasure, he persisted in his delusion, he might find his prize herd of cattle had been rustled, but one calf would always be left in the field with its legs broken.

If any local person was unwise enough to come forward as a witness to such happenings, and so break the strict rule of *omerta*, or silence, which held that it was dishonourable for even the victim of an outrage to reveal the name of the perpetrator, this witness could either be murdered, or, as a warning to others, have one hand hacked off.

Sometimes, witnesses brave – or foolish – enough to reveal their intention of giving testimony, would have their tongues torn out. They had been willing to talk too much; now they would talk no more. In graver situations, a man's genitals were as likely to be cut as his tongue, on the excuse that he had offended the wife of a 'friend'.

To such Mafiosi as the police were able to convict, the Italian authorities gave free passage to the United States, to rid Sicily of them. And no sooner had they landed in New York than they began to prey on their countrymen – many of whom had emigrated earlier to avoid their attentions in Sicily, and all of whom desperately feared and resented their activities, which continued and prospered.

The virus of extortion, *omerta*, the state within a state, built on fear, greed and superstition, travelled with them. In the New World, this malignancy was at first largely unrecognised and undiagnosed. It therefore spread with the speed of poison in a well.

Other minorities and immigrants adopted its methods – Jews, Irish, blacks, Chinese – but the Sicilians remained the innovators. They grew strong in local and national politics, local and national government; their voice was equally loud in the councils of the unions, such as the Tunnel Workers, the Water Pipe Extension labourers, the Sewer Diggers, the Macaroni Manufacturers' Union.

Pastellini had just received a visit from a dark-skinned young man with bitten finger nails and mean eyes set too close together, who introduced himself as Franco, 'a friend'. He informed Pastellini that the old man would have to pay thirty dollars a month to *La Mano Nera*, the Black Hand Gang, to ensure protection of his shop during the coming twelve months.

'I have no money to pay,' Pastellini protested. 'My shop is poor, as you can see. So are my customers, and so am I. Often I do not make that amount in a week. Look in my books, and see for yourself, my friend.'

'I see what I am told to see,' Franco replied enigmatically. 'Pay by Tuesday or we cannot guarantee that enemies will not damage your shop. If your glass window is broken, it will cost you that amount to replace, and you possess no insurance.'

Pastellini sighed. He knew what he knew; he could not speak against the unspeakable. The police would be bribed, and he had no powerfu political friends to combat such a threat – if indeed anyone could.

'I will pay what I can as I can,' he agreed bitterly. 'But I cannot run my shop without a glass window. If you break my window, you will have nothing. '

'We could still have you,' said Franco, and to show what he meant h kicked Pastellini twice on the shin, not hard, but as a warning. The ol man collapsed in pain. Franco looked down at him on the floor as thoug wondering whether to kick him again. He decided against it; he had made his point. He went out of the shop, pausing at the door.

'I will be here on Tuesday,' he said. 'Six o'clock.'

Pastellini gave him ten minutes to be away, then crawled painfully to his feet. He sat down at the table, feeling his bruises. The paper was open in front of him, and that was when and why the advertisement seemed to leap out of the page at him.

He knew that his son Leone had an idea which they both considered brilliant, and if he could meet this Captain Ross, that might be the means to make them both rich. Then surely they could escape this mesh of blackmail and violence, as in his boyhood he had seen starlings escape through an unnoticed hole in a net.

Pastellini picked up his glasses and re-read the advertisement. He was still reading it when his son returned.

Belize Town

At the same moment, another man read the advertisement and sat pondering a problem of a different kind. He wished to see Captain Marvin Ross for private and intensely personal reasons, but first he wanted to make sure that the Marvin Ross in the advertisement was the man he remembered. It would be unbearable to make a mistake after such a long time, and yet there might conceivably be two men with the same name.

He sat in a mahogany rocking chair on the verandah of a two-storey wooden house in Belize Town, the capital of British Honduras in Central America. The house faced the southern foreshore and the brilliantly blue Caribbean Sea. Nearby stood Government House, the repository of British authority. The Union Jack hung languidly at its white mast, and behind this was St John's Cathedral. On its site, in years gone by, kings of the Mosquito Coast had been crowned with long and complicated ritual.

The man, Jack O'Brien, was neither a loyal subject nor a Christian. His gods were not those of bishops and prelates. He owed allegiance to no-one, but he realised the importance of such matters in a colony, and it was wise to live close to these two shrines of English God and English power.

O'Brien's chair was placed for coolness under an attap roof that extended from the wall of his house above the verandah. A beach of blindingly white sand burned like flame in the heat of the sun. A toucan flew past with a great flurry of flamboyant wings. Butterflies, so large they seemed to swim through the air rather than fly, fluttered delicately above him.

O'Brien was in middle life, hard and tall, dark-skinned, with cold eyes and a mouth twisted tight as the cut of a knife. He sat recalling another ocean, and a voyage in a ship commanded by the captain he wished so desperately to meet again. The memory was painful, but he drew perverse pleasure from it, as a man can suck on a hollow tooth.

He pressed a brass bellpush. A black servant came out on to the verandah and bowed. O'Brien commanded respect from everyone, even from the English Governor, so it was said.

'Bring me my notes on Captain Ross,' he ordered his servant.

The man was small and limped slightly. Within moments, he had returned carrying two flat wooden boards bound together with pink ribbon. O'Brien undid the knot, parted the boards and began to read notes he had amassed over half a lifetime.

There were faded cuttings from old newspapers; items from trade and shipping journals; pages from personal letters with paragraphs ringed in red. He knew that the Captain Ross he wished to contact had traded between Calcutta in India and Canton in China. He had interests in the East with Trinity-Trio. His birthplace was Boston. O'Brien knew why he had left the United States – but nothing about his present whereabouts, or that he might be in New York.

Surely this *must* be the same man? No two sea captains with the same name and background could work at the same time for one company?

He replaced the items carefully between the boards, re-tied the ribbon. Then he poured himself a rum, added a measure of lime juice and stood up at the window, staring out at the familiar view. Colours blazed and glowed like living fire. Flying fish scudded across the water, glittering briefly in the sunlight like golden dagger blades. He regarded the scene with content. He felt certain he had found someone he had sought for so long. Now, he had to meet him. He finished his drink and recalled the servant.

'Get Gonzales here,' he ordered brusquely. 'I have work for him to do.'

London

The Panhard landaulette jolted on between the rows of new electric street lamps, towards Guildhall. Jackson turned to the companion who had invited him, as a mark of his esteem, to the traditional City banquet held in honour of the newly elected Lord Mayor of London.

'It is most agreeable to be sitting next to the governor of one of London's largest banks, on the way to dine with the capital's first citizen,' said Jackson. 'And only what seems a few years ago, as a general practitioner, I was being shown to the back door when I called to visit a patient!'

'And where was that, sir?' asked Sir Thomas Fulwood, expressing polite interest.

'In Gravesend. The house was owned by a Mr Piggott.'

'Really? Oddly enough, one of our managers was speaking to me about a Mr Percy Piggott of Gravesend only this week. The same man?'

'I would think so.'

'I do not discuss customers' affairs, of course, but in view of our bank's rather unfortunate relations with that gentleman, and purely in the privacy of this motor, I entirely agree. A most untrustworthy person. In fact, our manager formed the impression that he was mentally deranged.'

The two men fell silent. Sir Thomas brooded on the iniquities of Mr Piggott, and considered Jackson's rise to riches.

These *parvenus* from the East, nabobs who had made fortunes in relatively few years, and mostly totally unused to wealth, were forever harking back to their humble, often impoverished beginnings. As the grandson of the bank's founder, Sir Thomas found this tedious, but Dr Jackson and Trinity-Trio were among the bank's richest customers, and consequently had to be humoured. He had done wisely in inviting him to this banquet. Here, he could introduce him to other customers of importance. Business might then be done between them, and more profit and prestige would accrue to his bank.

Sir Thomas, a hereditary baronet whose title had been bestowed on his late father by a grateful sovereign for his efforts in extricating a prince of the blood from the clutches of Levantine money-lenders, knew the basic rule of advancement in all spheres of life: you help me and I help you. That was the way of the world, his world, every world.

'This is, of course, primarily a social occasion,' he assured Jackson, trying to make conversation. 'But since you are considering expanding your company's capabilities in this country, I can probably introduce you to people who could help you. A good burgundy or a vintage port are vital lubricants on such occasions.'

'I am interested in the increasing power of newspapers,' said Jackson. 'With these new laws that will keep children at school until they are thirteen, a huge new market will open up of people taught to read and eager to be informed.

'I have seen how *The Times*, the *St James Gazette* and *The Enquirer* influence people – and often, when one knows the facts personally, in what I consider to be totally the wrong direction. For example, I have read articles about the so-called Opium Wars in the East, and the more recent conflagration there, which were completely erroneous. The inference was that Britain went to war with China out of self-interest. Totally wrong, of course.'

Sir Thomas nodded agreement.

'I myself was of the opinion that Britain went to war to force the Chinese to buy our opium, when they were anxious to forbid its importation as a pernicious drug,' he said. 'And, more recently, because of the slur to our national honour over what we call the *Arrow* affair, when they boarded the vessel of that name and tore down the British ensign.'

'The Chinese have continuously interfered with our legitimate trade,' Jackson replied quickly. 'Even Napoleon gave us credit for being a nation of shopkeepers, but the Emperor of China thought otherwise. The fact that you, sir, a banker of renown, should accept such an erroneous view, shows how strong can be the influence of the printed word.'

'I agree, sir,' said his companion hastily; it was never politic to disagree with a wealthy customer, especially over an unimportant matter.

'These penny-a-liners are never to be trusted. To be blunt, not they, nor their editors, nor even many of their proprietors, are gentlemen, sir. Not as *we* understand the word, at least.'

The car rumbled on.

After dinner and toasts and speeches, the guests sat smoking cigars, with decanters of port and bottles of brandy at hand. An aura of well-being hung about them, rich and fragrant as the smoke of a hundred Havanas. Peers of the realm chatted with shrewd Austrian Jews to whom indirectly their estates were mortgaged, and who would one day change their names and acquire estates and British titles of their own.

Owners of manufactories in the North of England discussed with Members of Parliament the iniquities of the relatively new taxes on income. If some of these ridiculous laws could be altered, there might be lucrative directorships for Members who saw where the real interests of their constituents lay.

Fulwood introduced Jackson to William Butler Ogden, the first mayor of Chicago and now one of its richest citizens. Ogden, so Fulwood explained *sotto voce*, had travelled West by stage coach when his brother-in-law had unwisely invested the family fortune of $100,000 in buying land in those parts without even seeing it. Ogden went West to try and minimise this loss.

'Chicago had just been incorporated as a town,' Sir Thomas explained 'It possessed exactly a hundred and eighty inhabitants, living in forty three shacks and hutments. William Ogden was horrified when he real ised that his brother-in-law had bought – totally on someone else' description – a vast and desolate swamp, thick with wild onion an weeds of every kind. The only living creatures he could see were bull frogs croaking in the reeds. A lesser man would have been defeated, but not him,' Sir Thomas added approvingly.

Ogden had cut down the reeds, and stayed on until summer, when sunshine dried out the swamp through the reed fronds. Then he put up notices to announce that he was auctioning sections of land. None of the strangers who bid knew that this could become a swamp when the rains arrived, and Ogden did not tell them. Within a week, he had recovered all the family money – and still owned two-thirds of the swamp.

He returned to New York to reimburse his brother-in-law, and then went back to Chicago. Swamp or not, streets were already being constructed across the land he had sold. He had done the pioneering work; others were happy to follow his lead. The price he received for the rest of the land made him a millionaire.

Ogden then decided that Chicago needed a railway, so he set out with a horse and buggy to sell stock for what he called the Galena and Chicago Union Railroad. *And* he built it.

'Vision, doctor,' said Sir Thomas. 'Vision. That is what a man needs to succeed – a quality you possess yourself, of course.'

He introduced Jackson to another American, Cyrus Hall McCormick, a tall, well-built man with a fringe beard and a Virginian accent.

'Mr McCormick invented the grain reaper,' Sir Thomas explained. 'Ogden invested some capital for a half share of his company, and, of course, made another fortune, for the invention totally revolutionised farming in the United States. And Mr McCormick was always absolutely fair with every customer.'

'That's the only way to do business,' interrupted Mr McCormick enthusiastically. 'I have proved it.'

'How?' Jackson asked him, remembering shady deals in Canton and Macao; the bribes, the threats, the fast cutters, hull down and heavy with illegal mud, the Chinese shells that always fell short of their targets.

'Mr McCormick is too modest to explain,' replied Sir Thomas. 'So I will tell you. He had a fixed price for his reaper – one hundred and twenty dollars, flat. No discount, no haggling. The farmer could have one delivered for thirty dollars down, and six months to pay the rest.'

'What if his harvest was bad?' asked Jackson.

'I gave him time to pay,' McCormick explained. 'And I never once employed any attorney to enforce a debt. If they were slow in paying, I waited. My competitors, on the other hand, would seize a man's machine and sue him for the debt. But what is the point of suing a farmer who has no money? That way you only make the lawyers rich.'

'Was it all as easy as you make it sound now?' Jackson asked him.

'Hell, no,' said McCormick. 'When the gold rush came, all the farmers went West to California. I thought I was finished.'

'So do you know what he did?' Sir Thomas interrupted in admiration. 'He printed posters pointing out to farmers that labour was going to be very short that year – so they had better buy a McCormick reaper, which could do the work of ten strong men!'

Jackson was secretly surprised and pleased that such men as these, about whose achievements he had previously only read in newspapers, accepted him as an equal, and listened to his anecdotes of the East with the same attention that he gave to their conversations.

Then Sir Thomas Fulwood, who had recognised another man across the room, drew Jackson to one side.

. 'There is someone else I would like you to meet,' he said. 'Gunther Lewis, an old customer of our bank. He comes from Manchester. His father was a jobbing printer, and Lewis's task as a boy, when he was apprenticed, was to find out lots of odd facts – what you and I would call useless knowledge.

'When they were setting a column of type for the local paper, and there was not enough copy to fill the column completely, they would drop in one of these facts at the bottom – only a paragraph long. What in their trade they call a "filler", I believe.

'Soon, Gunther became more interested in these facts than in printing. He collected a mass of them, you know the sort of thing – How does a fly walk on the ceiling? How do we hear? What is the moon, and so on – and printed them in a booklet which he sold for a few coppers.

'These items were all true, so he called the booklet *Strange Truths*. So many people bought it that he printed another booklet of odd facts. Soon, he was running a magazine of that name.'

'I remember it well,' said Jackson. 'But I haven't seen it recently.'

'He sold out. The buyer lacked his skill, and within a year it went into bankruptcy. But Lewis used the money he had received to found a newspaper. Since he was still enquiring into facts, he called it *The Enquirer*.'

'I would be delighted to meet him,' said Jackson. 'I cannot say I always agree with the policy of his paper – a bit too liberal for my mind. Always harping on the theme that we merchants are not much better than pirates, peddling a pernicious drug, and so forth.'

'His policy no doubt stems from his own background, North Country nonconformist. Do not take it too seriously. That paper could make a great deal of money – in the right hands.'

'Why not his?'

'A tragic story,' Sir Thomas explained as they crossed the room. 'Do not show any surprise at his appearance. He is suffering from a wasting disease, poor fellow. I fear he is not long for this world.'

'Who will own the paper then?' asked Jackson.

'That is what worries him. He is a widower, with a feckless son. From what I have heard tonight, he is looking for a buyer. A cash buyer.'

'From what you tell me, Sir Thomas, he's looking at one now.'

The messenger knocked at the door of the editor's office on the second floor of *The Enquirer* building in Fleet Street. He entered and placed Jackson's card on the editor's desk. The editor was bald-headed with a short grey beard and a grey moustache stained with snuff. He had been drinking from the bottle he kept in the drawer of his desk. Whisky had dampened his moustache and his face was flushed. He was a worried, irascible man who suffered from chronic indigestion.

'What does this fellow want?' he asked the clerk irritably. He had unwisely eaten two dozen oysters for lunch, and his stomach was paining him. Whisky and shellfish rarely went well together, he knew, but he liked both inordinately.

'He says it's a personal matter, sir. Of great importance.'

'To him – or to us?'

'He did not say, sir.'

'I suppose I had better see him. You say he seems to be a man of means?'

'He gives me that impression, sir.'

'Show him in then, dammit!'

Dr Jackson came into the cluttered office, noticed the dirty fly-stained windows and smelled whisky. The room had not been cleaned for weeks. Dust lay thick on the editor's desk between piles of manuscripts. The editor did not stand up to greet his visitor. But taking in his expensive suit, his starched linen, the pearl in his tiepin, the polish on his hand-made boots, he wished he had. Jackson exuded the success that had so unfairly eluded him.

'To come to the point, sir,' said Jackson as he introduced himself, 'I am a partner in Trinity-Trio, an Eastern company of which you may have heard?'

The editor nodded.

'We are establishing a branch in this country and another in North America, and would place considerable weight on advertising in your journal. Do I make myself clear?'

'Perfectly,' said the editor. 'I assume that in return you wish a favour of some kind? Well-disposed comment in our editorial columns?'

'That would be of value, but the favour that I have in mind now is that your newspaper's reporting of mercantile and other European activities in China and India should be more accurate. I would like to see reports of what is actually happening there, rather than to read inaccurate accounts, often tinged with soft and sentimental liberal views.'

'Our staff of reporters and correspondents is generally considered to be the best in Fleet Street, sir.'

'Who considers that to be so?' Jackson asked him.

The editor did not reply. No-one had ever asked him that question before, and he could not find a quick answer. The claim had been part of their advertising for years.

'To come to the present reason for my visit,' Jackson continued, 'I am about to travel north to Scotland with my partner, Mr Alec Douglas. He is the rightful owner of a vast estate, a distillery and a castle – Coupar Castle – all of which have been taken from him by fraud, forgery and deceit. I would suggest that one of your staff could find much of value and interest in reporting events north of the border when we arrive.'

'You make serious allegations, sir, both about our reporting of commercial activities in the East and your partner's alleged experiences at the hands of others. If he is a partner in Trinity-Trio, I am at a loss to understand how anyone could have swindled him so heavily.'

'That is a matter which would no doubt also exercise the minds of your readers – and about which your reporter could enlighten them in an entertaining fashion.'

The editor shook his head. He did not take to Dr Jackson. He held his hand in front of his mouth to conceal a belch.

'I must tell you, sir, we would not consider changing our policy towards enterpreneurs in the East, nor would we consider sending a reporter on such a journey as you propose without direct authority from our proprietor.'

'I am giving you that authority now,' Jackson told him.

The editor allowed himself a smile.

'You speak almost as if *you* were our proprietor,' he said sarcastically.

'I am,' replied Jackson.

Mr Macnamara, at his desk in his chambers in Lincoln's Inn, examined the visiting card as though he had never seen one like it before, then ran this thumb expertly over the heavily embossed black lettering to test its depth and hence its cost: *Dr Richard Jackson, Partner, Trinity-Trio, Calcutta, Hong Kong and Canton.* He looked across his desk at Jackson with more interest and respect.

Behind Jackson, on the cropped lawns of the Inn, yellow leaves from the plane trees turned handsprings. Two gardeners wearing green baize aprons swept them steadily towards wheelbarrows. The sight recalled to Macnamara his own rolling acres in Kent – and an under-gardener he must dismiss that weekend.

The man had dared to question Macnamara's judgement about a laurel hedge; he had stubbornly said that laurel leaves should never be cut roughly, whereas Macnamara was certain that this did not matter. The man did not realise that Macnamara could never accept a contrary opinion. For someone to disagree with him seemed a deliberate challenge to his authority, and, for a subordinate, a hireling, nothing less than a calculated insult. No matter that the man had an ailing wife and a sick child to support, and years in his service, he had to go.

Macnamara's thoughts returned to his visitor. He knew of Trinity-Trio, of course; one of those newish companies in the East, producing enormous profits for a handful of partners. Dr Jackson was clearly very wealthy.

'I am glad that you have received my letter, posted in Calcutta,' Jackson was saying. 'The post is not always so reliable.'

'It arrived only last week, sir,' Macnamara replied. 'What is the matter on which you wish to consult me?'

'I seek your help over a delicate issue. I quite realise that your very high professional standards may prevent your cooperation. In that case, I will fully understand your rectitude. But let me put the problem, and you can judge.

'It concerns a friend and partner, Mr Alec Douglas. After the death of his father, his mother married a Mr Pomfret. Shortly afterwards, she died as a result of a tragic accident.

'Pomfret then married again, but sadly he also died suddenly. Then this young widow discovered, to her understandable consternation, that he had made a will of which she knew nothing, not in favour of her, or of Alec Douglas, but in favour of a young friend of her late husband, one Claude Cartwright.'

Macnamara interrupted him.

'I should explain that I act for Mr Claude Cartwright,' he said tactfully.

'So I understand. Which is why I am here – purely in a private capacity, of course. Pomfret's widow died in India shortly before I left Calcutta. Mr Douglas is a very rich man, but he is naturally upset. An estate which has been in his family's possession for several hundred years, is now apparently owned by someone else, for whom it has no such long association.

'Can you tell me whether anything can be done to help him? The matter, as you can appreciate, preys on his mind. I ask this as one professional man to another, always accepting how you are bound by the rigid constraints of a lawyer and client relationship.'

'I appreciate your frankness, Dr Jackson, but I have to tell you there is nothing I can do to change the terms of the will. I may agree privately that had I been in Mr Alec Douglas's position, I also would have felt aggrieved. But, as a physician, you will know how rich old men sometimes have their fantasies and whims, and we have to accept that everyone has the right to do what they wish with their own property. I fully understand your friend's feelings, but I only administer the law. I do not make it.'

Jackson nodded to show his acceptance of the logic of this statement. Then he glanced enquiringly towards the back of an old man perched on a stool at a high desk in one corner of the room, assiduously copying some documents with a quill pen.

'Is this gentleman the Mr Ebenezer whose name I saw as witness to the will?' he asked Macnamara.

'That is correct.'

'Could I have a word with him?'

'You would be wasting your time, doctor. Most unfortunately, Ebenezer is a deaf mute. He possesses an excellent copperplate hand, however, and I am therefore pleased to employ him. Otherwise, he might have difficulty finding any work to which he is suited. I believe we should all help those less fortunate than ourselves.'

'A noble sentiment,' Jackson agreed warmly, standing up. 'Now, sir, how much do I owe you for your time? Let me settle at once since we may not meet again.'

'A nominal amount. I would suggest twenty sovereigns. Purely for a charity in which I take a close interest.'

Jackson opened a purse and took out twenty sovereigns, placing them in a heap on Macnamara's desk.

'Should you wish to contact me further – although in view of what you tell me, I feel that this is doubtful – I will be at the Albemarle Hotel in Albemarle Street for the next few days,' he said.

Then, on impulse, he crossed the room to Ebenezer. He placed one hand gently on the old man's shoulder. Ebenezer looked up at the doctor.

'I know you cannot hear me,' Jackson told him, 'but you can see. Here are two sovereigns for your time. As Mr Macnamara rightly says, we should all help those less fortunate than ourselves.'

Jackson bowed to Macnamara and left the room. Before he was down the stairs, the lawyer had crossed to Ebenezer's desk and pocketed the two coins himself.

Douglas was sitting in an easy chair reading *The Enquirer* in the drawing room of their suite, when Jackson returned to the Albemarle Hotel. He looked up at his colleague enquiringly.

'Nothing,' said Jackson, shaking his hand. He poured himself a measure of The Macallan malt whisky.

'Not a man I would trust,' he went on. 'Closeted with a poor clerkish creature, a deaf mute, one Ebenezer, who witnessed the will. And the will is binding. No argument about that.'

Douglas lowered his paper, and sighed. 'Thank you for your efforts,' he said. 'I am not greatly surprised. I expected this answer. Well, we cannot argue with the terms of a will, even if it is drawn up by a sodomite and executed by a charlatan. Let us therefore put this sad matter behind us for the moment. I see a new musical is playing at the Theatre Royal. Let us have supper at Romano's, see this show, and then dine at my club.'

'On any other evening, a capital idea,' replied Jackson. 'But not tonight. I am half expecting a visitor.'

'You did not say so,' said Douglas, surprised. 'Someone I know?'

'Someone you *will* know,' Jackson promised him. 'So, just on this one evening, let us order chops and claret and eat here. I would not like to be absent should this caller arrive.'

Douglas picked up his newspaper. Jackson poured himself another whisky and lit a cigar. Time passed. A servant came in, drew the curtain, and took their order for supper. Then a discreet knock at the door caused the two men to glance enquiringly at each other.

A porter entered.

'A gentleman downstairs to see you, Dr Jackson, sir. Without an appointment, he says. A Mr Ebenezer.'

'Show him up,' said Jackson.

Ebenezer came into the room nervously. Standing, he appeared taller than Jackson had imagined, but he stooped and gave the appearance of a worried and perambulating question mark. Jackson shook him warmly by the hand, and pulled up an easy chair for him.

'Shall I leave the room?' Douglas asked after Jackson had introduced him.

'Of course not. Your concerns are what brings him here.'

'You will have a whisky, Mr Ebenezer?'

'Thank you, sir,' replied the old man, surprise and pleasure lighting up his face.

Douglas looked at him in astonishment.

'I understood you were a deaf mute?' he said, almost accusingly.

'It is Mr Macnamara's explicit order that he will only employ me if I always give that impression while in his office,' Ebenezer explained.

He paused, his sallow face flushed with embarrassment.

'You may not be aware, gentlemen, but he knows something with regard to my past that is gravely detrimental to me and my family. Should I leave, he says he would publish this, with consequent distress, even ruin, to those most dear to me.

'He uses me as a silent witness to all manner of transactions. People talk freely when they believe they are not overheard. Many visitors do not even notice me – and if they do, a deaf mute is not a person of any concern to them. I therefore make a note of all conversations between clients and my employer, in his two identities as Macnamara and O'Hara.'

'But now,' said Jackson, handing him a large Macallan, 'am I right in assuming you may wish to leave his employ?'

'I would have left long ago, gentlemen, had the opportunity presented itself, and provided I could keep my secret.'

'I think I can guarantee you both the opportunity and the assurance. But the last word rests with this gentleman here.'

Jackson indicated Douglas.

'I believe, Alec, that Mr Ebenezer can prove that the will in favour of Claude Cartwright was forged. His evidence should be sufficient to guarantee his retirement – and the lawyer's silence. Am I right?'

Ebenezer nodded.

'Then you have my word, Mr Ebenezer,' Douglas assured him. 'A most handsome emolument and a pension if you wish. Or maybe you would like to be set up in a law practice of your own?'

Ebenezer's eyes filled with tears of relief and amazement.

'But how did you know, sir, that I was not as my employer described me, a mute?' he asked Jackson.

'Medical knowledge, my dear fellow. When I approached you and placed my hand on your shoulder, you did not start up with alarm at the contact. That meant you must have heard me walk across the room. Had you really been deaf, you would have been startled at my sudden proximity.'

'You will dine with us?' said Douglas. 'We have ordered a meal and can easily set a third place.'

Mr Ebenezer nodded, then unexpectedly he sat down and covered his face with his hands so that the others would not see him weep.

'Forgive me, gentlemen,' he said, when he had composed himself. 'I cannot explain what being treated with kindness means when one has not known it for so long.'

'I well know how you feel,' Douglas assured him gently, and poured another whisky for the old man.

Perthshire

The reporter was a stout man in his middle forties, wearing a frock coat, mustard and cress trousers and a shabby green bowler. He suffered from an adenoidal constriction. To try and conceal this he had taken to breathing in through his mouth and out through his nose. This gave him the impression of being permanently agape like a fish; his lips moved, but no sound emerged. He smelled slightly of camphor and stout, but he was a good journalist; Jackson had read his reports over many years.

Now the reporter knocked nervously on the door of the drawing room of a suite in the Fair Maid Hotel in Perth. When Jackson told him to enter, he came in hesitantly. He had heard that this new proprietor wished to brief him personally on a special assignment. Jackson stood up and shook hands with him, wanting to put him at his ease.

'I'm very pleased to meet you, Mister –?' He paused.

'Arbuthnott, sir. With two T's.'

'Well, Mr Arbuthnott with two T's, we are about to give an exclusive story with which I have no doubt the editor will lead his front page as soon as you can get it to him.'

'It will go south by the first available train to London, sir. Do you wish to read it first?'

'No,' said Jackson magnanimously. 'I leave its content entirely to you. But bear in mind that we have studied your career, and it seems that perhaps you have not risen as high on the journalistic ladder as I personally believe your talent deserves. If this story follows the lines I have discussed with your editor, I can say, as the owner of *The Enquirer*, that you will be in line for instant promotion. Are we understood?'

'Perfectly, sir.'

'Right. Now tell my friend here what you have discovered. I will not give you his name yet, and it is a condition of your continued employment that you do not enquire until we choose to reveal it. Also understood?'

'Perfectly, sir.'

The reporter bowed to Douglas.

'I went out to the estate as instructed, and under the guise of conducting a survey as to suitable crops in the area, I spoke to six tenant farmers and probably twice as many labouring men – the latter in the inn, The Douglas Clan.'

'And what did you find?'

'All the farmers were very grievously in debt.'

'To banks and usurers?'

'No, sir. To the present laird, a gentleman from London, Mr Claude Cartwright. The labouring men were equally dispirited and, sir, if you will pardon the phrase, I would say almost mutinous, certainly ready for serious insurrection.'

'Why?'

'Because of the policies and personal life and habits of Mr Cartwright. He thinks of nothing except his own enjoyment and his carnal pleasures. If you will excuse my frankness, he finds his pleasure in the most disgusting way and in the grossest manner with young boys, even animals . . . sheep, even hens, so it is said.'

'How does that affect the farmers and the labourers – apart from their natural disgust at such abhorrent practices?'

'Their stock, when returned, are uneasy, ill, nervous. This affects other animals and the prices they fetch at the market. Added to which Mr Cartwright is so intent on making as much money as he conceivably can that he has squeezed rents to the highest they will go, so now the farmers fear eviction.'

'Who is the worst affected farmer?'

'Mr MacDuff in Long Glen Farm. He has lost his only son, Alastair. The lad was taken into service in the castle to learn the position of under footman. He did not want to go, and his father did not wish him to go, because he was useful on the farm, but he needed the money, for Mr Cartwright offered unusually good wages. Twenty-five pounds a year, five pounds paid in advance, with two new uniforms every twelve months, and all linen.

'Then he discovered he was hired largely to be a creature for the foul lusts of Mr Cartwright and others. He had to parade naked. His private parts were rubbed with oil and manipulated in the presence of fine guests from London – including women, I would not call them ladies – who laughed at his shame. He had to pleasure them, too, sir.'

'He did not *have* to, surely?' interrupted Jackson.

'He was told that if he did not, he and his parents, and his step-sister, Fiona, would all be put out of their house and farm. That would have meant starvation for them, sir. And with their existing debts to Mr Cartwright, possibly prison. Fiona is the daughter of Mrs Pomfret, who married Mr Pomfret, the laird, on the death of his first wife.'

'What is she like, this girl?' Douglas asked him.

'Very blue eyes and unusually fair hair. A most attractive girl. Often, she goes to the castle gates and just stands there, looking up the drive. Everyone likes her – except Mr Cartwright. He will send a servant down to order her away. She goes, of course, but then she comes back. It's odd, the locals say, to see her there, standing still as a little statue. Especially after what happened to the boy. They were close. Just like brother and sister. She must miss him greatly.'

'What happened to the lad?'

'He endured his disgusting treatment for as long as he could, but finally he was asked to have connection with a ewe as part of a spectacle to amuse Mr Cartwright's guests. He refused. There was a struggle, and he struck Mr Cartwright.'

'Good for him,' said Douglas. 'And then?'

'Mr Cartwright ordered him to be stripped and beaten as a punishment. The boy fought back and was unfortunately hit on the head with a club or walking stick. He lost consciousness. It would appear he suffered severe internal injuries to the head, and died.'

'Did none of the guests speak for him?'

'They had a whip round, sir, and collected fifteen sovereigns, which they gave to his father. But of course, all denied there had been any untoward behaviour.'

'So how did MacDuff learn about this?'

'A maid had been watching at a key-hole, sir. She was the lad's sweet-heart. She told his father but, naturally, he could not reveal the source of the information. She would have lost her position immediately, and without a reference, would never have found another.'

'So MacDuff is distraught, eh?'

'More than that, sir. He plans to avenge his son's death.'

'Understandably,' said Jackson. 'Now, here are your instructions. Exactly this, no more, no less. Understood?'

'Perfectly, sir.'

Jackson began to talk quietly and the reporter took a shorthand note as he spoke.

The following morning, at a quarter to eight o'clock, Douglas and Jackson, in a hired carriage and four, with a second closed carriage following them, arrived unannounced at the front door of Coupar Castle. Douglas surveyed the once familiar scene with sadness. The wide drive lay weedy and unraked. On the steps, huge stone bowls, which he remembered filled with flowers, stood empty, except for dandelions and couch grass. Plantains and daisies disfigured the vast front lawn. The general air of decrepitude depressed and angered him: such neglect spoke of a place unloved, and he had loved this castle all his life.

Both men climbed down from the carriage, and strode up the front steps. Douglas pulled the bell chain. He wore a scarf around the lower part of his face, his hat pulled low over his forehead. Jackson was momentarily reminded of Major Forster, who had posed as Mr Brown in the inn near Gravesend so many years earlier. That mission had been crowned with success. Would the same outcome attend their visit today?

A creaking of bolts, the rattle of a chain, and the door was opened. The butler, pouch-eyed, his sallow face still heavy with sleep, looked at the two men enquiringly and without enthusiasm.

'An interview with Mr Cartwright, if you please,' Jackson told him.

'He is still abed, sir.'

'Then get him out of bed,' ordered Douglas roughly.

'I beg your pardon, sir, but he is a late riser. Who shall I say requests is presence?'

'Dr Jackson. Assure him we would not have come at such an unsocial hour if our visit were not of the greatest importance – to him.'

'And your friend, sir?'

Douglas let the scarf drop from his face, took off his hat.

'Mr Douglas!' cried the butler in delight. 'I had no idea it was you, sir!'

'Do as my friend asks. But do not tell Mr Cartwright I am here. Is he alone in the house?'

'He has his lawyer with him, sir, a Mr Macnamara, from London, and a young man also from London. A man, if I may say so, sir, of an effeminate type.'

Douglas was pleased that the telegraph he had sent from Perth to Macnamara in Cartwright's name, urging his presence at the castle with all speed, had made the lawyer come north. Cartwright had no doubt been puzzled at the man's arrival. The lawyer, probably equally mystified at Cartwright's denials of having sent for him, would have to stay at least until that night, before he could catch a train south. Two birds with one stone, Douglas thought. Why waste two stones on two crows?

The butler padded away, his long bunioned feet performing unlikely miracles of speed for such a portly man, up the marble staircase and along carpeted corridors, while the visitors waited in the hall. Douglas replaced his hat and scarf and stood still, a huge, brooding, rather sinister figure. Jackson lit a cigar. In one corner, between two suits of mail, a grandfather clock measured out the morning with its heavy metallic tick.

They heard a shuffling of slippered feet upstairs, a shrill querulous voice raised and as instantly quietened. Cartwright came down the staircase, wearing purple silk pyjamas beneath a brocaded dressing-gown with golden tassels. His hair was ruffled and there were marks of red lip salve on both cheeks. Behind him came a slightly built boy of sixteen or seventeen, similarly dressed, with his mouth reddened by salve. He had streaks of rouge on his face, mascara still on his eyelids. He looked at the visitors petulantly; this was clearly a very early hour for him to be awake.

'You wish to see me, I understand,' said Cartwright coldly. 'What is the nature of your visit so early in the morning?'

Jackson exhaled a cloud of cigar smoke.

'I do not like smoking in this house,' Cartwright said irritably. Jackson took another puff, and looked over Cartwright's shoulder to a third man who was following them downstairs. Macnamara was fully dressed in a dark suit, a gold watch chain across his waistcoat. He cracked his knuckles as he recognised Jackson.

'Why, Dr Jackson, sir,' he said in surprise.

'You know this gentleman?' asked Claude sharply.

'He called at my chambers earlier this month.'

'You are his attorney?'

'Not so. It was on another matter.'

'It is no secret to say what the matter is,' said Jackson, removing his cigar and regarding the glowing end. 'But I respect your professional rectitude. The fact is, Mr Cartwright, I came to see him about a will involving this property, and the disagreeable and most scandalous way in which my friend, Mr Alec Douglas, has been treated.'

'As I have already informed you, sir, the will in question has been proved beyond all possible contention,' said Macnamara quickly. 'My client, Mr Cartwright, is the main beneficiary. A certain sum was left for Mrs Pomfret, but since she left for India without informing anyone of her address, we have been unable to contact her. I see that news of her tragic death in India was published in *The Enquirer* quite recently. There is nothing more to be said on the matter.'

Douglas took off his hat, unwound his scarf and smiled at them. Claude took a step back in horror and disbelief. Macnamara's eyes narrowed.

'On the contrary, there is everything to be said and much to be done,' Douglas informed them. 'First, Claude – I find the name more suitable for you than Cartwright, which has connotations of an honest craftsman, while Claude has a soft, simpering, pansified, Frenchified sound – that will is a forgery. You both know it, and I will prove it in any court in the land.'

'I assume you must be Mr Douglas?' said Macnamara icily. He began to come down the stairs slowly, his face grave. His knuckles cracked like dry twigs with every step.

'Your assumption is correct.'

'You are making a most grave allegation,' Macnamara told him.

'You, sir, in whatever prison you may be detained, will have ample time to reflect upon its gravity – and your loathsome part in this fraud.'

'You are damned insolent, sir!' said Macnamara roughly. 'And I will have you answer for these absurd and baseless charges in court.'

'Whenever you please,' Douglas replied. Macnamara saw relentless anger burn fierily in his eyes, and withdrew a pace. Cartwright called to the butler.

'Wake two of the stoutest grooms,' he ordered. 'Bring them here at once with sticks. We will teach these impudent London swine a lesson they will long remember, and then the law can deal with them.'

'Before you become too free with your teaching of lessons,' said Douglas quietly, 'listen to this. You, Claude, originally dressed up as my mother, actually wore her clothes, when she was already dead – murdered, I suspect – only a few hours earlier.

'You put on gloves to conceal your hands, which, though effeminate, were not quite so dainty as hers. You wore a thick veil so that her attorney – who had not seen her in years – would not see your face too closely.

'It was not difficult for you to dress and act as a woman. You have done as much for money often enough in a certain house in Jermyn Street, so my researches tell me. It was a simple step to explain to an attorney not blessed with very good sight or hearing – although doubtless most learned in the law – that, as Mrs Pomfret, you wished to change your will in favour of your husband, Mr Pomfret.'

'Lies!' screamed Claude furiously. 'You cannot prove a word of it.'

'I can,' Douglas assured him. 'Every word. But I have no need, because Macnamara here, or O'Hara as clients of lower social degree know him at Seven Dials, forged the later will that so surprisingly left everything to you.'

'In a lifetime in the law, I have never heard a more absurd or more scandalous claim,' said Macnamara. 'And these allegations in front of witnesses here will cost you dear.'

Douglas did not answer. Instead, he put a silver whistle to his lips and blew. The front door opened and Ebenezer came into the hall. He had been riding in the second carriage.

'What brings you here?' asked Macnamara, his voice suddenly thin and shrill.

'To pay a debt of years of misery at your hands,' Ebenezer replied. 'And to prove that I am not the deaf, stupid mute you have told everyone I am. I am here for the best reason of all – revenge!'

He turned to Douglas.

'As I have already told you, I witnessed the will,' he said. 'It is a total forgery. I have signed an affidavit to that effect.'

Douglas turned to Macnamara.

'You see, I could sue you – and win. But the law takes too long. Instead, I will ruin you – now!'

'There has been a terrible mistake,' said Claude desperately. 'I think you are distraught, Mr Douglas. You are quite wrong in your assumption. But let us not argue here in the early hours. Pray let us discuss this calmly later this morning.'

'There is nothing more to discuss. I give you five minutes to collec your belongings, Claude, and *only* your belongings. Then, get out.'

'I refuse. This is my property, my estate, left to me legally.'

Douglas took a step towards him.

'Years ago, when you bore false witness against me to your fello pederast Pomfret, I knocked you down. This time I will knock you dow again. Then I will pick you up and repeat the performance until there not a tooth left in your head or a bone unbroken in your body.

'This prospect has sustained me many times during my time in Indi in a life to which your lies condemned me, but from which God has been pleased to rescue me.'

'You heard what he said,' Claude appealed to his lawyer. 'He is threatening me!'

'I hear it,' said Mr Macnamara. 'I think you are overwrought, Mr Douglas, as my client says. You are saying things you will later regret.'

'The only thing I regret is that I did not have the opportunity to say them long before this. I do not give a damn what you think, or what you do. As you told Dr Jackson, everyone has the right to do what they wish with their own property. And I wish you to get off my property. Now!'

He took his watch from his waistcoat pocket.

'Five minutes,' he said. 'No more, no less.'

The two men looked at each other. Macnamara shrugged. Then they turned and went back up the stairs, talking in low voices. The boy with the made-up face looked at Douglas pathetically.

'Get out and keep away from this creature,' Douglas told him. The boy nodded vigorously and fled away up the stairs.

Douglas whispered something to the butler, who bowed and crossed the hall to the kitchen quarters. Four minutes passed. Claude, Macnamara and the youth appeared together on the landing. Claude carried a portmanteau, and behind him a servant laboured under the weight of two huge polished leather suitcases.

'Open them,' Douglas ordered.

'They are locked, sir,' the servant replied nervously. 'I have no key.'

'Take a fire iron and break the locks.'

The butler did so. Clothes cascaded out: silk shirts and drawers, linen handkerchiefs, all initialled and scented, and, at the bottom, as much silver as Claude could collect within the space of minutes.

'Remove all that,' said Douglas. 'Let him take his clothes – and nothing else.'

He turned to Macnamara.

'If ever you have the effrontery to solicit any fee from some poor devil who seeks legal advice, I will lay my knowledge of your dealings before the courts and personally prosecute you, to the uttermost limit of the law.

'In the meantime, I will ensure that readers of *The Enquirer* are kept fully informed about your activities, public, private – and charitable. For a start, you have recently dismissed one of your gardeners, simply because his knowledge regarding laurel bushes exceeded yours. You will immediately reinstate him and double his wages. *Enquirer* readers will also shortly be treated to a full investigation into the financial structure of the charity known as St Agnes' Fountains.'

'You are taking my living from me,' said Macnamara hoarsely.

'You have taken much more from too many others over too many years. Consider yourself fortunate I am not taking your liberty – or your life.'

The servant picked up the suitcases to carry them to the front door.

'Put them down,' Douglas ordered him.

Claude turned as though to challenge this, then thought better of it, swallowed nervously and dragged the cases across the tiled floor towards the door. They were too heavy for him to carry.

'There were two carriages here,' he said petulantly.

'And they are not coming back for you,' Douglas told him. 'You will all have to walk.'

'Where to?'

'Anywhere. To the Law Courts in London, if your companion pleases.'

With Jackson and Ebenezer, he followed them to the top of the stone steps that led to the drive. Cartwright went down these steps first, pulling the cases after him. At the bottom, he turned and stamped his foot.

'You bastards!' he screamed. 'You bastards!'

A great wave of derisive laughter answered him. He looked up at the castle in surprise. Every window framed grinning faces: parlourmaids, scullery maids, pantry-boys, housekeeper, under-butler, grooms, ostlers, gardeners. The entire staff of a great country establishment were looking down at him, watching his departure with delight, revelling in his humiliation.

And as the two men and the boy walked away, the servants began to clap their hands slowly, in the way of a music hall or theatre audience that wishes to show its contempt.

Macnamara turned and shook his fist impotently up at them. Then they walked on. As they entered an avenue of rhododendrons, gardeners and labourers stepped from behind the bushes. They held sticks, rakes, forks, leather belts. At the sight, Macnamara, Claude and the boy began to run. But these men ran more quickly and belaboured them with blows until they reached the castle gates.

High in an oak tree on the far side of the lane, totally concealed by thick foliage, crouched MacDuff. A double-barrelled shotgun lay cradled in front of him, across a bough of the tree. He saw Claude pause and wipe sweat and blood from his face, and turn to Macnamara. In that instant, MacDuff took aim and fired.

Claude spun like a top and dropped to the ground. MacDuff fired again Claude's portmanteau burst open. Pink silk shirts billowed and fluttered in the early morning breeze like the wings of huge and delicate moths.

Macnamara and the boy kept on running. MacDuff reloaded and fired a third time. Macnamara faltered. The buckshot had caught him in th rear. Then, screaming with pain and rage, he stumbled on after the boy staggering out of sight like a drunken man.

MacDuff climbed down from the tree and approached Claude. He turned the man over with his foot. The creature was not dead, only stunned, as much by shock as the weight of shotgun pellets in his rump; MacDuff was the best marksman for miles around.

He stood looking down at Claude until he stirred and his eyelids twitched. Then MacDuff opened the flap of his trousers and urinated into Claude's open mouth.

Back in the castle hall, Douglas ordered whisky to be brought for everyone present. The servants drank thankfully, smacking their lips, wiping their mouths with the backs of their hands, holding out metal beakers for more.

Ebenezer drew Douglas to one side.

'If you have nothing else for me, sir, I will catch the noon train south,' he said.

'Do that,' agreed Douglas. 'But I have much more planned for you. Dr Jackson and I wish you to become our lawyer.'

'That is extremely kind of you both, sir, and I would dearly like to accept. But I am not qualified to do so.'

'Then become qualified. At our expense. And when you are, we will set you up in your own practice and with a special retainer to ensure that you will fight with all your abilities *any* case of legal malpractice or chicanery that comes to your notice.'

Mr Arbuthnott, the reporter, joined them and drained a glass of neat Macallan.

'You saw everything?' Jackson asked him.

'Yes, sir. But the shooting at the end – do you wish that included in my report?'

'Shooting?' asked Douglas in innocent surprise. 'Who was shot?'

'I saw Mr Cartwright fall. I think he will recover, though. He was hit in the rear, sir.'

'Where he has already suffered pain for his pleasure. And the lawyer?'

'He was hit, but could run away.'

'Your report must explain how justice was done here,' Jackson told Arbuthnott. 'I would not presume to dictate how it should be presented. Name the rogues, of course, *and* give their full addresses. Others they have wronged may wish to seek them out.'

'Perhaps you could say that MacDuff was out shooting vermin and these two strangers, not versed in the ways of the Scottish countryside, were wrongly placed for a morning's sport,' Douglas suggested.

'Are there any witnesses, sir?'

'You are the witness. The only witness. Understood?'

'Perfectly, sir. But my editor may not like that.'

'Your proprietor does. And in any case, if your story has the effect I hope, there will soon be a new editor, one more directly in tune and sympathy with my aims and policies.'

'And who will that be, sir?'

'You, Mr Arbuthnott, with two T's.'

Dr Jackson reined in his horse at the head of the glen and sat for a moment, breathing the scented air while miles of heather trembled before him in the wind like a wide and purple sea. As he listened, he realised he must have stopped because he had heard a cry – now repeated – so faint that it could have been the sound of an animal caught in a trap. But there were no traps here; Douglas had banned them all. This was a human cry. Someone was in great, perhaps mortal, pain.

Jackson spurred his horse down the path which wound through a small wood. In a clearing, he saw a carriage on its side, wheels still turning, sunlight reflecting from brightly varnished spokes. Two coachmen were struggling to calm horses which were kicking frantically to be free. On the ground, a man knelt by the side of a young woman in a white dress smeared now with dust, one shoe torn off through the force of the accident. The man was ineffectually fanning her face with a handkerchief. Jackson dismounted by his side.

'Richard Jackson, physician, at your service, sir,' he said. The man looked at him thankfully, and stood up. He had a weak aristocratic face with a receding chin.

'I am Lord Dalgoun, sir. I was accompanying Lady Priscilla Graham to Balmoral, where the Queen is in residence. One of the horses is young. It took fright at a bird that flew out in front of us, and bolted. This is the result.'

The girl on the ground opened her eyes and moaned feebly. Jackson knelt down by her side, felt her pulse.

'My leg,' she said faintly. 'My right leg.'

He raised her skirt; the leg was twisted below the knee, clearly broken.

'You have injured your leg, ma'am,' he told her. 'We will send a coachman off to get a hurdle to carry you to the nearest house.'

'Is it broken?'

He nodded.

'I was on my way to attend upon Her Majesty.'

She moved slightly, and cried out in anguish at the spear-thrust of pain.

'Have you anything to help her?' asked Dalgoun.

'I have no medicaments with me,' Jackson replied. 'But I think I can ease her pain to some extent.'

'Then I beg you to do so.'

'This is rather unorthodox treatment,' said Jackson. 'But I have been practising in China, and it can have remarkable results.'

'I don't care what the treatment is, if you can help her.'

Jackson put his hand in his fob pocket, took out a small crocodile skin pouch and opened it; Dalgoun saw three fine golden needles with their points embedded in a strip of cork.

Jackson removed one needle, rolled down Lady Priscilla's stocking on her uninjured leg and carefully placed the tip of the needle into the skin below her knee. He pricked the skin above her ankle with a second needle, her foot with the third.

'What the devil are you doing, sir?' asked Dalgoun in amazement.

'Ask the lady,' Jackson replied.

'There is no pain at all,' she told them. Her voice sounded relaxed now, almost soporific. 'It is amazing. I feel no pain whatever.'

'Help me to move her,' said Jackson.

He and Dalgoun carried her on to the soft grass at the side of the track. The horses were now quietened. One coachman held them, while his companion set off to the nearest house. Within minutes, he was back with a crofter. They carried a five-bar farm gate on which they laid Lady Priscilla as on a bed, and bore her out of the wood.

Dalgoun shook Jackson's hand warmly.

'Where are you staying, sir?'

'At Coupar Castle, with my friend, Alec Douglas.'

'I have never seen treatment like this in my life. Amazing. Truly amazing. Her Majesty will be most astonished when Lady Graham tells her.'

'Is she likely to do so?'

'She is a Maid of Honour, and Her Majesty is very curious about matters that are new, of interest, or strange. A legacy from the interest in scientific things shown by her late husband, Prince Albert.'

That morning, Queen Victoria awoke early. For a moment she lay still, eyes tightly closed, as was her custom, while she fondled the cold plaster cast of the hand of her husband, Prince Albert, the Prince Consort, who had died nearly forty years previously. Every night since then she had slept with that hand by her side.

Then, her eyes misting with tears at the memory of a love long gone, she stroked his nightshirt, which, although now threadbare, was still washed and ironed regularly and placed, neatly folded, on the side of the double bed he had once shared with her.

Every morning, the Queen also ordered fresh flowers to be put on his pillow, and a fresh jug of hot water was placed, with a new towel and soap and flannel cloth, on the marble wash-stand. Every evening, her dead husband's dressing gown, and a newly pressed change of clothes, were laid out as though he was only in the next room, not the next world.

The walls of the Queen's bedroom in Balmoral were dark with tartan wallpaper – her husband's choice. Tartan curtains hung at each window, tartan carpets covered the floor. Gilt-framed mirrors reflected the sightless eyes of antlered heads that faced each other, wall to wall, above the Royal arms of England and Scotland, together with those of her eldest and indolent son, Edward, Prince of Wales. Other panels represented St George of England, St Andrew of Scotland and St Hubert, the patron saint of hunters. Prince Albert – *dear* Albert – had been a great hunter, and this whole castle was now a huge granite monument to his memory. There had been a castle on this site long before he and the Queen had built the present one, but that had been small and insignificant. Albert had helped with the architectural drawings for its replacement, and personally supervised all the decorations, even to choosing plaid upholstery for the chairs. He loved flowers and at his wish the thistle of Scotland appeared above doors, in wall panels, on windows, with dirks and targes.

Lord Rosebery, who had briefly been the Queen's Prime Minister, once remarked to a friend, not imagining he would tell anyone else, that he personally had considered the Queen's drawing room in Osborne House on the Isle of Wight to be the ugliest room in the world – until he saw the drawing room at Balmoral.

But because Prince Albert had played such a part in the castle's construction, because his memory was forever sacred to his widow, nothing could ever be changed, criticised or altered. Her world had stopped turning on the Saturday night he had died at Windsor Castle.

For months – possibly years – before his death Prince Albert had been growing increasingly disenchanted with the subsidiary role he seemed forced to play. He was gravely disappointed in the sloth and slovenly appearance of the Prince of Wales, of whom he wrote bitterly to a friend: 'He is of no more use than a pistol packed in the bottom of a trunk if one were attacked in the robber-infested Apennines'.

Even worse, Queen Victoria was given to unexpected and uncontrollable tantrums and flights of hysteria, and the prospect of being tied by marriage to her became unpleasant to contemplate. Indeed the Queen's two personal physicians, Sir James Clark and Sir William Jenner, had long been concerned about her state of mind. Sir James wrote in his diary: 'Unless she is kept quiet and still, the time will come when she will be in danger. . . .' Both doctors feared she was suffering from what was discreetly known as the 'hereditary malady' of the Royal house – porphyria – but neither of them had ever been permitted to examine their royal patient thoroughly. They did not know, for example, that for years she had been suffering from a ventral hernia and a prolapse of her uterus. She had a dread of the stethoscope, and her doctors had to make do with questions and answers relayed through a personal maid or other female attendant.

Porphyria included symptoms which they believed – at second hand – were apparent in their patient: severe abdominal pains, which brought on insomnia, headache, and restlessness. The disease had apparently originally been inherited from Mary Queen of Scots, who passed on this genetic fault to sixteen generations of European royalty, including Queen Victoria's father, the Duke of Kent. George III was believed to have suffered from it, and became so deranged that he was frequently enclosed in a strait jacket, or confined forcibly in a specially constructed wooden chair with high back and arms, which he sarcastically called 'my coronation chair'.

When Prince Albert succumbed to typhoid, brought on by choked and stinking drains at Windsor Castle, doctors forbade the Queen to kiss his dead face in case she caught the fever, but they had allowed her to kiss his clothes. She then had the room thoroughly photographed, so that, however long she lived, she would know exactly how it looked that Saturday night, December 14th, 1861.

Now, many years on, a housemaid knocked delicately on her bedroom door, entered, curtsied and carried in a ewer of warm water for the Queen to wash her face and hands.

Other maids helped her out of bed. The Queen stood, dumpy, sullen and sallow-faced, barely five feet high. She had been in mourning ever since Prince Albert died, and nowadays little brought a smile to her set, morose countenance.

She found an interest in visitors of a type she might not usually have met, people whose lives or experiences she believed would have entertained her husband. Today she was expecting a subject who she hoped might fall into this category: Dr Richard Jackson who had worked in India 'of which country her shrewd and flattering Prime Minister, Disraeli, had declared she must become Empress), and later in China, where her forces had dealt severe blows to that country's infamous and impertinent rulers.

She never tired of hearing stories from people who knew the outer fringes of her enormous empire. Life there, with vast spaces, huge burning deserts and snow-topped mountain ranges, with spreading new towns and provinces (often named after her, as Victoria, or after her husband, as Alberta) seemed to be painted in primary colours, not the timid pastel tints of Britain.

She was continually reminded of this by the colourful native dress of her Indian servants and her *munshi* – a male Indian secretary who accompanied her on her journeys from Buckingham Palace to Windsor Castle, to Osborne, and then here to Balmoral in Scotland.

The Queen did not wish servants or courtiers to hear her conversation with Dr Jackson, for this would be a strictly private meeting. She had therefore arranged to see him not in Balmoral Castle, but at a cottage she had built after the Prince Consort's death, at the west end of the lonely Loch Muick.

The name of the loch meant darkness or sorrow. Here, in the cottage she called the Widow's House, she felt closest to her husband's spirit. Here, if anywhere, Albert's spirit would advise her on the value of whatever this doctor from the East might have to say.

She would never have heard of him had not one of her prettier Maids of Honour, Lady Priscilla Graham, asked permission to be excused her duties because of an accident in which she had broken her leg when her carriage overturned. She explained how she had been lying in agony, miles from any professional help, when a middle-aged man riding by announced himself as a physician, and immediately eased her pain – not with a draught of opium but, incredibly, by pricking her skin gently and painlessly with tiny gold needles.

Prince Albert would have been interested in this, thought the Queen. He had always been fascinated by science and new scientific discoveries, although even the best medical aid in the land had not been able to save him.

Jenner and Clark, cautious men both, were unenthusiastic at the Queen's proposal that she should actually meet this Dr Jackson.

'I am sorry to have to admit it, but there are many charlatans about in our profession, Majesty,' said Jenner dourly.

'Your Majesty must realise that while what Lady Priscilla says is doubtless true, she may not realise she fainted through sheer pain,' added Clark. 'That is not at all uncommon in the case of accidents.'

'It is our wish to see him, and our wish that you should both also be present,' replied the Queen. 'If we had ignored the advance of the steam engine – and now the horseless carriage driven by benzine – if we had not progressed with electric lights and the marvellous electric telegraph where would we be now? Progress is too often blocked by reactionary views.

'You will remember, gentlemen, that when railways were first proposed there was an outcry from landowners and farmers. The noise of the trains would turn milk sour in the cows. Physicians claimed that the rattle and shake of the carriage would affect childbearing. Smoke and fire from the engines would cause conflagrations and destroy woods and forests. But, in the event, these prophecies were all proved false.

'We have, therefore, invited the doctor to come here at ten of the clock tomorrow morning. We wish that one or two tenants or members of our staff, who have physical disabilities, are also brought here. Let him see what he can do – where other branches of more orthodox medicine have failed to provide a cure.'

'Majesty, if I may be so bold as to submit, this could be a dangerous precedent,' said Clark.

'Dangerous to whom?'

'Majesty, the art of healing is a noble one. I would not wish that any tenant or servant – however humble – should have his or her life placed at any risk by some stranger from China who claims the ability to heal simply by digging gold needles into their flesh.'

'We appreciate your concern, Sir James, which does you credit. But let me repeat a remark made by the American, Benjamin Franklin, which made a deep impression on Prince Albert. Mr Franklin, with several sceptical companions, was watching the ascent of a hot-air balloon. One asked him contemptuously: "What use is that?" Mr Franklin replied: "Of what use is a baby?" '

She nodded dismissal and at ten o'clock the following morning, when Jackson arrived at Balmoral, a courtier and a lady-in-waiting greeted him and escorted him to the cottage on the shore of the loch.

Queen Victoria, in widow's black dress, a white cap on her head, her face pudgy and pasty, mouth set in downward lines of self-pity and discontent, acknowledged his deep bow.

The courtier introduced Jenner and Clark to Jackson. They did not offer to shake hands with him.

'You understand, Dr Jackson, why we have asked you here?' asked the Queen. 'Our late husband, dear Prince Albert, would have wished to meet you and learn about your means of treatment. We would be pleased if you could tell our physicians here the nature of your cure.'

'I will do my best, Your Majesty,' said Jackson. He turned to the two men, who regarded him with hostile eyes.

'When I first went East, gentlemen,' he said, 'I believed that in medicine I had to follow the precepts of the learned physicians and surgeons with whom I had walked the wards.

'I was taught to regard any departure from the norm, as I would regard advertisements in the popular journals for quack cures for tuberculosis, cancer and dropsy, as being without credibility. But in the East, gentlemen, I met a Chinese physician, now unfortunately dead, and from him learned that as the Bible tells us, in Heaven, in our Father's house, there are many mansions – so in medicine there are many ways to the same goal of healing.'

As he spoke, he had a sudden recollection of Kuan Chung's bound body bobbing in the sea, the ship turning in a wide curve of foam. He had as good as killed the man. Who was he to talk of healing?

He cleared his throat and tried to drive the terrible memory from his mind. He explained about Yin and Yang, the plus and minus of man's makeup, which needed to be kept in equilibrium.

'I accept what you say, Dr Jackson,' said Sir James impatiently. 'But I find it difficult to accept that sticking needles in one part of the body can ease pain in another.'

'Lady Priscilla proved it, Sir James.'

'What do you think, Sir William?' the Queen asked.

'Majesty, I was trained, like Sir James here, in the arts of healing, according to the best healers in your kingdom. I must therefore frankly admit that I also find what Dr Jackson claims very difficult to believe.

'It is possible, of course, that many people *imagine* they are ill. They can be talked out of symptoms, even out of physical pain, because they were never really in physical pain. They only imagined it. I would suggest that this Chinese treatment would only be suitable for highly-strung, imaginative people such as this. What do you think, Jenner?'

'I agree. I have practised as a physician all my adult life, and I have never heard of cures like this. One might say they were almost miraculous. I really find it difficult to give them credence, your Majesty.'

'But you do admit Lady Priscilla was cured?'

'Not cured, Majesty, but momentarily relieved of pain. It would seem to me there may have been some element of hypnosis. Or perhaps there was some oriental drug on the needles?'

The Queen looked questioningly at Dr Jackson.

'Would you be willing to put your claims to the test, so that we can judge their value for ourselves.'

'Certainly, Your Majesty.'

'We have two servants whose condition has not responded to more orthodox treatment. Could you cure them now?'

'I would be pleased to attempt a cure for their malady with the needles,' replied Jackson. 'But I cannot guarantee that it will work. My colleagues here would be the first to agree there is no nostrum to cure every disease.'

'If there had been,' said the Queen sadly, 'dear Prince Albert would still be with us today.'

She picked up a handbell. An Indian servant materialised, turbanned and incongruous in the cold, bright, Scottish air. He bowed, backed out of the sovereign's view, and returned with a page boy and a middle-aged woman with a bunch of keys at her belt – a linen-keeper.

'Please do not be afraid,' the Queen told them. 'This gentleman is a doctor. We are told by the *munshi* that you have had headaches above your eyes, a dizziness and a choking feeling in your nose?'

'Your Majesty,' said the boy nervously, 'I am still fit for my job.'

'Of course you are. But please do as this doctor suggests.'

The boy looked at Jackson, his eyes wide and apprehensive.

'Have no fear,' Jackson said gently, shaking his hand in an attempt to calm the youth.

'With Your Majesty's permission I would like him to relax in a chair.'

The Queen nodded. The boy sat down, his head pressed rigidly against the back of the wooden chair.

'Now,' Jackson said, 'tell me exactly where the pain is?'

The boy pointed to his temples, his nose and under his eyes; he was too afraid to speak. Jackson nodded and made ready his needles.

'I am going to prick you with these,' he explained. 'Do not be alarmed. You will feel no pain, and they will not draw a single drop of blood. If they do, by any mischance, I will give you a golden sovereign for every drop you shed.'

He felt the boy's shoulders, then he inserted the tip of one needle into the skin on the back of his neck, and two others higher up his skull. The boy's body suddenly relaxed. His tensed muscles eased, his shoulders drooped as though he was about to fall asleep. Jackson waited for a few moments and then withdrew the needles.

'Stand up,' he said. The boy did so.

'Where is the pain?' Jackson asked him.

'In my head, sir,' the boy replied, and then paused and shook his head. 'But it is *not*, sir, it has gone! It has completely gone!'

'A very interesting exhibition,' said Sir James coldly. 'But from a medical point of view, inconclusive. The boy is obviously of a nervous temperament and susceptible to suggestion.'

'Let us see the lady,' said Jackson.

The boy bowed his way backwards out of the presence of the Queen as the linen-keeper curtsied and stepped forward. She explained she had slipped on a step while carrying out her duties and, as a result, complained of an aching back.

Jackson asked the Queen's permission for the woman to lie down on a sofa. He then rolled down her thick woollen stockings and inserted the needles on the inside of each knee joint, all the while talking to her with a calming voice. Then he removed the needles.

'Stand up,' he said.

She moved slowly, and then more swiftly. Her face was suddenly transformed. She smiled in delighted amazement.

'Your Majesty,' she said. 'It is a miracle! *I am cured!*'

The Queen gave her permission to leave.

'Well, gentlemen, what is your verdict?'

'A most interesting demonstration, Majesty,' said Sir James. 'But we

would like to discuss it between ourselves and with our colleagues before
we can give our considered views.'

'What a pity that dear Prince Albert could not be here,' the Queen
replied sadly. '*He* would have given us his views at once.'

New York

Captain Ross sat in the drawing room of his suite in the Fifth Avenue
Hotel on Madison Square, New York City, reading the replies to his
advertisement.

His ship had berthed in New York some months before. Hundreds of
shabbily dressed immigrants had lined the decks all the previous night to
watch in awed silence as the stars went down in the sky, and dawn came
up with a silver pinkish glow to reveal this new world of opportunity
whose shore they had finally reached.

Long Island Sound stretched away on one side, with the Hudson River
on the other. A steward obsequiously pointed out to Ross sights he
thought he might otherwise have missed, not realising Ross had seen
them many times before the steward was born. Ellis Island; the Battery,
taking its name from a fortification the British had built in 1693; even the
Statue of Liberty's statistics. ('Her finger nail is thirteen inches long by
ten inches wide, sir. Her nose is four and a half feet long. Altogether,
she's the largest lady in the world!')

It was many years since Ross had been in Boston, his birthplace, and
even longer since he had seen New York. The changes amazed him.
Everything was larger than he remembered – whereas, generally, streets
and houses visited after many years, appear much smaller in reality than
in recollection.

To Ross, after years in the East, New York seemed a city conceived
with giants in mind. Avenues lay straight as arrows and wider than any
road he had seen in any other country. The buildings were tall and th
sidewalks clean and well-swept. Most important to him, a strange almost
electric animation seemed to pulse in the air. Even the humblest, poorest
and most illiterate immigrant or refugee, unable to speak a word of
English, suddenly became infused with surging confidence. Here they
could at last be free. Here they could prosper, even grow rich. Here was
America, the land of opportunity.

Ross had placed his advertisements in several New York newspaper
and was agreeably surprised by the pile of replies that awaited him. Som

were crudely written messages on postcards; others were in thick envelopes addressed in copperplate; a few typed on one of the new typewriting machines. Most contained requests to fund schemes which were manifestly absurd: a method of extracting gold from sea water; a search for lost Inca treasure in Mexico; an appeal to fund an electric mechanism to send messages – even music, so the inventor claimed – from one place to another, without the wires which Ross knew were essential to electric telegraphy.

A few had some merit and he had examined these carefully, meeting the inventors or principals involved, but for one reason or another, he had eventually decided against them all. The letter that had most impressed him was from an Italian, Leone Pastellini, the son of an immigrant who ran a grocery store on Mulberry Street. Mr Pastellini proposed making a type of sweetmeat that could be chewed literally for hours without apparently diminishing in size.

Ross intended to buy controlling shares in a pharmaceutical company, or if this proved impossible, to start such a company, which would manufacture tranquillizing medicines. The use of opium in Britain for these medicines was so widespread now, whether publicly admitted or not, that Trinity-Trio already owned a chemical factory in North London, which manufactured sleeping draughts, cough syrups and pain-relieving pills. So far as the company was concerned, this was what they called repeat business. Opium was addictive. A child or a grown-up who became accustomed to taking one or two pills each night to induce sleep, soon could not sleep without them. Then they found they needed to take twice as many to have the same effect; then they could not face the day, as well as the night, without the comfort of these little white, sugar-tasting tablets. From that moment on, there was no turning back. The grave might mark the end of that road, but the journey produced continuing profits for Trinity-Trio.

News of Dr Jackson's successful treatment of Lady Priscilla Graham and two members of Queen Victoria's staff at Balmoral spread rapidly throughout the country. Within days, people were queuing outside his London house, seeking his help for all manner of illnesses. Within weeks, he was famous, and prospective patients were having to book appointments months ahead. He had never sought such acclaim, but he found he greatly enjoyed it – and also the fact that acupuncture could help many people whom orthodox Western medicine had not been able to cure.

His renown and, of course, the huge income that it generated, understandably infuriated other specialists in more traditional branches of medicine. But denigrate him as they might, they could not argue against the astonishing results he obtained. Jackson found their hostility as surprising as their closed minds; they simply could not admit that there might be areas in the art of healing which the West had neglected to explore. He also realised that he could only attend to a relatively small number of patients, while thousands, perhaps millions more, went in need of treatment. In an attempt to resolve this unhappy situation, he formed a trust through Ebenezer & Son, The Dr Richard Jackson Medical Foundation, with the aim of teaching other doctors about Chinese medicine, and any other branches of healing that had not received recognition let alone research in the West. All the income from his huge practice went into this project, plus a great many far larger sums from his share in Trinity-Trio.

Jackson had devised an ointment that cost very little to produce, but which, thanks to his name and the results it achieved, sold in tens of thousands of tubs every year. It was basically a harmless white cream, and with each tub came an outline sketch of the human body, showing what Jackson called the 'acupuncture points', with brief details of the parts of the body they controlled. A stiff elbow or shoulder might need ointment to be rubbed into a patient's neck; an aching back could be eased when 'Dr Jackson's Soothing Balm' was applied to the inside of the patient's knee.

The rubbing, and not the ointment, was what actually helped to relieve the pain – if anything did. But it was easier to tell a patient to rub the ointment into the skin because this ensured they would rub for at least a minute.

Results were spectacular, and while many doctors could not accept that a pain in one part of a patient's body could be cured by rubbing a totally different part, for the sufferers it was sufficient that they were cured, and they praised Soothing Balm to their friends.

North America was a new and enormous market for this and other pharmaceutical products, and relatively untapped, so far as Ross knew. He was also interested in any project involving the manufacture of pills or sweets which would not contain opium; the wider the range of Trinity-Trio's range of products, the greater the profit potential. It was also not impossible that the United States authorities might realise the incipient danger of a drug like opium and follow the Chinese in forbidding its use.

Leone Pastellini claimed to have access to some kind of harmless malleable substance like putty, which was without taste or any deleterious qualities. He proposed enclosing pellets of this chewable substance, whatever it was, with a trace of scent within a hard coating of sugar or toffee, and marketing these chewing sweets, or chewing gum, as he preferred to call the sweets.

He pointed out that many men already chewed unlit cigars or cigarettes. Why should they, and children and women, not chew sweets instead? They would be healthier, would sweeten their breath, and promote digestion because chewing increased the production of saliva. Th idea seemed ingenious and worth pursuing. Ross made a note of Pastellini's address and decided to visit him that day, but first he wished to take his wife on a carriage drive to see New York.

Many people had been surprised when Ross had married in Macao. Ross and his wife, Evelyn, whom he had originally met in Calcutta, had not been universally accepted in Macao. Evelyn even complained of receiving cruel anonymous letters, which she declined to show her husband. These letters referred to her background and her employment; several addressed her bluntly as a whore.

Sometimes, driving in their open carriage, with coachman and two footmen, and a spotted dalmatian dog running obediently beneath the axles, or in their new Mercedes-Benz car, she claimed she had heard people shout abuse at her, and even make rude signs. Ross wondered whether this arose simply from jealousy – they were probably the richest couple in the colony, and not Portuguese – or whether Evelyn's love of brightly coloured clothes and expensive jewels could be the cause. He never considered that there could be any other reason.

Evelyn grew to hate Macao, and so they moved to a great house in Calcutta, arriving some time after Douglas and Jackson had left. Here again they were unhappy. Surprisingly, they were not asked to the most important soirées and balls held in other great houses. European ladies did not leave their cards, and Evelyn complained of being ostracised.

This concerned Ross on her behalf, but not on his; he was too rich to care what people thought or said about either of them. His retort to his wife was that he could afford to buy up anyone in Calcutta – and ruin them. That was the power money gave him, but still this comfortable knowledge did not bring peace of mind to Evelyn. She wanted to be the belle of the Governor General's ball, to be the most successful hostess in the city, whose invitation to dinner was a command. She believed she had the looks, she knew that Marvin had the money, but somehow these two ingredients were not enough.

After much discussion, they decided to leave the East. All three partners now left the routine running of Trinity-Trio to others, but kept a sharp and critical eye on their decisions.

In the United States, Ross could start a branch of Trinity-Trio, and he and Evelyn would begin a new life in what was after all his own country.

Evelyn came into the hotel sitting room now, and he stood up and smiled a greeting. His wife was heavily made up, in the manner of a vaudeville star, with long false eyelashes, mauve eyelids, cupid's bow lips. He could never look at that figure without feeling the stir of lust and longing. Evelyn possessed the gift to arouse him, old as he was.

It seemed to him he had searched the seven seas and the ports of every ocean to find such a paragon – someone who could match her moods to his, her needs to his, someone who was never found wanting. What did her expensive tastes matter in such a situation? Expense was relative, and even her compulsive spending could never seriously diminish his huge fortune. He felt as though Evelyn was in some way a creation of his own; a companion he had designed to his personal, private and individual specification. Proudly, Captain Ross took her arm and they went out to the elevator and down to the car awaiting them at the front door.

Leone Pastellini paced his bedroom above the family shop. On a table brought up from the kitchen he had spread a white cloth and several plates. One contained spoonfuls of sugar; a second, the basic putty-like gum; the third, a selection of hard-shelled pellet-like sweets he had made, enclosing this gum in a white sugar coating. He was excited to learn that Captain Ross was coming to see him, yet he felt nervous. So much depended on the outcome of their meeting.

He would buy a house, perhaps even in the country, where the air was fresh and there would be no jeers from Irish or Jewish immigrants that he and his father were only greasy wops. No-one would insult him there in the hope of provoking a fight, which they would win, because he was slightly built, unable to stand up to a bully twice his weight. And he and his father would be out of reach of the Mafia.

On an impulse, Leone knelt down, as his mother had taught him, and said a quick prayer imploring heavenly help in his enterprise, promising to give a tenth of whatever his project brought him to his local church. As he made the sign of the cross, almost as though on cue, he heard wheels outside, and he stood up. Through the narrow window he could see a man, thickset and grey-haired, paying off a cab; this must be Captain Ross. Leone heard the tinkling of the bell above the front door as Ross came into the shop. Leone smoothed back his hair, cleared his throat and went downstairs to meet him.

Ross glanced around the room, clean but threadbare; noted holes in the linoleum, a single bed against the far wall, hastily concealed by a rug to give the impression it was really a sofa. He guessed his man needed money; he would pitch his spiel accordingly.

'I am interested in your product,' he said, taking off his hat and gloves. 'Please tell me more about it. What gave you the idea, and what is the stuff you propose to put inside your sweets that will not be swallowed?'

Leone took a deep breath, held it for a moment in case he spoke too quickly in his nervous eagerness, then he began.

'I was born in Sicily, sir, and came here when I was very small. I had to learn a new language before I could learn anything in school. I tried to learn ten new words every day, and their origin. One word was "masticate", to eat.

'I discovered that it came from Greek, from mastic gum, a resin taken from a tree or shrub common in Greece and Turkey. Greek women, years ago, used to chew this gum because it cleaned their teeth and gave a sweet scent to their breath.

'One of the early Greek pioneers of medicine, Dioscorides, discovered that chewing this gum actually helped people to digest their food. The action of chewing promoted an increase in saliva.

'This interested me, Captain, and I looked deeper into the subject and learned how early colonists here in America adopted a habit of the Indians in New England, and chewed resin that came from spruce trees, when they cut the bark. But the best gum came from the juice or latex of the sapodilla tree, found in the rain forests of Mexico, Guatemala and British Honduras.

'The Mayans, who built temples and great cities there a thousand years before the Spaniards appeared, called this *chicle*. The word means juice in the Aztec tongue.'

He paused.

'Can this material be marketed?' asked Ross.

'It is already being sold, sir. William Wrigley, Jr., from Philadelphia, has founded a very successful firm that produces chewing gum.'

'He is a friend of yours? You have approached him with your idea?'

'No to both questions, sir. He is a remarkable man. As a boy of nine, he used to earn pocket money selling soap from a basket at street corners in his home town. When he grew up, he bought a horse and wagon and sold soap from that.

'Then he moved to Chicago, and to promote his sales of soap, he offered various inducements to buyers. For example, if they would buy so much soap he would give them a packet of baking powder free. He then found that baking powder was easier to sell than soap, so he stopped selling soap and to boost sales of baking powder, he offered two packages of chewing gum with each packet of powder.

'The gum proved more popular than the powder, so he said goodbye to that and concentrated on making and selling chewing gum. Several other firms are also producing chewing gum, but my belief is that there is always room for one more – if it is the right product.'

'And yours is?'

'I think so, sir, yes. Please taste this.'

Leone handed Ross the plate of pellets. Ross chewed one and nodded appreciatively. It was flavoured with peppermint, and gave a freshness to his palate, jaded by years of cigars and cheroots.

'This is made using latex from British Honduras. If I had backing, I would find factory space here near New York, and hire key workers from other gum companies by offering them a better wage, and then buy the gum in bulk. It is so much cheaper that way.'

'How would you promote the product?'

'First, choose a name and a distinctive wrapper, both easy to recognise. I would call it Lion's Share. Lion is a play on my own name – and also everyone wants the Lion's Share of the good things in life.'

Ross nodded. He was already thinking that his pharmaceutical factory could easily produce these sweets. He might even introduce opium to some versions as a soporific, or maybe disguise medical pills as sweets to make them palatable to children. The profit potential was clearly very high. Also he liked the name – and this man's approach.

'What do you want for the idea?' he asked Leone.

'A share in the manufacture and the profits.'

'Have you been involved with a similar business before?'

'I have helped my father in his shop here since I left high school. I understand about buying and selling and something else -- colour. It is very important to have the right colours when you are marketing things to eat. Yet not everyone realises this. You would not choose a purple orange, for example, or a pink banana, even if they tasted good. Americans are a patriotic people. We are from all sorts of backgrounds and countries, from ghettos and slums and steppes. We all seek an identity, so the colours of this country, like its flag, provide a heart and core for this longing. We will put the gum in red, white and blue wrappers. I *know* that will sell. I feel it here – in my heart.'

He beat his chest dramatically.

'I think you are right,' agreed Ross. 'And I will back you. This is my offer. My company, Trinity-Trio, will put up whatever money is needed to form a company to manufacture and market the sweets and so forth.

'You will take nothing out of the company until this initial investment has been paid back in full with interest at five per cent – except, of course, necessary expenses, which I will approve in advance, and a small salary which we will agree. When we are in profit, we split everything down the middle, fifty-fifty. Of course, you will not work for any other company in direct or indirect competition. Have we a deal, Mr Pastellini?'

'Captain Ross,' Leone replied happily, 'we are in business.'

Ross went downstairs, humming cheerfully to himself. He had taken with him in his pocket a simple contract form with blank spaces for the names of those signing, and the figures involved; Leone had signed willingly. Ross hailed a cab, gave the driver the address of the Fifth Avenue Hotel, and sat back on the cracked leather seat to enjoy a Havana.

From where he sat, the future looked very good. He never once thought of glancing in the tiny oval rear window, or he would have seen a man step from a doorway near the Pastellini shop and hail a following cab.

When Ross paid off his driver at the hotel door, this man did the same

Entering the foyer at a discreet distance behind the captain, he was able to see the number of Ross's suite on the key that the reception clerk took down from its peg. Then the man turned and went out of the hotel and was almost immediately lost amid a myriad hurrying anonymous New Yorkers.

Captain Ross took a lease on a warehouse on the outskirts of Trenton, New Jersey, where rents were low because the mayor was eager to establish industry. Then he advertised for men with chemistry degrees or experience in the drug industry. He offered them ten dollars a week more on their present salaries, plus a month's paid holiday a year, with the opportunity of a pay review after twelve months. Within the week, he had hired an entire technical staff.

He then placed an order for medicine bottles and small cardboard pill boxes, and engaged a number of women on a part-time basis to fill them. They stuck labels on bottles of cough syrup and soothing elixirs, and counted twenty sleeping pills into each box. When he had built up a stock, he placed advertisements in magazines he knew were read largely by travelling salesmen.

From a box number, he offered these salesmen a fifty per cent commission on all sales. He was inundated with replies from men travelling in such diverse goods as corsets, brushes, boot blacking and ready-made clothes. All were eager to add a new and non-competitive product to their line, on such unprecedented terms.

Nothing could be easier, Ross assured them, than when they were selling a broom to a housewife to suggest she also bought a bottle of Dr. Jackson's Sleepyhead Elixir, for the baby who kept her awake because he was teething. He explained that all their medicinal products were guaranteed efficacious by a distinguished English doctor who had attended Queen Victoria. The word 'attended' was strictly accurate. After all, Jackson *had* visited the Queen at Balmoral, and since she had been dead for some time, any legal queries seemed unlikely. Ross thus built up a keen sales force with wide trade connections from coast to coast, without having to pay any of them a cent in salary or expenses.

At the same time, Leone Pastellini engaged a number of Italian Americans who had worked as cooks or waiters or served in family grocery stores, with some older workers from a chewing gum firm on the verge of bankruptcy.

They conducted experiments with trays and vats and pans until they reached the best method of making their sugar-coated gum sweets. William Wrigley, Jr., had several excellent brands of chewing gum already on sale: Lotta Gum, Vassar, Juicy Fruit and Spearmint. His company was doing extremely well, and six other competing companies had recently joined forces to form what was called The Chewing Gum Trust.

Leone was therefore a late starter in the race, but this did not deter him. If William Wrigley thought it good business to call one of his chewing gums after the famous university for women, he would do the same for men. He produced three different labels in college colours: Yale, Harvard and Princeton. In addition, he produced a line of larger tablets which he sold under the name of the military academy, West Point.

Sales at first were slow. Salesmen already carrying Ross's opium products were not all eager to sell chewing gum. They felt that one product might fight another, with the result they would not make any sales at all.

Ross advertised widely, especially in papers read by the unsophisticated, stressing the health-promoting properties of his gum and the fact that every wrapper carried a special number. Once a week, these numbers could be checked against the current newspaper advertisement for Lion's Share. If the numbers tallied, the buyer of that particular packet of gum won a prize – a Lion's Share, as he called it.

Sales took nearly two years to build up, and all this time he and Evelyn lived in their suite in the Fifth Avenue Hotel. From time to time, Ross thought he might buy a house or even an entire apartment block and keep one apartment for himself and his wife, but he felt reluctant to put down roots and become a servant to possessions.

Things should always be for him – never the other way round. He had travelled all his life, and now that he was older he did not wish to change this lifestyle totally. Also, the hotel was extremely comfortable. Like many rich people, he was reluctant to spend his own money, and had negotiated excellent rates with the manager for a permanent stay. This was his agreeable situation when he received a letter from Dr Jackson in London.

The demand here for mahogany has become immense. A whole new prosperous class of people has sprung up – shopkeepers tradesmen, merchants. Many have no idea of good or bad taste and so they ape the aristocracy. They cannot afford great houses, but they wish for symbols of solidity and prosperity that all may see and recognise.

This is most easily provided by heavy furniture – mahogany chairs, tables, sideboards. Also, the railways and shipping companies are prospering and huge quantities of mahogany are needed for railway carriages and ships' cabins.

I am told that there are whole forests of this wood in British Honduras in Central America. One of our ships is in passage

New York with a cargo of special medical essences of a type with which you are familiar, and a gentleman in Belize Town, the capital of British Honduras, one Senor Jose Gonzales, has written offering his services as our agent. I suggest you make contact with him.

He will introduce you to a Mr O'Brien, also of Belize Town, who owns mahogany forests and is disposed to make a deal with us. Please take passage to Belize Town and buy as much mahogany as you are able. You could be well placed to decimate all competition in this area.

Evelyn was unwilling to make the journey, so Ross decided to sail on his own. On the visit he would attempt to corner the market in sapodilla gum, as well as mahogany. The prospect of a trip, especially to a warm climate, sounded agreeable, and so with high expectations he embarked aboard Trinity-Trio's latest acquisition, the steam ship *Godolphin*.

Belize Town

On the voyage Ross took care to refrain from giving advice to the captain; a difficult decision because, although it was years since Ross had commanded a vessel at sea, he still believed he could do so better than any other sea captain.

Eventually, the water turned from grey-green to the translucent green peculiar to the Caribbean. Strange pink and silver fish with huge fins and tails swam in shoals on either side of the ship, clearly visible against the sandy sea bed. Belize Town from the sea appeared as a cluster of wooden houses with tin roofs and verandahs, where half-castes sat at ease in mahogany rocking chairs, drinking rum, their feet stretched out on boxes.

The harbour was silted up with mud brought down by the Belize River. Clumps of wiry grass stuck out of the water like spears. On shore, palm trees shook lazy fronds like giant green feather dusters.

Sailors lowered a boat and rowed Ross ashore to a wooden jetty. Here, a dark-skinned man, wearing white duck trousers and jacket, stood waiting for him. He had a drooping black moustache shaped like the horns of a buffalo, and he wore a straw hat. He was sweating in the heat of the afternoon.

'Jose Gonzales,' he announced as Ross stepped ashore. 'At your service, sir.'

The two men shook hands.

'What is your pleasure?' Gonzales asked him. 'As your newly appointed agent, I wish to make your visit here as pleasant and productive as possible. After all, I wrote to your company suggesting the mahogany trade.'

'We are much in your debt.'

'First, Captain, I would like to show you around Belize Town – the only town in the world built on a foundation of mahogany logs and empty rum bottles.'

'Which speaks highly of the abundance of your forests, your cane fields and your good taste,' Ross replied. 'I particularly wish to meet Mr O'Brien. I understand he owns mahogany forests?'

'That is so, sir. He owns many things, Mr O'Brien. But I am sorry to have to say you have just missed him,' said Gonzales sadly. 'He has gone into the interior, up to the mountains.'

'How long will he be away?'

Gonzales shrugged. On such a matter it was impossible to give a positive answer.

'He has many forests, many plantations to visit,' he said vaguely. 'To follow him there would be impossible. There are no roads. You would never find him.'

'Then I will wait here for him to return. I have come a long way to meet him. I will not go away without seeing him. Now, what about resin?'

'For sapodilla, you also want to meet Mr O'Brien.'

Ross nodded; he had guessed as much. He might be stuck here for days, possibly for weeks. Time in the tropics was always elastic; in India, the word for yesterday was the same as the word for tomorrow. He was therefore used to delays, and in the meantime the ship could take on fresh water and stores. There was no reason for haste. Or was there?

The day felt suddenly oppressive. Or was the reason this man Gonzales? Ross did not like his swarthy appearance or his greasy complexion. However, he obviously knew his way around; he had better prove his usefulness.

'Now, sir,' said Gonzales briskly, as though reading his thoughts, 'if you will honour me by visiting my humble home, I will be pleased to show you samples of the best gum and mahogany in all the wide, wide world. We have a saying, "Every man knows where his house leaks" we all know our own faults. But you won't find any fault with these. No sir.'

They walked along the jetty, up through the main street and across wooden bridge, under which cows grazed below on the banks of a river. few horsemen rode by on thin, spavined nags. Most people appeare black, or at least very dark-skinned. They must be mostly descended from slaves, Ross thought. He was surprised, because he had always imagine that slaves from Africa were sold in America, or Jamaica, where he had usually landed them, but many must also have landed here. He was also surprised to see several Chinese and Indians in the street.

'You British brought them over as labourers,' Gonzales explained. 'They are indentured to employers here.'

'I am not British,' replied Ross coldly. 'I am American.'

'Forgive me, sir. I forgot.'

'What is their period of indenture?'

'For life.'

'So they are still not much better than slaves?'

Gonzales shrugged.

'We all have to work for someone. In that sense, we are all slaves. They have regular food, they are looked after. But I know what you mean. They have really lost their liberty, because to be free costs money. And they'll never get rich on what they're paid. No, sir. Empty sacks don't stand upright and full ones can't bend. The poor are weak and the rich are strong. We have a proverb, "When black man steals, he steals *some*. When white man steals, he steals *all*." '

'All?'

'Yes, sir. All. Mahogany is our main source of revenue, so the workers depend on it – at fifteen dollars a month pay, and seven quarts of flour and four pounds of pork a week as rations.

'Every Christmas, their employers contract them to work for the next nine to eleven months and advance them some money against their wages. Naturally the workers spend this over Christmas, and so are in debt before they even start their new jobs. And, of course, they have to buy food for their families at a company store – and have this docked from their wages.'

'Mr O'Brien does this?'

'Oh, yes, sir. He is a very rich man, sir.'

Just for a second, in the flicker of an eyelid, Gonzales' dusky face clouded with resentment. Then he was smiling again, and showing Ross up a flight of wooden stairs to his house. This was built of wood, two storeys high, with an upper verandah.

They sat in cane rocking chairs, drinking rum and coconut milk, and examining pieces of mahogany and samples of sapodilla resin. Later, in a primitive restaurant with oil lamps on each table, they dined together off crayfish tails with fried rice, and then fresh mangoes, and again more rum. That night, Ross slept soundly aboard *Godolphin*.

Next morning, Gonzales provided a horse, and they rode around the town together. This did not take long; it was a small town. The day after that and the day after that, they did the same, and still there was no sign of Mr O'Brien.

This delay began to irritate Ross. O'Brien could be in any of several places, all miles apart and all impossible to reach, Gonzales explained patiently. He could not say exactly where he was, and there seemed no means of discovering his whereabouts. Captain Ross would have to wait; Mr O'Brien was a very busy man.

Ross curbed his annoyance; he had long ago learned the futility of attempting to hurry the East, and this applied here also. Fortunately, his sojourn was eased by the chance meeting with a young Belizean boy who was willing to be pleasured by an American for what was to him a large sum, five U.S. dollars a time.

On the fourth evening, Ross returned early to his ship in a bad humour; the boy had for some reason become sullen and off-hand. Ross felt a sudden revulsion against Belize Town and these long delays. He *must* see O'Brien, but how the devil could he, when he did not know where he was or when he was coming back?

He sat in his cabin brooding on this, safe from the mosquitoes which plagued the town. He poured himself a huge glass of rum. He had drunk a lot that day, and in the heat, which he knew was foolish. But then he was angry at being kept waiting like a door-to-door salesman, when he could probably buy up this bloody man O'Brien and scarcely miss the money. He poured himself another rum, and sat down in an easy chair. He must have dozed, because suddenly he was awake.

The night felt damp and warm as a Turkish bath. Rum beat in his head like hammers pounding on an anvil. For a moment he had no idea where he was. Then he realised what had roused him.

Someone was beating frantically on his cabin door.

Perthshire

MacDuff came into his cottage and removed his boots at the door; his wife was a very houseproud woman. In his stockinged feet, he sat down heavily by the fire and passed his hand across his face as though unutterably weary. A sheepdog thumped his tail on the floor in welcome.

'What's the matter?' his wife asked her husband; she knew her man and his moods.

'I think you should have a word with young Fiona.'

'Why, what is up with the bairn?'

'She is always hanging about the castle gates. Has she nothing better to do?'

'She helps me a lot in the house every day. She likes walking. She feels drawn to the castle. She has told me so.'

'Aye, and you know why.'

'I do that,' replied his wife. 'But no-one else does.'

'Are you sure? If rumours got about, we might be put out. And there is another thing,' her husband went on. 'I was talking to Campbell, the head gardener, and he says the laird quite likes the girl.'

'So he should,' said his wife. 'There is no law against that, is there?'

'None,' agreed her husband. 'But they are often seen walking together. He tells her stories about his life in the East, so Campbell says. Fills her little head with nonsense, no doubt. You have got to tell her that she does not belong to the gentry, she belongs to us. If you are taken up by the gentry, you are spoiled. You cannot come back to live in a bothy, not happily. You want fancy clothes and dainty food. And worst of all, fancy people.'

'That is her privilege,' said his wife. 'And Mr Douglas is no a fancy man.'

'I am no denying that but it is better to stop her getting ideas above her station. Can you no see that?'

His wife could see this very well, and the knowledge saddened her kindly, homely heart. She put down the plates of soup on the table for their supper, and then went out into the tiny kitchen so that her husband would not know she wept.

Calcutta

On the other side of the world, T'a Ki also heard the sound of crying.

It came from behind the closed door of her son Robert's room on the first day of his school holidays. He attended a local high school and, like other children, was taken there in a *gharrie* driven by a *sais* or groom, and collected again at the end of each day.

For some time T'a Ki had been wondering what to buy him for his birthday. She knew little about boys, but she felt concern that Robert appeared to have so few friends. There seemed no-one he really liked enough to ask to a birthday party, such as the English children gave, with candles on a cake; or one of the kind Indian children liked, with sticky sweetmeats and syrupy drinks and fireworks.

She paused and went back to the door, knocked on it. There was no answer. She opened it and went inside. Robert was sitting on the bed, hunched up dejectedly. He dug his fists in his eyes as his mother approached, and stood up, turning away from her so she would not see his tears.

'What is the matter?' she asked him.

'I have something in my eye,' he explained.

'In both your eyes?'

He looked at her then and nodded, all pretence of hiding his shame gone in the extremity of his unhappiness.

'Why are you crying?'

He shook his head violently.

'Are you unhappy?'

He nodded.

'I know what unhappiness is,' she told him gently. 'You might not think so. Children never think their parents have ever felt any of the emotions they feel, but we have and we do – all the time. Is it school?'

He shook his head again, and then, unexpectedly, he nodded.

'The boys laugh at me. They say I am a half-caste, a Chink.'

'What boys?'

'They are all English, or Scots or Welsh. They say I am yellow, and I have slit eyes. They make faces at me, pretending to be Chinese, and make funny noises. If I fight them – and I can, one at a time – they all set on me.'

'How long has this been going on?' she asked.

'Ever since I went there.'

'You never told me.'

'I did not want to. I thought it would stop. They sometimes bait their own kind, because they are a bit different – they have red hair or they are Jewish. One has a hare lip. He has a miserable time.

'I know that Indians have all sorts of castes, from untouchables, who empty lavatory pots, right up to the Brahmins, who are almost as high as their gods. But I did not think it was the same with the English. That is not what you taught me.'

'It is the same with everyone and every race,' his mother admitted. 'People are herd animals. They want to conform. Anyone who does not is an oddity, like a black sheep in a flock of white sheep, or a cow with only one horn. They take out their own unhappiness on this individual. You *are* a half-caste. I am Chinese, your father is English. But most of those boys who jeer at you are also half-caste.'

'What do you mean?' Robert asked, looking at her appraisingly.

'They are not all of true blood, English, Scots, Irish or Welsh. Some have a Scots mother and a Welsh father, an English mother and an Irish father. They are as much half-caste as you.'

'They do not have slit eyes.'

'No, but they have other characteristics – dark hair, pale hair, red hair. Tell them that. And there is something else I will tell you, which you must keep secret. Your father is so wealthy he could buy up *all* their parents, the entire school buildings, and never know he had even wasted his money.'

'Does he give us a lot of money?' asked Robert.

'He is very generous,' she replied. But, like many wealthy people, Richard Jackson would rather give money than his time; and his presence with her and their son would be so much more valuable than the largest gift.

'Why is he never here?'

'Because his work has taken him to England.'

'Will he come back?'

'One day,' she answered him. 'When you have lived in the East, you always come back.'

But even as T'a Ki spoke with such conviction, she knew that so far as she was concerned, this was only wishful thinking. Richard Jackson had gone out of her life forever. But he would never be out of her thoughts, nor out of her heart.

Bombay

In a huge house high on Malabar Hill between silken sheets in a scented room, Savina Sodawaterwallah lay dying.

Through wide windows, lights glittered along the shore like a necklace of stars, and beyond them darkness draped the sea like a vast crêpe shroud.

For many months, Savina's family had known, and she had guessed, that there was no cure for the illness from which she suffered. All that her doctors could do was to try and keep the gnawing pangs of pain at bay. But despite ever increasing doses of the opium with which they dosed her, she still felt agony beyond the reach of all relief, as of a ravening creature within her, tearing at her with sharpened claws. The sign of Cancer in the zodiac, the crab, was truly symbolic.

Savina was drowsy now, and lay with her thin hands outside the coverlet in that misty twilit land between sleep and wakefulness, life and death, when time dissolves and the past becomes the present, for the future has vanished away. One of the nursing sisters from a nearby convent sat patiently by her bed. The night light's tiny flame flickered as feebly as Savina's heartbeats.

She had already lost her sight. Now her hearing was going, and for days her voice had been barely above a hoarse whisper. Her husband, their daughters and their two sons would take it in turns to watch by the bed. When they saw her cracked, dry lips move as though to form words, they would lean over in an attempt to hear what she wanted to say, usually only disjointed fragments of memories that moved through her mind in a dream procession.

Savina's frail hands clenched into fists, her neck arched slightly as muscles tightened around her mouth. The nurse saw her lips move as she spoke one word, the name of her eldest son. *Edward.* The boy had been named out of loyalty after Queen Victoria's eldest son, now Edward VII, King of England, Emperor of India.

The nurse tip-toed hastily out of the bedroom. Mr Sodawaterwallah, who had spent most of the previous night by his wife's bedside, was dozing in a chair in his study. He guessed the end could at most be only hours away, and he did not wish to be absent when it came. Then would follow that final journey to the tower of silence, where Savina's body would be placed on a metal grid, high up within the tower, for birds to peck the flesh from her dead bones.

This was a melancholy prospect, for he had loved Savina, and he had been drinking steadily in an attempt to force the knowledge from his mind. The young never considered that death could ever threaten them, he thought. But the old knew it must always win the last battle.

'She is asking for Edward,' the nurse told him, as he started up out of his chair.

'Edward is not here. He has gone into Bombay.'

He was not certain exactly where Edward was, but he knew he had left the house. Edward had also been awake through most of the previous night; the boy needed some fresh air. Odd, how he still thought of a young man in his twenties as a boy. Perhaps this was the prerogative of every father?

'She is sinking fast,' the nurse continued. Mr Sodawaterwallah hurried out of the room, and ordered a servant to bring his second son to him immediately.

George was named after Prince George, King Edward's son. The Sodawaterwallahs were a loyal family, treasuring links with a country they had never seen. George was tall, and good-looking in a rather weak way. His hair was too long for his father's liking, and he carried himself imperiously. He had the air of a young man who had never experienced hardship of any kind – or hard work, either. The world not only owed him a living, and a very good one, he saw that it was constantly reminded of this undiminishing debt.

'Your mother is calling for Edward,' his father explained to him. 'He told me he was going to see a friend, I'm not sure who. But he will not be back for at least an hour, maybe longer. The doctor said his mother was stable. Now, it seems we may not have too long.

'You go into her room and pretend you are Edward. She cannot see, she is barely able to hear. She just wants to feel the presence of her eldest son near her, to know she is not alone.'

George opened his mouth to refuse. His father held up his hand.

'No excuses,' he said sternly. 'She has been a very good mother to you. Do this for her sake.'

George nodded reluctantly, and followed the nurse into the room.

Savina's eyes were open now, but cloudy with drugs. They stared blankly and sightlessly at the ceiling. George stood looking down at his mother, unwilling to enact the deception to which he had agreed, yet, seeing her condition, realising that it was justified.

He put out both hands and enfolded his mother's fragile fingers. They felt cold, lifeless. He pressed them gently to let her know he was there, near her, with her. The nurse went out of the bedroom and left them alone.

'Edward,' said Savina feebly, 'I want you to do something special for me.'

'Anything, Mama,' George replied, bending close to hear the words, scarcely above a whisper, and slurred together. The effort of speech was all but beyond her.

'In my bureau, second drawer down, there is a letter to someone you do not know. He was once dear to me. I want you to take this personally to him, not telling *anyone* here, especially not your dear father. It would only hurt him. You understand me, Edward?'

'I understand you, Mama.'

'He is a long way from here,' Savina went on dreamily. 'In Scotland. I have never been there. But I used to collect pictures of that country, and I imagined him in his castle. I want you to go to him.'

'Of course, Mama.'

'Now promise me you will tell *no-one* what I have told you? *No-one.* Have I your word?'

'You have, Mama.'

'I knew I could trust you. It would only cause pain to your father if he knew of this. One must always strive to avoid hurting those who love you.'

She paused, then added in an even fainter murmur, almost thinking aloud, 'Even if you have always loved another more.'

Savina lay silent for a moment and George thought that she slept – or, or a fearful moment, that she was already dead, her hand in his. Then she spoke again, but more feebly, each word now an immense physical effort.

'Tell your father you are going to London on business. Do not worry about the cost. I am leaving all you children a large sum of money each. But do this for me without telling anyone else. *Anyone.* You promise?'

'I have promised, Mama.'

'May God bless you and keep you. May His light ever shine on you, my son. May your way be one of happiness . . . and . . . love.'

Savina's lips were still moving, as though she had more to say, perhaps much more. But now there was no sound, and no time. Swiftly and silently, as George watched, Savina had died.

Belize Town

The knocking on the cabin door that had awakened Captain Ross from his rum-drugged slumber continued furiously as he fumbled with the lock, cursing the interruption.

The beating sounded imperative, impatient. His mind went back to African talking drums aboard slaveships, years ago. All gone; there were no slaves now. Only the memories of the voyages remained: sweat, dung, tears, misery, and the lonely beating of drums across an empty sea.

Ross opened the door. A thin, dark-skinned man faced him. He wore a shabby jacket and trousers. His feet were bare. One hand went up to grey, fuzzy hair in salutation, and he bowed. Ross recognised him as some minion he had noticed earlier that day in a warehouse belonging to Gonzales.

'I have come to tell you, on Señor Gonzales' orders, Mr O'Brien has returned from up country,' this man announced importantly. 'He would be pleased to see you this evening. *Now*, sir, if you so wish.'

Ross wanted to meet Mr O'Brien, but not now: he needed a bath, a change of clothes, a sleep to clear his fuddled brain.

'I do not wish,' he said shortly. 'This is not the hour to do business.'

'That may be so in your country, sir, but the cool of the evening in Belize Town is the best time to work. There is always siesta in the afternoon time. We start early, we stop early. We start late again, we finish late. I can conduct you to his private house. Señor Gonzales said you wished to see him urgently, or I would not have ventured to disturb you.'

'I will see Mr O'Brien in the morning.'

'In the morning, sir, I have to say he is taking ship to one of the Cayes.'

There were small islands several miles out to sea, where richer citizens maintained houses, totally remote from any interruptions. Standing in the doorway, Ross envied them this opportunity. Suddenly, he felt uncharacteristically tired of voyages and meetings and hotel food. He was too old to be doing this – and too rich, far too rich. After this trip he would retire and enjoy life; he had worked hard long enough.

'He is a busy man, then, Mr O'Brien?' he asked.

'He is that, sir.'

'All right,' Ross agreed reluctantly, 'I will come with you in these circumstances. You have a carriage?'

'I will conduct you on foot, sir. It is no distance.'

Ross poured out four fingers of rum to sharpen his mind, drank the spirit neat, picked up his hat and cane and followed the man up on deck. A local boat with two rowers was waiting alongside. They moved swiftly towards the jetty. The tide was on the turn and he smelled the salty slime of swamps that lay at the edge of the sea. Riding lights on cargo vessels dipped and rose uneasily. He wondered what O'Brien would be like. He had questioned Gonzales about him, but could only extract vague answers.

'Oh, a hard man, sir.'

'In what way, hard?'

'In business. We say, "Cows know where weak fences are" – the strong take advantage of the weak. Mr O'Brien very strong man, sir, but so are you. You are well matched. You want to buy more mahogany and resin than all the other merchants put together. And he owns more forests than any other man in British Honduras. Yes, sir.'

It seemed fitting that the biggest producer and the richest buyer should do business together; a lot of business, so Ross hoped. The rowing boat bumped against the jetty.

Ross followed his guide through narrow streets, with deep storm gutters on either side filled with stagnant, stinking water. Houses stood on stilts, as if to keep out of the filth. Pigs and goats were tied beneath them and dogs, growling behind picket fences, bared their teeth at the passers-by.

Candles and oil lamps guttered in open windows. From several houses Ross heard a faint sound of music – a guitar or some similar native instrument. In other circumstances, the sound would have been pleasing, but now it seemed off key, jarring, a lament – or a warning. But of what, and to whom?

As Ross picked his way through the dirty street, sweating with unaccustomed exertion, he thought for a moment of the men in the forests cutting down the great mahogany trees. Did they return after weeks at their back-breaking work to these squalid clapboard shacks? It seemed very likely. What did they want out of life? Simply to earn enough money to buy food to give them strength to go out and repeat the operation? At least they were technically free men, he thought; as slaves, all males above the age of ten had been forced to log mahogany.

They had worked then – and still worked now – in teams of ten, twenty, even fifty, and each man knew his own task thoroughly. Failure by any of the team could instantly endanger all their lives because the trees stood tall as church steeples.

The most important man in any team was probably the tracker, called the huntsman, who hunted groves of mahogany trees. He might have to search the forests for days or even weeks until he was successful. Each team was in fierce competition with every other team, and since all depended on the huntsman, his skill was vital.

When he located a suitable clump of trees, axemen climbed up to a branch about fifteen feet off the ground and then, swinging enormous axes which bit first into the bark, then into the heart of the trunk, they brought down the tree.

When it fell, others in the gang trimmed the logs and cleared a path so they could be dragged by cattle to the nearest river. Here they were lashed together into rafts and floated down to the mouth of the river, usually in the rainy season. A boom prevented them drifting out into the open sea, and they floated, acres and acres of tree trunks, until they could be squared into shape and shipped to England. And all this work, danger, separation, for a pittance to spend in the company shop!

The black man stopped suddenly. Ross, his thoughts still out in the forest, bumped into him and cursed him for blocking his way.

'I am sorry, sir. We are here.'

He beat with his fists on a door in a certain code, three loud blows, two soft.

The tapping again reminded Ross of that time aboard the slaver, when the drums had talked, and he had stood alone on the bridge, and was afraid. He shrugged the memory out of his mind. The stink of this man brought back the smells of slavers. These blacks were all alike, monkey men; they still kept to the patterns of their past in Africa.

Sweat trickled down Ross's back and he cursed himself for being fool enough to come out at this time of night, at the behest of some stranger with an Irish name who was probably just doing this to show his own importance.

The door opened into a surprisingly large hall. A black servant wearing white livery bowed respectfully. The outside of the house, like all the others, appeared shabby, run-down, nondescript. Inside, walls were covered with pictures – not Ross's choice, admittedly, but what he had heard described as primitives: fishing craft or native women, wearing brightly coloured bandanas, with children on their hips.

In a gilt-framed mirror he could see himself, hastily dressed and ill-at-ease. He looked dishevelled; his face shone with heat and sweat, and sleep had matted his hair. The black man who had guided him here had not entered the house with him, and the servant showed Ross into another room. This had wide windows covered by muslin curtains, finely woven to keep out the accursed mosquitoes.

The furniture here was mahogany, thick and heavy; even the walls were panelled in solid mahogany. There were wooden carvings of fish and birds, very graceful and smooth as glass on small plinths. He had seen similar ornaments in local shops, but none so well-made. He stopped opposite a wood carving on an ebony base. For a second it seemed that time stood still, and his heart stopped with it.

He was looking at his own face, carved in cedar.

How the hell had O'Brien got this thing done? Was it meant to be a present for him, a surprise?

This idea seemed agreeable; comforting, even. But why should he need comforting? Seeing a life-size likeness of his own face in the house of a stranger, in such a remote place, had disturbed him. His mouth felt dry and his whole body drained of energy. He would have given a fortune for a drink.

Across the room, a door opened and closed silently. Ross turned. He was facing a tall man, black as Ross had imagined he must be in this colony, wearing a white linen suit and a white silk shirt.

'I am Jack O'Brien,' said the man in a deep melodious voice. 'You must be Captain Marvin Ross?'

'I am, sir. At your service,' replied Ross insincerely. He held out his hand. O'Brien did not shake it, but opened and closed his own right hand as though flexing the muscles. The man obviously had something wrong with it, thought Ross; he lowered his outstretched hand. Wouldn't do to embarrass the fellow.

'I was admiring your works of art,' he went on. 'This one especially, this carving. It's of me. Did you know that?'

'I did. A good likeness, I think.'

'I was amazed to see it here. Who did it?'

'Someone who had the opportunity to observe you closely over a period of time.'

'Really? Well, he – or she – has certainly carved a remarkable likeness. Is it for sale? I would dearly like to possess it.'

'No. It is not for sale, Captain. But I am pleased you think it is faithful to your features. But enough of that. Before we discuss business, I hope you will join me in a glass of rather special rum we do not put on sale?'

'My pleasure,' said Ross. 'Always drink the wine of the country. Whisky in Scotland, beer in England, rum here.'

Even as he spoke, Ross wished he was not being offered more rum. Anything but rum, so long as it was cool and could quench his thirst and the dryness in his mouth. He had already drunk enough rum, probably more than enough, and he wished to keep his mind clear when they came to work out their deal. Still, he could not refuse. The fellow might feel offended if he did. You could never tell with these blacks.

'You are a much travelled man?' O'Brien asked him courteously.

'A seafarer, you know.'

'A girl in every port is your saying, yes?' asked O'Brien, with a smile. 'Or a boy?'

Ross looked at him sharply, eyes narrowed. What was this black bastard getting at? A boy? What did he mean, or, rather, what did he know?

A servant brought in a tray of hammered silver. On it stood two glasses, fresh lime juice, a silver bowl of ice, and a decanter of dark rum. O'Brien poured two generous measures into two glasses, added ice and lime juice, raised his glass in Ross's direction. Ross felt his anger subside; it was only this coon's idea of humour, nothing more. Nothing sinister in the remark at all. Why should there be? This was a business meeting, wasn't it?

'It is good of you to come to my house at such short notice,' O'Brien went on. 'But I must leave on other business tomorrow, and since you have been waiting patiently for several days, I thought you would wish to get the matter finished with. I do not want to trespass further on your valuable time, so I have had the agreement between us drawn up.'

'You have?'

Surprise sharpened Ross's voice.

How could O'Brien know how much mahogany or sapodilla resin he wanted – and over what period, and at what price? His mind felt clouded, woolly, thick. Had these figures been agreed with London through Gonzales? That must be it. Good fellow, Gonzales. He must have wronged him. It was always unwise to judge a man by his appearance. I mean, look at me now, he thought, and almost giggled. This rum was bloody strong.

But why hadn't London kept him informed? He was a bloody partner wasn't he, not a clerk? Irritation ran with the rum in his veins. He took another draught to soothe himself. No need to get angry; this black fellow was only trying to be helpful.

O'Brien crossed to a desk, opened a drawer, took out a large sheet of parchment. Ross sipped his drink. He knew the terms of the deal he wanted, but was not sure whether O'Brien had the same ideas. They were sharp, these characters. At least, he thought he knew the figures but extraordinarily the more he tried to remember details, the more they eluded him.

Did he want to buy resin on a three months basis – or was it for three years? How did Trinity-Trio propose to pay for the mahogany? Cash here or in London, landed, or F.O.B.? Ross strove to keep his face calm, unconcerned, as his mind frantically searched for facts and figures which only hours – minutes – earlier he had known by heart.

O'Brien handed him the contract. Ross read it. Percentages, tonnage, dates of shipment, methods of payment; all were here. But were these the correct figures? He should have written them down, instead of keeping them in his head. He must be getting old or sickening for something – and this rum was the strongest he had ever tasted. He pushed the paper back across the table, unsigned. As he did so, he noticed that his hand trembled very slightly. Perhaps he *was* ill? These tropical places were hotbeds of fever; must be as bad as India.

'How do you come to be called O'Brien?' he asked, trying to delay the moment of signature in the hope that this forgetfulness would pass. 'Not born in Ireland, I'll vow?'

'That is true,' agreed O'Brien. 'But perhaps I will go there one day. The name is, as you would say in your language, a corruption of another name. I believe that Jews who come to Britain from Europe sometimes change their names – Stein becomes Stone, Harvish is Harris. They wish to feel they belong to their new country. Similarly with me.

'I changed my name because I have found that an Irish name, especially when dealing with Catholics who are influential here in Central America, can be very useful. A Scots name also has value. But not an English one.'

'As an American, I would agree,' said Ross.

'Your name, Captain,' O'Brien went on, 'could be of Jewish origin – perhaps originally Rosenberg – or Scottish. And yet you are American. My original name can only have one origin – Africa. I was an Ibo. I was given a first name, Jack, at the same time as my father also received his first name, John.'

'Really?'

These names – Jack and John Ibo – brought back recollections from the long dim aisles of memory. A voyage he had almost forgotten, or thought he had. Now details surfaced from the recesses of his mind like corpses floating to the surface of the sea. The slaver. Jack and John Ibo. Buggering the boy – and punishing his father with the bamboo pole when he had struck him in rage and despair.

Now the names pealed in his mind, loud as cemetery bells. This man Jack O'Brien must be that boy, grown to manhood and prosperity. Well, what the hell did it matter?

Obviously, O'Brien was not concerned – probably amused by the recollection – just as Ross sometimes recalled his own encounters in the past with reflective interest.

Ross took another swig of rum. This must be 150° proof. You were warned not to open a bottle of that stuff near a candle flame in case the fumes exploded. Of course, O'Brien had said it was special. Perhaps it was his way of being hospitable – like showing him the carving. You had to give these bastards the benefit of the doubt: they were really only savages.

But of what doubt should they have the benefit? This question jarred his mind. Something was not right here, but what? Oh, God, *what?*

Sweat burst out on Ross's forehead. His shirt seemed suddenly starched to his body, a second, soaking skin. Yet only moments earlier, the room had felt cool. Now, it appeared oppressively hot. He was used to being in command of people like O'Brien, ordering them about, meeting them where he wanted and when – not where they wished, in their private house, late at night.

This put him at a disadvantage, but you had to move with the times, and the continuing profits from this contract could be enormous. Ross turned away to mop his forehead with a handkerchief. He felt embarrassed to be sweating like this when O'Brien appeared so cool.

O'Brien opened another drawer in his desk, took out an inkhorn and pen, passed the contract back to Ross.

'Your signature, sir, if you would be so good. You will see I have already signed and my servant will be witness. He writes good English. For an Ibo.'

Ross dipped the pen shakily into the inkhorn. He had better sign it. If any details were wrong or not to the partners' liking, they could wriggle out of them somehow. That's what lawyers were for, and Ebenezer & Son were very good lawyers. No doubts about that, and so no worries over this.

Ink splashed the green leather top of O'Brien's desk. Ross mopped at the stain apologetically with his handkerchief. Where the hell was he to sign? He screwed up his eyes and could just make out the name, Jack O'Brien. He signed above this and stood back triumphantly as though he had achieved something worthwhile, all concern about figures and quantities and other details gone, as a crab sheds its shell. He had signed; that was the main thing.

Another man now entered the room silently. Ross noticed that he limped. He seemed to have seen this man somewhere before with this distinctive limp – but where or when? Then he remembered. This man had interpreted for O'Brien's father aboard the slaver. What an extraordinary coincidence! But better not remark upon it. The fellow might be touchy; not everyone wished to be reminded of their past – especially when they had been slaves.

O'Brien shook some sand over the signatures.

'One copy for each of us?' asked Ross.

O'Brien smiled. His mouth seemed suddenly larger than Ross had noticed: it held as many sharp teeth as a shark's.

'That will not be necessary,' he replied. 'We can trust each other. After all, Captain, we have met before.'

'I don't understand you.'

Ross's voice was slurred. Of course he understood the bastard, but what was the point of admitting this too soon?

'Then I will make myself clearer, Captain. You do not remember my face?'

'I do not.'

Suddenly, O'Brien undid his belt, dropped his trousers, bent forward and presented his bare bottom to the captain.

'Perhaps you will remember this view of me better, Captain. You buggered me every day, at least once, sometimes more frequently, throughout the whole voyage, from the windward coast of Africa to Kingston in Jamaica.

'I was John Ibo's son. Remember me *now*? You punished my father, who despised you for what you were, and for what you did. You tied him up around a bamboo and then forgot him for a night and half a day. When they untied his bonds, he could never walk upright again.'

'I remember,' admitted Rose slowly, wondering desperately: Why is he bringing this up now? Of course I remember and so does he, because some things you never forget. But O'Brien had been very friendly; giving him a drink, talking rationally, so clearly he could not hold against Ross what had happened so long ago. Or could he?

Ross said stupidly, because his mind was too muddled to allow him to think clearly or to choose his words well: 'I lost money on the man.'

'You lost *money*, Captain Ross. My father lost his manhood, his health, his spirit. But not his ability to carve wood more brilliantly than anyone else I have ever met. When he became too feeble to work as a slave, he was allowed to carve little ornaments for sale.

'His master took the profit, of course, and all my father received was food and shelter. He could carve from memory – animals, birds, people from the old country – Africa. And in case I should ever forget who had done these things to him and to me, he carved the face of the man concerned. You, Captain Ross. There are a lot of proverbs in Belize, the wisdom of slaves, so they say. I give you one now. "Time is longer than rope. Justice finally prevails."'

'I could pay you back now in your own coin. Have you whipped or castrated or buggered by a man or beast and left to bleed to death. Or, as the Pathans on the North West Frontier of India treat captured British soldiers, I could cut off your private parts, ram them in your mouth and sew your lips together, and put you out in the burning glare of the sun to die – slowly.

'As we say, "The same knife that sticks the sheep, sticks the goat." The harm you do to others can also easily be done to you. But I will not treat you as many would. I will deal with you mercifully.'

'Mercifully? What the devil do you mean?' asked Ross. 'We are in business together. I don't know what you are talking above, slave ships and so on.'

His mind seemed filled with fog; he did not recognise his own voice; that drink must have been laced. No rum could ever be so powerful. Dear God, he prayed, help me now.

'Two things have ruled your life, Captain, lust and money. You have corrupted many young boys and girls and you have amassed a fortune. You have enjoyed your good days on many a long voyage. Now, all that is over. You are about to begin your longest voyage. Tonight.'

Ross swallowed. His throat seemed suddenly to have tightened. He tore at his shirt collar as though pulling away a hangman's nose. He smelled the sharp, pungent sweat of his own terror, and for a moment he was not standing in this scented room facing a black man who must have hunted him cold-bloodedly, untiringly, for years. He was back in that open square in Canton, and three sailors, trussed like chickens, were awaiting their punishment at the toss of a coin: castration or ceremonial death.

He was staring, not at O'Brien's black and shining and triumphant face, but at the face of the red-haired sailor, contorted with fear and horror and disbelief at the knowledge: the face of a man who realised that Ross had betrayed him.

Now, on the other side of the earth, a lifetime later, that sailor's words echoed in this elegant room, thundering in Ross's brain like a madman beating on a drum.

'*I curse you and all who bear your name! May you rot in hell, you Judas bastard!*'

And, as with that sailor long ago, in another country, Ross had no means of escape.

A door that he had not noticed began to open. Ross saw the silent movement and glanced towards it, wondering vaguely where it led, why it had been concealed as part of the mahogany panelling. In that moment O'Brien brought up his right knee into the captain's groin. Ross doubled up in agony and surprise at the fearful blow.

As he fell forwards, two men came in through the door, carrying a long rush mat. They spread this on the floor and rolled Ross up in it as he struggled feebly, gasping for breath, crying out for help. Then the drug in his drink and the lack of air combined to calm him. The pain thankfully receded, leaving a sense of almost unbearable desolation and loneliness.

The two men carried their snorting, wriggling bundle out of O'Brien's house and through the streets. Oil lamps still guttered in uncurtained windows; guitar strings still stroked the night with their lament. No-one paid any heed to the two bare-footed bearers and their burden, or to O'Brien following some distance behind. In Belize Town, it was not wise to enquire into what others might be doing after dark, especially when a man as powerful and influential as O'Brien was concerned. Whoever saw nothing and heard nothing was likely to live longer than someone who saw or heard far more – and told others about it.

The two men carried the body to the Belize River, wide and slow moving, liquid silver now beneath the stars. Thick reeds and jungle concealed each bank. They went down a narrow path, then swiftly tipped their burden from the mat into the water. Ross slid silently out into mid-stream. His arms and legs threshed the water into a brief flurry of foam as the chill of the river revived him. They watched for a moment.

A log floating near the bank moved towards Ross suddenly and in total silence. Alligator jaws opened and snapped shut on Ross's feet. The two men heard his choking scream of pain. Then they went up the path, carrying the mat. They did not look back, or they might have seen O'Brien on one bank watch the body of his old enemy drift between a dozen devouring jaws – and on the opposite bank, Gonzales watching O'Brien.

The captain of *Godolphin* paced up and down in his cabin; now looking out at the blinding sea through the porthole, now peering into Gonzales' swarthy face, wishing he was anywhere but here, wondering how he could best inform his principals of Ross's death with the least damage to his own prospects of promotion. Too often the bearer of bad news was quite wrongly associated with the news he brought, and the captain had an ambitious wife.

'So you tell me, Gonzales, that Captain Ross, one of the three founders of our company, has been found drowned in the Belize River, terribly mutilated by alligators!'

'It is most unfortunate, Captain, but that is so. I have personally seen the body. It has been moved to Mr Gomez's funeral parlour to await the last rites.'

'I will come and examine it myself to make sure this is the right man.'

'It is the right man, Captain, as God is my judge.'

'But how could he fall into the river? Was he drunk? Did he slip?'

'Some people in Belize Town say he could have been searching for his dog, which he thought was drowning.'

'His *dog*? What do you mean? Ross had not got a dog.'

'That is so, Captain. But maybe he decided to dive under the water so that he could see where his dog might be. *If* he had a dog, of course. And you say he did not possess such an animal?'

The captain pondered this for a moment.

'You mean he was murdered?' he asked Gonzales bluntly.

'That is not a word I care to use in my own town. Fish, we say, are hooked by the mouth. Loose talk can be dangerous.'

'I understand. Had he been to a whorehouse or something? Was there trouble over a woman – or a boy? You know what he was like, even though he was getting on.'

'I have heard of his preferences, Captain, but I have no personal knowledge of them. He left this ship in a small rowing boat to come ashore with another man. After that – nothing. Until his body was found. At least, what the alligators left of it.'

'Bloody extraordinary,' said the captain. 'Who was this other man who rowed ashore with him?'

'I have no idea.'

'I see. Well, we have all got to go some time. But that isn't a way I'd choose. What about the contract for mahogany and sapodilla?'

'That is still to be negotiated. I am meeting Mr O'Brien today to do that thing.'

'I thought Captain Ross was going to sign it?'

'He signed something else, Captain. Perhaps under the mistaken impression that it *was* the contract.'

'How the hell do you know this?'

'I have my sources, Captain. I was born here and have lived here for more than forty years.'

'So what are you trying to tell me?'

'I am trying to tell you, sir, that Captain Ross signed a form, which was witnessed and is perfectly legal – I have seen the original. In it, as a gesture of friendship, in payment of a debt incurred aboard ship on an Atlantic crossing many years ago, he has willingly made over all his shares in Trinity-Trio to a third party.'

'A third party? And who the hell is that?'

'A coloured gentleman, sir. Mr O'Brien.'

New York

Four chambermaids worked in shifts on the tenth floor of the Fifth Avenue Hotel on Madison Square. Two were Italian; one, German; one, Swedish. Franco had a friend, an under-manager, who gave him the names and addresses of the Italian maids.

He followed one to her lodgings and introduced himself as a friend of her father. He brought with him a two-pound box of chocolates as a present. The girl was surprised, flattered and slightly puzzled; her father had been dead for two years, but she still accepted the chocolates.

Their conversation turned to hotel guests. He asked who occupied various suites and steered the conversation round to Captain and Mrs Ross. The maid explained she was responsible for rooms on the opposite side of the corridor to the Rosses' suite and so she knew nothing about them.

Franco then followed the other Italian girl to mass at the Church of Our Lady of Mount Carmel on East 115th Street. He sat in the same pew and they came out together into the bright sunshine and, as he stood on the steps beside her, and others in the congregation filed past, he introduced himself as a friend of the under-manager's. Franco said his friend had spoken very highly of her integrity and ability as a chambermaid. Franco had recognised her in church and hoped she did not consider him forward in addressing her now.

He explained the reason; he was about to be appointed manager of a new family hotel soon to be opened on East 44th Street, and he wished to offer her – on the under-manager's recommendation – the post of housekeeper.

They had a meal together in an Italian café to discuss terms and the earliest date she could join him. He asked her not to tell the under-manager she was leaving until he could give her a definite starting date, and she willingly agreed.

Franco gradually turned their conversation into a discussion of the foibles of hotel guests, and how they invariably stole cutlery and ashtrays. The maid said she was surprised how the richest guests would steal towels, pillow-cases, even sheets.

'So who are the richest people you have got staying at the Fifth Avenue?'

She gave several names and then added, 'And, of course, there's Captain Ross and his wife. The housekeeper told me he was so rich he could buy the hotel.'

'Really? How interesting. What are they like as people?' asked Franco, pouring her more Chianti.

'He's pleasant enough. But he's not there at the moment. I think he is in Central America somewhere. But his wife. . . .'

The maid paused, embarrassed. Franco did not remark on this, but raised his glass in a toast.

'To you,' he said solemnly. 'And to our future, working together.'

They clinked glasses. The girl was already fuddled with wine and the exciting prospect of a new job, at better pay, and eager to show her appreciation of the compliment Franco had paid in asking her to join him.

When Franco asked casually: 'Well, what's his wife like?' she blushed and looked down into her empty glass for a moment.

Franco filled it.

'I don't know what to say,' she said. 'I've never had an experience like that before.'

'Like what?' asked Franco quietly, guessing he was now coming to the nub of the interview.

'It's not nice to talk of such things,' the maid replied primly.

'We will have to talk about everything in the hotel – if we are going to work together.'

She sipped her wine, made up her mind. Then, leaning across the table, elbows on the patterned cloth, she whispered to Franco what she had seen in the captain's bedroom. She explained that of course she had told her priest. He had said that either she was imagining things, or she must put such recollections out of her mind.

Franco patted the maid's hand in a fatherly way to show that he fully understood, and called for the bill.

Perthshire

Alec Douglas was being married at noon.

He and his best man walked across from Coupar Castle to the church, and waited in the vestry. The best man had thoughtfully brought a bottle of The Macallan and two glasses. They drank toasts to each other until the preacher arrived. There seemed a certain desperation in this drinking, a lack of genuine enthusiasm for the marriage about to take place. As Douglas drank, he pondered on the swiftness of events leading up to this ceremony, which he had neither anticipated nor greatly welcomed.

He felt like a man who has suddenly been overtaken by a whirlwind and which, almost incredibly, so he now thought, he had not ever attempted to avoid. But had he really wanted to avoid it? Or had he secretly welcomed it as a kind of challenge?

Quite unexpectedly, a letter had arrived from Emma MacTavish in India. Her husband had died, and she was returning to England. She invited Alec to dine with her on her arrival.

He had accepted this invitation, and discussion of past events then and at several subsequent meetings led to talk about their present situation – and future prospects. Within weeks, he had proposed marriage and been accepted with a speed that, too late, had alarmed him.

Did Emma really care for him as a person, a partner, or was the appeal his huge estate and his social position? Had he been attracted to her more by recollections of their passionate affair aboard ship and later in India than by the prospect of wedlock?

In recalling this past association, why had he not also considered that this had happened long ago, and the years between that had changed him, might also have changed the woman he was about to marry? Neither was young any more. Once, there had been sexual attraction, a mutual magnetism, but would that still link them now? However, such reflections were at this moment academic; there could be no second thoughts, no retreat or change of plans. The time for such prudent manoeuvres was behind him. Ahead lay – what?

Douglas and his best man followed the preacher into the church and stood facing the altar. The organ boomed, bells high in the ancient tower began to peal – and Douglas felt sweat bead on his brow and his back.

He knew he was on the point of living through the scene he had dreamed of so often, when he was standing in a church about to wed a woman whose face he could not see.

He heard sighs of appreciation from women guests and knew that Emma had arrived at the far end of the aisle. He did not look round, even when she was standing by his side. She lifted one hand in the gesture he had seen so often in his sleep, and removed her veil. Now he saw the face of his bride, and he looked at her with heavy heart and leaden spirit. He knew instinctively he was making the wrong decision. Lust and vanity had led him on. He was paying too high a price for someone who no longer greatly attracted him; worse, who could soon even repel him.

Their honeymoon, which he had somehow assumed would be a prolonged and totally satisfactory sexual marathon, proved nothing of the kind. Alec Douglas was discovering, late in life and at great expense in terms of treasure and content, the harsh truth that what seems sweet and delectable when taken illicitly, can lose much of its savour when enjoyed within the legal bonds of matrimony. And very strong bonds these soon proved to be.

In their relationship aboard ship, in stolen moments in MacTavish's house at Barrackpore when the colonel was away, even under the banyan tree, the risk they ran of discovery added an exquisite piquancy to time stolen from its lawful owner. Now that there was no risk, everything was legal; and, as a curious consequence, almost inevitably dull.

Also, Douglas found that his wife had apparently totally changed in character and outlook. (Like many men, he never considered the possibility that he might also have changed as much, or even more. The pursuit of wealth, and many affairs with other women, had moulded him in ways he did not even begin to comprehend.)

Aboard ship and in India, Emma had been warm, passionate, never critical – because then there was nothing to criticise: he was rich and she was eager. As his legal partner, she criticised him long and often. She was also relatively wealthy now, and wanted her wishes to prevail.

He was spending far too much time shooting; he should have put more fields down to pasture. Some of the tenants, whose houses he had refurbished, were ungrateful. It was foolish of him to spend so much money simply to make life more comfortable for such unappreciative people. They were not used to warm, dry houses; they would think less of him for imagining that they would value such comfort.

Emma's criticisms became steadily stronger, more strident and more constant, and soon Douglas noticed that, even by early afternoon, her speech was often slurred. He could not believe she was drinking heavily, and he did not wish to descend to the level of marking bottles of whisky. Even so, he could see for himself how their level dropped, and sometimes, when he drank a whisky and soda in the evening, he realised the spirit had been watered to conceal how much had already gone.

Gradually, they drifted apart – not physically, because they still lived under the same roof, although sleeping in separate bedrooms. They had been snared by the illusion of attraction, and now reality revealed two disparate people, without shared interests or even concern for each other.

So long as they could remain on civil, if platonic, terms, Alec Douglas felt he could bear the situation. After all, this must be the state into which many marriages deteriorated sooner or later, with both partners thankful to find their own basic level of communication and civility. What worried him was the very real possibility that, as they drifted farther apart, his wife's voice would become ever more strident, ever more critical under the influence of discontent, disappointment and strong malt whisky. There might come a time when this combination became insupportable – and what would happen then?

It was in these unhappy circumstances that he first became really aware of Fiona Pomfret. He had seen her often enough, with her strangely fair hair, her blue eyes and her slim boyish figure. At their first meeting, she had asked him shyly whether he would allow her to walk over the estate.

'Of course,' he had replied instantly, flattered that this young girl should be interested in something which had belonged to his family for so long. Soon, he was demonstrating to her the country tricks his father had taught him when he was her age: how to tickle a trout from beneath a stone; how to cast a fly; how to make a fire with two pieces of wood, when lacking match or tinder. He was gratified at the apparent pleasure she showed on being taught such things.

From Fiona's childhood, MacDuff had allowed her to ride his pony when it was not pulling the cart. Now Douglas took an interest in her prowess. He taught her, as the cavalry riding instructor had taught him in his early days with his regiment, how to ride without reins or using his hands; how to swing one leg over the saddle and turn a complete circle – again without reins and with the horse trotting; how to roll beneath the horse and swing up on the other side.

He enjoyed teaching her. She was a ready pupil, quick to grasp points and determined to succeed, although this might mean falls on the way to perfection. And Douglas enjoyed teaching Fiona for another reason he scarcely admitted to himself: the lessons brought back memories of his own youth, and in so doing made him feel young again.

One day she came to ask whether she could borrow a small saddle and a set of harness she had noticed in the tack room.

'Take whatever you want,' Douglas told her.

Fiona had been delighted, and in her pleasure dropped a stirrup. She was wearing an open-necked blouse, for the day was hot, and as she bent down he could see through the open neck her small pointed breasts with their wide dark aureoles.

As Douglas looked, he found himself wanting her as he had never wanted anyone since he had first seen her mother years before. He forced himself to look away. His mouth was suddenly dry, and when he took down the saddle from its tree on the wall his hands were trembling.

He noticed, also, a strange glow in Fiona's eyes, and she was suddenly awkward, and blushed, and bit her upper lip. She had not minded that he had seen her breasts.

In that moment, they both knew the surging strength of attraction each felt for the other. It had always been there. Now, it would not go away.

When George Sodawaterwallah arrived in England from Bombay, he was surprised and secretly distressed to find that people made fun of his name – people totally inferior to him in terms of family and money. And, as he kept asking himself, what other terms of reference can there possibly be?

When he signed the hotel register in London, for example, the reception clerk had difficulty in concealing his amusement. Later, George heard him talking to a hall porter.

'Sounds like a music hall comic's name,' the porter replied. ''Whisky and Soda'' – they're on at the Empire all this week.'

George could not understand what was so funny, but he decided to adopt an Anglicised version of his name, at least while in England; George Wallace sounded a useful compromise.

He travelled north to the Fair Maid Hotel in Perth under this name, and it was as George Wallace that the butler now announced him to Alec Douglas.

'You do not know me, sir,' George explained. 'Indeed, we have never met, but I bring a personal letter to you from my mother.'

'Your mother?' repeated Douglas in surprise. 'Where are you from?'

'Bombay.'

'It is many years since I was in Bombay. I knew a family there. Parsees. Name of Sodawaterwallah.'

'*My* family, sir. I have changed my name.'

Douglas looked at George more closely, then opened the letter and glanced at the date; it had been written many years previously. He read with a lump rising in his throat because it was as though he heard Savina's voice, and in the twilight, saw her grave and lovely face smiling at him.

Dear Scotsman,

If you have a memory for such things, as I have, you will see that I am writing this letter on the tenth anniversary of the sad evening when we said farewell.

I have followed your career over the years as closely as I could. I have diligently read the shipping intelligence in newspapers in the hope that a Trinity-Trio vessel might one day bring you back to Bombay and we could meet again. But in my heart I felt that our farewell was indeed our last meeting.

You have gone your way in a world that is, alas, not mine, but which I can imagine and appreciate, and for my part I am the wife of an increasingly successful man of business. But, sometimes, as on this day or on other of our anniversaries that are too secret and precious for me to put on paper, I remember, and I wish that our fates could have been different. But as a dream is only the shadow of a shade, what might have been once, now will never be.

I do not know when or even whether you will receive this letter which I am sealing and placing in my bureau, where it will stay until I die. I intend to give instructions to my son – your son, our son – when I am close to death, to bring this to you.

Please treat him kindly. He is part you, part me, and in his face and character I already see you, and pray that you will also see me. He has no idea who you are and I leave it to your judgement whether to tell him or not, always bearing in mind I do not wish to hurt my husband.

He and I have never loved each other as I believe you and I could have loved each other, but he has been true to me and generous, and it is little enough to hope that, after I am beyond answering any questions, he is not distressed.

Of course, my husband instigated our union, for reasons you know, but to introduce two people for one purpose is not to expect that another will result, and they will fall so deeply in love that every time I see a ship in the harbour I go down to the docks in the vain hope you may be coming ashore. And every time I read your name in a newspaper, my heart leaps.

I hope that you will like – nay, come to love – your son, and will approve of the way in which I have brought him up. If you have any advice or help to give him, please guide his feet into the path of righteousness, which, hopefully for him, if not for me, may lead to happiness. I sign this, not with my name, but with the lips of a woman who by the time you receive it, will have loved you all her life.

Douglas folded up the letter and put it in his pocket, thankful that Emma was in Edinburgh. He sat in silence for a moment to compose himself; he did not wish to reveal to this young man the extent of his emotion. It seemed strange to be looking at his son for the first time not as a baby or a boy, but as a man. He was quite good-looking, yet with a weakness about his face. His hair was dark, but of course that was to be expected; who had ever seen a red-haired Parsee?

'I knew your mother long ago,' Douglas began at last, instantly conscious of the unintended irony in the words. He had known Savina far better than her husband, far more intimately than this young man would ever imagine.

'I take it from this letter that she has died?'

'Yes. From cancer, after a long illness. She was very brave. My father brought in the best Indian and European specialists, but there was no hope. I was with her at the end.'

'I am sorry to hear the sad news. Tell me, is your father still alive?'

'Most certainly. He is very busy, but well.'

'You have a brother and a sister, I believe?'

'One brother, Edward, and a sister, Zarita. My brother has just finshed his studies in law at Bombay University. My sister is an accomplished pianist.'

'And what brings you over here, George – if I may call you this?'

'My mother suggested that I should come to see you. There was the matter of this letter to be delivered, and she thought it would broaden my outlook to see something of England. And, of course, Scotland. This was her last spoken wish – that I should come to see you personally and deliver this letter. She did not wish my father to know about it. She was very positive about that. She thought it would hurt him if he knew.'

Both men were silent, then Douglas spoke.

'Now what are your plans?' he asked George.

'I am booked for one week at the Fair Maid Hotel in Perth. After that, I have no plans at all.'

'Then I have some for you. First, cancel your booking. You must stay here for as long as you wish. You will be the most welcome guest. I would like you to meet my friends, and we can go fishing together.

'You must also meet a girl of about your age who lives locally. No doubt Fiona Pomfret will gladly introduce you to other young people of her acquaintance.'

London

Dr Jackson's manservant ushered the captain of Trinity-Trio's ship *Godolphin* out of the doctor's house in Harley Street in London.

From behind the curtain of his consulting room, Jackson watched him walk away smartly up the road, and envied the captain his youth, his ambition and his health; most of all, his health.

The captain had just personally reported the death of Captain Ross in Belize Town, and Jackson had listened, outwardly calm, while all the time his mind was in a ferment for another totally unconnected reason.

He had spent that morning with an eminent specialist on diseases of the blood, who had confirmed Jackson's own personal diagnosis as to the cause of a growing inertia that had gripped him for more than a year. He was suffering from a wasting sickness for which there was no cure. His life could at the most be measured now in months.

Soon, of the original trio, only Douglas would be left. Jackson opened his safe, and re-read the original document of association they had signed in the offices of Groves, De Souza and Bortwith, in Calcutta, all those years ago.

As he had thought, if one partner died, he could only leave his share to his widow – or to his two other partners if they were still living. Death then, when they were young, seemed very far away, something that happened to other people.

This clause had been included on the lawyers' advice, in order to keep full control of Trinity-Trio in their hands for as long as possible. This claimant Jack O'Brien would therefore receive nothing; Ross's share would to go his widow.

The whole business of Ross making over his share to O'Brien only hours before he died seemed most unusual, if not suspicious. If Jackson had felt better, he might have gone after O'Brien and tried to discover the reason, but now he lacked all energy to do so. And since time was his enemy, he felt he must consult Douglas and secure his agreement to his own intentions about his shareholding.

Jackson sat down at his desk. Its green leather top was bare except for his blotter and a small ebony plinth that supported a single penny. He picked up the coin and examined William the Fourth's head and the date. He turned the penny over in his hand, remembering Tom Gray, and his dying mother whispering how she saw mud in the doctor's future; and the little girl, Joanna, who had given him back the same penny.

His lucky penny, he had often called it jokingly. In the end, it might not live up to that description, but at least it might still prove lucky for others.

Jackson replaced the coin carefully on its base, picked up his pen and began to write.

New York

Every Friday evening, Leone Pastellini stayed late at the Lion's Share factory in Trenton, New Jersey. He was conscientious and ambitious and wished to make certain that all consignments promised for delivery that weekend were actually on their way. Late was a relative term so far as Leone was concerned; he remained in the factory on most evenings until eight or nine o'clock, and was always the first to arrive in the morning. He reasoned that if the boss was late, who would then bother to be early?

On this particular Friday it was nearly ten when he locked up. The night was dark, with a waning moon, and so he did not see another man standing in the shadow of the building until he came forward and introduced himself.

'My name is Franco,' he announced. 'I know your father.'

Leone could not see the stranger's face, but he smelled sweat and the scent of cheap hair oil, and instinctively disliked and distrusted him. Franco's hand felt clammy to the touch; he seemed a creature of the dark. If, as he claimed, he was a friend of his father, why had Leone never met him before?

'Some friends and I make sure nothing happens to his shop,' Franco explained.

'You mean, you work for an insurance company?'

'In a sense. A group of friends from the old country.'

This gave Leone the clue; he must belong to one of those secret societies he had heard about, but so far had never personally encountered: the Black Hand, the Red Hand, the Family. He had heard his father mention them, and always with bitterness. They were like leeches, the old man would say, they sucked your blood.

'What do you want from me?' asked Leone.

'I have been admiring your progress here. I read your advertisements in the newspapers regularly. Your sales are increasing all the while. You must be making a lot of money. It would be a shame if any setback befell you.'

'I do not own the factory, and so far we have not even covered our original investment. When you are selling packets of gum at a few cents a go, it takes a hell of a lot of sales to make a profit.'

'There are over a hundred million people in this country,' replied Franco, 'you will make a fortune.'

'My backer, Captain Ross, has first charge on any profits.'

'Of course. But he will not be claiming that right. He has died in Belize Town in British Honduras. A drowning accident.'

Captain Ross dead! Leone stared at Franco in amazement. He had been too busy for weeks even to look at a newspaper.

'Are you certain?'

'Positive.'

'How do you know?'

'A friend there has advised me.'

'Why tell me this now?'

'Because I admire your enterprise. Because we will do business together – soon. But see Mrs Ross first. Then I will be in touch with her – or you. Goodnight – and *arrivederci!*'

Next morning, Leone did not go into the factory. Instead, he travelled to New York to the Fifth Avenue Hotel. The bellboy took him up to Mrs Ross's suite. Evelyn had no idea who he was; Ross had always been secretive about his business life.

'A drink?' she asked Leone after he had introduced himself.

'A bit early for me,' he replied cautiously. 'But thank you all the same, ma'am.'

'Early or late,' said Evelyn, 'I find it steadies the nerves.'

'And your nerves, ma'am, must be frayed by the sad news of your husband. I only heard last night, or I would have been in touch before.'

'You have come to see me about that?'

'Yes. To offer you my condolences.'

Leone paused, reluctant to discuss business at such a time, but he had to know whether his arrangement with her husband would be continued.

'He financed me over Lion's Share gum,' he explained. 'I want to know if we are going along on the same basis – as I very much hope.'

'If that suits you, it suits me,' said Evelyn, shortly, lighting a cigarette. Leone was surprised; he had not known any woman who smoked openly.

'You want it in writing?' Evelyn continued. 'Just in case there is any trouble with banks and the law? You know what those bastards are like.'

Her language surprised him. He watched her scribble a note on a sheet of hotel notepaper, confirming their conversation. Huge stones in the rings on her fingers heliographed their value across the sunny room.

'Where is your factory?' she asked him, as she handed him the paper.

'Just outside Trenton, in New Jersey.'

'I must come and see you some day.'

'I would like that, ma'am. In the meantime, if I can do anything to help you, please let me know.'

'You are a nice, kind boy,' said Evelyn appreciatively. They shook hands.

Leone went out into the corridor, clutching his piece of paper, his heart fluttering with relief. The elevator was waiting and he stepped right into it – and so did not see Franco, who stood pressed into the next doorway. As soon as the illuminated arrow flickered to show that the elevator was going down, Franco knocked on Mrs Ross's door.

'Room service, ma'am,' he called crisply. As she opened the door, he pushed in his foot, and then was inside the room.

'Who the hell are you?' Evelyn asked angrily. Franco had entered with such force that he spilled the drink in her hand.

'A friend of Leone's.'

'Then why pretend you're room service?'

'Because I have something private to say which you may not wish anyone else to hear.'

'What do you mean?'

Evelyn backed away, watching him warily. Was he an accomplice of Leone's? Could they be working as a team to rob her? The bell push was only feet away. Franco saw Evelyn glance speculatively towards it.

'Ring if you like,' he told her. 'But *after* you have heard what I have to say.'

'I am listening.'

'You are Mrs Evelyn Ross. Your husband, the late Captain Ross, owned a third share in the international company, Trinity-Trio? Right?'

'Right.'

'Captain Ross and his two other partners had an agreement that if any of them died, and left a widow, the dead man's share would automatically go to that widow. You know that?'

'I did not,' said Evelyn. 'But it seems reasonable.'

'It is. But, of course, that agreement is dependent on the widow being a *genuine* widow.'

'Obviously.'

'But you are not genuine.'

'Not genuine? I was married to the man, wasn't I?'

'You were never married. You went through a *form* of marriage to him. That is not the same thing.'

'Are you mad? What the shit do you mean?'

'You know exactly what I mean, so listen – and listen hard. I will not repeat what I know about you, on one condition: that you pay half of what you will inherit to a charity in which I have an interest. It helps a lot of people.'

'You want money?'

Make-up dissolved into the tears on Evelyn's pathetic painted face. Her artificial eyelashes fluttered in fear and despair.

'No. Trinity-Trio shares. If you paid the charity in money that would be a single payment. In shares, dividends will be paid for as long as the company lasts. You may keep the shares in your name for the time being but we will have a private agreement whereby half are registered in favour of United Charities Incorporated. Fortunately, they have an office in Trenton – not far from the Lion's Share factory. That is my secret. And you must keep it – if I am to keep mine about you.'

'How do you know about the marriage?'

She did not query his accusation; there was no point. This man knew too much to listen to argument.

'It is my business to find out things like that. On behalf of my Family.'

'Your family? Who are they?'

'You will find out. Now, get your coat and hat and gloves. You are coming with me to see a lawyer who will draw up this agreement between us.'

'My attorney?' Evelyn asked him hopefully, in a thin small voice. There might still be a chance of thwarting this stranger. She had the pathetic belief of the poorly educated in the ability of lawyers to extricate clients from all manner of calamities – if they paid them well enough.

Franco smiled, but only with his mouth, not his eyes.

'No,' he said. 'Mine. The Family lawyer.'

Calcutta

T'a Ki was brushing her hair in front of the long mirror in her bedroom in Park Street when her personal maid came in to tell her that a European gentleman had arrived unannounced to see her.

The maid handed T'a Ki an embossed visiting card on a silver tray: 'Mr A.B. Groves, Partner, Groves, De Souza and Bortwith, Attorneys-at-law, Chowringhee, Calcutta'.

'What does he want?' T'a Ki asked the maid, letting the card drop on to the tray. She had never heard of this man or his firm.

'He said it was a private and most important matter, mem.'

'I will see him in ten minutes,' T'a Ki told her, and went on brushing her hair. If people appeared without an appointment, they could not expect her to rush to meet them – especially if they were English.

Mr Groves was short and fat and undeniably English. He sweated heavily under his armpits; the stains showed as white-rimmed dark patches on his cotton jacket. He prowled about the drawing room where the maid had left him, examining the spines of books in a glass-fronted case, peering at china ornaments, and especially at a photograph of a young man in his twenties.

He had a slightly Chinese cast of countenance, yet his features seemed basically European. He was holding a scroll of some kind. Possibly the photograph had been taken to mark his graduation at school or university?

Groves turned as T'a Ki entered.

'You wish to see me?' she asked him, ignoring his outstretched hand.

'Archibald Groves, mem. At your service,' he replied, bowing. 'I understand you have a son, Robert Jackson?'

'That is his photograph you are looking at.'

'I thought as much. He is of age?'

'Yes. But why these questions?'

'We have been favoured with instructions from a London firm of solicitors, Ebenezer and Son, who are acting on behalf of the late Dr Richard Jackson.'

'You mean Dr Jackson is *dead*?'

'Unfortunately so, mem. I am sorry to be the bearer of such bad news.'

'What did he die of?'

'Pernicious anaemia. It was quite painless. My own father died of the same, so I speak with some knowledge.'

T'a Ki's hand went up to her throat. For a second, the room spun like a demented wheel. Mr Groves was speaking with a disembodied voice. She steadied herself with an enormous effort. She had been right; Richard would never come back to the East. As in a dream she remembered the words of the Lord Buddha: 'Sons are no help, nor a father, nor relations; there is no help from kinsmen for one whom death has seized.'

Nor was there any comfort for those whom death had left behind.

'Why do you wish to see me?' she asked. 'Just to give me this news?'

'My news principally concerns your son Robert, mem. Dr Jackson has left him one-half of his estate.'

'You mean an estate of land?'

'I mean, mem, your son now owns one-sixth of the capital of Trinity-Trio, the largest British trading company in the East.'

'Oh, my God!' cried T'a Ki in total amazement.

Mr Groves stepped forward to catch her as she fell to the floor in a faint.

Perthshire

A servant took the coat from Alec Douglas's shoulders as he came into the castle on his return from London where he had been to attend Dr Jackson's funeral. He poured out four fingers of The Macallan for his master.

Douglas drank thoughtfully. He had never felt particularly close to Jackson as a friend, but his sudden death had shocked him. He could accept Jackson's dedication to the acquisition of wealth by any means whatever, but not the way in which he had ruthlessly abandoned the Chinese woman T'a Ki and their son, Robert.

Then Douglas remembered Savina; he was in no position to criticise his partner. It had seemed prudent to take the Parsee's money and leave, because he was young then and hardened by the knowledge that his birthright had been stolen from him. Now he was older, he realised that life has more important gifts to offer than possessions.

He knew now, too late, that Savina had loved him and, even more disturbing, he had loved her. He had thought he was not capable of that emotion, and now he was consumed by regret at the years of possible enchantment that had passed him by. Savina was dead, and Ross and Jackson were dead, and he was on his own.

He sat down in the great drawing room of his castle, the last survivor of the original three partners. Emma had not accompanied him to Jackson's funeral, although she was in London, staying with some new friends she had made. She could stay away for as long as she cared; forever, so far as he was concerned.

Douglas suspected that she was being unfaithful to him; he had noticed a new sparkle in her eyes when a certain man's name was mentioned, and had counted the trunks of dresses that accompanied her on her trip. He did not greatly care whether she was faithful or unfaithful. Too much was made of a simple chemical and biological reaction, a brief fusion of flesh. And, as he had often heard in the army in India, a slice off a cut loaf was never missed.

What Douglas did miss was his freedom. He was tired of watching his wife's face for any advance inkling of her mood, and then adapting his conversation accordingly. To be married to the wrong woman was like making a long march in ill-fitting boots. He longed for the ease and comfort of slippers, for the sight of a young fresh face, the pleasure of sharing his life with an uncomplicated character. But life was like a narrow street. You could go on; you could stop; you could never go back. If he had his time again. . . . Ah . . . if. There was no sense in looking over one's shoulder; the road lay ahead.

The butler entered.

'Miss Pomfret to see you, sir,' he announced.

Douglas stood up as Fiona came into the room.

'I saw your motor car return,' she explained. 'So I knew you would be in.'

'And delighted to see you,' he replied warmly. 'You have a problem you want to consult me about?'

Why was it, he thought, even as he spoke, that people only seemed to visit him if they had some problem on which they sought his help? They wanted their rent reduced, they had suffered a bad lambing season, the fish were not rising.

'No, I am glad to say, absolutely nothing at all. It was simply to tell you I have been offered a saddle by someone else, and so I thought I should return the one you so kindly lent me. You might be needing it.'

'That is unlikely, my dear. It is for a smaller horse than I will ever ride. Anyhow, it was a gift.'

'Oh, I thought it was a loan.'

'So now, my dear, you know that it was not.'

'You look very sad,' Fiona said gently, watching his downcast face. 'You liked Dr Jackson?'

'I respected him,' Douglas corrected her. 'And he and Captain Ross were my two original colleagues in the company. As you grow older, Fiona, it is distressing to find fewer and fewer people left who remember earlier days. This is obvious to anyone else, of course, but curiously, not to the people involved. We are all growing old – but we do not feel old. That is the odd thing.

'I remember first meeting Jackson in Calcutta, as clearly as if it happened yesterday. Neither of us had much money, only the idea of joining forces to attempt to build something out of nothing. And if someone came to me now with such a proposition, I would say it was totally impossible.'

'But you three proved it possible?'

'Yes, but it was easier then, looking back. Now, everyone is very respectable. Full accounts must always be kept. Offices are packed with clerks adding up sums in ledgers. Taxation is so complex. Then, we pooled what we had and simply pocketed the profits. And if we saw a business elsewhere we liked, or we thought could be useful to us, we simply bought it. I am not interested in newspapers or magazines but Dr Jackson was. He was attracted to them – and so bought *The Enquirer*. If he had had to explain to bankers and lawyers and people like that he wanted to borrow money for the purchase, they would not have lent him a penny. And rightly so, for he had no experience in that field at all.

'Fortunately, he had enough money without having to try to borrow anything. And he *knew* he could make the paper pay. Confidence, that's what we all had then.'

He paused.

'And not now?' Fiona asked him softly.

'Oh, yes, still. But not quite so much. When you are older you realise the pitfalls and the dangers. You don't even think of them when you are young.'

Douglas sat for a moment, recalling images he thought he had forgotten. The thirteen factories at Canton. The Hoppo. The thrill of each deal. That was what he missed now most of all: the excitement. Others might still be enjoying it, but he was not involved. The river of time was running swiftly past him, and he was on the bank, watching it go when he should be riding on that tide.

'Dear Mr Douglas,' said Fiona gently, 'you are like a little boy, always wanting to be taking part in a game, not liking being left out.'

She sat down beside him, put her hand on his and squeezed it. He looked at her as though seeing her for the first time: long blonde hair, wide blue eyes, a slight smile on her lips. He felt a deeper affinity with her than he had ever felt for anyone else. Even Savina? Even Savina, he told himself.

He felt protective towards Fiona, as well as attracted; that was the difference. He wanted to tell her how he felt, but he could not find the words. And were words really necessary? He remembered the brief sight of her bare breast, the look in her eyes, the knowledge in his heart.

He moved slightly towards her, as though to reply to what she had said – and within seconds, his arms were around her, his mouth on hers.

For how long they kissed, he had no idea. It seemed beyond all measurement of minutes or the deep metronomic ticking of the clock in the corner of the room. Drawing away, he felt relaxed for the first time in years. Here was someone – less, much less, than half his age – someone he could understand and who, he believed, could understand him. Here was someone with whom he could be himself.

Douglas felt an almost immeasurable sense of freedom: home at last was the wanderer from the hills, the sailor home from the sea. The memory of Savina, so sharp and sad in his mind, faded like a face in a rising Highland mist. Still there – her memory would always be there – but now of the past, in the past, a loving, tender spirit, but no more than that.

Douglas stood up, and Fiona stood up with him, as though already they were not two people but one. Again, they kissed. His hands caressed her small proud breasts and he felt the nipples stir beneath his touch.

How many times had he felt this with unnumbered women, married and single, black, white and brown? But never with any of them had he experienced the full flood of feeling that now surged from his heart. There was no word spoken between them, for neither felt the need to speak. Their bodies spoke for them.

In silence, Douglas led Fiona from the room, up the wide staircase to the even wider bed.

Stewart MacDuff tucked his napkin into his collarless shirt and, without any appearance of enjoyment, began to eat the haggis and neeps his wife had prepared for him.

'How were things today?' she asked him across the scrubbed table, looking at him with the shrewdness of a woman who has lived with a man for a quarter of a century, and senses his moods even before he speaks.

'Much the same,' he replied shortly.

'Something wrong?'

Her husband shook his head, and sawed at the haggis. The oatmeal burst out in a savoury cloud of steam. He took a mouthful, then lowered his knife and fork.

'Fiona,' he said abruptly. 'She is up at the castle far too often.'

'She likes it there. She gets on with the laird.'

'Too well, if you ask my view. I had a dram with the butler the night, and according to him, they spend a lot of the time together. Alone.'

'Of course they do. There is no-one else in the house, except for staff. His wife is down in London again. Has been for the past three weeks.'

'He would not want anyone else there.'

'What are you trying to say, MacDuff?'

'What I *am* saying, woman, is that they are together – in bed.'

'I cannot believe it! He is a gentleman, Mr Douglas. He has always reated us very fairly – and everyone else on the estate.'

'I grant you that. It is the girl I fear for.'

'She can look after herself.'

'You said that about our boy, and look what happened to him with that English swine Cartwright.'

'You are not suggesting there is anything like that?'

'I am suggesting nothing more than I say, woman. But if a man goes to bed with a girl young enough to be his daughter, you can judge for yourself what he is about.'

'No,' said his wife, shaking her head in horrified disbelief. 'No.'

'Aye,' replied MacDuff, and pushed away his plate. He had lost his appetite.

On the 12th of August – the glorious twelfth, so called because it marked the first day of grouse shooting – and at that darkening hour of evening when a man can be alone with his thoughts, Douglas was strolling along the terrace of Coupar Castle. Its lichened walls beat back the residual heat of a summer sun in which they had been basking all afternoon.

The sound of a discreet cough made him turn. MacDuff was standing nervously by the stone stairway that led down to the rose garden. He held his hat in both hands and was twisting the brim awkwardly.

'You wish to see me?' Douglas asked him.

'I feel I should, sir. I did not get a proper chance to talk at the shoot today. It is something rather personal.'

He paused.

'Tell me what it is,' said Douglas.

'I am very reluctant to do so, sir, but Mrs MacDuff says I must – or she will. I would rather you heard it from me than from her, if you understand.'

'I'm sorry, but I don't. What is this all about?'

'About Fiona, sir. I must ask your indulgence before I speak.'

'Be assured I will treat whatever you say in total confidence.'

'I do not wish to give you any offence, sir.'

'You will not cause me any offence, whatever you say. You have my word.'

'In that case, sir, I have to tell you that when Mrs Pomfret left Fiona in our care years ago, she was not sure when she was going to return. She gave us money for the bairn's keep, which she had raised by selling jewels. She also left an envelope, sealed with red wax, which we were not to open unless we were in dire trouble, sir. In these circumstances we could open it, and then we were to tell you – and no-one else – what it contained.'

'Me?' asked Douglas in surprise.

'Yes, sir. We did not open it until recently, when my wife became very concerned about Fiona's feelings for you, sir.'

'In what way, concerned?'

'I would rather you read this than I should speak the words, sir.'

MacDuff handed over the letter. It was signed by Jane Pomfret, witnessed by the Writer to the Signet who Douglas had visited before he went to India, and dated after his departure.

I swear on oath that the child, named as Fiona Pomfret, is not the child of my husband, the late John Pomfret. Fiona's father is Alec Douglas of Coupar Castle. So help me God.

Douglas looked up at Macduff in amazement.

'Is this genuine?' he asked.

'Yes, sir.'

'But Fiona does not look at all like me. For one thing she is fair, and everyone in my family has red hair.'

'So does she, sir. But we thought a girl with exactly that same shade of red hair as yours might cause talk in the village as to who her father really was. My wife kept it bleached so that no-one could suspect anything.'

'I see,' said Douglas slowly. 'I am greatly surprised to hear this news. In fact, I am overwhelmed. I need time to think what I must do. You will keep your own counsel about this, of course?'

'Of course, sir.'

Hardly had MacDuff left him, than Douglas heard the drum of running feet on the path. Fiona caught up with him. She was breathless, eyes shining like stars, hair cascading about her shoulders.

'I have been trying to see you for days,' she began.

'You cannot have searched very hard,' Douglas replied tartly. 'I have kept to my usual routine: a walk in the morning, then work with the factor.'

'Well, *I* could not find you,' she said. 'I so much wanted to see you before George did. He has asked me to marry him.'

'*Marry* him? But you have only just met him.'

'Not really. He has been here for weeks, although it only seems like days. I wanted to explain to you how I feel, how we both feel.'

'But there is nothing to explain,' Douglas assured her, striving to keep the anguish out of his voice. 'You have fallen in love with a pleasant young man of your own age. I wish you both every happiness.'

'It is not really as simple as that,' Fiona replied. 'You see, I love you, too. Our time together has been wonderful. You are like no-one else I have ever met.'

'Except George?'

'Well, George *is* different. But it is silly to think that a woman can only love one man. I love you both – in different ways. You must see that?'

'You *like* me,' Douglas corrected her. 'You were very good for me, and perhaps in a way I was good for you. But age and youth do not get on together for long.'

'*We* got on together.'

'Yes,' he agreed. 'We get on very well. But in ten years' time, I will be very old, and you will still be young. It would be like marrying your father.'

As he spoke the words, he could have bitten his tongue, but Fiona saw no irony in them.

'I like you better than *any* father,' she answered him warmly. 'Which is why I am so glad that at last I have seen you, and you are not angry.'

'I am not angry,' said Douglas. 'I am very pleased for you and for George. But perhaps I feel just a bit sorry for myself.'

Fiona kissed him, not with passion, but gently; a sister kissing a brother, a daughter kissing her father. Their affair was over, locked away; not forgotten, never to be forgotten, but equally from now on never to be spoken of between them.

'We are going into Perth tomorrow to buy a ring,' she said. 'George says it must be a sapphire to match my eyes. Isn't it fun!'

Douglas nodded. He could not bear to speak. He watched her as she ran down the path, skipping now and then with sheer happiness.

Fun. That was not the word he would have used to describe it, but then, he had enjoyed what some would describe as fun with her. He walked on, but now with a less resolute step. The evening suddenly felt cold, and he felt lonely and more than lonely, alone. For the winner in every race, there must also be a loser. He had won so many races in his time, for money, for power, the acquiescence of other women. Now he had lost the prize he wanted most of all, which, even if George Wallace had not arrived, must still have been denied him in view of what MacDuff had just revealed.

For a father to love his daughter as he had loved Fiona was bad enough. To lie with her again and again, to bring her and himself to raptures of sexual ecstasy was far worse. But then to allow this daughter to marry his son, what would be said – what *could* be said – of a father who did this? But whatever punishment the law might inflict could never approach the agony of the guilt he felt, would always feel.

He had often heard people assure him earnestly that money could not buy happiness. Of course it could not, for happiness was priceless, a gift of the gods, or rather a loan from the gods. He had also been told equally often that even if you were rich and unhappy, you could be miserable in comfort. This was also true, but Douglas knew that no comfort coul ever assuage the black misery in his heart. He faced a bleak future, alone with Emma and her increasingly shrill and venomous criticisms. Perhaps she was ill, or it was her age – or, worse, perhaps he was ill himself, and only imagined her hostility?

He wondered whether anyone else suspected that Fiona was his daughter. He had been a fool not to guess that this affinity between them must be as much the cause of their closeness as any physical attraction. He felt an immeasurable sense of loss and regret at having missed the precious years when Fiona was growing up; when his advice might have been of value; when his money most certainly would have been.

Jackson had told him once, shortly before he died, how greatly he regretted never keeping his promise to return to see Joanna and old Tom Gray in Gravesend. He had meant to go back, of course, but other matters had always taken priority, and by the time he was rich and successful, he had postponed the visit so often that it had lost all meaning, and by then it was indeed too late.

Douglas was undecided as to his own decision now. Should he do everything in his power to stop Fiona's marriage? He could afford the best legal counsel in the country, and he had the strongest possible case, but again he could never reveal its full strength. To do that would ruin him, and probably the lives of two young people, his own children.

Equally, to do nothing could ruin them in a different way. Could he – dare he – allow Fiona and George to build what he felt could only be a terrible future for themselves?

If Fiona conceived a child by her half-brother it might be born deformed or imbecile. Could he stand by and risk this happening to his grandchild? As he had often heard the minister in the local kirk assure his congregation, the sins of the father shall be visited unto the third and fourth generation. No, please God, not that.

Dare he tell Fiona and George of their relationship and risk the effect it might have, not only on them but on their feelings for him? In the end, all these possibilities came back to what *he* thought, what *he* felt, what best suited *him*.

In a lifetime's pursuit of his personal satisfaction, Douglas realised now that he had never given much thought to the consequences to others of his actions or his liaisons. He had secured the return of his estate because that was what he wanted. He had seduced countless women, married or single, for the same reason, without any thought or concern for their feelings or their future. If he suspected they might make trouble, he would buy them off. If they left his life with dignity, he might give them a present; or, again, he might not.

One, a shrew, he had been unwise enough to marry; again, not because he cared for her, but because it suited him then, because he thought that marriage was in his best interests. Selfishness had been his guiding star. What other star could now guide him through the lonely years ahead? He despaired that Fiona and George had fallen in love but, more than that, he despaired for himself.

Douglas went up to his room, poured himself half a tumbler of The Macallan, drank it and then poured himself a second. For a long time he sat on the edge of his bed, drinking and brooding on the problem, white shadows stretched across the floor to meet him and the room grew as dark as his thoughts. Then he arrived at his solution.

Douglas visited the office of the Writer to the Signet, overlooking the myriad chimneys of Edinburgh.

'Under Scottish law,' the Writer was explaining, 'in your will, you must leave your wife sufficient for her needs.'

'By my standards or hers?' Douglas asked him.

'By yours, having regard to your position in life, and the standard to which she has become accustomed. But you can leave everything else to anyone you like.'

'She is already well provided for by her first husband,' Douglas replied. 'I therefore intend to leave my estate here and all my shares in Trinity-Trio to Fiona Pomfret on these conditions: that she changes her name to Douglas or at least incorporates that name with her married name, if she marries; also, she must occupy the castle when she is in Scotland, and should she have any sons, they will also bear my name. The Douglas motto is "Never behind". I would like the family name to go forward.'

'A most generous provision for a fortunate young lady.'

'In all the circumstances,' Douglas replied, 'I feel it is no more than just and fair. Please have the will drawn up while I wait, and I will sign it here and now.'

That evening, after dusk, Douglas took down his favourite shotgun from the rack, broke it, inserted two cartridges, and poured himself a long drink of malt whisky.

He stood, while the spirit moved like warming fire in his blood. Then he picked up a pistol, slipped six cartridges into the clip, and with the loaded shotgun in the crook of his arm, and the pistol in his jacket pocket he went out into the darkness, leaving his dogs behind him.

Next morning, a white-faced ghillie came into the servants' hall of Coupar Castle. He had found the body of Mr Douglas by the river, shotgun and pistol by his side. The top of his head had been blown away

Part Two

The 1900s to the 1920s

London

Joanna Gray faced Samuel Ebenezer in the law office of Ebenezer and Son in Lincoln's Inn. Samuel, now senior partner, was the grandson of the man whom Mr O'Hara had employed for so many years in his offices in Seven Dials and Lincoln's Inn, on the pretence that he was a deaf mute.

Samuel regarded Joanna Gray with a mixture of interest and surprise. When he had opened Dr Jackson's will, he at once wrote to ask her to attend at his office; the firm still handled Trinity-Trio's legal work. Joanna replied that she could not afford the train ticket from Gravesend to London, and so he dispatched a five-pound note to her by registered post.

Now that she had arrived, he was surprised to see she was so young; he had expected someone at the very least in late middle age. This *was* Joanna Gray, there could be no mistake? She had a cheerful, pleasant face, not pretty but agreeable and alert, and it was clear that she was as surprised at his urgent request to see her as he was by her youthfulness.

Plainly dressed, her face showing the concern and even secret apprehension she felt at this totally unexpected summons to meet a London lawyer of whom she had never heard, Joanna opened her purse and took out some notes and coins, putting them on his desk.

'That is what is left from your five pounds,' she explained. 'You had better have this change back at once.'

Ebenezer shook his head, smiling.

'Keep it, Miss Gray. It is yours. It came from your money.'

'I don't understand you. How can it come from my money? I have no money, or I would not have had to ask you for my train fare. And until you sent one to me, I had never even seen a five-pound note.'

'You are going to see many in the future, Miss Gray. And ten-pound notes, even hundred-pound notes.'

'Please,' she said, frowning, 'you are making fun of me. Why have you asked me to come up to see you?'

'To explain that you have been left a sixth share in a very large tradin company, with offices here in London, in Calcutta, in Hong Kong and in Canton.'

'*Me?* But how can this be so? There must be some mistake. You have confused me with someone else.'

'Did you ever know a Dr Richard Jackson?' the lawyer asked her.

'No,' she said, 'but my mother used to speak of him. He had been her grandmother's doctor. Apparently he was very kind to her.'

'There was something about a penny, was there not?'

'You are right. I think he gave my mother a penny when she was a little girl and he was going to take out a tooth. She gave it back to him when he was leaving for India.'

'That penny brought him luck,' Ebenezer explained. 'Or at least, he thought it did, which is much the same thing. Dr Jackson became a very rich man, Miss Gray. He left half of his estate to your mother or, should she not be alive, to any children she might have. You are the only child?'

'Yes. I have to admit something my mother always wished to keep secret: she and my father never married. He was a sailor. They were going to marry, she told me, but on his way home from the Cape, his ship was lost at sea. She had a hard job bringing me up on her own, but she never complained.'

'Those days are all ended now, Miss Gray. Dr Jackson left a letter for your mother with his will. I would like to read it to you. I think it is applicable to you as much as to her.'

Dear Joanna Gray,

I am writing this hours after an eminent physician has told me I am under sentence of death from a disease for which there is no cure.

When a man receives news of this gravity, he looks back on his life and thinks of promises he made and never kept – not because he did not wish to keep them, but simply because other events intervened. He pushes those promises to the back of his mind, to be attended to at a more convenient time, as one puts unwanted luggage in an attic. Only now, when I am about to leave the house, I find myself sifting through items to which I should have attended so much earlier on.

I remember you so well, and your father, who literally saved my life on the night I left England for the East. I promised to come back and see you both, but I did not do so. To my shame, I did not even write to you. But now I am writing to repay a debt, belatedly, agreed – very belatedly – but at least, I hope, with interest.

I wish you well. I hope you enjoy the wealth I am leaving to you, and I hope you may do some good with it. I have used money to make more money, but, at the end of life's journey no matter how rich one becomes, one can carry nothing out through the lych-gate to eternity. There are, as the preachers say so aptly, no pockets in our shrouds.

I still have the penny you gave to me, and I hope you will also keep it – as a talisman, if you like, or as a mark to remind others of a little girl's kindness, and of a man, who, late in his life, as the sky darkened, remembered, and wished to God he had remembered sooner.

The lawyer cleared his throat; the letter moved him more than he cared to admit. His grandfather had frequently mentioned his first meeting with Jackson and Douglas, and the debt he owed to them both. Ebenezer looked at Joanna. Her eyes were moist with tears.

'If you would like me to help you administer this fortune, I would be happy to do so,' he said. 'But if you already have professional advisers of your own, please put me in touch with them, and I will hand everything over to them.'

'I would very much like you to help me. I do not understand these things. I do not even have a bank account.'

'So that is agreed. Good. Now, you would like an advance?'

'What can I have?' she asked.

'I could advance you over this desk five hundred pounds in cash. That is the limit – simply because it is all we keep in our safe.'

'A fortune!' she replied in astonishment. 'I find all this so difficult to believe. I would not know what to do with so much money.'

'You will soon find ways of spending it, Miss Gray, I assure you. We will open an account in your name in a bank in Gravesend, if you wish to continue to live there, and then you can sign a cheque, and draw out whatever you want. But, in the meantime, I will advance you a hundred pounds in notes.'

'Thank you.'

She paused.

'Tell me, to whom did Dr Jackson leave the other half of his estate?'

'To his son.'

'I did not know he was married.'

'He was not, but he had a liaison with a Chinese lady, and I think would have married her. At least, I have letters in my possession that point very strongly to that possibility. But he was ambitious, and to have had a Chinese wife would not have helped him.'

'So he abandoned her?' asked Joanna. 'And her son?'

'He saw that they lacked for nothing,' the lawyer replied defensively.

'Except love,' said Joanna.

'Possibly he loved her, Miss Gray. But perhaps he loved money more. It is always difficult to pass judgment.'

'And the son? Did he keep in touch with him?'

'Only by letter.'

'I see. Where is this son now? I would like to meet him.'

'I thought you might. As a matter of fact, he is waiting in the next room. He said he wanted to meet you.'

Samuel Ebenezer pressed the bell for his clerk to show in Robert Jackson.

Perthshire

Fiona came into Dr Drummond's surgery. She had known the doctor from childhood, and she admired him, not so much for his gifts as a healer, which now she was grown up she realised relied heavily on common sense and purges, but for his kindness. He had been treating Mrs MacDuff for an internal growth for more than two years, and never once had he suggested that she pay anything at all towards his weekly visits or her medicine.

'Is this a professional call?' he asked Fiona, looking at her over the tops of his horn-rimmed glasses. 'You look very well, I am glad to see.'

'I am, doctor. I have come to pay a debt.'

'You owe me nothing, my dear,' he told her, puzzled.

'I owe you for years of kindness to me and to the MacDuffs. I do not think you ever put in a bill?'

'They could not have paid it if I had,' the doctor replied, 'so why bother to write one out?'

'I have done that for you,' she said. She opened her purse, took out a cheque and handed it to him.

'But this is for five hundred pounds,' the doctor said in amazement. 'A fortune.'

'You forget, I am a rich woman now, doctor,' said Fiona with a smile. 'Mr Douglas left me his estate. And all his shares in the company, Trinity-Trio.'

'I heard something about that, but only rumours,' the doctor admitted. 'But I could not possibly accept this, whether you are rich or not.'

'You will hurt me very much if you don't,' she replied. 'And I am sure you would not wish to do that.'

'Of course not. Well, I will take it and put it towards the bills of other good people who cannot afford to pay me. Thank you again and again. Now, tell me, what are your plans, Fiona? Are you staying on here?'

'This village will be my home, as it always has been. I also intend to renovate Mr MacDuff's house, and see that he and his wife want for nothing. I wish you to call in whatever specialists you feel could help her. Spare no expense at all – and tell them to send their bills direct to me. Then I want to take a part in the running of the company.'

'But you know nothing about business matters, my dear. You have hardly ever left this village.'

'Now is the time to do so.'

She paused.

'I am also going to marry George Wallace,' she added, almost defensively. Yet why be defensive when she was in love?

'I have seen you with him,' said the doctor carefully. Instinctively, Fiona knew he did not like George. Could it be because of his brown skin, his half-Indian background, or simply the air of indolence he cultivated?

'After all,' George had told her on more than one occasion, 'there is no *need* for me to work. I have enough money to last me the rest of my days if I don't do a hand's turn. And if one does not positively *have* to work, I cannot see any point in doing so.'

'But, George, a man gets satisfaction out of work, out of doing something worthwhile. You cannot just moon your way through life, doing nothing!'

'Why ever not?'

'Because that is a waste of a life. You are only killing time. There are so many better things to do with time than just kill it.'

'This is the Presbyterian work ethic I have seen affect so many Scots in India. They build bridges and railways and hospitals and factories – and never once do they relax and enjoy themselves. Result? They die young.'

'Maybe they die happy in the knowledge that they have built these things.'

'Maybe. In the meantime, I will let you know when I grow tired of doing nothing. . . .'

'And then?' asked the doctor, cutting into her thoughts.

'Then I am going to London to meet the staff and the other partners. I also plan to sail to America. I see a great deal of mahogany furniture on sale in Perth and Edinburgh. The company imports mahogany from British Honduras, where it grows. I want to go there and visit other places which, until a few weeks ago, I had not even heard about.'

'I wish you very well,' said the doctor. 'Now, is there anything I can do for you? Any medicines you need for the journey? Chlorodyne? Purges?'

She smiled.

'I think not. But there is one question I would like to ask you. I was very fond of Alec Douglas, as you know. He was kind to me, took an interest in me, almost like a father. I hope he did not suffer pain when he died as he did?'

'I would think his death was instant. The ghillie who found him summoned me. He had discharged a pistol at his head.'

'But he had a shotgun? One was found by his side.'

'I know. I let it be thought there could have been an accident, that the shotgun went off by mistake. It is now back in his gunroom.'

'And the pistol?'

Dr Drummond opened a drawer in his desk and handed a small pistol to Fiona.

'Keep it,' he said. 'He left you everything else, so no doubt he would have liked you to have this, too. But tell no-one what I have told you. I did what I did to try and protect his name. He was my friend.'

Fiona put the pistol into her handbag; it felt very light.

'You are sure it *was* suicide? It could not have been murder?'

'No. It was suicide. I am certain of that.'

'Was there anything odd about his death?' Fiona asked, watching him closely.

'Only that he should kill himself. He was in good health. He had no money worries. He had a wife, but no family, so far as I know – and that is not always a hardship. Children are not all a comfort in your old age. But one thing did surprise me. The force of a single round from what you see is a very small weapon.'

'What exactly do you mean, doctor?'

Dr Drummond took a cartridge from a drawer.

'He had these made up for his shotguns as well as the pistol, all filled with Chinese powder,' Drummond explained.

'We used to have long discussions about his days in the East, and he told me how far advanced the Chinese were in making gunpowder. He brought back a couple of pounds of the stuff and had it put into cartridge cases. He always maintained that if the Chinese had any sense, they could have blown our warships out of the sea during the Opium War, before they ever came in range of our guns.

'But they lacked strategy, or common sense – or maybe both. They painted guns on their vessels, as though that was any use – when they had actually produced the most potent explosive in the world.'

'Have you any more of this powder?' Fiona asked him.

'Not here. In his gunroom, you will find a wooden box with his name on the lid. He kept several packets of powder there, and a number of cartridges. Why do you ask?'

'I would like to have it analysed, to find out why it is so powerful.'

'That is no problem. I know some very fine medical and chemistry students at Edinburgh University who would gladly do the work for a few guineas.'

'Pay them whatever they ask for the fullest examination. I will reimburse you.'

'What have you in mind?' the doctor asked her.

'I am a businesswoman now,' Fiona replied. 'If this powder is so strong, there must be other people who would like to buy it, individuals, maybe companies – even governments. I might build up a profitable trade.'

'You might indeed,' agreed Dr Drummond sagely. 'In fact, knowing you, I am sure you will. And to think I said you knew nothing about business!'

London

Robert Jackson knocked on the door of his mother's suite in the Carlton Hotel. She was sitting up in bed, reading, a silk shawl around her shoulders. She wore half glasses and their thin, rimless lenses accentuated her Chinese appearance. For the first time in his life, Robert realised that his mother was old – or ill. She looked frail, almost defenceless.

'You had an enjoyable evening, my dear?' T'a Ki asked him, motioning him to a seat. He sat down, not relaxed, leaning back as he usually did, but shifting uncomfortably on the edge of the satin-covered chair.

'Yes, Mama. I took Joanna to the theatre. We saw Cyril Maude and Madge Titheridge in "Lady Flirt" at the Haymarket. Then we went on to Kettners in Romilly Street.'

'A nice restaurant?' she asked with deceptive casualness.

'Delightful. We had a private room, all red plush, with everything brought in by our own waiter. We even had a lock on the door.'

'I trust you did not need that?'

'Not yet,' he agreed, smiling. 'But I find her very attractive.'

'She is what we would call a *pleasant* girl,' said T'a Ki carefully, 'but unversed in some things we consider important. Possibly even in the art of love?'

'I could teach her,' suggested Robert gently.

'It is better if others tutor an inexperienced girl. Then she is not nervous and gauche and frightened, like a mare approached by a stallion for the first time.'

'Joanna is not like that at all, Mama,' he replied. 'You must realise she has never had any money of her own, until quite unexpectedly she inherited all this from my father.'

'Which bears out what I am saying. She does not know how to behave with money. We have never been rich, *really* rich, but your dear father saw that we were, in the English expression, very comfortably off. Do not rush into some emotional attachment you may later regret.'

'I would like to ask her to marry me,' he admitted.

'Then you are a fool. You have known her for barely six months.'

'We have been out on numerous occasions. We went to Ascot in our own carriage. We have been to the theatre almost every week, and must have dined in every pleasant restaurant in London. I feel I know her well. I am relaxed with her. I *like* her, Mama.'

'Liking is not sufficient. If you are setting off on a journey through high mountains and deep ravines, over frozen rivers and across rough seas, with only one companion, you have to do more than *like* that companion. You have to trust them, rely on them – and they on you. What here in Europe they call love, soon fades. Remember the Chinese saying, "Nightingales only sing in the spring. They are silent when they have hatched their eggs." '

'You may be right, Mama. But I know how I feel.'

'You feel you want a woman,' said T'a Ki crudely. 'There are plenty in London with private rooms in Jermyn Street. You can meet them in the Trocadero or when they ride in their carriages and cars in the Park. You only have to doff your hat and they will stop.'

'That is not what I want.'

'You do not know what you want.'

'I do,' her son replied, and paused. T'a Ki looked at him sharply over the top of her glasses.

'Do you mean you are seriously contemplating marriage soon, but are reluctant to tell me?'

'I mean just that, Mama. I can afford to keep a wife. I feel at ease with Joanna, as I say. Every morning, I look forward to seeing her. If she is not there, it is as though the sun has not shone that day. She says she feels the same about me.'

'Of course she would, you fool! Women can be as false as a feather in the wind. You are a rich young man, Robert. A great catch for a woman.'

'She is as rich as I am. She does not seek my money.'

His mother pursed her lips, searching for a further argument against his marriage. She was reluctant to let him out of her orbit. He was all she had to remind her of a man she had loved; more, the only man she had loved.

'There is another thing,' she said. 'You are not wholly English. You are half Chinese. You are more in sympathy with the Eastern way of life than Western ways. After all, you have lived far longer there than here.'

'I can adapt, Mama.'

'Possibly you think you can, but you do not know the English as I do. Your father had to abandon you – and me – because his countrymen, and especially his countrywomen, would not accept the marriage of an Englishman of his class and qualifications to a Chinese. He would have lost face, as we say – or money, which was probably more important to him.

'He took the easy way out. Men do. He bought us off. He and I were not married. I had no rights in law. But I realised that even if I had been his wife, I would never have been accepted in England – and neither will you be. They will laugh at you behind your back – call you chinky-chinky Chinaman, make jokes, ask you where your pigtail is, call "Chop, Chop". You may attempt to find that humorous at first, but, believe me, the joke soon dies.

'They are an insular race, living on a small island, certain their way of doing things is the only way, that they have some divine right to rule – and they are very good at that. They believe their Empire will last forever, and that they will always be, as they say, cock of the walk.

'You have been taught differently. You know that history is like a slowly turning wheel. When one country is on top, another is slowly sinking, a third ascending. It has always been like that, and it always will be.'

'You may be right, Mama. You have been right in so many things, but this I will tell you: I *will* be accepted here, and I will prove it.'

'How? You speak like a child.'

'I will get myself elected to the most exclusive club in London, the Coliseum.'

'That you never will! They are all dukes and lords and earls there, men with heads so small they have no room for brains. They have inherited whole towns and great estates and live off them, like animals living off their own fat. They do not create anything – not even money. *They* will never accept you. Cannot you see that?'

'I appreciate what you say, Mama, but they *will* accept me. As you tell me, I am also rich.'

'Rich! Money does not count with these people. They have always had it, and their ancestors before them. What counts with them is what they call breeding. Blue blood. Lord this marries Lady that. That is what is important in this country, my son.'

'Well, time will tell,' said Robert cheerfully. 'But if I am elected, will you believe me then?'

'I will believe what I believe,' said T'a Ki shortly. 'Knowledge comes but wisdom lingers.'

* * *

When Mr Arbuthnott, the editor of *The Enquirer*, heard that Robert Jackson was on his way upstairs to see him, he hastily closed the drawer in his desk from which he had just taken a bottle for a pull of whisky. Arbuthnott followed the custom of his predecessor in always keeping a bottle of spirits nearby; the hours of an editor were long and the pressures high. And he claimed the whisky helped his breathing. He rose to greet his new proprietor with feigned enthusiasm.

'You have been all round the building?' he asked him, not knowing quite how to take this young man, who appeared half Chinese. 'You still want to take a personal hand in running things here?'

'Of course,' Jackson replied, as though surprised at the question. 'I know nothing about newspapers, but I know what I like to read, and there must be many like me.'

Arbuthnott hoped that the young man could not smell whisky on his breath. He might be less than half his age but he knew his own mind, and since he was so wealthy, his whim would be Arbuthnott's order.

'I have checked your figures,' Jackson continued. 'They are, unfortunately, accurate. As you told me, we are losing £30,000 a year on *The Enquirer*. Perhaps rather more this year.'

'That is substantially less than when your father bought the paper – and I became editor.'

'Agreed. But it is still a very large loss to sustain. My aim is to make a profit.'

'We have a very high reputation with the readers, sir.'

'Agreed, again. So we must attract more readers. Now, tell me, what do you think a newspaper is for, Mr Arbuthnott?'

'To provide accurate news and reports, with articles of general interest. To tell people what is happening in this country and in the world.'

'That may be your aim as a professional,' Jackson allowed, 'but so far as I am concerned, I want *The Enquirer* to have power and influence. To say what *I* think, to print points of view in which *I* believe.

'Then, through its influence – and your editorial skills – we can move the masses politically. Put ideas into their heads – our ideas, *mine*. We can promote the products and policies of our parent company, Trinity-Trio. The only way to achieve this is through wide circulation – and big profits.'

'I agree with you, sir, but already we are printing 7,000 copies a day.'

'I want 70,000 minimum. And then on to ten times that number.'

'Our presses could not possibly cope with that.'

'Then we must have new presses, more presses. Now, does anyone here know who I am?'

'No-one, sir. It is not known that Dr Jackson had a son, or, indeed, that he had ever married.'

'He had and he hadn't,' Jackson told him shortly. 'So explain vaguely that I am hired as a general dogsbody for whatever reason you care to give. Then I will tell you how we will make *The Enquirer* pay.'

'As you wish, sir. You are the owner.'

'You are the only person who knows that, Mr Arbuthnott – for the time being. Now, for a start, give me every day's issue for the past week, and a corner of some office where I can look through them.'

Jackson carried the newspapers out to a table in the reporters' room. Mr Arbuthnott introduced him vaguely as a new employee on the management side. There was a strict division between editorial and management employees, and he calculated that the information would arouse neither interest nor suspicion.

The editorial staff felt total contempt for the penpushers of management. They, in turn, strongly criticised reporters' expenses, their indolent ways and drinking habits. No-one had ever explained to both groups that they were all members of one team, and that their continual denigration of each other might be more productively reserved for rival newspapers.

Jackson read through the back numbers, then threw them into a wastepaper basket. The news stories had mostly been copied from other papers; sometimes they had been lifted almost verbatim. At the best, accounts from several rival papers had been amalgamated by a sub-editor to produce a new version carrying points from all of them.

The editorials were cautious and dull, with too many bows in different directions: 'It may well be. . . .' 'On the other hand. . . .' 'This fact notwithstanding. . . .' Flabby writing like this irritated Robert Jackson, and he did not think it would impress the readers whose custom he sought: men and women of taste and money.

The richer the readership, the more profitable the advertising. He could make more profit from a single-page advertisement for mahogany furniture suites than from a page of small advertisements for grooms and housemaids.

From now on, he decided, the editorials would be short, written in sharp, vigorous sentences.

They would introduce a far more comprehensive coverage of police court cases. Local correspondents in the provinces would be paid a bonus for every report they sent about matrimonial disputes, so long as they were detailed, and the more salacious and scandalous the better. They would increase the number of photographs in the paper. Men who found difficulty in reading could always enjoy a picture of a pretty woman.

'Ordinary people are interested in three things,' he told Arbuthnott 'Sex, money and food, probably in that order. So, tell them all you can about these subjects without, of course, infringing the rules of modesty

Print articles on money. Not how to save it, like other papers do, but how to make it – how to spend it.

'Then, food. What is Royalty's favourite dish? How do the cooks' of earls and dukes cope with dinner parties for thirty or forty guests? What are the world's twelve most popular recipes? If you don't know, pick them out of a cook book and ask the views of actresses and politicians. They will give them gladly – and freely. They all love publicity.

'Now, sex. What foods are the best aphrodisiacs? Print the fullest details of every divorce case or society scandal, *every* day, *every* week. Don't sail too close to the wind, Arbuthnott. Sail right into it. We will possibly have a few libels, but who cares? I don't, and I will be paying the damages. And think of the publicity these lawsuits will provide. A lot cheaper than posters.

'Another thing. Everyone knows how King Edward has had a number of mistresses, Mrs Keppel, Lily Langtry, Sarah Bernhardt and others, but the papers are reluctant even to mention that these ladies are his friends – if nothing more. Forget that nonsense! Commence a series on "The Women in the King's Life".'

'But that could land us in court, sir.'

'Of course it couldn't, because we will include all sorts of women in his life – the Queen, his sisters, his mother, his aunts all over Europe and so forth! Just drop the real subjects of the piece in here and there. Royalty and religion, Mr Arbuthnott, make little sense to lots of people – but damned good reading for everyone.'

These ideas were not at all to Mr Arbuthnott's liking, and nor, he had to admit, was the new proprietor. How could this young man with his smooth, sallow face and his slanted eyes know so much about public taste? He had no journalistic training; he must sense these things instinctively. And, just as instinctively, Arbuthnott knew that he was right, if his object was profit and political influence. If readers agreed with him on some topics, they would fall in with his views on others. Such aims were understandable, but not to Arbuthnott's taste: he preferred respect, the membership of clubs open to him as editor of a newspaper often bracketed with *The Times*, not as a man running a scurrilous rag.

That he stood in the presence of a young man of prescience, if not genius, Arbuthnott could accept, but this did not make him like Jackson any the more.

Jackson, oblivious of the older man's feelings, was skimming through that morning's edition. Tucked halfway down a column on an inside page was a small, dull, desiccated account of a society divorce. A peer of the realm had taken an actress to bed – at the same time as his wife. The implications had so shocked Mr Arbuthnott that the paper had simply recorded this fact, without any details.

'Here we are,' said Jackson triumphantly. 'Three in a bed. Now, hire a good cartoonist, get him to do a sketch of a double bed with two pillows and a caption explaining that this is a true and accurate picture of Lord What'shisname's bed.

'On the next page, he prints a correction – the same sketch with *three* pillows. Understand me?'

'Perfectly, sir. But this sort of thing would not be what *The Enquirer* readers are used to.'

'Possibly, but it is what they – and thousands and thousands more – will be delighted to become used to. From now on.'

Jackson went down into the machine room. He knew nothing about printing machines, but the three ancient presses, with parts held together by wire and welding, aroused no respect. He would be rid of them and install a new Hoe, which he had seen advertised in a trade journal, and which could produce three times as many papers at half the cost. And when circulation grew, he would buy another.

The foreman in the machine room, a Welshman named Evans, clearly regarded his visit as an intrusion.

'It is not usual for new arrivals on the management side to come down here,' he said pointedly.

Jackson nodded and did not reply. He looked around at the twelve machine men – far too many for the work available. They had the bored, dissatisfied appearance of men with too little to do. A small man with bright blue eyes and a fresh complexion stood out from the others. He was alert, and, judging from his clean finger-nails, a non-smoker. Jackson inclined his head as an indication to this man to follow him out of the machine room. He did so reluctantly but introduced himself; his name was Joss Erskine.

'I am undertaking a survey of the plant for the owner,' Jackson explained. 'Come and have a drink with me.'

'I cannot do that, sir. I am on shift.'

'When do you take your dinner break?'

'Twelve o'clock.'

'Come out then. I will see you in the back room at The Cheese.'

Erskine was nervous when he arrived at the Cheshire Cheese public house in Fleet Street. He usually ate sandwiches his wife made for him and drank cold tea from an enamel flask. Jackson took him over to a corner where they sat down.

'What do you want to see me about?' he asked Jackson.

'Your promotion.'

'What do you mean?'

'There are far too many men down there. What are they all paid?'

'Five pounds a week each, on average.'

'How many men would you say are needed – with modern equipment?'

'Five,' Erskine replied at once.

'Then why are there so many?'

'Because Evans is Welsh. He thinks Mr Arbuthnott and the late Dr Jackson were against the Welsh. A ridiculous idea! These men Evans has hired all owe their positions to him, so he feels he has good friends around him if there is any trouble.'

'Could he lead them out on strike if he wanted to?'

'Of course, and that would be very expensive for the management. A daily paper is not like a factory producing hundreds of glasses, say, or candlesticks or chairs.

'Every day's edition of a newspaper is a totally new product. Its readers are fickle. If the paper doesn't come out one day, they will buy another or do without – and often are lost to it forever. I've seen that happen several times in Fleet Street. Also, if there is any dispute or hold-up in working hours, newspapers miss their train for the West Country or the North – and no-one buys today's newspaper that arrives late or next morning.

'This means that every advertiser has to be contacted and offered their money back for one lost day – or days. Newspapers are very vulnerable to stoppages. That's why newspaper managements all turn a Nelson eye to what goes on with the presses.'

'You have given this some thought, I see, Mr Erskine.'

'I have indeed. I enrolled for evening classes on the history of the Press but I couldn't keep up with them. Evans put me on the late shift so I had to drop out.'

'Could you do his job?'

'Easily.'

'Think about it,' said Jackson. He ordered two steak, kidney and oyster pies and two tankards of stout.

'For how long?' Erskine asked him.

'Until I invite you to take it over. Wages, ten pounds a week, and you to choose five men at six pounds a week each.'

'Are you joking?'

'No. I own the paper.'

'I thought you were only a young chap learning his job?'

'Years ago,' replied Jackson, 'people thought the world was flat.'

On the evening of Jackson's third day in the office, he went to see Mr Arbuthnott in the editor's office and told him of his impressions.

'The reporters I have seen are lazy and too fond of the bottle. From now on, every reporter will write at least one original story every day.'

'How do you propose they find them?'

'By using their brains – and their feet. This capital is alive with news, but they won't find any of it in the taprooms of Fleet Street. Run a page of London stories under some such heading as "London – the City that is Always News".

'Let them specialise. One can write on architectural matters, another on politics, a third on scientific discoveries.'

'I do not think they are qualified to do that.'

'Then sack them and hire people who are. We have mass education now. People are avid to read and learn – if the facts are presented attractively.

'Someone could write a series on other people's jobs. He goes down the mines, he rides on the footplate of a new locomotive, he follows a doctor on his rounds, that sort of thing. The wider the range of jobs, the better the series – and the more readers you will pull in. And I am surprised you have no women writers at all.'

'Fleet Street is no place for a woman, sir.'

'Then make it a place for a woman – several women, in fact. Half the world are women – so are half our readers. Let them answer problems on etiquette, children, marriage, jobs. I want all these points implemented by the end of this week.'

'This will cost a very great deal of money, sir,' said Mr Arbuthnott miserably.

'I have a very great deal of money,' retorted Jackson, and picked up his hat.

The first official meeting of the new partners who now controlled Trinity-Trio took place in Samuel Ebenezer's office in Lincoln's Inn. Fiona, who under the terms of her inheritance had changed her name to Douglas, greeted Robert Jackson and Joanna Gray with some reserve. None of them had experience of running any business, nor were they quite sure what the others had in mind.

They were now all rich enough not to work, but this course held no attractions for any of them. Equally, they knew they could lose their money if they expanded the company too quickly or in the wrong direction. What was essential, in Fiona's opinion, was to build slowly and steadily. The sale of opium had established the company, but this alone could no longer sustain it. Fiona thought that the solution lay in diversification – but into which other areas?

Before the meeting, she had asked to see the accounts for the previous three years, which Ebenezer explained to her. He was considerably impressed by the way in which she could grasp the essentials immedi ately, almost instinctively. She would put a finger on a debit for a large sum, and when he explained the reason for it, however abstruse the explanation, she would accept it instantly – but would then query a far smaller expenditure, which he had to admit had been a waste of money.

Ebenezer had been prepared to act as a father figure to her, guiding her gently, step by step, through a labyrinth of items in profit and loss accounts. Instead he discovered, not altogether to his liking, that she soon understood the most complex details, which he had expected would take a long time to explain to her.

He regarded her with new respect. Fiona was not interested in the figures as figures, as an accountant would regard them. Instead, they were to her arithmetical symbols, hieroglyphics representing large, complicated transactions, with human consequences.

They stood for cotton shirts and towels shipped from Lancashire mills to Calcutta, off-loaded on the docks, re-loaded on the same ship to defeat a landing tax, and then sent farther east to Hong Kong and beyond. They represented scrap iron from the Midlands hauled to the docks in trucks, lifted by giant magnets on cranes, or beaten brass ornaments by the hundred tons for India, where they would be sold – and often reimported to Britain – as genuine Benares wares. Opium balls were sometimes prudently described as putty or wax for pharmaceuticals, with bills of lading being changed on the voyage for political reasons.

She had a mind for money, the rare ability to understand how it could be made with a minimum of risk and effort, and with maximum profit. Neither of the other partners possessed this gift to anything like the same extent.

Ebenezer knew from Harold Arbuthnott, the editor of *The Enquirer*, and Joss Erskine, now head printer, how Robert had an intuitive sense for what the reading public wanted. This was already being translated into advertising revenue, which was important not only for the profit it represented, but for the way in which the advertisements in this paper and other journals he planned to publish could influence public taste – and hence their spending.

Joanna was still surprised and almost unable to comprehend she had inherited so much money, and with it, potential power. Ebenezer knew that Robert Jackson had taken her out to the theatre on a number of occasions and then had supper afterwards. He wondered whether their relationship would develop into anything more lasting, perhaps even marriage.

He had discussed this possibility with his wife; women were intuitive about such things. She thought it possible, but in her view it would be unwise. Wasn't Jackson half-caste? Wouldn't there be a risk of any children being throwbacks and of totally Chinese appearance? She had heard of such things happening when people of mixed blood married. It wasn't a risk she would care to take, she told her husband, and Ebenezer agreed.

Now, in his office, he looked around at the three partners; he was temporarily in the chair.

Fiona was the first to ask a question.

'Since I understand between us we own two-thirds of the company, what is the situation regarding the other third?'

'This was owned by the late Captain Marvin Ross,' Ebenezer explained. 'On his death in British Honduras, a Mr Jack O'Brien claimed that Captain Ross had signed a document shortly before he died, making his share over to him. That was quite true, but the document was not legal because the partners had earlier agreed among themselves that, in the event of any of them dying, the shares of the deceased partner would go either to his widow, if he had one, or would be offered to the other surviving partners. In this case, the Captain's widow, Mrs Evelyn Ross, inherited.'

'Does she still hold the shares?' asked Jackson.

'Not all of them, apparently. Our last address for Mrs Ross was an hotel in New York. I wrote to her there on a number of occasions, but all the letters were returned to me by the manager. She appears to have left without leaving any forwarding address.'

'What about her dividend income?' asked Robert Jackson.

'Dividends are paid into an account her late husband opened in London years ago.'

'That bank has no address for her either?'

'No. Money is apparently just piling up on deposit.'

'So who holds some of her shares?'

'A charity in the States. I have recently received a communication, which I have not yet answered, from United Charities Incorporated, with an office at Trenton in New Jersey.

'They enclosed a letter which purports to come from Mrs Ross – the authenticity of which they had attested by a first-rate legal firm in New York – to the effect that Mrs Ross has given half her shares to this charity.'

'Have you been in touch with this charity to see if they know where she is?'

'I have. They replied most courteously that she has given explici' instructions that her address is not to be revealed to any enquirer.

'I was waiting for this meeting, to have your views on the matter Legally, of course, Mrs Ross is entitled to do whatever she likes with he share of the company.'

'What exactly are the aims of this charity?' asked Joanna. 'Who are th trustees?'

'I have been in touch with a legal firm in New York we have used fc other matters, and they have given me some details. It was formed man years ago by Italian immigrants who had done well in the New World. They wished to express their gratitude in a positive way. It gives grants to organisations or individuals who they consider are worthy of assistance. They help immigrants start in business by investing in their enterprises and they do not take any interest on their investments, but a share in the profits – if there are any.'

'How rich is it?' asked Fiona.

'That is difficult to establish because it is a charity. The impression of our legal friends in New York, however, is that it is already worth several million dollars.'

'Why should Mrs Ross give to such an organisation? She is not Italian, is she?'

'Not so far as I know,' replied Ebenezer, 'but as a lawyer, I have to tell you that widows of means often give very generously to the most unusual causes. I have sat in this room and seen fortunes given to societies who seek to prove that the earth is flat, or that the hieroglyphics on the pyramids in Egypt contain the secret of human happiness and eternal life. Only yesterday, I was instructed by the widow of a prominent industrialist to give £100,000 to a consortium of people who claimed they could harness waves breaking on a beach to make electric current.

'I felt it my duty to introduce to this lady two eminent scientists who, with all the resources of our great universities, had been unable to achieve this success. She, however, remained convinced that three young men, without any scientific training at all, but who were friends of her son, on whom she doted, could be successful where Fellows of the Royal Society had failed.

'However, be that as it may, neither this charity nor Mrs Ross, as holders of a minority interest, can influence the direction of Trinity-Trio without your authority, and it is this direction which I think we should now discuss.'

'Can you tell us exactly the extent of Trinity-Trio's activities, apart from the trading activities you have already mentioned?' Fiona asked him.

'Certainly,' said Ebenezer. 'We have a pharmaceutical factory in North London near the village of Edgware. Mr Alec Douglas also bought a furniture factory in High Wycombe, a town with a long tradition of furniture-making. That is now producing solid mahogany furniture, and for the cheaper market, softwood cupboards and chests of drawers finished with mahogany veneer.

'In Trenton, New Jersey, we have a fifty per cent interest in Lion's Share chewing gum and sweetmeats. The other half of the same factory, which we control absolutely, is producing sleeping draughts, pills and so on, mostly with an opium base.'

'What is the profit situation on Lion's Share?'

'After a slow start, the growth is healthy. Steady rather than dramatic, I would say. The brand faces very strong competition in its field.'

'I think we should diversify into foods of various kinds,' suggested Fiona. 'It is a basic fact that people of every class want to eat – usually three times a day. There is thus a constant and, as the population increases, an ever growing market for foods. So far as furniture is concerned, a married couple may buy a three-piece suite or a big chest of drawers, but that is often a once-in-a-lifetime expense. Food is a daily expenditure.

'Also, I noticed on the train coming up to London that many gentlemen are smoking cigarettes. In popularity, they seem to have taken over from pipes. I counted cigarette smokers in several compartments. It was an average of four to one over pipe-smokers.'

'That is because people have taken a lead from King Edward,' Ebenezer explained. 'His doctors told him how harmful cigars were to his chest, and he has largely gone over to cigarettes. Society instantly copied him, and what had previously been acceptable only in the labouring classes became fashionable almost overnight. I am told that His Majesty now smokes twelve Havanas and twenty cigarettes every day. Before, he would smoke many more cigars.

'Cigarette smoking first started when British soldiers caught the habit from the Turks during the Crimean War. There is still an echo of this in society, because miniature cigarettes, known as Cigarette Turcs, are on sale in coloured boxes so that ladies can follow the lead of the monarch in smoking cigarettes after dinner.'

'*The Enquirer* is publishing a series of articles next week on the increasing popularity of cigarette smoking.' said Jackson. 'The editor told me that women actually collect cigarette stubs the King is said to have smoked, like holy relics.'

'Very good for the cigarette manufacturers,' said Joanna. 'Think of the publicity they will receive.'

'That does not help us in any way,' replied Fiona. 'We do not manufacture cigarettes. But I will tell you what we *can* make: the boxes and cartons to pack them in, and the paper that holds the tobacco.'

'An excellent idea,' said Jackson appreciatively.

'We can employ first-class designers to make them as attractive as possible. We will find out which cigarettes are the least popular, and then offer their makers a very good deal on new packets – so long as we control the design and marketing. If we can put up their sales by an agreed percentage, the arrangement will be that we can increase our prices to them. They are bound to go for that proposal because they simply cannot lose.'

'So it is agreed, then?' asked Ebenezer. 'We look into the whole matter and I will report back?'

'That is not agreed at all,' said Fiona sharply. 'We do not want reports, but action. We must find companies already making cardboard boxes, cartons and cigarette papers – and buy them. We can keep on supplying their existing customers while we branch out into this new field with other cigarette manufacturers.

'In the past, Trinity-Trio seems to have grown in a haphazard way. It would buy this company or that, almost on the whim of an individual partner. I suggest that from now on, we approach acquisitions in a more scientific manner. We look for a specific gap in some market and then we try to fill it before someone else does. Is that agreed?'

'Unanimously,' affirmed Jackson with enthusiasm.

Belize Town

Señor Gonzales, Trinity-Trio's agent in British Honduras, lowered his brass extendible telescope, closed it, and went down the stairs from the flat roof of Mr O'Brien's house overlooking the ocean, to report to his master.

'*Coromandel II*, flying the Trinity-Trio flag, is about to drop anchor.'

'I was not expecting a visit,' said O'Brien in surprise. 'What is the position over the last shipment of mahogany and resin?'

'We are still withholding one cargo on your instructions.'

O'Brien nodded. Without any warning, he had put a surcharge of thirty per cent on both items, blaming this on an unexpected increase in labourers' wages, and a hurricane that had swept Central America.

He calculated that the new partners controlling Trinity-Trio would not wish to query his figures so early in their relationship. Indeed, they seemed an unusual group to be in charge of so large a company: a half-caste Chinese, and two women. As the son of a slave, O'Brien sympa-hised with all coloured people but not with European women. They belonged to the race of whom Captain Ross had been the most hated examplar. And coloured men who married white women became, in his opinion, traitors, not to be trusted. The monotonous dirge of *dhobi* men, as they washed clothes by beating dirt out of them on flat rocks at the edge of the river to the rhythm of 'Black man, good man, white man, bastard', echoed his feelings – and especially so far as this woman Fiona Douglas was concerned.

He had been astounded to receive a letter from Ebenezer and Son informing him that the document Ross had signed was invalid because of a prior agreement of the partners that, if any were married, their widows would inherit their husband's holding. He had immediately consulted a solicitor in Belize Town, and when he told O'Brien that the captain's letter was valueless, O'Brien had insisted he obtain a second opinion from a law firm in New York, also with the same result.

Who but this white woman and her Parsee husband could have done this to him? Now they came to crow over his disappointment. He could have killed them slowly, painfully, for what they had done to him. She might hold the shares, but doubtless this Parsee was the real brain behind her action.

O'Brien was secretly surprised that his outrageous increase in prices had not produced any comment whatever from the London office. Perhaps they were sending someone over in this vessel to discuss the matter personally? That seemed most likely.

'Meet the ship,' O'Brien told Gonzales. 'Tell their representative it will be my pleasure if he – and any colleagues aboard – will dine with me here tonight.'

It would be instructive to assess them at first hand. Maybe they were such fools that they would wear a sixty per cent surcharge, not just thirty?

Fiona's first impression of Gonzales was not favourable. He smelled of garlic and sweat. His face shone as though covered with oil and his eyes flickered from side to side like the eyes of adders she had seen in the undergrowth of the Scottish hills. She did not trust serpents and instinctively she put Gonzales in the same category.

George Wallace held no strong views about the man. He had a darkish skin, which struck an immediate answering chord, for, like O'Brien, he was always prepared to view more sympathetically anyone who was clearly not wholly white.

He therefore accepted O'Brien's invitation to dinner without even consulting Fiona. She would have preferred to spend a day or two ashore, becoming acclimatised to the heat and humidity before she undertook any engagements, which, while ostensibly social, were in fact business meetings and discussions.

'You might have asked me first,' she told George irritably.

'You were in your cabin, and Gonzales was eager to be away. He said he was busy.'

'So he should be – about our business. After all, *we* employ him.'

'You mean *you* do,' George retorted.

'We are husband and wife – a team,' she reminded him. 'So next time please ask before you accept any invitation. We do not wish to appear to eager with this man O'Brien. There was something odd in the wa

Captain Ross made over his shares to him – yet he can only have met him once or twice.'

'Ross was odd in many ways, so I have heard,' replied George. 'We are hardly being too eager simply by saying we will have dinner with O'Brien.'

'Why can you not understand?' Fiona cried in despair. 'It is all a matter of prestige, *our* prestige. You should have let him wait. He would think far more of us if you had.'

She looked at her husband now, not only with disappointment but with growing distaste. She found it hard to believe she could ever have made such a mistake about him. In Scotland, before their marriage, walking across the heather-covered hills, he had seemed charming and pleasant, the companion of whom she had dreamed as a little girl, looking at pictures in the fire in the MacDuffs' kitchen.

George always appeared interested in anything she could teach him about the ways of country people and the lore of the countryside. But she knew that the MacDuffs, if not disapproving of him, at least found George difficult to communicate with. Fiona remembered Dr Drummond's non-committal reply when she told him she intended to marry him. George, she realised now, had represented something missing from her life: romance. He had travelled widely, he was rich, well-educated, and had met important people about whom she had only read brief items in the newspapers with which groceries were wrapped in the village store. George was someone she could look up to and admire – or so she thought.

They had kissed. He had caressed her, gently and kindly, and she had mentally compared this with Alec Douglas's vigorous and expert approach. She and George were married in the local kirk and he took her to Edinburgh for a honeymoon. Here, for the first time in an expensive hotel, in a bedroom with its own bathroom, with flowers banked everywhere, she had realised with a shock, physical as well as mental, that he was rather different to the man with whom she imagined she had walked in the hills. She had invested that companion with virtues she admired – but which the real George simply did not possess.

For one thing, George drank heavily; she had thought he was almost teetotal. What disturbed her now was his secret drinking: whisky, rum, gin. She would find empty glasses pushed out in the corridor with shoes to be cleaned, or bottles thrown into the wastepaper bin, hidden beneath deliberately crumpled newspaper.

Perhaps, in India, his religion had denied him the pleasures of alcohol? Now he was on his own in another country, he was not bound by any such discipline. But what distressed and disappointed her, and in the end repulsed her, was George's total inadequacy as a lover.

Douglas had years of experience gained with women of different colours and classes across the globe. Now, she found a fumbling, inexpert partner. He had no idea how to arouse her, and when, haltingly, she tried to explain, George took sudden and angry umbrage and swung out of their bed, naked, to drink a huge draught of whisky.

When he returned, she smelt the spirit on his breath, overlaid with rum and the sweet scent of gin. He was flaccid and useless, and he lay there, groping at her in an irritating and goatish way. When finally she had patiently stroked him into some kind of erection, he discharged before he even entered her, leaving her totally unsatisfied. Within minutes, he was asleep and snoring, mouth open like a hog.

Fiona attempted to rationalise this unexpected revelation. He had been strictly brought up in a religion about which she knew nothing; she had had the incomparable advantage of an older, extremely experienced lover. Eventually they must find a means of mutual satisfaction and respect. After possibly a few more unfortunate and unsatisfactory attempts, everything would be all right. But in assuring herself that this would be so, in repeating it in front of the bathroom mirror, in willing herself to believe it, Fiona knew it was a lie.

There was some flaw in George's character, in his mental and moral and physical fibre, that could never be overcome. He was weak and she was strong. She first realised this when a dispute arose over a bill at a restaurant in Edinburgh on their honeymoon. She pointed out they had been grossly overcharged, but George paid the money without querying the amount.

'We don't want to make a fuss,' he told her.

'Why not?'

'It's only money,' he said. 'Pointless to argue about it.'

'When you have been without money for as long as I have,' Fiona replied, 'you realise it is *never* pointless to argue if you are overcharged. These people think we are fools, throwing money away. The next time strangers come in here they may be overcharged, too. If we stopped it now, we stop it not only for us but for others.'

'To hell with others,' George retorted thickly. He had drunk four Drambuies, and was in no mood or condition to argue. 'It just is not worthwhile, my dear.'

'If you take that attitude,' she said, 'nothing is worthwhile. I do not expect people to swindle me, or for my husband to condone it.'

'No-one is swindling anyone,' he said as they climbed into the taxi, and he groped her ineffectually, feeling her breasts, kneading the nipple through her camisole.

'Please,' she said, drawing away. 'The driver will see you.'

'Don't you want me?' he asked her, ignoring her obvious distaste. Sh looked at him and under the flitting lights along the pavement of Prince's Street, she realised the answer. No. She did not want him; then, or at any other time. If she was being honest, perhaps she had never wanted him. She had assumed he was someone he was not; someone he had never been, who she had imagined would lift her out of her dull, safe, impoverished rut.

But with this realisation came another; there was no need now for anyone to lift her out. She could lift herself out – and she would. She realised with a shock as she paid off their taxi, that if she had met George after she had inherited from Alec Douglas, she would never have given him more than the briefest time of day. And in acknowledging this, she had to accept an even more basic and ironic truth: if this had happened, she would never have inherited at all. She disliked George, but without him she would still be the adopted daughter of the MacDuffs. She believed that because of her wish to marry George, her benefactor had shot himself, and as a result, she was rich.

She determined at that moment, as they waited for the lift in the foyer of their hotel, to be her own person. She was married, and outwardly she would be loyal and obedient. Inwardly, she would be as she had always been, but now fired by the desire to increase her inheritance.

She felt she was like a runner in a relay race. She had been given the baton. She could drop it, or run with it and hand it over so that the person on the next stage could beat their competitor. Thus and thus only would she feel worthy of the trust which a man whom she now realised had loved her to the point of death had placed in her.

O'Brien impressed Fiona even less than Gonzales. His eyes were heavy and hooded, like the eyes of a lizard. He addressed her without looking at her, as though speaking to a third person.

They dined on a verandah overlooking the sea. Candles and oil lamps hung from rafters entwined with bougainvillaea and night-blooming flowers. They had turtle soup, grilled lobster tails and fresh mango with ice cream. The wines were French and clearly expensive. As O'Brien and George drew on their cigars afterwards – neither had asked Fiona whether she minded if they smoked, and she hated cigar smoke – O'Brien, gauging his man, turned to her husband.

'I trust you will forgive me for speaking of business at a social occasion, sir, but I have to leave early tomorrow for the forests.'

'Please go on,' said George. He had drunk a lot of wine and several local liqueurs without realising that the rum they contained was 150° proof – so strong that if poured neat into a saucer the spirit would evaporate. He did not see Fiona glance at him sharply as he spoke. He was sitting too far away from her at the oval table, or she would have tapped his ankle as a warning. She sensed what their host was about to say, and she did not want to be committed too soon to any business agreements.

O'Brien went on: 'I expect you are wondering about that thirty per cent surcharge. It was quite impossible to keep down to our agreed price. I had either to pay or abandon the shipment.'

'But that is what you did, Mr O'Brien,' said Fiona. 'The goods are still on the docks.'

'Ah, but they have been invoiced,' said O'Brien quickly. She must be a sharp one, this white bitch. She must have spoken to some of his men – or had she bribed Gonzales?

'I am sorry to say this,' O'Brien went on, making up his mind now to come to the point immediately, 'but regrettably it will be necessary to increase the price by as much again.'

'Why?' Fiona asked him.

'Mrs Douglas-Wallace, I am in the unfortunate position of being pushed by spiralling costs.'

George nodded stupidly. The rum was surging within him now, swamping his brain, clouding his responses. He longed to be in bed, away from the heat of this room and the mosquitoes and this tiresome need to talk business, about which he knew nothing and cared as much.

'I understand, old man,' he said thickly.

'I do not,' said Fiona. 'We have a contract, Mr O'Brien, a written agreement. We guaranteed to buy wood and resin at fixed prices – which *you* fixed. Even if we can find no use for these products, we are still obligated to buy them. In that situation, it would be our loss. If you cannot supply them to us at the agreed price, that is your loss. Otherwise our agreement is void, and that I cannot accept.'

'I sympathise with your view, ma'am, but I cannot agree with you. There is another reason for this rise in costs, which I regret and deplore as much as you. The Governor of British Honduras has drawn me into a scheme to build a mechanism to produce electricity for the colony. My best men are working on plans at this moment. It is, as you will understand, essential that I do not let the Governor down. I have had to hire experts to help, it is such a complex affair. Believe me, I have many problems.'

'You find this new scheme a problem?'

'I rarely sleep without dreaming of it,' O'Brien admitted, shaking his head gloomily.

'And if you did not have this on your mind, taking up your time and the time of your employees, you could honour your contract with me – us?'

'I could at least come very much closer to your figure.'

'Well, come closer,' she told him. 'My husband and I will take over this electric scheme from you.'

'It is kind of you to suggest, but truly impossible.'

'Nothing is impossible. You are suffering sleepless nights through it, and as a result you cannot honour your commitment to us, which is extremely important to our company. We will take the matter out of your hands, and with it, all your worry. Is that agreed?'

'No, Ma'am, it cannot be agreed.'

Mr O'Brien leaned forward, and Fiona could see his eyes, cold and hard, and in them she read a message of hate. He loathes me, she realised with the shock that anyone feels when they suddenly discover that someone dislikes them with total intensity – and seemingly without any reason. She looked away, hoping that O'Brien had not seen the concern in her eyes. Then she glanced towards her husband. He lay back in his chair, eyes closed, on the edge of sleep. A patina of perspiration glazed his face like varnish. O'Brien followed her gaze. He smiled contemptuously.

'Your husband is tired?'

'Yes.'

'Perhaps my rum did not agree with him. It is known as charcoal rum, ma'am. What we call here, Slave Juice. My father was a slave, Mrs Douglas-Wallace. I never drink rum myself, perhaps because of that reason. The slaves drank it to take their minds off the terrible drudgery of their lives and the fact that they could never expect release.'

'But slaves were freed long ago,' Fiona pointed out.

'Freed in body maybe, ma'am, but never freed in mind,' O'Brien replied bitterly. And again hatred clouded his eyes like cataracts.

The Governor of British Honduras was a plump man with a receding chin and a large nose, soft and pitted as a pink sponge. He handled the visiting card his butler had brought in as though it might be infectious.

'You say a woman gave you this? A *white* woman?'

'Yes, baas.'

'A married woman? The card just says Fiona Douglas-Wallace, a director of some company or other.'

'She say she want to see you. She came in big boat, *her* boat.'

The Governor nodded. He had seen *Coromandel II* riding at anchor in the harbour and the vessel reeked of wealth. He felt a surge of envy; he was prepared to dislike this woman if she represented such fortune.

'I will see her,' he announced.

Fiona came into the room and introduced herself.

'I did not expect a lady director of such an important trading concern,' said the Governor. 'I know that your company already buys the largest amounts of mahogany and sapodilla resin from the colony. Do you wish increase these amounts? If so, I fear it is nothing to do with me, Mrs Douglas-Wallace. One of my staff can help you.'

'I came to see you personally on another matter. You are about to electrify the colony?'

Fiona made the question sound like a statement.

'Electrify sounds very grand. We have a great deal of work in hand to improve general living conditions, but yes, certainly, one of our most distinguished local citizens, Mr O'Brien, with a consortium, is going to build a steam-engine house to contain dynamos so that in due course we may have electric lights in our homes and in our streets. This will be an inestimable improvement.'

'Has the contract been placed?'

'We are on the point of accepting his tender. There were no competitive bids. Indeed, I know of no-one else here who would even undertake such a task.'

'Have you a copy of the specification?'

'One can be found. Your company is interested in tendering for the supply of electric light bulbs, or wires or material of that kind?'

'No. I am interested in supplying the whole service. Presumably you would accept a cheaper estimate?'

'That could be very difficult to achieve,' said the Governor uneasily.

'Why?' she asked him. 'Surely all colonies are keen to reduce costs?'

'Well, yes, they are. But we must be certain of the results. One tends to get what one pays for.'

'That is exactly what I intend to give. Now, if you will be kind enough to let me have the specification, I will tender on behalf of Trinity-Trio.'

Fiona sat in the day cabin on *Coromandel II* reading how many kilowatts the dynamos would have to supply, how many miles of wire were required, how many lamps and holders and posts and fuses and switches and meters would be needed.

It was impossible to tender with any hope of success without knowing what O'Brien's price had been, for to have any chance of securing the contract, they would have to undercut him substantially. She had formed her own opinion of the Governor: this would not be a fair contest with the deal going to the best and cheapest tender. She guessed he could be taking a percentage somewhere for himself from Mr O'Brien's estimate.

George was sitting on deck, a huge glass of rum and lime juice at the side of his canvas chair. He was reading a novel, sipping as he read. She looked at him with distaste and irritation, and took the book out of his hands. How could he laze like this when they faced a challenge of this size?

'A problem for you,' she told him as brightly as she could.

'I was reading a novel,' he replied petulantly.

'Read this specification instead. How do we find out what O'Brien quoting?'

'How do *I* know?' he asked her, putting the specification down on deck and reaching for his book.

'Ask him,' Fiona told him.

'He would not tell me. Why not ask Edward here? He seems to know everything. You keep wanting his opinion on everything else. How fast is our ship sailing? How long are her engines likely to last before they need servicing? Let *him* do it. Let *him* earn his passage.'

'I will,' she said in disgust, and went in search of George's elder brother, Edward.

George and Fiona had been spending a few days in London before they sailed to Belize Town aboard *Coromandel II*. To their surprise, walking along the strand one morning, they heard someone behind them call a greeting. They turned. A tall young man, rather better looking than George, with the same darkish skin, but with a smile on his face and a spring in his tread, was running to catch them up.

'George!' he cried.

'Edward!' said Fiona's husband in amazement.

'Who is this?' asked Fiona.

'My brother,' said George. 'I had no idea you were here.'

'I knew you were in Britain,' replied Edward, 'and I decided to come and see the heart of the Empire. Piccadilly Circus. Eros. The Tower of London. St Paul's Cathedral. All those places I had only seen pictures of in books in Bombay. What luck to meet you – and your wife.'

'What are your plans now?' George asked him.

'I really have none,' Edward admitted. 'I have been over here for three weeks. I thought I might go to Wales and Scotland. And then – who knows?'

'*I* know,' said Fiona suddenly, and as she spoke it was as though she was listening to someone else's voice; as though another person altogether was uttering the words.

'Come with us,' she said. 'We are going to British Honduras. I am a shareholder in Trinity-Trio. A man out there called O'Brien, whose products we buy, has suddenly pushed up his prices by a third. I want to ask him why, and at the same time look over the prospects for trade generally there, and possibly up in North America.'

'I do not want to be the third person on a honeymoon,' said Edward.

'No question of that,' said Fiona sharply. George's face darkened. He looked sullen. But Edward either had not noticed his reaction, or he diplomatically pretended not to have seen it.

'If you both are certain, I would very much like to join you. I promise you, I will keep out of your way.'

'You will be very welcome,' said Fiona. 'Our ship is lying at Gravesend. We leave in two days.'

'Now,' said George pointedly, 'if you will excuse us, we are late for an appointment.'

Fiona and he walked on. Edward stood for a moment in the busy street looking after them, wondering whether he should have accepted the invitation, hoping Fiona would look back.

She did not – but she wanted to.

Edward Sodawaterwallah walked into O'Brien's warehouse and stood for a moment, accustoming his eyes to the dim light in the cavernous building, savouring the subtle and agreeable scents of coffee, molasses, mahogany shavings.

Behind a plain wood counter, a black clerk sat on a stool, watching him. He had a morose, discontented face and regarded Edward without interest or welcome. He began to pick his teeth with a sliver of bamboo.

'Want something, baas?' he asked reluctantly, as though hoping the answer would be negative.

'To show you this,' said Edward. He took out a dollar bill, spread it on the counter, put a second on top and a third, a fourth, up to ten. Then he slammed the palm of his hand on them. The black man's eyes followed the movement greedily.

'Mr O'Brien been in today?' Edward asked him casually.

'Not this morning. He's coming in later this afternoon. You wan see him?'

'No. I came to see you.'

'Me, baas? You want see me?' Alarm creased the clerk's pudgy face.

'I want you to have these,' Edward told him.

'What for, baas? What you buying?'

'Your help.'

'How?'

Edward added another five bills, pressing them all flat on the counter

'I have been a bloody fool,' he began in a low and contrite voice. 'I ser boss man O'Brien a letter. And in it I was rude to him. Very rude. I'd ha one or two – or three – drinks too many. You know how it is?'

The clerk nodded, his eyes on the bills beneath Edward's hand.

'And sure as hell I'd have been more careful if I'd known how rich an powerful he is.'

'Sure is. He don't want for nothing, boss man. Sure can make life ha for you, man, if he wants to.'

'Exactly. Which is why I must get my letter back and give him this o instead.'

Edward took an envelope addressed to Mr O'Brien from his jack pocket.

'I can do that,' the clerk said confidently, holding out his hand for the envelope. 'I put it on his desk. Okay?'

'Sure you can – but you don't know what my other letter looks like. And I do. It's not in an envelope this colour. I want to go in, bring it out, and leave this. And, of course, these bills are for you.'

'No, baas. My job. Mr O'Brien would sack me. I'd never work again.'

'Mr O'Brien will never know. But if he opens my letter, he will make life so bad for me, I'll have to leave town. You understand?'

Edward added a five-dollar bill to the little pile on the counter.

'You only take one minute, then?' asked the clerk anxiously.

'No more. Probably less.'

'You won't do no damage, now?'

'Of course not. Come with me and see for yourself.'

'No way, baas. I gotta stay here, case Mr O'Brien comes in. Safer that way. If he does, there's a window open in his office. Go through it.'

Edward handed the notes to the clerk and went past him into a small inner room. He closed the door behind him, locked it. The room smelled of cigar smoke and beeswax polish. In one corner stood a polished mahogany filing cabinet. He opened the top drawer. Nothing but bills and receipts. The second drawer was packed with files of letters. The third contained folders in alphabetical order. Under "E" he found one headed Electricity Quotation.

He hastily copied down details on a piece of paper and replaced the folder. He came out, winked at the clerk in a conspiratorial way, walked out into the sunshine. The clerk picked at his teeth.

Aboard *Coromandel II*, Edward sat down with his brother and Fiona to examine the figures. They seemed very high, which would allow a generous percentage for bribes. Clearly, it would be impossible to buy the miles of wire, the pylons, insulators, generators and other gear locally, and very expensive and slow to ship them in from England. They would have to try the States.

'Do you know any electrical firms in New York?' Fiona asked him.

'None,' Edward admitted. 'I have never even been to the States. But pay my expenses and I will do my best.'

'Why should *you* go?' George asked his brother sullenly. 'You are not even a shareholder. My wife owns a third of the company. I can do a far better job.'

'You stay here,' Fiona told him firmly. 'Edward found the price we have to beat. Let him carry on with it.'

George poured himself a neat rum, shrugging his shoulders as though the matter was of little importance.

'Anyway, Mr O'Brien has asked me to go fishing with him,' he said petulantly. 'There are some mighty fine marlin around the Cayes. I will be away a couple of days.'

Fiona looked at him with distaste. So far as she was concerned, George could be away forever.

Before she met Edward in the Strand, Fiona had been willing to make the best of her life with George, largely because there seemed no alternative. She had married him, according to the service, for better or for worse, and the fact that their marriage was so much worse than she had ever imagined was something she had resigned herself to accept.

Now she realised how strong was the affinity she had felt with Edward as soon as she met him. This had prompted her to invite him to accompany them. She had never felt so close to anyone else; what Edward thought, she thought. When he was with her, or even simply in the vicinity, she knew she need never be alone again. She felt fulfilled, content, at ease.

She went out on deck. These thoughts and feelings disturbed her, and she feared them, for they were growing more powerful. Sooner or later, she knew she would go to bed with Edward, and from then on nothing could ever be the same between the three of them. But that was in the future, the indefinite future; she must do her utmost to keep it there for as long as possible.

The present was more immediately important. She had to beat O'Brien over this electricity contract or he would put another totally unjustified increase on his prices for resin and mahogany, and this running battle would continue until either Trinity-Trio gave in to his continual demands, or they pulled out from the trade and let their rivals win. If she could beat O'Brien now, early on, in his own town, on his own project, then she sensed he would not risk overcharging them again. She had to show him that any deal a man could do, a woman could do better but not just any woman – Fiona Douglas-Wallace. She had, of course, no idea that O'Brien blamed her and her husband for the fact that he had no inherited Captain Ross's share of Trinity-Trio.

Edward took passage aboard a mail steamer to New York and booked into a small hotel on 42nd Street. Next day he went out to Trenton in New Jersey and introduced himself to Leone Pastellini.

'You have a fine business here,' he said, as Pastellini proudly showed him round the works.

'Well, it's growing.'

Pastellini explained how, in the forests, natives cut vertical zigzag grooves on the trunk of each sapodilla tree so that the viscous resin or latex could slide down them to a metal container at the bottom of the tree. The resin was then filtered through a cloth into huge kettles over camp fires and poured into wooden moulds. When cool, the blocks from these moulds were shipped to the factory.

Here the gum was again melted and filtered and poured into large circular tanks. Flavours and sugar were added and the warm, creamy compound thoroughly mixed by a rotating paddle.

The gum was then squeezed out in the form of a long ribbon to be cooled and rolled flat. A machine stamped this into small rectangular pieces, to be coated with a hard sugar layer and packed automatically, half a dozen at a time, into red, white and blue Lion's Share wrappings.

None of the workers was allowed to smoke, and electric fans, running continuously, kept the air clear and clean. Edward was impressed by the factory's efficiency. All the women operatives wore white overalls and gloves and caps over their hair; the machinery was gleaming and new.

'We are not nearly as big as Wrigleys,' Pastellini admitted, 'but we are holding our share of the market – although we want to live up to our name and have the Lion's Share.'

'We want that, too,' agreed Edward. 'And if you need more finance or anything else, let us know. Trinity-Trio's aim is to expand into all kinds of fields. The more diversification they achieve, the broader their base, and the sounder the company becomes. So if you find any area you feel could be exploited, please remember that.'

Edward now explained the object of his visit, how Fiona and her husband were living in the ship off Belize Town until he returned; how it was important to gain the contract against O'Brien's competition.

'I am George Wallace's brother,' he added.

'With a name like Sodawaterwallah?'

'With a name like that, yes. He changed his. I kept mine.'

'Good for you,' said Pastellini enthusiastically. 'It has often been suggested to me that I should change mine to Pastor or something more Anglo-Saxon Protestant. But I was born a Sicilian Catholic, son of Luigi Pastellini, and that is how I stay. What I was, I am. A good enough motto for any man. So, let us get down to details.'

Within two days Edward had received several quotations for dynamos, wires, lights and switchgear, but only one was low enough to be interesting. The engineer, an Italian, pointed out a drawback which Edward had not envisaged: the cost of the coal necessary to fuel the engine that would power the generators.

'To light several hundred homes and miles of streets,' the engineer explained, 'you will need at the very least two large dynamos, with a third in reserve, because the demand for current will increase as more people discover its advantages in their houses, offices, factories and so on. These dynamos take a lot of driving, so you will need to have two stationary steam engines, one to use and one in reserve. Soon, no doubt, both will be running full time as the demand grows, but two should see you started. They are going to eat a lot of fuel.'

'There are forests of trees in British Honduras,' Edward told him.

'I know that, but boilers this size do not like eating wood. They feed on coal – which will have to come from the States, and is expensive. On my calculations, using the figures you have given me of the number of houses and shops and street lights, you will have to charge so much for your current that most of the users simply will not be able to pay.'

'They will have to, or they cannot use it.'

'That is so for many honest folk,' said the engineer patiently. 'But not all people are so upright, and it does not take long for even simple people to realise the benefits of electricity. Once they are converted, they will never go back to oil lamps. That means, if they cannot afford it legally, they will have it illegally. They will simply tap the lines, and light their houses and shops for nothing.

'Of course, you can sue them and fine them and imprison them, but not on the scale of the offences. And putting a negro in jail for a week does not pay for the current he has stolen – and which he will go on stealing as soon as he comes out. And remember, whoever is running the electricity company has to keep paying for the coal, or it all shuts down. Then you will have trouble from paying customers because they have paid but you cannot supply them.'

'Is there no way round the coal problem? Could we use a windmill, a water-wheel?'

'A windmill will only drive a small dynamo, and so far as I know, there are no rivers in that colony that could turn a turbine of the size you need.

'You will not beat my price for the installation, and I will bring my own men down to build it. But on these figures, you cannot make it pay. I have to be frank with you. I want the work, but it is no good me putting in the equipment if the company will run at a loss.'

'Let me think about it,' said Edward. This was a hazard that had not occurred to him. He came out of the engineer's office and walked through the wide streets of the little town. The neat houses were mostly of wood clapboard, painted white, with verandahs and hitching posts for horses. Many had flagpoles in their front gardens with the Stars and Stripes fluttering lazily in the afternoon breeze.

He found himself near a race-track where high-stepping horses were pulling tiny carts with huge thin spidery wheels. Hundreds of spectators were watching as the drivers crouched high up in these carts, almost over the shafts. The speeds seemed frightening, and clouds of dust from the track billowed up behind the carts. Edward was seeing the sporting speciality of the area – trotting-horse races.

The larger the wheels, the faster the cart would go, almost regardless of the size of the horse that pulled it. Time and again he saw a small horse pull away from a far stronger animal because the wheels of the cart it pulled were larger than the ones on the cart they overtook. This gave Edward an idea. He sat down on a bench, took out an envelope and made a pencil sketch of a huge wheel, with a very much smaller one meshed against its rim.

Assuming that the large wheel was made of cast iron, and perhaps weighed several tons, with teeth milled all round the edge to mesh with the teeth on the small wheel, a relatively small steam engine, running at high speed, could make the big wheel turn.

If he fitted a clutch to engage the two wheels until the engine had built up speed, and then cut out, the big wheel would then keep on revolving for a time by its sheer weight.

As it slowed down, the clutch could re-engage the small wheel until speed had once more been built up. This sequence could easily be made automatic, and could continue indefinitely. Such a wheel, if heavy enough, could drive the dynamo largely by its own enormous inertia – and at a fraction of the cost needed to power a steam engine coupled directly to the dynamo.

Sitting there, with the smell of horse sweat and newly-cut grass in the air, feeling the sun warm on his back, Edward Sodawaterwallah knew that their proposed electricity generating company could now show an operating profit.

The Governor of British Honduras hastily pulled a sheet of paper towards him across the desk, and dipped his pen in the inkwell to give the impression of having been disturbed at serious work as Fiona Douglas-Wallace was shown into his presence. He stood up, frowning slightly to show that while he welcomed such an unanticipated visit, he was nonetheless eager to return to what was clearly an infinitely more important task.

'Delighted as I am to see you, ma'am, you have unfortunately caught me at a busy moment for a social call.'

'It is not a social call,' Fiona replied. She opened a briefcase, took out a folder, and placed it on his desk. He looked at her in surprise.

'Trinity-Trio's tender to put an electricity system in this colony,' she explained.

'I have told you, we have already virtually agreed with Mr O'Brien,' the Governor replied sharply. 'I cannot see why a pretty lady like you wishes to become involved in such a complicated matter.'

'Even so, here it is – and roughly $100,000 less than Mr O'Brien's estimate.'

'How do you know that?'

'See for yourself,' said Fiona.

'The matter does not rest entirely with me,' the Governor said uneasily.

'Then put it before the person with whom it does rest entirely,' Fiona suggested.

'I have several advisers.'

'I am sure they will advise you to take this tender.'

The Governor's face creased with irritation. He pressed a brass bell on the desk and a servant entered.

'Mr Fanshaw,' the Governor said.

Mr Fanshaw, a tall, thin man with a prominent Adam's apple, glanced appreciatively at Fiona and then nervously at his employer. The Governor introduced them.

'This lady has put forward a specification from a British company which she says undercuts Mr O'Brien's tender for electrification. Please look at it.'

'Now, sir?'

'Now.'

Fanshaw took the specification to a side table, produced a notepad and began to scribble down figures, while the other two watched him. Then he turned to the Governor.

'A very fair tender, sir. Only one thing I would query.'

'What is that?' the Governor asked eagerly.

'The steam engine they propose using develops less than a quarter the power of the engine in Mr O'Brien's specification. It could not conceivably work generators of the size they quote.'

'You see,' said the Governor triumphantly to Fiona. 'Pretty ladies should *not* meddle in business matters.'

'I am not meddling,' she replied. 'I will personally guarantee that this system works – and at less than the operating cost of Mr O'Brien's engine. If you are not satisfied, then, at my own expense, I will put in a boiler and steam engine of the larger size that he proposes.'

'But why do you not specify that size here?' asked Fanshaw.

'Because, Mr Fanshaw, we have devised a scheme which enables a small engine to run extremely economically, using far less fuel and producing an extraordinary amount of power at very much less cost.'

'I cannot understand that,' said Fanshaw shortly. 'Not with generators of this power. Can you explain this scheme in detail?'

Fiona smiled.

'I cannot do that. Mr O'Brien might somehow hear about it and include it in his tender. Then where would I be? I have made my offer, gentlemen. You have nothing to lose.'

'I appreciate your interest in our problem,' said the Governor, 'but really we must go ahead with Mr O'Brien. We have to support local industry. And he is a black man, which is important here in a community overwhelmingly of that colour and background. Former slaves, you know.'

'I hear what you say. But surely the Colonial Office insists that the lowest tender, subject to quality, must always be accepted?'

'Cost is not always the only consideration. I am sorry, but you have heard the expert view. In all the circumstances, the contract must go to Mr O'Brien's consortium.'

'If that is your last word,' replied Fiona, 'I will give you mine. You have refused to save more than $100,000 on a system I personally will guarantee to be infinitely cheaper to run. Our apparatus will give employment to the same number of workers as Mr O'Brien's. There is no obvious reason for accepting what is a very much more expensive tender. On my return to England I will report this extraordinary decision to your superiors at the Colonial Office.'

Fiona paused and added: 'Unless – as the newspaper *The Enquirer* may consider – there could be a personal reason? Is someone being bribed?'

'You have no cause for making such a statement.'

'I am not making such a statement. I am asking a question.'

The Governor looked at her, hating her youth, her good looks, most of all her wealth and power. Here he was, stuck in this sweating backwater with a discontented, dyspeptic wife, while others – far inferior to him, in his view – had been knighted and promoted. What Fiona had suggested was true: there would be $10,000 U.S. in new bills for him if O'Brien won the contract. This young bitch could ruin him. If he accepted the $10,000, this newspaper might discover it and he would be instantly dismissed. If he accepted her offer, then O'Brien might become restive and remind him of past financial favours. But of the two diabolical alternatives, this seemed less damaging. He forced a smile to his unhappy face.

'I will discuss the matter in detail with Fanshaw and let you know,' he said.

That night, a messenger from Government House delivered his reply. Fiona had secured the contract for Trinity-Trio.

Mr Gonzales and Mr O'Brien were talking in the latter's office.

'The biggest wheel I have ever seen in my life is being unloaded now on the quay,' Gonzales informed him. 'Cast iron and painted bright red, with a polished solid metal rim and cogs all the way round. It is more than forty feet in diameter, so large they have had to bring it down from the States flat on the deck of a freighter. There was no hold wide enough to carry it. I can tell you, some of the crew were worried in case they ran into a storm and capsized with this dead weight.'

'What is it for, exactly?' asked O'Brien.

'They are putting it in the new engine-house they have built. That is why the house is so high and thin. The axle runs from one wall to the other, so the wheel revolves in an upright position. Extraordinary!'

'They will never turn it with the small steam engine they have,' said O'Brien confidently. 'Not if the engine has also to power the generators.'

'Mrs Douglas-Wallace thinks they will,' said Gonzales.

'That white cow,' said O'Brien bitterly. 'What does she know about engineering? Keep me fully informed of all developments. I will not be put down by this white trash.'

'They do not appear hostile,' said Gonzales. 'I think she simply wants to prove she is as good as a man in business.'

He did not add 'or better'; O'Brien was a cruel man and there was no point in antagonising him further.

O'Brien spat on the floor and did not reply.

Out in Belize Town, the giant wheel was already being manoeuvred from the quay into the new power-house building. This had been specially sited near the water-front because of the difficulty of moving such an awkward load through narrow lanes and between houses. Three cranes had been required to lift the wheel from the ship. Now it was too large to be carried on its side, although half a dozen trucks had been assembled to move it; it was far beyond the capability of horse-drawn wagons.

Edward organised a gang of men, forty on either side. They held on to ropes attached to a mahogany log pushed through the centre hole in the wheel to act as an axle. Their job was to keep the ropes taut and so hold the wheel upright. Twenty men pulled the wheel forwards, while as many more walked behind it with other ropes tied to the log to make a brake, to ensure that the giant wheel did not run out of control.

Its cogs crunched in the dust of the road and struck sparks from small stones as the strange procession began to move forwards. Children ran alongside, skipping and shouting excitedly. Women clasping babies stared at it fearfully. The more religious and superstitious crossed themselves in case the devil lived within the wheel.

A complex scaffolding system of tree trunks and bamboo poles lashed to metal girders and pulleys had been built outside the engine-house. Slowly, willing hands trundled the wheel into place. Giant bolts now slotted into holes bored around its hub: nuts and lock nuts were tightened with huge wrenches. The wheel was still upright and resting on the raw earth in the centre of the building.

A gang of labourers appeared, carrying picks and shovels, and began to dig the earth out from beneath the wheel to allow it to rotate freely. To one side of it stood the steam engine. Workmen now fitted a geared wheel to its main axle so that the cogs could engage with those around the rim of the wheel. A simple clutch mechanism meant that the steam engine would gather speed on its own, and when an engineer threw a lever the small wheel would mesh with the large one.

The wiring of street lamps had already been completed. Many of the richer homes had installed private switchboards with electric lights and switches in every room. All that now remained was for the steam engine to start and for the great wheel to rotate and drive the generator. The benefits to the colony would then be immense.

Circular saws could be driven by electricity; so could water pumps for irrigation and sewage removal. Electricity could also power the huge new American freezing machines which would enable locally-caught shellfish to be kept fresh for weeks or even months, and so fetch the best prices in foreign markets – a bonus for the fishermen. Fiona invited the Governor to perform the commissioning ceremony to start the steam engine and mark the beginning of a new era of prosperity for the entire colony.

He accepted Fiona's invitation, but hours before he was due to arrive he sent an apology. Unexpected and urgent business most unfortunately meant that he could not be present. He expressed the deepest regret.

No other official seemed free to take his place at such short notice, so Fiona herself declared the generating station open by pressing a button which activated a bell in the engine-room. Here, an engineer opened the main steam cock. The piston slid forward sluggishly in the engine's cylinder; the revolving flywheel drove it back. Steam hissed from the exhaust as speed increased. When a tachometer registered 350 revolutions a minute, the engineer lifted a lever so that the teeth on the two wheels meshed.

For a moment, under enormous strain, the engine slowed. As its head of steam built up, the huge wheel began to revolve, slowly at first and then with gradually increasing speed. Filaments in a thousand electric bulbs on streets, in houses and shacks, glowed dull red, then orange. Then, suddenly, they were ablaze with light.

Locals, who for years had been accustomed to carrying torches or oil lamps if they ventured out after dark, in order to avoid falling into ditches or stumbling over the carcass of a dead dog, cheered as the flickering electric bulbs lit up their streets, shops, houses.

O'Brien watched a single electric bulb glow amber, then blazing white, in the ceiling of his drawing room. As servants turned down the wicks in oil lamps, he sat brooding on the nature of this change and the fact that he had no part whatever in it, and hence no profit.

Gonzales watched his face for the slightest indication of his mood. When O'Brien glanced across the room at him, Gonzales instinctively stiffened with tension.

'We must stop this,' said O'Brien. 'And I have a way. This is what you have to do. . . .'

* * *

At four o'clock on the morning after electricity came to Belize Town, the engineer closed the steam cocks on the engine and damped down the furnace.

The giant wheel began to slow and then stopped. All over Belize Town, lights dimmed and died as the sky grew pale with dawn.

At that moment, the engineer heard an urgent knocking on the front door. He was not expecting a caller at this early hour, and had been brewing up coffee for his assistant and himself, using steam from the engine's exhaust to heat water in a saucepan. He went to the door, the pan of boiling water in his hand, and slid the bolts.

Immediately, two men with scarves wound around their faces leaped in. One punched him in the groin and, seizing his arm, flung the water over his face, blinding and scalding him. The second hit him over the head with an iron bar.

Behind these two came dozens of others – unemployed layabouts; chronic rum drinkers, wretched in shabby shirts and torn trousers – all carrying sticks and staves or *dahs*. Instantly, the engine-room was a riot of half-tipsy ruffians, high on *ganja*, eyes wide, mouths roaring abuse.

'What the hell is going on?' shouted the assistant engineer in astonishment as he came in from the generating room, wiping his hands with an oily rag. He saw the crowd, the open door and the blinded engineer, strips of scalded flesh hanging like ribbons from his face as he crawled in agony across the dirt floor. The assistant seized a wrench two foot long from a tool rack on the wall, and waved it at the growing crowd.

'Get back, you bastards!' he bellowed. A few nearest to him cowered away. The rest streamed past him into other rooms in the building.

'This engine is the work of the devil!' one screamed hysterically. 'It is stealing our manhood with its throbbing and hissing! It is taking the blood and seed from our balls! We must destroy it before it kills us!'

'You stupid idiot!' shouted the assistant engineer, turning towards him. 'You don't know what you are talking about!'

Someone hit him over the back of his head with a block of wood. The wrench dropped uselessly with an iron clatter on the floor, and he sank down beneath a rush of trampling feet.

Soon the machine-room was filled with the hiss and roar of escaping steam as the mob broke pipes, smashed junctions, tipped fire buckets of water over the furnace. Wires, cut with saws, hacked by *dahs*, exposing bright copper cores, hung impotently from the walls. Axes came down on standby electric cells, huge glass tanks filled with acid and copper and lead plates. Acid bubbled and frothed over jagged sections of glass. The entire switch-board was torn from the wall.

Within minutes, the whole building had been gutted. At a whistle from one man, the mob fled as quickly as they had arrived, leaving one engineer blinded, his colleague with a fractured skull and both arms broken. Outside, cocks crowed to announce the start of a new day.

For the third time since *Coromandel II* anchored in the bay, Fiona faced the Governor across his desk in Government House.

'I have been to see the chief of police,' she explained. 'He tells me he has no idea who could have committed this destruction. Therefore he cannot bring anyone to justice. I find that unbelievable.'

The Governor shook his head sadly.

'I deeply regret the terrible incident, Mrs Douglas-Wallace,' he said. 'But he has a fine body of detectives under his command, and if he cannot help you, how can I, much as I would wish to do so? The fact is, many of the people in the colony follow the old religions. Voodoo plays a very large part in their lives. The thrusting of the piston of this steam engine, the grunting and puffing of the exhaust are symbolic, in their minds, of the act of procreation. The men believe this engine will sap their virility.'

'That is rubbish.'

'You and I know that, Mrs Douglas-Wallace, but they believe what they want to believe.'

'Or what someone tells them to believe. But if Mr O'Brien and your Mr Fanshaw had their way, the engine and all the noises it makes, would be much larger and louder. How would you cope then?'

The Governor shrugged his shoulders.

'That is an academic question, ma'am,' he said unctuously. 'It is a very complex situation. I wish you had taken my advice right at the start and not concerned yourself with the matter. Far better to have left it all to Mr O'Brien. He is at home here. He knows these people because he is one of them, and you and I will always be white sojourners in a black man's land. What *can* I do?'

'You can place a guard on the premises for a start, Your Excellency. Or let us have six soldiers or policemen stationed inside the engine-house after we have repaired it. I am prepared to help defray their cost in any way you decide. But without guards, clearly we cannot run the company and provide electricity.'

'We have only one battalion of troops here, Mrs Douglas-Wallace. Their commanding officer says they are fully extended. There has been labour unrest over the price of chicle gum, which has cut wages, and which, of course, your company buys in large quantities.'

'We are easily the largest buyer of gum and mahogany, and I am surprised to learn of wage cuts. Mr O'Brien has just increased his price to us by thirty per cent. Without our contracts, the price would fall drastically and your troubles here would immediately increase. Owing to our unique position in bolstering this colony's prosperity, we have a right to protection – as, of course, does every other individual and company in any British possession.'

'Madam, in this world we really only have one right, which none of us is eager to exercise: the right to die.'

'So you will not help me?'

'I cannot,' replied the Governor.

'This is your last word, then? We can have no protection to enable us to engage in legitimate business, which will benefit directly or indirectly everyone in Belize Town? Even though we will pay for it until this agitation dies down?'

The Governor nodded.

'And you would have given the same answer to Mr O'Brien if he had won the contract?'

'He would have no need of guards, as I have explained.'

Fiona stood up and left the room. For a moment, the Governor sat at his desk, drawing faces on his blotter with his gold pen. The generator could be repaired, but then, he knew quite well, the locals would attack it again, and eventually they would destroy it altogether. These Trinity-Trio people could not keep on rebuilding it indefinitely.

What could he do to prevent this catalogue of ruin and rebuilding?

He could send in troops or police, but this would mean that Trinity-Trio's venture would succeed. He did not wish that to happen, for then O'Brien would not honour the promise he had made: $10,000 if he won the contract.

This woman Douglas-Wallace and her half-caste husband must accept that their machinery was not welcome, nor their interference, nor were they. The sooner they accepted these facts, the better, and then Mr O'Brien could move in, and the Governor's overdrafts would immediately be paid off.

Of course, Trinity-Trio might then abandon their trading operations altogether in the colony, with calamitous results for its economy. No matter, he assured himself, some other company would be bound to buy their wood and gum. He gave a sigh at the numerous complications of office, and rang for a servant to bring him a large rum and lime juice.

Mr O'Brien personally organised the second attack on the generating station although he was careful not to lead it. He told a huge crowd assembled in Gaol Lane that this slowly-turning wheel, and the regular pounding of the pistons required to drive it, was a direct and deliberate assault on the manhood of every man in Belize Town. If they did not stand against this, they would never stand again. His audience appreciated the play on words and, primed with rum and dollar bills, shouted their approval. The lane rang with cheers. He was one of them, he reminded his audience; he had been a slave once – at the command of the same company which now assaulted their basic rights to have children. Who were these strangers who dared to do this?

At O'Brien's call a hundred men – carrying staves, clubs, machetes – gathered outside the engine-house within an hour of the lights being turned on. They stamped their feet to the rhythm of the steam engine, shouting, 'No! No! *No!*'

More came from huts and hovels and shacks on the edge of the city, to gaze in wonder at the pulsing street lights, and they joined in the shouts. Most had no idea what they were shouting or why, but O'Brien was their man; he had told them so often enough. Now, at his command, they surged against the double doors of the engine-house. These had not been built to withstand such an assault. They swayed and creaked and then burst open with a crash of splintering wood. The crowd swarmed inside.

Within seconds, they were hacking at the braid and rubber insulation around the copper cables. Within minutes, the lights went out for a second time, and the control room with its fuse boxes and ammeters and switchboards was totally destroyed. Then the vandals vanished, taking what loot they could carry.

Fiona and Edward walked around the building, carrying hurricane lamps to inspect the damage. It was almost total. The only sound was the hiss of escaping steam. Someone had gouged bricks from one of the axle supports for the giant wheel, and this leaned drunkenly to one side. The glasses in all the instruments were hammered flat on to the dials. The destruction was much worse than after the first attack, because this time the mob had been told where and how they could inflict the most lasting and extensive damage.

Next morning, Edward accompanied Fiona to see the Governor.

'You really *must* give us protection, sir,' he told him bluntly. 'We won this contract in fair competition to provide the colony with electricity, and for the second time, the actions of a mob, who are drunk and harangued by O'Brien, have put all our machinery out of action.'

'Mr O'Brien sympathises with the men's fears. I regret there is nothing I can do,' the Governor replied coldly.

'There may be nothing you *will* do, but there is a lot you *could* do,' retorted Fiona.

'That is an unfair remark, Mrs Douglas-Wallace. You know my position. We have already discussed it in detail.'

'So you still refuse to help us?'

'My hands are tied,' the Governor replied.

Edward and Fiona went back to order new components and the complete rebuilding of machinery. Two weeks later, the generator was ready to start for the third time.

The Governor had meanwhile asked O'Brien to call on him privately. He visited him after dark, going through the back door of Government House where no-one was likely to see him. The Governor explained to him that on the official birthday of King Edward VII he was holding a huge garden party to mark this most auspicious occasion. Rows of electric fairy lights specially brought down from New York would be strung between palm trees; it would be absolutely unthinkable for such a loyal and important function to be disrupted. Socially and politically, it was of the greatest importance to the Governor and his lady that this reception was a success – and clearly it would be infinitely better to light the gardens by electricity than by candles and oil lamps.

O'Brien agreed and promised that he and his men would not attack the engine-house until the evening after this party. For one night, Belize Town, like the grounds of Government House, would blaze with lights. But on the second night, the lights would again be extinguished, and he hoped they would not come on until he was given control of the whole operation.

'That is a matter between you and Mrs Douglas-Wallace,' the Governor replied cautiously. 'A purely commercial matter. As you know, it is not my function to interfere in any way in matters of business.'

Workmen draped trees and hedges with wires from which hung red and blue and green and yellow electric bulbs. At a rehearsal, the effect was magical; these coloured lights transformed the grounds of Government House into an enchanted garden. Fountains appeared to spray red and green water. Palm trees stood in purple silhouette. The night was alive with colour.

Neither Fiona, George, nor Edward was invited to the party, but almost every other white resident of the colony received a formal invitation with the Royal arms embossed in gold; the Colonial Office could on occasion do these things rather well. Soon after seven that evening, guests began to arrive by carriage, or in the newly fashionable motor cars.

Despite the humidity, the men wore white tie and tails, with decorations. The women were in long and elaborate dresses, either made by local dressmakers from patterns from England, or ordered from New York. The band of the regiment on detachment to Belize Town played Strauss waltzes and lilting numbers from London musical comedies.

The Governor and his lady moved among their guests with a gracious word here, a smile there, the wave of a hand or a nod elsewhere. Everyone agreed that this was quite the most romantic and wonderful evening party anyone had ever given in the colony, made memorable by the coloured lights and floodlights on the Union Jack. All this, they told each other, could only have the most beneficial effect on the native population.

At half past eight precisely, the Governor climbed four specially built, red-carpeted steps to a dais decorated with red, white and blue bunting. Under a giant illuminated crown, to symbolise the British Empire and the Royal House, he stood for a moment, surveying the scene with total satisfaction. This must help him on his way to a knighthood. What other Caribbean colony could even approach this as a spontaneous and magnificent demonstration of loyalty and imperial splendour?

Hundreds of white faces – some perspiring in the humidity of the dark night, others with eyes glazed by alcohol – stretched, it seemed, to infinity. Blacks had not been invited; one had to keep these important functions exclusive, otherwise where would it all end?

The Governor cleared his throat, took from an inner pocket the paper on which he had written his speech and began to read.

'Ladies and gentlemen, loyal citizens of this colony, it gives me the greatest and most heartfelt pleasure. . . .'

At that moment, all the lights went out.

Darkness, all the more fearful because it was totally unexpected, seemed to leap at everyone from the trees. Women shrieked with surprise, some in fear. Against a background of whirring cicadas and croaking bull frogs, male guests cried out, at first anxiously, and then angrily.

'What has happened? Get the lights on! What is the matter? Strike up the band!'

The musicians began to play, faltered, missed a beat and stopped.

The Governor turned to his ADC.

'Go on your motorcycle to the electricity company and find out what has happened, and report back *immediately*,' he ordered.

The ADC was surprised to find Fiona, her husband and Edward sitting around a table in the control room. They were playing cards. Glasses of wine were at their elbows. They looked up at him without interest. In contrast to the darkness outside, the room was brightly lit from storage batteries, and through an open door the ADC could see the steam engine and the huge red flywheel, silent now and still.

'All the lights have gone out,' he explained without preamble.

Fiona nodded.

'I know,' she said, and took a sip of wine. 'Your bid,' she told her partner.

'Can you *please* put them on? We are in the middle of the Governor's reception. It is terribly important.'

'To the Governor, maybe.'

'But is there something wrong? Has there been a breakdown?'

'No. Nothing wrong. No breakdown, is there, George?'

'None. Everything is in fine working order.'

'Then, please, ma'am, what *is* the meaning of this? Why are the lights not on?'

'Young man,' said Fiona more sharply, 'go back and tell the Governor to come here. I will then explain to him personally what needs to be done to rectify this unhappy situation.'

'But I have told you, he is in the middle of his reception. He was just starting his speech. It is impossible for him to come. That is why he sent me, ma'am, to see you. Immediately.'

'And I am sending you back to see him. Immediately. He cannot see many people in the dark, let alone receive them. I doubt he can even see to read his speech – and from my impression of him, he will not have learned to speak without notes.'

'The Governor cannot come here,' said the ADC firmly.

'Why not?' asked Edward. 'Mrs Douglas-Wallace has been to see him three times. I have been once. Now it is his turn to return our calls. Please close the door on your way out.'

'His Excellency is the King's representative, sir. You cannot treat him like this.'

Fiona scanned her cards.

'Pass,' she said.

The ADC raced back through the darkened streets, his acetylene headlamp casting a feeble yellow path along the dust road. Government House servants had brought hurricane lamps and lanterns into the garden to stop guests falling over. The Governor was still standing on the dais, his speech in his hand. The band had begun to play music from memory. The ADC repeated Fiona's message to the Governor.

'It is impossible that he goes,' replied the Governor's lady at once. 'The cheek of it. These upstarts, absolute *nobodies*. Half-castes even! Geoffrey, *order* them to switch on the current.'

The Governor chewed a fingernail. If the lights did not come on again within minutes, he would have to cancel the whole party. This would make him a laughing stock, not only in the colony but in the Caribbean. Lewd calypsos would be composed and sung about his inability to get the lights switched on, hinting at what he might have done in the dark. Worse, news of this fiasco might reach the Colonial Office in London. It almost certainly would, since Trinity-Trio owned *The Enquirer*. This would not help his chances of promotion, or the knighthood that minutes previously had seemed within his grasp. His wife would dearly like to be called 'Lady'. He made up his mind; he would have to go and see these people. He had no option.

'I will be back in a moment,' he said, not meeting his wife's contemptuous gaze. He followed the ADC to his motorcycle, and climbed up on the pillion behind him.

The Governor, ill at ease in white tropical uniform, holding his plumed hat under one arm, stood framed against the darkness in the doorway of the engine-house.

'I have come at your request,' he told Fiona sharply. 'I wish you to get the generating machine working again as soon as possible.'

'I am sure you do, Governor,' Edward replied. 'But this is not a matter we can hurry. The first time it stopped because, under the influence of Mr O'Brien, it was deliberately wrecked. It took us a week to repair. The second time this happened, they did an even more extensive job. We took two weeks to put it in order again.

'After your party, the mob will doubtless wreck it for the third time. And so it can go on and on. We have personally paid for everything here, right down to the last nut and bolt, and we are not prepared to risk our investment for a third time. The engine does not start again unless you give us protection.'

'I cannot guarantee that.'

'Then we cannot guarantee you light. Tomorrow, we will begin to dismantle the equipment.'

'But *why* has it stopped so suddenly? Is there a breakdown you cannot repair quickly? I am host at the King's birthday reception. It is *most* important we have light.'

'And equally important that we provide it without any fear of future violence and disruption. There is nothing wrong with the mechanism that your assurance cannot cure. The lights went out because I switched them off. And off they stay until you give your word the mob keeps away.'

The Governor stood sweating with embarrassment.

'All right,' he said at last, in a choking voice, 'I will see you have a platoon of soldiers here within the hour.'

'Thank you. If you renege on your promise, the lights go out and stay out. And after reports about this reach London, I think the same will be said about you.'

'I have given my word,' said the Governor stiffly.

Fiona nodded to the engineer; he turned the main steam cock. Slowly, the big wheel began to turn. Lights came on, dimly at first, and then more brightly. In the distance, they could hear the military band begin to play more confidently, and people cheering. Trust the Governor to sort things out. Damn' good sort. He'd show these damn' upstarts who was boss here, eh?

The ADC's motorcycle was very noisy, otherwise the Governor, uncomfortably astride the pillion seat, would have heard the guests begin to sing, 'For He's a Jolly Good Fellow'.

Mr O'Brien climbed up the gangway of *Coromandel II*.

'You wish to see me, ma'am?' he asked Fiona. Nothing in his face betrayed his total loathing of the woman who, doubtless under her husband's prompting, had beaten him over the electrification contract, and who he was still certain had thwarted his intention of acquiring Captain Ross's holding in Trinity-Trio. He was determined they would never outwit him again, and somehow, somewhere, they would pay for having done so twice.

He also hated Fiona especially because she was white and a woman. O'Brien swallowed hard to control his bile and kept his eyes down in case Fiona should see the sullen hatred that burned in them like fire.

'I would like you to arrange a trip for me to the mahogany and sapodilla forests, Mr O'Brien,' Fiona told him.

'That will be very difficult, Mrs Douglas-Wallace. The jungle is a dangerous place, and a long distance from here. It is not fit for a white woman to visit.'

'Nevertheless, I wish to go. My husband will accompany me.'

'And the other gentleman, Mr Sodawaterwallah?'

'He will remain here.'

It was difficult enough for Fiona to be aboard the same ship with the man she was beginning to love. It would be infinitely more tantalising to be close to him in the warm, steamy atmosphere of the jungle. With her husband by her side, she would compare him continually with Edward; that comparison could soon become unbearable. And she had to take George with her. If she left him on his own on board ship, he would only make a fool of himself with drink. She could not bear to see him lose respect in the eyes of underlings.

'As you wish,' said O'Brien. 'But I counsel most strongly against it. Señor Gonzales will agree. It is not as in your country, ma'am. There are wild animals here – and even wilder people, descendants of runaway slaves. But if you are determined, the sooner we leave the better. The rains are due any day.'

'Then make all necessary arrangements as soon as possible.'

'I will do so immediately. I will be here to guide you personally to the forest at eight o'clock tomorrow morning.'

He and Gonzales arrived punctually with mules for the baggage and three young horses for O'Brien, Fiona and her husband to ride.

'You are not coming with us?' Fiona asked Gonzales in surprise.

'I am sorry, ma'am, but I must stay and safeguard the company's interests here,' he replied. 'We have a new shipment of resin to load. The company is now the biggest buyer and our rivals greatly resent this. Unless I keep a very close eye on it, we may easily lose several tons to them.'

Fiona packed in a pannier the few clothes she would need. She loaded

Alec Douglas's pistol, wrapped it in a scarf and put this in the saddle bag. As an afterthought, she put a clip of extra rounds in her sleeping quilt. If conditions were as rough as O'Brien claimed, to be armed could be a wise precaution.

The little group set off through the town, riding in single file along its narrow roads, built in a grid pattern with right-angle turns. Soon, houses gave way to shacks, and then shacks to rough huts, and all the time the jungle reached in greedily from either side. Mangrove swamps, thick and green, stretched as far as Fiona could see: they seemed without end and impassable. She shuddered at the thought of being lost or marooned there with alligators and serpents watching, waiting.

Within a mile, the track degenerated into a narrow path used by pack animals: as many as 300 would move in a single file out to the forests to collect loads of gum. Thick fleshy leaves brushed the horses' flanks and the riders' legs. The air felt very hot and humid, like moving through a steam room. Clouds of black flies hung around their faces, crawling into their noses, their ears and eyes. Sweat poured off their bodies; shirts clung to their backs like a second soaking skin. Fiona had brought a veil of the type used by women in open cars, but it was stifling in this heat. She put it back in her pannier.

Half a dozen Belizean labourers walked in front, and as many more came behind them. Their duties, O'Brien explained, were to handle the mules and horses, to pitch camp for each night's stop, and to cook. They marched silently, heads down, apparently as dejected as the slaves from whom they were descended.

They passed areas where giant cedars soared above the mangroves. A trade in cedarwood had already been established and Fiona had decided to investigate the possibilities of increasing it. All day they travelled, with only brief stops for mugs of smoke-laden coffee brewed over hastily laid fires of twigs, or to relieve themselves.

In the late afternoon, they approached a river that flowed wide and green and fast. The banks were so overgrown it was almost impossible to see exactly where the river began and the ground ended. The servants prepared a meal of jerk pork, meat cooked with strong spices. Smoke from several small fires, lit around them, kept some of the mosquitoes away. After dinner, they withdrew to their tents. They had endured a long hard ride; an equally arduous journey faced them next day.

Mr O'Brien's tent was pitched about fifty yards from the tent occupied by Fiona and her husband. George had brought his private supply of rum, in bottles wrapped with strips of sacking to prevent them breaking. He poured a huge measure into a tin mug as soon as he reached his tent, and squatting on the groundsheet that covered the earth, he lit a cheroot. He sweated heavily and as he finished one cheroot, he lit another. He wondered what Edward was doing and was thankful he had not accompanied them. Mosquitoes buzzed around his face and neck and ears, and he cursed them, slapping at them irritably with his hands. They retreated, only to return. The night was alive with their monotonous whine.

Soon, his tent was filled with acrid blue smoke, and still the mosquitoes pestered him. As the fiery spirit moved within him, surging through his body with his blood, George's brooding resentment of Edward increased. He had always been envious of him. Edward was the eldest; the boy who won most races at school sports days; the young man with an unusually shrewd eye for business opportunities. Edward could make money, while others said unkindly that all George could do was spend it.

As he poured himself another four fingers of rum, he wondered whether Edward had been to bed with Fiona. He thought not, because he believed his brother had an old-fashioned idea of honour. But no doubt he wanted to, and one day he might. His ill temper exacerbated by this thought, George quickly gulped down the rum and poured himself a third. As he replaced the bottle, he saw a small metallic glint beneath Fiona's quilt. It was a clip of cartridges.

For a moment, fuddled with alcohol and envy, he did not realise the clip's significance. Then he did, and his eyes narrowed. If Fiona had cartridges, she must have a gun. He felt through the thickness of the quilt but could not find it. So she had hidden it somewhere or kept it concealed beneath her skirt or belt. But why? It probably wasn't loaded; women, he believed, were afraid of loaded guns. For no real reason, save to annoy her, he put the clip into his pocket. If the bitch asked whether he had seen it, he would ask why she wanted a gun. Why had she not told him she was armed? Unless, of course, she planned to use the gun against *him*?

The thought, absurd as he knew it was, fuelled his anger and self-pity. When he first sat down, he had drunk to clear his mind. Then he drank because his mind became fogged. Soon he was drinking not to remember, but to forget. And what he wanted to forget most were the humiliations he had suffered in bed with Fiona.

How was it that with whores in Grant Road in Bombay, or in London in their scented rooms off Jermyn Street, he had been able to perform, if not brilliantly, at least adequately? Of course, he was paying them in cash, or with a present – a jewel perhaps, a silk shawl, trinkets of some kind – which immediately established their inferiority. They were not his equal, as Fiona was. They would smile, and stroke him to arouse him, and ruffle his hair and beg him to return, assuring him there had never been anyone else like him.

But with Fiona it was different; everything was different with her. She always seemed aloof, unapproachable. You could reach out and touch her physically, but never mentally. Was she in love with someone else? Had that old Scot, Alec Douglas, seduced her? Were those the tricks of the forest and glen she claimed he had taught her?

George suspected as much, but he had never cared – or dared – to ask her. And then there was Edward. Obviously, Fiona liked him. He could tell that by the way she looked at him, by the light in her eyes. But why should that matter when he pressed against her in bed, hands on her lithe, firm body? It mattered desperately because he was flaccid, useless, and then suddenly would come the surge, the quick warm rush of life from him to her, and all was over before it had properly begun, and she was turning away from him and saying in a resigned voice, 'Never mind, it will be better next time. Don't worry about it.'

But how could he not worry about it? He had originally been the rich man, the travelled stranger from the fabled East, and she the poor girl living in a tiny bothy on an estate in Scotland. Now she was far richer than he would ever be, and clearly frustrated and discontented. Whereas once she had been eager to learn from his experience of travel and people and strange cities, now she could go anywhere in the world – often in a ship owned by her company. He had nothing left to give her. But did he *want* to give her anything?

Ugly thoughts, bitter as bile, sharp as crushed glass, pounded in his brain; questions chased answers and never came near to catching them. He put the bottle to his lips – to hell with sipping the stuff from mugs – and made up his mind what he would do now in the heart of the jungle, what he had to do or admit forever he was less than a man.

Fiona stood alone on the bank of the river, watching the moon reflected on the rushing water, listening to the alien sounds of a jungle night: the ceaseless twittering and whispering of a myriad unseen, unknown insects. On the edge of the clearing she could see the tent, lit from within as in a magic lantern show, and her husband's outline moving like a giant, phantasmagoric figure in silhouette against the canvas. Mosquitoes hummed and whined around her ears. She brushed them away – and realised she was simply staying out by the river as long as she possibly could, to delay the moment when she must return to the tent to a husband for whom all affection was dead.

On board ship, they had occupied separate cabins. Here they would be forced to lie close together by the confines of the tent, and the thought of his soft, sweating flesh disgusted her. How could it be that only months ago he had appeared so attractive that she had married him?

Surely the main reason must simply be that she was unused to any social contact, and he was the first young man she had met in Scotland, except for the loutish, illiterate sons of labourers with tied tongues and raw red hands and heavy boots? What a fool she had been not to realise this before she married him! For what did her future with George hold but a growing dislike, and an equally increasing contempt for herself for being so unbelievably naive? There was another reason, she knew, but tried desperately not to admit, even to herself. Until they had met Edward, she had been prepared to accept she had made a grave mistake, and abide by it. But now, with Edward, the equation changed. How much easier everything would have been if he had not noticed her and George in the Strand! Minutes earlier or later, and they would not have seen each other. Yet deep down, whatever the result, she was glad they had met, if only to part again. His presence had already enriched her life.

Fiona had no idea how long she remained out in the warm, pulsing, steaming dark, turning over the problem in her mind. O'Brien's tent was unlit, which presumably meant he was asleep, and the Belizeans all slept on the ground, with only a shirt or a piece of cloth over their faces as a screen against the mosquitoes. From where she stood, they looked like a row of corpses. She might be the last person left alive, and she felt overwhelmed, almost to tears, by the inexplicable loneliness which only someone unequally yoked to a person they dislike can ever experience. Finally, she had to go back to the tent; the mosquitoes were unbearable. She walked slowly over the stubbly grass, undid the tapes of the tent entrance and bent down to go inside.

Cheroot smoke was so thick, it billowed past her in a choking cloud. She took a step backwards in disgust.

'Can you not smoke outside, if you must smoke those filthy things?' she asked him.

'No, I cannot,' George replied, his voice rough with rum. 'It is my bloody tent, and I will smoke here whenever I want.'

'In that case, I am sleeping elsewhere.'

Fiona picked up the quilt. The tent was not tall enough for them both to stand upright, and they faced each other angrily, shoulders hunched. George thrust his face into hers through the whirling blue wraiths of smoke. She could smell spirit, sweet and sickly, on his breath; see its effect in his bloodshot eyes.

'You bitch,' he said hoarsely. 'Is it because my mother was a Parsee? You think you are too good for me, don't you?'

'I don't think anything about you. I just want to get out of this tent and sleep on my own.'

George followed her into the sweating darkness. She looked unusually vulnerable, facing him, a slight figure, clutching the quilted bag. The sight excited him. In the dark, he was the stronger of the two. Blood surged like flame in his loins; he felt his body harden. By God, he would show this Scottish cow who was master, and if any of these bloody natives saw him, so much the better.

Rum had purged him of all doubt and inhibition. He tore the quilt from Fiona's grasp and flung it away. She stood, staring at him in horror, guessing what he was about to do and knowing she was powerless to prevent it.

Dimly, George could see some of the natives start up from sleep, wondering at the unexpected noise. He seized the neck of Fiona's cotton dress and ripped it from her body. Fiona took a step back, meaning to run. In turning, she tripped over a guy rope and fell heavily to the ground. He descended on her, tumescent with lust, tearing down his trousers, feeling the night air cool his sweating limbs.

Her long legs gleamed pale and exciting under the moon. She struggled desperately to rise, gripping the guy rope to pull herself up, and then he was on her, in her. No softness now, no apologies, no excuses. He drove with the force of a piston thrust.

Fiona fought him, screaming. She dug her fingernails into his back, gouging soft flesh. She scratched his face and bit him on the neck. George forced back her head, cursing her, further inflamed by her fighting spirit: this was not an act of love or even lust. This was naked aggression and revenge, the payment of a debt. And all the while, he plunged like a rutting beast, as though his whole life depended on it, and if he ceased, he died.

O'Brien heard the commotion, opened the flap of his tent and peered out sleepily, wondering at its cause. Then he heard George's cry of exultation and smiled, remembering other cries of satisfaction, or for mercy or release. And in remembering these, he remembered Captain Ross; how he had died, how convenient the river had been then, how useful it might be now.

George stood up for a moment, and looked down at his wife. She lay, legs still apart, half naked, head on one side, an arm held out before her eyes as though somehow she could blot out the memory and the shame of what she had just endured. Then – unsteadily – fuming with drink, heart beating like a demented drum, George began to stumble between the tents towards the river.

I did it, he told himself, I did it. I hated the bitch and that was the reason. He felt weary, drained of life and energy, and desperate for a drink of cold water; he felt so thirsty, he could drink the whole bloody river dry.

As silent as a creature of the night, O'Brien came out of his tent and watched them both. This was his moment, his chance; he would not let it pass by. He knew that Fiona had not seen him. She sat up, put her face in her hands, and then went into her tent. There, she poured water into a metal bowl and washed herself to try and rinse away the horror of her husband's assault.

One by one, the natives, aroused by the noise, went back to sleep. It was not their concern how white people behaved when in drink. Such occurrences were common enough in their own lives; why should whiteys be any different?

George crashed on through the thick bushes by the river, knelt down and scooped up some brackish water in his hands to splash his face. He bent down closer to drink. Too late, he heard a faint crackle of twigs behind him. He turned – and the hard edge of O'Brien's right hand came down on the back of his neck with the force of an axe.

For a second, a surrealistic vision of O'Brien's face – exultant, and filled with hatred – fused in George's brain against a rim of foam at the edge of the river, the bushes, the trees, a sky pricked with stars. And then he was in the river, thrashing feebly against the current. He cried out, once, twice, but water filled his throat. Choking and gasping for breath, still beating uselessly with his hands, the silent, streaming tide bore him away.

Next morning, the cooks had made breakfast and were ready to load the mules before Fiona appeared. She looked pale, with dark shadows beneath her eyes.

'Sleep well, ma'am?' O'Brien asked her insolently. She shook her head.

'And Mr Douglas-Wallace, ma'am?' he persisted.

'I have not seen him since –' she paused '– since last night.'

'I heard him going down to the river in the night,' said O'Brien. 'Maybe he wanted a drink.' Then he added contemptuously, 'Of water, I mean.'

'Probably you are right.'

Fiona looked at O'Brien more closely as she spoke, seeing hatred glitter in his eyes. She wondered how much he knew about what had happened during the night; what he had heard, what he had seen. But what did that matter now? She had already made up her mind: she was going to leave her husband, unless, incredibly, he had already decided to leave her. But where could he have gone in the middle of the forest?

She walked down towards the edge of the river. Perhaps, as O'Brien had suggested, he had gone for a drink and fallen asleep on the grass? She saw torn branches where some person or large animal had indeed been down to the water. One of the servants came towards her.

'I saw him, ma'am,' he explained. 'Your husband. I think he been drinking slave juice. He was at the river getting cold water drink, ma'am. Like Mr O'Brien said.'

'Did you see him come back?'

'I no see him come back, ma'am. I am thinking he did not come back.'

O'Brien came across to them, looked from one to the other.

'Perhaps he fell in,' he suggested. 'It is easy enough to do. You go

down on your hands and knees for a drink, and you lose your balance –
and that is that.'

'How do you know?' Fiona asked him.

'I have seen it happen, ma'am. The current is very swift, and if there is
no-one around to help, and they cannot help themselves – for one reason
or another – that is the end of it.'

Now Fiona saw footmarks on the river bank, a torn branch, trodden
leaves; O'Brien could be right. George had been drunk and probably was
unsteady on his feet. If he had crouched on the bank, he could very easily
have fallen forwards into the river. But did he fall – or had he been
pushed? If the latter was true, only one person could have pushed him, or
ordered someone else to do so.

O'Brien might have wanted George out of the way, partly for beating
him over the electricity contract because he would assume this had been a
man's idea, not a woman's aim; partly because he would think that, on her
own, Fiona would lack courage and resolve to go against whatever he
proposed.

Fiona smiled inwardly at the thought. O'Brien clearly did not know
her – or that she would now be even more alert for any action he might
take against her.

'Are we going back to Belize Town, ma'am?' O'Brien asked her.

'No. We are going on, to inspect the gum trees and the mahogany.
That's what we set out to do – and what we will do, God willing.'

'As you say, ma'am. What about your husband?'

'He has either walked back to Belize Town, or, as you suggest, he may
have fallen into the river. In either case, staying here cannot help him or
us. Nor could returning to the town. We leave as soon as all is packed up.'

They set off in single file; O'Brien in front, Fiona some way behind.
Heat lay like a lead weight on their backs. Humidity and the thick cloying
greenness of seemingly endless jungle all around them sapped the spirit.
The mules trudged forward, heads bowed. No-one spoke. It was as if they
had no energy to spare for speech.

Eventually, they came to a parting of the track which by now was so
faint that only the leading Belizean, who made this journey regularly,
could follow it. The column halted. Horses and mules put down their
heads and began to graze off the stubbly grass. O'Brien rode back to
Fiona.

'The best gum trees are some way along the left hand, ma'am,' he
explained. 'I suggest we ride on there while the main body goes to the
right. A mile along, no more, is where we usually camp on visits to the
forests. There is a clearing and they will pitch tents for us when we come
back. That way no time will be lost.'

Fiona nodded agreement. O'Brien gave the natives their orders. They set off, and almost immediately the jungle swallowed them. Within moments there was neither sound nor sight of men or mules; it had become as though they had never been.

'I will lead the way, ma'am,' said O'Brien. 'I know it well.'

He spurred his horse ahead of Fiona. She followed him. Trees now leaned in alarmingly close on both sides. Sometimes branches touched above their heads, so that they were riding through a long green tunnel. She lay flat on the horse's neck as brightly plumaged birds started up to spread frightened wings in a dozen brilliant colours.

They came into a small clearing, surrounded by enormous trees between 250 and 300 feet high and broad in proportion. The huge trunks were scarred by gashes cut at an angle in the shape of a V. These grooves were connected from high up the tree to within easy reach of the ground. Gum trickled down them slowly into a metal bucket at the base of each tree. Men were working high above their heads, tied to branches by ropes around the trunks, cutting new zigzag grooves with axes. They did not look down as Fiona and O'Brien rode into the clearing; they were paid by results, and to stop work even momentarily meant that they lost money.

'Each night, the resin is strained through a square of cloth into big kettles,' O'Brien explained. 'Then they heat these and pour the liquid into moulds carved from wood blocks. They cool the blocks in a stream and mules carry them to the quayside.'

'How far is the mahogany from here?' Fiona asked him.

'No distance on a good horse, ma'am. Please follow me.'

They rode on. The heat was now intense. Fiona could feel her body run with perspiration, and yet her lips seemed dry. She glanced at her face in a small mirror she carried and saw a rim of white salt around her mouth. The steady pace of the horses, the soft, almost constant caress of branches against her legs, and the pounding, hammering heat made her soporific. She was almost asleep in the saddle when suddenly O'Brien, ahead of her, cried out in alarm: 'Look out! Spur your horse!'

Automatically, Fiona dug the spurs into the animal's flanks. It surged forward. O'Brien was galloping ahead, apparently oblivious of branches that reached out on either side. Had some wild animal – a bear, a jaguar – frightened his horse? Why his sudden cry for speed?

Soon O'Brien was out of sight, and peering ahead between the trees in an attempt to see him, Fiona turned a sharp corner in the narrow path – and nearly rode headlong into the huge broken bough of a giant cedar that blocked the way only feet from the ground.

Instinctively, with a reaction born of practice in the yard at Coupar Castle, under Alec Douglas's eye, she rolled sideways as he had taught her. She hung on to the girth as the horse ducked its head, and passed so closely beneath the branch that the pommel tore away some small twigs and sprigs of leaves. Then Fiona swung herself from beneath the horse's belly, and reined in the animal.

The horse was panting in terror, ears flat back, saliva frothing at its mouth. She patted its neck soothingly and gradually the frantic breathing ceased and the pounding of its heart returned to normal.

But where was O'Brien? He had been ahead of her, out of sight. Had something happened to him? Had the fierce men of the forest he mentioned attacked him, and he had shouted to warn her?

On her own, the forest pressed in all around her, a living, breathing, sinister presence. Her horse whinnied nervously. Fiona unbuttoned the pannier, removed the pistol, pushed it into her belt, and pulled her shirt down loosely over it. If any wild man or animal came prowling past, she must be ready to shoot.

'Mr O'Brien!' she called. 'Are you there?'

No sound, no answer, nothing but the fleshy rustle of thick, oily leaves on unknown trees. Was he dead, unconscious, dragged into the bush by his frightened horse? He had been right: this jungle was no place for a white woman.

Her horse whinnied again and stamped its feet. Flies were beginning to annoy it, but such was Fiona's concentration, she did not even notice them. She turned her horse to face the way they had come. Then she dismounted and walked back beneath the bough. At first, the horse was reluctant to go, and trembled, rearing up, but she spoke soothingly to it. She understood horses; Douglas had taught her a great deal about them. If she could not find O'Brien, she would have to return to the junction of the tracks and take the other fork and hope to reach camp. All thought of examining mahogany trees had now left her; survival was her paramount concern.

She started to walk back along the track leading the horse. She would mount it again as soon as she sensed the animal was calm. Then, at the first bend, she saw O'Brien. He was on his horse, facing her.

'I was nearly killed,' she told him. 'Where have you been?'

'Looking for you, ma'am,' he replied. 'What happened? Why are you dismounted? It is very dangerous to walk in the jungle.'

'It is more dangerous to ride behind you,' she retorted. 'There was a tree across the track. I saw it just in time. Did you not see it?'

He shook his head, frowning.

'You must have missed your way, ma'am,' he replied. 'There was no tree across the path I took. You should have kept closer to me. You should have followed me.'

'Then why did you go away so quickly, and shout to me to spur my horse?'

'Because I feared you were falling too far behind me, ma'am.'

'You feared something else, O'Brien,' she told him quietly. 'Something much worse. You feared I knew too much.'

She did not know why she said this: the words seemed prompted by some inner force. Somebody else might be speaking them, but she knew intuitively she was right. That bough would have killed an indifferent rider.

O'Brien did not answer immediately. He licked his lips with his tongue, curiously long and pink in the black face, and somehow repulsive.

'You killed my husband,' Fiona said flatly.

'Of course not, ma'am. You are distraught. I am very sorry you have had this frightening experience. It was certainly not my wish.'

'It was not your wish that we should be talking here now, either. It was your wish to kill me, as you killed him. Am I right?'

Even as Fiona spoke, the accusation astonished her. She had no proof whatever that this was so, only a sudden feeling deep inside her that it was.

Mr O'Brien looked down at her, as though considering his reply. For a moment, she thought that he would continue to deny it, shake his head and shrug his shoulders and assure her of his friendship. But he did none of those things.

'You are *right*, ma'am,' he admitted. 'I killed him, and I will kill you.'

'Why?'

Fiona was again surprised – this time as much at the calmness of her voice asking the question as the equal coolness of his admission. They might have been discussing the weather, the merits of one brand of tea against another, not murder – and his intention to murder her, as he could so easily do. He was far stronger; also, he was on horseback, and she was on her feet. But surprisingly she felt no fear. Instead, she experienced a strange, almost dreadful, calm. It was as though she had realised from the moment they left Belize Town that this was what O'Brien intended. Now the Providence that had brought her so far would show her – or him – the way ahead. Events were out of her hands: she was only the instrument, not the player.

'Why? I will tell you why,' O'Brien replied. 'You came to my country, like all you white people, to grind us down. I came here as a slave, the son of a slave. I was caught like a wild hog in a snare and brought here in chains, against my will. I had no choice. You did.

'My father was a chief in the old country. I would have followed him. It was the decision of the elders, the tradition. But that was denied me. Your people bought and sold us both as you would sell a dog, a horse. On the voyage I was constantly humiliated by Captain Ross. My father, he ruined.'

'You killed Ross, too?'

'I waited a lifetime, and I killed him, yes. He made my father a cripple. As a result of Ross's cruelty, he was forced to live out his days in pain and misery. His only comfort came from his carving. And even that Ross tried to stop. I could have made the swine suffer as my father suffered, but I killed him kindly. Would that he had shown my father such compassion.

'Here, I built up my own business. I became wealthy. Of course, I was only a black man – not accepted by all the white people – but I would become richer in the colony than all of them put together. Then you arrived with your husband, a weak, drunken creature.'

'Do not speak ill of the dead,' said Fiona.

'I speak of people as I knew them, alive or dead,' O'Brien retorted. 'I hated Ross, I despised your husband. He stole away my plan for the electricity station. He bribed my clerk to get into my office. I know these things. I have watchers all over Belize Town – and others to watch them.'

Fiona was about to explain that he had mistaken someone else for her husband, but bit back the words.

'Fate put him into my power,' O'Brien went on. 'Now you accuse me, white woman, and I readily admit what I have done. Why not? No-one can hear. Only God, if there is a God. Who cares? That is for others to ponder. For months, I worked to light Belize Town by electricity. All was agreed with the Governor. Then you two arrive – and ruin every-thing. But that is the last harm you will do me, ma'am. I brought you down this track because I knew of this broken branch, and I did not think you could avoid it. But you did. So you will have to ride back into it again. This time you will not avoid it.'

'I am not riding,' said Fiona. 'I am walking.'

O'Brien slipped his hand into a wicker case behind his saddle and drew out a long whip.

'Get on your horse!' he ordered.

His whip cracked like a gun. Fiona's horse started, whinnying in fear, standing up on its hind legs, pawing the air. Fiona soothed it. Like one in a dream, as though she was watching this, taking no part in it, was indeed totally unconcerned by it, she swung herself up into the saddle. She allowed the horse to turn, and bent forward, patting its neck, her back to O'Brien. She was certain he could not see the movement as she withdrew the pistol from her belt, cradled it in her hand as she turned her horse to face him.

'You should have listened,' he said. 'The jungle is no place for a white woman.'

'Or a black swine,' she retorted.

'You bitch!' he roared, his face contorted with hatred. He flicked his whip across her horse's head. The animal panicked, rising up. O'Brien swung the whip again, only inches above her head.

Next time he would hit her, and such a blow would either blind or kill. She raised her pistol, fired once, twice.

The first bullet hit O'Brien in the chest, the second in the head. He flung up his hands like a straw dummy, and rolled back off his horse. One foot caught in a stirrup. The animal reared and then was away, dragging his body upside down into the bush.

Fiona replaced the pistol. The barrel felt warm, and the air was sharp with the peculiar smell of the Chinese gunpowder Alec had used. She wondered obliquely, possibly absurdly, had Alec had time to smell it that night when he killed himself? This pistol had killed one man she loved, and now another who hated her. Would she ever use it again – and if so, in what unimagined, unimaginable circumstances?

She rode on, partly because she could not face going back immediately in case she saw O'Brien's mutilated corpse again, but mainly because her resolution had returned. She had set out to see the mahogany trees and was determined to do so.

After about an hour, she reached a clearing piled with gigantic mahogany trunks, waiting to be floated down river to Belize Town. All around the clearing, other trees, still standing, had been marked with chalk signs; some would be felled before the rains, some afterwards. The gangs of woodmen had left and the whole area was deserted and eerie: a huge wound in the heart of a vast forest.

She turned her horse's head and rode back to the meeting of the two ways, then followed the other fork. Within half an hour she arrived at the camp site. Tents were already pitched and pots were steaming on a fire. She dismounted. A servant came up to take her horse.

'Mr O'Brien, ma'am?' he asked her.

'He has gone on ahead,' she told him. There was no need to explain further to these people. His horse would probably shake his body free, and wild beasts would do the rest. She had nothing to fear from discovery. What could anyone here deduce from picked bones in a shirt and trousers?

Fiona felt surprised at her own calmness. She had killed a man. But, then, if she had not, he would have killed her. That was the oldest law of all, the law of survival, the law of the jungle. She smiled slightly as she walked into her tent.

O'Brien had been right. The jungle was no place for a white woman.

London

Sir Thomas Fulwood, the banker who had originally introduced Dr Jackson to Gunther Lewis, the founder of *The Enquirer*, dozed at a horseshoe table in an upper room of the Coliseum Club.

He was on the committee that met every three months to select or reject candidates who wished to become members of this most exclusive club. Through the high windows he could hear the clop-clop of horses' hooves and the honk of motor horns in St James's. They were becoming more numerous now than cabs and carriages. Changes like these made him feel very old. He had lived through too many, but his mind was still alert to any issues that concerned him.

The club chairman, a duke who had gambled away one estate and was now busily re-mortgaging another in the hope of recouping his losses by applying a system for winning at roulette which a Russian prince had recently sold him, tapped the table with a leather-headed gavel.

'Well, gentlemen,' he said, 'we have only three candidates up for admission this time. One, I think, we all know. Jock Bridey's son, Jake. Damn' good rider to hounds, excellent fellow, will inherit the Leicestershire estate and also a great deal of property in South East London. Lives in Curzon Street when he's in town, where he keeps a damn' good cellar and table, as I know, and I think most of you do, too. Any objections?'

They shook their heads. The chairman struck the table with his gavel.

'The second is Lord Gridmore. I do not know him personally, but he comes with a very good proposer and seconder. And you have seen for yourselves the number of friends who have signed for him in the members' book. Nowadays, he lives most of the time in Spain, but he sends a very pleasant letter – I have it somewhere – in which he says he often wishes he were here, and able to join us.'

A few members smiled slightly and knowingly at this. Lord Gridmore had prudently fled to Spain two years previously to avoid charges of gross indecency with a succession of young footmen. He managed his huge estates at long distance. His agents and others would meet him on some neutral ground; in Seville, Madrid, Paris. He could never return to London, but his father and grandfather had both been members, and Gridmore wished to carry on the tradition.

'I would not think we will see much of him here, unfortunately. But he has been a very good friend of many members. An intimate friend, in fact.'

Another laugh at the unintended pun.

'Any objections? No? Right.'

The chairman's gavel struck the table for a second time.

'Now, gentlemen, the third, a young man, Robert Jackson. He owns *The Enquirer* newspaper and he and his fiancée are large shareholders in Trinity-Trio. I know we are all anxious to attract younger members. None of us is getting any younger ourselves. But. . . .' He paused. 'His mother is Chinese'

'Slit-eyes?' asked a noble lord, looking at the duke from under bushy eyebrows, as though he could not believe what he had heard.

'Jackson's father was a distinguished physician, totally British, and one of the founders of that most prosperous company,' the duke replied. 'I believe he also attended on Queen Victoria.'

'I knew him,' said Sir Thomas. 'He banked with me. Very sound fellow. He formed a liaison in the East – these things happen – and this is his natural son. I would say, gentlemen, that he is not alone in fathering a natural son.'

He looked at the duke who, to the knowledge of everyone in the room, had certainly sired two illegitimates, and very possibly a third.

'Agreed,' said an unmarried admiral. 'But white men and white women are one thing. This native stuff is a bit of a tall order, in my book. I mean, where will it all end? That's what I want to know. We'll have Indians in here if we don't watch out.'

'There are in fact several maharajahs on our waiting list,' the duke pointed out.'

'They can damn' well stay there,' said a general. 'I've served in India for thirty years. Too many babus. Bengali lawyers. Can't be doing with them.'

'This case is rather different,' the duke replied. 'Jackson is an extremely pleasant and able young man. I have met him on several occasions.'

'I would recommend him most strongly,' said Sir Thomas. Word that he had not done so could easily reach Jackson, who might then withdraw huge amounts from the bank with unhappy effects on their profits.

'Put it to the vote,' the admiral suggested.

The committee members stood up, and crossed the room to a small table. Here, a steward handed each man two balls, one black, one white. In single file they crossed to another table on which stood a small box of polished wood with a central hole, large enough to take a man's hand. Inside was a partition. The left of this was marked Ayes; the right, Noes. Each member put his hand into the hole, still gripping the black and white balls. If he put the white ball to the left, and the black ball to the right, he was voting for the candidate. If, however, he put the black ball to the left this would be a mark against the candidate.

The committee members returned to their places and the club secretary opened the box. On the left were five white balls and four black.

'That settles it,' said the duke. 'Black-balled.'

'It is the wrong decision,' said Sir Thomas. 'He would be an asset to the Coliseum. He has a great business future.'

'We're not concerned here with business,' said the admiral sharply. 'This is a *gentlemen*'s club. Business we can safely leave to people like Mr Jackson.'

The chairman tapped the table with his gavel to signify that the meeting was at an end.

Belize Town

The hut stood on the edge of a clearing on the banks of the Belize River, near the site of a derelict Mayan temple. Stones from the temple's stairway had been used to build its walls. Then locals had planted the clearing with Indian corn and tobacco, and thatched the crude building with husks of corn.

At the doorway, a native crouched low over a twig fire, above which was suspended a copper cauldron. He blew on the twigs through a hollow bamboo. The acrid smoke made him cough, and as he spat into the red glowing embers, something caught his eye in the water: a movement, a colour that was neither fish nor alligator. Instantly, with the reaction of a wild animal, he was alert. He stood up slowly, without a sound, his eyes on the place where he had seen the alien object, his right hand moving towards the knife in his belt.

Only feet away, stuck in the reeds, lay a man's face, eyes closed, mouth open. It was not white, like a European's or an American's, nor dark like his, but somewhere in between. Carefully, cautiously, the native went into the hut.

The missionary was sleeping on a crude bed with a bull's hide spread over him. He was a German in his forties, a bachelor belonging to an obscure Lutheran order. He slept with a loaded revolver beneath the wooden pillow. Propagating the Gospels was neither easy nor safe in Central America. It was better to be armed. Not all natives responded to his teachings; some preferred the old religions, and others simply hated all white men – American, German, British – and would kill to possess a watch or even a copper kettle. The missionary started up now, one hand instinctively reaching for the weapon. He relaxed when he saw his servant.

'Man in river, baas,' the native said laconically.

'Dead?'

'No knowing, baas.'

The missionary had been sleeping in his shirt and long cotton drawers. He pulled on a pair of denim trousers and followed the man down to the water's edge, calling for others to come out and help. Two servants came from the far side of the hut, hawking in their throats and rubbing sleep from their eyes. Together, they pulled the body from the reeds, up out of the water, into the clearing.

At first, the missionary thought the man was dead, but then his eyelids fluttered slightly. They rolled him on his front and pummelled his back. A great gout of filthy stinking fluid spewed from his mouth. They sat him up.

'Who are you?' asked the missionary, somehow expecting the man would answer in English.

'George Wallace,' the man replied feebly, his voice so faint they could scarcely hear him.

He fell back, exhausted by this effort of speech, and closed his eyes. The missionary motioned to the servants to carry him into the hut. They laid George on the hide bed and gave him a mug of soup, but he could not drink. Then the missionary undressed him, and although the day would soon grow warm, wrapped him in a blanket for he was shivering uncontrollably. He must have been in the river for a long time; his flesh was soft and puffy.

George slept, breathing heavily, snoring now and then or crying out and making weak motions of swimming. Sometimes he spoke a few words of English, then lapsed into a language the missionary did not know. Presumably, he was English, but very dark-skinned for an Englishman. He was clearly delirious, and what he said was unintelligible.

The missionary emptied the pockets of his jacket and trousers; a handkerchief sodden into a linen ball, a clasp knife with the initials G.S., a clip of cartridges suitable for a pistol, and ten American dollar bills in a metal clasp.

The missionary dried the cartridges in the sun and examined them closely. They did not fit his revolver. He wondered about them, why they had no number stamped on their base, no initials or insignia of their manufacturer. Thoughtfully, he put them on one side and sat down by George's bed, watching him.

Outside, warm rain began to fall, at first like fingers tapping tentatively on a drum, then a cascade as the heavens opened and the sky grew dark and water fell in a wall. George stirred at the sound and sat up.

The missionary put another pillow behind his back. George's lip moved. He was trying to speak but he could not form the words. Suddenly his body stiffened, then relaxed. His head drooped. The missionary lifted George's hand, felt his pulse. There was no beat: he was dead.

Thunder cracked like distant cannon and the wind changed, blowing spears of rain into the mouth of the hut. They would have to bury him quickly; a corpse putrefied within hours in this heat and damp, now that the rains had come. The missionary called out the natives, and with their primitive implements they reluctantly dug a shallow grave. The missionary said a brief service of burial.

Next day, the rain eased temporarily and they struck camp and left the hut. They were in Belize Town by the end of the week, where the missionary paid off his servants. When in Belize Town, he lived in the house of another German bachelor, Jan Bulow, who ran the general stores.

Herr Bulow, as he was always known, was small, plump, very correct, with waxed upturned ends to his moustache in imitation of the Kaiser, whose coloured portrait hung next to the portrait of Edward VII at the back of the shop. He sometimes thought, but was too discreet to say, that these royal relatives had much in common: small, mean eyes, soft faces, narrow foreheads and a love of colourful uniforms decorated with medals they had awarded themsleves.

Herr Bulow combined trade with a more devious profession. Any items of news he heard, which he thought could conceivably interest the Foreign Intelligence Department of the German Imperial Government, he passed in coded letters to an address in Munich, a subsidiary of a brewing company.

All over the world German tradesmen like him – barbers, butchers, importers, exporters – were performing the same service for the fatherland. They did this from patriotism and with a great willingness and wish to be of service to the Kaiser. One day, the German Empire would eclipse the British Empire. When that glorious moment arrived, Herr Bulow and all those others like him would feel proud that they had played their part.

'What sort of man did you say he was?' he asked, when the missionary reported the death of a man who said his name was George Wallace, but on whose knife the initials G.S. were engraved.

'Very dark-skinned, but he spoke English. His name, anyway.'

'Was he Indian? Not an Indian from America, but from India?'

The missionary considered.

'He could be a half-caste.'

'No marks of identification?'

'Nothing except this knife and handkerchief and these cartridges. There's no maker's name.'

'Really? Is that important?'

'I suppose not, but shall I say, unusual.'

Bulow turned the clip over in his hand.

'They have an unusually long case,' the missionary pointed out.

'I would not know about these things,' said Bulow. 'I will send them to someone who does know. In the meantime, as you religious people say, the labourer is worthy of his hire. Here are ten American dollars to buy hymn books or whatever you want.'

'Thank you,' said the missionary gratefully. He would put the money to good use in the service of Our Lord, along with the ten dollars for which George Wallace had no further use.

In cane chairs around a cane table, under a canvas awning on the afterdeck of *Coromandel II*, Edward sat facing his visitor, a plump, perspiring, middle-aged man. His card lay on the table between them: Mr A. B. Jobbledebhoy, Proprietor, Great Bombay Emporium, Belize Town, British Honduras.

Mr Jobbledebhoy was speaking earnestly, hunching his shoulders, spreading out the palms of his hands to emphasise each sentence.

'When I heard that you were also of our faith,' he was saying, 'I thought you might like to meet other Parsees who have settled here.'

Edward nodded agreement.

'We have quite a community,' Jobbledebhoy continued. 'Small but devout, with our own priest who instructs the children and takes marriages and funerals. We have a new fire temple and have recently built a tower of silence. I know everyone here would very much like to meet you.'

'And I would like to meet them,' replied Edward courteously.

Jobbledebhoy nodded. He had expected this reply. Now he came to the real object of his visit.

'I know Señor Gonzales represents your company here, but I do not know with what success. Should you ever contemplate making a change in your representation, Mr Sodawaterwallah, I would be honoured if you would consider my qualifications.'

'I will bear that very much in mind,' said Edward. 'I will discuss it with Mrs Douglas-Wallace – who I see is arriving now. I will be in touch with you before we leave.'

Mr Jobbledebhoy stood up, bowed respectfully and went down the gangway. He climbed into the boat that had brought him out as the one conveying Fiona from the quay tied up alongside *Coromandel II*.

Edward could see from Fiona's face, drawn and pale and tired, that something terrible had happened.

'Where is George?' he asked her. She shook her head and grimaced, drawing a hand across her face as though to wipe away some terrible memory.

'Give me a drink,' she asked him weakly. 'Then I will tell you.'

Edward poured her a large whisky and she slumped into a cane chair and drank gratefully. Then, haltingly, she explained what had happened.

'Poor George,' said Edward softly. 'My only brother, dead. We were never close, and I do not know quite what I feel. Sorrow, yes. And regret that I never took the trouble to know him better, perhaps to like him better. But that is about all, if I am honest. And one must be, over something like this.'

Fiona nodded in sympathetic agreement. She felt no sorrow whatever at her husband's death, only relief – and the hope he had not suffered as he died. It was as though he had been someone else; as though she had heard of the death of someone she had not been personally involved with. Two other people had once walked hand in hand across the hills in Scotland. Not her, not him, not together.

She had felt almost euphoric after she shot O'Brien, and this had driven all other thoughts from her mind. She knew that O'Brien meant to kill her and so she had killed him first. It was as simple as that; an equation of survival. But now, each time she closed her eyes, she could still see his mutilated, almost headless trunk, spouting blood, reeling backwards off the horse.

'You are certain O'Brien would have killed you?' Edward asked her after she had told him everything.

'Positive.'

'Did anyone see you shoot him?' Edward asked her.

'No. We were a mile or so into the jungle, away from the others.'

'You are positive O'Brien pushed George in the river?'

'He admitted it. To get even with us.'

'What about his body? Will that be found?'

'Unlikely, I would think. But, in any case, it will already be eaten beyond all recognition by wild animals and red ants. His horse made its own way back. I sent out two natives to search for O'Brien, but they found nothing. I would not think they went too deeply into the jungle to look. He was not well-liked.'

'So, in the end, you never saw the mahogany trees?'

'Oh, yes I did.'

'But it was risky for you to go there on your own, surely?'

'Maybe,' she agreed. 'But I had to go. That's what I went out there for.'

'You are a hard woman,' said Edward admiringly.

'I have had to be. I was brought up in what in Scotland they call a butt and a ben, a two-roomed cottage. Often, food was short. Money was even shorter. And I did not know exactly who I was. I used to hang about the castle gates, feeling an immense affinity for the place. I felt somehow, and quite absurdly then, that the castle was where I belonged.

'You were born rich, Edward. You do not know what it is like to be poor. Alec Douglas would lend me books about things I had never heard of, myths of the Greeks, the Romans, the Norsemen.

'There was the theory of the wheel of fortune that always intrigued and frightened me. Life is like a wheel, perpetually turning. You may go up to the top, and become rich and successful. But the wheel is never stationary. It keeps on turning – and you can lose it all.

'There was a man, Claude Cartwright, who tricked the estate from Alec's stepmother. He rode high on that wheel – for a time. Then Alec came back from India and the wheel turned and Claude lost everything!'

Fiona paused.

'But all that is over now,' Edward assured her, and took her hand. Despite the warmth of the day, it felt cold.

'Do you want to go back to find George's body, to bring it back for a proper burial?' she asked him.

Edward shook his head.

'In my religion the dead are taken out to high towers on the edge of Bombay. They are open to the sky, and right up on top, out of sight of everyone, are metal grids. The bodies are placed on these, and birds pick them clean. Then the bones fall through the spaces in the grid to the base of the tower. In George's case, the fish and the alligators will do the office of the birds. In any case, he was really only my half brother.'

'How do you mean? He always spoke of you as his elder brother.'

Edward explained the custom among some in his community to keep the complexions of their offspring fair.

'Did your father arrange this deliberately with your mother?' Fiona asked in amazement.

'I understand so, yes.'

'Do you know who your real father is?'

'I have no idea.'

'Did George know who his father was? I mean, was he the same man?'

'He could be. I just do not know. It is purely a commercial transaction. Money is paid and the contract always stipulates that the man keeps total silence on the matter. He must never attempt to find out whether he has sired a son or a daughter, let alone contact them.'

'But what sort of men would do this?'

'Army officers. Professional men short of money. Others who are not short of money, but who are intrigued by the idea. Many bachelors welcome the opportunity of proving their virility with an attractive woman. No problems, only a bonus when she becomes pregnant – no responsibility for the child. It proves something they feel is important to them. Men are vain, you know.'

'There is a lot I have yet to learn about men.'

'I could say the same about women. But I would like to spend my life learning more about you.'

'What about me?' she asked.

'How to make you happy, for one thing,' Edward told her. 'How to make you smile every day of your life. How to make you realise I love you. Fiona, I am asking you to marry me.'

'It is too soon,' she said, looking away, shaking her head.

'It is never too soon. You or I might have a fatal accident tomorrow – today. Then it would be too late. Life is too short to delay.'

'But what would people think?'

'If you wait a month, a year, they will think the same. Let them think! I am not proposing out of pity for you, but out of love. The first time I met you in the Strand, in London, when you were already married to my brother, I felt an instant and total affinity with you. Since then I have sat in a room with you, and many times known what you were going to say next.'

'The same with me,' she agreed. 'It is amazing.'

'I had never experienced that feeling of closeness with any other person in the world. But you were my brother's wife, and I put behind me all thought and hope of having any relationship with you other than that of a friend. Now you are free, I want you to marry me. By your religion in a church here in Belize Town. By mine in Bombay. In front of a magistrate, the Governor, the captain of this ship, anyone you wish. They can all hold ceremonies that would make our relationship what they call legal. But real relationships come from inside. The contract, my dear Fiona, need never be written on paper, if it is written in our hearts.'

And as he spoke, he reached out towards her, took her hands in his and looked at her face close to; at her wide mouth, her blue eyes, at the flame-red hair she had stopped bleaching after her departure from Scotland.

As she smiled tremulously, and nodded her head, bewildered at the depth and speed of her changing emotions, Edward knew that in her he had found the happiness all men seek and so few ever find: the gift that is beyond assessment, comparison, valuation or dispute; the priceless, ageless gift of love returned.

Señor Gonzales dipped the bristles of his hairbrush in the bowl of scented green pomade on his dressing table, carefully scraped off the excess against the side of the bowl and then brushed his hair slowly, paying particular attention to the parting.

He examined his reflection closely and critically in the mirror. He was about to keep what he considered could be the most crucial appointment of his career, and he wished to look his best. If he handled the meeting with aplomb, panache and exquisite timing, he could be on his way to a fortune by the end of that day.

All his working life Gonzales had been subservient to others. He had taken orders from merchants of low intelligence and grasping minds, and for years had been humiliated by O'Brien. He had, of course, attempted to make money on the side, but never very successfully, never as his employer seemed able to do. He had even been reduced to selling information to policemen and, latterly, to an Italian family who ran Palermo, the only restaurant and guesthouse in Belize Town.

Gonzales had no idea why they should want such snippets of news or gossip that he could provide, or what good it did them, but, in return for telling them in advance that Trinity-Trio had won the contract for electrification, for informing them that Captain Ross had left a widow in the States, and that Mrs Douglas-Wallace was the dominant partner in her marriage, the proprietor allowed Gonzales several free meals a week for himself, his wife and their four children. He was not allowed to choose the more expensive dishes on the menu, because, as with everyone else for whom he had worked, touted or ponced, even the restaurateur treated him as an inferior, a hireling, a second class of person.

Sweating slightly, with a combination of nervousness and anticipation, Gonzales walked through the bustling early morning streets, past cows grazing under the bridge over the Belize River, down to the quay. Two American merchant ships lay at anchor, and beyond them, *Coromandel II*. He hailed a fisherman, tossed him a coin to row him out. Edward watched his progress through a telescope. He turned to Fiona.

'Have you asked to see Gonzales?' he asked.

'No. I don't like the man. There's something about him. I just don't trust him.'

'Well, he's coming out here.'

'Then let us see him together.'

They greeted him on deck – after all, he was their company's local agent – and ushered him into a saloon. A steward set out glasses and a jug of fresh lime juice.

'I have to go up-country unexpectedly on company business this afternoon,' Gonzales began. 'I have therefore taken the liberty of coming out to you without an appointment. I know you plan to sail within the week, and I may not be back before you leave.'

'Have you a problem you wish to discuss?' asked Fiona bluntly. She had the direct approach of many people with red hair.

'Not a problem, ma'am, but an opportunity which I think could benefit you, your company, and which I must admit would also benefit me greatly. With the sad disappearance of Mr O'Brien, his company is without direction. It makes a fine profit. I know, because I have examined the books. I am suggesting to you that you buy it and allow me to run it – in all our interests.'

'What would you want out of this deal?' Edward asked him.

'An emolument commensurate with the responsibility, and a half share in the equity.'

'An interesting proposition,' said Fiona slowly. 'You were close to O'Brien, weren't you?'

'No-one was close to him, ma'am. But I worked for him for a long time. He was a bad man.'

'I am sure,' agreed Edward. 'But how specifically bad?'

Gonzales paused, then made up his mind; he was playing for high stakes.

'I think he killed Captain Ross, ma'am.'

'What makes you think that?'

'I knew the captain was going to O'Brien's house at night. An hour later, I saw two men carry a rolled-up mat through the streets to the river. O'Brien walked behind them. I followed, taking care he didn't see me. A man's body was slid out from this mat into the river.'

'You are certain?' Edward asked him.

'I saw what I saw,' Gonzales replied enigmatically. 'And I never saw Captain Ross again.'

'Was this man dead?' Fiona asked him.

Gonzales shrugged.

'If not then, soon afterwards. The river there is thick with alligators.'

'What did you do then? Did you report what you had seen to the police?'

Gonzales shook his head vigorously; the scent of pomade suddenly filled the saloon.

'Ma'am,' he replied gently, 'I have lived here all my life. I know the police. They take more money in bribes than they are paid in wages. It is not safe to say such things to them.'

'So you did nothing?'

'What could I do? It would be one man's word against mine. A very rich man's word. I am not rich, and I did not want to end up in the river myself. There is a saying here, "When the cockroach holds a dance, he does not invite the fowl." That means, do not go looking for trouble.'

'So you stood by and saw a man whom you think was one of the founders of our company, either dead or alive, being pushed into the river at night from a rolled-up mat to be eaten by alligators? Why did you not tell us before?'

'It was not opportune.'

'Why is it opportune now?'

'We say, "Every day the bucket goes to the well – and one day its bottom drops out." Secret misdeeds continue until they are exposed. I want to show you the sort of man O'Brien was – worse than any other merchant here. And why you need someone now who understands the background of the colony to run his company – in your interests.'

'You speak of O'Brien in the past tense,' said Edward slowly. 'Are you certain he is dead?'

Gonzales nodded.

'Why are you certain?' asked Fiona.

For a moment, Gonzales did not speak. Then, with a great sigh, as though the words were being forced reluctantly from him, he spoke.

'When you left with him to go up-country, ma'am, I stayed behind, explaining I had work to do. But in fact I feared for your safety with O'Brien, knowing how he hated you both. So I sent after your party the best tracker in the colony, someone I have used before.

'I ordered him to watch over you and report to me. No-one knew he was there. He followed at a discreet distance, and when you and O'Brien took one route, and the others went on to pitch camp, he followed you. He saw you ride beneath a fallen tree. Then –'

Gonzales paused as though some words were too painful to utter. Edward prompted him.

'Then?'

'Ma'am, I am reluctant to say this, so please forgive me, but he says he saw you shoot O'Brien and kill him.'

The words, spoken in a soft voice, hit Fiona like a blow. For a moment, she could not speak. Gonzales watched her reaction closely and triumphantly. The tracker had not lied; she *had* killed O'Brien.

'That is a very serious allegation,' Edward said. 'How can this tracker prove it? If Mrs Douglas-Wallace denies it, it would simply be his word against hers. And I think that spies have a habit of telling their paymasters what they most want to hear. Am I right?'

'Of course, sir. There is no question about that. But every fowl ends up cooked for dinner some Sunday. Retribution comes to everyone, and here there was – and is – can I say, another silent witness.'

'What the devil do you mean?'

'O'Brien's body, sir. The tracker located it. I sent out men who have brought it in. The corpse has been out in the rain for days and is in a rather unpleasant state. It is now in Mr Gomez's funeral parlour. The coffin has been sealed, of course, and stays that way until. . . . Until you decide what to do.'

His voice tailed away to silence.

'About what? Buying O'Brien's company?'

'About that. And the matter of my running it.'

'So your evidence is buried with the body if you get the job. Is that it?'

'That is it, sir.'

'In effect, then, you are blackmailing us?'

'I would not use that word, Mr Sodawaterwallah. I simply seek an accommodation, a business arrangement.'

'I suggest you seek it with someone else,' said Edward. 'And speedily. Trust is essential in all business dealings. To be blunt, Gonzales, what you have told us about the death of Captain Ross, and about the spy you sent out after Mrs Douglas-Wallace, and who made no effort to help her when O'Brien threatened to kill her, does nothing to make us eager to put further trust in you. Nor does your attempt at blackmail. And so that there can be no possible misunderstanding, your arrangement with Trinity-Trio is cancelled. As of this moment, you no longer represent their interests in British Honduras.'

Gonzales shrugged. He had played his biggest card, but he was not beaten yet.

'As you wish,' he said. 'There is a saying, "Don't call the alligator big-mouth till you have crossed the river" – do not antagonise people in whose power you are. And I must tell you that Mrs Douglas-Wallace will not be allowed to leave the colony. She will be arrested on a charge of murder. To use your own words, Mr Sodawaterwallah, I tell you this so that there can be no possible misunderstanding about the matter.'

'You have two minutes to get off this ship,' said Edward, coming towards him. 'Or I throw you into the sea.'

Gonzales stood up hastily, and backed out of the saloon. The fisherman sat waiting for him in his boat. Gonzales climbed down the gangway.

'You will be sorry!' he shouted. 'You will wish you had taken a different course!'

Edward watched him go, then returned to the saloon. Fiona sat at the table, her head in her hands. She looked up as Edward entered.

'I thought no-one saw me,' she said wretchedly. 'I did what I did in self-defence. This tracker may say anything, his word against mine, with O'Brien's body as Gonzales says, a kind of dead witness. Oh, it is all too horrible! Can we get a lawyer out here from London to help me?'

'Of course. I will telegraph Ebenezer at once,' promised Edward, 'but the matter may not come to court.'

'What do you mean?' she asked him. 'The Governor will insist it does – if only to get even with us.'

'I will go ashore and cable Ebenezer now, and then make some enquiries of my own.'

'Will I be all right here?' Fiona asked him miserably. 'Can they arrest me, lock me up?'

'They can,' he said, 'but they won't. Not yet. They will expect me to telegraph for a lawyer, and they will wish to read the cable and wait until we have a reply, and read that.'

'And then?' she asked.

'And then we will see what happens,' he said, smiling, and kissed her.

The telegraph office was crowded. Birds flew in and out of high unglazed windows, and messengers and clerks besieged the apertures in the wire-netting screens on the counter, shouting for attention, waving money orders and letters to be stamped.

In one corner, a telegraph operator ignored them all as he tapped a Morse key. Edward wrapped a ten-shilling note around the message he had written aboard ship, and pushed this through the wire to him. Instantly, the operator stopped transmitting, took Edward's money and his message, glancing up at him sharply after he had read it.

His instructions were to delay any message from anyone aboard *Coromandel II*. He counted up the words laboriously. Edward paid him. The operator took the message form to the back of the building and copied it.

TO EBENEZER & SON LINCOLN'S INN LONDON ENGLAND STOP MOST URGENT STOP PLEASE CABLE SOONEST AVAILABILITY KINGS COUNSEL BEST SUITED TO DEFEND PRINCIPAL ON MURDER CHARGE IN BRITISH HONDURAS STOP EXPENSE UNIMPORTANT BUT EARLY AVAILABILITY ESSENTIAL STOP CABLE REPLY DOUGLAS-WALLACE COROMANDEL TWO BELIZE TOWN HARBOUR BRITISH HONDURAS

He folded up the copy, put it in an envelope already addressed to Señor Gonzales, came back to the front office and went on sending his original, interrupted message.

Outside the telegraph office, Edward stood for a moment in the sun. He lit a cheroot and then walked slowly along the pavement to the town centre. Here the Indian community had stores selling cloth, wooden carvings and spices. As he went into the Great Bombay Emporium, Mr Jobbledebhoy rose to greet him from behind a desk in the dim recesses of his shop.

'This is an unexpected pleasure,' he said warmly, extending both hands. 'What have you come to buy?'

'Your help,' said Edward with a smile. 'Can we talk privately?'

'In my room,' said Mr Jobbledebhoy instantly.

He unlocked a door at the back of the shop and led the way into a storeroom, piled high with bales of cloth and sacks of scented herbs.

'Now, sir,' he said, 'How can I help you?'

Edward told him.

Mr Gomez's funeral parlour stood a little apart from other buildings, as befitted the sombre nature of Mr Gomez's trade. Its walls were pink, and a wooden cross surmounted the red tiles of the roof. A single window faced the street. The parlour's double doors were at the rear; neighbours did not care to see the melancholy traffic in coffins or bodies wrapped in blankets. At all other times, these doors were locked and padlocked.

Behind the building was a small wooden shack for the funeral carriages, with stables for their horses. Clients who had probably endured poverty from birth were adamant that their remains should travel to the grave in a carriage with silver fittings and purple drapes, drawn by horses with plumes tossing and heads bowed down by martingales.

These patient, elderly animals now stuck their heads over the stable doors and watched with mild curiosity as three men, each carrying a folded blanket, came out of the shadows that evening. They went straight to the service chute behind the parlour, and pulled to one side bales of hay which covered the manhole lid.

They lifted the lid carefully, then, one after the other, climbed down into the cellar, and pulled the lid in place again over their heads.

Inside the cellar, Edward lit a small hurricane lamp he had carried concealed in the blanket. The cellar smelled strongly of damp coal and freshly cut wood. He and his two companions wore gloves and rubber-soled shoes. They moved silently behind this light towards a wooden staircase. He climbed the stairs first, slipped the bolts on a trap door and led his companions out into the rear of the mortuary on the ground floor.

The smell here was of embalming fluid, beeswax polish and wood varnish from newly assembled coffins. Along one wall coffin lids and coffin sides were neatly stacked, ready to be assembled. Elsewhere, small piles of lacquered brass handles and nameplates winked in the gentle light of Edward's lamp. Near them stood carboys of embalming fluid, rubber pipes, syringes, kidney-shaped enamel basins and other paraphernalia of the undertaker's most private arts. In the centre of the room three coffins rested on trestles. The men crossed the floor to them.

Edward directed the hurricane lamp on to each of the engraved nameplates. The plate on the left-hand coffin read: 'Jack O'Brien'. He nodded. One of his companions produced a ratchet screwdriver. They undid the six brass screws that held down the lid and lifted it off.

The putrefying stench of the rotting headless corpse within made them all choke and stand back, swallowing nausea. One of the men spread out his blanket on the floor. Edward put his lamp down beside it and then helped him to lift out the suppurating body, which was wrapped in a crude winding-sheet. They placed the body on the blanket and folded the fabric around it carefully.

The other man produced two mule-loading ropes and trussed it firmly, while the first man filled the coffin with logs of wood from a pile near a boiler at the other end of the mortuary.

They replaced the lid, tightened the screws, then carried the body down the steps, closed and bolted the trap door above their heads, walked through the cellar and lifted the manhole cover.

The horses whinnied and stamped their feet as the three men climbed out with their bundle. They replaced the manhole cover carefully, pulled the bales of hay back across it, and within moments were carrying their burden through the back alleys of the town.

The new tower of silence stood in a clearing in the jungle half a mile away. Edward produced a key. They let themselves in through a metal door, and climbed a ladder to the huge grid fifty feet up. This was shielded by a wall a yard high, so that no-one at ground level could see the cadavers stretched out on the iron strips – or how the birds disposed of them.

In the distance, over the feathery branches of the trees, electric lights glittered like glass beads in Belize Town. The wind carried the thumping noise of the steam engine turning the big wheel; it sounded like the beat of a distant drum.

They undid the loading ropes and rolled the corpse out on the grid next to two other bodies already picked nearly clean. Then down the ladder they went thankfully. Where three men had been carrying something heavy, now three people set off on their own, walking in different directions, each carrying a folded blanket.

Next morning, a steward woke Edward at seven o'clock.

'A police officer to see you, sir,' he said, 'with a member of the Governor's staff.'

Edward dressed and went out to meet his visitors. One was a police superintendent in uniform, the other a middle-aged civilian with a florid face blotched by drink.

'Mr Edward Sodawaterwallah?' he asked brusquely.

'Yes. Who are?'

'Attorney General of the colony. This is Superintendent Pine, head of the police force. We wish to see Mrs Douglas-Wallace.'

'She is not yet awake. What is your business?'

'I am sorry to have to tell you, sir, but we have reason to believe that on a day last week, several miles out of Belize Town, in the jungle, she deliberately shot and killed Mr Jack O'Brien.'

'And what gives you reason to hold such an extraordinary belief?'

'I know how much you and Mrs Douglas-Wallace have done for the colony over the matter of giving it electricity,' said the Attorney General awkwardly, 'and I am therefore reluctant to say what I have to say. But I must tell you there is an eyewitness, and, of course, Mr O'Brien's body bears evidence of two shots having been fired at close range from a pistol of a type Superintendent Pine believes is in the possession of Mrs Douglas-Wallace.'

'I fully understand your reluctance to make such an astonishing allegation, but justice must of course be done.'

'You will then wake Mrs Douglas-Wallace, sir?'

'In due course, yes. But first, who has identified O'Brien's body?'

'A close member of his staff, Señor Gonzales, has done so.'

'No-one else?'

'That was sufficient, sir.'

'With, of course, the witness who, you say, saw the shots being fired?'

'Yes.'

'Then I propose, gentlemen, that we examine O'Brien's body together. I met him on several occasions and would recognise him, if only from his general build and his clothes. Where is the body?'

'In Mr Gomez's funeral parlour.'

'Before we wake Mrs Douglas-Wallace and alarm her with this astonishing reason for your visit, let us also find Señor Gonzales, and we can all go to the funeral parlour.'

'This is highly irregular,' said the Superintendent uneasily.

'So is life,' replied Edward. 'I appreciate what you say, but I am sure you will both agree that if we all identify the mortal remains of Jack O'Brien, and satisfy ourselves he was shot and killed by a bullet, we can save a lot of time.'

The Attorney General nodded. The Superintendent pursed his lips in disapproval, but followed them down the gangway into the waiting boat.

The town was stirring into reluctant wakefulness as they walked through the streets. Mr Gomez, a small, round-shouldered man of Mexican appearance, was tightening the girth on one of the horses hitched up to a mourners' carriage; he had an early funeral. He looked up in surprise as these three serious-faced men approached him. The Attorney General spoke.

'I understand you have in your mortuary the body of the late Jack O'Brien?'

'A body was brought in from the jungle yesterday,' Gomez agreed cautiously. 'Señor Gonzales said it was that of Mr O'Brien. It was several days old, wrapped in strips of cloth. I did not examine it closely. We put it straight away into a coffin because of the unpleasant condition it was in.'

'Then please fetch Gonzales,' said the Superintendent. 'We need to identify the body positively, and establish how he died.'

Gomez called to a groom and gave him instructions. The four men stood waiting in the shade of the building until he returned with Gonzales.

'We wish you to identify the body of the late Jack O'Brien,' the Attorney General explained.

'That I can do.'

'You must be certain it *is* his body because a charge of murder depends on this evidence,' Edward warned him.

'I realise that.'

Gomez now led the way into the mortuary, picked up a screwdriver, unscrewed the lid of the left-hand coffin and opened it.

The others gathered round it – and stood looking at a mass of wooden logs sawn into firewood lengths.

'Where's the body?' asked the Attorney General angrily.

'It *was* here, sir,' Gomez assured him. 'I helped to put it in this coffin.'

'Then where is it now?' Edward asked him. 'Has a miracle taken place in your funeral parlour, Mr Gomez? Has there been a resurrection from the dead within these walls?'

'I cannot understand it. I saw it come in with my own eyes.'

'And perhaps with your own eyes you saw it go out,' the Superintendent suggested ironically.

'No, sir. I assure you all, no.'

Edward lit a cigar.

'The body of a prominent citizen of this colony is not something easily mislaid, gentlemen,' he said conversationally. 'So let us examine facts we know, and thus perhaps discover the answer to facts we do not know.

'Yesterday, this man Gonzales was dismissed from the service of the company in which Mrs Douglas-Wallace owns a third interest. Quite clearly, this is his clumsy attempt at revenge. He wishes to punish her for what he feels she has done to him. He wants her to hang for murder.'

He paused and turned to the Attorney General.

'Your knowledge of the law, sir, is infinitely greater than mine. So doubtless you will tell me if I am wrong, but I believe that, without a body, there can be no charge of murder. Am I right?'

'That is so,' the Attorney General admitted grudgingly.

'So I suggest you address your enquiries to Gonzales here. There is presumably some charge on your statute book of wasting police time spreading malicious rumours, attempting to bring a charge of murder without a body to back it up.'

'There is the witness,' said Gonzales. 'He saw it all.'

'But that would simply be his word against Mrs Douglas-Wallace's.'

'He is right,' said the Superintendent. 'It would only be one person's word against another's. No jury would convict on that evidence.'

'I take it then, that you do not still wish to interview Mrs Douglas-Wallace?' Edward asked him.

'In these circumstances, no,' replied the Superintendent. 'We would, of course, if and when we discover the body.'

'Ah,' said Edward. 'If and when. Short words, but ones on which so many great issues can depend. Do not bother to take me back to my ship. I will hire a boat from the quay.'

He walked out from the mortuary into the brightening sunshine, and he did not look back until he was sitting in a rowing boat with two oarsmen rowing him out to *Coromandel II*. Then he glanced casually towards the forest and the tower of silence. Above it, a flock of birds was already wheeling and diving in the shimmering sky.

Fiona was waiting for him in the saloon. She had seen the visitors come and go. Edward smiled and gently put his hands on her shoulders.

'You have nothing to worry about,' he told her. 'Nothing at all.'

'They are not going to arrest me?'

'No-one is going to arrest you.'

'You are *certain*?'

'Positive.'

'Thank God,' she said fervently, and added: 'And you.' She smiled and kissed him lightly on the cheek.

For a moment, he held her close to him.

'There is something I should tell you, though,' he said casually, almost as an afterthought.

'That you still love me?'

'In addition to that, of course,' he replied. 'Since we have sacked Gonzales, Trinity-Trio needs a new agent here. I have found one for you, and I think he will prove an excellent choice. Since we are sailing so soon, I have signed him up right away. I hope you don't mind?'

'Of course not. If you think he is right for the job, that's good enough for me. Who is he?'

'A Mr Jobbledebhoy.'

London

The secretary of the Coliseum approached the chairman diffidently as he stepped from his Rolls-Royce at the front door of the club.

'I wonder if I could see you for a moment, Your Grace?' he enquired obsequiously.

'Only for a moment,' growled the duke reluctantly. He did not like to be side-tracked from the half bottle of Krug he always drank before luncheon, and the club secretary usually had such dull matters to discuss. Also, the Russian count's system had most unhappily not proved infallible. Indeed, through using it, his debts had increased alarmingly. He was in no mood for other problems, and so followed the secretary unwillingly into his little hutch of an office.

'I have just received a disturbing letter from a firm of solicitors, Ebenezer and Son,' the secretary began.

'Jew boys?'

'Oh no, sir. Theirs is a Biblical name, of course, but they are, I believe, a nonconformist family.'

'Are they now? There was an Ebenezer once my father knew years ago. Distantly related, I believe. Not close. Got in some kind of trouble with a crafty lawyer. Macnamara, I think the man was called. Well, what do they want that concerns the club?'

'They act for a property company. They are writing about the club's lease.'

'What about it?'

'It runs out next month.'

'Well, renew it.'

'That is the problem, Your Grace. On what terms?'

'Same as before, of course.'

'I fear it will not be as simple as that. They do not give us the option to renew on those terms.'

'Well, what terms do they propose?'

'Ten times the rent we are paying.'

'*Ten times!* The damn swine! Why is that?'

'I have no idea, Your Grace, but we either have to pay or go.'

'Go? Are you serious?'

'Unfortunately, I am, Your Grace.'

'Have you been on to this Ebenezer fellow and asked the reason?'

'He says this is the decision of the new owners. They have recently bought the freehold of the whole block of property. They are putting up all the rents as the leases fall in. We are only one of many tenants affected.'

'We are, are we? Who are these damn' new owners? Jew boys, eh?'

'I do not think so, Your Grace. But I am seeing Mr Ebenezer this afternoon to find out positively.'

'You do that. And tell him to tell this company, whoever it is, that we are not going to be held to ransom in this way. Dammit, we have three cabinet ministers as members. We will show them what's what, eh?'

'I very much hope so, Your Grace.'

New York

Edward and Fiona sailed north to New York from Belize Town on their way back to England. She had an appointment to keep, but first they inspected the Lion's Share factory in Trenton, New Jersey, and were extremely impressed by Leone's commitment to the project.

He had introduced several new flavours for the gum: root beer, sarsaparilla and mint leaf being the biggest sellers. Profits were still low, but increasing. This whole enterprise was not one in which Fiona personally would have become involved, but since they were, they must see that it became highly profitable as quickly as possible.

'Any problems you want to discuss with us?' Fiona asked him.

For a moment Leone thought of telling them about Franco and what he had been forced to agree with him, but then he decided against it. They were from England or India, the old world. They could not be expected to understand what it was like to be an immigrant in a new country, a new world, and to see the evil tentacles of the past reach out after you – and be powerless to avoid them.

He would have liked to confide in someone, but he did not trust the police and, anyhow, what could policemen do? They might provide him with protection for a few days, or even for a few weeks, but not forever; and when they left he would be on his own again, alone, and more vulnerable than ever because he had spoken of matters about which he should have kept silent. So Leone shook his head, but Fiona saw the flicker of doubt in his eyes and wondered what was troubling him, and why he declined to discuss it.

'There *is* one thing,' he said suddenly. 'Toothpaste we manufacture in the other part of the building is selling steadily, but somehow no amount of advertising seems to improve its sales. They remain static. We are running two shifts in the factory but we could easily manage three.'

'Why not try new advertisements, a totally new approach to those I see on the hoardings now?' Edward asked him.

'We have,' Leone replied, 'with even worse results. So we went back to the original campaign. The trouble is that a tube of toothpaste lasts, on average, for twenty days, and then the customer buys another one – either our make, or someone else's. Usually, they stay loyal to one brand. Our problem, if we cannot persuade more people to use our product, is to make our buyers use more paste – and that seems impossible.'

Edward opened a glass-fronted display cabinet of Trinity-Trio pharmaceutical products and took out a tube of toothpaste. He unscrewed the top, squeezed half an inch of the paste on to a piece of paper.

'That is the amount everyone uses on their toothbrush, right?' he asked. Leone nodded.

'Yes. Our survey on the matter shows that they rarely use more, and almost never less.'

'Then I will show you how to double your sales – and the profits,' said Edward. 'Simply make the hole in each tube twice as large. Then double the amount of paste will be squeezed out – but to the same length. Customers will have to come back every ten days, and not every twenty.'

'Great!' said Leone in admiration. 'Have you any other good ideas like that?'

'I have one,' replied Fiona with a smile. 'In this cabinet there are tubes of different sizes, even different shapes, that you have never used. Why not?'

'They are simply dummies. We thought of using them and then decided against it. They looked wrong, somehow.'

'For Lion's Share products, maybe,' agreed Fiona. 'But get out to the stores. See the buyers. Offer to fill these tubes for them and then they put *their* names on them. That way, you make nearly as much profit without any advertising costs, and they have an advertisement for their store on hundreds of thousands of bathroom shelves, week after week after week.'

'Mrs Douglas-Wallace, you should come here more often,' said Leone admiringly.

'Mr Pastellini,' said Fiona, 'we intend to. But right now, we are looking into the possibility of manufacturing explosives in the States.'

'You mean gunpowder? That sort of thing?'

'Yes. We have a Chinese formula for an explosive which no-one outside of China seems to be using. It is phenomenally powerful.'

'The du Pont people in Wilmington, Delaware, are masters at explosives. You should see them.'

'We will,' said Fiona. 'I have already made an appointment with them for the end of next week.'

* * *

Fiona had read the extraordinary history of the du Pont family, and been impressed by their remarkable dedication and achievement. Irenee du Pont had arrived in the United States after the French Revolution and settled, with his wife and family, on a 95-acre farm at Brandywine Creek, near Wilmington, Delaware.

When Irenee was a boy in France, he had been interested in chemistry and biology, and as a hobby had grown a number of pot plants from seeds. One day, a family friend, the scientist and chemist Antoine Lavoisier, gave him a packet of saltpetre to mix with the soil in the flower pots to make the plants grow more quickly. He explained to Irenee that saltpetre possessed unusual qualities. While it was an excellent fertiliser for the soil, a more important application lay in the manufacture of explosives.

Lavoisier was in charge of the French government's gunpowder factory at Essonne, and he took young Irenee along to the works to see how saltpetre was mixed with sulphur and charcoal to produce gunpowder.

Irenee was fascinated, and in his teens became Lavoisier's laboratory assistant. Here he learned how to refine saltpetre and sulphur, then to mix them with willow wood charcoal, and to polish and grind and press the mixture into the product known as black powder or gunpowder. Lavoisier was greatly impressed by the young man's abilities, and even saw him as his successor, when he retired.

But after the French Revolution, life became difficult for people of culture and ambition in France. Lavoisier was transferred to other work, and Irenee, who was married by then, with a young family, emigrated to the United States, where relatives had already settled. Out shooting with some friends one day, they ran out of powder, and had to buy some more at a country shop. Irenee du Pont was so disgusted with its poor quality and high price that he decided to manufacture his own, and with capital from other immigrants, he set up a small factory.

The market for gunpowder was large. Hunters and trappers, who supplied animal furs for export, used a great deal. Much larger quantities were needed to blast away rocks to build roads and railways as more and more people moved west to California.

The du Pont company grew over the years as the demand for commercial explosives increased dramatically. The Panama Canal, begun in 1904, used 61,000,000 pounds – 27,232 tons – of du Pont dynamite. The New York City subway system and Grand Central railway terminal, and water supply systems, such as the Los Angeles and the Catskill aqueducts, and other huge construction projects, needed 300,000,000 pounds – 133,928 tons – of dynamite and almost as much black powder every year.

The du Pont concern had produced gunpowder for the United States armed forces for many years. Initially, the government asked them to investigate the possibilities of acquiring secret formulae used by the French and British for their high-efficiency military explosives.

This proved impossible, so the enterprising du Ponts built a special laboratory to perfect their own. They were successful, but their success as the largest United States producer of all manner of explosives for use in peace and war inevitably brought criticism. It was claimed that competition in the industry was negligible because the du Ponts held a virtual monopoly. Against this background of success and the criticism attendant on it, Fiona and Edward arrived in Wilmington for their appointment with a senior manager of the company.

Fiona explained to him that Trinity-Trio held the formula for an unusually strong and effective explosive powder.

'We have come here to propose that our two companies collaborate to make this powder in the United States – as eventually we hope to manufacture it ourselves in England.'

'I am fully aware of the success of Trinity-Trio as a trading company, ma'am,' the manager replied, 'but, with respect, I think it is unlikely that your powder will be superior to powders we are already producing. I cannot find any instance of your company inventing explosive powders or manufacturing them, whether alone or in collaboration.

'On the other hand, we at du Pont maintain very large technical and development departments, staffed by chemists with the highest qualifications. They are working continually on new products, as well as refining our current range. Our policy is one of constant improvement and we spend a great deal of money every year on research. So before we could discuss any fusion of interests, we would, of course, have to analyse your powder.'

'I understand your reasons,' replied Fiona. 'But I do not think we could allow that at this moment.'

The manager was used to letters and visits from strangers who claimed to have invented secret explosives of unprecedented power, but who were reluctant to put them to analysis. Here, however, he was surprised at this hackneyed response.

'If you suspect, ma'am, we would steal the formula, I can assure you we would not. But I think you will agree that, as a result of our position for very many years as leaders in this industry, it seems possible – I would not put it higher – that our chemists may already have been working on at least a similar formula.

'They might have abandoned it for technical or other reasons, or we may even be about to put it into full production – if indeed we are not already producing it commercially.'

'I accept that, sir,' said Edward. 'But I believe that actions alway speak more conclusively than words. Could I give you a simple demonstration with a target and a revolver, using your best powder for a weapon of that kind and calibre?'

'By all means.'

They went deep into the heart of the building, into a concrete room which contained a small arms firing range. An employee set up two targets against the far wall and handed a .38 revolver to Edward. He put two of his own cartridges into the cylinder and fired at the left-hand target. Then he removed the cartridge cases, slipped in two cartridges the manager handed to him, and fired at the second target.

The manager took down both targets and examined the bullet holes through a magnifying glass.

'Your powder certainly *appears* very strong,' he admitted cautiously. 'Perhaps even stronger than the one we used against it. But we will still need to analyse it.'

Edward nodded.

'I will discuss this with my wife,' he said, and turned to Fiona.

Suddenly, he saw her eyes flutter, her head loll to one side. She collapsed on the floor at their feet.

'Quick!' cried the manager. 'She needs air.'

They carried Fiona into an office, and laid her down on a sofa.

'I will call our first aid department,' he said.

'There is no need,' Edward replied. 'I think the noise and smell of the powder in that confined space overcame her. We have been travelling for several days and she is tired.

'I will take her to our hotel, where she can rest. We have a car outside. I apologise for this, sir, but I will be in touch with you as soon as possible.'

Back in the hotel, Edward gave Fiona a brandy.

'What a fool I feel,' she said as she sipped it. 'But at least I got you out before you agreed to have our powder analysed.'

'So you only pretended to faint?'

She blushed.

'It is a very obvious step for du Pont to take,' Edward argued. 'When people offer Trinity-Trio merchandise to sell, you always test everything to make sure it is of the stated quality. The du Ponts are only doing this, too. You must see that?'

'I do. But even if they agreed to manufacture our powder, it would be only one very small item out of dozens they make. Let's do it *ourselves* – for *our* country.'

'We would save a lot of trouble and money if we did it here with them first,' Edward replied practically. 'They have the best technicians and the finest plant in the world. On our own, we would have to start from scratch, and about two hundred years behind them.'

He paused, looking at Fiona closely.

'You are sure you didn't *really* faint?' he asked her. 'You certainly looked very pale.'

Fiona smiled.

'I have been keeping it from you,' she said. 'But now I must tell you. I am going to have a baby.'

Fiona and Edward were married quietly as soon as they returned to England. Clive was born eight months later, a premature baby, and after such a difficult birth that the doctors told Fiona she would never be able to have another child. When she looked at Clive, pink-faced and wrinkled in his bassinet, she could not be absolutely certain whether she was sorry about this or relieved.

She had nursemaids to look after him, and so his arrival did not impinge in any way on her social life or, more important, on her business involvement with Trinity-Trio. She admitted to herself (but not even to Edward) that she felt happiest in the middle of complex negotiations, such as the take-over of another company or the expansion of an existing concern.

It seemed to her, but again she kept these thoughts to herself, that while many women were pleased to find fulfilment in their children, or at least gave every appearance of doing so, she found equal – if not more – satisfaction in expanding the firm in which she had inherited such an important share.

She saw Clive every morning in the nursery and again in the evening. So long as she was at home and not at the theatre or attending some official dinner with Edward, the boy was brought down by the nursemaid on duty to the drawing room for them to say goodnight.

Fiona tried to love him but found this extraordinarily difficult. She had seen so many mothers pick up their children, cuddle them, coo over them, and kiss them, but she never felt drawn to such displays of affection with Clive. He seemed too plump, often bad-tempered, always self-centred. He was not the sort of child who would relish being picked up – and she was not the sort of mother to want to do so.

From a very early age, he would petulantly throw toys out of his cot, and scream if he could not get his own way, tearing the legs and arms off a teddy bear in paroxysms of temper. Looking at him during these tantrums she felt little affinity with him, but again these were feelings she could not discuss with anyone, not even with her husband.

After their experience with the du Pont Company, Fiona and Edward, on behalf of Trinity-Trio, attempted to interest British factories in producing explosives based on the Chinese pattern. Fifty-odd years earlier, a Swiss scientist, Professor Christian Schoenbein, had produced nitrated cotton, to which he gave the name guncotton, and around the same time an Italian, Professor Ascanio Sobrero, working in Turin, invented nitro-glycerine.

These two discoveries were soon attended by disasters on a colossal scale. In Faversham, in Kent, a factory built to manufacture guncotton blew up with such heavy casualties that for the next twenty years no-one attempted to produce it commercially. Nitro-glycerine was even less stable than guncotton. While it would withstand warmth, sudden heat could cause it to explode without warning.

Although guncotton could be used for military purposes, to blast a fortification or breach a dam, it was unsuitable for propelling shells or cartridges. Scientists discovered that the addition of picric acid partially solved the problem, but again the resulting product was dangerously volatile. Because of spontaneous combustion in the ship's magazine, the Japanese battleship *Mikasa* blew up in September 1905, and 599 lives were lost. In the following January, the Brazilian battleship *Aquidaban* exploded off Rio de Janeiro with 213 deaths, and two months later, the French warship *Jenna* disintegrated in Toulon harbour with 114 dead.

The Chinese powder that Fiona and Edward had to offer could be stored without the risk of such catastrophes, and handled safely by untrained personnel, while combining the best qualities of guncotton and nitro-glycerine. Quite simply, they believed that it was the world's most powerful – and safest – propellant for cartridges and shells.

The managing director of an explosives factory in Erith, in Kent, only a few miles from Gravesend, from where Dr Richard Jackson had originally sailed to fortune, readily admitted its unique qualities.

'We are totally committed to contracts we already have,' the director explained to Fiona and Edward. 'I am sorry, because your product is infinitely superior, but we have to honour our bond.'

'I appreciate that,' said Edward, 'but we feel so strongly about the merits of this explosive that our company is prepared to underwrite building a special factory to produce it. Our powder is smokeless, which means it would be impossible for an enemy to see the telltale puff of smoke that can give away an artillery site – or even a sniper's position. It is safe to handle – and far more efficient than present powders. And neither you nor the government would have any development costs to bear whatever. All we would seek in return is a small commission on powder made and sold.'

'An interesting proposition,' the director agreed. 'But I fear you already have my answer.' He had never done business with a man and woman team; he was not quite sure how to proceed. 'Most interesting. But, sadly, not for us.'

'What if we sold it to a foreign power?'

'I think you would find the same lack of interest,' he said. 'Have you tried the Americans, du Pont? They are the leaders over there.'

'Yes,' said Fiona. 'We have.'

'With what result?'

'We did not wish them to analyse our powder, and so our negotiations broke down.'

'That is the considered opinion of a first-class firm in private hands, ma'am, dedicated to making a profit, not a government concern. I fully understand their point of view, just as I appreciate the patriotic motive behind your offer, but I am sure you will understand that we simply cannot take advantage of it.'

Fiona and Edward received the same response from the heads of all other explosive factories they visited. Their product was everywhere admitted to be vastly superior to anything in production, but paradoxically, no-one wished to produce it.

The Riviera

Robert Jackson and Joanna Gray were married that autumn, despite T'a Ki's displeasure. They spent their honeymoon on the French Riviera, not yet popular in summer, but from September onwards, a magnet for the wealthy. King Edward VII had made the Riviera fashionable; hotels and roads were given such English names as The Bristol, The George, the Promenade des Anglais.

For the journey, Jackson had bought one of the new London-Edinburgh Rolls-Royce Silver Ghosts, a magnificent machine with a body of polished aluminium that glittered in the sun like a travelling heliograph. The car took its name from a demonstration Rolls-Royce made, driving from London to Edinburgh in top gear, a remarkable feat for any car. Its huge silver-plated headlamps had mirror reflectors, and a swivelling searchlight that enabled the driver to read signposts when travelling unknown roads at night. They took a chauffeur with them as far as Paris, then sent him home and Jackson drove the rest of the way.

With the scrubbed canvas hood folded back, their splendid barouche travelling down sun-bathed roads, straight as the poplars that lined them, Joanna knew she had never been so happy. In the years ahead, whenever she saw a poplar, or admired the Parthenon shape of a Rolls radiator, or its silver mascot, a young girl, loosely draped, gracefully leaning forward into the future, she knew she would remember this drive.

'We have been sitting behind that mascot for hours,' she remarked dreamily. 'We should give her a name.'

'She already has one,' Robert replied. 'The Spirit of Ecstasy. Somehow, she symbolises everything I admire in England. The beauty of the countryside, the feeling you all possess that because you are British you are somehow superior in outlook, intellect – everything – to all other nations. Grace. Youth. Endeavour.'

'All qualities you also already possess in abundance,' Joanna answered him with a smile. '*And* you are British, too.'

'Only half,' he replied, and for a moment she saw a twinge of pain in his eyes. He was remembering sneers at school in Calcutta, the fact that he still secretly felt he was somehow an alien, on sufferance; one of them, not one of us. Then his face lit up as he remembered something.

'I didn't tell you,' he said, 'but the very day we got married, the absolute actual day, I had a wonderful surprise. I was elected a member of the Coliseum Club.'

'I am delighted,' Joanna said, putting an arm round his shoulders. 'You should have told me.'

'I had other things on my mind,' he replied.

She blushed.

'That really means something to you, doesn't it, belonging to the Coliseum?' she said, looking at him proudly.

'You have no idea how much,' he admitted. 'I feel that it is somehow an accolade, a welcome to England. All those famous men, lords and dukes and goodness knows who else, have voted that I should join their club. They accept me, not as a half-caste but as an equal.'

'I can't see why that matters so much. With our shares in Trinity-Trio, you must be as rich as any of them.'

'It's not a question of money,' he replied, remembering his mother's opinion. 'It's a question of being wanted. You have always been English. You have never had people smiling behind your back at your accent or your looks, or the fact that your mother was Chinese. I have. Often. But now I can forget all that. It's all behind me. Forever.'

Joanna leaned back against the buttoned leather upholstery. The sun, growing stronger with every mile they drove south, warmed her face and her bare arms. As the great car soared on, silent as a passing cloud or the ghost from which it took its name, she felt bathed not only in sunlight but in happiness. This was a time to treasure, to store in the safe places of the mind. It must never be allowed to wither, never grow dim.

'You say our mascot, the Spirit of Ecstasy, sums up for you everything you like in England,' she said dreamily. 'For me it sums up something else – my life since we met, since we both became so incredibly fortunate. I will always remember this drive, and the sun on my face, and you by my side, and the hum of the engine like the surge of the sea or a great swarm of dreamy bees.'

She decided that when they returned to England she would order a Rolls mascot, have it mounted on an ebony plinth and keep it on her writing desk. Then, should she ever feel unhappy, or should life ever offer less than she hoped for, it would remind her of this journey, and her feeling of total contentment.

Each evening, they stopped at a small auberge. The impressive opulence of their car, and their expensive hide luggage, brought special deference from inn-keepers to whom Jackson was immediately *Milord anglais*. The inns were invariably simple: a small restaurant, sometimes simply part of the kitchen, and a bedroom with scrubbed floor, print curtains and bowls of newly picked flowers – everything clean and fresh. Joanna had grown accustomed to sparseness in her upbringing, but this was something new; simplicity with style.

She was surprised at the sheer size of France, its rolling miles of fields and forests and hills between each village, the ungainly farm carts with huge wheels and shaggy horses, the smell of pine woods and garlic and pungent French tobacco.

In Nice, Jackson had booked a suite at the Negresco, overlooking the Mediterranean. Across the Promenade des Anglais and the beach, lay the glittering sea.

'I could never imagine a sea as blue as this,' Joanna said in amazement. 'In England, it is green and cold – or grey and cold.'

'Probably the same here out of season, when it's raining,' replied Jackson. 'But I'm told it is rather like the Danube in one respect. The Danube is generally a pretty dirty river, but it becomes the blue Danube – if you look at it when you're in love.'

'That *must* be the reason,' she said, and laughed.

She found it difficult to accept that she could order anything she wanted on the menu; that she could buy any dress, any jewellery. She could even buy a house by the sea.

'Let's do that,' said Jackson impulsively. 'We'll buy a chateau a mile or so inland, with the hills behind us and the sea in front.'

'But we can't *live* here,' said Joanna, being practical, remembering the cottage by the Thames where she had lived all her life.

'We can,' he told her. 'For as long as we want. Whenever we want.'

'But who will look after it when we're not here? Who will keep the garden tidy?'

'My dear Joanna, there are any number of people here aching to work for us, and have everything ready for us when we come on our own or with our friends – maybe, in the future, I hope, with our family.'

'But I can't see how we will pay for it,' she protested. 'It will cost such a lot of money.'

'Darling,' said Jackson softly. 'I had to tell Arbuthnott at *The Enquirer* this, but I don't expect to have tell to you. We *have* such a lot of money. Both of us. . . .'

After three weeks in the sun, they drove north through Switzerland. The passes were still open, and Joanna was delighted to see snow and yet sunshine so strong she had to put on dark glasses.

Their return journey had the same timeless enchantment about it that had marked the drive south. Every day seemed more than just another day, another drive; it became a totally new adventure. Tiny villages; cattle wearing leather thongs around their necks and polished metal bells; little wooden houses perched high on hillsides, bright with flowers; men and women in quaint peasant costumes that seemed out of the Middle Ages.

'What other countries can we go through?' she asked, wanting the journey to continue indefinitely.

'I suggest we should motor through Germany, follow the Rhine north, and then turn west through Belgium. We could then go along the French coast to Boulogne, where we can find a boat to carry the car and us back home.'

'*This* is home,' said Joanna gently, looking around the sitting room in their hotel; at heavy waxed beams, blackened by smoke from the fire in its iron grate; at thick ornamental candles; wrought iron carvings.

'Nice and all the little places we stayed at on the way down were also home, because you are with me, because home is where we both are, where love is.'

'Darling,' he said, 'no-one has ever said that to me before.'

'And I've never said it to anyone else. And I will never say it to anyone else, only to you.'

The Rhine, when they reached it, stretched in a wide proud sweep of glittering water, between high rocky cliffs covered with shrubs. Jackson stopped the car opposite a solid wall of rock.

'The home of the Lorelei,' he announced grandly, like a theatre impresario. 'A siren whose voice was so enchanting and her beauty so unbelievable, that to hear and see her bewitched sailors in their ships. They forgot the dangerous rapids and reefs, and their boats would sink and they'd be drowned.

'She even lured the son of the local ruler to his death. His father called out the army to catch this witch. She knew she could not escape, so she called on *her* father, the Rhine, for help. The river sent huge waves, higher than anyone had ever known, and they carried her away safely.

'She was never seen again. But sometimes, in the moonlight, her voice is still heard.'

'Is that true?' Joanna asked.

'An interpretation of a truth,' replied Jackson diplomatically. 'That rock has an extraordinary echo which sounds exactly like a voice. Even in the last century, ships passing up river would sound a three bells warning here to tell the crew it was time to pray that they might avoid the hidden rocks.'

'Why was the Lorelei a woman?'

'Because sailors are men.'

They laughed, and Jackson started the car. It slid forward, the silver mascot silhouetted now against the glitter of the river, now against the green of the hills.

'The Spirit of Ecstasy,' Joanna said raptly. 'Our Lorelei.'

'I wonder if the model for the mascot would think so,' said Jackson.

'Who is she?'

'A very pretty girl indeed, Eleanor Velasco Thornton, who comes from Stockwell in south London – not a very fashionable address. The head printer of *The Enquirer*, Mr Erskine, lives there. He knows her father, a telegraph engineer. Her mother is partly Spanish, hence the middle name, Velasco.

'When Eleanor was sixteen she became secretary to Claude Johnson, then the secretary of the Automobile Club.

'Johnson went on to become managing director of Rolls-Royce. Rolls was an aristocrat who dabbled in selling cars and was killed flying in a gas balloon. Royce is a North Country engineer, a perfectionist. Johnson is a business man, who accepts the basic fact that the company must still make a profit. He is nicknamed "The Hyphen" between Rolls and Royce.

'Through him Eleanor met the present Lord Montagu, then John Scott-Montagu. She became his secretary and helped him to launch *The Car Illustrated* magazine, the first motoring magazine. They started an affair – more than an affair. They fell in love, and she bore his daughter.

'Last year, Rolls-Royce decided they needed a mascot, a special symbol of elegance and speed, so they offered Charles Sykes, the artist, £30 to design one. He knows Eleanor and asked her to pose. At first the result was called the Spirit of Speed, now it is the Spirit of Ecstasy. Motor dealers refer to it more bluntly as "Miss Thornton in her flowing nightie".'

'How do you know all this?'

'I was introduced to Claude Johnson in the Coliseum a few weeks ago. He told me himself.'

'Two legends, two loves,' said Joanna.

'Make it three,' suggested Jackson. 'Ours. *Damn!*'

He swung around a corner on the gravelled road – and then swerved violently to avoid a stationary car parked at the roadside. A tall man with a waxed moustache, its ends twisted into points and slightly upturned, was standing by the bonnet, watching his chauffeur work on the engine. He looked on in horror as Jackson missed his car by inches.

'Damn' silly place to stop,' said Jackson angrily.

'They probably had no option. They appear to have broken down,' Joanna pointed out.

'Then I'll see if I can help him push his car forward a bit. If we had been going fast we could have ploughed right into it.'

He stopped the Rolls, climbed out, and walked back.

The tall man clicked his heels together and bowed stiffly from the waist.

'Colonel Obermann,' he said in English. 'At your service.'

'Robert Jackson, sir. Perhaps I can be of service to you? It's a dangerous place to stop.'

'We had no choice. There is something wrong with the ignition. Our engine just went – phht!'

'Can I help you and your man to push it farther off the road?'

'You are very kind, sir, but there is no need. My driver has located the fault.'

'I have an extensive tool kit if that would be of use?'

'That is extremely generous of you, sir, but that will not be necessary. My driver is fully competent.'

'Very well,' said Jackson. He bowed and walked back to his car.

The colonel watched him out of sight.

'Damned insolent, condescending English swine,' he said to himself.

Jackson and Joanna drove to the next town, Boppard, on the bank of the Rhine. A double row of chestnut trees grew along a wide promenade by the river, with pale green metal railings, and red geraniums in boxes. They ate lunch in a restaurant overlooking lines of slow-moving barges, propelled from behind by sturdy tugs. Seagulls dipped and wheeled above paddle steamers packed with tourists. Brass bands in the stern of each steamer played military marches.

Robert and Joanna left Boppard at about the same time as Colonel Obermann was entering the town. He had been delayed much longer than he had anticipated and sat by his driver, clenching and unclenching his hands in his irritation.

He ordered the driver to stop outside a house off the Casinostrasse, near the eighteenth-century monastery building now used for meetings of the town council. A servant, watching out for him, had seen the car and already the front door was open. He bowed obsequiously as he took the colonel's coat and hat. Two men wearing white coats came out from the back of the house, clicked their heels respectfully and bowed. The visit of Colonel Obermann, the Inspector General of Armaments of the Imperial German Government, was a rare honour; these two scientists from the Department of Explosives were nervously conscious of its importance.

Usually, they dealt with underlings; Colonel Obermann was only a name to them. Now he was here in this house which contained their secret laboratory. Who knew what promotion, even honours, could flow from such a visit?

They led the colonel to an upper room of the house. This was empty, except for a solidly built table with a polished aluminium top. On this table, in a small saucer, was a tiny pyramid of black powder crystals. A number of revolver cartridges of different sizes and two pistol-shooting targets peppered with holes were ranged beside the saucer.

The senior scientist cleared his throat nervously, anxious to make the best possible impression. He picked up one of the cards.

'You will see, Herr Colonel, an army marksman shot at this card with cartridges of government issue for the Mauser. He fired at this second card with the same pistol, but using cartridges we had made up, having analysed the powder found in cartridges of unknown make received from our contact in British Honduras.

'You will observe, sir, that the penetration is very much deeper on the second card. Gramme for gramme this is a far superior explosive.'

The colonel picked up the two cards and put them down again.

'Most interesting,' he said insincerely.

He was never at ease with scientists; they might have brains, but they lacked breeding. Why, these two weedy, nervous characters would run like stags if they heard a single shot fired in rage, yet they could spend their lives pottering around with saucers of explosives like alchemists. No gentleman would do that; or could – or should – do that.

Colonel Obermann owed his own position of authority to the fact that he had served in the same regiment as his predecessor, and that he was also due to inherit from his elderly and ailing father an estate of 60,000 hectares, where the boar shooting was generally considered to be the best in Bavaria. He had originally been scheduled to visit Boppard a week previously, but had managed to postpone the journey because a brother officer's wife, with whom he was on the closest and most shamefully intimate terms, had been away with her husband in Baden-Baden.

Now she was home, only three kilometres from Boppard, and her husband was absent on manoeuvres. The rest of the afternoon could be better employed on a chaise longue than in this bleak laboratory. He glanced at his gold hunter. He was very late already; he could not afford to spend any more time here with these people. He had seen all he needed to see, such as it was.

'Well, gentlemen,' he said briskly, 'this has been a most instructive visit. I will make my report accordingly.'

'I cannot stress enough, sir, that this is an extremely powerful explosive. It contains saltpetre of a much higher quality than we are importing from Chile. I suspect it is even better than the superior saltpetre used by the English, which they import from Bihar in India.

'My belief is that it may come from China, which I know has large deposits, but which it has always been impossible to export because of difficulties with their rulers.'

'Quite, quite,' said the colonel. 'I will phrase my report to that effect.'

The two scientists accompanied him to the door of the house. The second scientist had been nervous of expressing an opinion in front of his superior but now he said urgently: 'If I may speak, sir, this is the strongest explosive powder we have *ever* analysed. We have arranged a special demonstration to show its strength for other military purposes. It will only take a few moments of your time to see this, Herr Colonel, I assure you.'

'That is very good of you, but I regret I am pressed for time. My motor broke down on the way here. Please be assured I am much impressed by what I have seen already. Should any members of the Imperial Staff wish to see this demonstration, I am sure they will be in contact with you through the proper channels.'

The colonel was bored by these dull, earnest fellows. His thoughts were racing ahead to the prospect of an afternoon, an evening, perhaps even an entire night with his brother officer's wife. The chauffeur saluted, and the colonel stepped into his car and sat back thankfully on the buttoned leather seat.

A week later – because the husband of his mistress was away for much longer than anticipated, and so the colonel was able to prolong his stay – he dictated his report from memory. He had not taken notes, although the scientists had offered him a note pad. He thought that scribbling away was demeaning, ungentlemanly; like a policeman at the scene of a crime, or, heaven forbid, a newspaper reporter. As a result, he lacked formulae and figures and could only couch his report in general, and hence unconvincing, terms.

> 'This day in Laboratory No. 14, I saw a demonstration of the power of a new smokeless cartridge powder. The demonstration was impressive, but, in my opinion, does not warrant further detailed investigation. Its penetration power at short range was slightly better than the powder in present service, a point to which both scientists drew my attention. No experiments were made in my presence with longer range penetration. My recommendation is therefore that, at present, no further action need be taken. The results would not warrant the cost of changing to this powder in view of our present contracts with suppliers.'

Back in the laboratory, the two scientists had written their own reports and pinned the targets to them. The cartridges they had made and which had not been fired, were put in a cardboard box in a cupboard, ready in case – as they hoped – the Imperial Staff should ask to see a further, more extensive demonstration. They locked the door and put the key in a drawer in the senior scientist's desk.

The laboratory was cleaned early every morning by an old man, Wilhelm Chotek, who did other odd jobs around the house and garden. He augmented his larder by shooting hares, which on his meagre pay he could not always afford to buy in the market. The scientists therefore allowed him to take any cartridges for which they had no further use. If they did not give him any, he would sometimes help himself; he knew where they were all kept in their neatly labelled boxes.

It was, of course, important that he did not remove too many without permission, because then the theft would be noticed. A majority of the boxes held at most a dozen cartridges of different types, and he passed them by. The exception was this last box, in which he counted 25. He put six in his pocket, two for himself and four for his nephew, his sister's son, who had descended unannounced upon him and his wife for a few days. Years ago, his sister had unwisely married a Hungarian who had been a waster, and in Wilhelm's opinion, their son, Petar Princip, was no better: a thin, pale, round-shouldered youth, who claimed to be a student but who early on had found the discipline of scholarship too strict. He did odd jobs, by the day or even the hour, and scrounged any items that he could sell, or exchange for a meal. The cartridges he asked for were doubtless intended to pay the bill of some café owner who had given him food or drink.

The old man had no use for such layabouts, and he envied Petar his youth and his opportunities to better himself. He could not understand why he did not take advantage of them. However, he was his sister's son. He would give him the four cartridges that he could trade for a drink or a cup of coffee. Then he locked the cupboard, replaced the key in the senior scientist's desk, and went home.

London

When the last guest had left Robert Jackson's house in Belgravia, he stood for a moment in the hall, adjusting his black tie in the gilt-framed Louis XI mirror. The knot was as perfect as the fold of his silk-faced lapel, and the cut of his jacket. He was not really concerned about these things at the end of the evening; he simply wanted to check whether he looked as depressed as he felt. He rather thought he did not. At least, he hoped he did not.

Joanna came into the hall from the drawing room.

'What's the matter, darling?' she asked him.

'Why should anything be the matter?'

'Well, something is. I felt worried at giving our first important dinner party, and you have been depressed all evening, ever since you came back from the office. I wondered whether it was a total failure?'

'The reverse. It – and especially you – were a total success.'

'Then why the gloomy looks?'

'I am sorry, I did not think you'd notice. I tried my utmost to keep my feelings concealed. After all, you had twenty people for dinner tonight, including the Foreign Secretary, and God knows who else, and it was all magnificent. Congratulations.'

'Thank you kindly. So now will you tell me what is the problem?'

'A familiar one in the newspaper business,' he explained. '*The Enquirer* is losing money. Heavily. Much more than I realised. I have dismissed the editor and the advertising manager, and I am sorry to say that the women journalists writing for us are simply not attracting new women readers, as I had hoped.'

'I can believe that,' Joanna said at once. 'They probably live in semi-detached houses in Clapham or Penge, yet they write articles about who takes precedence at a dinner party if the guests include a bishop and an ambassador. *Enquirer* readers don't *go* to dinners like that. Not many of them, at least.

'You have to interest all sorts of people who may never have bought a newspaper before. Make *them* regular readers. They will tell their friends how good the *Enquirer* is, and the effect snowballs.'

'Agreed. But how do you suggest we do that?'

'I will do my own research,' Joanna promised him, 'and come up with an idea by the end of the week.'

Robert kissed her.

'I should have told you earlier on,' he said gratefully. 'Next time, I will.'

'Promise?'

'Promise.'

Early the following morning, after Robert had left for the office, Joanna changed into her oldest clothes, wrapped a scarf around her head instead of a hat, and let herself out of the house. She hailed a passing cab.

'Victoria Embankment,' she told the driver. 'Stop opposite Cleopatra's Needle.'

She paid off the taxi and began to walk along the wide pavement, watching barges on the river, without any plan in mind. But she had been brought up near the Thames, and found the flow of the water peaceful and reassuring. The river had the power of all familiar things to soothe – and stimulate. Rows of plane trees along the Embankment were weeping yellow leaves, tears for a summer that had all but gone. She walked slowly, like someone without any aim. Tramps and vagrants sitting on the benches all ignored her. Some tried to sleep, hands tucked under their armpits for warmth, heads sunk on their chests. A few were wrapped in old newspapers, looking like huge parcels waiting to be delivered.

Children with thin, pinched faces followed her hopefully, wondering whether she would give them a coin, but Joanna shook her head dispiritedly to show she also was without money or hope, a derelict like the Embankment people.

She reached a bench which had one middle-aged man sitting at the far end, reading a copy of *The Enquirer*. She saw from the front page that this was three days old and stained with mud. He must have picked it out of the gutter, or maybe he had slept under an archway with it wrapped around him.

He glanced up at her briefly and without interest as she sat down. He seemed a cheerful enough person, unshaven, with a red face and a bright eye. A brass collar stud gleamed like a precious stone in the neckband of his shirt. She guessed he had probably come up from the country in search of a job and found nothing. Now, he had nowhere to go. This, she suddenly realised, could be exactly the sort of person to solve their problem: willing to work, but with no work to do, and none in prospect.

'It is very cold today,' she began tentatively.

'It is that, Ma,' he replied. 'Especially when you've had no breakfast.'

'I am lucky enough to have had breakfast, *and* I found a florin.'

She passed the coin to him. He looked at her in surprise. Why should she give him money? What was she after? Where was the trick?

'Buy yourself something,' she told him. 'Money is made round because it is meant to go round.'

'Are you sure you don't want it yourself, Ma?'

She could see reluctance fight anticipation in his face. His cheeks were hollow with hunger; their rosy colour came more from cold than health.

'Certain,' she said.

'Then thank you very much indeed, Ma, bless you.'

A hand creased with dirt closed firmly over the coin like a claw. Behind them, trams groaned and ground their way along the rails towards Blackfriars Bridge, spitting sparks from their overhead power lines. Chauffeurs driving City merchants to offices blew imperiously on the horns of their limousines.

'All right for some,' said the man, nodding towards them, not bitterly simply stating what appeared to him to be an obvious fact.

'I suppose it is,' she agreed, as though willing to talk. 'If that is what you want. I don't really know what I want. Tell me, what do *you* want most out of life?'

He looked at her then, as if seeing her for the first time.

'Money,' he said. 'Not a lot, mind you. Not like those rich people in their big cars, but enough *never* to be hungry or cold again. Never to have to sleep rough under the arches by Charing Cross station, or near a hot air vent outside an hotel up West. That's what *I* want.'

'How much money?' Joanna asked him curiously. 'I heard someone say once that people either had nothing – or not enough.'

'I'd never say that,' he replied instantly. 'If I could get a quid a week, that would be marvellous. But a *fiver* a week – that's riches. That's what I'd like, five pounds a week until the day I die. I'd do anything for that, Ma. Well, almost anything.'

'A wonderful idea,' she told him. 'Do you think lots of other people would agree?'

'Millions of 'em,' he assured her. 'It's a fortune, Ma, nearly twice what a skilled man gets for six days' hard work out of every seven. *And* I'd have it for doing nothing at all!'

As he spoke, Joanna realised she had found the answer to *The Enquirer*'s circulation problem. That night she told Robert of this conversation.

'Run a competition,' she said. 'Offer a prize to the winner of five pounds a week for life. Not for a month or for a year, but for as long as they live. That's only two hundred and fifty pounds a year, and if you award it to an old man or woman, you will probably have less than a thousand to pay.'

'A brilliant idea,' said Robert enthusiastically.

'I am glad you think so. And here's another one: you make it a condition that everyone who enters the competition agrees to buy the paper every day for at least one week. If they take it for a month or more, they become eligible for full life insurance. Not the penny a week pittance they may already be paying to friendly societies and so forth to make sure they receive a decent burial, but to give them a nest-egg after so many years – twenty pounds, perhaps, maybe even a hundred – to spend as they like.

'Trinity-Trio could fund it easily enough. Think how that would boost circulation, and also actually help readers who have not the money to help themselves. I know what it is like to be in that situation, remember. And my mother experienced it all her life.'

'Joanna,' said Robert admiringly, 'you're a genius.'

'I'm happier to be called Mrs Jackson. And there's one other thing.'

'What's that?'

'Send a reporter down to the Embankment. On the bench near Cleopatra's Needle he'll find the fellow I had a talk with this morning, who gave me the idea. Give him a present, something generous. Say twenty pounds.'

'I'll give him much more. I'll give *him* his pension for life! He has just made our fortune.'

Sarajevo

For the last half of June, 1914, the hills of Bosnia, between the seedy city of Sarajevo and the Adriatic, in the southernmost part of the Austro-Hungarian Empire, had been alive with troops.

The weather was unexpectedly poor for the time of year: snow covered many peaks, and in the foothills horses dragged gun limbers through a slush of snow and mud. Cannons fired angrily at each other from the higher hills, and their thunder echoed and reechoed in the chill air, while white smoke from their mouths hung low in the grey skies like storm clouds.

The 14th and 16th Corps of the Austro-Hungarian Empire's ramshackle army were on their annual manoeuvres. Sarajevo tradesmen welcomed the end of this exercise; the soldiers might not have much money to spend, but there were 30,000 of them, and trade had not been brisk that spring. It was never outstanding: the religious groups – Moslem, Jewish, Christian – that comprised the population meant that every week had three holy days, Friday, Saturday and Sunday, when some shops had to close.

By Sunday, June 28th, the manoeuvres were finally declared over. Archduke Franz Ferdinand, heir to the Austrian throne, who had been observing them, cabled to his father, the Emperor, praising the high morale and efficiency of all ranks. In fact, he thought the troops a rather ragged lot, in shoddy, ill-fitting uniforms, using antique equipment and led by officers keener on the cut of their tunics than the sombre arts of war. But Franz Ferdinand feared his father, who in turn despised him as a weakling – he suffered from a recurring cough – so he thought it politic not to criticise.

Franz Ferdinand now had only two duties left to perform before, with his morganatic wife Sophie, he could depart thankfully in the royal train to join their three children on holiday by the sea. Neither of these tasks was onerous, and indeed both were in his opinion equally unnecessary. But he was advised that not to carry them out would cause offence to people loyal to the throne – of whom there was not a majority – and so he readily agreed to do as he was asked.

First, he had to drive to the Town Hall in Sarajevo to receive an address of welcome from the mayor. Next, he had promised to visit the local museum. The first duty seemed even more pointless than the second because the mayor had been with the Royal party throughout their three day visit, but the Archduke was told that it could not be omitted without causing personal offence to local dignitaries and their wives.

Franz Ferdinand, his wife and their entourage of equerries, valets and ladies' maids had arrived from Vienna by train, without a motor car. A member of the court, Count Franz von Harrach, who lived locally, instantly put his own vehicle at their disposal. This was a four-year-old Graef und Stift, an open car, known as a *doppel phaeton*, a double phaeton, because it had two huge open cockpits. In the front, one passenger could sit beside the driver; the rear compartment carried four passengers, the two most important ones occupying the main seat while the others sat on folding 'jump seats', facing them.

Von Harrach's chauffeur had been driving the Archduke to the manoeuvres every day, and early on this Sunday morning, he was washing his car in preparation for the royal procession. He would be glad when the visit was over; by five o'clock every morning he had been out in the motor house cleaning the vehicle, which was thick with mud churned up from the rough farm tracks he had used to follow the troops.

As he worked, church bells tolled for early services. The Archduke and his wife were already celebrating a special early mass in the private chapel of the Hotel Bosnia, where they were staying.

Elsewhere in the city, others were also making preparations for the procession.

Six former students, lately of the Bosnian High School, were determined to commemorate this particular Sunday in a very special way. It was the 525th anniversary of the start of the Turkish conquest of their country. On June 28th, 1389, Sultan Mourad and his Ottoman Army had defeated the entire forces of Serbia, and for the next five centuries the country had suffered under oppressive and corrupt Turkish rule. These students belonged to a revolutionary order, the Narodna Obrana, or National Defence, which held that the Austrian royal house, which now ruled Bosnia as part of the Austro-Hungarian Empire, was equally abhorrent.

On this anniversary they planned to show the Austrian Emperor that even after so long as a subject nation, Serbians possessed power and policies of their own, and wished to control their destiny without the guidance of foreigners. The method these six young men had chosen to demonstrate this intention was to assassinate the Emperor's son, Archduke Franz Ferdinand, in Sarajevo.

They were earnest, lacking in humour and social graces, and came from poor families. They still thought of themselves as students, although they had all either failed their examinations or been expelled for revolutionary activities. They now faced lives of unrelieved drudgery as filing clerks or in similar obscure, repetitive jobs. The dream of achieving a patriotic master-stroke, which would immediately make them famous, had brought them all to the city.

On the way, they collected arms for their purpose. This was easy enough, since groups who claimed to be professional terrorists, but who limited their activities to discussing revolution and political assassination over coffee and glasses of water in open-air cafés, had gathered stocks of armaments against just such a need. They were pleased to pass them on to any who actually wanted to use them.

The six young men each carried a bomb the size of a small orange under their shirts and above their belts. The serrated edges of these grenades scored their flesh as they walked, and so constantly reminded them of their purpose. Four of them also had revolvers of various sizes. Ammunition for these had been more difficult to find, but Petar Princip had brought a pocketful of cartridges from his uncle in Boppard. He handed them out to the others, and kept four without markings for himself.

The sluggish Miljacka River, 25 yards wide and spanned by six bridges, bisected the city. The main road through Sarajevo, the Appel Quay, followed one bank of this river. The Archduke's procession would go along the Appel Quay to the Town Hall, and on the way back, the cars would turn right at the Latein Bridge to Franz Josef Street on the other side of the river. They would then go on to the museum and back to the Hotel Bosnia.

The conspirators walked through the streets, still almost empty of people, and took up their positions in pairs by the three bridges nearest to the Town Hall. They were spaced apart in case one couple found it impossible to fire or throw their bomb – or in case they did both and missed their target. They reckoned they would escape easily enough in the commotion that would follow the killing. But such was their naivety – or stupidity – that they did not reconcile escape with fame. If they escaped – as they were all convinced they could – then no-one would know their names. They would still be as unknown as they were now. If they did not escape, then their future did not bear contemplation. Their fame would certainly be posthumous.

The rain stopped and the sun began to shine. Pavements steamed, and with others of their age, they leaned against walls, already warmed by the sun, enjoying this change in the weather. It was a day for a stroll, or to spend on the river, Princip thought, not for politics and shooting. If he had been on his own, he would have abandoned his mission – postponed it, would be better – and indeed others of the group were already doing just that, melting away prudently into the gathering crowd. The whole task seemed suddenly much more complicated than when discussed over a café table: that was theory, this was fact.

Princip's companion was dour and earnest, however, and Princip did not wish to sink in his estimation. So he waited, arms folded, feeling the hard outline of the revolver under his shirt, against his stomach.

Unknown to them, a seventh visitor was also preparing to watch the procession by the Latein Bridge. He was neither Austrian, Serbian nor Hungarian, and while the six were young and amateur, he was middle-aged and professional; a German of deliberately undistinguished and indistinguishable appearance.

He wore a light suit, a pair of spectacles with thick tortoise-shell rims, and had a neat dark goatee beard. This beard was not his own, and indeed his eyesight was extremely good, but if local police should for any reason seek a bearded man with heavily rimmed glasses, they would not necessarily assume that a red-haired man, clean-shaven and without glasses, could be the same person they sought. This spectator was a German secret agent. His brief was to report in detail on the popularity of the Austrian royal family in Serbia. Were they better liked than they had been – or was national hostility towards them on the increase?

The Kaiser had expressed a personal interest in this matter, and so expenses were lavish. On the previous evening, the agent had entertained his local contact, the deputy head of the secret police, at a café where a popular act, The Dancing Dervishes, was the main attraction. While these dancers leaped in the air and flung themselves about in a frenzy, the German had presented his contact with a box of Havana cigars. The bottom layer of cigars could be removed to reveal gold coins in payment for past assistance, and in full expectation of more to come.

This agent had already sent a coded message to his office in Berlin, reporting that although 30,000 Austrian troops had returned from manoeuvres, they were all confined to barracks. He explained that the authorities saw no reason for them to line the streets, as troops had done on previous royal visits. His contact assured him that the local police force of 150 was quite sufficient to protect the visitors from any hostile demonstration. It was therefore clear that nationalistic feelings on the part of the Serbs had subsided; the Archduke could be assured of a genuinely cordial farewell as he and his wife drove through the streets that Sunday morning.

The agent also relaxed in the sunshine, so very welcome after the rain. He smoked a cheroot and pondered on the excellent lunch he would have, after the procession, in the Europa Hotel, famous for its crayfish à la Parisienne, chicken grilled on a spit with asparagus hollandaise, and wild strawberries. He would order them all.

The sound of distant cheering scattered these pleasant thoughts. People suddenly appeared at windows overlooking the route. They looked excited, he noted professionally, and waved yellow and black flags, the personal colours of the Hapsburg family, and national flags with red and black stripes. Not much happened on any Sunday in Sarajevo; the visit of the heir to the throne was a great event. In the distance, approaching at little more than walking pace, the agent could see a line of seven open cars. Their thin diamond-treaded tyres threw up plumes of dust behind them, so that the cars at the end of the procession appeared to be travelling through a fog of dust and blue exhaust smoke.

In the first car he recognised his contact, sitting with other police officers. Franz Ferdinand's own personal detectives should have ridden in this car, but the local policemen had turfed them out at the barracks. They did not want foreign interlopers leading such a distinguished procession in their city.

In the second car, he saw the mayor and his party, very conscious of their importance; plump, serious men in tight dark suits that emphasised their obesity. Then, some way behind them, with the Count's chauffeur slipping the car's clutch to try and ensure smooth progress at such a low speed, came the double phaeton.

Count von Harrach sat in front next to his driver. Behind them, on one of the two jump seats, sat the city's military governor, and an ADC, facing the Archduke and his wife. Following these cars came more vehicles carrying members of the Archduke's entourage and the military governor's staff.

At the side of the high windscreen of the Archduke's car, the Hapsburg standard flew proudly. The gear lever was outside the body and the chauffeur kept one hand on this in case the engine overheated and he had to throw the gear into neutral. The car was not built for such a funereal pace; it was at its best on the open road.

One by one, the leading cars passed the German agent. He noted that Sophie wore a white dress with a wide-brimmed hat held by a veil. She bowed to the crowds and waved one hand. She was a pleasant, agreeable woman and she smiled as though genuinely enjoying the drive and the sight of an unexpectedly large number of spectators on the pavement. Franz Ferdinand saluted first to the left, then to the right. He had a pale rather sad face and kept swallowing hard to prevent himself coughing; to bring up blood on such an important state occasion would be unthinkable.

A man standing near the agent casually knocked what appeared to be his pipe against an iron post. Too late, the agent saw with horror that it was not a pipe the man was tapping free, but the detonator of a primitive bomb or hand grenade of obsolete design.

As the German stared at him in disbelief – but unwilling for obvious reasons to become involved in a scuffle – the man threw this bomb at the royal car. His aim was poor. The bomb bounced harmlessly off the car's scrubbed canvas hood, folded down behind the royal visitors to give the public a better view of them, and rolled away into the gutter.

In his haste the man had totally forgotten he should count ten before throwing it, to allow the fuse sufficient time to burn. Now the bomb lay spluttering and smoking like a damp firework. It exploded as a following car passed it.

The governor's adjutant was cut badly in the back of the hand. He ducked forward, screaming with pain and shock. His driver slammed on the brakes. Tyres smoked on the road as he instantly reversed the car and, without waiting for orders, set off for the garrison hospital.

Spectators were now shouting angrily and waving their fists. Only a few knew what had happened, but all realised something was terribly wrong. Had the car's engine exploded? Could someone have thrown a bomb? The former student, realising he had missed his target, ran across the road behind the procession and jumped into the river. In his panic he had given up all hope of escape. In his hand he carried a twisted paper containing a cyanide powder to swallow rather than face capture. In his haste and terror, he dropped this in the water. He attempted to swim to the far bank but spectators and policemen followed him into the filthy water, dragged him out and beat him insensible with truncheons and fists. The white paper of cyanide drifted away harmlessly on the current.

The mayor, in the second car of the procession, had heard the bomb explode behind him, but thought the noise was part of a planned royal salute from a ceremonial artillery unit. He did not even look back, and so had no idea that there had been an assassination attempt. He drove on to the Town Hall, climbed the steps, unfolded the sheet of paper on which he had written out his speech, and waited for his royal guests to arrive.

The other cars in the convoy had also re-started. There was no sense in remaining stationary in the centre of a milling, shouting crowd. That way they could all be sitting targets in case the bomb-thrower had any accomplices. These, apart from Princip, who still waited by his bridge, left the scene in haste.

They had seen how their colleague had fared; thoughts of personal survival instantly overcame all wish to make history. They held their arms across their chests as they walked as quickly as possible. To run would draw attention to themselves – as would the outline of a bomb or revolver bouncing about beneath their shirts. The cars trundled on to the Town Hall and stopped in a line outside the building. The drivers remained in their seats, leaving engines running. After so long in low gear they were very hot and could be difficult to start.

As soon as Franz Ferdinand climbed the steps, the mayor began his address of welcome.

'Your Imperial and Royal Highness,' he declared pontifically, 'our hearts are transported with happiness at your gracious visit.'

The Archduke took him by the arm.

'Mr Mayor,' he interrupted heatedly, 'we visit Sarajevo, and we have a bomb thrown at us! It is *scandalous*! Now carry on with your speech!'

The mayor re-started his speech.

'Happiness fills every soul in this capital city,' he declared. 'The entire population greets the Most High visit of Your Highness with the most cordial of welcomes.'

The mayor was not clear what the Archduke meant. Was he joking? Yet he did not appear to be in a humorous mood. But then one never knew with royalty; they often had a peculiar sense of humour. Why, the German Kaiser, as was well known, would deliberately humiliate his staff when aboard his steam yacht by making them drop their trousers and bend over, like English schoolboys awaiting punishment, so that he could cane their buttocks.

An aide handed Franz Ferdinand the manuscript of his reply. It was stained with blood. The aide apologised for this. The Archduke waved the paper in the air.

'Let these gentlemen see that blood has been spilt already!' he shouted and began his reply.

As soon as he had finished, police and army officers held a hurried conference while Franz Ferdinand and his wife waited, impatient to be on their way. Because of protocol, and what had happened, no-one wished to open conversation with them, either to congratulate them on a most fortunate escape, or to seek their wishes in view of the incident.

One officer suggested that the streets should be cleared by the military before the royal party left in their cars. Another thought this to be too complicated, because the troops were in barracks and it would take at least an hour to deploy them. As a compromise, the visit to the museum was cancelled, but instead, the royal couple would visit the governor's adjutant in hospital. This would show their compassion to an officer wounded in attendance on them – and also demonstrate that they remained unafraid.

In this new scenario, the first two cars in the procession would turn right over the Latein Bridge, as though going on to the museum as originally planned, but the Archduke's car would keep straight on to the hospital. After the visit to the officer they would drive to their hotel and then on to the station. This change of plan was explained to the Archduke with much saluting and clicking of heels. He nodded his agreement. He could not disagree, of course, because all arrangements were in the hands of his hosts.

Everyone now took their places again in their cars. This time, Count von Harrach stood on his car's running board to keep a better eye on the crowds. If he saw any suspicious movement, he would shout a warning.

The cars set off slowly. No-one had thought to tell the Archduke's chauffeur of the change in plan. His original orders were simply to follow the car in front, and this he continued to do. Thus, when the convoy reached the Latein Bridge, and the leading two cars turned right, he made to do the same. For a moment, the Count, scanning the crowds along the route for any sign of anyone drawing a gun or preparing to throw a bomb, did not notice this mistake. An officer from a following car did, and shouted warningly: 'Get back! *Reverse!*'

The Count's chauffeur looked at his master in bewilderment for confirmation. Why go back? What was happening? Von Harrach nodded frantically.

'Back!' he cried. '*Get back!*'

The driver heaved at the gear lever. Teeth grated, jammed. He raced the engine, stabbing the clutch, unable to engage any gear, either to go forwards or back. The car remained stationary, engine roaring impotently.

In the forefront of the crowd across the road, Petar Princip took his revolver from under his shirt and aimed carefully. A policeman in plain clothes standing next to him, puzzled at the shouting in the royal car, suddenly saw Princip's gun and struck out at his arm to deflect his aim.

Another spectator saw the policeman do this, and not yet aware of Princip's raised revolver, thought that the policeman was a ruffian, attacking a harmless and loyal spectator. He kneed the policeman in the groin as Princip fired.

His first bullet hit the Archduke in the neck. Von Harrach felt a sudden unexpected warmth on his own cheek. He put up his hand; perhaps a bird had soiled him. Then he saw his hand was crimson. Blood had spurted from the Archduke's mouth right across the car into his face. He believed that Franz Ferdinand suffered from tuberculosis, and thought he must have coughed too energetically, and had a haemorrhage. He was understandably prepared to ignore the incident, and wiped his cheek with his silk handkerchief. As he did so, the Archduchess leaned forward towards him. She saw blood streaming down his face.

'In heaven's name, what's happened to you?' she asked him in anguish – and instantly collapsed in a flurry of silk on the floor of the car. Princip's second shot had hit her in the abdomen. Her white dress was suddenly soaked by blood.

Count von Harrach shouted desperately: 'A doctor! Quick! A doctor!'

Two doctors in the crowd ran to the car and jumped on to it as the driver managed to engage gear.

'To the military hospital!' they cried. 'As quickly as you can!'

The car raced along the road, scattering pedestrians on its way. Despite the speed at which the chauffeur drove, the Archduke and his wife died within minutes of each other, without regaining consciousness.

The German agent melted back into the crowd that now surged forward towards the following cars. He had seen everything, but he could not risk being called as a witness. Also, he had to cover himself quickly for sending his first optimistic message about the Archduke's popularity. Next, he had to find out who had killed the visitors – and with what kind of cartridge. To kill two people with two shots at that distance, firing a small revolver over the heads of a crowd, was remarkable. Not only was the assassin an extraordinarily good marksman, he must be using cartridges with a propelling force of astonishing strength.

The agent's contact, the deputy head of the secret police, had already arrived back in his office at police headquarters, greatly agitated at what had happened, and especially worried as to how it could affect his own career. He had been one of the police officers who had taken the places originally reserved for the Archduke's personal guard. This would take some explaining in view of what had occurred. But at least the assassin had been caught; that must be a bonus, even if only a minor one.

'Where is he?' the agent asked him.

'In the cells. Beaten up, but still conscious.'

'Who is he?'

'A student, or ex-student, called Petar Princip. We have a file on him. Usual agitator type. No good at his studies. But up to now, all talk, no action.'

'I must see him.'

'Impossible. Absolutely out of the question.'

'Say I am the Archduke's personal physician. Say anything. It could be worth more than another box of Havanas.'

'You don't understand . . .' the deputy chief of police began, and then he shrugged his shoulders. He might be very grateful for this German's help if everything went against him in the enquiry that was bound to follow.

'I'll do my best,' he promised.

Ten minutes later, the agent was in the cell with Princip. The Judas hole in the door was open. He could see the guard's eye watching them closely, ready to rush in if there was any trouble.

Princip was in no condition to make trouble. He lay on the stone floor. His face was battered and raw and bleeding. He had lost several teeth and one eye would not focus. His jacket hung in shreds, where people in the crowd had seized him. His shirt was stuck to his arms with congealing blood from sabre cuts. A tin mug of water lay untouched on the floor. The agent held this up to Princip's swollen and bloodied lips.

'I am a doctor,' he said. 'I want to help you. Tell me about those bullets you fired. Were they poisoned?'

'No,' Princip said weakly.

'Where did you get them?'

'My uncle.'

'Who is he?'

'Wilhelm Chotek.'

'Where is he? It is most terribly important – for your life as well as the Archduke's.'

'He lives in Boppard on the Rhine. He works for two scientists in a government office. I can't remember the street. I am dizzy. I cannot think properly. But Boppard is a small place. Everyone knows everyone. You can find him easily enough.'

'Thank you for helping me. I will do all I can to help you. I will speak personally to the governor.'

The agent left the cell. Half an hour later, he was in the telegraph office with another urgent coded message for Berlin.

Two hours later, Wilhelm Chotek was arrested in Boppard.

Three hours later, detectives were interviewing the two government scientists in their laboratory.

Yes, they had missed six cartridges. Yes, again, the powder was remarkably strong, but they had passed on all details to Colonel Obermann, Inspector General of Armaments. He had visited them, and doubtless had already made his report to the Imperial Government. In their own considered opinion, this powder was the most effective they had ever analysed. It possessed stupendous power.

Two days later, Colonel Obermann was relieved of his commission. The reason given – but never made public – was not that he had reported adversely on such a sensational advance in explosives, but that he admitted misconduct with the wife of a brother officer. He was given a chance of redeeming himself by way of a single cartridge in a pistol. He accepted this release from disgrace, and after what was described as a tragic shooting accident, he was buried with full military honours.

Within the week, the powder was in production in three German ammunition factories.

The Emperor, Franz Joseph, informed the Kaiser that his aim now was to eliminate Serbia from being what he called 'a Balkan power factor'. The German ambassy in Vienna advised the government in Berlin to be cautious in their reply. The Kaiser would not accept such advice. He told his diplomats curtly: 'Stop that nonsense. The Serbs must be cleaned up – now or never.' He pledged that Austro-Hungary could count on full German support in whatever measures they took.

In Vienna, the Emperor's cabinet met. They favoured a surprise attack on Serbia, or at least giving them an ultimatum they would find impossible to meet. The exception was the prime minister of Hungary who prophesied that to attack Serbia would bring in Russia and start a world war because of the treaty Russia had with France. His prophecy was fulfilled. With Germany and Austria allied against Serbia, Russia came in on Serbia's side, and France with Russia, and then Britain joined with France, by reason of other treaties and obligations.

Petar Princip, of course, knew nothing of all this. He was still in his cell awaiting trial. He waited for weeks, latterly strung up by chains around his wrists in the belief that this might persuade him to incriminate others on the promise of more lenient conditions for himself. Sometimes, in his increasingly few periods of consciousness, he wondered about the German doctor who had assured him he would speak for him. Where was he? What was he doing? He never discovered.

Princip had done what he did to mark an anniversary and to make his name. He did not live to learn that he had indeed achieved fame of a kind, not for killing an alien archduke, but for firing the first shot in a world war. Twenty million more would die before it ended. If, indeed, it ever ended.

London

The butler showed the regimental medical officer into the drawing room of Fiona's house in Belgrave Square.

'Captain Ponsonby, ma'am,' he announced.

The captain stood, looking about at the elegant furnishings: paintings by Matisse, Corot, Pissaro; a bronze bust of Mr Jackson by Epstein. To stand in the centre of such evidence of wealth and good taste made him feel uneasy; it was worlds away from the crude casualty clearing station in a barn outside the French town of Etaples, to which he was returning.

He bowed to Fiona.

'I was in London,' he began hesitantly, 'and I thought I should visit you. I hope you do not mind this short notice, but I am going back to France tonight, and, well, there may not be another chance. Edward and I were pretty close, you know. I treated him when – when he was wounded.'

He waited a moment; he had liked Edward very much. He did not wish to hurt his widow.

'He often mentioned you in his letters,' Fiona told him. 'It is all so very, very sad. But then, nearly every family in the land has lost someone.'

She paused.

'I have been very pleased to receive quite a procession of officers who knew my husband. It is a great comfort and pleasure to see them. The adjutant was here, yesterday. Poor fellow, he is being invalided out, he told me. He lost an arm. And the colonel has just this minute left.'

'I know, ma'am. I saw him on the way in. It is raining, and he was waiting in the hall.'

'I had no idea – I would have rung for my car. Taxi-cabs are so short in wartime.'

They talked awkwardly, avoiding the real object of their meeting – Edward's death.

The captain could not tell her how he had died. A mangled red mess of blood and flesh and bone and sinew with both legs blown off, his trunk raw as a carcass in a butcher's shop, had been brought in on a stretcher – and still conscious. There was nothing Ponsonby could do except to pump morphia into his collapsed veins. He remembered Edward's gasping voice, trying to make a joke of this.

'My money mostly came from that stuff,' he whispered. 'Opium. I never liked that. Mud, they called it. Now, I can't get enough myself.'

Ponsonby did not understand, and nodded until Edward's eyelids closed. He began to snore as the drug took hold, and then he gradually stopped breathing altogether. At once, the body was carried away to make room for another casualty.

'Did he say anything before he died?' Fiona asked Ponsonby.

'He made a little joke, ma'am. About opium. Said he never liked the fact that his money – family money, I suppose – came from it. Now he didn't mind. We used a lot of it in the clearing station.'

'On him?'

'Only a touch.'

The medical officer lied unconvincingly. She did not pursue the point.

Someone knocked on the door and entered. A nanny brought in Fiona's son, Clive.

'I am sorry, ma'am,' she apologised. 'I did not realise you had company.'

Clive looked from one to the other.

'This is Captain Ponsonby, a friend of your father's,' Fiona explained to her son.

The boy shook hands gravely with Ponsonby, who was surprised at the weakness of his face, how close his eyes were together. There seemed little of his father in his appearance.

'It is late for you, I expect?' said Ponsonby, trying to be pleasant. He was unmarried, and always felt awkward in the presence of children; he never quite knew what to say to them.

'I am twelve,' said Clive shortly, as though that settled the matter.

'Of course,' said his mother. 'Now go to bed and I will come and see you in a moment.'

The nanny hurried the boy away.

'Well, I will also be going, Mrs Douglas-Sodawaterwallah.'

Fiona smiled.

'It is a strange name, isn't it? I should think Edward had a lot to put up with in the mess?'

'We always asked him to take whisky with it.'

'And he did?'

'Invariably. He had a nickname, actually. All popular officers do. We called him Sodasplash.'

They both laughed, glad to discuss anything which would relieve the tension. Ponsonby bowed.

'I can see myself out,' he said. As he reached the door, he turned to her.

'If there is anything I can do to help, please do write to me, care of the regiment.'

'Thank you. I will.'

She watched him go, and glanced at the clock. It was late, nearly ten. She wondered why her son was still not in bed. She would go and see for herself. Nanny was far too lax, and Clive was so headstrong, sometimes almost absurdly difficult to control. He was too old to have a nanny, in any case, but she had been with them since his birth and seemed almost one of the family.

Edward had sent the boy to a prep school as a boarder; to several, in fact, but within weeks he was home again from all of them. The school matron would explain that he couldn't settle down; that he cried so much in the dormitory, he upset the other boys. So Clive was now living at home, going to a local day school.

The war made things so difficult, Fiona told herself; it would all have been different in peacetime. Now, with Edward dead, she sensed she would have trouble with Clive unless she was firm. This was not easy when the boy had just lost his father, but if he was so wilful at twelve, what would he be like when he grew up?

She went out of a side door, along a corridor and up the service staircase to Clive's bedroom. To reach this, she had to pass briefly along a gallery above the hall. To her surprise, looking down, she saw Ponsonby and the colonel still standing by the front door. A thunderclap and a blue flicker of lightning gave her the reason. It was still raining heavily and they did not wish to be soaked. She would order up her car for them as soon as she had seen Clive.

As she walked, she heard the colonel ask Ponsonby, 'What did you tell her?'

Immediately, she paused, her back against the wall to stay out of their sight, sensing he was speaking about her husband – her late husband.

'Nothing much, sir,' Ponsonby replied. 'I could not explain what he looked like. You can't. People at home have no idea. They imagine their sons and brothers and husbands all die quietly, falling asleep. That's the impression the newspapers give, and they believe it.'

'You did right. It's what they want to believe, anyway, and it only causes pain to tell them the truth. Tell me, was that Sodasplash's boy I saw with a nanny? Bad-tempered, pampered-looking kid, I thought.'

'He was introduced to me as his son. But, of course, he can't be.'

'Why ever not?'

'Sodasplash could never father a child. He'd had malaria very badly when he was young in Bombay.'

'One of these bloody medical things, eh?'

'Yes.'

'But how do you know?'

'He wanted another child. We have a lot of really top specialists in the Base Hospital. They did every kind of test on him to see if it was possible. But, no. No cure. No hope.'

'So his wife must have had it away on the side, eh? Women! You never can tell, can you? But I would never have thought that of her. She seems such a, well, you know, a *lady*. I wonder if old Sodasplash knew?'

'If he didn't earlier on – and of course he wouldn't – he must have done after the results. But I'm sure he would never let on. Perhaps that was why he asked for all the tests, he wanted another child – his own, this time.'

'Poor devil. And I thought he had everything going for him. The old saying's right, isn't it? Never envy anyone until you have walked a mile in their shoes.'

Fiona's hands were trembling. For a moment, she thought she was going to faint. She leaned weakly against the wall until the feeling passed.

So Clive was not Edward's son. Captain Ponsonby could be mistaken, of course; all doctors made mistakes, and it was wrong of him to reveal medical details to someone else. But they were men under enormous stress, going back to France with the strong possibility they would not return. She had to forgive him. She knew they had both liked her husband, and that Ponsonby obviously did not realise she could overhear him. And while he, as an individual doctor, might be wrong, the specialists who carried out the tests on Edward were unlikely to have made such a mistake. Could it be that when Edward heard Clive was not his son, could not possibly be his son, and that he could never father a child of his own, he had not greatly cared whether he lived or died, and so took risks that resulted in his death?

Surely not. They still had each other and they loved each other – unless, of course, he believed she had been unfaithful to him.

What hurt almost as much as the knowledge that Clive was not Edward's son, but George's, was the fact that Edward had never mentioned the matter to her. His attitude towards Clive had never altered. He had accepted him as his son, and treated him as his son. But what must his thoughts have been about her? How could he have remained so tender and loving when he had what must have seemed incontrovertible evidence that Fiona had borne another man's son?

Fiona's feelings overcame her. Love and admiration and longing for Edward welled up in her heart, but she would never be able to tell him of her adoration for him. She remembered that night of near rape in the jungle on the edge of the river in British Honduras. How ironic that the only occasion when George succeeded in entering her, he had made her pregnant. That he was Clive's father could account for the boy's slothful disposition, his mean character, the fact that Clive possessed none of the qualities of the man she had loved.

She turned back from the door of Clive's bedroom. She felt she could not bear to see him just then, or even speak to him. She knew none of this was his fault, that her reaction was totally unfair, but then so was life.

Now Edward, like George, was dead, yet ironically it was as though George still lived – in the person of his son, their son. She walked on to her own bedroom, and threw herself on the bed, weeping uncontrollably.

The colonel stepped out from the sheltering evening shadows as Robert Jackson arrived in his Napier at his home in Eaton Square. He waited until Jackson went up the steps and then called out to him softly. Jackson turned.

'Yes?' he asked impatiently.

'Excuse me, sir,' the officer began diffidently. 'I did not like to come to your office. Someone might recognise me, and that could be very embarrassing for me. I wonder if I could see you for a few moments in your house? Privately. On a most important matter.'

Jackson looked closely at the man. He was in his early forties, wearing the red band of the General Staff around his cap, and a British warm overcoat. He carried a malacca cane. Under the gas light, his face seemed grey and lined. He was clearly under great strain.

'I am rather busy,' Jackson told him. 'Could you not send a letter to my office? Someone there will deal with whatever you wish to discuss.'

All kinds of people arrived at *The Enquirer* building, every day, claiming that they had been wronged, or that they possessed a unique war-winning idea in which authority was not interested, and they sought the newspaper's help in presenting their case. Most were harmless enough. Some were recovering from mental breakdowns. A few, shell-shocked from gunfire in France, had been invalided out of the services. This colonel could fit into any of these categories. But did he?

'It is an extremely sensitive matter, sir, involving national security – possibly even national survival,' the colonel went on desperately. 'I have to see you – or no-one.'

'Really? Come inside then.'

Jackson was unenthusiastic, but the man seemed genuine. He would give him the benefit of the doubt – and five minutes. He had a dinner to attend that night in the City, and he was already late.

He poured two whiskies.

'I will endeavour to be brief,' said the colonel, 'and I have to remain anonymous for obvious reasons. I am on leave from France. I was on the staff at the battle of Festubert in May this year.'

'I read the report of that in *The Times*. Unsigned, of course, but I believe it was from their very able correspondent, Colonel Repington?' said Jackson.

'You are right,' agreed the colonel. 'He had been the guest of Sir John French at headquarters. I met him there. In his published report, he stated, and I quote from memory: "Our want of an unlimited supply of high explosive was a fatal bar to our success." You cannot have much more damning evidence than that. And remember, Mr Jackson, that is only the weak, emasculated account which the censors allowed to reach the public.

'I can tell you privately that in a single day in that battle the French fired 276 rounds of high explosive from *every* gun in their batteries, while we had not sufficient high explosive to blast even a relatively narrow path through the enemy parapets for our infantry. We could only fire a fraction of the French bombardment.

'Our infantry did splendidly, as always, but to die by tens of thousands, through the criminal fault of others in whom they trusted, is not to win the day. It is neither magnificent, to paraphrase the French Marshal Bosquet, nor is it war. It is simply murder; deliberate, unnecessary murder.'

'I lost a friend and a business partner, Captain Edward Sodawater-wallah, in that battle,' said Jackson.

'So did thousands of other families,' the colonel replied bitterly. 'A whole generation of our finest young men – most of them volunteers, officers and rankers alike – is being decimated for a few yards of disputed mud, already thick with a million corpses. Why? England will pay dearly for this folly for a hundred years, and all due to the total inadequacy of our shells.

'If we must fight, we must fight to win, not just, as it seems, for the sake of sacrifice. The Germans put down a barrage that lasted for eight hours in that battle. Our artillery was restricted to *one* shell every *half* hour – because that was all they had.

'The men who go over the top are dead before they have taken a dozen paces. Slaughter, day after day after day. It is happening still – and it will go on happening. Unless. . . .'

The colonel paused.

'Unless what?' Jackson asked him. 'What do you wish me to do?'

'I wish you to do, sir, what Lord Northcliffe is doing most patriotically in his *Daily Mail* and *The Times*: exposing our almost incredible lack of shells. Even the shells we have in any quantity are mostly the wrong type. Our field pieces might as well be in museums for all the good they are. People in Britain simply do not realise what is happening across the Channel. The truth is being withheld from them because it is too awful. There would be red revolution if they knew the facts.

'Every day in every newspaper – yours included, sir – I read dispatches from Flanders that are total fiction. Reporters calling themselves war correspondents write about happy troops dying for God, King and Country. This is rubbish. They are dying needlessly, for nothing at all, through the scandalous unpreparedness of the government.

'The reporters are miles from the front. They know nothing and they see nothing. They make up their stories, which is quite literally what they are. *Stories*. Inventions. Fiction. The authorities are delighted, so long as they keep the terrible murderous truth out of their dispatches.

'Half the London theatres are full of musical shows with silly actresses prancing about, waving Union Jacks and singing songs about war, as though we had something to celebrate, not to mourn. But out there, just over the Channel, thousands more have died, during each performance – and *while we are talking here*. And all to no purpose whatever. The cream of our young men are dying, all believing that they are risking their lives for honour – when they are simply losing them for lack of guns, shells, proper strategy.

'If we are to continue fighting this war with any hope whatever of ultimate victory, without haemorrhaging the entire Empire of its best and bravest young men, we need more shells, of the right sort: ones packed with powerful explosives, not the old-fashioned stuff too many of them contain.'

'And if that is not forthcoming?'

'In that case, sir, prepare for a German victory.'

'Have you any documentary proof of what you tell me, Colonel?'

'I have made copies of relevant paragraphs in secret reports on the production of high explosives. Here are some figures for you.'

He took a paper from his pocket and spread it on the table.

'You cannot keep it, Mr Jackson,' he said. 'But perhaps you can memorise the figures.'

'With your permission, I will write them down,' said Jackson. He scribbled details on a sheet of notepaper.

'The British are used to fighting what are relatively minor colonial wars, either over vast open spaces – as in South Africa – or in the hills of the Khyber,' the colonel continued as Jackson wrote.

'Their weapons are designed for more of the same – and for nothing else. We have large supplies of shells for use against such an advancing army, literally in the field. But for a war being fought in trenches across no-man's land, the desperate need is for heavy guns and high-explosive shells filled with shrapnel that can rip apart barbed-wire entanglements.

'We have virtually none, and in the second year of this war, the biggest in history, we still have no plans to produce them on anything like the scale required. Armour-piercing shells, of which we possess large stocks, can blow a round hole in the wall of a fort or in the hull of an ironclad, but they create only localised damage outside that particular area. Shrapnel kills and maims over a wide area.

'The Germans, by contrast, have the right artillery, with the correct ammunition and an enormous quantity of machine guns specifically designed for trench warfare. One belt of that machine-gun ammunition can decimate a battalion of a thousand men advancing with rifles and bayonets. That is a terrible sight to see. I know, I have seen it too often. In addition, observers up in aircraft, in wireless communication with the gunners, can direct and concentrate German fire.

'Not only is our weaponry totally wrong but, for the first time in the history of warfare, guns are firing day and night, week after week, virtually all the time, along hundreds of miles of front. This means that one day's firing can use more powder and shot than has ever previously been used in an entire battle.

'Nor are the only inadequacies with the politicians and the high command. Do you know that trades union restrictions on unskilled labour in the Clyde are worse than they were before the war?

'I was in Glasgow early last week, visiting a factory where output has been pathetic. I was astonished to see, in mid-morning, hundreds of idle men standing by idle machines. I asked why, when the need for what these machines should produce could literally be a matter of life and death for thousands of our men, possibly the difference between defeat or victory on the Western Front.

'The management was quite open about it. The engineers' union had forbidden its members to touch the machines, while new rates for working them were being discussed!

'If anyone had laid a hand upon any of them, Mr Jackson, all the engineers in that factory – and half a dozen others nearby – would have immediately walked out. Yet there was no reason at all why they could not operate the machines while negotiations went on. Then, when new rates had been agreed, any adjustments in their pay would be made. But, no. The union jacks-in-office must savour their little moment of power. It made me want to vomit!

'The Clyde isn't alone in this attitude. We have a tramway strike here in London. Hundreds of thousands of people have to walk to work every morning. Two thousand workers are on indefinite strike in south Staffordshire. All over the country it is the same. But, except for *The*

Times and the *Daily Mail*, this incredible state of affairs largely goes unreported.

'I think, sir, that if you also publicised such acts of treachery fully, day after day after day, the public would be shocked – and things would change. At present, they are like ostriches, heads deep in the sand of illusion, because life is always more comfortable if you don't really see the unpleasant things going on all around you.'

'You have a great faith in the power of the Press,' said Jackson.

'To be blunt, sir, I have now little faith in anyone or anything. But I believe that, of all the institutions in the country, the Press is the only one which can alert the people quickly to the appalling danger that faces us.'

The colonel paused, finished his whisky.

'I have taken up too much of your time,' he said, almost apologetically. 'However, I feel I have done my duty. But, for talking like this, my superiors could have me court martialled. I could even be shot if they learned about the figures I have given you from the reports.'

'Why?' asked Jackson.

'Because they are true, sir. Truth is a very dangerous commodity – and the first casualty in this war. Thank you for giving me so much of your time.'

Jackson followed the colonel to the door, meaning to ask for his name, or an address where he could contact him, but thought better of it. Instead, he watched him walk away along the empty street. Then he returned to his study, and telephoned the editor of *The Enquirer*.

'What are you leading with tomorrow?' he asked him.

'An imminent breakthrough on the Western Front, Mr Jackson. A great victory is in the air. The War Office is jubilant.'

'I hope they are as jubilant in the trenches,' Jackson replied grimly. 'Put a shorthand writer on the line. I will dictate a new lead. But first, get local reporters out to every public house near ordnance factories in Bristol, Glasgow, Woolwich, Crayford, and wherever else they are. Let them talk to the workers. You will find that everywhere production is very low. I want facts, figures, instances of this. The whys and the wherefores.'

'That's what the *Mail* and *The Times* are hammering on about, sir.'

'I am aware of that,' Jackson replied. 'I also read the other newspapers. Now we will put our hammer on the same anvil – and we will hit harder.'

'That policy has made those two newspapers very unpopular with the government.'

'Popularity – or the lack of it – with any government is not something that has ever bothered me.'

Jackson began to dictate into the telephone.

'Behind the story of this long awaited, frequently delayed breakthrough lies an even more important account of inefficiency, sloth and lack of direction in high places. For example, how many people in this country know that for every shell the Allied artillery fires, the Germans can fire at least twenty?

'How many people know that a very high proportion of our shells fall short? That the explosive which propels them is old-fashioned? How many appreciate the full and terrible indictment that can be made of British war production?'

Jackson continued for several minutes on this theme, then spoke again to the editor.

'We'll have to put this to the censors, sir,' the editor told him nervously.

'Put it to whom you like, but answer me this: since when has it been wrong to ask *questions*? That is all we are doing – tonight. Tomorrow, when the reporters find facts, we will print answers. Do I make myself clear?'

'Abundantly, sir, but. . . .'

'But what?'

'It is very contentious, sir. The public are all for the breakthrough. There has been so much bad news recently. They *want* a victory.'

'So do I,' retorted Jackson. 'So does everyone, but a real one. Not just a newspaper story about one.'

'I see your point, sir. But I must confess, I am not very happy.'

'Then I can easily make you happy,' Jackson told him pleasantly. 'If you do not agree with my new policy – *our* new policy – you can resign at any time. Now, if you wish.'

'I did not mean that exactly, sir,' the editor said hastily.

'I did,' Jackson told him, and put down the receiver. He finished his whisky then walked upstairs to bathe and change for dinner.

The next day, as his car arrived outside *The Enquirer* office, he was surprised to see a crowd milling across the pavement, and thought at first that there must have been a street accident. Then a woman angrily broke her umbrella over the Napier's bonnet. Others kicked the tyres in rage. A few spat at the windows. Several men seized the mudguards roughly and began to rock the vehicle from side to side on its springs.

'Traitor!' people were shouting.

'Half-caste bastard!'

'Go back to China, where you belong!'

'Chinky-chinky Chinaman!'

The commissionaire cleared a way for Jackson to reach the building. Policemen were standing in a row in the entrance hall, truncheons drawn.

'I had to let them in,' the managing director explained apologetically. 'They fear a riot. The crowd out there want to smash the presses because of the story we ran today.'

'Really?' replied Jackson grimly. 'Then we shall have to see what they want to do when they read what we will print tomorrow.'

Next day, the Stock Exchange suspended business while brokers in swallowtail coats and stiff high collars ceremoniously burned copies of *The Enquirer* in bonfires in the streets. The editor and the circulation manager came into Jackson's office, their faces white with concern.

'The telephones have been going all morning, sir,' the manager reported. 'Readers in their thousands are stopping taking the paper. Already we have lost fifteen thousand circulation. I have girls on every outside line taking more cancellations all the time. This is costing us a lot of money.'

'I *have* a lot of money,' Jackson replied. 'And I am willing to spend it all in the interests of my country – as I see them.'

'I'll be up at the Bailey,' the editor said miserably.

'Not you, me,' Jackson corrected him. 'I am the proprietor, and I started the campaign. If I am charged, I will insist on appearing in person. I can then say in evidence what I cannot say in print – because court reports can be printed under privilege of reporting a legal case. Indeed, I would welcome the opportunity of naming people and companies who are letting down our country and our cause. We are collecting a lot of very serious evidence.

'And if I do go to court, we will lead the paper with what happens there every day for as long as the case continues. Here, read these letters for yourself.'

From his briefcase, Jackson took a pile of letters that had been sent to his home, some by special delivery, from workmen in munitions factories, from servicemen home on leave, all applauding what he was doing. Many gave detailed instances of inefficiencies in factories and mistakes in planning and tactics that had cost many lives, sometimes entire regiments.

'Truth,' said the editor nervously. 'You know what Pontius Pilate said about that. "What is truth?" he asked.'

'What indeed?' Jackson retorted. 'We could have told him. Get a leader written on the subject. Truth is what we print. And tomorrow we run the whole front page on this true issue, with another article inside attacking generals who never go near the front, profiteers who produce substandard gunpowder – and other newspapers that subscribe to the fiction of British supremacy, when actually the country and the Empire stand on the brink of ruin and defeat. Do I make myself clear?'

'Perfectly, Mr Jackson. Perfectly.'

At that moment, a uniformed messenger entered carrying a small carton bound with brown paper and tied with a ribbon in a bow.

'For you, sir,' he told Jackson. 'A lady brought it into the front hall and asked me to bring it up to you right away. She said it was a present. You would understand, she said, sir.'

Jackson cut the ribbon and opened the carton, wondering what it could contain and who had sent it.

Inside, nestling on a bed of red velvet, was a sealed envelope. He ripped it open, read the unsigned note it contained.

'If you feel so strongly on the matter, why don't you put your manhood where your mouth is, you coward?'

A white feather fluttered out on to the red carpet.

As Fiona stepped from the Rolls-Royce outside Ebenezer and Son's office in Lincoln's Inn, wearing a long black dress, hat and veil as befitted a widow, she suddenly noticed how many other women she passed in the street were similarly dressed. Like her, they were in mourning for a husband, a father, a brother, a fiancé. Like her, many were wearing regimental badges or brooches.

The casualties on the Western Front had mounted steadily. On some days, a whole page of *The Enquirer* was taken up simply with names of officers; other ranks died anonymously, otherwise their names would have filled the whole paper. A generation was being systematically destroyed to gain a few yards of mud, which would in turn be abandoned within hours, then repossessed, and fought over day after terrible day, week after week. She felt conscious, as never before, of an immense sense of loss, not only of her own husband Edward, but of all those other young men, who to her were simply names on casualty lists, whose only memorial was a little notice posted in the front window of too many homes: 'A man from this house died fighting for his King and Country.'

The clerk showed her immediately into Ebenezer's private office. He stood up to greet her.

'How kind of you to visit me,' he said. 'I thought it best if you signed your late husband's share certificates, which are now yours entirely, in this office, where my clerk can be a witness.'

'Of course.'

Fiona drew off her black gloves. Ebenezer handed her a pen, then blotted her signature. The clerk signed beneath her name and withdrew.

'That is all?' she said, pulling on her gloves again. 'I did not realise it would be so quick. I sent the chauffeur off to collect some parcels from Harrods.'

'There is something else,' said Ebenezer hesitantly, not looking at her but over her shoulder out of the window. He was in the same room where his grandfather used to sit on a high stool, working for Mr Macnamara.

'Yes?' said Fiona. 'No problem, I hope?'

'Not a problem,' he said, 'but something I have to tell you personally, which may come as a shock. As you know, we have been refurbishing a number of the old cottage homes on Coupar Castle estate. One of these, you will remember, was where you lived with the Macduffs.'

'I know. What about it?'

'The builders had to do rather more work than they anticipated because the roof was faulty, and up in the rafters they found an envelope. It was unsealed and just addressed with your name, "Fiona". I think Mr MacDuff probably put it there for safety. Then he had his stroke, poor fellow, and was unable to retrieve it.'

'What was inside it?' she asked, anxious to get to the root of the matter. She disliked legal circumlocution: it usually ended inconclusively and was always expensive. Ebenezer opened the drawer of his desk and took out a cheap manilla envelope. He shook two papers out on to his desk.

'This first one,' he explained, 'is signed by your mother in the office of a Writer to the Signet in Edinburgh. It says: "I swear on oath that the child named as Fiona Pomfret is not the child of my husband, the late John Pomfret. Fiona's father is Alec Douglas of Coupar Castle. So help me God." '

'Give it to me,' Fiona said hoarsely. 'Let me read it myself.'

She looked at the copperplate hand-writing on the thick folded sheet of legal paper. On the bottom, in an illiterate hand she recognised as that of MacDuff, was a note: 'I showed this to Mr Douglas on August 12th, glorious twelfth. He asked me to keep it quiet.'

Fiona let the paper fall on to the lawyer's desk.

They sat in silence for a moment, looking at each other. Fiona was seeing not him but Alec Douglas on the evening of that day when she had told him she and George Wallace were going to marry.

She recalled the weekly washings of her hair with the bleach on which Mrs MacDuff insisted. She had been red-haired all along – like Douglas, her father.

She thought of Douglas making love to her; his body on hers, in hers, mouth upon mouth; his words of endearment, and she felt a physical coldness around her heart.

This letter had tarnished the memory of a man she had loved. Surely he had not known their relationship? He could not have done, she realised thankfully. Their association had been finished before August 12th of the year she became engaged. Indeed, that was the date she had accepted George's proposal. She remembered Douglas's face, shocked and drawn as he tried to congratulate her. Until that day, almost that moment, he was as innocent of this knowledge as she had been. He had not known how to explain it to her. And because of that, he had taken his own life – and she had inherited everything.

'What is the other letter?' she asked Ebenezer tonelessly.

'It appears to have come from a Mrs Sodawaterwallah, a Parsee lady in

Bombay. It was addressed to Mr Douglas and brought over to him by her
son, your first husband. There is a note on it from Mr Douglas, explaining
how he received it.'

Ebenezer handed Fiona the letter that Douglas had read before he made
his will. She read it.

So George had not been Douglas's son. He was the younger of the two
boys. Edward, the elder, the man she had loved and married second, had
been his son. Now Edward was dead, and she was alone with his brother's
son.

For the first time, she began to realise why Douglas had shot himself.
The knowledge that he had seduced his own daughter – who was then to
marry a man he thought was his son – must have been too much to bear.
And yet there was no-one with whom he could share what he believed was
his fearful secret. There was one small comfort. Clive had not been born of
an incestuous union. But did that matter? Did anything matter now? She
felt drained of all vitality, all initiative.

Ebenezer watched her face closely. She was deathly pale. He pressed the
bell for a clerk.

'Bring brandy and a glass, quickly.'

He handed her the drink. She sipped it, then put it on a side table.

'I will go now,' she said.

'But your car has not arrived. We will be told when it is here.'

'I would like a walk in the fresh air.'

'I'll come with you,' said Ebenezer. 'It must have been a terrible shock.'

'I will be all right,' Fiona assured him. 'I will go on my own. I want to
think over what you have told me. I am sure you will understand.'

'Of course. Is there anything you want me to do about these papers?'

'Nothing. What can you do? The people they refer to are all dead. Everyone whom I cared about is dead. I am the only one left.'

She stood up. Ebenezer opened the door for her.

She went down the staircase, out into Lincoln's Inn. The sun was
shining and a small band of wounded, discharged soldiers with trumpets
and fiddles, walked in the gutter, playing 'Roses of Picardy'.

She opened her purse as she paused, took out a handful of sovereigns and
gave them to the leader. It was an automatic reflex action, brought on by
the music. He saluted smartly.

'God bless you, ma'am. Got the old Beds and Herts badge up, I see.
My old mob, that is – what's left of 'em not on the old barbed
wire.'

Fiona did not even hear him. She stood for a moment, wondering what
she should do, where she could go until her car appeared; anywhere but
inside that office, with those papers.

She waited for an omnibus to pass, and when the way was clear, stepped out to cross the road. In her anguish, she had forgot that tramcars ran in the opposite direction.

The tram that hit her carried her beneath its chassis for nearly thirty yards before it stopped. Police and ambulance men took an hour to free her body.

Someone found her diamond brooch of the Beds and Herts Regiment crushed beneath an iron wheel, and laid this on the blanket with which the ambulance crew covered her. She was obviously a war widow, poor soul; smelled a bit of brandy. Can't blame her, really, just had bad news. That must be why she never saw the tram. The driver wasn't to blame. No-one was. It was just one of those things. She was a war casualty, like the rest, like her old man.

By late each afternoon, the smoking room of the Coliseum Club in St James's was usually almost empty. The fire was allowed to burn low in its burnished grate beneath the magnificent marble mantelpiece on which an eighteenth-century ormolu clock gravely measured out the members' lives.

In red leather-buttoned armchairs, two elderly members slept, mouths agape like stranded fish, oblivious to its ticking. Across the room, two more were engaged in deep and earnest conversation over a bottle of port. A miasma of cigar smoke hung in a blue cloud above their heads.

Jackson sat alone, his chair half turned away from the others, its high wings on either side totally concealing him. He did not want to be approached to make up a four for cards, or to exchange conversational banalities. He wanted to be on his own. He was saddened by Fiona's death, coming so soon after Edward had been killed in action. He felt drained of emotion; it was almost impossible to realise he would never see them again, or hear their voices. And then, on top of this, the white feather.

He had put it in the breast pocket of his jacket and thrown away the box in which it had arrived, with the note that accompanied it. He had never thought of himself as a coward or a war dodger, principally because he had never considered himself a naval or military man. Courage was their prerogative. He believed he could achieve far more for the country through the power and influence of his newspaper than with a rifle in his hand. He recalled the Chinese proverb: 'All are not soldiers that go to the wars.' Now, he wondered; both at the identity of the sender of the white feather, and at his own reaction on receiving it.

He was on close terms with several Cabinet ministers, all of whom assured him – at least until he had started to criticise government policy on armaments – that his newspaper was doing an invaluable job in keeping civilian and service morale at a high level. He had believed them because, of course, this was true.

Now, for the first time, he realised there was another dimension to life: he might have been sleeping, oblivious to it, until this feather had arrived. It was one thing to exhort others to action, altogether another to go into action oneself. He had been doing the first to the best of his ability. Now perhaps it was time to attempt the second. He felt required to prove himself, to show that, like the majority of his generation, he also could bear the mark and scars of a warrior.

Only that day, at the head of *The Enquirer's* leader column, where the editor ran a quotation each morning, he had read Dr Johnson's familiar words, 'Every man thinks meanly of himself for not having been a soldier.' Now Robert realised that this was essentially true, especially in time of war. To live with himself, he required to be tried, like steel, in the fire; the rest was only rhetoric.

A sudden angry voice broke into his thoughts.

'You've spilt the bloody port, Forbes! Get a waiter! Quick!'

One of the two men who had been talking together crossed the room and pressed the bell for a servant. No-one answered his summons. He pressed it again and again and again.

'Dammit! We could all be burning to death here and no-one would come. Are there no bloody club servants left?'

'They're in the services,' his companion explained. 'And those who aren't are no damn' good. Bloody shirkers, most of 'em.'

The other man grumbled, his voice thick and slurred with drink.

'Not the sort we used to have here before the war, eh?'

'That goes for a lot of the new members, too. I've seen people in here I wouldn't have allowed through the tradesmen's entrance at my home in the old days. Not past the lodge gate.'

'Where *is* that bloody waiter?'

'Gone home, most like. Here, let's mop it up ourselves. Port makes a deuced nasty mark on any carpet – and we'll be liable.'

'Use this newspaper, then. *The Enquirer*. Best use you could put it to, if you ask me.'

'Fellow who owns this rag, Jackson – half-caste Chinese apparently – he's one of the new members. The sort I was telling you about. Wrong type, altogether. Rich, of course, but when all is said and done, what is money? By itself, I mean.'

'Absolutely. It's breeding that counts. No question. You can tell a *proper* person easily enough by their whole attitude, their behaviour. Always have done, always will.'

'I asked the secretary how it happened. Jackson getting in, I mean. He hummed and hawed, said his name came up and he was proposed and seconded and that was that. Went through on the nod, apparently.'

'There's more to it than that. I happen to know that several candidates were elected at one go, so a selection committee member told me. Some were very decent fellows. Most of them, in fact. He said questions would have been asked about one or two others, in the normal way, I understand. But the owners of the freehold threatened to put up the rent steeply if there was any quibble. Tenfold increase, so the word goes.'

'Really? I thought old Braithwaite owned the place. He's been a member here for years, you know.'

'I know. But he sold it.'

'To whom?'

'That's the odd thing. To a property company, nominally. Actually, it was Mrs bloody Chinese Jackson. She's loaded with money. Bought the whole block here. Of course, she owns a third of Trinity-Trio, so I'm told, and they must be making a fortune out of the war. She's said to be English, but what does she see in a slit-eyed fellow? You tell me that.'

'You mean she bought this whole block, offices, shops, everything, just to get her husband elected to the club?'

'Can't think of any other reason. Can you?'

A waiter arrived with a sponge and pail of water. He went down on his hands and knees and began to wipe the carpet.

Jackson took advantage of the fact that the two members immediately began to give him loud and contradictory instructions, and left the room. They had not noticed that he was there, and they did not see him go.

His car was waiting outside.

'I'll walk home,' he told his chauffeur. 'You have an early night for once. But pick me up at eight tomorrow morning, at the house, as usual. I may want you then. I am not quite sure yet. Good night.'

'Good night, sir.'

Jackson walked along St James's, up into Piccadilly. Nothing had cheered him more than being elected, seemingly on his own merits, a member of the Coliseum. This represented to him an accolade he had believed could not be bought by money or influence; it was awarded by other members because they genuinely wanted him to join them, because they wished him to know that he was accepted. Now, he realised bitterly, this had been illusion: his place had been bought by his wife's wealth. Of course, Joanna had acted with the best intentions. Buying an entire block of property simply to give her husband the distinction he wanted above all others was surely proof of her love for him. Equally, it was one more proof, in his mind, at least, that money was the key which opened doors which he had naively assumed would stubbornly resist its influence.

He felt unutterably depressed. He had been so certain that the Englishmen he admired had accepted him, but because he did not look English, was indeed only half English, he realised he might never entirely be approved of by those he most admired. To them, he would always remain an outcast, someone to be tolerated, toadied to because of the power his newspaper gave him, but kept firmly on the outside, never allowed into the heart of the family; always on the outside, looking in, never on the inside, looking out.

Did this matter? Surely, like rich foreign Jews, who are fawned upon by reason of their wealth, and laughed at behind their backs because of their names and accents, he could rise above this? He had overheard a remark in the office earlier that day; someone had said that Jesus was a Jew. There had been a pause, then came the qualifying reply: 'But only on His mother's side.' Well, he was Chinese on *his* mother's side, and from now on, he would not be reluctant to admit it.

He walked along Piccadilly, barely conscious of the young officers in uniform home on leave, pretty women by their sides, the cars, the cabs, the buses – all the pulsating life of the Empire's greatest city.

These people, even the humblest newspaper-seller or boot-black, possessed something that could never be his unless he proved himself, starting from scratch with them. Then, and then only, he could look everyone in the eye, for money must always play a poor second to manhood.

He paused at a lighted window filled with brightly coloured posters for regiments of the line, for artillery, for the Navy. Kitchener pointed a finger at him from a wall: 'Your King and Country need You'. Perhaps, thought Jackson, I also need them.

He went into the recruiting office. A handful of thin youths with pinched, pale faces and shabby clothes stood patiently in line in front of a desk while two sergeants laboriously wrote out their particulars. A third sergeant approached Jackson, noted his expensive suit, his silk tie, the spats and beautifully polished shoes. This was no ordinary recruit from a clerk's stool or from behind the plough: this one had style, money, and, doubtless, influence.

'Can I help you, sir?' the sergeant asked respectfully.

'Yes,' said Jackson. He glanced at the posters on the wall behind the desk. A picture of Canterbury Cathedral caught his eye, with an invitation: 'Join the Buffs, Third of Foot, The East Kent Regiment, Pride of the Line'.

'I want to enlist in the East Kents,' he said slowly.

'Officer entry, sir?'

'No. Definitely not. As a private soldier.'

The editor of *The Enquirer* sat in his office high above Fleet Street, facing his New York correspondent, who had arrived in London earlier that day, bringing with him a report written in the United States.

'Since I was coming on leave, I thought it best to bring this with me personally,' he explained. 'I thought it a bit too sensitive to send by any other means.'

'I agree,' said the editor. His face was grave.

'I have read it with the greatest interest, but at this stage in the war – three years old and still no sign of victory – it would be dynamite to publish it.'

'It is all true,' the correspondent replied defensively.

'That is the trouble. The censors will absolutely castrate it, and if they didn't, then I think we would face charges of spreading alarm and despondency. *The Enquirer* could even be closed down.'

'You stood up over the shell scandal,' the correspondent pointed out.

'We had to. The proprietor insisted.'

'And he was right. Events proved that.'

'I know. But things were different then. People were more – how shall I put it? – idealistic. The war was still young. People believed what they were told. What we said was the truth. What the other side said were lies. Also, we could have lost the war then, easily. With America in, we could not lose it now.'

'Maybe not,' said the correspondent, 'but we are still losing millions of men, and millions in money, through a total lack of preparation for any conflict. With our Empire, we are like a man who has inherited a huge estate, with farms, villages and so on over a vast area. Then one day he faces a dispute over a boundary – and does nothing. Thieves see he is weak, so they break in and rob him. He has neglected to pay his insurance – as an economy, of all things – so when he has these losses there is no compensation.

'When gypsies occupy an outlying farm, he lets them stay. When a barn full of hay burns down, he has to write it off. That was Britain's situation. She was totally unprepared. There is no future at all for this country or the Empire if we do not learn the basic lessons of conservation and the consolidation of our national assets. When we needed new shells in tremendous quantities, we had to buy them in – largely from America, which has grown rich at our expense.'

He picked up his report and began to read from it.

'Look at these figures. On October 8th, 1914, when the war was only three months old, Russia ordered nine hundred and sixty pound weight – less than half a ton – of TNT for high-explosive shells from the du Pont concern. Within a week, France had ordered eight million pounds of powder – 3571 tons – and one and a quarter million pound weight – 558 tons – of gun cotton. That was as much as du Pont normally produces in a whole year.

'By the end of 1914, the Allies had placed orders with du Pont for fifteen times as much smokeless powder again, and nearly three times as much gun cotton and TNT. Within less than three months these colossal orders had increased a further three and a half times. Within a twelvemonth, we gave them another order for seven and a half *million* pounds of powder – 3348 tons – and twenty-two *million* pounds – 9821 tons – of TNT

Why couldn't we make this stuff ourselves? We have the resources and the scientists.

'Remember, this happened at a time when the du Pont company was only producing eight million pounds of smokeless powder in a year – not in a few months.

'To cope with our orders, they had to build new plants, so they said: "We *can* produce all the explosives you need, gentlemen. But the factories we must build to do so may only be scrap when the war is over and the demand exhausted. You are asking us to contract for raw materials that may not be needed next month – or even next week – if the war ends suddenly. It is *your* war, gentlemen. The risks must also be yours." '

'A very reasonable attitude,' said the editor.

'Of course – from their point of view it was common sense. But from ours, it only showed how unprepared we were. Not only did the Allies pay enormous sums for explosives they could have manufactured themselves more cheaply, they even had to build factories for rivals to produce them! And after the war, those factories, every one modern, with the latest, most up-to-date plant, will be far more efficient than ours, which date from the middle of the last century. Isn't that a story worth printing?'

'I'll speak to Mrs Jackson,' said the editor. 'She deals with policy matters in the absence of the proprietor in France. If we cannot use the stories now, they will hold. We could use them later.'

'Later?' retorted the correspondent bitterly. 'That's England all over. Wait and see. Sleep on it. Don't rush things. Tomorrow is another day. There are better fish in the sea than ever came out of it.

'The tide of that sea is on the ebb. If we don't move now, the country will be left high and dry on the shore. That is what I learned from my time in the States, but no-one is prepared to heed it. Not even you, on whom I pinned great hopes. Do you know what I'm going to do? I'm going out to the Press Club to get drunk!'

Joanna Jackson kept one hour free every evening for a telephone call from the editor when he gave her a brief outline of the contents of next morning's front page, or a visit from him, if the war news was serious.

She received him that evening in the drawing room of her house. Although everything was still elegant, the editor noticed that the paint on the skirtings was slightly scuffed. Dust lay on the book shelves, and silver ornaments were missing, locked away in a bank vault. The exception was the Rolls-Royce mascot, mounted on a plinth, which he had seen so often. He nodded towards it.

'She died, you know,' he said. 'The model.'

'I didn't know. When did that happen?'

'She was accompanying Lord Montagu on a ship, the P & O liner, *Persia*. It was torpedoed off Crete on the way to Port Said.'

'So many deaths, so much sadness,' said Joanna softly.

For a few moments, she was not in this drawing room in Belgravia. She was back on her honeymoon on that enchanted drive through Europe, in a sunlit world of happiness, hearing from Robert about the mascot's model, Eleanor Velasco Thornton.

Joanna poured a whisky for the editor, and he sat watching her face as she read the correspondent's report. Joanna seemed pale and tired. For the first time at their regular meetings, she was wearing reading glasses. Even the very rich are feeling the strain of the war, he thought. They have managed to conceal it until now. He wondered how it would end; when it would end; and then, *if* it would end. There had been a Thirty Years War once, hadn't there, and a Hundred Years War? Why should this one be any different?

Joanna handed back the papers to him, removed her spectacles and put them on a side table.

'A very disturbing story,' she said. 'The irony so far as I am concerned is that Mr and Mrs Douglas-Sodawaterwallah tried to interest the du Pont company in the States in manufacturing Chinese Powder that Mr Douglas, one of the founders of Trinity-Trio, had brought from Canton. They had no success, so they took it to powder factories here in this country, to try and persuade them to produce it. But while everyone agreed that it was the strongest explosive they had ever encountered, no-one would manufacture it.

'I was speaking to Lord Moulton, the Director General of British Explosive Supplies, the other day. He told me that the Allied Armies simply could not have held out at all in 1915, if it had not been for du Pont supplying the explosives. All our factories could not manufacture anything like enough – and a lot of what they did make was of very indifferent quality.

'The chief of the British Munitions Board goes even further. He says that the du Pont company is entitled to claim the credit for saving the entire British Army in Flanders – which was something British companies should and *could* have done.

'At a dinner party here the other evening, one of my guests, a general in the Engineers, said it was common knowledge that German explosive companies were using exactly the same Chinese formula that we could not sell in the States – or here. An extraordinary thing! Apparently, the Germans also turned it down at first, then something, I don't know what, made them look at it again.'

'With disastrous results for the Allies,' pointed out the editor.

'Yes,' Joanna agreed. 'I very much fear so. Now, and also in the future. This country appears to lack vision. We live too much in the past, believing what worked well then will suit equally well now. That is not necessarily true, yet no-one in authority – and few out of it – seems to realise this.

'But, as you say, we cannot publish this report now. It would be far too provocative. Russia, so the Foreign Secretary tells me, is on the verge of revolution. The Americans are claiming they have come over to win the war for us – three years late – and the whole temper of the country is tired and edgy. Every family has suffered.

'I was speaking to a mother the other day who has lost three sons, and that terrible loss is by no means uncommon. The mutilations of the wounded are fearful, too grave even to be reported. I work for the Red Cross, and I can tell you that the sight of young men without arms or legs – known as basket cases – but still with all their mental faculties unimpaired, is harrowing. And for what? Why?'

She paused, poured another whisky for the editor.

'About your husband, ma'am,' he said. 'Have you heard from Mr Jackson lately? We all admired him. There was no need for him to go, especially not as a private of the line. He could have obtained an immediate commission in something like, well, Intelligence or Information.'

'He preferred to do it the hard way – like his readers have to do. I had a letter about him only yesterday.'

'*About* him? He has not been wounded, I trust?'

'Yes, he has,' said Joanna quietly. 'He expects to be invalided home by the end of the month. He was gassed and has lost his sight in both eyes. He will be permanently blind.'

King George the Fifth sat at the head of a small table in the Blue Drawing Room overlooking the rear garden of Buckingham Palace. He was smoking a cigar. Now and then he stroked his beard. Through the window, he and the three elderly men in frock coats who sat with him could see gardeners in green baize aprons sweeping up leaves on the lawn with almost military precision.

The sun glinted weakly on the lake, and autumn had already painted the trees old gold. Only the roofs of buildings in Piccadilly and the top of the war memorial at Hyde Park corner were visible above them. They might have been sitting in a country house, miles from the capital.

These three men were members of the Honours Scrutiny Committee. They had brought for their sovereign's eyes – and signature, if he approved – a list of people whose service to King and Empire the government considered should be recognised by a title. A long initial list had been whittled down to a relative handful: the King was only concerned with the qualifications of candidates for baronetcies and above.

One man read out a name, with a brief description of the man's qualifications, and the King, cigar in hand, nodded acquiescence, or sometimes asked a question.

'Didn't he win the Victoria Cross?'

'Yes, Majesty. He was attached to the Tank Corps in one of their early engagements. He realised there was a great risk of them losing their way and so jumped out of his tank and guided them on foot to their objective. He was gravely wounded, Majesty, but recovered. Now he is managing director of a number of very old Midlands companies. A most enlightened employer.'

'Oh, yes. Excellent choice. Most gallant officer. And the next? An inventor, you say?'

'Yes, Majesty. A distinguished scientist. Fellow of the Royal Society. Carried out remarkable work in arranging that a machine gun mounted on an aircraft could fire between the blades of the propeller as it revolved. This gave much better aiming for the pilot.'

'Why didn't the bullets rip the blades of the propeller to pieces, eh?'

'By a most ingenious set of gears, which he helped to design, Majesty.'

'Remarkable. Most deserving fellow. Well, we're getting on. Who's next?'

'Robert Jackson, Majesty. A partner in the Trinity-Trio empire. Volunteered as a private soldier. Awarded the Military Medal for gallantry. Then he was blinded.'

'I remember,' said the King, drawing on his cigar. 'Gallant fellow. In the early days of the war, he was very outspoken about our shortage of shells. Suppose he was right. But Kitchener couldn't stand him at any price. Nor could Haig. Thought he was a *parvenu*. Wasn't his mother Chinese or something?'

'Yes, Majesty.'

'Any family to carry on the title?'

'His daughter died in childhood in the influenza epidemic just after the war. A son is still at Eton. His wife has been very active in the Red Cross and war charities, and she has contributed large sums to hospitals. Anonymously, of course. She is also a trustee of the Richard Jackson Foundation, set up by his father, a doctor, to study what one might define as unorthodox medical treatments. He is in poor health himself as a result of his wounds.'

'Very well,' said the King. 'Most deserving. Terrible to be blinded. Least we can do. Next?'

So Robert Jackson was created first Baron Jackson of Gravesend in Kent.

When the time came to design his armorial bearings, Garter King at Arms was puzzled by a request he made.

'He wants two golden lilies in the design of his arms. But there's no such thing as a golden lily.'

'Well, he must have his wish,' replied a colleague. 'Perhaps it means something special to him?'

'I believe his mother had something to do with it. She died just after his baronetcy was announced. Very vigorous old lady. Chinese, I believe.'

'Even so,' his companion replied, 'I wish these people had even a basic knowledge of heraldic symbolism. There may be *some* good reason for it, but I can't think what.'

There was no reason why he should, of course; neither the Garter King nor his colleague had ever visited China.

Oregon

The Abbess of the little convent on the Oregon coast stood by the narrow bed, looking down at the dying nun. Outside, breakers thundered on a pale, deserted beach. Trees, brought down by storms long past, raised bare, bleached arms to the afternoon sky. The effect was eerie; ethereal; a moonscape rather than a foreshore.

The nun lay, her eyes closed, her hair grey and thin, face wrinkled as the neck of a tortoise. Her worn hands plucked feebly at the rough sheet. All around her bed stood other nuns, holding crucifixes to their flat chests.

They had not known the dying nun for very long, and in their tiny world of silence, as members of the Sisterhood of Heaven, they could only communicate with a smile, a bow or a nod. It was impossible in these circumstances to know anyone well in the true sense and meaning of those words.

Their lives were hard. Every morning, they woke early to bake bread, milk cows and churn butter. In due seasons of the year, they gathered honey from hives, fruit from the trees, and made preserves. They gave generously of these products to the poor and ill in the community. At dusk, they said their prayers and then went to their cold beds.

In their small province of peace and good works, time not only stood still, it simply did not enter their calculations. An old nun died, a novice arrived; the wheel of youth and age, life and death, kept turning against the grey mists of ocean. Time was, time is, time will be.

As they looked now at the nun on her truckle bed, some of them wished there had been more time to know her, and permission to speak. One day, each of them would be in her situation, life ebbing away. As she was now, so they would be, while others, possibly strangers, would gather around their beds, mute, mourning someone to whom they had never spoken a word.

What good could fifty spinster women, from the age of nineteen to probably eighty-five, achieve that could not be improved and increased if they were only allowed to talk? Had God not given them the power of speech for a purpose? The Abbess was the only one who was permitted to talk, but even she invariably elected silence.

She had seen many nuns die, and the signs were familiar; a rattle in the throat, the sudden frantic gasp for breath as a tired, sometimes lonely, heart laboured, and lungs refused to expand. And then the long slow sigh of release as the spirit left her body to soar, so she prayed, to Heaven, for its just reward.

This nun had been different from many of the other novices. They were usually either very young, reared from childhood by pious parents who wished their daughter to take her vows – for could she not then intercede with the Almighty on their behalf? – or poor, wretched, middle-aged women.

To flee from the world outside, they would accept silence in a nunnery as better than speech with those they hated, or at the least could no longer bring themselves to endure or pretend to love.

Love was a word the Abbess mentioned frequently but she knew its meaning in only one sense; to love the Lord, her God, her Creator, so that she would willingly submit her whole life to doing what she felt He might wish. There were other interpretations of the word, she realised and accepted, but they stood beyond the vows that limited her experience like high, unscaleable walls.

The old nun had admitted to the Abbess she had enjoyed love in many ways, with many people. Her face could have been pretty years ago, but it had been rouged too often, and the shadows on her eyelids had been purpled too much, and her hair was brittle from years of dyes. She was not at all the sort of person the Abbess would usually have accepted as a novice, but what made her all the more remarkable, and even welcome, was the fact she was wealthy. At their first meeting, she had shown documents to the Abbess that proved this conclusively.

'And I will leave all this money, either to you or to your Order, whichever you wish,' she had promised.

'Why?' the Abbess asked her. There must be a reason. The rich not only paid late; generally, they gave little and seldom, and always on strict, even harsh, conditions.

'That question takes one word to ask,' the woman had replied, 'but it could take me a year to answer. I have done terrible things in my life, Abbess, things I would not – could not – wish to discuss with you, a Sister of the Cloth, a Bride of Christ.

'I have been to places you could not begin to imagine. I have sinned in every sense of the word. I have lied, given false witness many times. I have fornicated with men, lain with women, even with beasts. I have been a voluptuary. I have taken drugs to inflame my basest lusts. I have used my money to buy who I wanted – not simply *what* I wanted – and when I wanted them.

'I have never been concerned with any consequences of this selfish and wicked behaviour, either to others or to myself. I considered myself to be above all morality, and the risk of being required to pay any price whatever for my pleasures. And then, slowly, I began to realise I was nothing. I did not belong to anyone, let alone to myself. I had no friends, and I experienced great fears both of this world and the next.

'Like you, I was born into the faith, but while you believed, I abandoned its teachings early on. As a child, I went to church regularly. I prayed every night. Now I want to go back to those habits, but I cannot go back on my own. I need your help and your prayers. Will you admit me here?'

'You sound as though you have humility,' the Abbess admitted. 'But to say something is not necessarily to mean it, or, much more difficult, to do it. You may change your mind when you realise how spartan and disciplined our life is here, without the comforts of the world outside, even without speech. But I will accept you – on one condition. That on admission here, you at once make over all your money to the Order. Irrevocably.'

The other woman looked at her with tired, unhappy eyes.

'I agree,' she said. 'You strike a hard bargain, but you force me to accept, because only by doing so will I *have* to stay here. There will then be no way out for me. Money can always buy an escape route. It is the key to open every door but the last. I may come to hate your Order and your silence. I may even come to hate you, although I trust not, and you may even hate me. But we will then have to bear with each other until my life's end.'

And now the spirit was escaping from her wiry, tortured body. The final door from this world to the next was about to open. The Abbess glanced enquiringly at her deputy, who had been a nurse before she had taken her vows. She nodded almost imperceptibly. When they looked again, it was as though nothing had changed on the face of the nun in the bed, but those assembled around it knew that everything had. They were no longer looking at a sister, a novice nun; they were gathered around a corpse. Instinctively, they all knelt down, and the Abbess led them in prayer.

'Accept, O Lord, the soul of this our sister. Have pity on her, as on us at the day of Your Judgement. May her sins, whatever they were, however grievous they have been, be washed clean by Your Son's most precious blood. We ask this in His name, Thy Son, Jesus Christ, to whom be glory, honour, power and dominion, world without end.'

They all said 'Amen', and stood up. Some of the nuns made the sign of the cross, then bowed and backed away from the corpse to go about their duties. Nothing must delay the work of the convent. Their concern was always with the living; as it was written, let the dead bury the dead.

The nun who had been a nurse and the Abbess were left with a third nun of feeble mind, who was usually engaged in carrying in logs chopping wood or drawing water from the well. At a word from the Abbess she pulled away the sheet that covered the dead nun. She would wash the body, dress it in a shroud, and then others would help her to carry it to a mortuary on the edge of the convent garden.

Here, lay brothers from a monastery nearby were allowed to visit. They would dig the grave, and a priest would read the burial service. Then the dead woman's wooden plate and enamel mug, her crude metal spoon, fork and knife would be washed and put on a shelf to await the next arrival.

The Abbess undid the buttons of the shift in which the nun had died, slipped it off one shoulder and pulled it free. Suddenly, the feeble-minded sister began to shriek and jump up and down as though demented. Her eyes started from her head like onions; froth gathered on her lips.

'What is the matter, child?' asked the Abbess, shocked and shaken by this sudden, unexpected, unseemly disturbance. The nun was jabbing her finger frantically towards the corpse, mouthing unintelligible sounds, like an animal in an extremity of fear. The two other women followed her gaze.

The shift was now wide open. They were not looking at the body of a dead novice, Sister Evelyn, but at the naked corpse of an elderly man.

London

On December 20th, 1923, *The Enquirer* newspaper printed its front page with a black border, a distinction usually reserved for the death of the Sovereign. The main article on the page was headed *LORD JACKSON DIES: A man who spoke for England.*

> The death is announced of the first Lord Jackson of Gravesend at his home in Belgravia, London.
>
> Lord Jackson was the proprietor of *The Enquirer* and the Enquirer Group of magazines and provincial newspapers. While serving as a private soldier in the East Kent regiment in 1915, he was awarded the Military Medal for gallantry. He was later blinded in a gas attack and never regained his sight or the robust health he had previously enjoyed. His wife and son were with him at his death.
>
> Field Marshal Earl Haig said last night: 'Robert Jackson must be regarded as a casualty of the war. He joined a regiment of the line as a private soldier, serving in Flanders for eighteen months before he was blinded as a result of a German gas attack. I did not always agree

with the policies of his newspaper, but I must pay tribute to his courage and his patriotism.'

Mr Clive Douglas, the well-known racing motorist and joint managing director of Trinity-Trio, said from Le Touquet, where he is on a brief holiday: 'With the death of Lord Jackson, a link with earlier days of the great company of which his father was one of the three founders, has been severed. He was a brilliant man of business and a warm and steadfast friend. The worlds of commerce and public life in this country and elsewhere have lost a man who can ill be spared at this time.'

Lord Jackson was elevated to the peerage two years ago at the personal wish of His Majesty as a direct result of his efforts, as proprietor of this newspaper and joint chairman of Trinity-Trio, to bring to public notice the grave shortage of artillery shells in the earlier years of the Great War, and then to remedy this grievous cause, which was the direct and indirect root of so many Allied casualties.

He was the only son of the late Dr Richard Jackson, whose public benefaction, The Richard Jackson Foundation, has investigated the claims of comparative medicine with beneficial results to innumerable people whose diseases and disabilities had confounded Western orthodox medical science.

With the late Mr Alec Douglas of Coupar Castle, Scotland, and the late Captain Marvin Ross of Boston, Mass., USA, Dr Jackson founded, in the last century, what has since become one of Britain's most prosperous and influential trading companies. It is said that the name Trinity-Trio grew from the fact that these three remarkable gentlemen were joint and equal founders. Each certainly contributed disparate and special talents to the outstanding growth of this commercial group.

Robert Jackson was born in Calcutta where he was educated at the High School and later at the University. He came to England on the death of his father when he inherited one-sixth of the shares of the company. Within a year of landing on these shores, he married Miss Joanna Gray, to whose mother Dr Jackson had also bequeathed an equal share in the company. Their marriage was extremely happy and there were two children; Isobel who died tragically in the influenza epidemic of 1919, and James, who has already let it be known that he does not wish to use the title.

Lord Jackson had an intuitive sense of what the public wished to read in newspapers and magazines, and on this, he built the success of The Enquirer Group. He had no formal training whatever in this field, but in the words of the late Sir Harold Arbuthnott, a former editor of this newspaper, 'He was a born journalist. He had an open and enquiring mind. He reasoned – and the circulation of *The Enquirer*, which far outstrips that of all other daily organs of the first rank, is proof of his gift – that whatever interested him would also interest other people.'

No subject was too obscure or too esoteric for him to publish an article about it. He established the largest and highest paid and best qualified corps of foreign correspondents in British daily journalism. Every one of them and every home affairs reporter was required to contribute at least one story to the newspaper every day.

Lord Jackson maintained an office in *The Enquirer* building and from this directed a constant stream of ideas and memoranda to his editors. After he lost his sight, he would have the newspaper read to him every day by relays of readers, and would then dictate his comments, views and ideas to stenographers.

His greatest contribution, as the Prime Minister says in his special tribute [page 2], was 'his tireless and patriotic campaign to redress the imbalance of British and Allied armaments in the early days of the war. Into this he threw his prodigious energies, working selflessly day and night without thought of reward. Totally and courageously, he disregarded personal criticism and contumely heaped upon him from ill-informed people who, unlike Lord Jackson, utterly misunderstood the essential gravity of the situation.'

This campaign – with which, of course, the late Lord Northcliffe was vigorously and brilliantly associated through his own national group of newspapers – was successful. Lord Jackson then decided that he would join a fighting service. Why he suddenly decided to take this step, he never revealed. Perhaps the motto he chose to go beneath his arms of two golden lilies provides a clue. It was 'Beyond the dreams of avarice'. And that is where Lord Jackson's dreams could be found. Wealth he had in abundance, and with it, power, influence and fame. Yet it is doubtful whether he cared greatly for any of these things.

He could easily have obtained a commission in any of the Armed Services and put his great talents to use in some Intelligence or informative capacity. But with typical courage he neither asked nor sought special consideration. Instead, he joined up as a private soldier in the East Kent Regiment.

A close family friend said last night, 'His decoration, along with membership of the Coliseum Club, was something of which, disregarding his peerage and the enormous success of all his commercial enterprises, Lord Jackson was most proud.'

A memorial service will be held in St Bride's Church, Fleet Street, at a date to be announced.

Part Three

The 1920s to 1945

Brooklands

Clive Douglas – he had dropped the Sodawaterwallah part of his name as soon as he came of age – waited until the last race of that afternoon at Brooklands, the Junior Car Club's two-hundred-mile event – before he set out for home. He usually did this to avoid the worst of the traffic. After a race meeting, many spectators, especially middle-aged men of generally mild demeanour, drove their Morrises and Standards and Singers as if they were actually competing in a race themselves. Sometimes this delusion led to crashes on such fast stretches of road as the Portsmouth Road or the Great West Road. It saved time – and was safer – to let these people get out of the way.

He stood in the restaurant overlooking the huge upturned concrete saucer of the track. The entrance through a tunnel to the road was still jammed with spectators' cars on their way home. A few racing cars were being started in the paddock. They moved with snorting, barking exhausts like expensive bright blue, red and green toys. Some would be driven home by racing drivers. The richer competitors, like Clive, used car transporters, converted trucks or single-decker buses.

The sun flashed heliograph messages from a hundred windscreens, and girls wearing short skirts squeezed into the back of open tourers, and waved their floppy hats at friends fifty yards away, shouting messages they could not hear.

Clive had not been racing that Saturday. He had been watching others race, and betting on the results. Long Tom, the track's bookmaker, was a great character, and apart from betting arrangements, motor racing in Britain owed much else to horse racing. Initially, when Brooklands opened in 1907, on the private estate of Henry Locke-King, who wished to provide a testing ground for British cars, competing drivers wore coloured silks like jockeys. Races were started by a member of the Jockey Club, and bets were placed in guineas. The area where the cars were prepared and warmed up was still called the paddock.

Clive had been offered three to one on Salamando's supercharged Fiat, four to one on a similar car driven by Malcolm Campbell, and seven to one on a Bugatti win. He had bet on them all and lost £2,000. The two Fiats had been unable to stay the course, and Leon Cushman's yellow Bugatti exasperatingly came second behind an Alvis. If Clive had put anything on that car – the odds had been around a hundred to one – he would have cleaned up, but added to earlier and as yet still unpaid gambling debts, he was now thousands of pounds down. He did not like to admit even to himself exactly how much he owed, but the total was far more than he could possibly afford, more than he could ever hope to borrow (on top of his other loans) from any bank or moneylender, on their increasingly harsh and usurious terms. In the circumstances, he reacted in the only way he knew: he snapped his fingers at a passing waiter.

'Half a bottle of champers,' he told him brusquely.

'On your account, sir?'

'Of course.'

'Very good, sir.'

Within minutes, the waiter returned, not with half a bottle of champagne in a bucket of ice, as Clive had hoped, but with the restaurant manager.

'I am sorry, sir,' the manager said, as though he meant it, 'but we cannot give you any more credit.'

'What the hell do you mean, no more credit?' said Clive angrily. 'You know who I am.'

'I do indeed, sir, but you already owe us £217 on the bar account, and we simply cannot afford to let it go any higher. Those are my orders, sir. Not, I may say, of course, my personal decision.'

'I've been betting thousands out there on the track,' shouted Clive, 'and now you won't sell me a drink! It's bloody scandalous!'

He hated to have any wish thwarted; any refusal of his instructions was a deliberate personal affront. He was being 'got at'.

Some spectators, leaning on the bar drinking cocktails, raised their eyebrows at his outburst. Women with them gave silent thanks that they were not Clive's guests. Wouldn't it be awful if that had been Jackie or Duggie or Frank, behaving like that? My dear, I wouldn't know where to look.

'Having a bit of trouble, old boy?' a man in a check suit asked sympathetically.

'Not really. Only this clown won't let me buy half a bottle of champers on the slate.'

'Have it on me,' suggested another man in a blazer with brightly polished brass buttons. He took a pound note from a wallet of imitation alligator skin.

'Thank you very much, sir,' said the manager gratefully, and nodded to the waiter, who poured the champagne.

'Cheers, Reggie,' said Clive. 'Have one on me next meeting, eh?'

'Glad to,' said the man in the blazer, and winked at his companions. Old Clive Douglas was rich as bloody what's his name, that Greek bloke, Croesus, but he always seemed hard up.

Clive knew his promise rang hollow as an empty gin bottle. He had made it too often for anyone to believe it any more, and the champers tasted like acid on his tongue. He drank one glass quickly and poured himself another, while he considered his financial situation.

He had spent a fortune since he came into the estate, and owed as much again. In his hands, money just seemed to dissolve, to melt without trace. The bank manager in Perth, whom he had visited after his mother's death, had brought a bottle of Long Glen whisky from his cupboard and poured out two glasses as they sat discussing money.

'So you see, Mr Douglas, we drink your local brew,' he said. 'I would like to wish you every success in the future, both personal and financial.'

'Thank you,' Clive replied. 'Since you mention it, that's why I came to see you. About some money.'

'No problem at all, sir. You leave the deeds of a farm or two with us and it will be a pleasure to accommodate you. How much have you in mind?'

'Well, I have great plans for the estate,' Clive answered him vaguely. He wanted to say he would use the money for something which the bank manager might conceivably consider worthwhile. That way, he should advance him more. After all, it was really his, and his security was huge. 'I would like a tidy sum,' he went on briskly. 'Say £10,000. For a start.'

'For a start? A nice round figure. If you'll just sign this form, I'll see that it is made available for you. But, for a sum of that size, the bank will require the deeds of more than one farm, as I am sure you appreciate. Land up here is not as valuable as it was, you know. One can buy an estate for as little as £2,000 these days, with all this talk of slumps and so on. It may be that they will require a lien on the whole property. But it will be purely a formality, of course. Simply for the record, to satisfy head office.'

'I see. Well, I will sign whatever I have to. Quite a lot needs doing on the estate. Not much was done during the war, so I will be improving it – and increasing its value.'

But he had not spent a penny on any improvements. The money had gone on expensive motor cars and on gambling, for which he developed an obsession. The anticipation of a huge win, spent in advance, far outweighed the depression which followed almost constant losses.

That £10,000 had gone within the year, and he still had interest to pay. He then sold fifty acres at the end of the glen to a recently demobbed sergeant from the Army Service Corps, who wanted to start a motor garage. This paid the interest for a few more months. Then bookmakers to whom he owed money stopped sending him letters about payment and instead sent messengers. These were men in light blue suits with bowler hats and well-polished shoes. They looked like retired policemen or Army warrant officers; some were both.

Clive was persuaded to sell a painting, then a silver tea service. Prices were very low. After a feverish post-war boom in 1919, the market was poor. Factories were closing, laying off thousands of workers. The future looked bleak, and people with savings took them out of shares and then even out of the banks in case there was a sudden financial crash, not only in Britain, but throughout the world.

Clive toyed with the idea of selling some of his master shares in Trinity-Trio, but this was easier to talk about than to do. There was a slump in rubber in Malaya, where they owned plantations; the chewing gum business in the States was facing strong competition. Leone Pastellini had been killed by a hit-and-run driver. His successor lacked Leone's dedication: under his management there had been strikes and lock-outs. Far Eastern trade seemed fraught with difficulties Clive did not understand or care about. Making money was so boring. He was content to leave it to his directors and managers and their staffs. That was their affair. He only wanted money for what it could buy – fun.

Now that he had spent far more than he could possibly repay, he would have to sell something else. But what?

He finished the champagne, waved goodbye to the others still at the bar, and went out to his Hispano-Suiza. Once behind the wheel, looking along the polished aluminium bonnet to the elegant stork mascot above the broad shoulders of the silver radiator, he felt more relaxed, more secure. He always felt like this when surrounded by his own possessions, even if they were mortgaged. Without visible evidence of wealth, he felt naked and oppressed. The feeling was illusory, fanciful, like the name of this huge car with its crocodile-skin upholstery, its dashboard inlaid with mother-of-pearl. Would it sound anything like so impressive if its name was translated into the more prosaic Spanish-Swiss, chosen to honour the nationalities of the car's financial backers and designer?

Clive drove out of Brooklands through Weybridge to London, effortlessly overtaking slow-moving streams of traffic, and racing cars being driven without mudguards or even number plates, drivers crouching behind the wheel in leather coats and helmets. He spent that night at the Coliseum Club, where credit arrangements were agreeably lax. On the Sunday morning, he drove up the Great North Road to Coupar Castle. There was little traffic about and the twelve-cylinder car ate up the miles so swiftly that he was enjoying a Long Glen special malt before dinner.

'Two gentlemen called this afternoon to see you, sir,' the butler informed him.

'What about?' he asked. They were probably some swine sent to dun him for a debt. Who else would call on a Sunday, believing, no doubt, that on this day of rest he must be at home?

'They did not say, sir. They were American gentlemen. They said they would be here at ten o'clock tomorrow morning.'

'Where are they from? What bloody cheek to say they will come tomorrow! I might be busy. In fact, I *am* busy. I will get in touch and tell them so. They left their names, an address?'

'No, sir.'

'Well, you should have insisted on it,' Clive told him angrily. 'Remember that next time. *Always* get their names. Not even a telephone number? Ridiculous.'

'I am sorry, sir.'

The butler withdrew. He did not care for his new master. He remembered Mr Sodawaterwallah. There had not been any shouting or bad-tempered banging of doors then. He had been a gentleman.

At ten o'clock on the following morning, Clive, never an early riser, was still eating breakfast when the butler announced that Mr Schoenbach and Mr Logan had arrived to see him. They were waiting in the library.

'Who the hell are they?' Clive asked irritably.

'The American gentlemen who called yesterday. They said they would be here at ten, sir.'

'Oh. Them. Let them wait,' said Clive shortly and poured himself another cup of coffee. They were probably only tourists, claiming that their ancestors had lived here, or some such rubbish. To hell with them. He finished his breakfast, deliberately not hurrying, buttering a third slice of toast he did not really want and glancing through the racing notes in *The Scotsman*. Then he went out to meet his visitors.

Mr Schoenbach was small and round, with strikingly thin legs covered in tight tweed trousers. He wore highly polished brown boots and a gaberdine sports jacket. Mr Logan was taller and thinner and wore a dark business suit. He held a grey Homburg with a rolled brim.

As soon as Clive saw them, he wished he had not kept them waiting. There was about them an air of power, almost menace, quite out of keeping with what he considered their comical appearance.

'You must excuse us calling without an appointment,' said Mr Schoenbach in a strong American accent, 'but we found ourselves in Edinburgh, and it seemed easier to hire a car and driver and motor out here rather than to write or telephone.'

'What did you wish to see me about?' asked Clive, looking from one to the other.

'A business matter,' said Mr Logan. He had a strong Irish accent, soft and persuasive. 'We understand, Mr Douglas, that you own Long Glen Distillery?'

'That is so.'

'Well, we have always liked Scotch whisky, and having some money to spare, the stock markets in Montreal and New York being pretty buoyant, we want to make sure we never run short of the stuff. We would like to buy your distillery.'

'Buy the distillery?' Clive repeated in amazement. 'But it is part of the estate. It really is not for sale.'

'Everything and everybody is said to have a price,' said Mr Schoenbach smoothly. 'As your Cecil Rhodes said, "Tell me a man's ambitions, and I will tell you his price." A joke, naturally. We would not wish to dismiss any of the staff. Rather, we'd take on new people and produce more whisky, much more. And, of course, we will pay you in cash – quickly and without any fuss.'

'But you are Americans, surely,' said Clive. 'You've had Prohibition for years. Speakeasies. People making gin in bathtubs. That sort of thing.'

'Exactly. You are well informed, sir. We wish to import whisky of the highest quality, not some concoction brewed from commercial alcohol and potatoes and so on, and not to the States. Our market is Canada – not, I am glad to say, affected by the Volstead Act.'

'I see. This is very sudden and totally unexpected,' said Clive. 'How did you hear of Long Glen? We do not export much of the stuff, if any.'

'That is true, Mr Douglas. But what you do sell overseas is highly thought of. So here we are.'

'I am flattered, but I have never thought of selling the distillery. It is very old, you know,' he added lamely. 'It has been in my family's ownership for many, many years. I will have to discuss it with my lawyer.'

'Please do that. Put us in touch. We will negotiate with him if you change your mind, and decide to sell.'

'One thing, however,' added Mr Schoenbach. 'We do seek a quick decision. We are looking at half a dozen other distilleries in this part of Scotland. All much the same size and some producing more spirit than Long Glen, although not in my opinion of the same high quality. If we do not finalise a deal with you this week, then we may have to look elsewhere. Do I make myself clear?'

'Perfectly,' said Clive.

He wrote the address of the Writer to the Signet on a piece of paper.

'I will speak to him on the telephone now and advise him you will contact him.'

He watched their hired sleeve-valve Daimler drive up the long road to the end of the glen, trailing its distinctive frond of blue exhaust smoke. Then he went to the telephone and asked the operator to connect him with the Writer's number. The Writer drove out to see him that evening.

'A strange couple,' was his verdict. 'But they mean business. They came to see me this afternoon. They have been into the prospect thoroughly. They know all sorts of facts and figures. I don't know how, but they do. Most impressive. A bit disturbing, actually. They have really done their homework.

'They are prepared to offer you £25,000 in cash now, for the distillery and two acres of land around it in case they may wish to expand. A very high price indeed, I need hardly say, in the present financial climate.'

'A great deal of money,' said Clive, impressed.

'Indeed, yes, Mr Douglas. But in relation to your debts, not really such a lot. In fact, if you accept this offer it will pay off your debts, and possibly leave you a few thousand or so – no more.'

'I lost £2,000 on Saturday at Brooklands. If I accept, I will have nothing.'

'Not exactly. But you would certainly have no debts. I could not discuss your financial position with them, naturally, but I had the strong impression that they already knew a great deal about it, and were not unsympathetic.'

'You mean they offered more money?'

'Yes and no. They are prepared to pay you a further £15,000, making a total of £40,000, if you will also give them the option to buy, at today's value, half of your shareholding in Trinity-Trio any time during the next ten years.'

'Is that good or bad? I never understand money, except how to spend it.'

'It's a good offer for the distillery and for the shares – as things are now. They can, of course, fall in value. We have some harsh times ahead of us in this country, as anyone who reads the papers must know. Also, Trinity-Trio is a private company, and you cannot sell your shares on the Stock Exchange, although the company could be floated at some future date. If that happened and the shares rose, they could be buying them for well under their real value, and these are voting shares. The decision is up to you.'

Clive poured out two Long Glens and gave one to the Writer.

'You know my position,' he said. 'The bookies are after me. Although they can't issue a writ for a gambling debt, they can make life very uncomfortable. You have no other suggestion as to where I could get more money?'

'Short of working for it, no,' said the Writer wryly.

Clive frowned.

'I think I will take their offer, on condition I get the money this week.'

'They have every intention of that, Mr Douglas. Indeed, they have already engaged their own lawyers in anticipation of your answer. There is one other condition attaching to their offer, which I have to tell you. After ten years, they can renew their option on your shares for a further ten years on payment of £1,000. When the second option runs out, they can renew on the same terms.'

'For how long?'

'For as long as they wish. You get another £1,000 each time, of course.'

'Seems fair enough,' said Clive, already spending the money in his mind. 'Do I have to tell the other shareholders?'

'It is your duty. You are seriously diluting the company's voting shares. One-third is, I understand, already owned by American interests, and now others – also Americans, oddly enough – want a further one-sixth. The merits of Trinity-Trio have certainly impressed people on the other side of the herring pond. No doubt about it.'

'What if I don't tell the others? I only meet them at partners' meetings every three months. We send each other Christmas cards. That's about all the contact we have.'

'I can only advise you most strongly to be frank with your colleagues – as you would wish them to be with you.'

'I'll make my own decision,' retorted Clive, and poured out a further four fingers of Long Glen for each of them.

'Which is?'

'That I don't sell them 50 per cent, but 49 – so I still have the controlling share. What do you say?'

'It is your decision, Mr Douglas. I will put it to the Americans tomorrow morning.'

He did. They agreed.

London

The quarterly partners' meeting of Trinity-Trio, held in their new London offices in Queen Victoria Street, near the Thames, was all but over. The partners had reached the final heading on the agenda: 'Any Other Business'.

Clive had chaired the meeting, and now he looked around enquiringly at the others present. Was there anything further to be discussed?

'Yes,' said Ebenezer, the company secretary. 'There is one matter on which I want your collective opinion.'

He took a letter from a folder.

'I have received this,' he went on, 'from the Abbess of a convent outside Oregon, on the west coast of the United States. The religious order of the Sisterhood of Heaven. As you will recall, Evelyn Ross retreated there shortly after the death of Captain Ross. Before that, she had seen fit to give away to an American charitable trust, United Charities Incorporated, based in Trenton, New Jersey, half her shareholding in our company.

'We would naturally have welcomed the opportunity of buying these voting shares from her, but we were not offered them. There was, of course, nothing we could do to prevent her giving them away. But it is not in the best interests of the company to allow any outsider to hold as much as one-sixth of the total voting shares.

'However, that is all in the past. The Abbess now writes to tell me that Evelyn Ross died, apparently of heart disease, some time ago. The will has only recently been proved. She has left the remainder of her shareholding to this religious organisation.'

'Which means then that we around this table now only hold two-thirds of the voting shares?' asked Clive sharply.

'Exactly. We are in no danger whatever of any outsider taking over the company – so long as we keep these shares. But our position has been weakened, and we must always keep this in mind.'

'And there is nothing we can do about this latest bequest?'

'Nothing whatever – so far as the bequest goes,' said Ebenezer, 'but the Abbess adds a most extraordinary fact. She says that only when Evelyn Ross's body was seen naked for the first time was it discovered that she was not a woman *but a man*. Captain Ross had gone through a form of marriage with a transvestite.'

'So his marriage was not legal?'

'Exactly. It was not a marriage at all.'

'In that case, Evelyn Ross had no right whatever to the shares in the first place,' said Joanna. 'Since she had no title to them she could not give them away to this charitable organisation or to the convent or to anyone else – because they were not hers to give away.'

'That is also my reading of the situation,' agreed Ebenezer. 'I have taken counsel's opinion, and he corroborates this view.'

'Then let us get these shares back – at once.'

'Again, that is my feeling, but this will not be as simple as it sounds. It would involve long and complex litigation. While Trinity-Trio could stand this easily enough financially, in view of this most unfortunate sexual connotation, I think it might be unwise to pursue that course.'

'Why?' asked James Jackson.

'Our opponents would understandably use every means of attracting publicity, possibly of the lowest kind, in order to discredit us, and keep their very valuable holdings. The company could be held up to ridicule if it came out that one of our three illustrious founders was so perverted that he deliberately went through a form of marriage with another man. Other revelations might come to light of an equally unsavoury nature. Opium smuggling, the death of three British sailors in Canton in the early days, even the mysterious deaths of O'Brien and Mr Wallace in the jungle. Our past has not been altogether blameless.'

'Nor has the past of any company of comparable size and success that has traded in the places where we have traded,' Jackson replied.

'Agreed. But they would not be subjected to a rigorous examination of their murkier areas. We would. We might win the case – *eventually* – but in the meantime we could have lost credibility on a world-wide scale. Our name would have been dragged through the mud.'

'I do not agree,' said Joanna. 'The whole matter would be forgotten in a week. People's memories are very short.'

'And we have *The Enquirer* and our other magazines,' said Jackson. 'We could print stories about the proprietors of any journal that made fun of us. That would give them pause to think.'

'Possibly, but dog should never eat dog. The diet is indigestible and dangerous. Such a tit-for-tat situation would leave us with very few friends in Fleet Street – and one day we might need them even more.

'My considered opinion, which counsel shares, is that we should ignore the matter, but write to the Abbess and say we are pleased that money Captain Ross made at such personal effort and risk to himself – which even cost him his life, poor man – has been given to such a worthy cause.'

'It's a lot of money,' said Clive. 'And it is legally *our* money.'

'Agreed again,' said Ebenezer. 'But if the chairman will put it to the vote we could see what the opinion of the board is.'

The motion was carried by his casting vote.

'Bloody ridiculous,' said Clive angrily. 'We should have gone after them.'

'A worthy sentiment, with which I agree,' said Ebenezer. 'But I do not think that would work in this instance. There is another more sombre reason I did not wish to raise until you had voted. I have looked into the background of United Charities Incorporated. All the officers appear to have Italian names.'

'They are not Italian on the letterhead,' said Clive, taking a sheet of paper from a file. 'There's Frank Castle, Bernard Andrew, John O'Malley. You can't get more American names than that.'

'Possibly,' said Ebenezer. 'Which could be why they chose them. But my researches show that Frank Castle was once Franco Costello. Bernard Andrew was formerly Bernardo Andriola. And Mr O'Malley's father was Mallinici, all late of Palermo, Sicily.

'If we went after these people they might not even resort to the process of law. They might show their displeasure in far cruder – and more permanent – ways.'

'What exactly do you mean?'

'We are dealing with men who are making fortunes bootlegging during Prohibition in the States. They were originally in small gangs, working in different cities and areas. The gigantic profits on offer now from bootlegging have shown them the wisdom of consolidation – just like other commercial concerns. They are still criminals of the worst and most violent type, but no longer isolated. They have combined, become organised.

'We would not be entering into a legal dispute with a charity, but fighting the immense wealth and huge political and judicial influence of something infinitely more dangerous – organised crime.'

Brooklands

When the chequered flag dropped to mark the winner of that afternoon's Mountain race at Brooklands, all the cars came down, one by one, off the concrete banking.

Clive Douglas had watched Dorothy Stanley-Turner's M.G. overtake the Hon. Peter Aitken's Alfa-Aitken, with an engine nearly four times its capacity, and beat it by 14.8 seconds – and cursed his luck. He had put £1,000 on the Alfa to win.

Exhausts crackled and snorted angrily and asthmatically, engines backfired as their drivers decreased speed. One behind the other, the cars – red, green, blue – one painted with yellow and brown stripes like a huge mint humbug on wheels – drove into the paddock.

Immediately, crowds of enthusiasts gathered around them. Men wearing plus-fours and flat tweed caps or trilbies were eager to be seen with drivers whose names and photographs appeared in the newspapers usually under such headings as 'Dicing with Death' or 'Girl driver in 100 m.p.h. race pile-up'.

Pretty girls in short skirts that showed a lot of silk stocking leaned back against the hot, louvred bonnets of the cars, hoping that their drivers or mechanics or at least *someone* remembered their names: Petal, Mavis

Susan. They chattered, thought Camille Douglas, not unkindly, like excited, brightly plumaged birds – which, in a sense, they were: decorative, but in her view useless in a crisis. What would they do in her situation, for example? Or would they have recognised the type of man Clive was early on in any relationship and not let him get too close?

Mechanics wearing white or blue overalls with the name of their car or its driver carefully woven into the cloth – Bentley, Riley, Sir Malcolm Campbell, Clive Douglas, B. Bira – pushed the cars away. Bonnets were opened, plugs expertly removed, oil levels checked. They worked quickly, quietly, unobtrusively. They were the professionals; this was their job. Wives, children, their rent and rates, depended solely on their skills. The drivers were the playboys, the amateurs. This was their fun. The social gulf between the two groups was wide and often unbridgeable. The mechanics were here on a Saturday afternoon because they needed the money. The drivers were here because they had the money and needed the excitement. Brooklands was a staging post on every year's social round, with Henley, Ascot, Wimbledon. It was justifiably proud of its discreet claim, 'The Right Crowd and No Crowding'.

Camille stood a little apart from the girls because she was slightly older, and also she had seen all this before many times; too many times. Clive went back to his blue Delage in the paddock, pulled off his white leather flying helmet and the blue-tinted goggles he always wore because, like the colour of all his cars, they matched the blue of his eyes. He stood, leaning against the rear wheel, smiling his perfect toothpaste advertisement smile, while the girls and schoolboys in school caps and blazers pointed their Box Kodaks and Brownie cameras at him.

He had won one race that day. Of course he had. He always spent more preparing his car, more on the mechanics who tuned and serviced it, more on everything to do with his hobby than probably any half dozen fellow competitors; if he couldn't win, then who could?

Clive was at his best like this, she thought with grudging admiration, at the centre of attraction: a god, handsome, young, rich, unattainable, stepping from his chariot to mingle briefly with his followers, and then to vanish.

Camille had no idea where he would vanish to that evening. Nor, she had to admit, standing in the Saturday afternoon sun, breathing the amalgam of scents – petrol and Castrol R, burning rubber and scorched paint – that wafted in waves from the hot concrete, did she greatly care.

Clive might go back to the flat in Curzon Street (to which he pointedly had never given her a key) with one or other of the several girl friends she knew about, or maybe with one or more she did not know about. Alternatively, he might decide on the whim of the moment to jump into his Bentley and drive north to Coupar Castle. He was as unpredictable as his moods; now gracious and charming, now morose and irritable.

He had no idea she was coming to Brooklands. She had given up going motor racing after their son, John, was born. The boy had a nanny, of course, and then a governess, before he went off to his prep school, but his arrival had provided Camille with an excuse she realised she had wanted for some time. As Clive's wife, she had known early in their far too hasty marriage that his world was not hers, and never would be. She did not like the raffish atmosphere of motor racing: men in sports jackets with Norfolk pleated backs and pockets, light grey flannel bags, the 'old boy' conversation, jokes only really understood by rich and extravagant young men.

Ages ago, so it seemed, but actually only a few years previously, she had been one of the fascinated, almost adoring crowd of girls attracted by Clive's personality as planets are drawn towards the sun. His interests had been racehorses then, and they had first met at Ascot. One of his horses had won – again, he had spent a fortune on bloodstock – and she happened to be standing next to him when a newspaper photographer asked him to pose for a picture.

'Come into it, too,' Clive invited her, and before she could reply, had put his arm protectively around her shoulders. She had been delighted, almost overwhelmed – and was photographed like that. ('Speed ace with mystery girl'.) He was so charming, so handsome, and he smelled delightfully and very subtly of expensive after-shave which no other young men she knew could afford. He had introduced himself and invited her up to his box. There, a crowd of other young people were enjoying champagne, cold salmon, strawberries and cream. The Prince of Wales, with Mrs Simpson, his friend whose name only rarely appeared in any newspaper, had called cheerfully to Clive as he went past: 'Damn' good show!'

Camille had not given a second's thought to who was paying for the food and drink then, or at half a dozen other parties. Only when they were married, and she happened to see the bills arrive after similar outings, did she discover to her horror that Clive was invariably the host. By then it was too late to remonstrate or criticise. He needed adulation as an actor needs applause. Without it, he sank, wilting and bewildered. Lacking the personality that attracts friends naturally, he did what seemed to him the next best thing: he bought their presence, if not their loyalty.

They had married only months after this first meeting, too soon for her to discover that his charm, the bonhomie and the ready smiles were only on the surface, sweet icing on a darker cake. She had no idea then of the mortgages, re-mortgages, the charges and second charges on the estate and farms, even on the castle, which he had taken out to finance this expensive lifestyle. Two racing cars – a Delage, and a Bentley with an Amherst Villiers supercharger – a Hispano-Suiza for his everyday use, two full-time mechanics and his own workshop at Brooklands did not come any more cheaply than the racehorses with their attendant bills for trainers, vets, blacksmiths.

And all the time Clive was borrowing more money at ever increasing rates of interest, first from bankers, then from brokers, finally from individuals she instinctively distrusted. They would arrive unannounced at the castle, lacking charm or conversation, spend one brief night there, complain about the cold and country life in general, and then depart. They had thick accents and rodent eyes, with more gold in their mouths than teeth.

After each of their visits Clive would enjoy a sudden brief rush of expenditure – a new car, a dozen new suits, a trip on the *Empress of Britain* to New York, until the transfusion of money he had borrowed yet again had melted away and only its repayment remained: another farm to sell, a painting, a terrace of houses in Perth.

Camille never accompanied him on his trips to the United States.

'It's all business, dear,' he would say. 'You wouldn't like it. Lots of boring meetings and things. Not your line at all.'

'What sort of meetings?' she asked him once. 'You have no directorships out there.'

'I have associations,' he replied carefully. 'Americans bought the distillery, remember. We keep in touch. Must do that.'

'A great pity you ever sold the distillery,' she said. 'They have spent money on the place, put in new equipment – which you could have done so easily yourself – and trebled the production.'

'Horses for courses, my dear,' Clive replied. 'I don't ask them to drive my cars at Brooklands, because they couldn't. And they don't ask me to get involved with the business of buying bottles and labels in bulk and so on, because I couldn't do that. And I wouldn't want to do it even if I could.

'Money is to spend, Camille, to have fun with, not to be reduced to items in ledgers and account books full of profit and loss figures. Might as well be a clerk and live in a semi in Streatham or Balham as do that. It's so *boring* – and I am not here to be bored. Ever.'

That was the basic reason, Camille knew: Clive had no staying power, no gift of concentration. He was lazy, weak and a spendthrift, with the lowest threshold of boredom she had ever encountered. Also, he could not bear to be alone. He had to surround himself with people, and he could only do that if he bought their companionship with drinks, dinners, theatre tickets. She had married an illusion, a handsome actor with a sawdust brain.

She stood apart now, slightly behind the crowd, not expecting that Clive would notice her. But he did. He had a sharp eye for strangers: he had been dunned once for a debt, and publicly, to his shame, simply because he hadn't kept an eye out for the process-server. He would never let that happen again.

Camille saw him frown slightly, and then smile as he signed autograph books thrust at him by eager schoolboys. A crackle of exhausts and a crescendo of accelerating engines announced that the next race had begun; thirteen cars of many colours taking part in the Outer Circuit Handicap.

The crowd drifted through the paddock to watch. Clive crossed over to her.

'You didn't say you were coming,' he said, almost accusingly.

'You haven't been home for a week, and I didn't know where you were, so I couldn't very well tell you, could I? But I thought you might be here, as it's Saturday.'

'Well, what brings you along?'

'I was in London. I thought I would take the train down. It's not very far.'

'Any particular reason today?'

'Not really. But Johnny, as you know, had his appendix out last week in the Middlesex, and I took a room to be near him.'

'Oh, I'd forgotten all about that. How is he? All right, I hope?'

'Yes. But he misses you.'

'Well, it's a very simple operation nowadays, appendix.'

'Come back and see him tonight, he'd love that. He adores you. Wants me to tell him all about the races today. You could do that so much better than me – and the visiting hours are pretty flexible on Saturdays. The sister's sweet. Even if we got there late, she'd let us see him.'

'I would like to very much, Camille, but I'm sorry, it's no go. Old Fruity Thurlowe has got a big thrash on down at his place near Brighton. I promised to be there. A whole crowd of us are going. It should be fun. Why don't you come down with me? You'd enjoy it.'

'No, I couldn't today. Not with Johnny in hospital. I told him I'd visit him. He's expecting me. But thank you for asking me, though. Some other time.'

'That's what you always say,' said Clive, fitting a cigarette into his long tortoise-shell holder. 'Some other time. Always got something else to do. Something better, eh?'

'Oh, you know I haven't. But there *is* so much to do, Clive. You don't take any part in running the estate now. You're away so much and someone just has to take the decisions. We've cut down such a lot on staff, it's very difficult to keep things running efficiently with so few left.'

'Don't let's start all that again, for God's sake,' Clive said irritably. 'I'll sell the bally place if necessary.'

'But can you? The last time we discussed this, we found there were three mortgages on it. Maybe there are even more now.'

'We could sell part of it, then. These money-lenders don't know *exactly* how much land I have – I hope. But we can't talk about that boring business here. Give Johnny my love. I must dash. Want to see this race – it's the last of the season, and I've got £1,000 on the Talbot to win. Lost a bit on the Mountain race, blast it. I should have cleaned up. I half thought that M.G. might do it. But, well, there it is. Staying to watch?'

'I'd better get back,' said Camille. 'I'm sorry you can't see Johnny.'

'So am I,' he said. 'But . . . well, life is full of disappointments, isn't it?'

He paused.

'Oh, I nearly forgot. I've got to go to New York next week.'

'Why? Business?'

'Well, not exactly. Fellow I've been seeing a bit of these last few weeks has asked me to his place in the Bahamas. Name of Denver, Paul Denver.'

'What to do there?'

'Oh, a bit of game fishing, sailing, you know that sort of thing. Should be great fun.'

'I see. You will be back by the fifteenth, Clive? We're taking Johnny to the Isle of Wight for two weeks, remember. It's all arranged.'

'Well . . . that's a bit awkward. Fact is, when old Paul asked me, I forgot all about that. Can't *promise* I'll be back, but I'll do what I can. Anyway, you and he will have a wonderful time on your own, you get on so well together. Well, 'bye for now.'

Camille watched him walk away into the crowd. On either side, people nodded to him, waved, bowed. A pretty girl blew him a kiss. It was more like a royal progress than a walk, she thought, and sighed. Soon the crowd had swallowed him up, and she was on her own. She did wait until the end of the race, simply to see who won. The Talbot was second to a Graham-Paige. Clive Jackson had lost another bet, making a total loss on that afternoon of £2,000.

Nassau

When the Pan American Clipper landed on time at Nassau airport on the edge of the cobalt Bahamian sea, Paul Denver, wearing a blue blazer with the badge of the Royal Nassau Ocean Yacht Club, was there to meet Clive Douglas.

'Great to see you,' he said enthusiastically as they shook hands. 'Weather's a bit better here than in England, eh? Last time we met at Brooklands, I almost froze to death – and in summer. Remember?'

Paul Denver had inherited a fortune from an American aunt who he described casually as 'big in breakfast foods'. He was the kind of playboy that Clive would have liked to be. It seemed impossible to diminish his enormous fortune to any serious extent, no matter how much he spent on racing cars, yachts, polo ponies, his homes in Manhattan, Connecticut and here on Cable Beach, Nassau.

Clive had been delighted to be invited to spend as long as he cared yachting and fishing with him. He had been even more delighted when Paul Denver enclosed a first-class return ticket aboard.the *Queen Mary*, and one for the return flight from New York to Miami and Nassau.

'You gave me such a great time when I was over in England with your lovely apartment in Curzon Street and your castle in Scotland, when your wife was away staying with her mother, I felt I had to show you how the poor live here.'

He roared with laughter at this. Clive smiled dutifully, but could not bring himself to laugh. His bank had been in touch with him on the eve of his departure. He owed huge sums on all his accounts, and while they were secured on Trinity-Trio quoted shares, the bank manager pointed out tactfully but firmly in his letter that with the present unsettled international situation, the value of all shares had been falling rapidly.

But how could Clive possibly pay the debts? He could sell more shares, but he had already sold far too many. To sell more now would mean taking even larger losses. How agreeable, how unbelievably pleasant, to be like Paul here, with his avalanche of money from millions of people who started each day with a plate of his aunt's obnoxious cereal.

Denver's house was built in the colonial style: huge stairway, porch, pillars, flag mast, and around it miniatures of the main building.

'For our guests,' he explained. 'We get together in the main house for meals, or if you want to eat out, we have an arrangement that you just sign the check and we settle up. No hassle, no expense. It is my pleasure to make you happy.'

'You have succeeded,' said Clive, looking around the set of rooms in the miniature house. 'This is perfect.'

'Great! If you're happy, then I'm happy.'

Now began days and nights of enjoyment: yacht races, barbecues, game fishing. There was a dance for which Paul took over the ballroom at the best hotel, the British Colonial, engaging the band there. Champagne flowed, as one guest remarked appreciatively, 'like the fountains of Rome'. And best of all there was Maria.

Clive met her on the second evening: dark-haired, sun-tanned, with a slight foreign accent, witty as well as beautiful. She seemed quite simply the loveliest, most ravishing creature he had ever seen.

'I think you've already met my uncle,' she said.

'Where? If he's as good-looking as you, I would remember him.'

'Thank you. He'd be flattered. It was years ago, in Scotland. He bought your distillery – Charles Logan.'

'Why, of course. He was with another man, Mr Schoenbach. How is he?'

'Not around, I fear. He died suddenly. Heart attack.'

'I'm sorry to hear that. And you are Charles Logan's niece. It *is* a small world.'

'You have no idea just how small,' she said, and smiled and raised her glass.

On the morning of the third day, the butler brought Clive two letters which had been sent airmail from England to Trinity-Trio's New York office and forwarded on to him. The first one was from his bank: not any manager now, but a director. Mr Douglas would no doubt wish to regularise the present situation regarding his indebtedness. The combined overdrafts were now so far above the agreed limit that unless he responded immediately, it would be their unfortunate necessity to call in the debt or possess the collateral.

Clive took a sip of fresh orange juice from the breakfast tray before he read the second letter. It was from Ebenezer.

> Dear Clive,
>
> I regret I have to give you very sad news about your wife Camille. As you will know, she was in the habit of visiting John every day.
>
> His doctors tell me that on her last visit she was rather concerned about John's condition – he was not responding to treatment as well as they had hoped – and this might have caused her mind to wander as she drove away from the hospital.
>
> Her car was involved in a collision with a lorry just outside the gates. I am very sorry to tell you she died instantly. You will at least be comforted in the knowledge that she felt no pain. The good news is that John's condition is now improving. He may be discharged from hospital within the week.

Clive let the letter fall on the table, walked out on to the patio, and stood looking across the lawn between palm trees to the sea. He was booked from New York on the next but one return voyage of the *Queen Mary* to Southampton. He should go back earlier, of course. That was his first thought. Then his second was: why?

Camille was dead, and John coming out of hospital. His secretary would see the boy was looked after. There was no need to hurry; he could do nothing if he rushed back. Paul was anxious he should meet a guest coming down from Miami – Bill Carlotti, an old friend, who was big in property and owned a chain of restaurants. Maybe they could do business together? Clive had no idea what, but the prospect seemed alluring. For this reason, he decided not to tell anyone about Camille's death. That evening, however, dancing to a calypso band on a floor especially laid on the lawn behind the main house, he did tell Maria. Not that he had just heard the news, but as if Camille's death had happened fairly recently, and he thought she should know about it. Maria clung more tightly to him in sympathy and understanding: two lonely people under the glittering stars.

'I am sorry,' she said. In fact, Clive was so captivated by her warm, caring attitude that when the music stopped, he realised with embarrassment they were the only couple left on the floor.

The evening was marked by a characteristic display of generosity from Paul. He had ordered from New York a dozen watches of a totally new design. Each had a little window on its face to give the calendar month, the day of the week and the date. Clive had never seen such an ingenious arrangement. He strapped one of these watches on his wrist, and all through the rest of the evening, he kept checking the date: Thursday, August 31st, 1939.

Clive was swimming in a warm and deep translucent sea. Indigo merged with blue, and blue with gold, as he moved slowly, weightlessly, timelessly, so it seemed, to a surface burnished by the sun.

He opened his eyes. He was in bed, naked. His left arm had been under his body, and the watch had dug into his wrist. He glanced at the time and date: 9.30 in the morning on Saturday, September 2nd.

What the hell? Had the damned thing gone mad? How could he have missed a whole day? Was this some joke played on him by Paul? He held the watch to his ear. It was ticking healthily. He tried to wind it up: it was already wound. He glanced across the room towards the window that overlooked the sea. Maria's head was on the next pillow.

He pulled down the coverlet. She was also naked. At the movement, she rolled over and snuggled against him, warm with sleep. His hands searched her body; he felt her nipples harden as her mouth sought his. Her leg moved over his, her arms went around him, as, tongue on tongue, they lay for a blissful, timeless moment.

She drew away slightly.

'Hello, Mr Douglas,' she whispered dreamily, and kissed him again.

'Hello, Maria.'

'No. Not just Maria. *Mrs* Douglas, darling.'

He sat up instantly and looked down at her in astonishment.

'What do you mean?'

She reached out, picking up a sheet of paper from the bedside table next to her.

'That's what it says here, darling. Read it aloud to me. I just love the sound of the words.'

Bewildered, he stared uncomprehendingly at his own marriage certificate. He was married to Maria. Desire left him; he suddenly became conscious of a breeze from the sea on his bare body. He wrapped the sheet around him. What did she mean? What the devil was this certificate? It must be a fake, part of some preposterous jest in the worst of taste. Why, Camille was not even buried. But who else knew this apart from Maria?

'What is this, a joke?' he asked her roughly. 'It isn't April the first.'

'No, darling. We were married the day before yesterday, remember?'

'Where?'

'Here. By special licence. The Bishop of Nassau.'

'The Bishop of Nassau? What the hell do you mean? Where have I been for the last day? I can't understand it,' he said. 'My wife is hardly in her grave.'

'You sound very ungallant for a new husband, darling,' said Maria chidingly. 'Your wife's *very* much alive. And here.'

She reached out towards him again. This time he moved away, put on some clothes, went out into the sunshine. His mouth felt dry. He must have been drinking too much. Married? What did she mean?

He saw Paul climbing into his car, and ran across the lawn towards him.

'Hi, Paul!' he called. 'Maria says we're *married*.'

'I know. Congratulations!'

'But I know nothing about it.'

'You'll learn,' said Paul. 'I've had five wives. Now that *is* the triumph of hope over experience. Twice is nothing, believe me.'

'But how can I be married?'

'Guess you're of age and you wanted to be – that's how. Maria's uncle, Charles Logan, came down. Maria wanted him to arrange it. I must say, you had taken liquor to some extent, but you said your vows.'

'Where is Charles Logan now?'

'Back in Miami. He is in a consortium trying for permission to open a casino here, but the Legislative Assembly isn't so wild about the idea. They think it will corrupt the locals and bring in the bad boys – as in Prohibition. But Charles will get his permission eventually – somehow. He's a trier. Never gives up.'

'You know him well?'

'As well as anyone.'

'But why did I get married?'

'I've told you – you wanted to. Sure convinced me!'

'Did you hear me ask Maria to marry me?'

'I wasn't there, but Charlie was very concerned about it. That's why I helped him with the Bishop.'

'My God,' said Clive hoarsely.

'You sure don't make a living advertisement for a new bridegroom,' said Paul in mock disapproval. He started his engine, waving cheerfully as he drove off.

Clive walked back across the springy turf, already warm against his bare feet. He went into the kitchen, mixed himself a rum and lime juice, drank it, then mixed two more and carried them into the bedroom.

Maria was dressed, combing her long black hair in front of the mirror.

'Satisfied I really am Mrs Douglas?' she asked him, smiling. He handed her the drink.

'Two against one,' he admitted. 'You and Paul against me. You must be right. I'm a democrat. I believe in the majority vote.'

They're mad, he thought to himself. It must be some kind of joke. These Americans have a crazy sense of humour. I had better play along with it.

'Too late now for a wedding breakfast,' Maria said. 'So we're having a helluva celebration tonight. Paul's giving a dinner party – especially for us. And tomorrow we're out fishing. All day. Oh, and I almost forgot – Uncle Charles left you a present.'

'Me? A present?'

She handed him a sealed envelope. Inside was a greetings card, on which was written one word: 'Congratulations'. Pinned to it was a cheque for $50,000.

'What *is* this?' he asked, staring at it in amazement.

'I told you. A present from Uncle Charles.'

Clive picked up the telephone.

'Who are you ringing?' Maria asked him.

'The bank. I want to check it's real. It's drawn on the Occidental-Oriental. I've never heard of that.'

'I have. So has Uncle Charles. He's the controlling shareholder.'

For the following day, Sunday, Paul had engaged two motor boats complete with crews, swivel seats in the sterns, sockets for rods, and a magnificent buffet lunch with bottles of champagne in ice boxes.

'I'm going to split up you two newly marrieds,' he told Clive and Maria. 'You'll see each other day and most nights for the rest of your lives. I'm putting you in one boat, Maria, and your husband is coming with me. Like the man said, absence makes the heart grow fonder.'

The sea lay calm and smooth, as though its surface had been specially polished for the greater enjoyment of the very rich. Despite a peaked yachting cap and sunglasses, Clive had a headache. He was usually a good sailor, but the sudden surge of the boat as the throttles opened, and then her lazy soporific roll when they cut the engines to start fishing, made him feel queasy. Had he eaten something that disagreed with him, or could this be a hangover from that day and night of which he could remember nothing? Could he conceivably have been drugged? The idea was ludicrous – but so was hearing his wife was dead one day, and next morning, it seemed, waking up married to someone else.

Earlier that morning, he had telephoned the office of the Bishop of Nassau, not giving his own name, to ask whether the Bishop had solemnised a marriage service between Clive Douglas and Maria Logan.

He had not taken the marriage service, he was told, but the couple had been married in a register office, and later the Bishop's chaplain had certainly blessed the union.

'Where did he bless it?' asked Clive. 'In the cathedral?'

'Not in the cathedral. He came to the house of a parishioner, Mr Denver.'

Clive rang off. So he *was* married. But why?

The fishing trip was not a success. The fish did not rise, the engine on one boat gave trouble, and after hours of rolling about on the slow Atlantic swell under a burning sun, no-one felt like drinking champagne. They came back in the late afternoon, earlier than Clive had expected, to the strains of dance music from Miami radio station. Suddenly, as the Andrews Sisters started the second chorus of 'Three Little Fishes', the music stopped abruptly.

An announcer interrupted with the brisk breathlessness of his kind.

'Newsflash. We have just heard from London, England, that the Prime Minister, Mr Neville Chamberlain, at 11.15 this morning, Greenwich Mean Time, announced that as of then, a state of war exists between Germany and Great Britain. As more news comes in, we will interrupt programmes with it. Stay tuned for our next news bulletin, every hour on the hour.'

Clive looked at the others in the boat, guests he only knew by first names: plump men in shorts and short-sleeved shirts; women in bright cotton trousers and sun tops too tight for them. Their accents cawed in his ears like shrill parrots. The news hadn't affected any of them, of course. They had probably not even heard it. Programmes were so frequently interrupted for the most trivial items of local information that the stream of words usually went unnoticed. The fact that Britain and Germany were at war for the second time in a generation was of no importance to them here. He was the only person aboard with a British passport.

As he walked up the jetty, the other cruiser came alongside and Maria jumped ashore.

'Catch anything?' she asked.

He shook his head.

'Only the news that Britain is at war with Germany.'

'Well, it's a long way away. Won't affect us.'

'It will me. I'm British.'

'So what are you going to do? Go home, join up, follow the flag for King and Empire – all that stuff?'

'Yes,' he said.

'You're too old for it, buster. Anyhow, let's not worry about that. We're having cocktails at the Van Deusens' at seven.'

'I'm going to see if I can get back to New York and then on to England.'

'*You?* What about me? I'm your wife. Be reasonable. We can't just leave our friends and everything here at the drop of a hat.'

'No-one's dropping hats. But they may be dropping bombs soon.'

Maria shrugged, and went over to the guest house alone.

Clive took a taxi to the British Colonial Hotel, which had a travel desk. A number of people were already crowding around the clerk.

'Every seat to Miami is taken for the next six flights,' he told Clive. 'I can only put you on the waiting list.'

Clive turned away. He would ask Paul Denver what strings he could pull. With his money, he must have some connections. As he turned, he bumped into another man and apologised. This man was middle-aged, wearing a lightweight suit, with the tie of the British Racing Drivers Club.

'You're Clive Douglas?' he said, smiling a welcome. 'You own that blue Delage I saw at the last Brooklands meeting?'

'Yes. You were there?'

'Of course. I live quite near, in Byfleet. My name's Clarke. Rex Clarke.'

They shook hands.

'Trying to get on a plane?' Clarke asked him.

Clive nodded.

'Yes. Only on the waiting list so far.'

'I might just be able to help you. Come up to my room. We can talk about it.'

Rex Clarke's room had a balcony overlooking the hotel gardens, with their huge king palms, and the shimmering sea beyond.

'I've had enough sun for today,' said Clarke. 'Let's sit in the shade.'

He mixed two pina coladas. They took them to the back of the room and drank. For the first time that day, Clive felt relaxed, at ease.

He was with his own kind, someone British, someone who understood his world.

'Now. Two things. First, I have two tickets for the three o'clock Miami flight tomorrow. You can have them – if you want them.'

'I want them,' said Clive.

'Good. I've been booking and cancelling seats ever since you came here.'

'But why?'

'Because I thought you might need them in a hurry.'

'But how could you guess?'

'A process of deduction; not disinterested, of course. I don't know what you plan to do in this war when you get back home, but unless you've something already lined up I would like to make you a rather special offer of work.'

'Doing what? Where?'

'In Switzerland. Basle, to be precise. In a bank.'

'Thanks. But I know nothing about banks – except that I owe them too much money. I'd rather be in the Army.'

'So would I. But we're both too old for that,' said Clarke. He pulled up his right trouser leg. Clive saw to his surprise that he had a metal ankle.

'I got that last time,' he explained. 'So now I have to work, as one might say, behind the lines.'

'What sort of work?'

'Shall we say, attached to one government department or another? In one name or another.'

'You mean you're a spy or something?'

'Something. Shall we leave it at that?'

'If you like. But how can you offer me a job in a bank in Basle? I'd be no good at it – and, anyway, how could that help anyone?'

'Because right now I have a brief from the Treasury.'

'A brief? What do you mean exactly?'

'I want you to work for us. The government. Your country. Our country.'

Clarke poured another drink.

'Probably without knowing it, you have had quite a bit to do with the Family since the 1920s. According to my information, you sold the Long Glen distillery on your estate to Mr Logan, the same man who virtually owns the Occidental-Oriental bank, and Mr Schoenbach. He had a very nasty accident. Some family friends thought he wasn't being friendly enough, so they gave him a present. They bought him an overcoat made of concrete. Then they dropped him in the sea. He didn't float.'

'My wife said he had a heart attack.'

'Wouldn't you, in that situation?'

'You mean he was murdered?'

'Precisely. Some of your host's friends have rather shady pasts. They belong to the Honoured Society – like the man who bought into Lion's Share chewing gum.

'I expect that your employee, Leone Pastellini, knew this, but he just *had* to sell. You presumably did not know anything about such matters when you accepted an offer for your distillery?'

'Of course not.'

'You thought you were selling the distillery to Canadians. They had Canadian passports, but Sicilian fathers. They wanted good stuff to run over the border into the States. And they did so – at a phenomenal profit. Most of the people down here in Nassau shared in those good days. Even the old women you see today sitting on the pavement outside the market making straw hats for tourists – they made canvas bags to put the bottles in to stop them rattling.'

'But that's all finished now, Prohibition.'

'Sure. But the rum runners made a lot of money, real money, millions and millions, all tax free, and you can't keep that sort of money under the bed. You invest it. When they were making hooch they needed bottles by the thousand.

'Obviously, they couldn't just buy them in such quantities openly, for the police could have got on to them – those who weren't taking bribes. So they bought bottling factories. They needed labels, so they acquired printing firms. They needed trucks to carry the stuff round the country, so they went into trucking. They had to store tons and tons of booze somewhere, so they went into warehousing and property. And now they are into almost everything. The wheel was turned right round. The bads have become the goods. Why rob a bank when you can own one?

'You put as much hot money as you can into legitimate operations and it all comes out clean and legal. Now they are making money both sides of the street – that way and in casinos. They control all the gambling in Cuba. They are trying to get a foot in here. One day, gamblers will come down by the shipload, be parted from their money and go back quite happy.'

'But all this has nothing to do with me. What could I do in Basle?'

'A place will be found in the Bank of New World Indemnities, possibly the world's most interesting financial organisation. This again you have probably never heard of, but it was started nine years ago in 1930, with the world's major central banks each holding a share.

'Dr Schacht, now the Nazi Minister of Economics and, incidentally, president of the Reichsbank in Berlin, was its inspiration. Three years before Hitler came to power, he calculated there would very likely be a war, and to wage war takes money. Not too many people at Schacht's level were thinking along those lines then in world banking. Certainly not the First National Bank of New York or the national banks of Italy, France and England. They saw his proposal for the Bank of New World Indemnities as an instrument of peace, where bankers of every major country could meet and discuss financial and other related problems and hopefully find solutions. Schacht and the Nazis saw it simply as a way of funnelling money to Germany to help them prepare for war.

'But now war has come, what happens?' asked Clive.

'That will be one of your tasks – to find out. All governments whose central banks are involved agreed when the bank began that it must be immune from ever being seized or closed – even criticised – in the event of any war involving those countries.'

'But I can't see that Britain and France will allow money to filter through to the Nazis now.'

'You don't read Plutarch?'

'Not frequently,' Clive admitted.

'You should. One of his apothegms is worth remembering. "In war, it is not permitted to make a mistake twice." And the Allies have already made a very grave mistake here. In March last year, when the Nazis marched into Austria, they seized all gold deposits, and transferred them to the bank I hope you'll join.

'The Nazi members of the bank's board refused to discuss the matter – not surprisingly, since the bank's director Emil Puhl, was also the Reichsbank's vice-president. He took personal charge of this vital transaction.

'Last September, the Nazis seized Czechoslovakia. In Prague, they held the directors of the Czech National Bank at gunpoint until they agreed to hand over the country's gold reserves, which amounted to $48 million, a huge sum from a small country.

'The directors explained they no longer held the gold in the country, so they couldn't surrender it. They had already put it in the care of – guess who? Why, the Bank of New World Indemnities, with instructions to forward it immediately to the Bank of England.

'The Nazis told them that they either handed over the gold within two days – or they died. The Czech directors telephoned the bank. A Dutchman was in charge that year and his general manager belonged to the Bank of France. Both were very sympathetic to their colleagues' situation. After all, within months they could find themselves in a similar one. So they asked Sir Montagu Norman, chairman of the Bank of England, to return the gold. He did so.

'Nazi Germany at once put it to good use, and doubtless it will all come back to the British, the Dutch and the French, in the form of shells and bombs.'

'That seems incredible. But there was no war on then. Surely it is all different now?'

'Very different. The main difference is there will now be twice as much pressure to channel all kinds of things to Germany. Gold doesn't move round in bars from country to country. Often it doesn't move at all. But its influence does, in a coded message, a letter, a telegram, a teleprinted message. And those bits of paper will pay for oil for Germany, magnesium, wolfram, copper – you name it. Unless you help to stop it.'

'What can I do to help? I know nothing about banks – except, as I've told you, I owe them money.'

'You will be told in London. If you take the job.'

'I'll think about it.'

And then Clive remembered something he had totally forgotten.

'But I'm married,' he said.

'I know. To Charles Logan's niece. Which is why I have reserved two air tickets for Mr and Mrs Douglas. There is one further thing I should tell you. If you accept, you will not receive any salary, but you will be given expenses. And all your bank debts will be paid on the day you sign the agreement. Thus not only will you be helping your country, you will be helping yourself.

'So remember this. When the British Treasury spends money with such prodigality it shows what value some people place on you. Now, another drink to toast the future, *your* future.'

The Arakan, Burma

As the patrol came out of the jungle, Corporal Johnny Douglas paused, eased the webbing straps on his pack that bit like teeth into his sodden shoulders, and wiped rain from his eyes. In the monsoon downpour, it was impossible to read a map; in any case, his map had long since disintegrated into a number of folded squares of soaking paper. Grid lines and contours were meaningless. He was lost and he knew it, and the other men in his section knew it, too.

They spread out on either side of him, still sheltered by the trees, scanning the open stretch of paddy field ahead. Spears of rain punctured a vast leaden sheet of water that covered it. For a mile or more on either side, Douglas could see more paddy, also covered with rainwater, and cut into squares by mud ridges two feet high, built by Burmese farmers to retain water to help the rice to grow. There was no cover, no trees, until the far side; only water in between. Against this bleak and empty expanse they would be naked targets to any Japanese. But across the water he could just make out vague shapes; bamboo *bashas* in a tiny village.

Rain dropped like a solid wall. Their feet were swollen from days of marching through water. Leeches clung, bloated with blood, to their knees and ankles, squeezing in through the eyelets of their boots. One man ripped away the soaking green cotton of his trouser leg as he waited, lit a cigarette and burned away the largest leech with the red hot tip. It squirted blood as it fell.

'Where we heading for then, Corp?' asked the Bren-gunner. 'What's it to be, Piccadilly, Old Kent Road or a bit of how's your father?'

He was the joker in the section; there always was one, cheerful, untiring, who chirped away like a Cockney sparrow. No-one paid much attention to him, but they would miss him if he wasn't there.

'The other side,' said Douglas. 'There's a village.'

'How do you know?'

'I can see its outline. And it's marked on the map.'

'When we last had a map,' said someone else tartly.

'Bugger the map,' said the joker. 'We've no cover if we cross this lot. I'm all for waiting here until it's dark.'

'Too risky,' Douglas told him. 'There's no moon, remember. We won't be able to see a thing. And there's no shelter. We can't even light a fire for a brew-up.'

They had been on patrol for five days and nights. Their rations, carried in packs, were all but exhausted. They had filled their water bottles by dipping them in the flooded paddy fields. They must reach the village, and get under cover and find their bearings, because it would be impossible to move after dark. Douglas knew he had only minutes to make up his mind to risk crossing now in the fading light, or to wait and then risk floundering in the dark without bearings.

He disliked the prospect of going into any village with so many men; they presented too easy a target. It was always safer and wiser to go in alone or with only one other man. That way, you had a better chance of escaping from an ambush. There was the chance that he might find a friendly headman – but it was just as likely the headman would be hostile. However, they could not possibly stay where they were.

Thunder rumbled and blue lightning split the sky. The rain increased until the lake that covered the paddy fields steamed and fumed. Spray hung in the air like fog.

'Come on,' said Douglas shortly. 'This downpour will give us some cover. Five minutes and we're there.'

'Where?' asked the joker facetiously. 'Home or away?'

They set out, wading through water over their knees, sometimes slipping in deep soft mud, tripping over unseen stones, picking themselves up, forging on again, silently and as fast as they could.

Four minutes across, and Douglas saw between the trees they had just left, the little sparks of flame he had dreaded. Seconds later, they all heard the familiar kok-kok-kok of a Japanese machine gun; they had not moved a moment too soon.

They started to run now, all need for silence gone, cursing the weight of their equipment, splashing through muddy water, falling, rising again, running on, always running. Japanese bullets hissed through the rain all around them. The welcoming shelter of the trees lay only yards away when the joker screamed and fell.

He dropped face down in the water, and lay writhing and heaving in agony, blowing into the water, choking with it. The pack on his back gave him the appearance of some humped sea-beast half submerged, eager but unable to rise.

Four men ran ahead past him into the trees. Douglas and the others knelt down in the water, rolled the joker over on his back. Rain drummed down on them. The joker had been shot twice near his spine. Streaks of blood were already turning the water red. His dark green cotton battle-dress blouse streamed with water and blood. He was gibbering in pain, retching out water and bile over the front of his blouse. They half carried, half dragged him, still gripping his rifle like a talisman, a totem, to the relative shelter of the trees.

As the corporal in charge of the section, Douglas carried only a small glass phial of morphine. He bit the neck with his teeth, spat out the glass and dug the jagged edge of the phial into the joker's neck, hoping he had punctured a vein. Gradually, the man's moaning ceased. Douglas threw away the empty phial, brushed grains of glass from his lips. If anyone else was wounded, they would have to endure the pain.

'What are we going to do, Corp?' one of the section asked nervously. This was a question only Douglas could answer. The easy reply was to leave the joker where he was, to let him die. But everyone would then know that this was all anyone else could expect if they were badly wounded. Their morale would vanish – and with it any stomach for further action. They had to try and save the joker's life – probably impossible, but, at the least, vital to attempt.

'We'll carry him into the village,' Douglas said. They could now all see the group of bamboo huts only yards away. Someone picked up the joker's rifle, while others carried him, like a drunk being removed from a dance hall, through the trees. The village hardly deserved the name; simply a handful of bamboo shacks built up on poles out of the water. Beneath these miserable hutments, hogs snorted nervously. A goat tied to a pole reared away in terror, and chickens on a raised bamboo platform cackled disapprovingly at the unexpected disturbance.

There was no main street, only a muddy track, pitted now with the spears of rain, between the houses. If they could find shelter somewhere for half an hour, Douglas could examine the joker's wound, patch him up or make a stretcher with bamboos so they could take turns in carrying him. But half an hour was too long to hope for. The Japanese would know they were here, because there was nowhere else for them to shelter. They would be on their way after them; not perhaps at first, in case other British or Indian troops might be in the area, and this section was only the rearguard of a much larger force. But it would not take them long to discover that the section was on its own. Doubtless they would have an informer in the village. At that moment, he could well be on his way out to tell them. Douglas had nothing like thirty minutes; at the best ten, at the worst, perhaps three.

A few children came out hesitantly on to bamboo verandahs to stare at them. They were pot-bellied and naked except for strings of glass beads dangling around their navels. They stood, sucking their thumbs, watching the men silently, eyes bright as their beads.

Douglas did not like the look of the village; it seemed empty, and except for these children, deserted, dead. British and Indian troops did not care for Burmese villages. They had been betrayed too often in them, and even if they were not betrayed, the Japanese could simply destroy the village and all who lived in it as a warning to others who might be friendly. He must prevent such a massacre if he possibly could.

A Burmese man appeared on the verandah of the nearest house, and looked down at them. He had a beard and wore a red skull-cap. There was something patriarchal in his appearance. He would either help them or he wouldn't. The choice was as simple as it was stark.

Douglas called up to him.

'You speak English?'

The man nodded.

'We've a man badly wounded. Can you give us shelter in your house while I try to put him right?'

'The Japanese are behind you and in front of you,' said the man. 'You know what they do to us if we help you people?'

'I have money,' said Douglas.

He patted the breast pocket of his blouse. In an oilskin pouch inside it, he had five hundred one-rupee notes. Patrols often carried money because where appeals to loyalty to a King Emperor thousands of miles away might fail, the rustle of notes could sometimes produce helpful results.

'We do not help for money,' said the man proudly, 'but because someone in need seeks our help.'

'Then will you help us?'

This bloody conversation could go on forever: a minuet of manners when there was no time for such niceties of Eastern behaviour. Douglas wanted a quick yes or no, not maybe or later.

The man pulled his beard thoughtfully and then made up his mind.

'There are stairs at the back,' he said briefly.

They walked around the stilts and climbed up a crude ladder made of bamboo rungs lashed with creeper to two long poles. Their boots creaked and slipped with every step. Even in his drugged condition; the joker groaned as they heaved him up with them.

On the verandah they halted in an awkward group until the man ushered them inside. The room seemed surprisingly comfortable, but then any shelter must be an improvement on outside conditions in the Arakan. There were no chairs, but several thick rugs covered the floor. A hubble-bubble pipe stood by the door and polished brass ornaments reflected a glow from a hurricane lamp. Rain hammered angrily on the bamboo roof. A calendar with a garish picture of the Shwe Dagon, the golden pagoda in Rangoon, hung on a wall. Opposite hung another brightly coloured picture of the Imam; this family must be Imfalli Muslims.

A middle-aged woman peered at them nervously from behind a crude partition. A baby cried, and a younger man came round the partition and nodded to them.

'My son-in-law,' the bearded man explained.

Douglas held out his hand to the older man.

'Johnny Douglas,' he said.

'Ahmed Akbar.'

'You are the head man of the village?'

The old man inclined his head. 'You want hot water for your friend's wounds?' he asked.

'If you have any.'

Douglas posted two men out on the verandah, arms at the ready, and two more looking through a window on the other side of the building. There was no glass, only a flap of plaited bamboos held up by a pole to deflect the rain. The old man clapped his hands, said something in Burmese. The woman brought out a Primus burner, pumped it up, lit it, set an aluminium bowl of water on top.

Outside, lightning flickered briefly, turning the sodden paddy fields to lakes of purple and indigo. No-one was crossing them – yet. The Japanese must be only minutes behind – if they had not gone around the paddy and were already on the far side of the village, waiting for them. Either way, time was running out fast for Douglas and his section.

Douglas bent down, undid the joker's blouse, rolled him gently over on his stomach. The flesh, pale and soft with rain, was blue around two jagged holes, one on each side of his spine. A little blood dribbled and oozed from his mouth as he breathed noisily, like an old man climbing up a long hill.

'Is he conscious?' the old man asked.

'No.'

'It is well. He will not recover.'

'How do you know?'

Ahmed Akbar moved the joker's body slightly.

'You can see, one bullet has gone right through,' he said. 'It will have hit a kidney or the spleen. He is a Christian?'

'C of E,' replied Douglas mechanically.

'May Allah the ever merciful show compassion even on an unbeliever who has died in battle.'

He leaned across the dying man and turned off the stove; the joker would not be needing warm water now.

Douglas felt his pulse. It was very feeble and erratic. The old man was right. The joker was dying, and the rest of them were trapped in this house. Within minutes they also could be dead – and with them this head man, the woman, the son-in-law, even the child he had heard crying. He turned to the lance corporal, second-in-command of the section.

'I'll stay with him until he goes,' he told him. 'You take the others on. Go south for a mile at least to put the Japs off the trail before you head for base. Here's my compass. It's set. March on the needle. The battalion must be no more than ten miles away.'

'We can't march anywhere in the dark,' said the lance corporal.

'Get out now before it's dark,' retorted Douglas, 'or you'll never get out at all.'

'What about you?'

'I'll follow.'

'How, without a compass, in the dark?'

'Never mind that. Just get out – *now!*'

The lance corporal called the men together, gave them their orders. They filed downstairs. No-one looked at the dying man, but the lance corporal made the sign of the cross as he passed him. Once, years ago, in another world, another life, he had been a server in his church.

'I have some tea,' said the Burmese when he and Douglas were on their own. 'Would you like a bowl? There is also fish and rice.'

'Thank you, but not now. There is no time.'

'I am sorry. It is not good to leave without food or drink.'

'Agreed, but it's better than not leaving at all. Now, what can we do with the body when he goes?'

'We will deal with that,' the old man assured him. 'We will say he was wounded and forced his way in here and then died.'

'The Japanese will come here, then?'

'Of course. They come every night to check every house. Once they found an Indian soldier hiding. They killed him.'

'And the son of that house,' said the son-in-law.

'Another time, they saw my daughter run away,' said Ahmed Akbar. 'They thought she had gone to warn your people. At least, that is what they said. They shot her. That is her son – my grandson – you hear in the next room.'

'He cries for his mother,' explained Akbar's son-in-law.

'Won't someone in the village tell them he wasn't on his own?' asked Douglas. 'Aren't you all in great danger now?'

Akbar nodded agreement.

'But it is written that we must always help those who are in need. One day we may also seek the help of others. If we abandon one in his hour of need, how can we expect others not to abandon us?'

'You are a Muslim?' asked Douglas.

'Yes. Of the Imfalli sect. That picture on the wall is of our leader, the Imam. I bought it when I was in Calcutta years ago. He has a palace there.'

'I know.'

'How do you know, Englishman? You are not of our faith? Our Imam does not interest himself in race-horses like the Aga Khan. His name does not appear often in your newspapers, if at all. So how do you know of him?'

'From boyhood, I was told how my great-grandfather used to speak of the Imam of those days,' Douglas explained, bending over the joker, feeling his pulse. It was all but still, trembling now, erratic and feeble as the wings of a captive moth.

'He was in India, then, your great-grandfather?'

'Yes, one of the founders of a big company, Trinity-Trio.'

'In what way did he speak of the Imam then? Did he speak well?'

The old man sounded wary, expecting criticism from a foreigner, an unbeliever.

'He spoke well. My great-grandfather, Alec Douglas, was, I understand, largely instrumental in seeing that he became Imam, but I am not sure of the details. It was all a very long time ago, remember.'

'In human terms, yes, it was long ago. But against the measurements of eternity, it was less than the flutter of an eyelid. Your name is also Douglas?'

'Yes. John Douglas.'

'Alec Douglas – that is a name to be revered in our community. We remember it in our prayers. May Allah the all-seeing, the ever merciful, bless his name.'

Douglas unbuttoned his pocket and took out the oilskin pouch of rupees.

'These are for you,' he said, changing the subject. The present was more pressing than the past.

'Hospitality is not for sale,' said the old man. 'We of the Imfalli sect know much about your great-grandfather. Allah, who sees the unseen as clearly as all that is visible, has sent you here. It is therefore my duty and my honour to help you. Not for money, or for any thought of earthly reward, but in praise and thanksgiving that the one true god and his messenger have afforded me this opportunity.'

'Even so, you may find the money useful, and it is no good to me.'

Douglas appreciated Ahmed Akbar's words but words alone could not help him. But what – or who – could? Like the waggoner in Aesop's fable, he knew he had to help himself.

The son-in-law put out his hand silently, shook the notes from the pouch, counted them carefully and put them on one side. Ahmed Akbar suddenly leaned over the joker, listening for his breath.

'He has gone,' he said, standing up. 'May Allah the compassionate have mercy on his brave spirit. May he already stand at the Gates of Heaven and walk tonight in Paradise. That is the reward for all who die honourably in battle, believer and unbeliever alike.'

Douglas knelt down near the joker. His pulse had stopped. The joker was dead. Douglas slipped the sweaty string with its two maroon fibre identity discs over the dead soldier's head, felt in his pockets, took away a letter still unopened with his mother's name as sender on its envelope, a pen-knife. Apart from a handkerchief, a sodden rain-soaked ball, there was nothing else. Patrols always travelled light.

He stood up. Akbar and his son-in-law stood with him.

'If I could have got him out, he might have lived,' said Douglas wearily. 'An M.O. could have saved him.'

He felt he had failed the joker; after all, he had been in command. The ultimate responsibility for the survival or death of any of his section must be his.

'No, Englishman,' said the old man. 'When our time comes, no-one can save us. It is written in the holy book, our Koran, that God who created man from clay, determined a term for all our lives. Nothing will ever befall us but what God has already decreed for us. Our lives are but a journey, following His chart. It is not for us to determine whether we go this way or that, or when our journey starts, where it will end. That is for God only.'

Douglas shrugged. He had no wish to argue: he must start his journey now, before the Japanese entered the village. He had waited long enough, perhaps for too long. If he could cover even half a mile before dark, he might hole up somewhere in the jungle until dawn, and then use his watch to take a compass bearing, and possibly catch up with the rest of the patrol. But now every minute counted, every second.

As he looked out at the streaming rain, the saturated landscape, the brief tropical twilight dropped like a curtain. One moment it was day; the next, dusk. He had left his departure too late. And yet he could not leave a comrade to die alone, although the joker had not even realised he was not alone. But Douglas felt to do less would have been to fail. Now he could look the other men in the section in the eye. He had done what he could; he had done his duty.

'I must thank you for your kindness,' he told Ahmed Akbar. 'You have given great help to strangers. May Allah reward you. And tell me, what is this village?'

'Ngaunglebyin.'

'I cannot very well write and thank you.'

'No,' said the old man, and smiled. 'We have no postal service. But what is your address? Maybe, when this war is over, we can communicate? I would dearly like to talk to you about your ancestor. It is a rare honour to meet one of his blood and line.'

He took down the Shwe Dagon calendar from the wall, tore off one sheet and handed it to Douglas with a stub of pencil.

Douglas wrote: 'Ahmed Akbar saved my life. He is my friend. Help him if he needs your help. Corporal John Douglas, First Lincolns, 26 Division, Ngaunglebyin, Burma, March 18th, 1944.'

'That could be useful if another of our patrols calls,' he told Ahmed Akbar. 'You might need it. Show it to them.'

At the bottom, he wrote Trinity-Trio's address in Calcutta.

'That will find me,' he said. 'One day. When this is over.'

'May the one true God and Mahommet his prophet guard you and guide your feet into the path of safety and righteousness, all the days of your life.'

'Amen to both those wishes,' said Douglas. They shook hands. The old man and his son-in-law watched him go down the stairs. Behind them, unseen, the baby began to cry.

Rain still poured down and Douglas shivered after the dryness of the house. Perhaps he was sickening for a fever? He had been wet for so long it seemed impossible he could ever feel properly dry again. He slung his pack into a more comfortable position, automatically checked that the safety catch on his Tommy gun was set to Fire, and set off.

He walked out through the village, carefully keeping in the shelter of the houses on one side of the track. He saw no-one, but he did not doubt that others could be watching him. Nights in Burma were alive with eyes, most neither friendly nor hostile, simply wary, observing.

As he moved cautiously through the rain, grateful not only for any cover the houses might provide against the enemy but also for the slightest shelter from the ceaseless downpour, he was reminded of sheltering in the rain only a month previously in Calcutta.

He had been on leave and dining at Firpo's, the Italian restaurant on Chowringhee. There had been some doubt in his mind as to whether a corporal would be given a table, because the place was patronised overwhelmingly by officers. He had therefore bought a pair of lightweight trousers and a check shirt in the Army and Navy Stores a few blocks away, and gone as a civilian.

It was his first monsoon in India and he was surprised how warm the rain felt; not cold like in England. Taxis, old open American cars painted bright green and yellow, splashed past crammed with passengers under flapping canvas roofs. Then one slowed and stopped. Three American officers climbed out and paid the driver. Douglas ran across the streaming pavement towards it. As he told the driver his destination, the Great Eastern Hotel, a girl appeared at his side.

'I saw it first,' she said.

'I'm sorry,' said Douglas. 'I didn't see you. But come in, we'll go wherever you're going. First come, first served.'

They sank back on the shiny rexine cushions.

'Alipore,' she said. 'Do you know it?'

'Never been near it in my life,' said Douglas cheerfully. 'But my great-grandfather had a house there.'

'Really? What was his name?'

'Same as mine. Douglas. Alec Douglas.'

'I've heard that name. Didn't he have something to do with one of the big firms in the early days?'

'Yes. Something. Let's introduce ourselves. I'm John Douglas.'

'Me Jane,' she said with a laugh. 'Well, not actually. Monica Reeves. Are you a civvy?'

'No. In the army. On leave. Going to Burma next week.'

'My brother was there. In the air force. He was shot down six weeks ago. We haven't heard a dicky bird since.'

'I'm sorry,' said Douglas. 'But it's amazing how many people do trek back to base. Don't give up hope. It's early days.'

'I'd like to think so,' she said. 'We were twins. What are you in the army?'

'Nothing very special. A corporal.'

'Napoleon was a corporal.'

'So was Hitler,' said Douglas.

They laughed and liked each other. Rain beat down on the roof so it seemed they were in a travelling tent, warm and young and happy. The Sikh driver watched them in his mirror, picked his teeth with a toothpick, and wondered about the size of his tip.

They reached a large white house set back from the road behind a wall. A *chowkidar* in khaki uniform, carrying a long stick and a hurricane lamp, came out of the shadows.

'It's all right,' Monica called out to him. '*Thik hai.*'

Then, to Douglas: 'My father is a widower – he'd be glad of some masculine company. Do come in and have a coffee or something. We can telephone for a cab for you later.'

'Thank you,' said Douglas gratefully.

He paid off the taxi and went inside. He had an instant impression of polished tile floors, waxed furniture, armchairs with white canvas covers. Her father poured Douglas a brandy while Monica rustled up a servant in the kitchen to make coffee.

'Where are you staying?' Monica's father asked.

'The Great Eastern.'

'Expensive.'

'Well, it's better than sleeping on the floor surrounded by Hindu statues in the museum, which is the only leave centre with any vacancies.'

'Then move your stuff in here,' said Mr Reeves. 'We have a spare room.'

'You're very kind,' said Douglas.

'I can lend you pyjamas tonight. I can even provide a razor. Collect your gear tomorrow. It's too wet to go out in this weather.'

So he moved in with this pleasant man who worked in the government arsenal at Barrackpore, and his daughter of eighteen. Douglas warmed not only to her and her father but to the whole relaxed atmosphere of their house. He had grown up in a divided home. Some school holidays he would spend with an aunt, and some with his father – when he was in the country.

He accepted this dichotomy of affection because he had to, and because other boys at school were in the same situation, with parents dead, divorced or separated, but he dreaded staying at home with his father when his second wife, Maria, was there. Johnny Douglas did not like her as a person; he did not trust her as a stepmother. He could not forgive his father for marrying her even before Johnny's mother was buried. There was something unseemly about that haste. He had asked his father about it several times, but he could never get a conclusive answer. Excuses about a party and having too much to drink could not be the real reason. So what could it be?

When he and his father met, they were like two strangers trying to find some common interest, any shared background. He had not liked his father's friends before the war, and since then he had scarcely seen him. It was probably a reaction against his father's extravagance, his need to spend money to assure himself of companions, that made Johnny refuse the chance of a commission. He wanted to find his own place.

To be here in this big, polished homely house with two uncomplicated, friendly people, bound by the sorrow of a brother and son missing, was a new and welcome experience. Perhaps this was, at last, his place? He felt his spirits expand. For the first time in his life, he realised how much he had been missing emotionally, and he determined never to lose the happiness and contentment he had so suddenly and unexpectedly discovered.

Within hours, Douglas and Monica thought they could be in love. By the next day, they knew they were. Within two days, he asked her to marry him, and with her father's blessing, she agreed. They were married by special licence in the garrison church.

'When is your next leave?' Mr Reeves asked him afterwards.

'Probably in six months,' Douglas told him. 'Do look after Monica until I come back.'

'I've looked after her for eighteen years,' replied her father with a smile. 'I think I'll cope for another six months. You look after yourself.'

He paused.

'Forgive a new father-in-law's questions, but when all this is over, what do you intend to do? Go up to the university, or have you something else in mind?'

'I will go into the family firm,' Douglas explained. 'I might qualify as a chartered accountant first, but in the end I'll join the firm.'

'A local business, is it, in England?'

'Well, a bit bigger than that,' said Douglas non-committally. He suddenly felt embarrassed, comparing his family's wealth with Mr Reeves'. He was afraid that their attitude towards him might change if they knew the firm was Trinity-Trio. He had seen that happen before with new friends; they had thought he was slumming, might put on airs. He could not bear this to happen here.

'My father owns a third of it, I think. I'll find a place there, and rest assured I'll look after your daughter. Don't worry about that, sir.'

'I won't,' said the old man, and turned away so that Douglas would not see the tears in his eyes. 'But again, look after yourself, my boy. . . .'

In the rain now, outside shacks stinking with hogs, goats and chickens, the memory of that brief stay in Alipore warmed and cheered him. Thinking of Monica – not Monica Reeves any longer, but Mrs Douglas, Mrs *John* Douglas – he stepped out with a new vigour towards the empty paddy and the welcoming shelter of the trees beyond.

At the far end of the village stood a tree near a clump of bushes. In the army jargon, used when giving troops a visual target, this would be 'a bushy-topped tree'. Beyond them stretched the paddy, dull as a vast sheet of lead under the hammering rain. Fifty more yards across the paddy field, and he would reach the jungle that crouched, immense and menacing, but offering cover, shelter, brief safety. He had never thought of the jungle being welcoming before. Now, it was just that.

He looked behind him. Light was all but gone. *Bashas* glistening with rain were only deeper shadows in the shade. A few miserable animals grunted, and hens stirred uneasily on their perches. Douglas took a deep breath and set out briskly across the paddy while he could still see his way.

Twenty yards out, the Japanese sniper's bullet hit the base of his spine.

Douglas dropped. Instantly, the flood waters of the paddy field surged over him and concealed his body. If the bullet had not killed him outright, he would have drowned within seconds.

Up in the tree at the end of the village, the sniper carefully wiped the lenses of his telescopic sight and tucked it for safety against his chest inside his uniform tunic.

As was the custom, he had roped himself to a branch among the thick leaves. Then, if he was wounded or killed, he would not fall out humiliatingly at the feet of his adversaries, but die privately and unseen to the greater honour of his Emperor.

He waited for ten more minutes in case this single enemy soldier had been a scout, and a larger body of troops was following him. Then he decided it was safe to leave. Rain had caused the rope to swell and he struggled with the knot for several minutes before he could loosen it.

The sniper climbed carefully and stiffly down the tree, crossed the paddy field until he stumbled over Douglas's body. He bent down, and with a clasp-knife cut the string on which the soldier's two identity discs were threaded, putting them into his pocket. His lieutenant liked to have proof in support of all snipers' claims, and these would be total confirmation. One round, one enemy dead; a perfect score should deserve a toast of sake, measured in the cap of a mortar.

He was looking forward to this and to the praise of his officer with almost childish anticipation, when a blow on the back of his head ended his life instantly. He sank down beside the body of the English corporal. The waters rippled and splashed and then subsided. Within seconds it was as though nothing had disturbed them, nothing at all.

Basle

Late every afternoon, when Clive Douglas left his office in the Bank of New World Indemnities, he would walk through the streets of Basle, an ancient city orientated towards wealth: its acquisition, its retention, but rarely its enjoyment. The city fathers were excessively proud of the fact that more than half the millionaires in all Switzerland lived there, but discreetly: no show, no flamboyance, no outward evidence of opulence.

Sometimes Clive would watch the giant barges chug up the Rhine, and the strange ferry boats, like tiny gondolas, which were attached to overhead wires and relied on currents to propel them across the river. Occasionally, he would sit in a quiet courtyard off the Frierstrasse for the length of time it took to smoke a cheroot, contemplating, without pleasure, his life – past, present, potential.

He had been in Switzerland for four years now with only brief leaves, which he spent either in neutral Portugal, or less often in London; the journey from Basle to England was difficult in wartime. Also, his wife Maria was in their flat in Grosvenor Square, and while she remained beautiful and elegant, and no doubt in every way desirable, his feelings for her had cooled. He still could not understand how one day he had been a widower and two days later had woken up married to her. He had the uneasy, uncomfortable feeling that he had been deliberately trapped. But why? She was rich in her own right; surely she did not need his money?

Equally, he had no idea why Clarke had chosen him for his present job. He was grateful to have his debts paid, of course, but what exactly *was* his job? True, he was attached to the bank under the vague title of adviser, but he knew nothing about money, except how to spend it, and he found the meetings he attended with German, Italian, Japanese and American directors not so much bizarre as almost unbelievable.

He had been brought up in the simple, patriotic belief that everyone should help their country in any time of need. The labyrinthine negotiations between directors, whose countries were at war with each other, totally negated this creed. How could he be genuinely helping his country here?

From time to time, Clarke, or someone else, would call on him at his flat near the Wettstein Bridge overlooking the Rhine. These callers never discussed anything of importance in case what Clarke euphemistically referred to as 'the other side' might have some listening device – and they always limited their visits to several minutes, in case he might forget this and ask any incriminating questions.

'Why shouldn't I?' Douglas would sometimes ask in exasperation. 'I am sitting down every day with these Nazi bastards! We discuss millions of dollars in their accounts all around the world. It's obscene.'

'But that is banking,' Clarke would reply. 'This is something else.'

His visitor would pass a small piece of paper to him. On this would be typed a single question in capital letters. Under this would be a figure, 2, 3, 7 and so on. Clive would read it, memorise it, then tear up the paper, flushing the pieces down the lavatory. The number referred to the days he was being given to discover the answer to the question.

Then, on the second, third or seventh day, or whatever it might be, another caller would arrive, and Clive would hand to him a similar piece of paper, unheaded, with no date, but with the answer typed as briefly as possible. Most questions referred to the ultimate destinations of millions of dollars; others to shipments of oil and wolfram and manganese, all paid for by huge sums of money passing through the bank to Axis accounts around the world.

Clive had no idea whether the items of information he supplied were put to any use or even who required them. He never received any acknowledgment, thanks or criticism: it was an exclusively one-way traffic.

His work depressed him because of this and its almost unbelievable cynicism. While the Nazi empire stretched triumphantly from the Black Sea to the French Atlantic coast, from the Arctic to the Mediterranean, enslaving more than four hundred million people, with Switzerland the only remaining unoccupied sovereign state between Spain and the Ukraine, representatives of the Allies were daily sitting down in the bank building with their enemies to discuss the one subject uppermost in all their minds: money.

How could this be morally right? Clive wondered. How could it be defensible at any level, for example, that one of the largest makers of electrical equipment in the United States should supply, through a German subsidiary, details of the most modern ground-to-air radio sets, submarine communications gear, radar equipment, artillery fuses?

On what grounds could anyone logically defend an international oil company buying oil from the Allies under one name, and selling it under another to fuel Nazi aircraft, tanks, ships, while the tanker was still at sea? What was he *doing* here?

While young men – and women – were fighting a war on fronts as far apart as Russia and the Pacific, while bombs rained down on largely defenceless cities, these careful men with pinched, pale faces and rimless octagonal spectacles moved pieces on a world-wide chessboard, with dividends their god. The aim was that British and American companies and their counterparts in France, Germany, Italy and Japan, could almost incredibly carry on with business disturbed as little as possibl throughout a global war, secure in the knowledge that their ultimate profitability would in no way be diminished.

Clive felt he should have the courage to denounce these men and their policies. But to whom? Who would believe him – and was he not in fact one of them himself? And, in the last analysis, all the governments concerned presumably knew what was going on and condoned it.

This ultimate feeling that he was wasting his life, and not only that, but actually aiding the enemy, depressed Clive beyond measure. But he had no-one to whom he could express this view, no-one with whom he could even discuss it, however guardedly.

He wrote to his son Johnny, who had joined the Army as a private soldier and who was now in Burma, but obviously he could tell him nothing about his work or his doubts. In any case, he had never been close to Johnny; he had never really been close to anyone, that was the trouble. He lacked the gift for making friends or even acquaintances, and true friends, he knew now, could never be bought by cases of wine, a roomful of flowers, or dinner at the Café Royal.

This discontent, sometimes almost amounting to pain, continually fumed and fermented in his brain. And every day, when he finished his cheroot in the square, as he stood up and smoothed down his jacket before walking back to the office, he would examine the murals on one wall together with the inscription, curious indeed for this Calvinist country: *Freiheit ist über silber und gold* – Freedom is above silver and gold.

But whose freedom, and how much silver and gold, was not stated, and he knew no-one who could give him an honest answer.

London

Clive Douglas let himself into his flat in Grosvenor Square and stood for a moment in the hallway, listening to unexpected music. The radio was playing 'Room 504'. He had not told Maria he was coming home; he had wanted to surprise her. He had brought with him from Basle two bottles of whisky – he still drank Long Glen out of loyalty, although the distillery was no longer his – a smoked ham and a tin of pâté de foie gras. An odd mixture, but this was all he had time to buy after he had quite unexpectedly been offered a flight. Air seats were so rare that any such offer had to be accepted immediately, or someone else would seize it.

He walked down the hall and opened the drawing-room door. Maria was sitting in a silk-covered armchair in front of an ornate electric fire, a glass of champagne in her hand. The mantelpiece was thick with invitations. She stood up, staring in amazement – was it also horror? – as she saw her husband.

'Why, *Clive!*' she said, simulating pleasure, smiling with her mouth but not her eyes. He could not remember seeing her eyes show welcome or warmth. How had he ever become involved with such a person?

An American colonel, dark-haired, wearing a beautifully pressed uniform, stood up slowly from an armchair on the other side of the fireplace. He looked at Clive, then enquiringly at Maria.

'My husband,' Maria explained, kissing Clive perfunctorily on the cheek. 'Clive, I'd like you to meet Colonel Bill Carlotti.'

'The name rings a bell,' said Clive slowly, and then the memory fell into place in his mind. 'Of course, we were going to meet in Nassau back in 'thirty-nine.'

'Nassau?'

'Yes. Paul Denver's house.'

'So we were. Hell, that's a long time ago. But you flew off before I arrived. Glad to meet you now, sir,' said Carlotti insincerely, smiling, like Maria, with his mouth, not his eyes. 'Have a drink? I got two bottles of champagne from the PX.'

'Thank you, but no. Not yet,' said Clive. 'I've brought some Scotch. I think I'll stay with that.'

'Why didn't you let me know you were coming?' Maria asked him, almost accusingly.

'I simply hadn't the time. I was suddenly offered an air seat – the man who got it had gone sick – and it was take it or leave it. I took it.'

'Bill here is an old family friend. We grew up together in the same town, more or less.'

'More or less,' Carlotti agreed.

He was good-looking in a soft Mediterranean way. He could have been a stand-in for Clark Gable or Victor Mature or some beefcake actor, thought Clive. His eyes were too small, but when he smiled, you didn't notice this; not at first. Carlotti's charm, his smile, the general impression of easy affability that surrounded him negated such a small criticism. But if he was such an old friend of Maria, why had she not mentioned this in Nassau?

'Your wife and I were going out to talk over old times,' Carlotti continued. 'I've just been posted here – Eisenhower's staff – so I'm looking up all my English friends. Do please join us. We've booked a table at the Savoy. She's really got something to celebrate now you're home.'

'And being American,' Maria added, 'he also has a staff car – with petrol. We won't have to hike about the streets looking for a cab and then share it with half a dozen others.'

'But perhaps you two would like to be together?' asked Carlotti solicitously.

'No, no,' said Maria quickly. 'You go and have a wash and change, Clive. There's a pile of mail in the study to keep you busy and I'll pour you a whisky. There's masses of time. It's just half past seven. The table's booked for nine.'

Clive went into his study. He had not expected any warmth from his wife, but neither had he anticipated being invited to join her and a total stranger to make a threesome for dinner. Was this Bill fellow screwing her? Possibly, but did it matter? Did anything matter?

He wondered whether any letters had arrived from Johnny in Burma. They came as airgraphs, written on a sheet of light-sensitive paper, photographed in India and reduced to the size of a postage stamp, then developed, enlarged and dispatched from some central address in London.

There were two, both dated several months earlier. Maria could at least have forwarded them on to him in Basle, he thought, but she hadn't, so that was an end of the matter. He read them through quickly, but neither contained any real news. They would have been censored, in any case. He read remarks about the heat, the leeches, and a mention that he had met a most unusually pretty girl in Calcutta – 'but more about her in my next', Johnny had added coyly. Clive smiled for the first time since he had come back. The boy was a chip off the old block all right.

He put the letters in his inside pocket to read again later on, and went through the rest of the mail: bills, dividends, a few circulars, and a cheap envelope of porous brown paper. He opened this, read the letter first without interest, then with total disbelief, and finally with horror.

It was from the War Office. The writer had to inform him that 6300414 Pte. Douglas, J., at present serving with an infantry battalion, First Lincolns in 26 Indian Division in Arakan, Burma, was missing, believed killed.

Missing? How could he be? And who believed he was killed?

Clive thought that commanding officers sent personal letters of condolence, but perhaps that was coming by sea mail? Or perhaps this report was already outdated and Johnny was now safe and well? Burma was so far away, and communications so primitive, letters took weeks to arrive.

Only that week he had been sitting opposite Japanese delegates at the bank in Basle. The President that year was an American, and the meeting with German, Japanese, British, American and Italian executives had an important matter on the agenda. After the attack on Pearl Harbor in December, 1941, the Nazi leaders had transferred $378 million in gold into the custody of the bank. No-one at the discussion thought fit to mention the origins of this precious metal. Much had come from deposits in the national banks of Czechoslovakia, Belgium, Holland and Austria. The rest had been transferred from the Reichsbank, augmented by the melted gold content of cigarette cases, teeth fillings, spectacle frames and the wedding rings of Jews in concentration camps.

Clive Douglas hated all such meetings, but this one especially. It seemed unclean, bizarre, that rich middle-aged men should be moving gold and securities and deeds and patents across the chasm of a world at war, while every day young men, totally ignorant of their activities, were dying for such vague abstracts as freedom and democracy. It might even be, although it was of course very unlikely, that some relation of a Japanese delegate had actually shot Johnny Douglas. Absurd to think such a thing, but Clive's life in Basle had been conducted at such a level of disbelief. He pushed this fantasy from his mind.

For no particular reason, he suddenly remembered Camille. He had never even been to see her grave; that was how much she had meant to him. But now, for the first time, he began to realise the extent of the loneliness, the aloneness, she must have felt during their marriage. It was too late now for regrets. Everything was too late: if it wasn't, he would make amends to Johnny for all the time he should have spent with him, and hadn't. If there was another world, an after-life, were Camille and Johnny together? But that was presupposing Johnny was dead, and he refused to believe that. Not yet; not until he had absolute irrefutable proof.

He noted the Whitehall telephone number under the address. He must ring that number in the morning, first thing. Lots of people went missing, yet they turned up weeks, sometimes months, later. He had read stories about them in the newspapers. They had been shipwrecked and thought drowned, but somehow they had survived. They had been bombed, buried alive, shot down in aircraft over enemy territory, given up for dead, but, like Mark Twain, rumours of their death had been greatly exaggerated. It would be like that with Johnny, he was certain. Well, not quite certain, but very nearly. Anyway, he could do nothing now. Nothing at all. No-one would be at the end of a telephone in the War Office at this hour, war or no war. Might as well go out with the others, look on the bright side. He went into the bathroom and ran a bath.

In the drawing room, Carlotti was saying, 'He seems a nice guy.'

'You're not married to him,' said Maria shortly. 'He's a waster.'

'You should know. But he was born rich. It's harder to achieve anything when you don't *have* to struggle. However, you are sure about the will?'

'Absolutely certain. I leave everything to him, he leaves everything to me. We agreed that just after we married. No problem.'

'Well, now he's here, the sooner the better,' said Carlotti. 'I didn't expect him, did you?'

'No. I don't want to be involved,' she added vehemently. 'I was never going to be. That was all your concern. And now he's come back like this, suddenly, I can't.'

'You can and you will. It's so much easier with two. You must drive the car. You know London. I don't. We've talked it over often enough. There's nothing to it.'

'Will there be any – mess?'

'Nothing. It's a Family business. All quiet and clean. No fuss, no trouble, no . . . mess.'

Maria poured herself more champagne. It tasted flat on her tongue. For the first time in her life, she felt afraid, a deep-down fear and an overwhelming distaste for what she knew she had to do. She had enjoyed years of good living, expensive clothes and cars and trips. Now she was overdrawn at this bank of pleasure, and the debt was being called in.

'I don't like it,' she said slowly, hoping Carlotti would be sympathetic. 'I've never been at the sharp end of these things before.'

'You feel like this the first time, sure,' Carlotti agreed. 'But soon you don't even notice it. Everyone must get involved once at least in their life.'

His face was hard now, not charming; not even smiling with his mouth. 'That is the rule. Then we both have a secret – we share the same secret – and we both know exactly where our true interests lie. In keeping quiet. Silence. *Omerta*.'

They sat listening to the radio. Alan Breeze was singing the Hubert Greg song, 'I'm going to get lit up,' with Billy Cotton and his band.

Clive came into the room.

'I've just had some very bad news,' he said thickly, wishing Carlotti wasn't there, hearing it, but unable to keep it to himself. 'Johnny is missing in Burma, believed killed.'

Carlotti's face showed immediate concern, like an actor registering emotion. Initial incredulity was denoted by his wrinkled forehead; mouth turned down at the corners showed his sharing of another's grief.

Maria stood up.

'How terrible!' she said.

'Yes.'

'Shall we call off the dinner?' Carlotti suggested.

'No,' said Clive. 'Life has to go on. Communications are so bad out there, it's quite likely he's a prisoner and alive. That's what I'm counting on. Anyway, there's nothing anyone can do here and now. So let's go. That's what Johnny would say, I'm sure, if he were here.'

He went into the hall. Behind his back, Carlotti and Maria exchanged glances. Carlotti nodded almost imperceptibly. They went out of the flat into Grosvenor Square. A black Chevrolet was parked outside the door, up against the kerb.

'I'll drive,' Maria said. 'I know the way blindfold. An advantage in the blackout.'

Carlotti and Clive sat in the back. The big car bowled through empty, darkened streets, past signs Clive had forgotten in his time in Switzerland: 'Emergency Water Tank', 'Air Raid Shelter'. Sandbags were still piled, rotting now and spilling their sand, outside front doors; empty office windows were still criss-crossed with sticky tape in case of bomb blast. Even in the gloom, he could see how many 'For Sale' notices sprouted from railings remaining after an earlier patriotic drive to remove them and melt them down to make tanks and guns.

London must be almost empty. This was not as he liked to remember Mayfair: lines of shining limousines parked outside a nightclub, fun, fast drivers, forfeits, pretty girls. . . . That brought back the mention Johnny had made of the pretty girl in Calcutta. Would he ever hear more of her now? Did he really want to – if Johnny was not coming back?

'I've been reading about the doodlebugs,' he said to try and rid his mind of such thoughts.

'Yes, we've had a few nasty moments,' replied Carlotti. 'But they've eased off right now, given we've over-run their launching bases.'

'Trouble is,' said Maria, 'there's no warning. You just hear a noise and then they cut out and that's it.'

'One day they'll fight wars by remote control like that. Pilotless planes. Rockets,' said Clive. As he spoke, he thought that this might be no bad thing if it saved the lives of other young men like Johnny, whose fathers had never bothered to get on more than nodding terms with them.

The Savoy was packed. As Carroll Gibbons led the Savoy Hotel Orpheans into 'After You've Gone', a waiter steered them expertly to their table on the edge of the dance floor.

After the flight in a Dakota and the whisky, the surprise of meeting Carlotti and the shock of the War Office letter, the sudden noise of the band beat into Clive's brain like hammers on his head. Everyone seemed to be laughing and chattering, but inside all he felt was a gnawing emptiness, a misery that spread like melting ice. He wondered about his son, wished he had spent more time with him, realising, despite his professed optimism, that it was probably too late for such thoughts. Whatever he thought or wished now, the chance had gone, passed him by forever. The fact was, he had to admit, he could hardly have spent less time with his son or shown less interest in him. Johnny had joined up straight from school and had not even attempted to get a commission. Odd that, for someone of his background, he thought, but there it was. Life was odd, damned odd.

Carlotti called for drinks. He was a regular customer, and whiskies appeared, disappeared, re-appeared. A meal was ordered. Clive did not notice what he was eating; it was food, as the whisky was drink, and that was all. He felt disembodied, a spectator, someone looking on, not taking any part in the brittle conversation, while just across the Channel young men were killing each other, and farther away, much farther away, in a land he had never really heard of until his son was posted there, perhaps – possibly, probably – that young man was also dead. How? Why?

He excused himself, went out to the telephone, rang the War Office number, but of course there was no answer. He was mad to think there would be, but he felt he had to ring, to try and make contact, any contact. He came back to the table and sat down.

Carlotti had ordered coffee and brandy. Clive drank the coffee: it was cold in his cup.

'Sorry,' Maria said. 'I didn't think you'd be so long or I wouldn't have poured it out.'

'That's all right,' Clive answered her. He did not care whether it was cold or not. He did not care about anything.

'I'm not drinking any more,' she went on. 'I've got to drive you two home. It's bad enough trying to see in the blackout when you're sober. You've been spoiled in Basle, Clive.'

'Yes,' he agreed. 'I have been spoiled. Lots of food and lights. Not like here.' For all its French description the main course he had just eaten was only a rissole disguised under a heavy sauce. He had been hopelessly spoiled, of course, not just in Switzerland, but all his life.

The drink and the warmth and the music were dulling his mind. He felt half asleep. The journey and the letter had tired him – shocked him – more than he had realised. He would be glad to get to bed. Tomorrow, first thing, he would ring the War Office, find out what he could. The thought cheered him: he felt he would be doing something, however little. He would get *The Enquirer* people on to it, too. They'd ferret out the facts, if anyone could. He was damned lucky to have the resources of a newspaper group at his command.

Clive climbed thankfully into the back of the car with Carlotti. As they drove west along the Strand, past Charing Cross station, drowsiness overcame him. He dozed, head back, mouth open. He began to snore. Carlotti shook him.

'Wake up,' he said, and repeated the words more loudly. Then he shook him like a dog worrying a bone.

'He's out,' he said to Maria. 'I put the pill in his coffee when he was 'phoning.'

'What are you going to do?' Maria asked, knowing the answer but hoping he would give a different one. Driving slowly, she watched his face in the rear mirror. Her mouth felt dry, her stomach like a stone.

Carlotti leaned forward, jabbing the mirror so she could not see her husband lolling back against the seat, mouth open like a corpse.

'Don't ask damfool questions,' he told her roughly. 'Tread on it.'

She accelerated around Trafalgar Square. The fountains had long been boarded up, and old tattered posters flapped in the amber glow of the car's masked headlights: 'Dig for Victory', 'Warship Week', 'Careless Talk Costs Lives'.

'Where to?' she asked.

'Regent's Park Canal. I'll tell you exactly where to stop when we get there.'

He guided her to a side road.

'Now put out the lights.'

Carlotti, she noticed, was wearing gloves and galoshes over his polished shoes. Idly, she wondered whether these had been in the car all the time. They must have been; he was a professional.

He opened the rear door. Clive lay across the seat like a sack, legs and arms at unnatural angles. He was now snoring loudly, choking in his drugged sleep. Loosening Clive's collar, Carlotti pulled him out on to the pavement. His head struck a paving stone with a crack like a chisel blow. He groaned in his stupor and moved his legs feebly.

Maria winced, turned away and was violently sick.

'Get a hold of yourself,' said Carlotti harshly. 'Pick up his feet.'

She did so obediently, still choking. They carried him to the edge of the canal, grateful for the blackout. The water lay dark as a river of ink. There was no moon.

'Don't let go quickly. It will make a splash. Let him in gently.'

Clive's body slid into the canal, turned over and floated, head down. Carlotti held him under as he writhed feebly, choked, gurgled. A great gout of air blew into the water from his mouth, then he was still. Carlotti stood up, still watching as Clive's body drifted slowly away on the gentle current.

They climbed into the car, Carlotti at the wheel. They did not look at each other or even speak until he stopped outside her flat in Grosvenor Square.

'See there's no mud on that dress,' he told her. 'And clean your shoes. I'll ring you after he's found. Not until then.'

Carlotti let in the clutch. Maria stood watching the car's twin dimmed tail-lights diminish around the Square behind the trees, then she let herself into the empty flat. As she did so, she remembered that neither Clive nor Carlotti had said goodbye.

Reuben Ebenezer stood up to greet Maria Douglas as she came into his office. He had recently taken over as senior partner from his father, and dealt personally with the private matters of Trinity-Trio's partners.

'I hope you received my letter of condolence about your husband's tragic death?' he said.

'Thank you, yes. It was most kind of you to write.'

'The coroner at the inquest seemed to think there might have been foul play, poor fellow. Traces of some soporific drug were found in him, I believe?'

Maria nodded, her lips pursed.

'Well, he had been on rather secret business in Switzerland,' she admitted. 'He never spoke about it, of course. And one never really knows with these things, does one?'

'Quite so. And I understood from you at our last meeting that he had only heard on the night he died that his son by his first marriage was missing in Burma? Is there any further news about that young man?'

'None, I am sorry to say. I fear we have to accept that he is dead. Clive had just arrived home, and the War Office letter was waiting for him. It was a terrible shock. Poor Clive. Poor Johnny.'

Ebenezer nodded sympathetically.

'Now, how can I help you?' he asked.

'I am naturally reluctant to mention money at this time, but now that the war seems finally to be on its last legs, I really must try and make plans for my own future.

'I think I will return to the States – when I can get a passage, of course. But, in the meantime, you know how both our wills were drawn up. I left everything to him and he did the same for me.'

'Yes,' agreed Ebenezer slowly.

'You don't sound very certain about it,' Maria said sharply.

'Actually, there has been a change in that arrangement. I expect your husband spoke to you about it?'

'No,' she said, puzzled. 'Never. But he was in Switzerland for a long time, remember. He came back very rarely. We had little time to talk about such things. What sort of change do you mean?'

'He made another will while he was in Basle. It was drawn up by the attorney in Geneva who represents Trinity-Trio, Laurens Gustav. Witnessed, I think, in the British Embassy, to make certain it was valid under English law.'

'Really? I had no idea.'

'I am surprised, Mrs Douglas. I have a copy here if you would care to persue it.'

Ebenezer took some documents from a file.

'You will see that, having regard to the fact that you are already very wealthy in your own right, he decided to leave everything to his only son, John.'

'*Everything?* All the Trinity-Trio voting shares?'

'Everything. I can let you have this copy of the will, if you wish to discuss it with your own legal adviser.'

Maria reached out mechanically for it. Then relief flooded through her.

'Even so,' she said, 'if his son were proved dead, killed in action, it would all revert to me, as the next in line, surely?'

'In the normal course of events, yes, Mrs Douglas. We would, of course, have to wait for a statutory period of six months to suppose him dead – assuming confirmation of his death has not reached us before then from the War Office.'

'We can't have very long to wait. Notification of his being missing had already taken a long time to arrive.'

'That is true. But there is something else I have to tell you, Mrs Douglas. John Douglas married in Calcutta shortly before he was posted to Burma, from where he has been reported missing, believed killed.'

'*Married?* He was only a boy.'

'He was considered old enough to fight, possibly to die, for his country, so he was certainly old enough to marry.'

'His father didn't know?'

'I have no idea. I should not think the young man had much opportunity to tell him. Perhaps he wrote and that letter is still on its way. Communications with that theatre of war are very poor.

'Anyhow, we have been in touch with his wife in Calcutta as the next of kin. She informs us that she is expecting John's baby. Her child – his child – boy or girl, will therefore inherit everything. Including, of course, the fifty-one voting shares in Trinity-Trio.'

Hong Kong

That day started like almost every other day in the forty-four months Jackson had been a prisoner of the Japanese. He had no reason to imagine it would be any different, certainly no better; but, hopefully, no worse.

He awoke in his cell inside Stanley Gaol, queued at a tap to wash, brushed his teeth with the frayed end of a piece of bamboo, and then prepared to pass the dreary hours as best he could with 2,324 other British, American and Canadian civilian internees.

He had counted each day by scratching a small line on the distempered wall of the cell with his thumbnail. Now he drew his nail across the wall for the 1349th time. Sometime during the previous few months – he had no precise idea when, or else he convinced himself he hadn't – he had begun to cough blood.

Not much, often simply phlegm with a faint pinkish streak, in the way marbles he had played with as a boy had such a streak. Each morning, when he visited the latrine he coughed deliberately, hoping the phlegm would be green, not red for danger. He did this again; it was still red. He felt his spirits sag. He had recently felt better.

The camp doctor had told him he had tuberculosis. This could be cured, of course, but not as a prisoner of war of the Japanese on a bowl of rice a day.

He looked at his companions in the cell. Once they had been rich merchants, senior government servants, accountants, lawyers. Now they were all reduced to shrunken bags of bones, wearing the cast-offs of the dead: shabby shorts, loin cloths, rotting shirts, searching the ground for a cigarette butt.

None of them had any means of knowing how the war was going, who was winning, who losing. The Japanese had a radio, of course, and a woman announcer gave regular bulletins in English. These were too distorted to be called news, and the constant stream of propaganda month after month had a peculiarly deadening effect. It might be true, though most likely it wasn't, but since there was no way of knowing, its power had long since dwindled. It was only an irritant, the mental equivalent of a broken finger nail, a thorn in the foot.

They counted time by the rising and setting of the sun, by such small mercies as a Chinese former employee bringing a bowl of rice concealed in rags, for which someone would solemnly write a chit. Because Trinity-Trio had employed many Chinese at its Hong Kong branch, Jackson calculated he must have written hundreds of such chits. Would they ever be honoured? He hoped so. Not only because honouring them would mean he was free at last, but also because these humble clerks and their families, most of whom he had never previously heard of, were loyal to a company that had treated them well in the good years.

Gratitude was at best a rare quality, and in these circumstances, one to be treasured. He had never worked in Hong Kong, only visited it as a tourist. He remembered how the family knew how old Dr Jackson had never liked Hong Kong. It was indefensible, so he had said, thinking of an attack by the Chinese, an expendable commercial outpost at the farthest stretch of an empire. This had proved an accurate prophecy though the attack, when it came, was by the Japanese.

Jackson vowed that never again, if he survived – it was noteworthy, he thought, that he had long ago given up saying *when* he was released, but now, *if* he survived – would he treat his employees as ciphers. They would all be members of a team. His imprisonment had taught him many things, but none more important than this: in pain, in suffering, all men were equal.

He stood, barefoot, arms folded, in a corner of the yard, wondering what was happening in that larger world beyond the wall. He did not know whether his first wife was still alive, or Esmerelda in Colombo. Perhaps Ceylon had been captured and India invaded, as the English-speaking Japanese propagandist assured them time and again. Perhaps these two women were both dead, or alive but believing him dead, and in any case, had given him up long since.

For no reason at all, he suddenly remembered seeing the penny that his grandfather claimed was lucky, a coin his grandmother, Joanna Gray, had given to Richard Jackson on the night he sailed East for the first time. Had it brought him luck? Was there such a thing as luck, or was good or bad joss simply a consequence of something one had done – or not done?

Had it been luck that his first marriage had failed, and he had met Esmerelda in Colombo? He remembered that first wedding at St Margaret's, Westminster, so well; six bridesmaids, two pages, a line of Rolls-Royces strung with white ribbons and a thin, acidulated woman – she had been much older than him – standing by his side at the altar.

He had doubts before the marriage, and many more afterwards, but she was the only daughter of a man who boasted that his estates in the Midlands ran for ten miles in each direction from his house. The family were Norman, so his father-in-law assured him, and Jackson felt that somehow he was vindicating his father's wish to be accepted. After all he was a peer even if he refused to use the title, and a partner in Trinity-Trio with huge interests in the United States, British Honduras, England, Scotland, India and the East. Any children his wife Laetitia bore would also inherit an estate that had been in her family for nearly a thousand years. Jackson was therefore surprised at his mother's opinion.

'I am pleased you are getting married, and I hope you will both be very happy,' she told him. 'I must admit that almost every mother feels that the girl her son marries is barely worthy of him, but you must be worthy of your wife.

'However, I must take issue with your prospective father-in-law over his constant reiteration of the fact that he can trace his ancestors so far back.

'When Napoleon wished to marry Josephine, her parents asked him rather dismissively: "Who are your ancestors?" And Napoleon, who had no idea, replied instantly: "I am my own ancestor." '

'Remember those words, my dear. Be your own ancestor. And more important, whatever you do, always be your own man.'

The marriage had never been a success. Looking back, he realised that their characters were too disparate, their backgrounds totally different. He wanted to press ahead with new schemes for Trinity-Trio, broadening its base so that even such cataclysmic financial disasters as the 1929 slump could do no more than cause a tremor in the company; barely a shock, never a crash.

Laetitia was more concerned with being seen in the right places: at Ascot, Henley, Wimbledon. And she was annoyed that James Jackson would not use his father's title.

'That belonged to *him*,' he replied, attempting to explain. 'He helped this country enormously and had abuse heaped on him for it. Then he served as a private soldier in Flanders and was blinded in a gas attack. His health never recovered. He earned that title, I didn't. I was simply born to it. If I ever do anything that merits an honour, I'll accept one, obviously. But not now. That, to my mind, is rather like wearing someone else's suit.'

'If we have a son, he must inherit the title. I insist,' said Laetitia sharply.

'Of course,' Jackson agreed. 'But again, whether he uses it or not will be up to him.'

'Well, I want to be known as Lady Jackson.'

They drifted apart. He grew tired of spending empty weekends in cold country houses, with huge rooms that smelled of musty leather armchairs and stale cigar smoke. He liked houses that were homes; warm, friendly, expressing the character of people who lived in them, not stage sets, uncomfortable and archaic. While he travelled widely for Trinity-Trio, Laetitia would only travel to the south of France or Italy, because 'everyone who is anyone goes there'.

'Everyone is someone to themselves and their friends,' Jackson pointed out.

She just shrugged her shoulders.

'You know what I mean,' she said irritably. 'You're hopeless.'

Their life together soon became just as hopeless. Was it to continue like this, with ever-increasing bickering and arguments, hastily hushed before the servants? Would it not be better, more honourable, to admit the failure of the marriage and each go their own way? This, so easy to propose, was unfortunately more difficult to execute, because of the absurdity of the law.

It ended with an unpleasant divorce case, in which Jackson admitted having spent a night at an hotel in Brighton with a chorus girl. Everything about this confession was a charade. The chorus girl paid £10 to give false witness; the chambermaid at the hotel paid the same amount for saying she entered with the breakfast tray and they were in bed together; the judge who passed stern comments on the collapse of morality in high society which should set an example to those less exalted; the newspaper moralists who wrote so eloquently about the urgent need to return to basic old-fashioned values – and then went out to get drunk and spend their nights with mistresses or lovers.

It had all been very unpleasant and unbelievably expensive, but in the end he was free; a single man. After that he was cautious of involvements, and in any case since the war he seemed to be travelling almost constantly on government business. Nearly all Trinity-Trio's factories were on war work. As war with Japan seemed increasingly likely, he was asked to set up a new office in Colombo and to bring out to it all the documents from Hong Kong in case the colony should be attacked.

Colombo, before Pearl Harbor, possessed an almost dream-like quality. Not only the war but the rest of the world seemed to have passed it by. There were no shortages of food or petrol; the only difference he noticed since his last pre-war visit was an increase in servicemen, especially the Navy. There were cinemas, new cars and ENSA touring concert parties, which gave shows every night, at theatres or halls or in hotel ballrooms.

Jackson had never been a theatre-goer, he had never had much time, but now he enjoyed not only the shows but the company of the actors and actresses afterwards. In particular, there had been two girls, Esmerelda and Barbara, vivacious, cheerful, a total antidote to Jackson's problems.

They had met waiting for a taxi outside the Galle Face Hotel. Jackson had his own car and took them on to a restaurant, and from there the friendship had blossomed. Sometimes he took out Esmerelda, sometimes Barbara; sometimes one or other would bring along a male member of the cast, and the four of them would go out together.

The girls had never been abroad before, so everything was new and exciting. With palm trees and the pounding surf, the Galle Face restaurant looking over the sea staffed by waiters in traditional costume, they felt they were living out a Dorothy Lamour film of the south seas.

Jackson went to bed with both of them and liked both of them, but he married Esmerelda.

He had not really intended to marry, but when he found he had to go personally to Hong Kong to try and sort out on the spot further complications after the Japanese attack, he knew he would miss her. He could not bear to think of her going out of his life.

There were rumours that the show would be posted to New Zealand, Australia, the Middle East, Bombay, almost anywhere. He had wanted to make sure that wherever they went, wherever he went, they could be certain of finding each other afterwards. Standing now in the sun in the courtyard of Stanley Gaol, he wondered what had happened to them all.

Another prisoner, thin, yellow-faced from malaria, his shirt and shorts no more than threadbare strips of faded cloth, came through the crowd of men who stood, lacking all energy, faces turned to the sun – like cattle, or horses in a field at home, he thought, eager for any warmth.

'Gimson wants to see you,' the man told Jackson.

'What about?'

'He'll tell you.'

Franklin Gimson was in his fifties and by general admission the leader in the camp. He was a tall, austere man, the son of a Leicestershire clergyman and married to a clergyman's daughter. He had read mathematics and history at Balliol, Oxford, and then joined the Colonial Service. Gimson returned to be commissioned in the Army during the Great War, and thereafter served abroad, largely in Ceylon.

His wife and daughters were in England when war broke out, and so had been unable to join him overseas. Then, in December 1941, he had unexpectedly been posted to Hong Kong as Colonial Secretary. On his arrival, knowing no-one and with no-one knowing him, he had literally only time to introduce himself to Sir Mark Young, the Governor, before the colony surrendered to the Japanese on the afternoon of Christmas Day.

Jackson had felt immensely sorry for Gimson during the months that followed. He was a difficult man to know intimately; reserved, withdrawn. Their backgrounds were quite dissimilar, but as the senior government officer, Gimson had been treated with astonishing and open hostility by many other internees. In times past, they would have been honoured by an invitation to his home. Now they ludicrously blamed on him the surrender of Hong Kong. This was obviously nothing to do with him; he had only arrived in the colony hours before it happened, but the shock and misery of being prisoners of small yellow men they had always despised, had warped their outlook.

'Why hadn't more been done before the war to make us defensible?' he was asked.

'Because it's totally indefensible,' said Jackson before Gimson could reply. 'My grandfather, one of the three founders of our company, refused to have our headquarters here because of that. How can anyone defend this tiny island?'

'Then why did we ever colonise it?' someone asked.

'Why did we colonise anywhere?' retorted Jackson. 'Because we have an ability to run these remote places, to make them pay. Not only for ourselves, but for the locals.'

'Pity we didn't also have the gift to see what was going to happen.'

Jackson shrugged. These arguments went on endlessly, regurgitated in bitterness and anger, born out of frustration, misery, the agonising humiliation of defeat at the hands of those they regarded as inferiors.

In June, 1942, many Americans had been repatriated to the United States in exchange for a number of Japanese nationals interned there, largely on the West Coast. As they said goodbye, Gimson told them seriously, 'When you are drinking the victory toast, remember the hardships you shared with us here in Stanley.'

'Be careful,' said a former banker nervously. 'These fellows are going home, but we've got to stay. You don't want to annoy the Japanese.'

'I don't mind whether we annoy them, or don't annoy them,' retorted Gimson. 'We're stuck here now, agreed, but not forever. *We are going to win.*'

'How do you make that out?'

'Because what he says is true,' said Jackson. 'Positive thinking. If you set out to cross Niagara Falls on a tightrope you concentrate on reaching the other side – because the alternative just doesn't bear contemplation. That's the same with us here. We are going to win and get the hell out of here.'

The others melted away, muttering that he and Gimson were both mad. Jackson admired Gimson – and so did the Japanese. He was a man they could respect, not some captured *taipan*, half resentful, half fearful of his fate, bellicose and maudlin in turn. He realised the extent of this admiration when he first accompanied Gimson to an interview with the commandant, Lieutenant Kadowake.

Gimson had sought a small concession for one of the internees; that he might be excused, on account of age and ill health, standing in the sun for hours during regular roll-calls.

The commandant shook his head.

'No concessions,' he said briefly. 'None. The matter is finished, Ended.'

'You are wrong,' Gimson replied. 'This is by no means the end of the matter.'

The Japanese commandant gazed at him in surprise.

'What do you mean by that?'

'Exactly what I say. Your refusal will be raised after the war at the Peace Conference. I will be interested to see then what will be their reactions – and yours.'

The commandant looked at him for a moment. Gimson stared him out. The commandant bowed his head.

'Request granted,' he said gruffly.

Day after day, in the heat of the sun or under the driving spears of monsoon rain, Gimson, with Jackson and an interpreter, was made to stand outside the commandant's office, awaiting his summons to report on some matter about the administration of the camp. Sometimes, the commandant would eventually see him, sometimes he did not bother. But every day for forty-four months this charade continued, and every day Gimson remained stoic, uncomplaining, unyielding.

And then, on the morning of August 15th, 1945, Lieutenant Kadowake did not keep them waiting. The moment Gimson and Jackson arrived, he ushered them into his office.

'I have to tell you, His Majesty the Emperor has taken into consideration the terms of the Potsdam Conference and has ordered hostilities to cease,' he announced in English.

Gimson and Jackson exchanged glances. They had never heard of the Potsdam Conference. What did the man mean?

The commandant saw their bewilderment and rephrased his statement.

'In other words,' he said simply, 'you have won. We have lost.'

'The war is over?' asked Jackson. The commandant nodded.

The misery and uncertainty, the hunger, the needless deaths from malnutrition, fever, inoperable illnesses, all this was at an end; too late for many, but not for those left alive. He wanted to cheer, and then he started to cough. The rag he used for a handkerchief came away bright red with blood.

Word of the Japanese surrender spread throughout the camp: many simply could not believe it. There had been rumours before, but all had been false. Was this also just gossip, a canard spread by desperate men? Or could it at last be true?

A car drove into the camp as the prisoners discussed the situation. A Japanese colonel climbed out: they recognised the officer who commanded all prisoner-of-war and civilian internee camps in Hong Kong. With him was a member of the Japanese Foreign Office. They greeted Gimson like old friends, even attempted to embrace Jackson. They might have been arriving for cocktails. Gimson and Jackson drew away from them. They could not endure this sickening hypocrisy that mocked years of imprisonment, humiliation and torture.

Gimson, as the most senior civil officer left alive of the pre-war Hong Kong government, insisted he should immediately take charge of the colony's administration.

'We need an office for this,' added Jackson. 'And access to the radio station. Mr Gimson must broadcast that the war is over, and the British are again in control.'

The Japanese colonel bowed and washed his hands thoroughly without water.

'You gentlemen are out of touch,' he said. 'We have heard from Tokyo that the American President, Mr Harry S. Truman, agrees that since Hong Kong lies in the Chinese sphere of influence, this former British colony will be handed over to the Chinese generalissimo, Chiang Kai-Shek, not back to the British.

'He will make all the arrangements for the handing over of authority and the surrender of Japanese forces. I must tell you that there is no certainty whatever that Hong Kong will continue to be British. Indeed, it is almost certain the reverse will be the case.'

'That is only your opinion,' said Gimson. 'What you hear has nothing to do with me. I am not concerned with it. I repeat, I will carry out my duties as appointed by His Majesty's Government in London.'

The colonel shook his head.

'Gentlemen,' he said gravely, 'the Chinese National Army is already waiting on the mainland to enter Hong Kong and take over the colony.'

'If they do that,' said Jackson, 'they will never leave. The Chinese and the Americans have done a deal together over this.'

'That is my opinion, too,' the Japanese colonel agreed. 'It is bad when allies fall out. But the Americans do not like colonies or colonists. They were once a colony of the British, too, remember.'

'The world is never allowed to forget,' replied Jackson. 'American foreign policy is dictated by the memory.'

'If the Chinese take over Hong Kong,' Gimson told the Japanese colonel, 'you are all dead men. The Chinese will settle old scores with you. After all, China and Japan have been at war for ten years.'

The colonel nodded wretchedly.

'It may be as you say.'

'It will be exactly as I say,' said Gimson, *'unless I assume control.'*

He insisted that the Japanese release from the officers' POW camp in Kowloon, Claude Burgess, a scholar in Chinese, and two other officers, Douglas Heath and Iain MacGregor, whose family wine firm, Caldbeck MacGregor and Co., had been trading in the East for more than eighty years. All these men knew pre-war Hong Kong well. They commandeered the French Mission building for what Gimson called the British Provisional Government, and above this they ran up the Union Jack.

It was essential that all civilian internees and prisoners of war should remain in their camps until the situation was resolved. The internees listened to Gimson as he insisted on this measure, for their own protection, first in silence, then with mounting criticism. Their homes and offices were in many cases within walking distance. They wanted to carry on with lives that had been interrupted so painfully for so long. Why was this further delay necessary?

'We are all weak from years of undernourishment,' Jackson explained. 'We are out of touch with events. Out in the streets are Japanese troops who may not even know the war is over, and thousands of Chinese soldiers are on the mainland waiting to seize Hong Kong. It is imperative for our own safety – everyone's safety – that we get the situation sorted out before anyone leaves the camp.'

As he spoke he started to cough again. He could taste salt blood on his tongue. He leaned against a wall, saying to himself it was from the heat, excitement and exhaustion.

'You're crook, mate,' said an Australian.

'It's nothing,' said Jackson, but he crouched down in the shade, his head between his knees, fighting off waves of nausea. How ironic to feel so ill on the eve of freedom.

In other prisoner of war and civilian internment camps, they were singing 'Abide With Me' and then 'God Save the King'. Someone who had kept concealed throughout the years of imprisonment a Royal Navy White Ensign and a Union Jack, now brought them out and they were run up on the camp flagposts.

A Chinese came into the camp, and explained to Gimson that his name was Leung, and he had come from Macao which, as a Portuguese possession, had been neutral throughout the war. He had brought two messages for Franklin Gimson from the British Consul in Macao. The first authorised him to take over the administration of Hong Kong on his release from imprisonment. The second said that permission from the American Chiefs of Staff was being sought to release a British naval force from the British Pacific Fleet so that it could head for Hong Kong. When this arrived, Franklin Gimson should hand over his authority to the senior British naval officer in command.

Two things puzzled Gimson and Jackson. First, why should American consent be necessary for what was entirely a British concern? Secondly, how long would this naval force take to arrive – and where was it sailing from?

If it was delayed for more than a few days, the Chinese would march into Hong Kong, and were most unlikely ever to march out again. It was essential to discover more information and as soon as possible. The only source was the British Consul in Macao who had a powerful radio transmitter and receiver. But he was forty miles away.

'I'll go to see him,' said Jackson.

'You're ill,' said Gimson.

Others looked at Jackson, speculating on his chances of success. He was, of course, part Chinese. He could be more easily disguised as a Chinese than any European. He spoke the language and he knew Hong Kong and Macao.

'I'm going,' Jackson repeated and that night, dressed as a coolie, he and Leung went out of the camp, down to the docks. Within a hundred yards Jackson realised how unfit he was, and how weak. For years, he had been cooped up in a yard, living on a handful of rice a day, not knowing whether this incarceration would ever end. Now he found it difficult to accept he was free, and even more difficult to keep up with his wiry, lean-muscled companion.

Leung had bribed the captain of a small fishing boat to bring him to Hong Kong from Macao. This was still tied up to the quay. Protracted negotiations took place. Leung promised the man money to carry them to Macao.

'But when will you pay me?'

'On our return,' Jackson promised. It was unthinkable that the future of Hong Kong could hinge on a few dollars.

The fisherman wanted his money now, which was impossible.

'Listen,' said Jackson finally, 'I am a partner of Trinity-Trio. You *must* trust me.'

At once the captain relaxed. He nodded.

'Trinity-Trio? I did business with your company pre-war time. They treated me fair.'

'They will do so again,' Jackson assured him and shook hands.

The two men climbed aboard. The little craft with its slatted sail set out to sea. They reached Macao at dusk on the following evening. Jackson went ashore near the lighthouse beneath Fort Guia.

The British Consulate was closed. He beat on the front door. It was opened by a Portuguese servant.

'I must see the Consul,' Jackson told him.

'Come tomorrow at nine o'clock.'

'To hell with that. I'm from Hong Kong.'

He pushed his way past the man. The Consul was in his study.

'It's after hours,' he said shortly.

'Not for me, it isn't,' said Jackson. 'I've come from Stanley Gaol in Hong Kong. I've been waiting years for this moment.'

'Goodness me! So you're not Chinese?'

'I am a British subject,' said Jackson, 'come to take a message back to Franklin Gimson.'

As he explained the situation, the Consul poured him a whisky.

'When is the fleet due?' asked Jackson.

'Heaven only knows,' said the Consul. 'You know the background to this?'

'Of course not. This is my first day of freedom. Everyone else is still behind the wire.'

The Consul opened a safe, and took out a sheet of deciphered documents.

'We haven't time to go through all these,' he said, 'but they are Most Secret and Most Immediate telegrams between Whitehall and our ambassadors in Washington and Chungking, copies to me.

'First, London has told our people in Chungking that Gimson would restore British sovereignty and administration immediately.'

'He is doing his best to,' said Jackson. 'But we've heard nothing from Chungking.'

'Understandable. The Chinese aren't being very helpful about letting messages through. President Truman wants Hong Kong to be a free port with consequent advantages to American trade. The American Vice President, Henry A. Wallace, was in Chungking last year and he assured Chiang Kai-Shek that this would happen. The Americans have consistently done what they can to diminish British standing and interests in China.

'The Chinese – you probably don't know – continually ask for more military equipment, which they cannot possibly use. We tell the Americans that it's nonsense giving it to them. The Communists will take over eventually and it will all fall into their hands.

'Chiang Kai-Shek is corrupt, and his influence in decline, and these weapons will simply be used against the West. The Americans won't listen. The U.S. Treasury will not consult the British Treasury in arranging financial exchange rates. Consequently, we lose out all down the line.

'General Wedermeyer, the American Chief of Staff to Chiang Kai Chek, has produced a plan for Chinese forces to capture Hong Kong. Ludicrous – and bloody hostile when you remember that Britain still has a fifty years' lease on the colony.'

The Consul paused and sipped his drink.

'That's the bad news, then?' said Jackson. 'And it sounds pretty grim. But when you've been inside as long as I have, the good news is that we are free, and we intend to stay that way. What's the message for Gimson?'

'Hold out,' said the Consul bluntly. 'We've tried to send a colonel as a military adviser to him from Chungking by aircraft. But we are told that Kai Tak air field is too heavily mined to accept aircraft, so that's out.

There is another snag. It has just been declared in Washington that Japanese forces within China will surrender to Chiang Kai-Shek – no-one else.'

'But Hong Kong is not within China.'

'Agreed. But the Americans say it is, so the Chinese are insisting that this order is carried out. There's another cable here about them, asking us to refrain from landing forces anywhere in the China theatre without getting permission from General MacArthur.

'Mr Attlee, the Prime Minister – you probably haven't heard that he won the General Election – has sent a personal telegram to President Truman, saying that while we will welcome Chiang Kai-Shek's personal representative when the Japanese surrender in Hong Kong, Hong Kong is British territory and cannot be included as being within China.'

'How did the President reply?' asked Jackson.

'Prevaricatingly. There is no objection to a British officer accepting Hong Kong's surrender so long as this is cleared with Chiang Kai-Shek first, etcetera, etcetera.'

'If we delay any longer,' said Jackson, 'the Chinese will be in the colony, and that's it.'

'Then hold out and contact the first British ship you see. Now, can I give you a bed here?'

'No,' said Jackson. 'The boat is taking on a cargo of dried fish for Hong Kong. I'll go back on it. I may not get a passage at all otherwise.'

'But you're ill. You are coughing badly,' said the Consul sympathetically.

'I'm lucky to be alive to cough,' retorted Jackson. 'So many who went into Stanley three years ago with me would have liked that chance.'

'It must have been terrible?'

Jackson shrugged. Some things could not be talked about, not yet. They were too close, the wounds in the mind too raw and open.

'Now please radio London what is happening – or not happening. Every hour counts. Stress the extreme urgency.'

'Will do,' the Consul promised.

'And give me a pencil and some paper,' Jackson asked him. 'I have a Chinese courier here with me. I'll write down your message for him to be able to hand on – in case I don't get through.'

When Jackson arrived back in Hong Kong, he was dismayed to see that nearly every building was displaying a Chinese national flag and Chiang Kai-Shek's picture at their windows. Where they had come from, he had no idea, but they were there; that was all that mattered. And the Japanese, who only days earlier had been eager to collaborate with the British, were now aloof.

A radio announcement had said that Chiang Kai-Shek's forces would occupy Hong Kong, and the Japanese wanted to keep their options open. Their only hope of survival if the Chinese did arrive was to collaborate fully with them. The British had no power and power was what counted: men in uniform, warships in the bay.

Time was running against the internees like a tide. Gimson broadcast over Hong Kong radio, which the Japanese still controlled, saying that British survivors from internment camps had taken over the administration of the colony. But had they? There was nothing now anyone could do but wait – for what? For some British naval force to arrive? Or for the Chinese Army to march in?

Many of the internees could now see less reason why they were still living behind wire, but they reluctantly accepted Gimson's argument that they were safer where they were. If the Chinese entered Hong Kong, their future could be as precarious as that of the Japanese occupying forces. To Jackson, coughing blood almost constantly now, it seemed that the effort to get a message to London had been totally useless.

Then two weeks after the Japanese had first admitted the war was over, a British aircraft flew low over Hong Kong. It dropped a small weighted bag on the runway at Kai Tak airfield. This contained a message to the Japanese commander from Admiral C.H.J. Harcourt, commanding the British fleet, still unknown miles over the horizon, but on its way. The message instructed the Japanese commander to send out an officer by boat to meet the fleet immediately, bringing full details of any minefields off Hong Kong. If he had no vessel, a British plane from the aircraft carrier in the fleet would fly into Kai Tak and collect their representatives personally.

The Japanese liaison officer came to see Gimson and Jackson.

'We cannot allow the British to land,' he said firmly. 'We have no authority to negotiate with you. The Chinese are taking over.'

'I cannot accept that,' Gimson told him.

'Anyhow, we have no suitable boat,' said the Japanese.

'In that case, you will radio acceptance that a British plane will land.'

'It is impossible,' said the Japanese. 'The airfield is water-logged.'

'Rubbish! No rain has fallen for the last three weeks.'

'But I have no authority to send anyone out with this information.'

'In that case, your refusal will be treated as a criminal offence after the British land. I am giving you authority now. More than authority – a direct order.'

The Japanese radioed the fleet that no arrangements could be made for any surrender because General Tanaka, the Japanese over-all commander, was absent in Canton.

Back from the fleet came a reply: Admiral Harcourt intends to enter Hong Kong and take over the naval dockyard tomorrow.

The internees watched them sail in: ten capital ships, an aircraft carrier, six Australian minesweepers, a submarine flotilla. Down came the Chinese flags, and the pictures of Chiang Kai-Shek from buildings and windows. Up in their place went hastily made Union Jacks. On the mainland, the Chinese Army suddenly marched away. Hong Kong had been saved by the determination and courage of Franklin Gimson, and a handful of others of like mind and calibre.

As Jackson watched the sailors come ashore, the moment seemed almost an anti-climax. They had waited so long for this, and now, what did the future hold?

No-one could be totally certain. They did not know whether wives and families were still alive. Some had left Hong Kong before it surrendered. Had their ships been torpedoed? Had they reached safety? Where were they now? In India? Australia? In England?

Everyone felt a curious and unexpected feeling of total desolation. They had been cooped up, wretchedly fed, abominably treated, for years, and now they did not know how to start finding their families or relations.

Some, of course, had no wish to do so. They accepted their incarceration as an excuse never to return to their previous lives, or wives. They had survived where thousands had died. This surely was the only moment they would ever have to start again, perhaps in a new country, in a new career, even with a new name?

Jackson had sympathised with them because he was so much more fortunate: with the branches of Trinity-Trio in Calcutta and London, he could soon establish where his wife was. He had a future made all the more attractive in comparison with the past three and a half years.

He walked through Hong Kong's crowded streets to his office. This was on the second floor of the building. He had forgotten about the stairs. He used to climb them two at a time, but now he waited for the elevator. This took him up as slowly and wheezily as it had done in pre-war days. He was rather surprised that it was working at all.

He came out onto the marbled floor of the reception room. A Chinese girl sat at the reception desk. He remembered her. She had been there in 1942. He looked around the room, astonished that so little had changed. Why had not the Japanese looted the place? But what could they do with their loot, where could they sell it? It was obviously better to keep it intact.

'Can I help you, sir?' the receptionist asked him politely.

'Yes,' he said. 'Is Mr Lin in today?'

'Mr Lin, sir, is down at the dockyard seeing the fleet come in. But he will be back in a few moments. What name shall I say?'

'Jackson.'

'*Lord Jackson?* I didn't recognise you.'

'I'm not surprised,' said Jackson. 'But no "Lord" stuff, you know. I've never used the title.'

'Why, I *am* glad to see you back.'

She stood up and came round the side of the desk and took both of his hands.

'Please come into your office. It's just as it was.'

So it proved. He sat down thankfully in the swivel armchair behind his desk, pressed the buttons on the intercom, picked up the telephone.

'The lines are down, sir, and the teleprinter isn't working,' the girl explained.

'Of course not. But it will be soon.'

He would have to send a letter to Calcutta asking them to find out his wife's address. Or perhaps she was in Calcutta or New York? She could be anywhere. He suddenly felt almost nervous about contacting her again. To marry someone after three weeks and then to go away for three years was not a recipe for guaranteed happiness. But then, what is?

He turned to the girl, meaning to ask, absurdly, if there was any mail, a purely reflex question, when suddenly he started to cough. He saw the girl's face register concern, then horror. One hand went up to her mouth.

Jackson was now coughing uncontrollably, gasping for air. Taking out his handkerchief to wipe his mouth, he noticed it was saturated with blood. More blood was running down the front of his threadbare shirt.

'My God!' cried the girl. 'I'll get a doctor.'

She fled away, shouting to a colleague in another office. Clerks emerged, men in white shirts and linen trousers. The room suddenly seemed full of strange faces, all staring at him. He was dying among strangers.

He called to the nearest man. The words were unintelligible; he was choking with his own blood. The message from his brain failed to reach his mouth. He sank back in his chair. He could not even see the faces clearly now, only as though viewed through frosted glass or a dense fog.

He heard voices distantly, speaking about him, behind him, around him. He managed one word: 'Esmerelda.'

He closed his eyes and then opened them, and for a moment he saw more clearly. The strangers were looking puzzled. Who was Esmerelda? Of course, they couldn't know he had married her. How could they possibly know where she was, if they did not know who she was? He knew he had a message to pass on, but who would listen, who would understand?

'My grandfather was right,' said Jackson thickly, speaking with a mouth full of blood. 'He nearly always was. Hong Kong was indefensible. Totally.'

His voice tailed away. He was conscious, but only vaguely, of someone lifting his hand, taking his pulse. There was a faint smell of anaesthetic in the air, the crispness of a voice of authority, and then he was drifting out through mists beyond the Peak, beyond the bay, beyond everything.

'He's dead,' said the Naval doctor. 'Poor devil. Survived all those years, just to die today. Well, better tell his next-of-kin. Anyone know who they are?'

Part Four

From 1945 to 1988

Manchester

The Australian was nine when he first made a puzzling discovery – and exactly one year older when he achieved his first profit on a business deal, and he found in this a deep and total fascination beyond all imagining.

He had been born in Australia, where, even during the last years of the Second World War there was no shortage of milk or eggs, and where sunshine was a constant bonus.

His mother lived in a small town, Katherine, seven hundred miles from Alice Springs, on the Stuart Highway to Darwin. This road had been built hurriedly during the war, about the time he was born, by Australian and American engineers to enable troops to travel north to Darwin to hold off the Japanese, who were already in the Dutch East Indies and expected to land on the north coast of Australia, and then to surge south.

The Australian didn't remember too much about Katherine, but he never forgot the anthills outside it, maybe eight or nine feet high, like domes. They were totally quiet, of course, but inside they teemed with millions of white ants.

These ants would eat anything dead or inanimate: the bones of a wallaby hit by a truck, the beams of a wooden house; always silently, and successfully. Nothing could stop them. The Australian feared and admired them. They had qualities he valued: persistence, lack of any ostentation, unswerving determination.

His mother brought him to England just before his ninth birthday. She had been in vaudeville, and decided that England offered more opportunities in what she always called 'The Profession'.

They lived now in a terraced house in a suburb of Manchester, opposite a nineteenth-century cotton mill, a grim, barrack-like block with a very tall chimney.

They moved in temporarily with a relation, Uncle Rob, a bachelor in his sixties.

The Australian – as Uncle Rob always called him, and then the boys and girls at school – did not take well to his surroundings.

From the back yard, with its washing line, a wooden door opened on to an open cinder-strewn space. Other houses around this had similar doors, and in the summer children would play cricket using an oil drum for a wicket.

He could not equate his earlier life under a wide blue sky, with plenty of steaks and prawns and the casual cheerfulness that seemed part of living in Australia, with this chill, gritty, narrow-shouldered existence.

His mother read *The Stage* newspaper every week and replied to advertisements that required many abilities: 'Blonde actresses needed for contract in Japan. Must be under five feet tall. . . . Good all round dancing needed, plus tap. . . . Attractive girl singers with acrobatic ability. . . . Light comedy essential.'

Week after week, she went for auditions. She treated dance directors to drinks in pubs near the stage doors of music halls, but she always came back rejected and dejected. Then she would make herself a cup of tea in the kitchen, pour in Nestlé's sweetened condensed milk from the tin and sit down to read the evening paper or listen to the radio.

'It's a ring,' she would explain to Uncle Rob. 'It's not what you know, but who.'

'Better luck next time, Amy dear,' Uncle Rob would invariably reply. He greeted almost every family happening with similar remarks: 'Not to worry', 'Mustn't grumble', 'Look on the bright side', 'Every cloud's got a silver lining'.

The Australian knew that his father had been killed serving with the Australian Army in New Guinea. He seemed to have left no other relations, but his mother hinted that he had been well-connected.

'You'd be surprised,' she said once when she came back after two or three port and lemons with the director of a touring show. 'You really would be. So would everyone else around here. He was a real gent, a hero. Not like these pansies I have to kow-tow to.'

For the Australian's ninth birthday, his mother brought home a cake she had bought at the corner shop on her way back from another unsuccessful audition. It was covered in pink icing with nine small candles set in imitation flowers. He chewed one of these flowers, thinking it might be hard icing. It wasn't, but some gummy substance that made him feel sick. He went out into the lavatory in the back yard to vomit, because this was nearer than going upstairs to the bathroom.

This outside lavatory was a relic from Victorian days, in a brick outhouse, with a wooden door opened by a coal-house latch. A wooden seat fitted neatly on top of a wide earthenware pipe. By shining a torch down this pipe, the Australian could see water in the drain beneath and sometimes, frighteningly, the baleful yellow eyes of a sewer rat looking up at him.

On a nail behind the door hung squares of newspaper, used instead of bought toilet rolls, to save money. On this particular visit, a headline caught his eye: 'Trinity-Trio announce record profits'. The name stayed in his mind. Holy Trinity Church across the road. Trinity House which, he had been learning at school, controlled lighthouses around the English coast. A Trio meant three people; he had heard announcers on the radio say that this or that violin trio was about to play.

But this newspaper story had nothing to do with religious matters or lighthouses or musical trios: it was a report on a company of which he had never heard, and there was no reason why he should ever hear of it again.

But he did – that same day, and then he made the discovery that when someone came across an unusual name or learned an unusual fact, almost immediately they encountered other references to it.

He kept repeating the name to himself as he went into the house and there, to his astonishment, he saw it again, in the local paper this time: 'Trinity-Trio in bid for Northern mills'.

He looked through the paper. Usually he only liked the cartoons, but now he read that a country estate of fifteen hundred acres bordering on Shap Fell had just been sold for £25,000 by a local estate agent acting for the trustees of Lord Jackson.

'Lord Jackson, who is eight years old, and who attends a fashionable prep school in Hertfordshire, will, on his twenty-first birthday, inherit a large shareholding in the London-based international company, Trinity-Trio. Starting as a small trading concern in the East in the last century, this is now one of Britain's most successful groups. Lord Jackson, when he inherits, will be one of the country's richest young men.'

There it was again, Trinity-Trio. And a new name to look out for: Lord Jackson.

'What are you reading?' Uncle Rob asked him. As he came into the kitchen, he took from his pocket the little machine he carried to roll cigarettes, filled the paper with tobacco, licked the edge with his tongue to seal the joint. For the fourth time that day the Australian saw the name, 'Trinity-Trio Paper Mills, Bristol and Cardiff'. It was extraordinary.

He told his mother about this, expecting her to be interested, but she was in a bad mood. She had drunk too many port and lemons with another dance director who promised her all kinds of jobs in future shows, but nothing at present. She read the items her son pointed out and then tossed the paper on one side.

Later that evening, when he looked at the paper to see the cartoons he had missed, the Australian saw that these stories had been carefully cut out. Why? Uncle Rob was out in the pub, and his mother was next door having a cup of tea and a gossip with a neighbour.

He searched unsuccessfully around the little room, under cushions on the sofa, down the sides of armchairs, behind the clock on the mantelpiece. He went upstairs to his mother's bedroom, began to open drawers, driven by a curiosity he had never previously felt. He could not wait for his mother to return. He wanted the cuttings *now*. He was always impatient. The prudent procrastinations urged by Uncle Rob – 'Wait and see', 'Sleep on it', 'Give it second thoughts' – always irritated him.

Standing on a chair to reach the top of the cupboard, he saw a small flat box marked 'Nylon stockings: a Trinity-Trio Product'. (Again, that name. What did this company not make or own?) He opened the box. Inside were the reports he had just read, with several newspaper cuttings, yellow and curling at the edges.

They referred to Trinity-Trio, to young Lord Jackson, to his late father; still others to a dashing-looking man, Clive Douglas, who was pictured standing by a racing car. Why hadn't his mother mentioned these when he was telling her about Trinity-Trio?

He heard the latch click on the yard door, hastily put the cuttings back in the box, replaced the box on top of the cupboard. He went downstairs as she came into the kitchen.

'Have you cut out those bits in the paper about the company, Trinity-Trio?' he asked her. 'They're in a box on top of the cupboard in your room.'

'You've been messing about in my things,' she said menacingly.

'No. Only looking. I was interested. It's funny, but I'd never heard of that company till today – and then several times.'

'I don't know what you are talking about.'

His mother went upstairs.

'Come and show me,' she called down to him.

The Australian followed her into the bedroom, put the chair next to the cupboard and climbed on it. There was nothing now on top of the cupboard. The box had gone.

'You see?' she said. 'You're making it up.'

'I am not.'

'Don't lie to me,' she said sharply and smacked him round the face.

He was sent to bed early, but he kept the name locked away in his mind, to be brought out as some people will take a piece of silver from a safe to turn it over and admire.

For his tenth birthday, Uncle Rob gave him a wrist watch. It had only cost seven and sixpence when new, and was very clearly second-hand. He would rather have had the money; he could have bought a Lucas dynamo lighting set for his bicycle from another boy at school.

The Australian decided to sell the watch, but no-one in his form had the seven and sixpence he asked for it. He divided the sum into pennies.

There were thirty boys in the form. If they each gave him three pennies he would have his seven and sixpence.

He decided to ask for sixpence from as many boys as possible, write each boy's name on a bit of paper, put the papers in a hat, and let the head of the form draw the winner.

He canvassed the proposition. Most boys paid their sixpence with varying degrees of willingness, except one, Micky Cohen, who said that it represented too big a gamble. His old man was a bookmaker. He would only bet on certainties.

There was a fad then for any dispute to be settled by tossing a penny. Heads you won, tails you lost. Micky Cohen was usually on hand with a penny. He would never give anyone the chance of best of three: it was heads or tails, win or lose with one spin of his coin.

One evening, when the Australian was walking home, he saw a light in the school's metalwork room and went in to see who was working late. Micky Cohen, wearing protective goggles, was using a grinding machine. He had no time to conceal what he was doing, grinding down one side on each of two pennies. He now glued the sides together. The Australian turned over the new coin in his hand. It weighed as much as a single penny. The main difference was it had a head on each side.

'A doubled-headed penny,' said the Australian. 'You said you only betted on certainties.'

'Well, this does cut the risk,' Cohen admitted. 'Some jerk stole my other double-headed coin.'

'You can't trust anyone,' said the Australian gravely.

The Australian could admire Cohen for totally destroying the risk of a tossed coin landing tails up. He did not admire the others in his form. Only one could win the watch – so twenty-seven would lose sixpence, a week's pocket money. For what? The *chance* of a win. Like Cohen, he did not want the chance; he wanted certainty. The draw raised fourteen shillings and sixpence. He then offered five shillings for the dynamo set and his offer was accepted. It was all so simple. Afterwards, some of the more affluent boys came up to the Australian and said they wished they had another chance; they wished they had bought *two* tickets.

'That would have doubled your chance of winning,' he replied.

'Of course,' they said. 'That's why we wish we'd bought them.'

He bought another watch from a junk stall at the market on Saturday and auctioned that the next week. This time, he made twelve shillings profit.

While other boys were content to earn sixpence a week by running errands, popping round to the bakers, or carrying bets to one of the illegal bookmakers' runners in the street, he had made the equivalent of months of spare-time errands in a matter of hours. Others in his class, in his school, might be good at games or woodwork or maths; he knew he could beat them all at a subject not taught in any classroom: how to make money.

The Australian left school at sixteen with most of his contemporaries. Cohen went to help his father, to learn the business. The Australian was not sure what he wanted to do. Making money excited him. Some of his friends found excitement other ways; in furtive stories of feeling up girls' skirts or inside their blouses behind the pavilion in the public park on summer nights, or lying with them in the long grass by the side of the canal, kissing, but this did not attract the Australian. Others boasted of the size and frequency of their erections, or the fact that they had bored a hole in the women's changing room at the public swimming baths. Such matters did not concern him at all, but he remembered these claims. One day he would capitalise on this strange need for such activities – and how even those who clearly did not take part, loved to hear about them. There must be money here, he knew, in letting people see – for a price – something they were not expected to see.

He also accepted that something was missing in his make-up, but he was content as he was. He did not spend the money he made by running little auctions. Soon he had over a hundred pounds in a Post Office savings account. His mother had no idea he had anything. He had to forge her name as his parent or guardian. He did this quite easily.

He spent Saturday mornings in the public library reading room, looking through the week's newspapers; not for news but for movements in company shares – the little pluses and minuses. He also read the lists of people who had died, giving brief details of their wills.

Those who left the most money seemed to be Lloyds brokers, whoever they were, and solicitors. One in Cheltenham had left nearly a million pounds, another in Warrington, £200,000. He looked more closely at the name. Why, it was old Pendlehulme. His grandson was at school – a thin, spotty boy. Next day he read of two more solicitors who had left large sums, and wondered how anyone became a solicitor. He saw Pendlehulme in Woolworths one morning and asked him.

Pendlehulme was on his way to his father's office; the Australian went with him. Pendlehulme's father, a short fat man with a shiny serge suit and a frayed collar, and hot angry eyes – he had lost the only pair of spectacles that suited his near sight and was too mean to buy another – agreed to hire the Australian as an office boy for two pounds a week.

'You could go on to become a clerk,' he told him. 'Then you might even pass your exams and become a solicitor.'

'How long would that take?' asked the Australian, dividing in his mind already – how long he had still to live into how much he would need to make to become a millionaire, his aim.

'Eh, I don't know. It all depends. Be several years, though.'

'And then?'

'Well, then you'd be qualified, like I said. You could set up on your own, or work for me, eh? Become a man of consequence, even a man of property?'

At about the time the Australian started work, his mother began to say she must go back to Australia. She showed no real wish to go; it was as though she was waiting for something – or could it be someone? – to persuade her either to go or to stay.

The Australian did not like Pendlehulme's. He did not care for the dirty office with its rolltop desks, and electric lights in old-fashioned white china shades, that shone into his eyes. But he kept his head down, as his Uncle Rob said they used to do in the army during the war, and he listened and hoped he was learning. One day, he knew he was learning.

That morning, he had to accompany Mr Pendlehulme on a visit to a large building on the edge of town. It stood in about five acres, once a formal garden but now running to seed.

'This is the recreational club,' Mr Pendlehulme explained. 'We have looked after it from the start.'

'How do you mean, looked after it?'

'Our firm was instrumental in founding it. There were a hundred founder members. Each took one share, and those shares still control it. Remarkable thing, tradition, my boy. Remarkable. You don't get so much of that these days, more's the pity.'

Everything was solid inside the club: fine panelling, oak staircase, heavy doors. He went into a bathroom: the nickel-plated taps could have come from a steam engine. He had never been in a house of this size, and although he had grown used to space in Australia, he had forgotten how important it was.

An idea formed in his mind. When he went back to the office with Mr Pendlehulme, he kept very quiet, because instinctively he knew that when you had a good idea you had to keep it to yourself.

He deliberately stayed late copying a will, and as soon as he was alone in the office he went into Mr Pendlehulme's room. He knew where he kept the key to the filing cabinet, quickly found the file for the recreation club, and a reference to another earlier file in the attic. He went up into the attic, searched until he found a list of the hundred original founders members. They were nearly all local people. He copied the names and addresses on a piece of paper and took it home.

At the weekend, he called on Micky Cohen. The Australian explained that he needed to find the descendants of a number of local people. It was a matter, he said vaguely, of wills and debentures – all dull legal stuff. He would pay Micky five pounds for his help, half now, half when he found fifty, another two if he could find sixty. Within a week, Cohen came up with sixty-two.

Nearly all the original founder members had died, as was to be expected, but their sons, daughters, grandchildren were living, often still in the same house. The Australian called on the first, a woman in her fifties. She looked worried and tired; she had a huge lump growing through the hair on her head. Her skin was stretched tightly across this tumour, giving it the appearance of a white and shining egg. He could scarcely take his eyes from it. Any physical oddity that others might find repulsive – a hare-lip, a hump-back, a wall-eye – fascinated him.

He explained he was raising money for the local scouts. In case anyone checked up on him, he had found out who the scoutmaster was, so he could mention his name, but he didn't need to. He was looking for old items, photographs, anything that he could buy and sell at a profit for this good cause. She had nothing really, she told him, and prepared to close the front door.

Then he added quickly: 'Oh, Mrs Ramsey, there is one thing you *might* have. A share certificate of an original founding member of the Recreational Club.'

'Never heard of it,' she said shortly.

'It's a very old club outside the town,' he explained.

'Well?'

'Well, your grandfather had a certificate. Worth nothing in itself, but in London I hear people collect these things. I would pay a pound for it.'

'You would?'

'Not a London price, I know, but you would be helping the local scouts a lot.'

The woman considered the matter. This tall young man could be very persuasive.

'Eh,' she grunted, 'there are some things Grandpa kept in an envelope, in a suitcase under the bed. Might be there. You'll know what it looks like.'

He followed her up the stairs and into the shabby, cold room; gas fire against one wall, a chamber pot under the bed on a threadbare carpet.

Mrs Ramsey went down on her hands and knees, opened the case, shook out the contents of an envelope on the floor. The Australian sifted a faded newspaper report of a funeral, another of a wedding, a letter in an envelope with a ha'penny stamp, then, in front of him, was the certificate for a one pound share in the Recreational Club, Ashton.

'That's it,' he said.

'One pound, you said?'

'Aye.'

He gave her a pound note.

'Funny,' she said musingly. 'It must have been there nigh on fifty years. Think of that.'

'I am,' the Australian answered her.

It took him a month of evenings and weekends to collect fifty-four certificates. Some people would not sell them; they had them framed as decorations. Others had lost them. Several had never heard of them.

With fifty-four out of a hundred, a majority of four, he caught a tram to the other side of Manchester, and walked the streets until he came to a solicitor's office. This was in the front room of a terraced house with frosted glass in a bay window, and the firm's name printed in black and gold letters. The solicitor kept him waiting; the clerk thought the Australian was only an office boy from another firm, delivering or collecting documents.

'Well?' the solicitor asked petulantly, when finally he saw him. 'What do you want?'

'Your opinion, after looking at a document.'

'On what? Who are you acting for?'

'Myself.'

'It will cost you two guineas. Have you that amount?'

The Australian took out a wad of pound notes, flicked a thumbnail over them, put them back in his pocket.

'Who are you?' asked the solicitor, more polite now. 'That's a lot of money for a young fellow to have on him.'

'And he has a lot more in the bank. Now, you've asked me enough questions. I will only ask you one. Will you look at this document?'

'All right.'

The Australian had copied out the deeds of the foundation of the Recreational Club, and given it a fictitious name, in Bournemouth on the south coast.

'I have come into an inheritance,' he explained as the solicitor read the copperplate writing. 'A number of shares in this club.'

'How many?'

'Fifty-four out of a hundred. Do I own the club now?'

'Yes. You are the majority shareholder. You own the club.'

'I haven't got any deeds, though, or title to it.'

'Are you in the law?'

'I have friends who are.'

'Well, according to this deed,' said the lawyer, much more civil now that he scented money, 'all you need to do is present this document and your shares to the secretary. You can keep the club going. Close it down. Sell it. Anything. It's all yours.'

'Are you sure of that?'

'My dear young man,' the solicitor had been going to say 'boy', but stopped himself just in time. There was something about the Australian which, even at sixteen, and in his cheap ready-made suit, commanded grudging respect. 'If this is an accurate copy of the document, I can only repeat, the property is yours.'

The Australian took over the Recreational Club the following week, but in his mother's name because he was too young to sign a contract. Mr Pendlehulme was furious, but there was nothing he could do except dismiss the Australian which, naturally, he did at once. The Australian sold the clubhouse and half the grounds to a speculative builder. The other two and a half acres he kept. England was a small island. More people were arriving every day, refugees from Germany, Poland. The birthrate was bound to rise – all the newspapers said so.

They were making more people, building more houses, but no-one was making any more land. He did not guess, he knew instinctively that the price of land would double within ten years, if not before. Anyhow, he had come out of the deal with nearly £20,000 profit. From that moment, he decided never to work for anyone else, but only for himself. But now he was sacked, people felt concern about him. He was an odd fish, they said. Cold, almost heartless. Not interested in games or girls or anything, really.

They were wrong: he was interested in making money and in nothing else.

Uncle Rob could not understand why he did not take a steady job like other young men of his age. He would cut out advertisements from the local paper for 'young lads' or messengers.

'Be the making of you,' Uncle Rob assured him.

'I'll only work for someone else when they pay me what I can pay myself,' the Australian told him politely enough. You had to say that for him; he was always polite.

'But how will you *live*?' asked the old man. 'Work is a discipline. All my life, I went into the mill at seven thirty in the morning, stopped for dinner at twelve and then back until the hooter blew at six. Saturdays, half day.'

'And what did you get out of it?' the Australian asked him, not trying to score points off the old man, just wanting an answer.

'When I retired they gave me a clock,' Uncle Rob said proudly.

'So you could see what time it was and how little time you had left?' the Australian asked him.

'You're bloody rude, boy,' said Uncle Rob angrily, and then he paused. Amy's boy was quite right. He *had* spent his whole life working, earning just enough each week to pay his rent and buy food to give him strength to keep on like this, year after year.

'You see,' the Australian told him, not unkindly, 'when you work for someone else, you only earn money. When you work for yourself – and maybe have other people working for you – you *make* it. That's the difference.'

'I don't know where you learned all this. Not from Amy, I'll be bound.'

'I just knew it. I didn't learn it from anyone.'

Actually, the Australian had his own discipline for each day. He always got up early, ate breakfast, then walked through the town looking into the windows of estate agents. He had £20,000 – which no-one except his mother knew he had, and she kept quiet because it was too large a sum to mention to Uncle Rob or the neighbours. He thought vaguely of buying empty houses and renting rooms as bed-sitters, and then one morning, in the public library, looking through the paper, he read that the Labour Government had passed a law that instantly interested him. If a house had been used during the war as temporary offices, this use could continue, and any change-of-use clause in local council rules would not apply. He read this through a number of times immediately to make sure he had not misunderstood its meaning. Then he went out and made the rounds of estate agents' offices.

'I am looking for an old house that has been derequisitioned by the services or civil defence. Anything like that on your books?'

Three agents had nothing, the fourth had a run-down block of flats on the Manchester Road.

'They're pretty rough,' the agent admitted. 'I'm selling them because the owners had the Admiralty in for five years, and they've really left them in shit order. They'll pay some dilapidation, of course, but everything needs doing – redecorating, replumbing, rewiring.'

'What's the price?' asked the Australian.

'Twenty-five thou. is what the owner's asking.'

'He'll never get it,' said the Australian. 'Offer him twenty.'

'That's a big drop.'

'It's a big sum, and it's cash. And you don't seem too keen on the property yourself.'

'I'm not – as it is, I have to be honest. But it's got *potential*.'

The Australian looked over the building: it was in poorer shape than he had imagined. He cut his offer to £17,000 – and told the agent it would lapse after six o'clock that evening.

He had been impressed by an article in *The Enquirer* describing how Dr Richard Jackson, one of Trinity-Trio's founders, had bought that company's second ship very cheaply, largely by saying that his offer was only valid for the time it took to row ashore from another boat. This good sense appealed to him – and the psychology proved foolproof: by six o'clock he owned the block.

He advertised the flats at once as offices in need of repair with low rents for the next two years, and rent reviews after every three. In two weeks he had let them all.

He now owned a freehold block of property producing an income of £5,000 a year (much paid in cash) with the tenants paying rates and all other outgoings.

Describing this as an investment in an office block 'let to substantial commercial tenants', he put it back on the market, advertising a ten per cent return: he sold it for £50,000 to a trust fund seeking a safe investment. There was no tax on this profit, and after deducting lawyer's fees, the Australian put roughly £47,000 in the bank in his mother's name. As he was coming out of the bank, he met his former maths master going in.

'Not found another job yet?' the master asked him sympathetically.

'Not yet, sir.'

Odd how he still called him 'sir', although he had left school nearly a year earlier.

'Well, I hope you find something soon. You always had a good head for figures. Pity you can't get a job where that would be useful.'

The Australian nodded, not having the heart to say that he had already made more money through reading a newspaper report than his former teacher and Uncle Rob had earned all their working lives.

Calcutta

Ahmed Akbar paused uncertainly outside the new Trinity-Trio building in Calcutta; he had not expected that it would be so imposing. There had been nothing about Corporal Douglas's appearance in Burma to indicate such prosperity. Hesitantly, he went up the wide, scrubbed steps into the marbled entrance hall, cool after the sweating humidity of the street.

An Indian receptionist in a white sari looked at him enquiringly from behind a desk. Ahmed Akbar pressed his hands together in greeting, and took from his pocket the piece of paper Johnny Douglas had signed in the upper room of his bamboo house in Ngaunglebyin so many years earlier. It was smudged now, and ragged through many foldings.

'I wish to see someone in connection with the late Corporal Douglas,' he said importantly.

Travel from Burma for several years after the Second World War had been extremely difficult. When the country became independent, it was ravaged by roving gangs of thieves and dacoits. The Japanese had supplied them liberally with arms before they surrendered. Burma, which once boasted the first air-conditioned railway service in the East, from Rangoon to Mandalay, now could not guarantee a safe journey for anyone on that line. Trains were ambushed, drivers shot, goods vans pillaged.

The oil refinery at Syriam, near Rangoon, destroyed in 1942 to deny it to the Japanese, was not rebuilt. Forests that had previously provided huge quantities of teak for world markets, had now gone back to the jungle. Paddy fields, which had grown thousands of tons of rice every year for other countries in South East Asia, now produced barely enough for the needs of local villages. Burma had become a country in turmoil and retreat; clocks had been turned back a hundred years, and not wound up.

Armed gangs would rob travellers on the roads, and then fight each other for the spoils. War lords, who controlled huge areas of jungle and hills, with platoons of armed guards, had grown rich because they catered for an entirely new and voracious market, for a crop forbidden when Burma was under British rule: opium. Ahmed Akbar owned uplands where he grew acres and acres of the white poppies, and because he could afford to distribute bribes where they were needed, he had been allowed to leave the country. For such small and expensive but essential mercies he gave thanks to Allah the all-compassionate.

The receptionist read the tattered, faded message, blurred by the rain of years ago, and pointed to the far wall. On this, a bronze plaque listed the names of Trinity-Trio's staff around the world who had died during the Second World War. Ahmed Akbar read the name: J. M. Douglas.

'I was with him just before he died,' he told her. 'He was a brave young man. He could have saved himself, but he felt duty demanded that he stay with a dying comrade.'

'There is a partners' meeting upstairs,' the receptionist replied. 'His widow is there. She is a partner, of course. I am sure she would very much like to meet you. Would you please take a seat, and I will telephone her?'

In a wide room on the second floor, overlooking the race course, where stable lads were exercising a string of horses, the partners sat around the oval table, which had come from Trinity-Trio's office in Canton. Oil paintings of the three founders, Alec Douglas, Dr Jackson, Captain Ross, looked down on their successors.

It had been agreed that at each partners' meeting, a different partner or their proxy would take the chair. Today it was Bill Carlotti's turn. He represented the interests of the American concern, United Charities Incorporated, which held one-third of the voting shares.

Opposite him, sat Lady Esmerelda Jackson, present as the trustee of her son, Roderick, born while his father was interned in Hong Kong. Next to her was Reuben Ebenezer, the company secretary, with Monica Douglas whose daughter, Jennifer, had been born six months after John Douglas had been killed.

The meeting was all but over. They had been discussing the advisability – and the feasibility – of moving their headquarters from Calcutta to London or elsewhere. Now that India was independent and the sub-continent brutally divided between India and Pakistan, the trading future here seemed uncertain. Indian government policy was apparently to allow all Western partners, directors and senior staff to fulfil existing contracts, but when these ended, or when they retired, Indians must be offered their jobs.

If the company moved to London, taxation problems would be considerable, and New York seemed inappropriate for a company with many of its interests still in the East and Europe. They had agreed to defer a decision and, as Ebenezer suggested diplomatically, to 'keep the matter under review'.

A buzzer sounded by Carlotti's elbow. He pressed down the switch on the intercom.

'Reception, sir,' said the girl in the front hall. 'I have a gentleman here who says he knew the late Mr Douglas – Corporal Douglas – in the war.'

'Where did he know him?' asked Carlotti.

'In Burma, sir. Apparently he was with him just before he died.'

'What sort of man is he?'

The receptionist lowered her voice in case Ahmed Akbar could hear her.

'Very civil. Grey-haired gentleman.'

'Wait a minute.'

He put the machine on 'hold' and turned to Monica Douglas.

'You heard that?' he asked her. 'Do you want to see him?'

For a moment, Monica considered the question – and her answer. She had known her husband for so brief a time that now he was barely a memory. He was someone she had met in the rain and married and briefly loved; someone who had died within months and, incredibly, left her a fortune. Yes, she owed it to him to meet this man. She also owed it to her daughter. She could tell Jennifer so little about her father that any further facts would be welcome.

She nodded.

'Let us all see him. It may just be a try-on for some money, or something.'

'You're becoming as hard as me,' said Carlotti, smiling as usual with his mouth only. He was thinking: I am about to meet someone who was with young Douglas when he died. What would they all think here if they knew I had murdered his father? The thought was quite out of keeping with this formal, panelled room with its old-fashioned air-conditioners humming away on each window sill, and the wide view of the watered turf of the race course beyond. He pressed the button quickly and put the thought out of his mind.

'Show him up,' he told the receptionist.

Ahmed Akbar came into the room, and bowed to each of the partners in traditional greeting.

'Please take a seat,' said Carlotti.

Ahmed Akbar sat down, pushed the piece of paper across the polished table to the American who looked at it, smoothing it with his big brown hands. Then, without a word, Carlotti passed it across to Monica Douglas.

'That is my husband's writing,' she said.

She looked up at Ahmed Akbar. Here was a man who had seen Johnny long after she had said goodbye to him. He knew a part of Johnny's life of which she was ignorant; a spirit from the past had joined them at their meeting.

'When did you last see him?' she asked, surprised how husky her voice sounded. She was totally unprepared for this meeting. As she spoke, she realised how much she had loved her husband, how much she still missed him. She hoped she would not weep.

Akbar explained about the rain and the patrol and the dying man. How Douglas had waited so that his comrade would not die alone. How Douglas had given Akbar five hundred rupees. He took an envelope out of his pocket as he spoke, and placed it on the table.

Carlotti shook out the notes, thumbed through them. He saw the overstamping: they had been issued for use only during the war. It might be difficult to change them now. He pushed them back towards the old man.

'They are yours,' he said.

'I did not offer shelter for money,' replied Ahmed Akbar with dignity. 'It was my privilege to help someone whose ancestor had helped my Imam. May Allah the ever merciful lavish blessings on them both as they walk together in the eternal light.'

'After my husband gave you this money, what happened then?' Monica asked him.

'It was raining very heavily, mem, and growing dark. Your husband knew he could not stay. If he had stayed and the Japanese found him, as they almost certainly would have done, they would not only have shot him and my family and me, but probably destroyed the whole village. They had done such things before.

'He left, hoping to reach the safety of trees across the paddy fields before night fell, because then it would be too late. He could not have seen his way. A Japanese sniper had tied himself to the branch of a tree on the edge of my village. He shot Corporal Douglas in the back as he passed by. He died instantly. May his spirit enjoy the peace of every brave warrior.

'Next day, my son-in-law and I took in his body. We buried him next to the man who had died only moments before. They are together now as they were together then.'

For a moment, no-one spoke. Each was trying to visualise the scene in a country they had never visited, about which they knew nothing. Carlotti was the first to speak.

'What happened to the sniper?' he asked.

'He came down from the tree and went to Corporal Douglas's body to take the identity discs, as proof of the kill for his superior officer. My son-in-law did not greatly like the Japanese. They had killed his wife, my only daughter.

'My son-in-law took the dead soldier's rifle and clubbed the sniper with it. Life for a life. Death for a death, as it is written, so it was then, so will it always be.'

Ahmed Akbar put a hand in his pocket, took out Douglas's two fibre identity discs, laid them on the table. Monica picked them up, fascinated.

'Proof,' said the old man quietly.

He stood up, leaving the money on the table.

'Give it to the poor,' he said. 'There are many about us always.'

'Where are you going now?' Monica asked him.

'I will go back to Rangoon by ship, and then up country to my village – if the dacoits allow me.'

'What are you growing now?' Carlotti asked him. 'Rice?'

'No. Things are not as they were. My own opinion is they will never be the same. The country has no leadership, no aims. We have retreated into ourselves, like the head of a turtle. We take no part in world affairs, we take no interest in them – and little enough in our own. Our only export now is opium. I, who have grown rice for forty years, and my father before me, now plant poppies for this.'

'This company was founded on the opium trade with China in the last century,' Carlotti said thoughtfully.

'So I understand,' said Ahmed Akbar. 'But there is not a large market for that product now, although it is growing.'

'It is still used in medicines,' said Carlotti. 'We – this company – might be able to find more outlets for it. Medical ones, of course. We have a pharmaceutical division with factories in the States, Britain and West Germany. I think your kindness to a brave young man who, but for the ill fortunes of war, would be sitting here today at this table, a partner with us, deserves some reward, Mr Akbar.'

'As I have said, I did not do what little I did for money,' Ahmed Akbar replied.

'We know that,' Monica answered him gently.

'That is why,' Carlotti went on, 'I would like to suggest – subject, of course, to the approval of all the partners here – that you become Trinity-Trio's representative in Burma.'

'That is a great honour, sir,' said Ahmed Akbar. 'But there is nothing I can do for you in the way of trade in Burma. There are so many currency restrictions, export and import permits, licences, forms, dockets. Every kind of bureaucracy. So many reasons for not doing something, so few in favour. The only activity the government turns a blind eye to, and even helps in a feeble way, is this new trade in opium.'

'Exactly,' said Carlotti. 'That is what, after this meeting, I wish to discuss with you in detail.'

Manchester

The Australian was only twenty when his mother announced definitely that she was going back to Australia.

He was surprised at her decision, although hinted at for so long. He never thought she would actually go. He did not greatly care whether she stayed or went; he had never felt close to her. Indeed, he had never been close to anyone, and had no need for companions of any age or either sex.

'What will you do there?' he asked her. 'Go back to dancing or acting?'

'No. I have had a proposal of marriage,' she said, and blushed. 'Mr Crabtree's wife has died. I always liked him, you know.'

The Australian nodded. He remembered once going into Crabtree's shop in Katherine, as he often did, when he was seven or eight, because he was allowed to take sweets from a bowl on the counter. The front door had a bell that rang when anyone opened it, but he knew how to slide it sideways without operating the switch. He took a handful of Smarties and, for some reason, walked on through the back of the shop into Mr Crabtree's parlour.

The door had been pushed to, but not properly closed. Something made him pause. Perhaps the noises he heard, alien sounds which because of their strangeness could be private, or dangerous, or both: a gasp, a groan, the creaking of sofa springs. Instead of opening the door, he just peered around the corner. His mother and Mr Crabtree were lying on the sofa. He was on his back, jacket off, collar loosened. His mother was astride him, as the Australian used to sit astride her knees when they had played 'Ride a cock horse to Banbury Cross', whatever that meant, wherever Banbury Cross might be.

But now his mother's skirt was pulled high up around her waist, her flesh strangely pale in contrast to its red and green check. Mr Crabtree's trousers were down around his ankles.

The Australian thought at first this must be some sort of game, but they seemed to be so serious and Mr Crabtree's face was red as though he was thrusting up at his mother with all his energy. Then he heard his mother give a cry of pleasure or pain, he was not certain, and lean forward over Mr Crabtree's chest and Mr Crabtree gasped as though suddenly short of breath, and then they lay together, one still on the other, panting as though exhausted.

Then his mother lifted herself off Mr Crabtree, and the Australian saw what he had been thrusting with. He went back into the shop, saddened and sickened. What had they been doing? Had Mr Crabtree been hurting her? As he reached the shop, he heard his mother's voice, anxious, querulous.

'The door's been open all along. I thought you said you locked it?'

'No,' Mr Crabtree replied. 'You've got to push it to. It blows open.'

'Do you think he saw us? He's wandering around.'

'Who?'

'The boy.'

'No. The bell didn't ring. He's not in the shop.'

'Darling,' the Australian heard his mother say, her voice soft with relief, an enticing, appealing whisper. 'Let's do it again. You on me this time. But for goodness' sake, do something about that door first. It would be too awful if he saw us.'

The Australian heard Mr Crabtree pad to the door in stockinged feet, shut it noisily. Then he went out of the shop. Mr Crabtree could never understand why he stopped calling in for sweets. His friendly feelings towards the man had suddenly run out, like stuffing from a wounded doll.

Years later, when the Australian had his first breakdown, psychiatrists assured him that this could have been a major cause for his dislike of women or for sexual activity of any sort. Perhaps they were right, perhaps not: all that still lay in the future. Now, his mother was going to marry this man.

'There's quite a lot of money in the bank in your name,' he told her.

'I know,' she said. 'I want to talk to you about that.'

'It's my money,' he said defensively. 'I made it.'

'Of course, darling. But you couldn't have made anything without me signing the paper to open a bank account, and all the legal documents, now, could you, eh?'

'No,' he agreed, 'But you have had anything you wanted – clothes, the car.'

'It's only a Ford Consul,' she said, aggrieved.

'That is what you wanted, Mother.'

'That's what I *said* I wanted. We could have had a Zephyr or a Zodiac on that money, easily. Mr Crabtree has a Jag. He told me so in his last letter. A green one.'

'What do you want to talk to me about, then?'

'I want my share of the money. Half.'

The sun was shining outside, just as on the day he had seen his mother straddle Mr Crabtree on the sofa, and again, he experienced a peculiar sensation of loneliness: the sun had light but now it lacked warmth. He felt cold and angry and hurt and defensive.

'I can double that within the next year, if you leave it with me,' he told her. He felt infinitely more gloom at the thought of losing the money, any part of it, than of losing his mother.

'No,' she said. 'I have to book a passage, and buy clothes and put something towards a house. Mr Crabtree thinks we should buy one in Alice Springs. He wants to move from Katherine.'

The Australian looked at her as though seeing her for the first time. She was a stupid woman. First, she had got herself pregnant by some unknown soldier, then when she came to England, she had not landed a single job. She would be better off back in Australia with Mr Crabtree; he could look after her.

'All right,' he said, 'we'll go to the bank and see the manager now. You can have a cheque for half of whatever's in the account.'

He knew how much it was, to a penny, but saw no reason to tell her.

'You sound a bit cold,' his mother said petulantly.

'No,' he lied. 'It's a business deal. As you say, without you – or someone else over twenty-one – I couldn't have made it. I hope you and Mr Crabtree will be well-suited to each other.'

He had meant to wish them happiness together, but he sensed that happiness was something beyond their reach, just as it was totally beyond his. Happiness and love were words film stars spoke to each other and to audiences from the wide screens of Odeons and Essoldos. They were only words, whereas money was real. You could buy things with money, translate paper into motor cars, buildings, shares.

He would be better off on his own; then he would have no-one to worry about, no-one ready with stupid criticisms or sudden outbursts of caution, when what you needed was encouragement, lots of it.

'Where will you live?' his mother asked him, suddenly showing a belated concern.

'Here, with Uncle Rob for the time being. Pay my keep.'

'Why don't you get a proper job, proper digs somewhere?'

He did not even answer.

His mother had already made an appointment with the bank manager. He wondered what would have happened if he had refused to give her half of what he had made? There would be trouble, argument, a scene; she could be very determined. He took after her in that. Had his father – whoever he was – been of similar character?

They walked down together to the bank. On the way, at a crossroads, he saw 'For Sale' boards from estate agents outside a pre-war ice-skating rink that had been on the market for years. One board had become two, and now two were seven. He counted them, and as he counted, an idea grew in his mind like a flower. He began to feel happier.

The bank manager shook hands with them both perfunctorily: his mind was on that day's Rotary Club lunch. He hoped they would not make him late. Al Read, the radio comic, was guest of honour and his little daughter was pestering him for the man's autograph. They sat down on rexine chairs opposite him.

'You have in your credit, madam, the very considerable sum of £62,000 17s. 6d,' he told the Australian's mother gravely, in the tone of voice bankers used when discussing death or other people's balances. 'It is my understanding that you wish to draw out half this sum and leave the other half in the care of your son here?'

'Yes,' she said. 'I told you on the 'phone.'

'Not in my care,' said the Australian. 'No strings to my half. It is mine. I made that money.'

'Well, really,' said the bank manager sharply, looking at the mother for her opinion. 'It is in your mother's name.'

'Put my share in my name then,' the Australian told him.

'You are not of age.'

'Do you want the account here or do you not?'

'Of course. We are very pleased to act for you.'

'Then put it in my name. Now.'

'I will take a cheque for half,' said his mother quickly. The manager called in a clerk; a cheque was produced, made out, signed. He handed it to her with a flourish, as though she had won it as a prize. In a sense, she had. She stood up, putting the cheque in her handbag.

'Are you coming with me?' she asked the Australian.

'No,' he told her. 'I'm staying here for a moment.'

His mother left the room.

The manager looked at the Australian questioningly. This young fellow knew his mind all right, but he did not care for him. There was something odd about him, cold-blooded. Reptilian was the word that came first to his mind.

'The ice-rink,' the Australian said. 'Who is selling it?'

'There are a number of agents involved.'

'I know. I saw their boards. Who is the owner?'

'Actually, he banks with us,' said the manager. 'Mr Ramsbotham.'

'Why is he selling?'

'He wishes to.'

'Look,' said the Australian, 'I have asked you a question. I also bank with you. I want an answer.'

'He feels he is financially extended.'

'You mean he owes money?'

The manager nodded. He felt he was not actually disclosing a client's business if he did not speak, but this young man had such strength of will, he seemed to squeeze answers out of him like toothpaste from a tube.

'Also,' he added, 'the place costs more to run than it takes at the gate. Have you ever been inside it?'

'No.'

'It's twice the size of the local swimming baths and about as deep. A huge hole to fill with water. Massive pipes, thick as your thigh, have ammonia pumped through them constantly to freeze the water and make ice.'

'That must be expensive.'

'Very,' agreed the manager soberly. 'Twenty-four hours a day, remember. For most of each day and, of course, all night, the place is empty. Mr Ramsbotham only gets people in of an evening, and at sixpence or a shilling a time, that doesn't even pay for the electricity, let alone the rates and staff and so on. He's had the devil of a job trying to get anyone interested in it, once they have gone into the figures. That's why so many agents have it on their books.'

'You could sell it for him?' the Australian asked.

'He has his agents, as you know. But as I say, he does bank with us.'

'What is he asking?'

'Twenty thousand for the freehold.'

'He'll never get that,' said the Australian firmly. 'A buyer will lose money all the way. If he can't make it pay, how can they?'

'That's what I tell Mr Ramsbotham. He would, I feel, be open to offers.'

'Offer him £15,000.'

'On whose behalf?'

'Mine. Cash. I have twice that in the account. You have just told me.'

'It is not a purchase I would recommend,' said the manager, shaking his head.

'I'm not asking you to recommend it. Just to buy it. The understanding being that Mr Ramsbotham pays all legal fees, and the deal is concluded one week from today.'

'That would be very difficult.'

'Life is difficult,' said the Australian bluntly. 'That is my offer. If you do not wish to pass it on, please say so now. The bank across the road will take a different view.'

So the Australian became owner of the ice-rink on the following Saturday, and visited it for the first time that evening.

A mass of rusting and ancient machinery littered waste ground behind the building. The changing rooms were bleak, with graffiti scribbled inside their doors. Most of the locks and electric light bulbs, even their holders, had been stolen. The place was simply a giant, very cold and unattractive hangar built above a huge hole. Into this, people had thrown empty cigarette packets, sweet papers, and other rubbish. The sight of this litter gave the Australian an idea.

He put an advertisement in the local paper the following week announcing that rubbish could be dumped in the ice-rink at £1 a load. Within two weeks it was completely filled, and he had £700 in his back pocket. He took the money in notes, no cheques or postal orders. That way there was no record and no tax.

He engaged a contractor to pour liquid concrete over the rubble to give the building a flat floor. Then he advertised for painters, plasterers, carpenters, electricians, willing to work at nights and weekends. An art student from the local polytechnic painted huge flowers and birds on the walls. The result was cheerful, if bizarre. The Australian then offered spaces in a covered market to local traders with stalls.

The chairman of the planning committee contacted him. This would be a change of use, he pointed out; it would be difficult to get this through his committee. At the Australian's suggestion, they met in the car park of a public house. He did not wish to be overheard.

'How much to make it easy?' he asked bluntly. 'Let's get down to basics.'

'A contribution to the welfare fund would help,' the chairman replied at once. 'Say two fifty pounds?'

'Notes?'

The chairman nodded, and put the notes into his wallet. No further criticism of the change of use was mentioned. Within a month, what the Australian called The Rink Market was thriving. He offered cheaper rents for cash; he never saw any need to pay income tax unnecessarily. After all, stall-holders dealt in cash for this same reason. Why should he be different?

A newspaper reporter from the local paper wrote a glowing account of the transformation. The fact that the Australian gave him a ten-pound note in a plain envelope showed him where his emphasis must lie.

'How did you succeed when others failed?' the reporter asked him.

The Australian smiled and shrugged his shoulders.

'Luck,' he said.

He knew instinctively even then that it was much easier – and infinitely wiser – to attribute personal success to providence, chance, luck, instead of to vision or ability or hard work. People believed in luck. They could accept that you could be luckier than they were, but never that you might be cleverer – especially if results proved you were.

He had made the ice-rink pay because while other potential bidders thought that what had been an ice-rink must remain an ice-rink, he realised that nothing and no-one ever stayed the same for long. They suffered from tunnel vision: what had been, must be. He knew differently, he knew better.

He thought about the next and, it seemed to him, most logical step ahead. The Rink Market brought together a collection of stall-holders – fishmonger, butcher, greengrocer – under cover. People could now shop out of the rain in the worst of weather. Would it not be even more lucrative to have entire shops, not just stalls, with their wares attractively laid out, so that housewives could buy everything they needed in one huge market place beneath a single roof? This could be pleasantly decorated and warm and they would have no necessity to queue for vegetables in one shop, and then to walk across town to buy a pound of cod or coley. Everything would be here in one huge market. It would be a complete market, a superior market, a *super* market. He liked the sound of that. If he did, he knew others would, too.

Next morning, he rang up Mr Pendlehulme and told him to form a new company for him and register its name: Rink Supermarkets.

On the Australian's twenty-third birthday he received a single birthday card from Micky Cohen, with whom he had been to school. The Australian had almost forgotten about him, but now he was touched that Cohen remembered.

The Australian had no particularly warm feelings about Cohen, but then he had no particularly warm feelings about anyone. He was, however, always almost absurdly pleased at any unexpected kindness shown to him, especially if it did not call for any reciprocation.

For example, Uncle Rob, who had died suddenly that year, left him £50 in his will. This was a total surprise. The money was nothing – only loose change, petty cash – but the fact that the old man had remembered him momentarily made the Australian want to weep.

He did not weep, of course; men did not weep, and indeed he could not recall ever shedding a tear for anyone or anything. But within his icy heart a tiny warmth glowed briefly, sparked by the gift and a puny prompting of regret. He wished he had been nicer to the old man – kinder, more friendly. But the thought passed as quickly as it arrived. The pleasure at Micky Cohen's card remained. He telephoned Cohen to thank him.

'Come and see me,' he added.

Cohen did so at once; he recognised the knock of opportunity. If he let this invitation pass, he might never have another from the Australian, and he had heard how prosperous he had become.

They sat in the front room of the house where the Australian had lived with his mother since they arrived in England; he had bought it from the executors of Uncle Rob's will. Now he had living quarters upstairs and his office on the ground floor.

'What are they paying you as a bookie?' the Australian asked Micky Cohen after the initial greetings were over.

'Too little. Forty pounds a week,' Cohen told him, doubling what he actually received.

'You own a share of the business, though?'

'Yes. My father and I are partners. But he would really like to run it on his own – as he did till I joined him.'

'Then let him. I'll give you fifty a week to join me.'

'Doing what?'

'Helping me in all sorts of ways. Generally keeping an eye on things. Sending rude letters to any punters who may want to make trouble. Whatever comes up. Interested?'

'Yes. But what about a share in the profits?'

'What about it?' queried the Australian, his voice suddenly quiet, with an adamantine edge.

'Just a joke,' said Cohen quickly. 'No offence meant.'

'And none taken,' replied the Australian smoothly. 'I think about sharing profits the same way I think about getting closely involved with anyone else over anything. I've been reading Kipling. "Down to Gehenna or up to the throne, He travels the fastest who travels alone." I'm travelling alone.'

'Where's Gehenna?' asked Cohen to try and warm the atmosphere which had suddenly chilled in a disconcerting way.

'Hell,' replied the Australian. 'I looked it up in the library. You should have known that, Micky.'

So Micky Cohen joined him, setting up his office in the back parlour. He bought a typewriter and hired a girl even younger than either of them to type and do the filing. She was recommended by the teacher in charge of the secretarial department of the local technical college.

'What's the next deal, then?' Cohen asked the Australian briskly. He thought that if he showed keenness, the Australian might change his attitude towards giving him a share of the profits.

'I've been thinking,' said the Australian slowly. He liked the phrase; he had read it somewhere. He was an avid reader of books borrowed from the local public library; that way, he could read them without buying them, and he was never a generous spender. He thought these words added dignity to whatever proposal he was about to make. Later, television interviewers and journalists would make great play of this; it became a catchphrase.

Cohen waited.

'Motor cars,' said the Australian. 'I've been looking into profits in the second-hand market. Astonishing. Sometimes a hundred per cent. Mostly in notes, of course. No tax. Or very little. Declare a bit, just to keep the tax man off your back.'

'It isn't all jam,' Cohen told him. 'They have a lot of hassle from buyers who think they've been done.'

'There is trouble everywhere,' the Australian assured him, philosophically. 'And they *still* make a fortune. I am going to make more – and with no aggravation at all. I am going to rent a bomb site with an option to buy for an agreed price within a year. The owner will see this as a wonderful chance to be rid of an eyesore, so the price will be nothing. I see it as a site for a car auction every Saturday. We advertise in local papers – and each week award a cash prize for the car entered in the best condition, whether it's sold or not.

'That'll make the punters clean their cars before they try to sell them. Saves us doing it ourselves. For a ten quid prize, we will have one hundred clean cars entered – and bigger commissions on the higher prices paid.

'We charge two quid entrance fee for each car and take five per cent of the sale, buyers to have the chance of seeing the cars run before they bid. No hard sell. No guarantees at all – except we guarantee the used cars we auction *are* used!'

At the first auction they sold seventy-three cars for a total of £18,250; their five per cent commission was £912.10.0. for an afternoon's work. Soon, the Australian was making a clear £1,000 a week profit, and sometimes a great deal more.

He kept the auctions going every Saturday afternoon for a year, then he bought the bomb site and applied for planning permission to put up a six-storey building.

The local planning committee expressed doubts about giving

permission for such a change of use. These doubts were happily resolved when the Australian reminded the chairman, who had the casting vote, how he had earlier given him a donation to charity. Now he gave him a Wolseley car which had not reached its reserve at the previous week's auction.

'I don't like the sound of renting flats to private tenants,' said Micky Cohen. 'With all the laws passed by the last Socialist government, you can't ever get the buggers out. And I mean that. Even if they leave because they want to go or because they die, their leases can still be taken over by a relation, and so you're back to square one. They're there forever.'

'I *want* them there forever. We're not going to rent the flats to them – we're going to sell them.'

'But how can you do that? No building society ever lends money for anyone to buy a flat. It has to be a house.'

'These buyers will not have to ask a building society. We're going to lend them money ourselves – from the auction profits. After all, it will be largely only a paper transaction. Then we'll have a steady income from these people for the next twenty-five years. We'll try and slip a clause into each agreement, giving us the right to buy back each flat at what they paid for it, at any time up to the twentieth year, say. The buyers will see this as a kind of safety net, because they'll never imagine the flats could ever be worth more than when they're new. They can't lose. They'll sign. I'll have old Pendlehulme do the legal stuff for them and us. That way they are less likely to quibble than if they hire their own solicitors. He hates me but he likes my money.'

'Can you afford to do this?' Cohen asked him.

'I can't afford not to! In twenty years, those flats will be worth ten times what they paid for them, maybe twenty times what they cost us to build. It's a double-headed penny. Remember that, at school?'

'I remember,' said Cohen thoughtfully. The Australian never forgot a trick.

'Anything else for me?' the Australian asked him.

'Oh, there's one letter for you,' Micky added. 'Marked personal. From Australia.'

The Australian opened the envelope slowly, wondering whether it was worth keeping the stamp; there might be a market for it somewhere. The letter was from his mother. As he read, it was as though she was there in the room with him, prattling on.

Well, I wanted to tell you that you have a half-brother. Isn't that wonderful news? Ian Bruce – for that's what we are calling him – was born six months ago. A fine, sturdy fellow with a good pair of lungs. The doctor says he's got a very large head for a child. I told him, must be all the brains in it!!! We are delighted and hope you will be, too.

I meant to write before, but you know how it is. So much to do here in the sun. Thought you would be glad to hear this.

Love, Mother.

The Australian read this little note several times and put it away in the locked drawer he kept for personal papers. He felt curiously sad, as though he had suddenly been bereaved in some remote and inexplicable way. He had never been close to his mother, never admired her, nor even particularly liked her, but he had been her only son.

Now there was another son, his half-brother, a boy growing up in a wide, uncomplicated country under the sun, as he would have liked to grow up, with a father as well as a mother. He envied this boy his future, which would not be here amid rows of grey slate roofs shiny with rain, and smoking chimneys and sooty laurel hedges behind rusting iron railings. It was as though he was hearing about someone who would live a life he would have given all he possessed to have known: he was hearing about himself as he would have wished to be.

He opened another drawer, took out an Alka-Seltzer, went into the bathroom, poured a glass of water and drank the fizzy mixture. He suffered from sudden bouts of indigestion, often after good news when he had done a deal – and sometimes when one had gone wrong, although not many did. He had a pain in his guts now, a feeling of foreboding.

For some reason, he sensed that this letter brought him bad news, very bad news indeed.

London

Lord Jackson's Rolls was approaching the last exit for London on the M1 when his car telephone buzzed.

He had been in Hertfordshire inspecting a site for a hypermarket, about which the property wing of Trinity-Trio thought highly. But, although he had been assured that the deal was all but signed, and therefore he felt he should show an interest in something he did not really understand, the agents for the owner had now informed him – actually on the site – that Rink Supermarkets had offered half a million on top of his bid, an offer instantly accepted. Jackson's early morning journey had been pointless.

He had immediately telephoned his extreme displeasure to his office and so was expecting some suitably chastened subordinate to be ringing back with explanations and excuses. He was wrong. His personal secretary said, in the expressionless voice she adopted when she had to pass on controversial news: 'Lady Jackson has been trying to reach you for the past half hour. I have told her you are travelling and speaking on the car 'phone.'

For a moment, Jackson considered letting this explanation stand while indecision and irritation ate like etching acid into his mind. What the hell could Corinne want, ringing him up? He could not remember when she had last telephoned him in office hours. She had a social secretary who might occasionally ring if there was some change in plans for an important dinner engagement, or a visit to the opera but, on checking his pocket diary, he found that evening to be clear.

'How does she sound?' he enquired carefully.

'Distraught, I would say.'

Jackson grimaced in resignation.

'All right,' he said. 'Put her on.'

He glanced at the clock set in its walnut frame beneath the glass division. Exactly nine fifty-two; early for Corinne to be calling anyone. She was rarely awake, certainly never dressed, when he left home each morning. They slept apart and, except for unavoidable social or official functions, they lived entirely separate lives.

Corinne's day usually began well after ten with breakfast in bed. Then followed a discussion with her social secretary about which invitations to accept, which to reject, with possibly a visit from the cook to decide a menu if she were holding a dinner party. After a long lazy bath, and a cursory look at her correspondence, a chauffeur would drive her to the Connaught for cocktails with one or more of her women friends. A light lunch somewhere – she was terrified of putting on weight – then an afternoon sleep wearing a face mask, to prepare herself for whatever the evening might offer. So the hours passed, filled with the expensive emptiness of a rich and discontented wife, always preparing for pleasures she seldom appeared to enjoy. Now Corinne's familiar, resentful voice, sharp as broken glass, shrilled at Jackson from the earpiece.

'I've been trying to get you for *ages*,' she said accusingly. 'You've been engaged all morning.'

'Not really,' he assured her mildly. 'I've been out looking at a site. Anyhow, you've got me now. What do you want?'

'Nothing for me. It's about Elaine.'

'What about her?'

Jackson's voice was guarded. Elaine was their only daughter, now twenty-two and living with a part-time guitar player in a flat Jackson had bought for her off the King's Road.

'She's been picked up by the police. Lying in the gutter.'

'What d'you mean? Was she run over?'

'No, you fool. She'd blown her mind, as they say. She's a druggie. Didn't you know?'

'I had no idea,' he said, shocked. 'Had you?'

'Hardly ever saw her, but I suppose the signs were there if I'd been looking for them.'

'Where is she now?'

'The police took her to the nearest hospital's casualty department. Luckily, they didn't know who she was, or by now we'd have had the papers on to it. She had my 'phone number engraved on a bracelet, so someone rang me.

'I've had her moved, of course. She is in a private clinic in Surrey that handles these cases – discreetly. Can't have this in the newspapers. But it has taken me *hours* fixing it all up. And I was so looking forward to lunch with Rosie Traherne out at Windlesham. That's all been ruined, of course.'

'I'm sorry,' replied Jackson mechanically, meaning he was sorry not only for her disappointment, nor even for Elaine's condition, but for being married to someone with whom he had nothing in common, and having a daughter they hardly ever saw. Why Elaine and he seemed so dissimilar, why he actually felt awkward in her presence, he had never discovered – and he had deliberately not delved very deeply for possible reasons in case they proved too painful. As a child, she had been pleasing enough, but even then their relationship was remote, sometimes almost wary.

Could this be because, as she grew older, he sensed she might be far shrewder than he would ever be, with a business potential of which Dr Jackson would have approved? Or could it simply be that Elaine appeared to side with her mother in any argument or decision? Often, afterwards, Jackson had to acknowledge to himself that they were right and he was wrong, but he could never admit this to them; that would have been a climbdown, and so in his mind almost a public humiliation. His whole waking life was clouded by the need to avoid such confrontations with employees better qualified or just cleverer than he was. He could not afford them at home.

Jackson knew that his main asset was simply being born rich. Without that fortunate accident, he might now be sitting behind the wheel of this car, on the wrong side of the partition – and the chauffeur in his place. Come to that, the fellow might not make a bad job of things; he and his wife had brought up two sons who had won places at university. One was now in Canada, the other something in computers and both were doing well, while Elaine, on whose education, expensive holidays and passing enthusiasms he had lavished uncounted thousands, was in a home for drug addicts.

He sighed at the perverseness of life.

'Give me the address,' he said, putting such unhappy comparisons behind him. 'I will drive there right away.'

The nursing home was an Edwardian house with Gothic pretensions: turrets, attic windows, sharply pointed gables. Half a dozen cars were parked in a drive green with moss behind a high, untrimmed laurel hedge. As the chauffeur reversed the Rolls, Jackson pressed the doorbell, and noticed that the porch gutter was blocked, the brass letter box unpolished. A middle-aged woman wearing a nurse's uniform, but with wrinkled tights and scuffed shoes, opened the door and looked at him enquiringly.

'I have come to see my daughter, Elaine Jackson.'

'We have no patient of that name here.'

'She might have been admitted under another name. I understand she was taken to a London hospital by the police last night. My wife had her transferred here this morning.'

'Elaine Jones then,' said the woman. 'That's the name we were given. Surprising how many of our patients are called Jones or Smith. How do I know you *are* her father?'

'You don't, but I am. Elaine has dark hair, blue eyes, a brown mole on the back of her left hand. She is twenty-two years old.'

The woman nodded. He followed her through the hall. A young man in a white coat came out of a side door.

'This is Dr Graham,' the nurse told Jackson. 'Our resident physician.' Jackson introduced himself.

'Roderick Jackson. I've come to see my daughter Elaine.'

'Have you seen her recently?' the doctor asked him.

'A few months ago. Why?'

'You may find her changed.'

'How do you mean, changed?'

'She is very strongly addicted.'

'To what?'

'Heroin. By a familiar route, Mr Jackson, one that starts with what seems to be the harmless fun of smoking a joint, and ends. . . .'

He shrugged his shoulders dismissively.

'Can you cure her?'

'I will try. But you have to remember that often drugs are an escape route from unhappiness or unfulfilment, to what seems – for a time – a sort of happy valley. Not all wish to come back to reality.'

'Does she?'

'I don't know – yet. It can be a very painful and prolonged process. But please do see her. I'll be here for another ten minutes if you want to talk things over later.'

Elaine Jackson was in a small room, narrow as a telephone kiosk on its side, partitioned with plywood walls from a much larger room with a very high ceiling. It contained a single bed, a chair, a rough white-painted cupboard with a Mickey Mouse stencil on the door; a job lot bought cheaply from a children's home. She looked up at her father with a dull, uninterested gaze. Her face was as empty of expression as a carnival mask.

'I heard you were ill,' Jackson said hesitantly, not knowing how to start the conversation. It was a long time since they had discussed anything more demanding than the merits of a dress, a book, a play.

'Self-inflicted wounds,' Elaine replied shortly. Her skin was pale and greasy. One eye seemed totally out of focus; the other had a gimlet stare, its pupil small as the point of a sharpened pencil. Her arms outside the coverlet were punctured with tiny marks like insect bites, ringed with bluish bruises. Her skin was blotched, her mouth slack, the lips loose and puffy. Jackson sat down carefully in the chair, hoping that the feeling of shock at his daughter's condition did not show in his face.

'I'm sorry,' he said.

'What about?'

'Everything. Especially that I had no idea you were on drugs or in trouble.'

'Why should you have? We almost never see each other.'

'We did. Last March, I think it was. In Oxford Street. You were with that guitarist fellow. I never took to him.'

'Rodrigues,' she said. 'He's gone.'

'Why didn't you tell me?'

'About Roddy?'

'No. The drugs.'

'Why should I? You couldn't have done anything to help.'

'Your mother and I could have tried. After all, she got you in here.'

Elaine shrugged. Silence hung between them like a soiled shroud.

'So what are you doing?' Jackson asked, just to say something, not to sit there.

'Spending money. I have an allowance of twenty grand after tax, remember. No reason for me to work for ten, is there?'

'It might be better if there was.'

'Lots of things might be better if, if, if. For you and Mummy as well as me,' she replied without rancour, merely stating a fact.

'True. So perhaps we could all make them better if you came back and lived at home? We could see more of each other then, like a proper family.'

'What *is* a proper family?' she asked him. 'Certainly not ours, never ours. Mummy spends the best of each day in bed, or tarting herself up trying to look twenty years younger. You pretend you're running a company which would run just as well if you dropped dead here. Probably a bloody sight better.'

'You've had everything you ever wanted,' Jackson said stubbornly, trying to steer the conversation away from such controversial and sterile matters.

'Maybe that's the trouble.'

'You can't say you didn't *want* the things you had.'

'I'm not saying that. I have never said that. But every time I didn't get on at one school, you sent me to another. You meant well – but that was also the easiest thing to do from your point of view.'

'Well, what *did* you want?'

'How the hell do I know what I wanted? I had everything I *thought* I wanted, and now I've got this.'

'I could get you out of here into a proper place.'

'This *is* a proper place.'

'Looks a bit seedy to me.'

'Perhaps the patients are seedy, too. We're not here by royal invitation, you know. We don't have to be proposed and seconded for membership. We're picked up off the floor in public lavatories, or stoned out of our minds in telephone boxes. Or like me, literally in the gutter.

'Look at my left eye. I'm blind in it. Much of the smack we buy on the street or even from our own dealers is mixed with flour or chalk or talcum powder to make it go further. My regular supplier wasn't around and some goon sold me a packet mixed with yeast. The bastard! I went totally blind within an hour, though the sight has come back in my right eye. The quack here thinks that is a bit dicey, too, so the future is not much brighter than the present – or my past.

'They have all been very nice to me at this place, I must say. They're kind. They may not be smart, but they care. That's what's important to me. You and Mummy didn't care.'

'We tried,' said Jackson unconvincingly. 'Do they know who you are?'

'Mummy said I was Miss Jones. I'll stay with that. Why did you come here, anyhow?'

'Because you're in trouble. You *are* my daughter.'

Jackson paused. He had meant to say, 'Because I love you,' but he could not. Elaine would no more have chosen him as her father than he would have selected her as his daughter. But why did he think this? Did every father feel the same about his children – or was he simply incapable of responding with warmth and love to someone who desperately needed both, who was starved of true affection? Like an accountant who knew the price of everything but the value of nothing, Jackson had always bought off Elaine, as he had bought off his wife, with expensive, often unwanted presents. But all the time he should have given them more than money; he should have given himself, and this he found beyond him.

Jackson stood up. The tiny cell-like cubicle seemed suddenly too small for both of them. He wanted to get away. That was always his reaction to any problem he could not solve quickly: leave it, buy himself freedom, let the professionals cope; he would pay anything not to be involved.

'Have you any money?' he asked Elaine. 'I mean, for day to day things. Fresh fruit, newspapers.'

'Not a cent. I'm broke. Skag has been setting me back at least five hundred quid a week – every week. I've had to sell almost everything in the flat just to keep going.'

'I see. If there's anything extra you want here, any special treatment, anything at all, tell me. I'll pay. You do understand?'

'I understand.'

Jackson wished that he understood. How *could* this happen to his daughter? And why, when he had always given her the best of everything?

Dr Graham was waiting for him in the hall.

'Well?' he asked.

'She looks very thin and ill,' said Jackson. 'And she says she has lost the sight of one eye.'

'With the amount she's been taking by mouth, needle, and chasing the dragon – burning heroin powder and sniffing the smoke – that's not surprising. It's a miracle she's alive. She has a tough constitution. There is another problem regarding the injections that worries me. The risk of AIDS. They all use old needles, share them, pass them around, never thinking of the danger.'

'Have you tested her for that?'

'Yes. I'm waiting for the results.'

Jackson scribbled a telephone number on a piece of paper.

'My private line at the office,' he explained. 'Ring me as soon as you know.'

'Of course. But about the drug problem, which is why Elaine is here. Do you know much about heroin, Mr Jackson?'

'Almost nothing.'

'Then let me fill you in briefly. Heroin comes from morphine, which is derived from opium. When the East India Company got the monopoly of trade with India in the eighteenth century, the moguls' monopoly of the opium trade came with it. They built up a huge illegal market in China. The Chinese Emperor resisted desperately, just as governments are doing now in the West, but without any success. The bribes and the profits have always been too big.'

'I do know something about the early background,' Jackson admitted carefully.

'I fear you may learn a great deal more about its effects, before Elaine is cured. A British scientist, Alder-Wright, first combined morphine with acetic anhydride in the last century. This produced a product we use in medicine – but sparingly. Diamorphine. A German chemist, Heinrich Dreser, marketed this new substance, giving it a new name – heroin, from the German word *heroisch*, which means something heroic, or having a powerful effect.

'At first, this appeared to be a panacea for coughs and pneumonia, the wonder drug of the day. No-one realised quite how addictive it was or what addicts would do just to get a fix to last a few hours. Or how terrible are the agonies they endure when they try to kick the habit.'

They came through the hall, into the porch. Jackson's chauffeur had brought the Rolls to the front door.

'Yours?' asked Dr Graham, impressed.

'A company car they let me have to come down here,' Jackson explained evasively. He did not want to admit that he had any part in Trinity-Trio, or give any clue as to his identity.

'You have been working here long?' he asked, to change the subject.

'Long enough to know that the problem is timeless and universal and getting worse all the time. How can it be otherwise, when at Heathrow at mealbreaks one Customs man may have to check one thousand arrivals? And at Dover, only about one in every hundred passengers from the Continent is checked – and one in five hundred at peak times? Coach traffic there is up nearly ninety per cent in the last three years – but only four extra officers have been taken on. And all round the coasts private yachts and motor boats come and go without any proper check.

'Do you know that at night three Customs men have to cover the entire east coast of Scotland? Two more have to watch the coast from Fleetwood to Caernarvon – with only one car between them. What can so few do against a determined army of drug-runners? Almost nothing. I've had about enough. I'm thinking of leaving. I have been offered a hospital job in Hong Kong.'

'One of my forebears was out there,' said Jackson. 'He was also a doctor, an idealist in his way. Then he went into trade.'

'Not the opium trade, I trust?' asked Dr Graham, meaning it as a joke.

Jackson smiled, but did not reply: the remark was not funny to him. He climbed into the car, and was instantly and thankfully cocooned by the softness of rich Connolly leather and burr walnut, by thick tinted windows, security locks and air conditioning, from the harshness of a world where a rich man's daughter lay half-blind in a narrow bed, and dust and verdegris coated unpolished brass. He lit a cigar, forcing such unpleasant realities from his mind. Then, on impulse, he pressed the intercom button.

'Gravesend,' he told the driver. 'I'll tell you where to stop.'

'Very good, My Lord.'

The huge car sighed through shabby suburbs of south Surrey and northern Kent, until they reached Gravesend, where the Thames flowed grey as pewter under a lowering, leaden sky. A tug towed three barges of litter down river, pursued by a flock of greedy gulls. Jackson had never visited the town and vaguely imagined that it might still be recognisable from the eighteenth-century print, 'A View of Gravesend, Kent', that hung in Trinity-Trio's board room. He thought he might even discover the shop once owned by Mr Stapleford, the apothecary, or the cottage where Dr Jackson had treated old Mrs Gray, but this was fanciful. Like many towns and cities in southern England, Gravesend was drained of its original character by high-rise buildings, betting shops, Pakistani take-aways. On Thursday Hill, where Dr Jackson had once ridden in haste to treat Miss Piggott, a journey that had led to wealth immeasurable, a hoarding now offered Georgian-style executive-type town houses.

Every vestige of a past about which Jackson had heard so often, had disappeared, been obliterated, overtaken. He felt overwhelmed by this realisation, and lonely, as though time had also changed him beyond recognition. Somehow, absurdly, he had expected to find some sign or message from the past to help him shape the future with his daughter, his wife, himself. But there was nothing, and of course there could never be anything.

Old Dr Jackson had solved his problems himself, and he must do the same. Perhaps that *was* the message? Or could it lie in the ultimate irony, that from forcing the East to accept a forbidden and deadly drug because the profits were so huge, the East was now forcing the same drug and even more dangerous derivatives on the West – and for exactly the same reason? Sellers had become buyers and buyers were now selling.

He climbed gratefully into the safe, familiar shelter of his car for the drive back to his office, but this time unease travelled with him.

The foreign editor of *The Enquirer* came into the editor's office.

'About those applications we've had for the post of roving foreign correspondent,' he began.

'What about them?' asked the editor curtly. His stomach ulcer had resented a lunch of three whiskies and a Porterhouse steak with a bottle of Beaune. He sucked an indigestion tablet.

'Most of them are no good, but there is one who's a possible. A woman, Anna Lu-Kuan. From Hong Kong. Here's her CV.'

The foreign editor handed a single typed sheet across the desk. The editor skimmed through it, noting the main details. Age, 26. Educated, Benenden; Girton, Cambridge; first class honours in History.

'Actually, she's Chinese,' explained the foreign editor. 'Been on the *South China Morning Post* in Hong Kong, and *The Straits Times* in Singapore, and then several women's magazines here. Her father is stuck in Red China, poor sod. She sends him money.'

'What's she look like?'

'Dishy. I'd say a great lay and nice to boot, to coin a phrase. Easy to get on with. She has also written a thesis on Trinity-Trio's history for a Ph.D. I glanced through it. Extremely readable, I thought.'

'Friendly?'

'Very. Apparently the Chinese rather admired the founders. She said that pre-war employees in Hong Kong regularly risked their lives to bring extra food to the internees in Stanley Gaol during the war. Especially to Jackson, the one who wouldn't use his title, who died in Hong Kong.'

'The present noble lord would approve, I'm sure,' said the editor. 'Let's have a look at her, and the history. When can she come in?'

'Now. She's in my office.'

The editor interviewed Anna Lu-Kuan briefly, to make sure she was articulate, that she could express opinions quickly and clearly. Too many reporters on his staff absorbed information like sponges but could not add any interpretation of their own. He hired her on a month's trial.

Two days later, Lord Jackson invited him to dinner to discuss the feasibility of having a midweek colour supplement as well as one on Sundays. The advertising potential seemed promising.

They ate in His Lordship's house in Belgravia. The editor thought enviously that Jackson had no need to paper the walls of his dining room, he had so many paintings. He had counted a Corot, two Monets and a Kokoschka, and was trying to work out their total value, when his attention was distracted by Lady Jackson. She was the daughter of the professor in charge of the Dr Richard Jackson Medical Foundation, and had been very good-looking twenty-five years ago, the debutante of her year. Since then she had become obsessed with the fear that her beauty was fading. Her hobby, to the considerable enrichment of beauticians, plastic surgeons, dieticians and others of that ilk, was to attempt not only to arrest this process but, if possible, to reverse it. The first aim was proving as difficult as it was expensive. The second seemed impossible, but her advisers constantly and earnestly assured her of their optimism.

She sat with a perpetual half smile on her face because she had been told that this caused less stress on the facial muscles and so delayed the onset of wrinkles, and took little part in any conversation beyond looking animated and uttering single words of appreciation or mild surprise, such as 'Charming' or 'Really?' Now she asked the editor how his wife was keeping. He replied as vaguely as he could. His wife had divorced him three years earlier and was at that moment sueing him for a larger share of his assets. After this, conversation died. The editor felt he had to revive it.

'I know your interest in the East, sir,' he said carefully, in case his proprietor wished to forget about his Chinese ancestry. 'I thought you might like to know we have just taken on a new and most promising young woman journalist, Anna Lu-Kuan. She has worked in Hong Kong and Singapore, and has also written a Ph.D thesis about Trinity-Trio.'

'Have you read it?' Jackson asked him.

'Yes. As a matter of fact, I've brought it with me in case you would like to glance at it.'

'I'll certainly look at it.'

Jackson did more than look at it; he read it thoroughly. And having read it, he sent for Anna Lu-Kuan. She came to his private office on the top floor of *The Enquirer* building in Fleet Street. Jackson thought that this seemed an apt day to interview someone from Hong Kong. It was the anniversary of his father's death there; the father he had never seen, and about whom his mother, Esmerelda, was sadly only able to tell him so very little.

He was standing by a huge window that gave a panoramic view towards St Paul's and the Old Bailey – the two poles of human success and failure, he liked to say, only partly in jest. He turned as the young woman entered the room. As he looked at her, he remembered hearing, as a boy, that when his great-grandfather, Dr Richard Jackson, first saw T'a Ki, he admitted to himself that he would never rest until she was his, and his alone. Now he experienced the same heady sensation. He felt physically weak with longing.

'Please take a seat,' he said, hoping his feelings did not show in his face – or his voice. 'I was most interested to read what you have written about Trinity-Trio. I don't agree with all your views, but that's probably understandable. Also, some of the details about how we acquired this or that concern are not quite right. But they are nearly right, and I congratulate you on that. Not an easy job to undertake without any help from the company, I imagine?'

'No, sir, it wasn't. But I enjoyed every minute of it,' Anna Lu-Kuan told him. 'Your company has had a long influence on my family and on me.'

'In what way?'

'My great-great-grandfather was an official at the Emperor's court in

Peking. In that capacity he had to observe rigidly all the codes of conduct of the court, but he could never bring himself to bind the feet of his only daughter. It was the custom then for girls of that class to have their feet bound in childhood to make them totally dependent on husbands, who also found erotic significance in the custom.

'My great-great-grandfather thought it abhorrent. He helped his daughter, T'a Ki, to escape this humiliation on various pretexts, but as she grew older, pressure on him increased to insist that her feet were bound. Then T'a Ki met a physician who wished to marry her. She agreed, if he could take her out of the country. Your great-grandfather, Dr Richard Jackson, gave them passage to Calcutta.'

'I have heard about that,' said Lord Jackson carefully. He did not wish to admit how much he had heard.

'I started from that basis,' Anna Lu-Kuan continued, 'and I became interested in the three founders of the company, and what had happened since.'

Something in the girl's frankness struck a sympathetic chord in Jackson's mind.

'So you must know I am descended from both T'a Ki and Dr Jackson – and that we are therefore related?'

'Distantly,' agreed Anna and smiled.

'Perhaps we can decrease the distance?' Jackson suggested.

'I would like that,' she said modestly.

'Now, to business. The editor speaks highly of your qualifications and your talents,' Jackson told her. 'What exactly do you want to do on this newspaper? What is your aim?'

'I applied for the job of foreign correspondent because I knew *The Enquirer* had a vacancy,' she said. 'But since you ask me, what I am really interested in is business. The people who take the big decisions, why they take them – and not always in the interests of the shareholders, or even their own. Perhaps for reasons they may not fully realise themselves.'

'I see. Is your family in Hong Kong?'

'My father is in Beijing, I think – what used to be Peking. I have a younger sister in Hong Kong, a teacher. My mother is dead.'

'You are a Communist?'

'Certainly not,' Anna replied vigorously. 'I don't think my father is, either, but he has to appear to be so.'

'You are close to him?'

'Very. He brought me up. He has been a mother as well as a father to me. Whatever I do, I do for his sake.'

'I see,' said Jackson, thinking about his own daughter. Would she ever have spoken so warmly about him? And in asking himself this question, he had to ask another: Had he ever done anything to warrant such loyalty from her? Soon, such matters would only be academic. The AIDS test had been positive; Elaine was living on borrowed time, and he had not yet told his wife. He dreaded this prospect so much that he kept postponing it, hoping that there had been some mistake. The wrong blood examined, two reports confused, anything. He must telephone the clinic and find out whether this could be so. Usually, he would have his personal secretary do this sort of thing, but this time, he could not ask her. The news that the chairman's daughter was a junkie dying of AIDS could leak out, the more people who knew of it, and was something the tabloids could not ignore. He forced his mind to reject this prospect.

'My father died in Hong Kong just after the war,' he told Anna. 'I rarely go there, perhaps because of that. I went back once, early on, to see his grave but, as I'd never met him, it didn't really mean much to me. A sad thing to say, isn't it? Perhaps, when I die, my daughter will feel the same way about me.'

Anna Lu-Kuan had lunch with him that day. On his way back to the office in his Rolls – Anna had left for an interview already arranged on the other side of London – he dictated a memo to the editor: 'I agree with your assessment of Miss Lu-Kuan's abilities. Move her to the City office. Give her a series of business articles to write. Try her on the great conglomerates and their future.'

He read the typescript of each article she wrote and discussed it with her. He arranged interviews with directors or the founders of several of these companies. Many would refuse to see any newspaper reporter or television journalist, but when Lord Jackson asked for such a favour, it was granted; one day they might want something from him in return, and they did not wish to ask in vain.

Jackson and his wife lived in his grandfather's house. Sometimes, after a dinner party when everyone had departed, he would walk on his own through the house, still lit for their guests, and imagine Robert Jackson, blinded and ill, dictating memos to his staff, having *The Enquirer* read to him, feeling his way through these same rooms, always refusing to submit to his disability.

And then he would wonder whether his grandfather's spirit, or his father's before him, ever returned to brood over the fortunes and follies of those who now controlled the company. The Chinese believed the dead could influence decisions of their descendants, and Jackson was part Chinese.

He came to appreciate the strength of this Eastern influence as his relationship with Anna grew and deepened. When he was with her, he felt completely at ease mentally, physically, spiritually. He was like a man who had been marching for too long in the wrong boots, who could at last relax in comfortable slippers. And yet he knew almost nothing about her. She was someone who had come from the East and into his life; now he was determined she should never go out of it. She had brought colour to a drab world and breathed life into his waning spirit.

They became lovers within a week of meeting. There seemed something almost predestined about this; it happened so naturally, so easily. When Anna first arrived in London, she explained, she could not afford to buy an apartment, so she rented a room in a mews cottage off the Cromwell Road. Jackson found out who owned this, and bought it for her in her name. This gave them a secret place to meet, an address that no-one on his staff knew, where they would never be disturbed.

He was a beneficiary of so many trusts, discretionary and family, that such an expenditure was easy and did not have to be accounted for. Money seemed to spring from unknown and complex sources unrecorded in any company accounts, to be filtered through companies with unlikely names registered in the Bahamas, the Caymans, the Netherlands Antilles, into a bank in Douglas, Isle of Man. He could write any amount of cheques that would never be queried, never need to be explained.

No doubt, all manner of lawyers and accountants, especially Laurens Gustav, Trinity-Trio's advocate in Geneva, who had set up these arrangements, took their percentage as money passed through (or even near) their hands, but that did not concern him. What mattered was that, at the end of its tortuous journey, laundered, sanitised, legitimised, it was there to spend as he wished.

As his relationship with Anna Lu-Kuan grew stronger, he realised he was coming to rely more and more on her opinions. He transferred her from *The Enquirer* City staff to what appeared to be a nebulous position in a subsidiary book publishing company, whose potential others had never appreciated.

She made a success of this and steered the company into profitability. He then promoted her to the New York office, largely because he could see her more freely there than in London. He guessed that his wife suspected their relationship, although she was too wise to remark on it or to challenge him, and it would be easier to continue the affair in another country.

And as they steadily grew closer, Jackson began to wonder how their relationship could be kept secret from the outside world – and how he would deal with the inevitable day when surely it must be discovered.

Manchester

Micky Cohen breezed into the Australian's downstairs room in his terraced house, smoking a large, torpedo-shaped cigar. The Australian frowned. He did not care for cigar smoke. He had read somewhere that smoking could injure the health of people simply in close contact with smokers, even more than the smokers themselves.

He read a lot of articles about health. He also kept a number of medical dictionaries at home and consulted them frequently. He was already a hypochondriac: not only was he his own doctor, he was his own hobby. He coughed now to show his disapproval of Cohen's behaviour.

'Oh, the cigar,' said Cohen casually, taking it out of his mouth and looking at it. 'Forgot you don't like them. Got given it today to celebrate something special.'

'What's that?'

'My old man has had an offer for the bookie's business he can't refuse. And since I own fifty per cent of it, I'm also unable to refuse.'

'What sort of offer?'

'You're not a betting man,' said Cohen, 'so you probably haven't been following all the changes in betting laws. Now that betting shops are legal, there's no need for bookies to have runners touting about in pubs. After all, why should the rich be able to telephone a wager while the poor, who don't have a bank account, or even a 'phone, have to slip bits of paper to men on street corners? It's all legal now.'

'We've a number of shops vacant. We can turn them over to betting, then?'

'Oh, sure, that's nothing. But what's happened to us is really something. We've had a visit from a couple of Americans who are staying at the Midland. They want to buy into our business, put in bags of money, and expand it. Their aim is that within the next six months our firm will have a betting shop in every town of over fifty thousand people, and then go public.'

'As Manny Cohen's?'

'No. They're going to give the shops a classy name. People trust class. These Yanks have gone into it in a big way, you know. In-depth research, they call it. Psychological stuff. For example, what would you say is the most trusted institution in this country?'

The Australian shook his head. He was not given to trusting anyone or anything. Uncle Rob used to say that an honest man had hair on the palm of his hand. He had still to find one, and if he ever did, he would check that the hair was genuine – and the hand.

'I'll tell you,' said Cohen, leaning forward conspiratorially. 'The Royal family. So we're going to call our chain Balmoral. Not bad is it, eh? Balmoral. We'll have a tartan motif – Royal Stuart. Why not? And a slogan something like "Bet on Balmoral".'

'What are they paying you?' asked the Australian.

'One million pounds down in a Swiss bank to avoid tax. Then twenty per cent of gross takings. They have the right to make spot checks on the books at any time, to see we don't fiddle, of course.'

'Of course,' said the Australian, considerably impressed. 'What was it you were saying about trust?'

Cohen shrugged.

'There's a hell of a lot of money involved, and most of it still to come. But that's not why I'm telling you: they want to meet you.'

'Why? I'm not, as you say, a betting man.'

'You've got the Midas touch,' said Cohen. 'They want people with that.'

'You can't eat gold,' said the Australian.

'What's this you've got, then? Philosophy? I've told them how you built up the company. The ice rink, car auctions, property. Think what you've done, even having to scratch around for a few pounds here and there from tight-arsed bank managers. These fellows have *millions*. If they put in their money, you would just take off.'

'What are the snags?'

'None, so far as I can see.'

The Australian was interested, but unconvinced; every offer of finance contained snags.

'How did they get so rich?' he asked.

'You'd better ask them,' said Cohen, aggrieved. 'Talk about looking a gift horse in the mouth – this is staring up its arse!'

'Sometimes a wise precaution. But let that go. When do we meet these philanthropists?'

Faro

On the far side of the customs barrier at Faro airport, on the Algarve in Portugal, now uncrowded as the season was ending, the guide was waiting as agreed: a girl in a blue and white Yves St Laurent dress. As the Australian approached, she signalled to a chauffeur to pick up his bags.

'Micky Cohen described you very well,' said the Australian.

'You, too,' said the girl, smiling. 'I recognised you at once. I am Gina Carlotti.'

She led the way to a Mercedes. They climbed into the back seat. The car felt pleasantly cool after the heat outside.

'Daddy is very proud of his yacht,' she explained. 'That's why he wanted your meeting to take place aboard it. And next week, he's off to the Caribbean.'

The Australian nodded, pricing her dress, her jewellery, the wrist watch encrusted with diamonds. They drove along the coast, past unfinished developments, hand-painted signs to restaurants, beaches, camping villages. In Portimão, they stopped on the quay. A motor launch, all white and blue paint and scrubbed canvas seat covers, bobbed elegantly and incongruously among the old-fashioned Portuguese fishing boats, the nets and winches and ropes.

A steward handed Gina Carlotti and the Australian aboard the launch which almost instantly carved a wide swathe of foam on the way to Carlotti's yacht, which gleamed in the mouth of the estuary.

They climbed up a varnished gangway. Another steward conducted the Australian to a huge air-conditioned cabin. The sun reflecting off the sea dappled its ceiling. The furnishings were all new and expensive, with little touches of luxury that intrigued him: that month's issues of half a dozen glossy magazines; four different brands of toilet water; even, in the bathroom, three textures of toilet paper. He smiled at this evidence of wealth, remembering the newspaper squares on the back of the door in the outside lavatory when he was a boy. And in remembering them, he also recalled seeing his first reference to Trinity-Trio on one of those pieces of paper. Was this another occasion when he would hear more about that company?

While the Australian had a bath, a valet emptied his suitcases, pressed his lightweight suit, laid out a clean shirt, underwear and socks.

The Australian dressed, went up on deck. Another steward brought him an iced orange juice, and he sat down under an awning. The deck trembled slightly as the yacht's engines started and they moved out of the estuary mouth.

A tall, dark-skinned man of indefinite age, wearing canvas yachting shoes, white trousers and a blue silk shirt, came out of a state room.

'Bill Carlotti,' he said. 'Pleased to meet you.'

He sat down beside the Australian. The yacht's twin propellers left a spreading wake, and the Australian was suddenly reminded of the advertisement he used to see frequently as a boy in the north of England for Reckitt's Blue: 'Out of the blue comes the Whitest Wash'. The sea in the posters then seemed too blue to be believed. Now, he realised it had not been blue enough.

'Micky Cohen speaks very highly of you,' said Carlotti. 'We have made a few enquiries and they all substantiate his warm opinion.'

'We?' asked the Australian, sipping his drink.

'Sounds royal or editorial, doesn't it? I should explain. I represent a charity in the United States. It was started originally to help immigrants down on their luck, and they proved very generous when their luck turned. They did not give donations, but percentages of their profits. So the charity prospered, because it invested wisely in people, in ideas, not just lending money. Never lending, always taking a share. That's why I wanted to meet you.'

'I'm flattered,' said the Australian, not altogether sincerely. This fellow Carlotti was a hard nut, not someone he would ever choose to cross. And he obviously wanted something from him. What would he give in return?

'I expect Micky Cohen has told you what we're doing with him and his father, financing a chain of betting shops right across Britain? Then we plan to go into casinos, bingo halls, all kinds of enterprises – what we in the States call leisure activities. You don't hear that phrase much in Britain yet, I guess, but you will, you will.

'Now I was very impressed with what Micky told me about your car auctions and property deals, and I wondered if we could get together on some future projects?'

'In what way? What kind of projects? Yours – or mine?'

The yacht was heading out to sea now, the coast rapidly falling away. Its rim of sandy beach, the long rash of white buildings on the cliffs diminished with every turn of the propeller blades.

'Both, I hope. Eventually. But first, some of ours. We always put up money, which we know about, and let others – like you – run businesses *they* know about. For instance, we have interests in hotel chains and casinos in the Caribbean, in Spain, South of France, in Italy. Tourism is becoming more and more important as electronics gradually take over much of the world's dreary work. People now have more time to enjoy themselves, and the money to do so.

'I have just spent several days cruising up and down this coast. We were in Spain, where we've bought huge areas of land. We will build houses on it, apartment blocks, condominiums, hotels, high-rise buildings.'

'Is it difficult to get planning permission for these things?'

'Not on our level. We have good friends in governments, and we employ the best architects, always local firms. We have not experienced any trouble so far. Sometimes, a few protesters, maybe. The odd cry that we're ruining the coast and so on. But they generally come round to our way of thinking. In the end!'

'Building that sort of thing isn't my scene,' said the Australian. He had never thought of it before, but didn't like to admit this.

'It could be,' said Carlotti.

'How?'

'What I would suggest to you,' Carlotti went on, signalling to a steward to replenish their glasses, 'is something in the States. And then Australia, where you were born, could prove virgin territory.'

The Australian nodded.

'You could be right,' he agreed. 'But what in the States?'

'Some years ago,' said Carlotti, 'the widow of a rich merchant who had made a fortune in the Far East, left our charity some shares in her husband's company. She later went into a convent and when she died she left the remainder of her shares to that religious order.'

'What was the company?' asked the Australian.

'One started by three men. An American, a Scot and an Englishman. English company. Trinity-Trio. Know anything about it?'

'Only what I read,' said the Australian. 'I was a boy when I saw that name for the first time in a newspaper, and then several times that same day. Somehow, it stuck in my mind. Still does.'

'These things do sometimes,' agreed Carlotti. 'One of the companies her late husband had financed through Trinity-Trio made chewing gum. It still does, but it's not big enough to stand up against the others. It's a sound firm, though. Could be the basis of a deal, if you agree.'

'Do Trinity-Trio want to sell?'

'Not yet. But I think they may have to. I feel there are going to be severe labour troubles in that section of the confectionery business. Machinery breaks down, deliveries aren't met, and then the banks get restive. Bankers never sleep easy.'

'You are sure of this?' asked the Australian.

'I should be. I am a partner – on behalf of the charity. I control a third of all the voting A shares.'

'I know nothing about chewing gum,' said the Australian thoughtfully.

'You don't have to. Business is business. It could be chewing gum or smokeless fuel or motor cars or bathroom fittings, cut-price holidays or holiday homes. Anything.'

'I get the drift.'

'I thought you would.'

'What would be the basis of any deal?'

'We would hold fifty-one per cent of the equity and you have the remainder.'

'So you could sell it over my head?'

'We could, but why should we – if it's making money? And if we did, you'd still have forty-nine per cent.'

'What do you want from me? Cash?'

'No way. That's our area. We want your brains and ability. You've done phenomenally well from nothing. Think what you could do with real backing.'

'How much money would you put at my disposal?'

'On the basis we have a lien on the sale of all freeholds, not to be unreasonably enforced, of course, and that you advise us – and only us – of any other possibilities of partnership, you can have as much as you goddamn' like.'

'You mean, millions?'

'Millions *and* millions,' said Carlotti and slapped the Australian on the shoulder before he shook his hand.

New York

Jackson proposed to Anna Lu-Kuan one night in his apartment overlooking Central Park. He had been thinking about doing this for weeks, possibly months, but suddenly he made up his mind. He was leaving for London in the morning, and if he let this opportunity pass, another might not come again for weeks.

They had been to the theatre, then on to supper, and now he stood in front of a big picture window, looking out at the dark heart of the park. The view seemed to him somehow symbolic of his own life: it was brightly lit around the edges but the centre was dark and lonely, uncharted, unsafe; not a place to linger.

He did not wish to fly out the next morning. No amount of complimentary champagne and caviare and smoked salmon, with air-conditioned limousines to collect and deliver him to and from the VIP lounges of international airports, could compensate for the fact that he always felt alone at the centre of a crowd.

In contrast, how pleasant it would be to wake up in the morning with Anna beside him, knowing he had no board meetings to attend, no decisions to make, no buying or selling of businesses about which really he knew nothing. And the only dividend he need ever declare would be one of happiness and content.

He often wondered what Dr Jackson would have said or done in his present situation. Then he realised he already knew. Dr Jackson had simply put T'a Ki out of his life, because making money was more important to him than any personal attachment.

Jackson was not cast in that mould. He would sit through partners' meetings, agreeing to proposals or raising some point which he knew was really irrelevant, simply because he felt he had to make a contribution, to say something that could be recorded in the minutes.

Did the other partners (apart from young Carlotti – Bill's son – who had graduated from Harvard Business School and M.I.T.) feel the same? He found it difficult to believe that Jennifer Douglas-Simmons really understood the infinite and arcane complexities of business today, but perhaps she did. She was a large, ungainly woman who had been married several times, always adding Douglas to her husbands' names. If not, she concealed her ignorance extremely well. Perhaps she deluded herself that she had a valuable contribution to make towards the running of the company, when, of course, she was totally irrelevant to its prosperity or decline.

On a recent business trip to the Middle East, Jackson had seen the seven-year-old son of an Arab potentate, dressed in a miniature naval uniform, prancing about on the deck of his father's sumptuous yacht pretending to be captain. The real captain and ship's officers understandably treated him with the greatest and most obsequious respect, but they were in command. The boy was only acting out a part, an illusion. Jackson felt that this was all he was doing: playing the role of a tycoon, without even wishing to be one. All he truly appreciated were the trappings of his role: the Lear jet, the house in Belgravia, the apartment on Central Park, the château in France his grandfather had bought on his honeymoon; everything money could provide – money made by the ingenuity, loyalty and efforts of others. This disturbed him; he felt he was living out of his league.

With Anna as his wife, all this would surely change. They would be a team. He would still be out in front, naturally, but she would be there to advise him, prompting him with the right questions to ask, the wise decisions to make. He could see nothing incongruous in this. After all, had not Confucius declared that the road to success was filled with wives – pushing their husbands along?

Anna came into the room.

'I've mixed two Brandy Alexanders,' she told him cheerfully.

They clinked glasses.

'I have an announcement to make,' he said. 'An irrevocable executive decision. We will drink to it. You are to marry me.'

'But that's impossible, darling,' said Anna. 'You're married already.'

'At the moment, yes. But not forever, nor indeed for very long. As you know – as probably most people guess – Corinne and I have only stayed together as long as we have because of our daughter. And the latest report on her condition is that, even though she has improved, reading between the lines, she'll never be much more than a cabbage.

'When the doctors told me this, I thought she is just one more of thousands and thousands of people Trinity-Trio must have ruined over a century and a half peddling opium. And I don't suppose any of my predecessors ever gave it a moment's consideration.'

'Alec Douglas did,' Anna replied. 'In my thesis on Trinity-Trio, I went into his refusal in some depth. He wouldn't touch a penny from the Coast Trade. That made a great impression on the Chinese – at a time when traders of every nation would say there were only two kinds of Chinese, those who gave bribes and those who took them.'

'Even so, Alec Douglas shot himself in the end, poor devil. His refusal didn't bring him happiness. Nor did money do much for Captain Ross, murdered, by all accounts, by the son of a slave he transported. But that is all in the past. Tonight, we're dealing with the present – and the future. I have telexed my solicitor to meet me at Heathrow. He has been working on my divorce for weeks.'

Anna kissed him gently.

'You are so sweet,' she said. 'But, even so, I cannot marry you.'

'But I love you,' Jackson protested. 'Is it because I am so much older?'

'That has nothing to do with it. Age is irrelevant when two people love each other. And I love you. But if I married you, everyone would say I had only done that for your money.'

'What the hell does it matter what everyone says or doesn't say? It's what *you* say that counts.'

'Agreed. But in the end, their remarks would get to you. I know. I've seen that sort of thing happen. Constant dripping wears away anything – even love. I want to marry you, but let me make a name for myself first. Let me make some money on my own. Then I will not be just one of your employees but a person in my own right.'

'You could make a name as the second Lady Jackson as easily as the first Anna Lu-Kuan.'

'Possibly even more easily. But you know how it is with members of every rich man's family – his wife, his children, even his distant relatives. If they succeed, it is always because *he* helped them and gave them the right introductions. If they still fail, it's because they're no good, even with all the wonderful chances they had. I want to make something of my life in my own way.'

'I can back you with money,' Jackson said earnestly. 'Whatever you need. Not a loan, a gift. Then you couldn't say it is a sort of Cophetua and the Beggar Maid situation, as you imply now. I would give it to you secretly. No-one would know.'

She kissed him again.

'You're such a dear, generous man, but in some things you are just like a little boy. *You* would know. *I* would know. God would know. As you said, it doesn't matter what others say, it is what *we* say. And I say I could not take your money like that. I don't love you because you are rich, but because you're you.'

'Then instead of money, let me give you a bank guarantee so you could borrow money yourself in your own right, in your own name, for any enterprise you wanted. Would that be different?'

She smiled at him. Her eyes seemed very bright. Had she been crying, or was she near to tears? For a moment, she did not speak.

'A variation, shall we say?' she said thoughtfully, considering this unexpected proposition. 'So long as it isn't money you give.'

'I've just remembered,' he said ruefully. 'The banks are being a bit touchy right now. There has been so much buying and selling of Trinity-Trio shares recently, and we are so damned extended at the moment. They might not even give me a guarantee. Mind you, I have various trusts and things all round the world. I can easily get money from them, and bank that and then give you the guarantee. No problem at all. A pleasure, in fact. What do you say now?'

'No,' she said. 'Not yet. Sometime, maybe. When the frenetic activity about the shares dies down. I know how you must feel, because on a far more modest level, when I first arrived in London and went only a few pounds into the red, the bank manager wrote at once, begging to have what he quaintly called "my advices".'

'I should have had a word with him.'

'No need to, now. When I was in *The Enquirer* city office, I met a director of the Occidental-Oriental for one of those financial interviews you suggested I wrote. I think they liked what appeared, for they've been very generous indeed since. On the understanding, of course, that they have a lien on everything that I deposit with them, which hasn't been much, I must say.'

'I've got the answer,' Jackson interrupted her triumphantly. 'As you know, I hold one hundred of the original three hundred voting A shares. I can easily put up, say, ten of those, which will give you an enormous guarantee. Then you can set up anything you want for yourself. What do you say?'

'No, again. I wouldn't dream of it,' Anna replied instantly. 'It's *so* kind of you to offer, even to think of such an idea. I just don't know how to thank you, but I couldn't possibly accept. Ten is far too much. It's a fortune.'

'What about five then? We seem to be bargaining in the wrong way. Most women would have asked for twenty.'

'But I'm not most women. I'm me.'

'I know. That's the difference – and the attraction. Well, what do you say to that?'

'I'm sorry, but I must still say no. I could not possibly take five, but if you are really serious, and you're going to be hurt if I keep on refusing your unbelievably generous offers, I would be immensely grateful for – well – one. That would be marvellous!'

'One's nothing. It would be lonely on its own. Have two. Two's company. The absolute minimum. You won't really get very far in business if you insist on bargaining the wrong way round.'

'This is not really business,' Anna replied. '*You* know that. It is kindness.'

'Well, show me kindness, then. Will you marry me now?'

'When you are free to do so, yes. I'm longing to marry you.'

'You mean that? Really and honestly?'

'Really and honestly.'

'Sounds like the wedding service already.'

'A good augury. But let's keep it quiet until you *are* free, darling. Otherwise you will only make totally unnecessary complications for yourself over your divorce. Wives are like that.'

'Are you?'

They kissed again gently, then drew apart.

'Ask me when I'm Lady Jackson.'

'I am serious.'

'So am I,' she whispered. 'I love you.'

'And I love you, now, today, tomorrow, always. And you will take these shares so you can forget the ridiculous idea you might be thought to be marrying me for money?'

'Yes, yes, you darling creature. If it makes you happy. Back me with one if you like – or none. I don't mind any more!'

'I've said two.'

'Say what you like about that, darling, but now now,' Anna told him huskily, and gently led him away from the window.

'I prefer the words of an ode attributed to Confucius two and a half thousand years ago: "If in my heart I love him, why should I not tell him? If with my body, I want him, why should I not tell him?" '

And then in the wide warm bed, under the dim glow of silk-shaded lamps, Anna told him.

Manchester and Hollywood

The Australian's middle-aged male secretary, neat in his well-pressed dark blue suit, with a white shirt and button-down collar to match his button-down mind, placed the sheaf of papers carefully on his employer's desk. The Australian opened them at random, read a few lines, then pushed the papers away.

'The accountants have checked all the figures,' the secretary said. 'They are accurate. If you buy the Lion's Share company, which you have good reason to believe Trinity-Trio would be willing to sell, you will get an eight per cent return, net.'

'Too little. I can get that almost anywhere, and Wrigleys are too big for us to take on. And if it is such a good investment, why do you think Trinity-Trio want to sell?'

'They need the money, sir. They are heavily extended. The banks are getting restive.'

The Australian nodded. If this careful creature did not know the reason, then it was unlikely anyone else did, either. The secretary's contacts were very wide. He looked at the balance sheet, working out in his mind percentages, written-down values of plant and buildings, write-offs, depreciations, bad debts and accumulated losses that could be set against another company somewhere else. That was all there was to business, really. You worked out figures and if they were good, you bought the company. If they were poor, you discovered a business to which they could relate. The rest should be profit. If it wasn't, you were a fool, and very likely down the hole.

The Australian could not understand how others had not learned this basic but essential truth. Perhaps this was because it was so simple that a child could do it – if they had the gift, of course, what he called the wheel in the mind, that never stopped turning over ideas with possibilities and figures, always figures. You had to have that, and he had it.

He had been reading an article about the conquest of Everest. Someone asked a climber why he had to climb it.

'Because it's there,' the climber replied simply. Everest represented a challenge he had to accept and beat. When newspaper reporters the Australian could not avoid asked him why he wanted to make more and more and more money, which he never spent on things they considered a man with money should buy – a Rolls, a yacht, even a private plane – he adapted this climber's reply and told them he wanted money to keep, 'because it's there'. And he believed something he had read in the newspaper section of the public library, naturally, because then he did not have to buy the paper, something Lord Beaverbrook had once said about money: 'You either have none, or you don't have enough.'

The Australian knew he could never ever have enough: there was simply not enough money in all the world to slake his thirst for more.

He looked up at the secretary.

'I have been thinking,' he said. 'We will buy Lion's Share. But offer Trinity-Trio ten million dollars less. The dollar is low against the pound. They could bite.'

'I do not think they'll take this figure. Not from my understanding of their situation.'

'You are not in their situation,' the Australian told him shortly. 'So how the hell can you understand it? Offer them the money. Dress it up a bit, of course. Say they have until six o'clock to agree.'

'But it is nearly noon now.'

'When I was a boy, I went to Sunday school. I was taught then that God made the world in six days and rested on the seventh. If we cannot buy this company in six hours, we are in the wrong business. Do I make myself clear?'

'Perfectly, sir.'

The telex accepting his offer arrived shortly before six. With the finances of United Charities Incorporated behind him, he could easily have bid much more for Lion's Share, but why spend money unnecessarily, even if it was someone else's?

The Australian flew over to examine the factory in Trenton, flying economy class, of course. The factory had been producing chewing gum for many years but, as with the ice rink, he realised it did not have to keep on doing what it had been built to do. Also, British Honduras was no longer the only source of chicle: countries like Mexico and Guatemala were also offering it, and chewing gum now contained tropical latexes from Colombia, Brazil and Malaya. As the market for chewing gum had increased, so had the sources of its main ingredients. If Lion's Share gum was being squeezed out of the market, he would have to find something else to make in its place.

He needed a product that staff skilled in producing confectionery could make: a sweetmeat or something of that kind which people wanted to chew or munch – and would keep on wanting to do so. He disliked sweet things himself, and so could never understand the extraordinary compulsion so many people possessed to keep their jaws moving. But it existed, and he must pander to it.

In Trenton, he walked into a confectionery shop that sold paperback books from racks, took out one book and looked at it, then at the other titles, really watching what the punters bought in the way of sweets. He was not so much concerned with older people because they had a limited buying life. He wanted to see what young people bought, who might keep on buying the same products when they grew up. He saw that three out of four children bought packets of popcorn. When the shop was empty, he turned to the girl behind the counter.

'I am a stranger here from England,' he explained. 'Why do these kids buy so much popcorn?'

'Pictures. They'd never go near the movies without a packet of corn.'

'That so? Thank you very much for the information. I have learned something most interesting.'

The girl thought he was a Limey nut; little did she realise that this reply had set her questioner on the road to another fortune.

He walked to the nearest cinema, bought a ticket. The film was indifferent, but he paid little attention to it. He was concerned with listening to the unattractive sound of people eating popcorn, the rustling of paper bags all around him.

Next morning he set up a meeting with the manufacturers of popcorn machinery. He ordered the most modern plant, had this installed immediately. It was wonderful what virtually unlimited amounts of money could buy, and quickly. It was also remarkable to see the effect of a casual mention that United Charities Incorporated was behind the purchase. This speeded up delivery and installation in a way he would not have believed possible if he had not seen it for himself.

Next, on the advice of the United Charities' trustees, he put in a bid for a small cinema chain, eight houses, in Michigan, Detroit and Des Moines. Ideally, he would have preferred cinemas around New York, but the trustees looked into the matter thoroughly and said there were no sellers, and anyway this was cheap at the price and one of the few chains still owned by the founding family and not a studio.

The cinemas were large but dilapidated. The Australian had them redecorated in nineteen-thirties style with huge black and white photographs of Ginger Rogers, Fred Astaire, Carole Lombard, Greta Garbo, Humphrey Bogart. People, he reasoned, liked the old stars; they had been around a long time, and the sheer familiarity of their names and faces was reassuring. People also liked to be reassured.

He sold popcorn in these cinemas, Lion's Share popcorn. He had called in food analysts to advise him on the most marketable taste; monosodium glutamate and other chemical additives improved it immeasurably. Soon, people who ate popcorn in his cinemas demanded it in their homes. Lion's Share produced West Point and Vassar popcorn to meet this demand.

Other cinema managers told him they would like to sell his popcorn – customers were asking for it by name – but they had contracts with other popcorn companies they could not break.

Then, as television became more popular, cinema takings fell steadily.

The studios were uncertain how to remedy this. Some made enormously expensive films employing armies of extras in the belief that size and spectacle were beyond the limits of the small screen. Sometimes these epics also proved beyond the limits of a studio's finances and it went into liquidation. Other studios sold off areas of land for property development and stayed in business but in a minor way. Several simply disintegrated. The founders were long since dead and so was the impulse of talent that had originally inspired them. The shareholders took fright and the studios were sold off in bits and pieces.

Soon, independent producers were making most of the pictures, and, as Sam Goldwyn asked, why would people pay good money to see a bad movie in a cinema when they could stay home and see a bad movie on TV? No-one had an answer to the question, but the Australian found that it answered his wish to buy not only a large chain of cinemas but the studio that owned them.

The owner, an old-timer – he had actually worked on the early Buster Keaton and Fatty Arbuckle pictures – had held on stubbornly until he could find a buyer for everything, all or nothing. Since the man was dying of cancer, the Australian knew he had to act quickly: the old-timer's successors might have different views. He bid for the lot and got them. Immediately, and again after consultation with the United Charities trustees, he hired talent for the studios. He put advertisments in magazines coast to coast, seeking directors, script-writers, cameramen, actors, actresses. His instructions were to make pictures (as cheaply as possible, naturally) but every picture had to have at least one scene common to them all, regardless of whether the films were in costume or outer space. The scene involved a girl climbing up a ladder, with quick shots of suspenders, a bare thigh and a flash of white panties. A variation could be to show her climbing into a car – but it must be an old car, because their doors were hinged at the rear – or on the upper deck of a ship, from the viewpoint of a voyeur on the deck beneath.

He had realised the unexpected value of this scene one day when he walked from his cheap hotel to the studio, something he was told no-one ever did; no-one walked when so many studio cars and limos were available. He walked because he wanted to see how long it took – and then as a result could cut down on the number of limos the studio ran.

On the way he passed the hotel swimming pool. Girls in bikinis were lounging about, and nobody paid any attention to them. They sat or lay provocatively, hoping to be seen, approached, maybe offered a part in a film. In this optimistic respect, the legend of Hollywood was still alive. Next to the pool were two tennis courts. Around one, a number of men of all ages were gathered, watching a match with avid attention. He joined them. The game was indifferent, but the four girls playing all wore ultra-short flared skirts. When they bent down to pick up a ball or leapt up to meet a high one, they showed an intriguing amount of small, tight, white knickers.

On the second court, four girls were playing much better tennis, but they wore shorts. There was not the slightest glimpse of knickers – and no men stood watching their game.

As the Australian walked, he pondered on these three sets of girls and came to the conclusion he remembered from his schooldays. Most people, and certainly nearly all males, are voyeurs. They want to see what others do not wish them to see; backstage at a circus, with the performers sweating nervously, the tightrope walkers rubbing chalk on the soles of their shoes; behind the Punch and Judy show, with the manipulator in shirt sleeves, pint of beer on a shelf, moving the puppets.

The girls' bikinis were designed, intended, meant to be seen, and therefore had little interest. The girls in the shorts had nothing forbidden to show and so aroused no interest whatever. But the tennis players in short dresses gave the – possibly illusory – impression that they did not realise their undies were showing. They were being taken advantage of, and here lay the value for voyeurs: they were seeing what it was not meant that they should see.

By the time the Australian reached the studio, he had decided on the scenes he wished to include in all his pictures. That morning he had to fire a veteran director on his way down, through poor box office returns, and out because of heavy drinking. The Australian had expected to shake his hand, wish him well and tell him to collect his cheque from the cashier's office. But something about the older man, the cast of his countenance, his grey hair, reminded him of Uncle Rob, who had left him £50 in his will. Despite his basic feelings of contempt for anyone unsuccessful or weak enough to drink to excess, he found himself drawn to the director. Perhaps he could keep him on in some advisory capacity – at a reduced salary, of course – but still working?

'Tell me something,' he said. 'What would you say was the classic film with points that have never been taken up fully since? Commercial ones, I mean, not artistic stuff.'

The director groped for a cigarette, and then, remembering how the Australian hated smoking, put away the case unopened.

'There are so many,' he said. 'The first action picture. Special effects. Comedy. And, of course, the Hays Office stopped so many things, after all the scandals, Fatty Arbuckle and the others. But I tell you one picture that I believe held the key to success but no-one dared to use it then because of the moral climate.'

'What is that?'

'*The Blue Angel*, the picture that made Marlene Dietrich. Josef von

Sternberg was the director and he had the touch. Hollywood never let him use the scene again.'

'What is it?' asked the Australian.

'A main shot,' said the director, all indecision gone, a professional talking about his craft. 'You see Dietrich low angle, sideways on, showing frilly white knickers. All the men in every audience expect her to swing round for a full frontal, but of course she never does. That would be too crude and would ruin the whole thing. You have to have style. You see what you're not meant to see, and you hope to see more, but you never do.'

'Check,' said the Australian. 'I want a scene like that in every picture we make from now on. Ten minutes ago, I was going to put you out, but you have got yourself a new job, working out angles on this theme. Are we in business?'

The director was too overcome to speak. He turned away so that the Australian would not see his tears of gratitude.

Articles now began to be written about the Australian as a new film czar; these little scenes, common to all his pictures, were analysed and discussed at inordinate length. Critics with beards and bow ties and horn-rimmed spectacles, who smoked cigarettes in tortoise-shell holders, declared that they were one ordinary man's protest about present-day values and hypocrisies. They praised the films for what they called their simplistic, natural content; they had all the fresh honesty of the wide sunlit spaces of Australia. A new wind of realism was blowing away old ideas.

It was all heady stuff. For a time there was even talk that the Australian should be given an extra Oscar or some special award to honour his contribution to the art of motion pictures, not only by buying the studios and the cinemas, but by providing a whole new output of films suitable for cinemas or TV, and each with its trademark as recognisable as the scenes in which Alfred Hitchcock cast himself in all his films of suspense.

No-one mentioned that the Australian had only bought the studio because he needed its cinemas to sell popcorn to pay for a chewing gum factory that no longer made gum. No critic noticed that to attract punters into the cinemas, where they could eat his popcorn, he had to have films to show them. And why buy other people's products when you could make your own with scenes which he knew men would like and women would at least tolerate? Certainly, no-one wrote anything about the part the ubiquitous United Charities Incorporated of Trenton, New Jersey, had played in all this.

If anyone had, the Australian would have sued them without hesitation. United Charities might also have sought redress, but not necessarily in the courts of law.

When the Australian left Hollywood, he hired a car and decided to drive across the United States on his own. He thought he might pick up a few new ideas; Americans were full of them.

He found he liked driving in the States because the highways were all enormously wide and straight, and the car radio offered a seemingly endless choice of dance-band music. This was totally different from anything in Britain, where roads were narrow and crowded, and the radio could only pick up one or two programmes playing the music he liked.

He sat at the wheel of his rented Mustang, while sugar-crested waves of Henry Mancini, Kennedy and Carr, Lerner and Loewe, lapped around him. He started to sing, as he sometimes did when driving on his own, loudly and out of tune, beating time with one hand, shouting the words, imagining he was what the 1930s magazines he collected called a crooner, out there in front of a band.

The boys – all dance-band musicians were called boys, regardless of age – would be wearing maroon dinner jackets, light gaberdine trousers, brown and white shoes, rimless octagonal spectacles. He was Dick Haymes, Rudi Vallee, Al Bowlly, Sam Browne, everyone and anyone who had ever crooned a number over the air. He was himself, as he would like to be.

In hotel bedrooms or in his own tiny office carved out of a former bedroom, his singing could be overheard, perhaps even smiled at, remarked on. He needed none of these attentions; only in the steel cocoon of a car on an open road could he be certain of escaping them.

A harsh, angry blast of air horns brought him back to instant reality and made him pull over sharply to the right. He had been edging out dangerously into the middle of the road, forgetting he was in the States. A truck and trailer roared past, festooned with coloured lights like a carnival float. He glanced down at the fuel gauge. The needle was almost on zero. He must stop at the nearest gas station; he never trusted these gauges.

The road was lined on both sides with the shacks and shoddy ribbon development and advertisement hoardings that disfigured so much of the American countryside: giant outlines of top hats, burgers, chickens. At night, they became a brash blaze of neon and simple invocations: 'Eat at Joe's, The Pizza King'; 'A Thousand Burgers Must Go – Tonite'; 'Botes f'r Hyre'; 'If You Lived Here, You Would Be Home Now'.

He passed a used-car lot with rows of brightly coloured sedans parked under strings of flapping orange and white plastic flags, but no pumps, then a gas station jammed with cars. So many customers were queueing up, they could not all get off the highway into the forecourt. He slowed instinctively, his attention drawn by the crowd. Had there been an accident? Was some TV personality there, as the adverts would say, 'in person' – although how could they ever be 'out of person'?

It was impossible to stop with the weight of traffic surging behind him, so he drove on more slowly to conserve fuel and pulled in at the next gas station, ten miles up the road.

Under a tin canopy stood half a dozen pumps – and not one customer. A man in dungarees came out of a shed, half an unsmoked cigarette behind his ear.

'Ten gallons,' the Australian told him and peeled off a ten-dollar bill. The man filled the tank, took the note into the shed, came back with the change.

'What's happening up the road?' the Australian asked him. 'Why the crowd? Last gas station was crammed with people. Here there's no-one.'

'Think you're telling me what I don't know, buster?' the man enquired belligerently.

'No way. Simply asking a question. I am a stranger here.'

'They're giving away stamps.'

'What do you mean? Postage stamps?'

'Hell, no. You a Limey or something?'

'Something,' the Australian agreed. 'I don't know what you mean.'

'Then you must be the only guy around here who doesn't. It's a sales con. Caught on in a big way. You buy ten gallons of gas, like you just done, you get ten free stamps a gallon or twenty or a hundred. The amount changes all the time. You collect five thousand stamps and you can get yourself an electric razor or a coffee pot or some other damn' useless junk.'

'Where from? Any shop?'

'Hell, no. You gotta go to a warehouse. The promoters have bought the stuff wholesale. So they make the retailer's profit without his overheads. Only the guys buying the stamps in the first place lose out. Gas stations, stores, supermarkets.'

'The stamps don't cost you a lot?'

'Hell, no. Not each one. But if you're buying them by the million, it all adds up. Makes another goddam' bill to meet.'

'But you probably sell much more gas – like the man up the road.'

'Yeah, that's so.'

'A new idea?'

'Naw, it's been around years. I thought it was dead. Then some wise guys just started it up again. It sure brings in the suckers.'

'Understandably,' said the Australian. 'Why didn't you take it on yourself? Were you offered it?'

'Guy came around the day I was in bed. A bad back. I get if off and on. Dumb guy I got helping me didn't have the sense to ask me if I wanted to join or not. He just told the damn' salesman to beat it, get his ass out. So he went right on up the road. And that cocksucker up there, who hates my guts, he jumped at it. He can make money and at the same time screw me. So he's happy both sides of the street.'

The Australian nodded sympathetically and started his engine. This was a parallel of the two tennis matches he had seen in Hollywood. One was crowded with men watching, the other hadn't one male spectator. He had acted accordingly. Now he must act again – before someone beat him to it.

Forty miles up the road he saw another gas station packed with cars, and a banner advertising free stamps for every dollar spent. He pulled in to the forecourt but not into the gas queue. Instead, he went into the office. The girl behind the cash machine looked up at him enquiringly.

'I'm from an English newspaper,' the Australian began, because with his accent he could not pass as American, otherwise he would have claimed he was from *Time* or *Newsweek*. 'I'm doing a survey across the States about improved trading results with firms selling stamps. How do you find them?'

'Great!' the girl said. 'Look at those cars out there. We just can't sell enough gas quick enough. And it's like that all the time.'

'What do you get for how many stamps?'

'Here's a booklet,' she said. 'Keep it. Feel free.'

The Australian put the booklet in his pocket, thanked the girl, bought a packet of Lion's Share popcorn, because he liked to support home industry, and went on his way.

That night, in his motel room, he thumbed through the pages. For two hundred and fifty stamps, you were entitled to a coffee percolator, and for a thousand you could have a hair dryer. He worked out that the stamp promoter must sell stamps in huge quantities very cheaply to shops and garages, priced to produce a small but steady profit on each sale. The traders then gave the stamps away in whatever quantities they decided. The punters collected their stamps, stuck them in little booklets, took them along to the warehouse. Each sequence of events dovetailed perfectly into the next, and the scheme had the similar and great attraction of chewing gum and eating popcorn; it could become a habit.

On the flight back to England he pondered on the choice of a name and logo. He wanted them to be attractive and reassuring to people with little money to spend, who had never heard of such stamps and so would approach them warily. No-one gave anything away; where was the catch?

Gold was his first choice. Gold spoke of wealth, security. Everyone wanted gold, if not for itself, for what it represented, what it would buy. He could call them Gold Star stamps, but that recalled the name of a BSA motorcycle. It could be Gold Sun, but that wasn't quite right; a touch of the Chinese about it. Gold Choice was no better. It implied there was a choice between his trading stamps and someone else's.

He thumbed through a glossy magazine, looking at the advertisements for U.S. Government Bonds. Immediately, he had the name:

Gold Bond. This spoke of wealth, integrity; my word is my bond.

He would have an artist to dress up this idea, to make an instantly recognisable logo; maybe two hands gripping each other in a firm, friendly clasp, or a castle on a hill-top; something to titillate people's imagination subliminally, with images of trust, integrity, friendship, mutual esteem.

He registered the company, Gold Bond Gift Stamps Limited, the day he landed and had stamps printed by the million (because the more he ordered, the cheaper each stamp became). Then, he discovered he could not interest a single shop, garage or company in buying them.

He visited potential outlets personally, carrying samples of the stamps, and notes about their operation. The managers of petrol stations he approached listened to his experience on the United States highway but shook their heads. It was different over there, they said. Trading stamps wouldn't go in England. No way. They'd tried them years ago and they were a flop.

'It's a load of rubbish,' he was told. 'Suppose the customer has collected a thousand stamps, what can they get with it? Some junk they don't want.'

'I'm changing all that,' said the Australian. 'We'll give them *good* prizes – things they need, or think they do. All backed up by a lavish advertising campaign.'

'What have you got to offer them now? Things you say they need?'

'Not yet. But I'll have them, you'll see. When we fix up with enough retailers.'

'Come back and see me then. But until then, no dice.'

When the personal approach failed, he sent out dozens of letters to the marketing directors of chain stores, chemists, grocery shops, drapers. Most did not even answer. Those who did, didn't want the stamps.

Finally, the Australian realised what he must do. He had been blinkered by tunnel vision, hoping to persuade some shop or group to use his stamps. But why should he bother? He had already registered the name Rink Supermarkets. He would start his own supermarket and give away his own stamps.

All the stallholders were on monthly leases. As they fell due, he refused to renew them. When the building was empty, he called in a firm of shop-fitters and gave specific instructions to copy the layouts of the most successful supermarket chains in the United States, incorporating the best points from all of them.

The colours must be those that gave people confidence – and at the same time, promoted their wish to spend: reds and oranges for excitement; greens and blues to calm doubts. There must be constant taped music to lull them, soothe them, reassure them. Sweets, chocolates, paperback books, loaves of bread – all things they might have forgotten or not bought on the grounds that they weren't really necessary if placed on the main shelves, but could be sold when the customers had change in their hands – these were to be stacked at the pay-out points.

When the first Rink Supermarket was ready, he hired a TV star for £500 in notes in a brown envelope to declare it open. He told the star, whose image had been fading recently and who was glad of the money, that he must also announce how for the first time anywhere in the world, Gold Bond trading stamps were going to be given away with each purchase.

He had photographs taken of vacuum cleaners, toasters, cameras, radios, garden furniture, and huge coloured enlargements were pinned up around the walls of the supermarket to show what people could acquire with their stamps – available only at the Rink Supermarket, of course.

The TV star was instantly mobbed by middle-aged housewives who groped him unashamedly, and stuffed cards with their telephone numbers into his jacket pockets. Children home from school for half term were each given a chocolate bar with a wrapper advertising the new stamps. The shop was a sell-out.

Next day, rival traders were on the telephone, asking the Australian where they could obtain these stamps. He did not let any buy them who could be in competition with him. That would have been foolish and he was never foolish, but he graciously allowed some other groups to buy them – but at twice the price he had previously asked.

He was on a seller's market, as he had been since boyhood, and where he determined to stay for the rest of his life. Gold Bond stamps were up and running.

Bill Carlotti's face creased in surprise as he came into the bedroom of the little house opposite the old cotton mill – now turned into a Rink Supermarket – which was still the headquarters of the Australian's financial empire. He looked in amazement around the simple room: two desks, shabby chairs, a single direct dial telephone. The wallpaper had been old when Uncle Rob was alive. Putty and paint on the window frames had cracked and flaked; under the Australian's desk he saw holes in the carpet made by his feet.

Carlotti said, 'So this is the heart of it all? I thought you'd have a splendid air-conditioned office, all anodised metal and black leather chairs in one of your high-rise buildings. I never expected this.'

'I started here,' said the Australian frankly. 'I know it. I like it as it is. Of course we have the computer elsewhere and an aerial for satellite transmission and all that. But this is where I feel at home. This *is* my home.'

'You don't have a yacht, a place in the country, anything like that?'

'Why should I?' the Australian asked him. 'I know people with yachts. You, for one. Other people here and in the States own country houses and ask me down if ever I want to go. So why should I pay indoor servants and a crew and gardeners and gamekeepers and so on? I am in business to make money, not to spend it.'

'Exactly. Which is why I wanted to see you before I go back to the States.'

The Australian motioned him into a chair.

'Would you like a cup of tea?'

'Thank you, no. I don't drink tea.'

'The typists have a tin of instant coffee outside, if you'd care for coffee?'

'Thank you again, but no. This is not a social call, it's business. Glad to see Lion's Share enterprises are doing well, and the properties, films, trading stamps. Everything.'

'We're covering our losses,' the Australian agreed cautiously.

'Now for the big one,' said Carlotti. 'When we were on my yacht I told you Trinity-Trio would sell Lion's Share because of their problems. This Lord Jackson has problems of his own. Wife trouble, a Chinese mistress, daughter hooked on snow. He's also worried about the buying and selling of Trinity-Trio shares. It's had an unsettling effect.'

'That's your suggestion, and your money,' the Australian replied. 'But Jackson still holds a majority of voting shares. One can buy all the non-voting shares and still have no control.'

'Yes. But . . . we are moving everything out to Nassau later this year,' said Carlotti. 'The charity would like you to take over some of their voting shares. On our money, of course.'

'How?'

'Like this. The widow of one of the original founders left his hundred shares to the charity. A trust with which I am also concerned has had an option for years to buy forty-nine per cent of another partner's shares. They are now taking it up.'

'However did they get that?'

'Clive Douglas, grandson of one of the original founders, needed money quickly in the twenties. He had the obverse of your philosophy, thought money wasn't to be made but spent. He lost a lot motor racing, gambling, fooling around. He just didn't know the value of what he was selling.'

'Most people don't. Until after they have sold.'

'So out of a total of three hundred voting shares, I will soon have one hundred and forty-nine. A few more, and Trinity-Trio has changed hands.'

'So why involve me? You can do it all yourselves.'

'Of course,' Carlotti agreed. 'But we don't want it to appear we are doing it ourselves. I have to be a white knight fighting off the infidel. Not the infidel.'

'So what do I get out of it?'

'Ten voting shares.'

'If I swing the deal?'

'Check. We'd like you aboard.'

'I'm coming aboard,' said the Australian. 'A few more shares are nothing if they've lost so many already.'

'In fact, they're everything,' Carlotti corrected him. 'For now none of the partners wants to sell even one. The weakest link is Mrs Douglas-Simmons. Her father was killed in Burma in the Second World War, months before she was born. Her grandfather, Clive Douglas, died soon after. So she inherited.'

Carlotti remembered the evening at the Savoy with Maria, then the drive through the blackout to Regent's Park Canal, with Douglas drugged in the back of the car. He put the thought from his mind. It was good to go back to the past occasionally; it was dangerous to stay there.

'This lady has had three husbands, all after her money. She's no looker, so that must be the reason. Last one, Simmons, was a boxer. She's now living with a Mexican film extra half her age.'

'Will she sell any?'

'Not unless the company lawyers, Ebenezer and Son, who have been with Trinity-Trio almost from the beginning, say so. She's given them power of attorney. On her own, I think she would. But they never will. They know the score.'

'Anything she wants?' asked the Australian. 'A younger, sexier Mexican?'

Carlotti smiled.

'We tried that,' he said. 'She likes to find her own men.'

'So. You want me to think up something?' the Australian asked him.

'Of course,' agreed Carlotti. 'But, in the meantime, here's something *we've* thought up. . . .'

Geneva

On winter evenings, Laurens Gustav usually stayed late in his office. He did not particularly care to be alone on the entire tenth floor his firm occupied, for he was not a brave man, but he liked going home even less. His wife would have been drinking, and if she came to meet him at the front door of their great house, overlooking the lake on the Quai Wilson, her voice would be slurred and her hair matted where she had run her fingers through it in the unattractive habit she had acquired.

She would begin to tell him something; there had been an important telephone call, or their son, who worked in Rome, was calling in on his way to Paris, but halfway through she would forget what the message was. The sentence would end with a shrug of her shoulders, and she would turn away from him, and slop back to the big room and throw herself in a chair and stare at him, as though she had never seen him before; and then he would wish she never had.

On summer evenings, when there was always the chance his wife might be out playing bridge or drinking, he would walk home slowly. There was no need for the chauffeur and the Mercedes. He would stroll past the shops selling expensive silk shirts, sable coats for men, gold watches for women. When he came to the end of the promenade by the edge of the lake, the water would often be surprisingly rough and he would stop to watch the waves, never so white as sea waves, but still strong enough to make the little boats moored along the edge bob up and down like toys.

From here, the road curved up towards the old palace, which had a plaque outside, because it had once housed the League of Nations. In the distance the lake stretched towards hills which wore haloes of clouds, although at that hour of the evening, the sun would still be bright and the sky blue.

On the left stood big *fin de siècle* houses, all meticulously clean; there was no smoke in Geneva. Their bricks and tiles were grey, and big glass windows like wide eyes looked across the choppy water towards the hills. Gustav was a lawyer by profession and a dreamer by choice. He liked to imagine people who might have lived in his house before he bought it – what famous statesmen, whose ghosts must surely gather on the steps of the League of Nations Palace.

As he walked on these evenings, breathing the fresh air, he felt nearer to happiness than anywhere else. On this first Tuesday in June, as he reached his house, he saw a man wearing a loose jacket and a floppy hat looking across the lake. Children were still playing, nurses pushed prams, couples walked arm in arm, but this man just stood. He was not

Swiss; he might not even be European. There seemed something vaguely American or Australian about the cut of his suit, the wide brim on his hat.

Gustav noticed him, then went into his house. He was thankful his wife was away. He poured himself a bols and turned on the hi-fi. Instantly, Beethoven overwhelmed the silence, but Gustav's mind was not entirely on the music. Twice he stood up and crossed the room to look out of the window. The man was still there. He had not moved. He might be a clothed statue. The third time, he had gone, and, for no reason he could imagine, Gustav felt uneasy.

Was this a hard man acting for someone one of his clients had sued? Could this be the beginning of a kidnap, someone casing the house? Surely not. Such people were professionals; they did not stand about like actors in a TV film, obviously watching, waiting. He was probably a tourist, nothing more.

But the man was there again on the next night, and again on the third evening. This time, Gustav approached him. The man did not turn until he was by his side and then he looked without surprise into his face; indeed, he was smiling. He was not American or Australian, but a Levantine of some kind; dark, oily-skinned, smooth, with a pearl pin stabbing a bright silk tie.

Gustav said, 'Excuse me, but I have seen you here for three nights outside my house. I wonder if you are looking for something – or someone?'

'You are quite right,' said the man. His voice was very soft, almost a whisper. 'I was looking for you.'

'*Me?* Why?'

'I wanted to show you something,' said the man.

'What do you mean, something?'

Could this be a prospectus for some company? He acted for so many national and multinational organisations that promoters or would-be entrepreneurs would sometimes accost him at parties or even in the street to ask if they could interest him in some project with which they were concerned. He always directed them to his office, and he did so now. 'You know where my office is. Please make an appointment with my secretary.'

'It is not a business matter,' said the man. 'More of a personal nature.'

'Who are you? Who do you represent?'

'I am what you would call a freelance,' said the man.

'A journalist? A salesman? Do you have a card?'

'No. I do not carry a card.'

'Then what is your name?'

'That is really immaterial. I have one name today, I might have another tomorrow, a third next week.'

'I do not think I wish to discuss anything with you,' Gustav told him, and turned away. The stranger was either being deliberately rude or he was insane; he would telephone a friend in the police and have the man questioned. It was ridiculous that such people should be walking the streets.

'That is not the point, monsieur,' said the man now, sharply. '*I* wish to discuss *this* with *you.*'

He took a small white envelope from an inner pocket of his jacket, handed it to the lawyer. Gustav opened it. He was holding a colour photograph of himself, naked, erect, with a boy stroking him while he felt the boy's pudenda. Gustav's mouth suddenly dried like a gourd. Someone threw a crust of bread into the lake and the seagulls squawked and flapped their wings and flew away, and he wished he could fly with them.

'What is this exactly?' he asked. His voice was hoarse and thin and querulous, not the self-confident, deep-toned voice that had forced so many confessions out of reluctant felons, either in his law office or in the courts.

'I would think it is fairly self-evident,' said the other man.

'Where did you take it?'

There was no point in denying it was genuine. He had a mole on his left thigh. If this photo was a montage, with his head added to someone else's body, that would have been missing. On that particular day, too, he had cut the little finger of his left hand; there was a sticking plaster round it. And any medical examination would only find further proof.

'I did not take it myself, but for your information it was taken in a house you visited in Amsterdam. You were over there on a legal matter involving Trinity-Trio's patents. Some medicines, I believe – I do not have the exact details with me – but you are doubtless cognizant of them. It was taken in March. You can see that from your little finger. You cut it on the third of March. An unhappy accident in your office with a pair of scissors.'

'Yes,' Gustav agreed. There must have been a spy in his office. His secretary, a clerk? It could be anyone. But surely no-one knew of the little house in Amsterdam he visited, where these young boys were paraded – washed, scented, hair brilliantined, some with their bodies slightly oiled, others dusted with talc, according to the preference of the client? Oh God, how could this happen to *him*? Where could that camera have been?

He remembered the room, small and warm, down near the canal. What an idiot to have been snared by this ancient trick – a concealed camera, a blackmailer – against which he had so frequently warned susceptible clients.

'I have others,' said the man. 'Or rather, *we* have others. You can keep that if you want, by the way. For your files, if you like.'

Gustav replaced the photograph in the envelope, licked the flap shut, and put it in an inner pocket. He would burn it as soon as he was inside his house.

'This is blackmail,' he said. 'You know the sentence for that?'

'Naturally. But this is not blackmail, only a matter of trade. On behalf of my principals, I will trade all the photographs we have, with the negatives, for your goodwill.'

'What do you mean exactly?'

'Come, let us walk. Everybody walks by the lake. It is so peaceful, so pleasant,' said the Levantine.

He wanted to walk because it was safer; you could never trust these lawyers. Gustav might have someone in the house, at an upper window, with a directional microphone that could pick up a voice at a mile range, or one of those gadgets that deciphered the sound waves of a voice from the minute reverberations on a window pane and played them back on tape.

This could still be done if you walked, but it was much more difficult, especially if you walked away from the house. Again, he might have a miniature tape recorder under his shirt or in his pocket, but he thought not. He carried a high frequency mechanism no larger than a cigarette lighter that would buzz discreetly if this conversation was being bugged. It remained reassuringly silent.

He fell into step with the lawyer. He had been a soldier once, in the forgotten army of some obscure country, and the discipline stayed.

'Well?' said Gustav.

'You act for a company in which my principals are interested. The Occidental–Oriental Bank in Zurich. Yes?'

'Yes.'

'You also handle many legal matters for Trinity-Trio, which is just moving to Nassau. Yes, again?'

'Yes.'

'We understand Trinity-Trio owes this bank considerable sums of money.'

The lawyer did not reply.

'I do not expect you to tell me how much, but I will tell you it is into billions of American dollars. If you argue, I will give you the exact amount, as at the close of trading today. In return for these photos, you can influence the bank.'

'To do what?'

'To follow your advice. Trinity-Trio's loans have a cross default clause. If they default on one – if they are one day late in repaying their interest or whatever part of the principal is due – the bank can foreclose. On your instructions, they would do so.'

'I cannot do that! I also act for Trinity-Trio, you know.'

'Of course. That is why I am here. I fully appreciate your moral dilemma, monsieur. But do you also appreciate your own dilemma – also moral?'

'I cannot influence one client against another. Not even if you ruin me.'

'I am relieved to hear that. My principals told me you were a man of honour, but with lawyers one can never be entirely certain. My own experience with them has not been conducive to trust.

'However, I only told you about the bank's loans to prove a great deal is known about the company and the bank.'

He took a second sealed envelope from his pocket.

'Your instructions are in here, typed out so there can be no misunderstanding. They are by no means onerous. They may even seem trivial to you, but that is because they are only a small part of a much bigger operation.

'Do as they say, and you will never see me again. All these photographs – and there are some others which are most remarkable – will be deposited in a sealed box that same day in your office.'

'If, however, you do not follow these instructions, copies of each one will be sent by registered post to all your clients, personally to the directors of every company for which you act – and, more important, to their wives.

'They are not all moral people, I know. But they would like to get their fingers round the throat of someone else to whom perhaps they have had to defer in the past, someone whose advice has possibly gone against their wishes, even their personal enrichment.

'By the end of the week, monsieur, not only will you have no clients left, you will have no friends.'

The Levantine saw Gustav hesitate, balanced on the high wire between indecision and despair. He put his hand in his pocket, took out another envelope.

'Four more photographs,' he said, 'and a telephone number. If you change your mind between now and tomorrow morning, ring the number. It is no good asking the police to trace it – it is a car telephone. The car is not even in this country. And again, there is probably nobody in the car, only an answering machine to tell you what to do if – as I hope – you decide to follow my advice. If you decide to follow your own advice, of course, I have told you what will happen next. Now, monsieur, it is chilly and I have no overcoat. I will bid you good day.'

He bowed slightly, doffed his hat in a curiously old-fashioned gesture and walked away.

I could have him beaten up, even killed, thought Gustav. He knew people who could easily arrange such things, but what good would that do? The Levantine was only the messenger, not the person who had sent the message.

Gustav walked back to his house. His wife was not at home. He went to his study, locked the door. Then he sat down behind the desk, and shook the photographs out on to the green blotting pad.

They were worse than the first. He was with boys of eleven or twelve, girls of the same age. How could he ever have got into this terrible situation? But he knew the strength of his need and even in the extremity of his misery, looking at these photographs aroused him; he felt himself harden against the expensive tweed of his trousers.

He tore the photographs into little pieces, put them in an ashtray, applied a cigarette lighter and watched until they burned, limbs, faces, smiles vanishing into curling charred paper. He looked at the number on the back of the envelope for a long time. It had an unusual number of digits. He wondered where the car was, who had arranged all this, whether, in fact, it could just be an elaborate bluff to terrify him. If so, it had succeeded. Then he opened the envelope, memorised the brief unsigned instructions and burned the paper. He put his head in his hands, and when he raised it, the room was dark.

He heard his wife call, 'Gustav, Gustav, are you in?'

He knew then he had only seconds before she found where he was. He took a deep breath. He felt an old man, ill, beaten, desperate. Then he picked up the telephone and punched out a number.

London

The head of production of the Australian's studio in Hollywood, with his financial director and assistant, and an independent producer with whom he had a contract, were sitting in a conference room at Claridges, in London. They all had planes to catch later in the day. The producer and the financial director were flying to Sydney, the others back to Los Angeles.

The Australian had asked to meet them before they left and now they sat, wanting to smoke but not daring to do so because the Australian disliked smoking, and wondering, but not of course discussing, whether there could be any sinister reason for this unexpected summons.

He came into the room with his male secretary and a large well-built man with very short hair who they took to be a bodyguard. They stood up respectfully. He nodded to them but did not shake hands; the Australian had an increasing dislike of touching someone else's flesh. He sat down at the head of the table, looking at them each in turn. It was impossible to tell from the expression on his face what he was thinking. Then he turned to the producer.

'You're making two pictures in Australia – *Boomerang Two* and *Captain Cook's Secret Voyage*, I see.'

'Yes, sir.'

'Give me the cast list.'

The producer opened his briefcase, took out two sheets of typed paper. The Australian glanced at them.

'In each of these pictures you have a good part for a woman in her late fifties or early sixties?'

'That's true, sir. As a matter of fact, we've already cast them both. They are pretty pivotal characters in each story.'

'Who have you got?'

The producer told him.

'I don't want them,' said the Australian.

'I'm sorry to hear that, sir. Can I ask why?'

'You can and you have. I have someone better in mind. One person for both roles.'

The producer and the financial director exchanged glances.

'We have, as a matter of fact, sir, entered into contractual arrangements with their agents,' said the financial director carefully.

'I don't think you heard me clearly,' said the Australian. 'I have someone better to play both parts.'

'Who is that, sir?'

'Amy Crabtree.'

For years he had resented the fact that his mother had taken half of his initial earnings, but now the sum seemed so minuscule compared to his present holdings that the memory had all but vanished from his mind. Not quite, of course; negative deals were never totally forgotten. But now he felt more kindly towards her. He recalled trips his mother used to make for auditions in music hall acts and touring revues; how she would come home despondent, with the smell of port and lemon on her breath, and complain to Uncle Rob that it wasn't what you knew but who.

It would be interesting to help her now when she would have no idea he was behind these films; his name never appeared on any list of credits. He wondered whether she would write and tell him that at last, and quite out of the blue, she had been offered two good roles. Maybe he was not so anxious to help her as to give himself the pleasure of exercising his power.

The producer took a directory of character actresses from his briefcase and glanced through its pages.

'She doesn't seem to be here, sir. What has she been in?'

'Lots of things. And she's playing in these films. Both parts. Do I make myself understood?'

'She may not be available, sir.'

'That is your problem, gentlemen,' said the Australian, standing up. 'Make her available. But she is in those pictures in these parts or there are no pictures. Good day to you.'

Geneva

Laurens Gustav stood in front of a mirror in his dressing-room and carefully brushed imaginary specks of dust from his Huntsman dinner jacket. Then he drew the curtain from the window. Outside, he could see his Mercedes, uniformed chauffeur at the wheel, interior lights already lit, waiting for him. Behind the car, the lake reflected the shimmering lights of the city like a necklace of fallen stars.

He called to his wife, 'I'll be back after midnight.'

She did not reply. He looked in the drawing room. She was asleep, sprawled inelegantly in an easy chair, glass in hand. Some gin had spilled out on to the Aubusson carpet. He frowned, took the glass from her hand and put it on a table. She snored and moved slightly in her sleep.

He glanced at his Piaget wrist watch. He was late, and the American ambassador did not take kindly to dinner guests who were late. He locked the front door carefully and went down the steps to his car. The chauffeur held open the rear door and saluted. His tinted night glasses fleetingly reflected the street lamps as he climbed in behind the wheel.

'American embassy,' Gustav told him briefly and sank back into the leather seat, soft as a glove. The interior light went out as the car started to move. Gustav picked up that day's copy of the *Financial Times*, which his secretary had seen was ironed and folded, with various shares marked. He switched on the reading light.

Across the top of the front page was written with a ballpoint pen in green ink to stand out against the pinkish paper: 'SIT QUIETLY. DO NOT ATTEMPT TO MOVE.'

What the hell was this? Some sort of joke? He glanced up angrily, saw the chauffeur watching him in the rear view mirror.

'Someone has written on the newspaper,' Gustav told him sharply.

'I know,' the chauffeur replied. He swung the car off the main street.

'What do you mean, you know? Who are you, anyway? You are not my regular driver.'

'He is indisposed, sir. He asked me to deputise.'

'I see. Hey – this isn't the way to the embassy.'

'No,' the chauffeur agreed.

Gustav grabbed the door handle. It did not move.

'Special locks,' the driver explained. 'For your protection.'

He pulled in to one side of the road, switched off the engine, turned to face Gustav.

'Why are we stopping?' Gustav asked him. 'For goodness' sake get on, man. I'm late already.'

'I am sorry to hear that. But I have something to say to you first. The other night you were advised to telephone a certain number. Instead, you telephoned another number. As a result, we had a visit from some ruffians. Not altogether unexpected, but unnecessary.'

'I don't know what the hell you are talking about. Take me on to the embassy, and let us have less of this ridiculous talk.'

Gustav's words were brave, but his voice sounded thin and nervous. He felt sweat dampen his back and his hands; he smelled his own fear.

'My superiors thought you might attempt something like that,' driver went on, 'so we took precautions. They asked me to give this.'

The chauffeur took out an unsealed envelope and passed it acro car to Gustav. In the bright, focused light of the reading lamp, more nude pictures of himself with children. The sight made hi and sick, uncomfortably aware of the heavy, dull hammeri heart.

'What do you want?' he asked. He had no bluster left in hi

'For myself, nothing. But in addition to doing what you been instructed to do, my superiors want you to undertal the United States.' He handed another envelope to Gust

'Here is a first-class return ticket, a hotel booking f name and address of the person you have to visit, a to do.'

'I'm a very busy man,' said Gustav. 'I can't and go.'

'If you do not, then everything and everyone w these photographs go into circulation. My super they are not eager to hurt you professionally, most unhappily, physically. But this is your be given another. Do I make myself absolut

'Yes,' said Gustav. 'But why pick on me

'Because you are uniquely placed to help my superiors. It is all a matter of business, Mr Gustav. Nothing personal, I can assure you.'

He adjusted his cap in the mirror.

'Now, sir,' he asked in a different tone of voice, 'shall we go direct to the embassy?'

Oregon

The senior lay sister of the convent opened the door of the abbess's office. She was not permitted to speak because of the strict rules of her order, but she bowed towards the visitor and extended her hand to invite him into the room. As Laurens Gustav came in, she closed the door silently behind him.

Gustav stood with his briefcase, facing the abbess. The room was sparsely furnished. Books on religious subjects lined one wall. Two upright leather chairs faced the desk, which was bare except for a crucifix, a rosary, a prayer book with a red silk bookmark.

The abbess shook hands with him.

'I greatly appreciate your kindness in seeing me at such short notice, ma'am,' he began, 'but I have something to discuss which I think is important to you and to your convent.'

'It must be, if you flew from Geneva especially to tell me. Please take a seat.'

Gustav sat down. He was unused to being in the position of mendicant salesman. Usually, in his magnificent office, all white carpet, black ther and anodised metal, he would lean back in his chair and listen impassive face to a client's halting exposition of folly or worse.

represent a world wide company, Trinity-Trio,' he went on, speakwly, trying to keep all trace of anxiety out of his voice.

ny years ago, Mrs Evelyn Ross, the widow of one of the founders ompany, joined your Order and, when she died, I understand she er her shareholding in Trinity-Trio to this Order. Can I take it till hold those shares?'

ess nodded.

ll this happened long before my time. But when we received naturally consulted with our own attorney and he confirmed say is accurate.'

Gustav.

ounted one hurdle; now came the second.

'I do not know whether you follow financial matters in the newspapers – I would rather think you do not have the time or the interest for such things – but I can tell you that Trinity-Trio shares are standing very high indeed. In fact, I think they are at their peak. This is because there has been very considerable buying in New York, and in London and Hong Kong.

'I have come to ask whether you would be interested in selling your shares at double their quoted price? This is a volatile market, and if you took your profit, which on your holding would be extremely large, your financial advisers could invest the money to bring a bigger and, if I may say so, less speculative return than you are receiving now.'

The abbess smiled.

'If the shares are so speculative, why would you wish to buy them?'

'Because the more of its own shares a company owns, the stronger it is against any hostile or predatory bid from outsiders, which is regrettably all too common nowadays. That sort of acquisitive person or group has no interest whatever in the wellbeing of the company they bid for, or the people who work for it, or its shareholders. All they seek is a quick profit – and on to the next takeover.'

'Your offer is extremely interesting, Mr Gustav. But as you can imagine, I do not know anything about such things – I have therefore asked our attorney to join us. He is in the next room.'

'I will be delighted to meet him,' said Gustav insincerely. 'Will that be the senior partner of Party and Secret in New York? A very distinguished firm indeed, with whom my company has enjoyed most felicitous professional relations over many years.'

'No,' she said. 'They used to act for us, and very well, too. But quite recently a charity that does a great deal of good work among immigrants has been extremely generous to us in paying for certain renovations to our building. At their suggestion, we have changed to their attorneys, Castle and Constance.

'Indeed, the senior partner with whom we deal, Mr Frank Castle, is also a director of the charity, which is most convenient.'

Gustav nodded. He knew about Castle and Constance; their original names had been Costello and Constancione. He stood up and did his best to smile a welcome as Castle came into the room.

He was a small, fat, swarthy man wearing a sharkskin suit and crocodile shoes. When they shook hands, Gustav noticed how many rings he wore and how big were the diamonds that studded them.

He repeated what he had just told the abbess. Castle nodded sympathetically.

'A very fair offer indeed, Mr Gustav,' he agreed. 'In other circumstances, I would have advised my client most strongly to accept it. With such an increase in the value of the shares, the profit to the convent could be very great. And very useful.'

He shook his head sadly as though unable to comprehend such greatness and usefulness.

'But in these circumstances?' asked Gustav too quickly, and cursed himself for having spoken at all. Had he given away his own desperate need for a deal?

'In these circumstances, sir, I have, with the utmost regret, to say that it would be impossible. You see, only yesterday – it must have been about the time your telex arrived – United Charities Incorporated, whose board I have the honour to chair, made an offer for these same shares, and as the attorney of Mount Carmel Convent I advised the abbess she should accept it. Irrevocably.'

'Perhaps we should have waited?' suggested the abbess nervously.

'How were we to know what Mr Gustav would offer?' asked Castle innocently, spreading his hands wide, palms uppermost.

'Was my price better than the charity paid?' asked Gustav.

'I cannot discuss clients' business, you must appreciate that.'

'In Switzerland, as I am sure you know, Mr Castle, oysters are considered talkative compared with bankers and lawyers. I can offer you on behalf of my clients a fifty per cent increase on what you paid, whatever that sum may be, to be paid to the charity or the convent or the Order, or however you may decide.'

'That sounds very generous,' said the abbess.

'It is *most* generous,' agreed Castle, 'but as the convent's attorney I could not advise it. We are not here to buy and sell like merchants in the market, Mr Gustav, as you will be the first to appreciate. I have to weigh very closely the interests of the convent *and* the charity. I must therefore decline your offer.'

'Would you put it to the board of your charity?' asked Gustav desperately.

'There would really be no point, Mr Gustav. You see, I take all executive decisions on these matters.'

He turned to the abbess.

'Now, madam, if you will excuse me, I have another appointment.'

He held out his hand to Gustav.

'A pleasure and privilege to meet with you, sir,' he said.

Gustav nodded and watched Castle go out of the room. He left a strong smell of expensive aftershave behind him.

'Well,' said the abbess abruptly, 'that seems to be the end of the matter.'

'Yes,' said Gustav. 'I fear it is.'

But he knew differently. For him, it was not the end; it was only the beginning.

London

The Silver Spirit, glittering like a giant jewel in Trinity-Trio's livery of dark blue and silver, came out of the tunnel at Heathrow and headed towards London.

Jackson checked that the electric glass division separating the driver from the driven was firmly closed. What he had to say to Ebenezer the lawyer was not for other ears.

'What progress have you made on the divorce?' he asked him.

'Enquiries, investigations.'

'I don't want private eyes following Corinne about.'

'If we could find anything against her, it would cut the alimony.'

'To hell with that,' said Jackson. 'We have been married for twenty-five years. I am not going snooping in dustbins or hotel bedrooms now. Anyhow, I don't believe she has anything to hide. What do you think she'll want?'

'Difficult to say. Her pride will be hurt, of course. Women – wives – always resent a younger woman. Understandably. Imagine how *we'd* feel if they went off with men – toy boys – half our age. Also, there is the element of incredibility. How could her husband suddenly attract a girl so young and pretty? What has she been missing – or what have you been denying her – all these years? The easiest explanation is that the girl is after money. So the wife goes after that, too. How much she asks depends on what lawyer she hires. Some work on a split, like the Americans, although that's frowned on professionally here.'

'You are talking in millions?'

'I would imagine so. She must know – or will very soon find out – just what your one hundred voting A shares could be worth. Everything depends on how amicable we can keep things. Trouble is, both sides get upset. Off with the old and on with the new is never a way to make friends with your wife.'

'I can imagine,' Jackson agreed dejectedly. Could such a situation ever arise with Anna? Surely not. The idea was absurd – but so would this conversation have seemed absurd before he married Corinne.

'You have discussed this with her?' Ebenezer asked him.

'Only in the broadest sense.'

Jackson put his hand in his waistcoat pocket, took out a small washleather pouch, opened it and slipped a copper penny into his other hand.

'Old Dr Jackson used to think this was his lucky penny,' he said. 'We Jacksons have carried it around ever since. Before we make a decision, we toss it – hoping to get at least two out of three heads.'

'And if you don't?'

'We keep on trying until we do.'

'I never realised you were superstitious.'

'Everyone is,' said Jackson. 'But about different things.'

He tossed it, and the coin came down tails. He turned it head up, on the back of his hand.

'Heads again.'

He tossed it once more. This time the penny came down heads.

'See? Two out of three. This divorce will go through all right.'

'Strange way of deciding it,' said Ebenezer.

'It's as good as any other,' replied Jackson defensively, putting the penny back in its pouch and into his pocket. 'How long will it all take?'

'It needn't take too long. Again, it all depends on who is acting for her, and whether we can come to an arrangement with them. Usually, we can. It's easier that way. Cheaper, too. And less painful for you both.'

Jackson nodded, looking out at the motorway.

'How's the move going?' he asked, deliberately changing the subject.

After many meetings and discussions, the partners had finally decided to move the headquarters of Trinity-Trio to Nassau in the Bahamas. With Hong Kong due to be handed back to the Chinese before the end of the century, plus increasing difficulties over trading in India, with a growing bias against firms of foreign ownership, strict exchange controls and a throttling bureaucracy, a move from Calcutta was already overdue. With the virtual certainty that if a socialist government was ever elected in Britain it would be violently to the left of any previous Labour administration, it seemed prudent to cut loose from past associations and attachments of an earlier, easier age, while they could do so. One day – any day, given the speed of political changes – this opportunity might no longer exist.

Nassau offered many advantages with its relaxed taxation system, pleasant climate, and the fact that physically it was closer to the United States and Canada, where they had made many acquisitions, although with satellite transmission, fax, computers and Concorde, it mattered less where the headquarters was physically, so long as it stayed well beyond the reach of predatory governments. Of course, the Bahamas had their own problem in the shape of heavy Mafia involvement with casinos and other leisure activities, but this was safer than political fluctuations. The Mafia merely wanted money, while politicians yearned for power and prestige; if a foreign company could be a scapegoat for their own failed policies, that was always useful.

'All the computers and other equipment have already been installed,' Ebenezer explained. 'The offices are furnished and we are two weeks ahead of target.'

They had bought a high-rise building near Bay Street, Nassau's main thoroughfare, overlooking the sea. The Senior Minister of the Bahamas had agreed to declare it open.

'Anything on the Athens thing?'

'Nothing concrete. The police out there say they hope to make an early arrest.'

'They would.'

The car in which he should have driven from the airport to his hotel had suddenly caught fire. His plane had been delayed, otherwise he would probably have died with the chauffeur. There was talk that some incendiary device had been planted in the boot, but there seemed no proof either way. Even so, it was unsettling; it could be a hostile act, and if one had failed, another might be attempted. He had guards now, former SAS officers, but although their presence was physically reassuring, it was also inconvenient, and never a certain shield against a professional terrorist or even some disaffected individual.

'Anything else?' he asked.

'Only one major thing: the Occidental-Oriental Bank.'

'What's their problem? I know we owe them vast sums, but the loans are all well secured, aren't they?'

'Oh, sure. It is not our loans that concern me, but theirs. I hear a number of rumours in the Square Mile about the bank's own liquidity position. It is one of the biggest banks in the world, but like many financial institutions, its past is a little dubious. It started in the States after Prohibition, when the gangsters decided to put away their guns – well, most of them – and hire lawyers and accountants instead. They discovered that one lawyer with a briefcase of documents could make far more for them than ten men with Tommy guns.'

'What are you trying to tell me?' asked Jackson, looking out at the dusty grass verges of the road. They were coming into the suburbs now, through the rash of Indian take-aways, mini markets and betting shops that disfigured the dreary western outskirts of London.

'You will remember we only went to them because other banks thought we were over-extended. The Occidental-Oriental agreed to accommodate us – if we agreed to cross default clauses in the loan agreements.'

'I know all that,' said Jackson irritably. Why the devil did lawyers, accountants, whoever, always talk in this roundabout way?

'For God's sake, get to the heart of the problem. What is the trouble?'

'This. Our loans have these clauses. Our people didn't like them, but it was a case of accepting them or doing without the money. Briefly, the clauses mean that if we default on any of these loans – even by one day – the bank can accelerate all our other loans. They may not call them all in, of course, but they have the power – and our agreement – to do so.

'If they do, the principal is due for immediate repayment plus what they call default interest. This can be two or three times LIBOR – London inter-bank offered rate. In essence, then, if – for any reason, and I mean *any* reason, not simply that we lack the money, which we don't – we delay repayment on any of these loans, Occidental-Oriental could take over the company.'

'But not our master shares?'

'I wouldn't say that they would be worth too much in such a situation.'

'But we haven't defaulted?'

'We came very near to it last month through human error. We pay different loans in different countries and thus in different currencies.'

'But surely all this is done automatically by computer,' said Jackson in amazement. 'It's not people posting letters with cheques in pillarboxes. How can we possibly allow any errors over such a vital matter?'

'Humans have to programme the most complex computers. They are only as good as their programmes.'

'Was this a rigged job?' demanded Jackson.

'I've no evidence of that. What happened was that unexpected currency controls in Brazil held up payments. This should have been allowed for, but somehow it wasn't. The person who didn't allow for this delay – only a matter of days, I must stress – is no longer in our employ.'

'I'm very glad to hear that. Make a stringent check on every other person who deals with these payments. Check their records, their background, the lot. Pay the money a month in advance if necessary to give us leeway, a safety net.'

'The bank itself has so many Third World debts they have to write off, they could use our assets,' commented Ebenezer.

'So don't give them the ghost of a chance,' said Jackson. 'What if they go under?'

Ebenezer shrugged.

'Sufficient unto the day,' he said drily. 'Let's cross that bridge when we have to.'

'Hmm,' said Jackson. 'Anything else?'

'Laurens Gustav. Geneva,' said Ebenezer. 'You remember he gave ill health as his reason for resigning? It was rather more complex. He was being blackmailed.'

'By whom?'

'I haven't discovered yet, but I am trying hard. There are so many cut-outs in the chain. Some Levantine fellow put the button on him. Our people gave him a going over, but he was only instructed by someone else and so on *ad infinitum*.'

'What have they got against Gustav?'

'Porn photos with young boys and girls.'

'Poor devil,' said Jackson. 'The Swiss are very moral about sex. Not about money.'

'He was loyal, though. Wouldn't act against you.'

'Wouldn't? Or couldn't?'

'Didn't, shall we say?' replied Ebenezer pointedly. 'He went over to that Mount Carmel convent in Oregon. Tried to buy back their Trinity-Trio shares.'

'For us, for himself – or for the blackmailer?'

'It doesn't matter now. They had already made over their share to Beechwood Nominees.

'Which means that people we can only call outsiders own one hundred and forty-nine voting shares out of three hundred. A very close run thing.'

'So was Waterloo – but we won.'

'Then there's this fellow the Press call the Australian,' continued Ebenezer.

'What's he up to?'

'He has been buying our shares very heavily.'

'He has to declare his interest if he gets over fifteen per cent,' asserted Jackson.

'Of course. And, in any case, he can't exert control over the company, even if he buys every single non-voting share in the names of hundreds of nominees.'

'Well? Perhaps he wants a good investment, as an investment, nothing else. We are paying a bigger dividend next year.'

'He's not interested in dividends.'

'What is he interested in, then?'

'Money. Only money, because that equates with power. I've heard some odd stories about him. He is worth millions personally, yet he lives in a terraced house outside Manchester and runs all his businesses from a front room. He's not interested in women. I don't really think he's keen on anything except making money – and then making that money make more.'

'How is he so rich?'

'He started on his own, but then he got backing somewhere, I don't know where.'

'If he buys enough shares, will he want a seat on the board?'

'Maybe. But wanting isn't necessarily getting. He is a very shrewd operator, though. I don't like this much. In my view, he wants to control the company.'

'That's an impossible aim. Originally, each of the three founding partners held one share each. Trinity. A trio. These shares were divided later to give each one a hundred shares. When we went public in the thirties, the Douglases and the Jacksons between them owned two hundred out of three hundred voting shares. Old Captain Ross had got rid of his shares before then. We control two-thirds of the voting shares. No-one can take us over – so long as we hold on to these.'

'So long as you do.'

'Who's selling?' asked Jackson sharply.

'The same finance group, Beechwood Nominees, claim they are exercising an option to buy just under half of the Douglas holding. Forty-nine per cent, to be precise.'

'What option?' asked Jackson in amazement.

'Something Clive Douglas got himself into in the twenties. It's true, unfortunately. I've seen all the papers.'

'What the hell do you mean? What papers?'

'Clive Douglas was a spendthrift and a gambler. He sold the Long Glen distillery for cash, to pay his debts, to two men who said they were Canadians. They weren't, as it turned out. They wanted to ship the stuff into the States during Prohibition. Better than bathtub gin – and more profitable.'

'But Long Glen was his own company. Nothing to do with Trinity-Trio. It was part of his estate.'

'Of course. But they dangled a little bait in front of him and he bit. They offered him £15,000 more in cash if they could have a ten-year option to buy forty-nine per cent of his shares at their value then, plus ten per cent.'

'But that's ages ago. That option expired fifty years ago.'

'That option, yes,' agreed Ebenezer. 'But built in was a clause that it could be extended, ten years at a time, for £1,000 a go, the money simply to be deposited into Douglas's bank. No need for any letters, just the cheques. And that's what they did. It was paid every ten years, as a dividend. Douglas was dead. The accountants accepted the money as a dividend from Beechwood.'

'So now they come and want what is theirs,' said Jackson.

'Exactly. They have been lying quiet deliberately. I never knew this document existed till they came over and showed me the original.'

'Do they have a case?'

'Watertight. They kept up the payments and they own the shares. We can delay making them over for a few months, maybe even a year, with legal stuff. But that doesn't alter the end. The bottom line is they will then own forty-nine master voting A shares in Trinity-Trio.'

'What does Jennifer Douglas-Simmons say?' asked Jackson.

'I haven't told her yet. I am seeing her this afternoon. The position, when we make over this forty-nine per cent, is that *you* are still in control – but only by two shares.'

'That's better than no shares,' said Jackson defensively.

'Just.'

The car entered the Piccadilly underpass and as it went down the steep slope, Jackson's spirits sagged with it. He felt sweat dampen his forehead and back. Those two shares he had promised Anna; he should tell Ebenezer about them. It was only a promise, of course, not a contract, not a definite deal, just a verbal agreement between two people who loved and trusted each other. Nothing to do with business. Not really. Well, not this business. But he must try and get out of it somehow, just for his own peace of mind.

He would back whatever project she put up in some other way; there were all kinds of ways. But would the lawyers need to know in the end, because of the settlement his wife would undoubtedly demand? Would they say he was disposing of assets to which she might have a claim? It was all becoming so infernally complicated. Best not to tell Ebenezer – not yet, anyway. Best to say nothing. Least said, soonest mended, and these things could get magnified, be taken out of context, distorted. That was how lawyers made a living; magnifying differences, and he had enough on his mind without this horrifying prospect.

Jackson was glad of the relative darkness of the tunnel so that Ebenezer could not see the concern on his face. He adjusted the air-conditioning: it suddenly seemed very hot in the back of the car. They came up on the other side into Piccadilly, bright under the sun, solid with traffic. He wanted to say something, to appear normal, unworried, unconcerned.

He said, 'This Australian. I'd like to meet him.'

'What for?' asked Ebenezer, surprised.

'See what he's about. What makes him tick.'

'No-one knows that. I doubt if even he does. As I told you, he just wants money. To own it, like others own paintings. He's dull and a bit squalid. Those films his studios put out – each one shows some girl's knickers. He insists on it, really for himself, so I'm told. They say he's not actively involved, though. Look, but do not touch, that's his motto with women. But not with deals. There he has the Midas touch – every time. He just has a nose for a profit.'

'Like my great-grandfather,' said Jackson enviously. 'They'd have got on well together.'

Manchester

Micky Cohen came into the room the Australian used as his office in his house outside Stockport.

'We've just had Lord Jackson's P.A. on the blower,' he said. 'His Lordship would like to meet you.'

'Good. I've wondered for years what Jackson was like.'

The Australian was remembering the newspaper cuttings in the shoebox on top of the cupboard in his mother's bedroom.

'How did you fix it?'

'Like those guys in your studios in Hollywood. Writer fellow suggests they make a film with a one-legged hero, say. He gives the producer a spiel about the immense world-wide interest in one-legged men – their virility, attraction for women, brilliant brains, etcetera. The producer isn't convinced, doesn't care a toss, in fact. But he goes straight into a meeting with the finance people, and they want a picture quickly because something else has dropped out. No-one has any ideas, so he pitched right in.

' "Have you ever considered the immense world-wide interest in one-legged men?" he asks them seriously. Some say, "Shit, no." But one says, "Sure, I was reading something about that. You're right. It's amazing the sex lives these fellows have. And one in ten is not a millionaire, or a billionaire, he's a goddamn' *trillionaire*."

'So they go to the boss man with a memo on the subject, and he can't say he's never heard of this – that's not how he got to the top – so he nods and agrees, and then they go back to the writer, having forgotten he started it off, and say: "We've got a great idea. We want you to write a script about one-legged men." In a word, it's bull.'

'Everything is,' agreed the Australian. 'Where do we meet, then? His place or ours?'

'Certainly not here. And if you meet in the Coliseum or at La Gavroche or in his office, someone is bound to see you and ring a gossip columnist, and that's the last thing either of you need. Leave it to me.'

Many people, perhaps most, who wish to discuss a business matter with someone else will meet in their office, in a boardroom, or a restaurant. But when the fortunes of multinational companies worth billions are at stake, such simple arrangements become impossible. Thus it came about that Micky Cohen and Jackson's P.A. planned the meeting with military precision.

The Australian, in a Daimler (snatched back from a defaulting customer by one of his hire purchase companies), was driven by his chauffeur, with the bodyguard he had recently felt necessary, to the Whitestone Pond on Hampstead Heath.

Here, a man none of them had ever seen before, but who had been briefed with the car's registration number, handed a sealed envelope to the chauffeur. On a piece of paper inside was written 'Savernake Forest. Two miles east of Marlborough. A4. Blue mini Caravette', and the van's registration number. The chauffeur instantly moved the gear selector to Drive, and the car sped away.

At the same time, Lord Jackson's chauffeur was driving him in his Silver Spirit out on the Cromwell Road extension, with instructions to go to Number Four Terminal at Heathrow. Traffic had thinned out after the morning rush, but a shabby red Cortina cut in front of them in an irritating and unnecessary fashion. The chauffeur was used to such exhibitions of envy from other drivers and so paid little attention to this behaviour.

At the Hogarth roundabout, the Cortina stalled, right in front of the Rolls. Neither the chauffeur nor Lord Jackson's bodyguard got out. This could easily be a hold-up, a kidnap attempt. The bodyguard moved his finger nearer the panic button, linked by a complex security system to the police, and eased his Smith and Wesson Airweight in its shoulder holster. The driver of the Cortina crossed to the Rolls, tapped on the chauffeur's window.

'Apologies,' said the driver cheerfully. 'But I wanted you to stop. A message.'

He handed an envelope through the window. It contained identical instructions.

East of Marlborough, on a wide grassy stretch where the forest begins a hundred yards away, the Australian's chauffeur saw a blue Caravette, checked its registration number, then pulled off the road towards it, stopping about fifty yards away.

The bodyguard got out first, and cautiously walked around the Caravette, holding an electronic instrument near its sides, pushing it underneath on the end of a long handle. The vehicle was clean – and empty. He nodded to the Australian who now climbed out, opened the Caravette's side door, and sat down inside. His chauffeur parked out of sight beneath the trees, with the car facing the road so that he and his companion could keep the Caravette in view.

Minutes later, Lord Jackson arrived, and the same cautious minuet of suspicion was gone through. When his bodyguard assured him that the van was neither bugged nor booby-trapped, Jackson climbed into it. The two men shook hands, and sat down awkwardly.

Each was secretly surprised at the other's nondescript appearance. The Australian, tall and thin, wore a ready-made suit from a chain of menswear shops he had recently acquired. Even the superb Huntsman suit that Jackson wore, his silk shirt and Sulka tie, could not disguise the fact that he looked quite ordinary.

It was as though the Australian had subconsciously expected a peer and part owner of such a world-wide concern as Trinity-Trio to look, well, *different*; and Jackson had rather imagined that the Australian, given his appetite for commercial acquisitions, would look like a Dickensian miser.

'I am very pleased to meet you after so long,' the Australian said. 'I first read your name in a newspaper when I was nine, and I have followed your doings ever since.'

'I could say the same. Your financial doings, at least.'

'There are no others,' the Australian assured him readily. 'I understand you wish to meet me to discuss something?'

There was no need to prolong matters: he had no small talk. Let's get this over and then on to the next deal, was his philosophy.

'Yes. As one of the partners in Trinity-Trio, I would like to know why you are buying so many of our shares. They're non-voting. They will never bring you control.'

'I do know that. But they are sound shares, as I am sure you will agree. And you pay a good dividend.'

'The fact that you buy them in such quantities and in such well-publicised forays, pushes the price right up.'

'Of course. Then I sell them and it comes down. Like a see-saw.'

'This does not help the company. It unsettles the work force. It really doesn't help your fellow shareholders, or, indeed, anyone.'

'It helps me,' said the Australian simply. 'It makes money for me. Let me explain my philosophy. We are the same age, but when you were going to prep school and then to Eton, I was at Salford Road Elementary School. I left there at sixteen. That was the end of my formal education – but the start of my informal studies. You went on to Christ Church, I joined the office of a local solicitor at two pounds a week.

'You have always had money. I have always wanted it. That is the difference between us.'

'Maybe. You have certainly been very wise in never having much written about you in the newspapers,' Jackson said with some feeling. 'If something hadn't been written about me when I was a boy, you might never have heard of Trinity-Trio.'

'Possibly. But I did. And here we are.'

'You always seem rather a shadowy figure. You don't appear in *Who's Who*. You are simply the Australian. Tell me, were you actually born in Australia?'

'Yes. In Katherine, a little town on the Stuart Highway going north from Alice Springs to Darwin. Now it's a tourist stop!'

'A Trinity-Trio subsidiary is doing a development just outside Darwin,' said Jackson inconsequentially. 'Your parents were Australian, then?'

'My father was in the Australian Army. Killed in New Guinea. My mother was an actress.'

'How interesting,' said Jackson. 'So was mine – in a sense. Never in the West End, or anything like that, though. She met my father in

Colombo when she was in an ENSA show touring service camps. Then he went to Hong Kong and died there.'

The Australian nodded. Jackson looked around the van. Neither of them had known their fathers, had never even met them: it was a curious link, and unexpected.

'I asked for the fridge to be filled with drinks,' he said, and opened the door. 'Taittinger. Krug. That can't be bad.'

'It is for me. I never drink alcohol,' said the Australian. 'But thank you for being prepared to be so hospitable.'

Jackson shut the fridge door.

'You're still going to continue buying our shares and selling them?' he asked.

'Why not? It's easier than working.'

'That's exactly what someone said years and years ago in the very early days of our company. The captain of a ship. It was about selling opium.'

Jackson wanted to find some mutual ground, to come on closer terms with the Australian, but apart from the fact that their fathers had died before they were born, he shared nothing with him. The Australian was a machine for making money, not for enjoying it, or putting it to any helpful purpose – except to make more. They both realised there was nothing more for them to discuss, and they had discussed almost nothing. They had made a wasted journey.

The two men stood up awkwardly and shook hands. As they walked into the sunshine, their cars came out from under the trees to meet them.

The Australian was in his office, checking box office receipts for the first of his two Australian films, *Captain Cook's Secret Voyage*.

There had been a Royal Première in Leicester Square, and almost immediately the film went out on general release. It was now playing all over Britain, and in more than twenty-five hundred cinemas in the United States. First returns were phenomenally good. Even the critics had liked it; not that their views counted for much. This wasn't an art movie, this was commercial.

A sure sign that the formula had been right was the number of letters that the company and individual actors and actresses received from people who had seen the film, and here the Australian had a strict rule. All letters from outsiders relating to any production or any business with which he had any concern, must be shown to him personally. He calculated that for every person who bothered to write a letter giving their views, and then buy a stamp and post that letter, at least a hundred, maybe a thousand, possibly many, many more, would hold identical views, but would not bother to write.

Therefore, if too many disliked a certain scene in a film, he would never incorporate anything similar in any future production. If they liked one piece of action well enough to write about it, then that would be repeated, augmented, revamped. The public, it was well known, liked old plots – look how enthusiastically the basic theme of *Romeo and Juliet* had been received as *West Side Story* and *Love Story*. In repetition of familiar items lay reassurance, and most people craved this as much as they needed food. Old plots, like old jokes, must possess unusual attractions or else they would not have lasted.

His male secretary placed a leather-bound folder on his desk with all the care and the reverence of a bishop at a cathedral altar.

'Twenty-seven letters this morning, sir,' he said. 'All appreciative.'

The Australian skimmed through them, then picked one out and read it more closely. The notepaper was expensive, heavily embossed with a Belgravia address.

My dear Barbara (or Amy as is),
I went to the Royal Première of *Captain Cook's Secret Voyage* last night, and imagine my amazement and delight when I saw *you* up there on the screen!!!

I thought you were absolutely *wonderful*, and seeing you again after all these years brought back so many happy memories of Colombo and then of our time in Bombay.

When the ENSA party broke up and we all went our different ways, I went on with a little show to Delhi, and you were going to Australia – I forget exactly where – but it was a town with a girl's name like Katie or Catherine, I can't remember it now. I had no address for you and so I didn't know how to contact you. Is Amy Crabtree your married name or your stage name? I always knew you as Barbara – you said you called yourself that after Barbara Stanwyck – but perhaps Amy – after Amy Johnson??? – is your real name. How little one really knows about anyone else, but we were very young then, and not together really for very long, though it seemed *ages* at the time, didn't it?

I am writing to you now care of the film company in your new name, and hope you will receive this letter. Funny, you starring in a picture, *and* with the Queen and the Duke of Edinburgh at the première, and guess what happened to *me*? James Jackson – you remember we got married just before he went to Hong Kong – was *Lord* Jackson!!! Of course, he didn't tell me till just before he left and the poor darling never came back. So I've been *Lady* Jackson since then – isn't it a giggle?

Actually, I always thought James was a bit keen on *you*. Remember how he eyed you when the top of your blue two-piece

swim suit came off in the surf on the beach near the Galle Face Hotel?
He didn't know I was pregnant when he left – neither did I – and it was only after the war that things became easier for my son Roderick and me. *He* is now Lord Jackson – *and* he's one of the partners in Trinity-Trio. How life changes!!!

I don't know whether you will be coming to England in the near future after the success of this film, but if so, please get in touch, otherwise I can easily fly out to Australia. It would be such fun to see you again.

Congratulations and love.

Esmerelda Jackson.

The Australian read the letter for a second time and then put it in a drawer of his desk which had a secret lock. Lord Jackson had told him that his mother had toured in an ENSA company; she and his own mother must have been in the same one. Perhaps this James Jackson had also gone to bed with both of them? It seemed highly likely. Pregnancy would have been a very strong reason for his mother returning to her family in Australia. They could easily claim her husband had been killed.

He pulled towards him a copy of *Screen International*. On the front page was a report describing the huge business his two films were doing, and beneath this a Hollywood correspondent cabled how critics across the United States thought Amy Crabtree's performance in both parts was outstanding. There was talk that she should be nominated for an Oscar as Best Supporting Actress. The mystery was that these seemed to be her first pictures. Offers were pouring in, so where had she been for so long? The Australian pushed the paper away from him. He knew the answer to that.

His mother's life had been a long struggle to achieve success in what she always called 'The Profession'. Now at last this was hers. But his Australian office had only that day informed him how she had concealed an illness while making both films, and indeed, on the last day of shooting, she had collapsed. She was now in intensive care; the belated diagnosis was inoperable cancer.

The strain of taking two parts in two films being made back to back could cripple someone years younger, and had understandably worsened her condition, but she had stubbornly postponed going into hospital until they were finished. This was her great opportunity, delayed for so long; she could not let it pass by, whatever the cost.

An even greater irony, so far as the Australian was concerned, was that Lord Jackson's father was probably also his. For a long time he had suspected that the account of his father dying in the Australian Army in New Guinea was rubbish. He had set researchers to find anything they could about this, and they had found nothing, because there was nothing to find. His mother had made up a better story than admitting the truth: that some Englishman had knocked up two girls and only married one.

And in the prison camp in Hong Kong Jackson could never have known he had fathered one son, let alone two. If he was indeed the Australian's father, this would explain his mother's hints that he had been well-connected. Perhaps she had really gone to England hoping to meet a relation and stake her claim for maintenance, and then had lacked the courage or the opportunity, or, most likely, the money necessary to fight her case. He could almost hear her voice: 'You'd be surprised. . . . So would everyone round here. He was a real gent, a hero. . . .'

The Australian's stomach had begun to pain him. He dropped an Alka-Seltzer tablet into a glass of water and as he watched the bubbles rise he wondered about his mother – and about himself.

Part Five

The Present – and the Future

Nassau

One by one, the guests at Trinity-Trio's lavish reception to mark the transfer of the company's head office to the Bahamas began to leave.

All were careful to say effusive farewells to Lord Jackson. He bowed graciously to each hesitant or oleaginous voice of gratitude. He had no idea who most of the guests were, and pondered briefly that many thousands of people around the world worked for Trinity-Trio, and he had never heard of any of them, and never would. Yet their jobs, minuscule in themselves compared to his authority and emoluments, were their lifelong careers; each small step of promotion was a matter of prime importance to the person concerned. Had he not been born to wealth, this was how he also could have been now – obsequiously bowing and shaking the hand of a man who did not even know his name.

The gradual drifting away became an exodus. Within minutes, the huge room was almost empty. Waiters moved in expertly and began to pick up dropped vol-aux-vents, crushed cocktail glasses, cigarette ends.

Jackson felt immeasurably tired. He ran a hand wearily across his face; despite the air-conditioning it came away damp with sweat. To grace these social functions required a great effort from him.

His wife said flatly, without emotion, 'Well, that's it. I've kept my part of the bargain, being here. Now, I'm going.'

She might be leaving for a visit to the cinema, he thought, instead of leaving his life after a quarter of a century.

'Thank you,' he said. 'I'm sorry it's ending like this,' not meaning the reception, but their marriage, thin and loveless as it had become.

'It's your choice,' she said bleakly. It was, of course. No doubt about that. And yet . . . and yet.

He watched her walk across the room. She did not look back. If he had spent more time with Corinne, and their daughter, would things be different now? If. . . . If. . . . As Churchill had said about the failure at Gallipoli in the First World War, 'The terrible ifs accumulate.'

A hand touched his arm, light as a butterfly's wing. He turned. Anna Lu-Kuan was smiling at him.

'You look so sad,' she said softly. 'You really loved her?'

'I thought I did. Once. But not now. Not for years, really. Now there's only you. But a parting is still sad, a mark of failure for both of us.'

She squeezed his arm.

'I tried to see you before the reception, but I didn't have the chance. You're always surrounded by so many people. It's like a court and you're the king.'

'An illusion. The truth is, I am where I am through an accident of birth, not through my own ability.'

'That goes for most monarchs, too.'

'Maybe, but while others make money for me, I can only make time. And from now on, I'm going to make all the time in the world to be with you. Anyhow, enough philosophising, what did you want to see me about? To tell me how good-looking I am?'

'Of course. But apart from that – those shares you've given me. I can't take them.'

'But you already have them, my dear. They are in your bank.'

'I know. And I'm taking them out tomorrow morning, just as soon as it opens. To give them back to you.'

'Why? Have you decided against a career now? They are a gift. You can't give a gift back like that.'

'I can. I'm giving a gift to you.'

Jackson glanced towards the penny on its plinth under the lights.

'My great-grandfather once gave that penny to a little girl,' he said musingly. 'She gave it right back to him. History, or a little bit of it, is repeating itself.'

'It generally does,' she replied. 'And there's something else I have to tell you now, because you must know. You will not like it.'

'Later, then,' said Jackson. 'We're having dinner together, aren't we? I have booked a table at Graycliffe.' This was Nassau's most exclusive restaurant. 'Tell me when we're on our own.'

Anna shook her head miserably. He could see she was biting back tears.

'Tell me then. What's the matter that is so important?'

'This,' she said, forcing herself to speak calmly. 'I must get it over with. You'll hate me and you'll leave me, but I have to tell you the truth or I can't live with myself another moment. Those shares . . . I wanted them, not because I hadn't any money – I don't care a damn about money – but because I was ordered to get them. Now you are having them back.'

'Ordered? By whom? What do you mean?'

'What I say. I was told to get ten at least. And you actually offered me ten, without any prompting. But you were so nice I just couldn't take them. I settled for two. You see, I loved you – that was the root of the thing. I came to London expecting to find a monster, a sort of cartoon capitalist, and instead I found you.'

She paused. Tears glistened in her eyes. She dabbed them nervously with her handkerchief.

'I have told you lies, too many lies. Now, please believe me because this is the truth. All the truth. I said that one of my ancestors was T'a Ki. I thought that would appeal to you – the idea of history repeating itself, as you just said. But that is rubbish. My family had nothing to do with T'a Ki. Nothing at all.'

'Then why did you say it had?'

'Because I was desperate to impress you. I only had a few minutes at that first interview. If I didn't, I would never have another chance. Like William Tell and the apple, I had to hit the target.'

'I would have liked you no less if you hadn't claimed to be someone you're not.'

'I did not know that. How could I?'

'What were the other lies?'

'About my father. I told you he was in Beijing. He is, but he's not a prisoner there. He is high up in the Communist Party. Hong Kong goes back to China in 1997, remember.'

'One of the reasons we've moved. But what has that got to do with all this?'

'China wants control of Trinity-Trio. They need it. Think of the foreign currency it could bring them – millions and millions of dollars every year. And companies and factories and everything else all round the world. So they checked out every possible person who might be able to use charm with guile to try and swing it their way. And they came up with me.'

'But how could they get control with only two voting shares out of three hundred?'

'Those two shares would just tilt the balance. Can't you see? United Charities Incorporated already has one hundred, and Beechwood Nominees, forty-nine. With my two, the Chinese Communists and the Mafia would have a hundred and fifty-one out of three hundred – and control! Neither could move without the other. Together, they'd control it. Then they could parcel out the drugs section, which is potentially the most profitable, and no-one could stop them. They'd have a company with a turnover greater than the revenues of many important countries. And that would just be the start.'

'The Mafia, you said?'

'United Charities Incorporated *and* Beechwood Nominees. Why do you think Carlotti is on the Board? He's not here tonight, either, is he?'

'No. He had a family problem in New York. Couldn't get away.'

'Family with a capital F, I should say. But you know who *is* in town? The Australian.'

'What is he doing here?'

'They will have to come to some agreement with him. They control the Occidental-Oriental Bank, of course. They thought of leaning on you through those cross-default clauses on the loans, and by getting the Australian to buy all the stock he could create a feeling of uncertainty about Trinity-Trio's future. You know how they work. They buy into a growing company and then grow with it, and use it. All the dirty money comes out clean. That's why he seems to have so much. It isn't all his, it's theirs.'

'Have you anything else to tell me?' Jackson's voice was very grave; he felt he could not take many more revelations.

'One last thing. When my controllers realised I really did like you – *loved* you – they couldn't trust me to go on with the matter of the shares. So they tried to get control another way. They leaned on Gustav in Geneva, blackmailed him.'

'So that's why he tried to buy the shares from the convent in Oregon.'

'Yes. But Beechwood nipped in hours ahead of him.'

'How do you know all this?'

'We have a lot of people who help us, for one reason or another. Money. Politics. Fear.'

'So why are you telling me all this now?'

'For the corniest reason of all, which after all the lies, you won't believe, which I don't even expect you to believe. But it is true. Because I love you. That's why I couldn't go on with this charade a day longer. I've a ticket booked to Miami on the late-night flight. I am going on it, out of your life – like Corinne. I did my job. I got them control – and when I give you back your shares, I will have taken it from them. Now I have no future anywhere.'

'You have with me.'

Jackson's mind was a mass of churning, contradictory emotions: surprise, anger, relief, love; unbelievably, yet cheeringly, mostly love.

He could feel his heart swell, his spirits soar. He was in command of his destiny now for the first time in his life. He was the controlling shareholder and from now on he would stay in charge. For too long, he had been coasting on the efforts of others, like the big wheel in Belize, revolving through its own inertia. Now he would supply the energy, he would give the orders, set the course, with Anna by his side.

Together they would see off all these predators circling like the hungry sharks out beyond the reef: the Australian, the Mafia, the Chinese, anyone, everyone. He kissed Anna then, not passionately but gently, a kiss sealing a bond of trust and love, a kiss of forgiveness and understanding.

'You are staying here,' he said. 'Never leave me. I need you with me, all the time. Without you there's nothing, I'm nothing. I love *you*, remember.'

'Excuse me.'

He turned. Ebenezer was standing in the doorway.

'Forgive me for interrupting,' he said, 'but I have just had some good news on the telex, and felt I had to tell you right away. Those cross-default loans. Whatever's due has been paid weeks before their deadline. We're in the clear, safe and solid for at least another three months.'

'Great,' said Jackson. 'Great. And by then we'll sell off companies we don't need. Have a share issue, two for one, three for one, *anything* to raise money fast and get them off our backs forever.'

'That's what I like to hear,' said Ebenezer enthusiastically. 'Fighting talk.'

Jackson crossed the room, flicked off hidden switches, lifted the protective cover from Dr Jackson's original penny and picked it up. The candelabra glittered on William the Fourth's polished face. He thought of all the people who had lived and died with the company, sometimes for the company, since this penny was minted. He had heard about Captain Ross's death; how Fiona had shot Jack O'Brien; the explosive mixture in the cartridges at Sarajevo; his own grandfather's attempts to be accepted by those who could never accept others not of their class and claustrophobic upbringing; Clive Douglas selling his shares to pay off gambling debts, and his mysterious death.

The original founders had been driven by goads of ambition and anger against injustice, and in rising to riches had in their turn been equally unjust. Their descendants, cushioned by inherited wealth, lacked this elemental motivation. They had turned aside to other pleasures, and like stumbling runners had almost dropped out of the race.

Now all that was behind them, as much a part of the past as this old penny. He and Anna would take the company on to heights as yet unimagined. Like Everest, they were there to be climbed; together, they would scale them.

Jackson walked over to the window, feeling totally relaxed for the first time in years. He had shed, like a needless skin, years of inferiority and guilt at living luxuriously on the efforts of others. He stood enjoying this moment. Yet despite his elation and the air-conditioning, the room felt fuggy. Maybe there had been too many cigars and cigarettes, too much smoke for even this sophisticated apparatus to cope with completely?

He felt the need to breathe fresh air; not humidified, deodorised, sanitised, triple-filtered and cooled.

The window was split into two parts with a horizontal anodised metal bar dividing them across their centre. The upper part was hinged at the top on a spring, and could be opened by moving a small lever in the wall. He pulled this down and at once the upper window swung outwards.

He stood breathing the warm, gentle scents of a Bahamian night. Somewhere, in an open-air sea-front restaurant, a local band was playing a vigorous calypso. Beyond the drumbeats and the singing, the sea stretched, smooth as glass, at first reflecting lights on shore, then out to a lost infinity of indigo where sky and water merged together.

Jackson stretched out his arms and gripped the top of the lower half of the window.

Far below, he saw palm trees, parked cars, floodlit buildings. And as he looked, they began to tremble, to waver, as though seen in reflection on rippling water, or through a shifting shroud of fog. He turned. His former SAS bodyguards were across the room, relaxing with glasses of champagne; any danger to Lord Jackson had gone with the last guests.

'It's been the most wonderful night of my life,' he told Anna. 'I mean that.'

His voice sounded strained and hollow: another man might be speaking. By some trick of acoustics – maybe the angle of glass in the open window – the words echoed as though he was calling down a well. He saw Anna's face clearly, not fuzzily like the cars and the palms. She was trying to tell him something, but although he saw her lips move, he could not hear her.

He felt slightly ill, fuzzy, almost faint. His knees sagged, and he gripped the horizontal edge of the lower window to prevent himself falling. Against his unexpected weight, this window also swung out on its weighted spring.

Anna shouted desperately: 'Help! Help!'

For a second, Jackson balanced on the slowly moving edge. Ebenezer and Anna grabbed frantically at his jacket, his ankles. The guards came running, but all too late. The window swung away, and he was over and out, beyond their outstretched hands, falling through the warm night, past coloured lights and palm trees and the hammering calypso, 'Yellow Bird'.

The Australian's hired limousine stopped fifty yards short of the entrance to the Trinity-Trio building. He always instructed his chauffeur or taxi-driver to do that; it saved giving a tip to any commissionaire.

He and Carlotti walked slowly towards the main doors. As they reached them, a mass of people suddenly streamed out: guests from the reception, employees and their wives and husbands, all shouting, screaming incoherently. Police sirens wailed a wake. Blue and amber lights flashed from the roof of a racing ambulance.

The two men looked at each other in astonishment. What the hell was going on? Then Carlotti recognised Ebenezer in the running crowd.

'What's happening?' he called out to him.

'It's Jackson. He's fallen.'

'Where from?'

'The reception room. Top floor.'

People were already threshing about in flowerbeds around the hotel, lit by shielded ornamental lights shaped like huge metal mushrooms. In their glow, bougainvillaea blossoms gleamed red as new-spilled blood. The earth seemed soft, damp from automatic sprayers, fresh as a newly dug grave.

Something glittered like a jewel on the pavement at the Australian's feet. He bent down and picked up a burnished penny. He turned it over, saw the sovereign's profile and the date. This must be Dr Jackson's special penny, the one he had heard about, read about. He put the coin carefully in his pocket. Lord Jackson would not be needing this any more.

By the time they reached the place where he had landed, and elbowed their way through a crowd, his body was already on a stretcher, covered by a red blanket.

'Poor devil leant on the window. Didn't know the bottom half was hinged. There's no notice about it in the room, no warning, nothing.' Ebenezer's legal mind was already thinking in terms of liability, damages, who could be responsible.

'A hell of a fall. Bounced off an awning over a balcony halfway down.'

'He's dead?' the Australian asked.

'Wouldn't you be?' retorted Ebenezer bitterly.

Anna Lu-Kuan reached them, and stood staring in disbelief at the red blanket. Her face was streaked with tears.

'We were so happy,' she said, almost to herself. 'I'd explained everything, and he understood. He wasn't angry at all.'

Nobody was paying attention to her now. She was only a minor executive, not a partner's mistress or his wife-to-be, simply someone they could all safely ignore, not kow-tow to. Already she belonged to the past, and they had their own futures to worry about, not hers.

'At least he'd *won*,' she said. 'He'd beaten them all. I know. I hold the two shares that made the difference.'

'I think you are mistaken,' said Carlotti quietly. 'To be accurate, the Occidental-Oriental Bank holds those shares. It has, you will recall, a lien on all your deposits.'

'A power,' the Australian added quickly, 'which I assume the bank will now exercise?'

'Immediately.'

'But they *can't*!' shouted Anna desperately. 'I promised to give the shares to him – tomorrow.'

'Possibly, Miss Lu-Kuan. But he is dead – today. And the shares are in the bank's possession.'

'Well, he *thought* he had won,' said the Australian easily, as though the question was simply academic, and of course it was; the dead draw no dividends.

'Not a bad way to go, I suppose, believing you've won. At least he didn't live to learn the truth. He's away from all that worry now. At last, as his motto said, he really is beyond the dreams of avarice.'

'You bastards!' shouted Anna Lu-Kuan furiously. She slapped the Australian across the face with the front of her hand and then the back.

'*Bastards!* Both of you! I hate you – and I despise you! That's all you think about – money, money!'

'What else is there?' the Australian asked mildly. No-one answered him. He was not a person now with whom it would be wise to argue, let alone contradict. So far as he was concerned, they were simply hired hands, and if he did not hire them, who else would?

Anna Lu-Kuan turned away. This was no place for her now.

'Let's go upstairs,' Carlotti said to the Australian.

'You come, too,' he told Ebenezer. 'We may need a lawyer.'

The three men did not speak to each other in the elevator, and walked across the reception room in silence. Waiters were still clearing up; there was a subdued clattering of plates and the clink of glasses, the discreet hum of a vacuum cleaner. Cold air, not warm any more, blew in from the ocean through the huge open window. Outside, the band stopped playing to a round of ragged clapping.

'Everybody out,' ordered Carlotti shortly.

Waiters looked at him and obeyed instantly. They recognised the voice of authority and the ultimate power behind it.

'So,' said Carlotti to the Australian when they were alone with Ebenezer. 'You've got it. The company you first read about on a scrap of paper hanging behind a lavatory door.'

'You mean *you've* got it,' the Australian retorted.

Carlotti smiled, his eyes dead as always like polished stones.

'*We've* got it,' he corrected. 'We're partners now. Let's have a drink on that.'

Several bottles of champagne were still unopened. He twisted the cork from one, filled three glasses, handed one to the Australian, another to the lawyer, kept the third himself.

'Not for me,' said Ebenezer. 'The media will be along any minute. I'll have to give them a statement. I want a clear head.'

'And I never drink alcohol,' the Australian said flatly.

'Make this an exception.'

The Australian shrugged, carried the champagne to the open window and looked out cautiously, keeping well back from it. He could see how easily Jackson had fallen. Only one pace back into the room – and he would still be alive. But life and death, success and failure, were often measured by much less than a single footstep: a line misread in a contract, the telephone call unanswered or unreturned, a glance misinterpreted across a boardroom table.

He raised the glass towards Carlotti, and for a second saw his face distorted through the stream of rising bubbles, into a mask of ageless evil. The sight shocked him. This man was his partner, and behind him stood unnumbered others, even worse. He was playing in the big league now; not his own man any more, but theirs. He had always shunned partners, but now he would never be free of them.

'Wait!'

The three men turned in surprise at the peremptory command. Anna Lu-Kuan was standing in the doorway. Her face was still puffy with weeping, but her eyes blazed.

'He's not dead!' she shouted hysterically, triumphantly. 'He's *alive!*'

For a moment her words did not register in the Australian's mind. He lowered his glass, staring at her in astonishment. He had been concentrating on his own future. Other people's pasts, recent or remote, had no place in his thoughts.

Ebenezer spoke first.

'You mean Lord Jackson?'

'Yes. I've been on to the hospital. They thought he was dead at first, but he's not. Apparently, that awning saved him. He has broken his back. He's in a deep coma, but he is breathing. He's still alive, that's the main thing. *And* he is going to get better.'

'Did they tell you that?' the Australian asked her sharply.

'No. I'm telling *you*. You haven't won, you see. You haven't.'

Her voice began to rise; she was very near to tears. Ebenezer crossed the room to her side.

'Please,' he said gently, 'you're overwrought. Come outside for a moment.'

He turned to the others.,

'I'll deal with this,' he assured them.

He led Anna out into the corridor, closed the door carefully behind them and put an arm around her shoulders. She was trembling.

'It's true,' she said, more calmly now. 'It *is* true. They wouldn't tell me a lie.'

She paused as a terrible thought scarred her mind.

'Would they?'

Ebenezer shook his head, not knowing how to answer.

'I must go to him,' she said.

'I'll come with you.'

'But what about the Australian and Carlotti?'

'I'll come back to them. I'll go with you now.'

'I hoped you would. I thought I could trust you.'

'We both owe him a great deal,' said Ebenezer.

Still with his arm around her, they hurried towards the elevator.

Inside the reception room, the Australian put down his glass of champagne, untouched. As he had said, he never drank alcohol; he did not wish to start now. The bubbles, he noticed, were still rising, but more feebly.

'What d'you make of that?' he asked Carlotti.

The older man shrugged.

'Women,' he said briefly. 'She is emotional. But so would we be if we'd been on the brink of making a fortune – and then lost it. Whether Jackson lives or dies, the two vital shares are deposited in the bank – which has a lien on everything she places in its care. And we own the bank. All the rest is wishful thinking, crap. Those are the facts.'

'Yes,' the Australian agreed. 'Those are the facts.'

But were they all the facts? Was this necessarily the end of the matter? Could it even mark a new beginning? Somehow this possibility, small as it might seem, soured his moment of victory. He turned away from Carlotti and walked towards the open window. As he moved, he felt something dig like a sharp thorn into his right forearm through the thin stuff of his lightweight jacket. What the hell could it be? Then he remembered. That morning he had received a letter from Australia, and put it unread into the pocket of his jacket. Now the corner of the envelope was reminding him. The letter inside was typed. He turned over the page to read the signature on the back: Ian Bruce Crabtree. His stepfather, nearly twice his age? No, his half-brother, barely half his age.

> I am sure you will be sorry to learn that mother died early this week. I would have written before, but I was in Canberra, tying up a deal, and returned too late to be with her at the last.
>
> She had been ill for a long time without telling anyone, and she was determined to make two films which came up unexpectedly. Ironic that she had waited all her life for recognition as an actress – and now this. The funeral is tomorrow and I will send flowers in your name.
>
> That's the very bad news. Now for something better. I have been following in your footsteps out here as best I could. As a result of a number of deals, which I won't go into now, I have made $500,000 Australian clear, so I'm coming to London to get into things there.

I don't know half the deals you've done, because you wisely keep your name out of everything. But now, look behind you! Another Australian is coming up in the fast lane. We've never met, but we will.

The Australian put the letter back in his pocket. He should feel elated at having acquired ten voting shares in Trinity-Trio for doing virtually nothing. But the news that his young and energetic half-brother was on his way, coupled with the likelihood that Lord Jackson and Anna Lu-Kuan could fight back, totally destroyed his pleasure.

He looked down at the gardens far beneath him, trying to marshal his thoughts. Men in white coats carrying portable spotlights were still searching through the bushes. A white tent had been set up to cover the spot where Jackson had landed. In the morning, the area would be thoroughly examined by police and lawyers and insurance assessors and anyone who could claim a financial interest in the accident; until then this tent would shield it from the curious.,

Looking down at the white canvas now, the Australian was suddenly reminded of the huge anthills around Katherine, where he spent his childhood. They had also been white, ghostly in the moonlight, just like this white tent, and silent, always silent. Yet inside they teemed furiously with millions of ferocious, voracious white ants that could devour the flesh of a dead kangaroo or the wood from the foundations of a house.

The Australian appeared calm, too, but, like these ants, his mind was in a frenzy. Over the years, ever since his mother had first told him of the birth of his half-brother, he had received regular letters from her about the boy's progress. From a very early age it was clear he also possessed the Australian's rare gift for making money. He had started by cleaning windows and washing a neighbour's car, then he had hired out bicycles borrowed from friends; little deals that with every letter had grown larger, more profitable, and so far as the Australian was concerned, more challenging – and so more dangerous to him.

He had hated having this news, and deliberately denigrated Ian Bruce's achievements to himself. That way, they were easier to accept, although this only kept from his mind the increasingly obvious fact that one day the boy might overtake him and, terrible, unthinkable thought, could even become richer. As he was now, Ian Bruce would surely be. And soon.

The huge anthills he remembered so well at Katherine had not always been so large. They had begun seven hundred miles south, around The Alice, as small, unimportant mounds. By Tennant Creek, they were already two feet high and still growing, and by the time they reached Katherine, they were enormous. This was how his own deals had grown, and now the achievements of his half-brother were growing at an even faster rate.

The Australian had travelled a long way since the day he saw his first reference to Trinity-Trio, but this was not the end of his road; because the road to riches had no end, only staging posts. You could never have enough money, not nearly enough: there was simply not enough money in all the world. With Ian Bruce behind him, overtaking him, this could only be the beginning of another, much rougher journey, and not really just a journey, but a race.

He had started out in search of money, and then money had come in search of him. He had taken over company after company, never caring – not even considering – that each company he acquired was not simply a name on an accountant's file, but involved people whose careers he had shortened, altered, often completely destroyed, and always without a thought or even a backward glance.

Now his half-brother could do to him what he had done to so many others – and with as little feeling or concern. He knew this with the certainty with which he had once instinctively identified which deal to pursue, which one to abandon.

When he was starting, back in the days of the recreational club, everything had been so much easier. Far fewer people were competing, and he had been young, single-minded, determined to succeed. But now that he had succeeded, this determination had diminished like sand in a glass; and he was no longer young. Also, machines – computers, fax, simultaneous transmission, satellite communications – had ruthlessly taken over from men. They could now produce complex answers before human brains had properly posed the questions.

Then, there had been room for one Australian in his field. But now could there be room for two? He already knew the answer, and it lay heavy as lead in his belly, beyond all help from any Alka-Seltzer.

No doubt, he assured himself, he could hold off Ian Bruce's challenge for a time. Experience counted, and he knew the short cuts, the people who mattered, who owed him favours. But many of them would not weep if he went under, for in the end the race and the battle must always go to the young, to the swift, to the sure. Rule-of-thumb decisions belonged to the past. Did he belong there with them?

Looking out over the shimmering sea, cold beneath the moon, the Australian felt his confidence ebb like an evening tide. A chill, unwelcome, unseasonable wind was suddenly blowing in on him from the darkness. And, for the first time in his life, he was afraid.